Down, down the heavy-lifter plunged, thirty thousand feet, twenty thousand feet, piercing the unknown planet's terminator. Day turned into night. Buffeting increased in the dense, low altitude air. Pieces of the hull began to break off.

There was no hope of a vertical landing on one of the small ring-islands, but Karr could ditch in the water—if he got the lifter down below one hundred and fifty knots. He checked the airspeed: four hundred knots.

Individual waves tossed on the surface of the platinum ocean. The lifter whooshed over an island covered in spindly trees, their puffball tops tossing in the vehicle's wake.

"Three hundred knots, two eighty. Slow lifter, slow."

Karr felt the world reaching up to swat him. The lifter was coming in way too fast and the physics were unforgiving. Here came the water, rushing up with frightening speed.

Whoop, whoop! Abort! warned a klaxon.

Karr grabbed a handle above his head and yanked down with all his might. Solid rocket cells ignited, flashing hot under his seat. Ceramite windows shattered overhead and Karr lost consciousness as he shot out of the cockpit into the bittersweet air of an alien world.

Also by Ivan Cat:

THE EYES OF LIGHT AND DARKNESS

www.ivancat.com

THE BURNING HEART OF NIGHT

IVAN CAT

DAW BOOKS, INC.
DONALD A. WOLLHEIM, FOUNDER
375 Hudson Street, New York, NY 10014
ELIZABETH R. WOLLHEIM
SHEILA E. GILBERT
PUBLISHERS
www.dawbooks.com

First printing, July 2002
1   2   3   4   5   6   7   8   9   10

ACKNOWLEDGMENTS

Most grateful thanks to everyone who assisted me with this book. Particular thanks to my scientist friends Garry Garrett and Randall Matthews, who took precious time out of their lives to answer many weird questions concerning the biology of Fugue, Scourge, and the entire New Ascension ecosphere. Thanks also to Steve Collins of the way cool Jet Propulsion Laboratory, to John W. Thomas for his inspired and inventive help concerning the use of Latin, to Peter Löfwenberg for his meteorological advice, and to dive master Bill Feller USN for explaining the intricacies of the Emergency Escape Assent and other underwater perils. Any mistakes in this manuscript are my fault and not theirs.

In the category of exhibiting patience well above and beyond the call of duty, the awards go to my editor Betsy Wollheim and my fiancée Marti Livingston.

And lastly, but definitely not leastly, my thanks to Ernie Sheldon, Jr., who is always willing to listen to a nutty idea.

THE
BURNING
HEART OF
NIGHT

No change without fear,
No destiny without dreams,
No wisdom without suffering,
No dark times without hope . . .
                    —Feral aphorism

PART ONE:

SACRAMENT AND FUGUE

I

The little girl fled across the vast floating island, the ground rolling under her feet like broad ocean waves. Shooting-star palms swayed in time to the undulating root mass, their sour smelling streamers silhouetted against a storm-churned night, and noble sailtrees bent, turning sheet-leaves into the oncoming fury with a *crack* and a *snap*.

Jenette Helena Tesla was the girl's name. She was six years old, slight of body and blonde of hair, but she was strong on determination—and she was angry—very, very angry.

Her daddy was mean.

Lights flickered and bobbed in the distance behind Jenette. Strobing red streaks and sweeping yellow beams flashed through the swaying trees. She must not let them catch her. She did not know where she was going, but she knew where she was not going: back to her daddy.

Her daddy did mean things to her friends.

Her daddy made her friends go to *Sacrament*. He said it was because of the sickness that killed all the grownups, but Jenette didn't care about mean grownups. She only cared about her friends.

That was why she was running away and taking her friends with her. Of course, no other human but Jenette could have seen her friends just then. Her friends were too good at hiding and nearly invisible in the dark. Only Jenette knew they were nearby.

Leaves rustled and brainturf squished in the jungle around her and not from the impacts of her own feet.

Jenette stumbled onto a heap of swollen puff sacks. A cloud of archerbush spines exploded. She fell. The spines didn't penetrate her olive-gray colonist's daysuit, but her exposed face and hands burned from a thousand pinpricks. Right away shadowy forms converged. She felt velvety muzzles nosing her back to her feet.

Her friends cared about her.

Not like her daddy.

Her friends were always nice to her. The heat of their bodies around her felt good that night. Jenette wanted to thank them, but she knew she must not talk, and she certainly must not cry out from the pain of the archerbush stings. If she or her friends made too much noise, they would be caught.

Jenette looked back. The lights were closing. Red patches and yellow beams spilled over the crest of a land wave and then disappeared into the depths of a following trough. The wind carried snatches of urgent, howling voices.

"Where? Where? There!"

They were getting too close. Jenette turned and splashed through a stretch of sinkhole bog. Its surface splattered from the passage of many four-legged shadows following her. Across the bog, Jenette dropped and squirmed under a thicket of iron-brambles. "Hide!" she whispered, unnecessarily; the pitter-patter of following feet had already ceased. Through the spiky brambles Jenette saw the hunting lights circle, confused, and then head off in the wrong direction. Jenette scrambled out of the thicket and ran the other way, her friends rustling along behind.

"We fooled them!" she hissed.

But not all of the lights had been fooled. One of the red patches had slipped away from the others, dim and invisible at first, then growing stronger as it sprinted nearer and became more distinct. The baleful red glow did not radiate from a human searchbeam or a torch, but shone from the body of a half-seen alien predator. It flashed like a glow-in-the-dark chameleon, racing four-legged along hook grass and then bounding over sweeping sailtree buttresses. Angry red and black patterns cascaded across its lethal form, like little avalanches of red hot coal.

Claws scraped and plant fronds crackled as the hunting form darted around ahead of Jenette. Leaves parted as the monster burst into view. Low and wide it was, like the legendary Terran wolverine, but it had no tail and it was much larger. The creature weighed more than four hundred pounds and stood over four feet tall at its massive, hunched shoulders. Leathery hide thickened into armor plate at its outer flanks, limbs, and back; on that hide and armor patterns of light glittered from thousands of tiny flashbuds. A bullet-shaped head hung low from the creature's neck. Black spheroid eyes glistened maliciously.

This was a Khafra, alien, ferocious, intelligent. It growled, aiming its ring of prehensile teeth at Jenette. "Bad Jenette, bad Jenette."

In response, dozens of patches of light flared into view around Jenette—where sophisticated camouflage patterns had been hiding her friends moments before. Each was a miniature version of the large Khafra, but with the gangly legs, oversized heads and eyes, and fat bodies common to young creatures on all planets. Arching their backs, they bared tiny teeth and growled at the older alien in small, shrill voices.

"Rrrrrrr, rrrrrrr-grrrrrr, grrrrrr!"

The larger alien growled louder. "RRRRRRRRRRR!"

Jenette stepped forward and bopped the large Khafra in the center of its forehead. "I'm not bad!" she said defiantly. "You're the one that's bad!"

The creature blinked its orb eyes deep into its head in surprise. "Urrr . . . Tarkas bad?"

"Yes, Tarkas bad!" Jenette said angrily. "I'm taking my friends back to their mommies and you're not helping!" This was why Jenette had broken the Khafra kits out of the Enclave nursery. Jenette didn't have a mommy. Jenette's mommy had died when Jenette was just one and a half years old. Jenette could cry all she wanted, but Jenette knew her mommy wasn't coming back, but the kits had mommies, somewhere, and she was going to take them back to their mommies before her daddy did any more mean things to them. "I thought you were my friend!" she accused the large alien.

"Am Jenette friend," the alien replied, hurt, "but Jenette must go back to Enclave. Tarkas must take."

"I'm not going back."

"But Enclave safe. Enclave good."

"No, it's not!" Jenette said fiercely, "and you know it because my daddy does mean things to you too!"

Tarkas hung his head, conflicted. "Yes, but . . . long time back, Jenette mother said for Tarkas to take care of Jenette. Tarkas promised."

Now Tarkas looked sad. That made Jenette sad. Tarkas was the closest thing she had to a mommy now that her real one was gone. He took care of her, not like her busy daddy who never had any time. For a moment on that cold, dark, and miserable night, she wanted to give Tarkas a hug. She wanted to cry and she wished for all the bad things that were happening to go away, but even at six years old, Jenette knew that wanting and wishing almost never made things come true. "My mommy wouldn't make me go back," Jenette sniffled. "You told me she always said to do the right thing."

Tarkas clattered his teeth in consternation, looking from the kits to the stormy sky, and then to Jenette.

"Are you going to help or not?" Jenette demanded.

"Urrkurrkurrk." The colors on Tarkas' flashbuds froze in a troubled pattern. The alien had made up his mind. "Hnrrrph . . ." he rumbled, "Tarkas, Jenette, and Jenette's friends must run away together."

Boom . . . boom, came thunder from ahead where the island ended.

Jenette ran with her iridescent friends, struggling to maintain her balance on the rippling ground. One moment they were deep in a trough, cut off from the rest of the world, the next they were high on a wave crest. Sheets of rain fell. It was hard to breathe. Her chest hurt. Her legs hurt. She needed to rest. But they could not stop running. They had to escape.

Boom . . . boom.

Jenette burst out of a waxy thicket onto a cliff top where the island ended. A wall of spray caught her and the aliens in the face. Salt water stung their eyes as a great black shape rose and fell a few yards away.

Boom . . . boom.

The thundering mass was another floating island, driven too close to Jenette's by wind and sea. *Boom . . . boom.* The two islands crashed together, thousands of tons grinding mercilessly. Showers of ghutzu—the gnarled, interlocking root that made up the islands' structure—splintered and fell into a frothing, platinum-colored sea.

Wherever that nutrient-rich water splashed, plant shoots and tendrils grew so fast that Jenette could see them move, like worms. To her this was natural—she had never seen the blue-green ocean that her mother had sung about in lullabies from another faraway planet—but the fury of the storm and the islands smashing together scared her nevertheless. And it scared the kits, too.

"What now, what now?" they trilled, huddling around her.

Jenette did not know. All she had thought about was running away from her mean daddy. She did not have a plan. She did not know where to go now.

Tarkas watched the rise and fall of the colliding islands. "That Feral island," he said, looking across the rift. "Ferals live there."

By *Ferals,* Tarkas meant Feral Khafra. Tarkas was a *domestic* Khafra, stolen from the wild when he was young, like Jenette's friends the kits, and raised in cages by Jenette's daddy and the other Enclave humans.

"Are Ferals nice?" Jenette asked, hugging the nearest kits for warmth and courage.

The large Khafra shook his head sadly. "Tarkas does not remember."

Jenette squinted at the other island, shielding her eyes from salt spray with one petite hand. "Are there Feral mommies there?"

"Urrr, Tarkas thinks so. Yes."

"Then we have to go there," Jenette decided. "How do we get across?"

"Jump," the adult Khafra said after some thought. "Tarkas takes Jenette and kits on back."

"Okay," Jenette agreed.

Tarkas wanted to take Jenette first, but Jenette made him take the kits first, three at a time. They scrambled onto his leathery back and clung tightly to his neck as he timed the rise and fall of the two islands. His strong rear legs coiled up as the Enclave island surged up. At its apex, he leapt, springing high through rain and spray. Jenette lost sight of him for a second. She tensed with the remaining kits. Had he fallen? He would be crushed! But then she spotted Tarkas, safely depositing the kits on the other side. Another carefully timed leap and he was back on her side.

"Jenette goes now?"

"No, not now. Later."

Tarkas loaded up another three kits and leapt again.

Tarkas made many leaps taking kits across. Soon most of the kits were across, but Tarkas was getting tired—and the searching lights were picking up Jenette's trail, getting closer again.

"There! There! Track! Follow track!" howled the hunting voices.

"Jenette goes now?" Tarkas huffed worriedly.

"Not now! Keep going!" Jenette urged the last three kits onto the large Khafra's back. With a last look at Jenette and the closing lights, he reluctantly leapt, but he mistimed his launch and arched through the air, thudding against the side of the far cliff.

"Hang on! Hang on!" Jenette cried as Tarkas scrambled with the claws on all four of his legs, trying to grip the crumbling root face. One of the kits on his back slipped. A wall of spray blocked Jenette's view as the older Khafra shot a forearm down to grab the youngling.

The pursuing lights homed in on Jenette. Eight large, domestic Khafra bounded out of the jungle and formed a semicircle around her and the cliff. They edged closer.

Jenette scrambled as close as she could to the cliff. She tottered, windmilling her arms for balance. Pieces of ghutzu broke free under her small boots and tumbled into the chasm.

"Not jump, not jump!" the domestic Khafra howled.

"Stop!" boomed the voice of a man.

The domestics froze. Jenette froze. A man strode out from the undergrowth, a great, bullish man, thick-boned with brutally short hair and eyes like cold iron. He towered over the domestics and the six-year-old human girl. One scowling glance sized up the situation. Meaty hands clenched a pulse-rifle.

This was Olin Tesla, Jenette's father.

Jenette froze as his voice boomed. "Jinny get away from the cliff!"

"No!" said Jenette, still searching for Tarkas.

"It's okay," her father said. "Daddy's not going to punish you. Daddy just wants you to be safe."

"Go away! I hate you!"

The large man's face flinched as the rain and spray abated for a moment. Jenette spotted Tarkas, safely atop the cliff; he had not lost any kits.

"Run! Run! Get away!" she yelled. "Get away!"

The kits hesitated on the other side. They did not want to leave her.

"Go! Find your mommies! Go!"

Finally, the kits turned away, but not Tarkas. He saw the other domestics and the grim featured human, but his legs still coiled for another leap.

Frowning, Olin Tesla cocked his pulse-rifle. "No!" Jenette yelled.

"No, Tarkas! Stay! Don't jump! Run away!"

Unable to imagine abandoning Jenette, let alone doing it, Tarkas sprang. The alien arched through the air as Tesla methodically raised his pulse-rifle and led his target.

Jenette loosed a shriek of utter, forlorn terror. "Don't hurt him, daddy!"

Tesla pulled the trigger. The weapon's shot-torque was set perfectly. There was no splatter of blood, no explosion of bone; Tarkas' skull cracked like a super-heated stone. His body cartwheeled, his flashbuds flaring and fading to black. Four hundred pounds of lifeless Khafra crumpled on the cliff beside Jenette. Jenette's mean daddy was quite satisfied—that is, until she lost her balance and tumbled over the precipice.

*   *   *

"No!" Olin Tesla cried, running to grab his daughter.

His two human legs were far too slow to carry him to the edge in time, but his domestics leapt after the little girl. Stinging spray obscured his vision as the vast islands pulled apart and slammed back together.

Boom! Boom!

Surely there was no hope. Numb horror swept over Tesla. What had he done?

But then paws, each with two pairs of opposed thumbs and no fingers, scrambled into view. The domestics pulled themselves back up. The fabric of his daughter's daysuit was pinched in their teeth. Tesla hurried over. A *huff* of fear shook his heavy frame as he checked the biosentry sewn into her garment. *"Blessed be the Body Pure,"* he prayed, fumbling to activate the tiny display. *"All contamination it purges. All faithful it protects. . . ."*

The display blinked green.

Alive! His precious Jinnybug was alive! He hugged her to his chest.

Jenette did not struggle, did not fight, but hung limp, tears streaming from her eyes. "I hate you. I hate you," she wept.

The domestics flushed crimson, nosing Tarkas' inert form. They shone accusing colors at Tesla.

"Hunter man."

"Killer man."

They pulsed in time. Two heartbeats on, two heartbeats off. The grisly scene strobed.

"Chaos man!"

"Quiet!" barked Tesla. "Quiet damn you, beasts!"

Blood pounded in Tesla's head. This was the disaster of weakness. It was all his fault. He knew what his daughter was like. He should have known. She was his flesh and blood, his responsibility. She was the last trace of his beloved wife Helena.

"Howarooooooooooo!" the aliens grieved.

"I said quiet!"

Tesla swiped wetness from his eyes. More weakness. He had been fond of the traitorous Tarkas. But he could not afford the luxury of grief. His feelings for what had been lost did not matter. He must be strong for that which remained.

The woods rustled behind Tesla.

The other colonists had caught up. They hung back, ghostly shadows in the night. Tesla tensed. What would be their judgment? Would they condemn or embrace?

As one, the colonists bowed their heads, stacking and kissing balled up fists. "The Body must be Pure," they murmured.

Another *huff* of breath shook Tesla's form, this one of relief. Without letting go of Jenette, he bowed his own head and kissed his own balled-up fist. "The Body must be Pure," he repeated.

Of course, there had never been a choice for the colonists of New Ascension. Not for him, not for them, not for his beloved Jinnybug; not since they had set foot on this new planet. Anything less than fighting tooth and nail to survive betrayed the Body Pure. They might succeed or they might fail, but they would fight.

That was why they had come.

And suddenly it was over. One by one, the humans disappeared into darkness, winding their way back to the Enclave.

The domestics looked across the rift where the kits had fled, and at their dead brother. "Tears must fall," they keened. "Tears must fall."

Tesla followed the other humans, clutching his daughter tightly and praying that one day she would find a way to forgive him.

She never did.

II

Location: deep space.
Velocity: 0.7 lightspeed.
Mission status: past the point of no return.

Sounds echoed in the dark, lonely corner of the ship.

Zik, shsssh. Zik, shsssh.

Worry twisted Fugueship Pilot Lindal Karr's face as he stood before the ailing airlock. The portal looked normal. Its skin was a healthy pink. But the circular inner door was irising open and shut inexplicably, twice in one second, then staying shut for two seconds, then the pattern repeated. The portal made about twenty of its strange cycles per minute, one hundred in the five minutes Karr watched.

Of course, Karr's bloodstream was saturated with *fugue*. His metabolism and perception were slowed so that only one subjective day passed for each realtime year. Karr did a quick calculation in his head. The airlock cycle took a languorous eighteen minutes in realtime, not the rapid three seconds that he saw.

Zik, shsssh. Zik, shsssh.

Karr tilted his head, as if a different viewing angle would explain the malfunction. Dark hair, cut short on the sides and long on top, flopped from one side of his dour face to the other, but he did not notice. Neither did he notice the blocky kilnsuit's weight on his tall, lean body. *What was wrong?* Mercifully, the outer airlock door was not malfunctioning, otherwise Karr and everything else not bolted down would have been sucked out into space. But if the inner iris-portal could malfunction, so could the outer one. It was just a matter of time. Karr pondered. There were nine other airlocks. One potential solution was to simply seal off the malfunctioning lock and use an alternate, but then that was not Lindal Karr's way. If there was a problem with the ship, he would not rest until he found out what was wrong and corrected it. He must take care of his ship.

Karr inspected a pulsing hose, which pierced an adjacent plump bulkhead: nothing out of the ordinary there. The hose swelled rhythmically as a small life support unit pumped atmosphere in and out of the airlock. The life support unit itself was sealed and, theoretically, never needed service, but Karr gave it a once-over anyway. He depressed a red knob atop the unit to shut it down. Pumping stopped for a few seconds, but then a green knob beside the red one mysteriously clicked down and the machinery chugged back to life.

Karr blinked. How odd.

He pressed the red knob again, then again and again as the green knob kept depressing by itself and reactivating the small unit.

How very odd. And a little bit creepy.

Karr stepped up and ran his hand across the iris-portal itself. It was leathery and warm, no abrasions or other signs of trauma. No clues to what was wrong there, either.

It took a moment before Karr realized that the unusual cycle had stopped. He watched a few seconds longer. The portal remained shut.

On impulse, Karr stepped aside.

Zik, shsssh. Zik, shsssh.

Step in front of the portal. No activity.

Step aside. The cycle began again.

Karr frowned. Airlocks were not supposed to behave like this. They were not triggered by proximity sensors. The iris-portals were manually activated. Karr blocked the door again, determined to stand there until he figured what was wrong. The cycle stopped. Seconds, then minutes ticked by.

Suddenly, an invisible impact knocked the wind out of Karr. The interlocking plates of his kilnsuit locked up, as they were designed to do against impact or pressure, and he found himself airborne, shooting down the organic passage and colliding with its far end.

Karr wiped deck sweat off his face and looked back. The undulating passage was empty. There was no sign of a pressure rupture in the iris-portal or its surrounding membranes, nothing that could have propelled Karr through the air with such force. Karr did notice unusual blurring motions at the corners of his vision, but he quickly forgot about these as he stood up to get a better view of the passageway.

The problem with the airlock was not limited to just the airlock. Unhealthy purple veins were visible through the translucent passage walls and angry bruises were developing along its entire length. Karr leaned into one of the large veins and took a pulse. The rhythm felt deep and tentative where it should be shallow and firm. And it was too warm. Whatever was affecting the iris-portal was spreading.

Zik, shsssh. Zik, shsssh.

Karr patted the ship walls nervously. "It's okay. I'll take care of it." Karr knew the ship could not hear or understand him, but expressing the bond between them made Karr feel better.

He hurried back to the airlock. The cycle stopped again. Determined to get to the bottom of the problem, Karr pulled on his kilnsuit gloves. He picked up a bubble helmet and locked it on. He also retrieved a five-foot-long chrome implement with six rotating barrels and a cluster of chrome spheres on one end: Karr's Colt & Krupp AB-8 Gattler. Each of its long barrels had a different function. The chrome spheres were binary propellant tanks and munition clips.

Grasping the Gattler's handgrips, Karr thumbed a selector. Barrel number one rotated into position and he shot a slow-resorbing *qi* needle into a muscle group beside the airlock. *Pffft.* The fatty bulge quivered around the long needle, then relaxed. The inner portal irised open and stayed open. Karr stepped inside. Ten seconds later, the needle dissolved and the portal irised back shut.

The interior of the lock appeared normal. Scarring circled the chamber where the outer iris-portal had been grafted on to form the airlock chamber. There was nothing else in the space except a reserve kilnsuit locker. Karr shot another *qi* needle into a nerve cluster controlling the outer portal. It dilated. Karr slung the Gattler over a shoulder, hooked a safety tether around his waist, and stepped outside into space.

For a moment, Karr was awestruck. No matter how many times he saw it, the fugueship took his breath away. He grasped a handhold as the airlock closed behind him.

Karr was a flea on the midsection of an immense, grub-shaped body, a living creature four kiloyards long and two kiloyards thick. Wart-encrusted hide stretched away fore and aft of Karr, narrowing to engine orifices at either end. During the first twenty years of Karr's present mission, knotty stern bulges had spewed fusion fire, accelerating the fugueship. Now, after the mission's halfway point, they were closed. Ahead of the ship, an aurora danced where five hundred kiloyards of electromagnetic field met with faint ripples of solar wind. Rainbows pulsated against the stars of deep space, like oil on water, as interstellar hydrogen swept down the cone-shaped field into a gaping maw. The fugueship digested the hydrogen in fusion furnaces deep in its belly and spit the atomic fire back out through engine orifices on its bow. Karr felt the rumbling fury through the palm of his glove on the handhold. He also felt the subtle g-force of deceleration tugging his inner ear *down* toward the bow, giving him the distinct sensation that the ship was falling headlong into the bowels of the universe on four shafts of star-hot flame. This was Karr's astounding companion. His fugueship. His *cosmosaurus planetos*. His *Long Reach*.

A string of tumbling beads arched out from the airlock, trailing down as the fugueship slowly decelerated and they did not. Karr did not at first know what they were. Was *Long Reach* shedding some part of itself? Karr's throat tightened as he began to understand what he was actually looking at. The irregular shapes were not beads. Each shiny object was a part of Karr's cargo: a human body. Each body was swathed in a hermetically sealed membrane, each one having somehow been ripped from the safety of a dreamchamber deep within the ship and ejected. Karr counted hundreds—no, thousands—of bodies spinning into the void.

Frozen-solid death was transforming the victims' peaceful fuguesleep into nightmares that would last for all of eternity.

The airlock twitched behind Karr. He twisted around, but not fast enough to keep from being bowled over by the ejection of another body from the airlock. Karr was not hurt, the plates of his kilnsuit locked up protectively. But he tumbled away from the ship, plunging down toward the ramscoop along with the string of dead human bodies. Karr grabbed frantically for his maneuvering thrusters, however by the time his fugue-slowed reactions kicked in, his realtime rate of fall had yanked him to the end of the safety tether. Karr spun on the end of the pendulum. When his fingers finally hooked into thruster controls inside his gloves, a shot of acceleration swung him inward at *Long Reach*. Karr hit hard, grabbing a rope-thick hair so as not to bounce off. After taking a moment to catch his breath, he began the arduous climb back to the airlock.

Every three seconds the lock shot another victim into space.

Something was very wrong. Sick or not, fugueships did not eject dreamers into space. As Karr climbed he wrestled with an unthinkable, improbable theory. He couldn't believe it. He didn't want to believe it. But Karr could think of no other explanation that made any sense.

There was a stowaway on his ship.

Back in the airlock, Karr stripped off the heavy kilnsuit, revealing a skintight ghimpsuit, which augmented his human muscles. Karr didn't take the time to don his white Pilot's uniform, but picked up the body of a dreamer, which had just mysteriously appeared in the airlock with him and which he had grabbed before it could mysteriously be ejected into space. Then Karr exited the airlock and hurried down springy passageways toward the center of the ship.

Karr's mind raced. The odds of a stowaway inside *Long Reach* were a billion to one. The vast majority of humans who entered a fugueship immediately succumbed to *fugue,* the vessel's immune defense system, and fell into suspended animation. Without the protection of a hermetic membrane, foodyeast would then absorb these victims the same as it would attack any other intruding organism.

Except Lindal Karr.

Karr was different. He did not fall into fuguesleep, but slowed a varying amount depending on how much *fugue* was in his bloodstream. Just breathing fugueship air, Karr moved half as fast as realtime.

One subjective day for every two realtime days = slowtime.

And Karr could go one step further. Artificially saturating his blood with *fugue,* the present forty-year mission would elapse, from Karr's point of view, in forty days.

One subjective day for every realtime year = fuguetime.

It was a perfect solution to the problem of sub-lightspeed travel between stars. Unfortunately, individuals like Karr were extremely rare. One in a billion. Humanity, spread across its many colonized worlds, spent vast amounts of time and energy searching such individuals out and training them to be fugueship Pilots, but few were found. The last time two *fugue*-resistant humans had been together inside *Long Reach* had been on Karr's apprentice voyage, when a retiring Pilot had taught Karr the finer points of fugueship husbandry.

For all these reasons, a stowaway was unlikely, but Karr was convinced it was the only explanation for such strange events. Which left the unsettling question of why the stowaway was murdering Karr's cargo.

It was an unknown sensation for Karr to feel ill at ease inside his ship. The ship was his world. The ship was his reason for existence. It might be a great, dumb beast, but *Long Reach* was also the closest thing to a friend that Karr had. Now, for the first time in centuries, the jasmine scent of *fugue* gave Karr no comfort, and neither did the grandeur of sweeping ivory archways, or wallfields of beautiful follicle flowers. There were kiloyards and kiloyards of passages inside the ship, meandering around colossal internal organs, ducking under girderbones, squeezing between broad sheets of muscle. It was a maze in three dimensions with a thousand places for an interloper to hide and Karr just could not search them all. Even with his experience in the labyrinth, Karr had to be careful in remote areas or risk getting lost. He hurried past a series of air-scrubber pillboxes with funnel intakes protruding from their tops. It occurred to him that the stowaway might be lurking behind one of the human-implanted devices at that very instant. Or the stowaway could be hiding in the next overhead bile duct waiting to pounce down on him.

It was unsettling.

More unsettling was that fact that unhealthy blotches and purple veins were now swelling up throughout the ship. Whatever the stowaway was doing was not limited to the airlock.

Karr turned onto Wendworm Way, a cathedral-shaped passage that spiraled through *Long Reach*'s massive hull from stem to stern. Karr followed its gentle slope through towering fuel bladders. Some of the bladders held reserve hydrogen. Others stored reserves of oxygen, carbon, and all other substances necessary for a fugueship's survival. Cargo netting held stacks of crates in the spaces between the bladders.

Karr observed that several stacks had collapsed where nets had somehow become unfastened.

Karr tapped the back of his left wrist. Three sets of numerals glowed subdermally. The first two, which counted slowtime and realtime, scrolled unreadably fast. The third counted fuguetime. It was almost time for Karr to resaturate his blood with *fugue*. Karr sped up, carrying his human cargo to a cockeyed intersection where Wendworm Way met up with an internal iris-valve. There, Karr unslung the Gattler, shot a *qi* needle to open the portal and stepped through.

The dreamchamber appeared tranquil at first glance. Salmon-colored glowbars bathed the curving space between the ship's inner and outer hulls. Broad girderbones kept the layers apart. Sprinkled between those rib humps was a profusion of human-sized capsules. Each was supposed to contain a dreamer, sealed in a hermetic membrane.

Karr's second glance around the chamber was more disturbing. Most of the capsules were open, lids sticking up like violated shellfish, and the dreamers were no longer inside. Some, like the body Karr carried, had been removed with their membranes intact.

Many more had been ripped free. *Fugue*-rich blood seeped from torn membranes.

And the horror continued to unfold. Before Karr's very eyes. Approximately every three seconds another capsule opened, another body disappeared. Karr did a quick scan of the chamber: out of thousands of capsules, only a few hundred still contained dreamers.

The peculiar motion blurs were back.

Smearing shadows danced around the dreamchamber. With a sinking feeling, Karr realized what they were. The stowaway was not dosed up on *fugue* like Karr, but merely breathing the *fugue* in *Long Reach*'s atmosphere. That meant the stowaway was only moving half as fast as realtime—one hundred and eighty times faster than Karr! The blurs were the stowaway moving in the chamber around Karr, ripping dreamers from their capsules and stealing them away to eject into space.

Putting down the body he carried, Karr turned to the dreamchamber entrance and adjusted the Gattler. Metallic spheres rotated, changing the multitool's load to long, permanent needles. Looking over his shoulder, he watched the capsules. The next step had to be timed just right . . .

Snap went a capsule lid. *Blink,* a body disappeared.

One thousand and one, one thousand and two, Karr counted in his head. Then he fired metal needles into *qi* points all around the iris-valve. Bap, bap, bap. Karr drove the shafts deep with the heel of a boot. Now the portal would not open from the outside and it would be very hard to get the needles out, even from the inside.

But had he succeeded?

Hairs prickling on the back of his neck, Karr turned back to the chamber. *Snap,* one more capsule sprang open. *Blink,* another dreamer disappeared. But then no more capsules were violated. Karr waited nervously. The body of a dreamer reappeared a few yards from its original location—*pop!*—carelessly discarded between two empty capsules.

The stowaway was trapped in the chamber.

Of course, that also meant Karr was trapped in the chamber with the stowaway, which was not a pleasant feeling. Even though

Karr had known that this would be the consequence of his actions, he could not suppress a sense of growing dread. The lightning-fast intruder could attack at any time, with no warning at all. And by the time Karr's *fugue*-slowed brain registered the pain of a mortal attack, Karr would have already been dead for five minutes.

Wait a second, Karr thought, cold sweat forming on his brow. *Long Reach* was at the midpoint of it present mission. At any time in those preceding ten years, the stowaway could have killed Karr. The stowaway must need him alive. Yes, of course. What good was a fugueship without a Pilot? No good at all. If the stowaway killed Karr, he was signing his own death warrant.

So be calm, he said to himself. There has to be a way to stop this mass murderer.

Karr considered the enormity of the problem. The killer would have to hold still for three slowtime minutes in order for Karr to get a mere one-second glimpse of him. And what could Karr do even if that unlikely event happened? Karr was virtually petrified compared to the killer.

They couldn't even exchange insults.

The killer's speech would be a high-pitched squirt of noise to Karr. Karr had pitch-translators in his ear canals, but the inefficient things had trouble translating simple sounds, like that of the malfunctioning airlock or the pulse of the Gattler injecting needles. Voice synthesis was right out. Karr could not speak, either. His vocal cords could not make sounds at the slow realtime rate at which he spoke, not enough air passed through his throat. A voice emulator, implanted in Karr's neck, was capable of reading nerve impulses and, working in conjunction with the pitch translators in his ears, recreating his voice for his own benefit, but the stowaway would hear nothing. Because of the difference in speed between Karr and the stowaway, even gestures and sign language were impossible.

The obvious answer came to Karr as his heart rate calmed a little: he had to out-think his opponent. As a Pilot, he was presumed to be of high intelligence. Now he had better prove it.

Eerie smears of motion flittered around Karr. The murderer was within arm's reach. Karr inhaled a whiff of bitter body odor.

Inspiration struck. Karr dug a stylus and mindercard out of his ghimpsuit pockets. He scribbled a message on the card's memory surface and held it outstretched at eye level.

"Who are you?" it read.

Karr felt pretty silly, but he had to engage his enemy, to learn what that enemy's weaknesses might be.

Blink! The stylus disappeared from Karr's fingers.

Blip, something was stuck to Karr's nose. He reached up and pulled off a quickfood wrapper. Lines were scraped out of its printed surface. Karr puzzled, turning the scrawl sideways.

It was a winged stick figure with a squat oval above its head.

Karr frowned. What did it mean?

The wrapper pulsed away and back onto Karr's nose. Examination revealed that there were now words under the drawing.

"I'm your guardian angel."

The stylus reappeared in Karr's hand. He wiped ink scrapings off its tip, cleared the mindercard and wrote, *"My what?"*

Again, the stylus disappeared. Another wrapper popped onto Karr's nose, with more ghostly writing.

"Your guardian angel, friend."

Karr crumpled and tossed the wrapper. He wrote, *"Do I know you?"*

This time Karr offered the mindercard so that the stowaway could respond without sticking garbage to his face. Karr's message cleared and another appeared

"No, but I've met you. I know all about you. We have enemies in common, you see. But don't worry about them. I'm making them pay."

The dialogue gave Karr the creeps. It was more of a séance really. He glanced around the dreamchamber. The violated capsules were testament to the stowaway's form of payment.

When Karr did not quickly respond, the message lengthened. *"I know how they fucked you on this mission. The bastards. They fucked you just like they fucked me. You see? We're just like two fleabhps in a pod."*

The motion streaks began to coalesce as the paranoid note continued. In the split second that the apparition hung around, Karr got a glimpse of an emaciated, male frame.

Karr wrote, *"You need to stop. Don't kill any more dreamers."*

"You're the one who wanted them dead."

"I want them alive," Karr scribbled, underlining *alive*.

"Oh no you don't. I've spent a lot of time watching you, getting to know you, Lindal. I know how you think, what you think of them. I read it in your personal logs."

Karr flushed red. This mission from Sheldon's World to Evermore had been cursed, even before the stowaway began to murder Karr's cargo. Karr had put in at Sheldon's World to resupply *Long Reach* for the next tour. *Long Reach*'s dreamchamber should have been refilled with twelve thousand dreamers, and six large seed-colony containers should have been strapped around its mid-section, each one stocked with the supplies and equipment necessary to found a new colony world on a new, virgin planet. That had not occurred. Imminent collision with a freak swarm of comets was about to wipe out all life on Sheldon's World. Therefore, the planet's political elite had packed themselves into *Long Reach*'s dreamchamber for evacuation to Evermore.

Karr had protested. It was a violation of Karr's sacred duty, to find and seed new human colonies throughout the galaxy. As a Pilot, Karr was not allowed to weep for failed colonies. The death and suffering bothered a deep, buried part of Karr, but consciously he could not allow himself to think about such sorrows. That would only lead to the misuse of his precious *Long Reach*—as was the case on the present mission. No one knew how long fugueships lived, but a twenty year trip to Evermore was a significant chunk of realtime, considering that there were only three fugueships in all of human space and no way to replace them. To make matters worse, *Long Reach*'s dreamchamber was not even full. Sheldon's World politics forbid intermingling elite and lower classes. Short of abandoning everyone on Sheldon's World and flying empty to Evermore—an even greater misuse of *Long Reach*—Karr had no control over who was or was not loaded into it. So *Long Reach* had left Sheldon's World with its dreamchamber less than half full.

That was why Karr had written vengeful words in his personal logs, but it was only to vent his frustration. He didn't love his present cargo of dreamers, but he didn't literally want them dead. In fact, it was his duty to keep them alive.

"*They tricked you,*" The stowaway was writing. "*You're an honorable man. Good thing I can't be tricked.*"

"Listen, 'Angel'—"

The stowaway snatched the mindercard. "*Call me Bob. We're friends, remember?*"

Friends. Foodyeast must be getting to the interloper's brain. Cursing inwardly, Karr decided he had better humor the psychotic killer. "*Sure, Bob.*" Karr tried a different tack. "*What happens when we get to Evermore? The authorities won't be very happy with you.*"

"*Don't worry. I'm taking steps.*"

Karr didn't like the sound of that. "*What sort of steps, Bob?*"

"*You write too slow,*" Bob scrawled, not answering the question. "*Can't you write faster?*"

More quickfood wrappers appeared on the deck, reminding Karr that in the two or three fuguetime minutes of their correspondence, Bob had been trapped in the dreamchamber close to half a slowtime day. He must be getting tired. If Karr could keep him answering questions, maybe Bob would make a mistake and stay in one spot too long. Karr took his time with his next words. "*Bob, I'm upset. You read my personal logs. Friends aren't supposed to do things like that.*"

Bob took the bait. "*I'm very sorry about that, really, very sorry. But it's so BORING on this ship. You know what I mean. . . .*"

Karr most certainly did not know what Bob meant. Karr loved his job and his ship, and it was encounters like this which reassured him that a life with minimal contact with other human beings was a good life, even if it was a bit lonely at times. Karr forced a smile and let Bob prattle on for a while.

Bob began to coalesce.

Karr felt for his Gattler. It was slung over his shoulder, with its barrels pointing down, set to fire *qi* needles. All he had to do was yank the Gattler up and autofire in Bob's general direction. While it was not specifically designed as a weapon, Karr figured that a volley of six-inch steel needles would immobilize Bob long enough for Karr to subdue him.

Bob kept apologizing. *"It was so easy. At night I could just walk into your quarters and do anything I wanted. It's a good thing we're friends, Lindal."* There was an ominous pause. *"I looked through your stuff. I even tried on your clothes, but they don't fit."*

Bob had been in the same position for a long time and he was still writing. Karr's finger closed on the Gattler's trigger. He should have fired right away, but morbid curiosity stopped him as the image of Bob unfolded. Bob was a sorry angel. His limbs were gaunt, muscles atrophied from too much time in low gravity without a ghimpsuit. Ribs showed under pasty skin. Bob's hands were blurred from writing, but his head was more distinct. Fishy, malignant eyes bulged over a hooked nose, withered mouth, and receding chin.

Bob's ghoulish monologue waxed sentimental. *"You look so peaceful when you sleep. I always tuck you in if you toss your blankets off. Four months is a long time to sleep without blankets, don't you think?"*

The idea of Bob prancing around Karr's quarters, wearing Karr's clothes—tucking Karr in!—alarmed Karr in the extreme. Never again would he get a wink of sleep until this maniac was locked up tight.

Karr yanked the Gattler up as fast as he could and squeezed off a volley of shots. Bap, bap, bap, bap, bap! Bob streaked away. The mindercard hit the deck. Karr held his breath. Had he hit?

No.

The Gattler abruptly ripped out of Karr's hands and disappeared. An angry gnat screeched around his head and the same force that had hurled him away from the airlock earlier now hoisted Karr into the air. *Blink—WHAMM!* Like a jump cut in a video recording, Karr instantaneously smashed into a wall five yards away. *Blink—SLAMM!* Invisible force ground Karr into the deck. *Blink—CRUNCH!* Karr hammered into a dream capsule, sudden fire in his ribs. *Blink—CRACK!* Welts raised under Karr's ghimpsuit. *Blink—WHACK!* Karr was in the air, falling. Then colliding. Tumbling. The violent montage escalated. Karr's mind fogged over with pain. His body was a rag doll in a tornado, waiting for a killing blow. Would it come in the heart or in the head, Karr wondered numbly? No, in the back. That was the kind of guy Bob was, a backstabber.

But no mortal blow came. *Blink.* Karr was on the deck. The angry buzzing went away. *Blip.* The mindercard reappeared in Karr's hand.

"That wasn't very nice, Lindal. Not very nice at all. I didn't want to do that, but you made me. Don't make me do that again. Don't make me do something I'll regret." There was a pause. When Bob resumed writing, the tone of his words changed with no apparent logic; Karr reminded himself that the schizophrenic switch was actually occurring over many slowtime minutes. *"You've been a bad boy, Lindal. I should punish you, but I forgive you. Know why? Because I love you. So much that it hurts. That's why I forgive you. Love. It's a special thing. Don't you think? I'm tired now. I'm going to take a nap."*

The motion blurs disappeared. Karr did not waste any time cooling off, but hauled his bruised body erect and hurried around the dreamchamber, scrambling over girder-ribs and around capsules in search of Bob. Sleeping humans didn't move much; all Karr had to do was find Bob. Karr searched furiously for three minutes, but then the mindercard called attention to itself again.

"I feel much better now. Bob's just not himself without eight hours of shuteye. It's been nice talking to you, Lindal. Let's do it again real soon. I have to get back to work."

"Wait—!" Karr scribbled hastily, but Bob cut in.

"Time's a-wasting. Bye."

There was motion at the dreamchamber entrance. Karr watched in utter horror as chunks of fugueship flesh ripped out where he had injected *qi* needles. Blood gushed from the wounds and the dreamchamber shook with *Long Reach*'s pain. Karr fell to his knees as the aperture opened with a spasm.

Dream capsules began popping open. Dreamers began disappearing. And the first dreamer to disappear was the one Karr had hauled all the way back from the airlock.

III

A human's first duty is to his other humans. A Pilot's first duty is to his fugueship. Any other consideration is distraction: without the ship, all is lost. A Pilot's execution of duty must become instinctive. Pilots whose training and discipline depend upon conscious thought become helpless in crisis. To train such Pilots is folly. To send them forth in fugueships is murder—of the ship, the Pilot, and those entrusted to his care. In creating the Pilot, we must strive to instill proper instinctive reactions, so that in the midst of the extreme distraction, the Pilot will always function to preserve the ship.

—Major A. Vidun
Founder, Pilot Academy
Post Terran Interdiction

Bob had hurt Karr's ship. Karr saw red.

Karr rushed to the wounded portal, wishing he had the Gattler that Bob had stolen. Barrel number two dispensed molecular adhesive, intended to suture and dress wounds just like these, but all Karr could do was press the torn flesh back into some semblance of its original position. It helped, a little. Searching around, Karr found two of the needles dug out by Bob and, carefully locating the nerve meridians, thrust them by hand into pain-killing *qi* points. The spasms of the chamber settled as *Long Reach*'s pain subsided.

Karr pressed his palms against his temples, remembering Bob's words, *"Don't worry. I'm taking steps."* It was now clear to Karr that those steps were the cause of the fugueship's spreading sickness. Bob was killing his cargo. Unchecked, Bob would obviously kill *Long Reach*, too.

Bob must die.

It was simple as that. Every fiber of every muscle in Karr's body desired to eliminate Bob. *Long Reach* must be preserved and Karr must use any and all measures to carry out that duty. But he must focus. Rage would do no good. Bob could act erratically, but for Karr every second counted. Karr forced himself to sacrifice a few hundred of those precious seconds and gather his thoughts. Soon Karr's steely calm returned and he strode out of the dreamchamber with the beginnings of a plan in his head. *Where* he had to go and *what* he had to do was suddenly very clear, but not the crucial *how* he was going to do it.

Karr was out in the winding passages of *Long Reach* before he noticed his hands. The edges of his fingernails were yellow-brown.

Karr looked closer. It was foodyeast. Small amounts of it were everywhere in the fugueship, seeping from inner hull chambers next to *Long Reach*'s fusion furnace. Foodyeast grew there in the waste heat. *Long Reach* fed the foodyeast oxygen and basic organic building blocks from storage bladders, then ate the yeast. That was how the cycle worked, just as Terran termites fed inedible wood chips to fungus cultivated in their lairs and then ate that fungus.

Karr had just become part of that food cycle.

Karr berated himself. He had lost track of time during the dialogue with Bob. He consulted his subdermal chronometer. He was overdue for decontamination. Very bad. Unchecked, foodyeast would drive Karr mad, as it had Bob. Very, very bad. Now he must make a fifteen minute detour. Bob would wreak a lot of havoc in that time and *Long Reach* would suffer for it.

Karr hastened to a lonely collection of cube modules, which were nestled between crimson pipelines of fugueship artery.

"Door open."

Nothing happened. Karr adjusted the voice-emulator at his throat and tried again. "Door open."

This time a crack formed on a blank cube wall, describing a

man-high rectangle, then that rectangle shifted back and slid aside. Karr stepped into a small airlock.

"Door close. Airlock cycle."

Crisp, dry air replaced humid fugueship atmosphere, then the inner door formed and slid aside. Impatient, Karr stepped through before it was fully open and he began unfastening the catches on his ghimpsuit as he strode down the sanitary white hall. Karr entered a cubicle at the end, unbuckling chest and waist straps while kicking off his left boot. Economy of motion was imperative. Every second was minutes less for Bob to do his dirty work. Karr peeled off a ghimpsock as he kicked off the other boot, then the other sock came off.

Ochre fur lined the cracks between his toes.

The rest of the ghimpsuit required full attention: wrist seals, ankle seals, neck seals. Karr looped his arms over support brackets in the stall and pulled the muscle-like bodysuit inside out in his rush to disrobe. Overtaxed muscles complained at the loss of support, but Karr ignored the pain. He wouldn't be unsuited long. A sweeping kick cleared his clothes into the hall.

"Door close." A frosted panel slid shut. Karr swabbed his mouth and nose with sterile fluid and fastened a rebreather over them.

"Shower on."

Stinging disinfectant sprayed from holes in the walls, ceiling, and floor. In the low gravity, the air quickly filled with unbreathable mist. Karr did not see the realtime droplets, only an eye-jangling stroboscope, like interference patterns on a viewscreen with no signal. He twisted around on the supports, careful to ensure that the disinfectant reached every part of his exposed skin. Twenty-four seconds was the minimum time to decontaminate if Karr did it just right. Arms up, arms down. Left leg up, down, right leg up. . . . Karr pegged the sequence without wasting a beat. The jets stopped. Different holes sucked the stall clear and three cycles of warm whirlwind tossed him dry. The stall door opened.

Karr stepped out rubbing his burning eyes. He had forgotten the protective goggles. It hurt, but he knew from experience that the burning would subside. Karr swallowed an antifungal pill, checked himself over—no sign of yellow fuzz—and slipped on a new ghimpsuit.

The hull shook and a windy groan rushed outside the walls of Karr's quarters. More of Bob's doing, no doubt.

"Hang on," Karr said to the ship. "Just a few more minutes." He crossed the small hall and unreeled two hoses from the *fugue* purifier, a large, clear globe filled with fugueship blood. Multi-colored filter spheres floated in the vat, extracting and concentrating the vital fluid.

As Karr prepared to insert the hoses into his sinuses, inspiration struck him and the missing *how* of his plan to deal with Bob became clear. But it was risky.

Just then, the shower door mysteriously slid shut. The shower hissed. The door slid open again. A counter on the pill dispenser clicked down.

Bob had taken a disinfectant shower.

The airlock cycled him out.

Bob hadn't even waited for Karr to sleep this time. Karr felt violated. It was apparent that Bob could go wherever he wanted, whenever he wanted. No place in the fugueship was safe.

Karr bent over. The hoses went into his nostrils and his hand reached to open a spigot and start the procedure of dosing up. That uncomfortable necessity lasted another five subjective minutes.

Bob finished that day doing things to *Long Reach* that his friend Karr would not have approved of. Bob used the Gattler he took from Karr. A needle in a fuel bladder here, another in a flow constrictor there. Bob didn't know what he was doing, specifically, but he didn't care either. These tricks worked for Karr, so why not for Bob?

Besides, they were necessary. As Karr had pointed out, the shortsighted authorities on Evermore would not understand Bob's divine purpose. They would condemn him. They would lock him up. They might even hurt Bob, and that would never do. Authorities were to be avoided.

Bob slept again before checking in on his buddy.

Karr was *still* under the fugue purifier with the hoses in his nose. Bob twitched, recalling the icky rush of fluid through his own sinuses.

"You'd think they'd come up with a better way to do that," Bob said lightheartedly. "Ah, never mind." Of course *they* would not figure out a better way. Nobody cared about what he and Lindal had to go through.

"See you later, buddy."

Bob spent the next day shoving backstabbing bastards out through the airlock. *The backstabbers thought they had the last laugh on Bob, but they were wrong.* Trip after trip went by, carry a load out, eject, and return for more. *It was Bob who laughed the loudest.* Once in a while, Bob took a break, to rest in his empty fuel bladder hideout. Items pilfered from storage made a jumbled nest around his bed mat. At these times Bob's mind would race, like a rodent retracing the same maze over and over.

Bob remembered Sheldon's World. He remembered the coming Armageddon: a freak swarm of comets on collision course with Sheldon's World. He remembered thinking they would all die. But he also remembered his discovery . . .

They thought they were so clever. *They* thought no one else saw their plans to flee Sheldon's World and leave everyone else to fry or get squished. But Bob saw. Bob was a cargo boss at the time, restocking *Long Reach* with a crew of grunts, who worked in spacesuits to protect them from dropping into *fugue*-coma. One day when he was alone, Bob opened a bunch of crates and saw what was inside. Booty. Art looted from public galleries, hordes of precious metals and gems, storage cubes full of technical secrets that would set *them* up in style on a different world.

Bob kept this discovery to himself. No one willingly challenged authority on Sheldon's World. It was clean and orderly because laws were harsh and punishment harsher. The citizenry liked it that way, so twenty million pairs of peeking eyes kept a lookout for boat-rockers. Any revelation of what Bob knew would at best lead to martyrdom and Bob was not into that. So Bob did nothing until the day he fell and cracked his helmet.

To his shock, Bob did not black out as *fugue*-laced atmosphere hissed into his suit.

No one had to tell Bob what to do then. When *Long Reach* accelerated out of system bound for Evermore—a suitably cushy destination for fleeing cowards—Bob stayed on board. At first, he didn't feel much guilt over abandoning the rest of the planet's population to die, but about halfway from Sheldon's World to Evermore, when Bob knew beyond a shadow of doubt that everyone on his homeworld had been wiped out, he did begin to feel shame. After all, if he hadn't been so concerned with saving his own precious skin, he could have warned someone about what the backstabbers were up to. Bob began to feel cowardly and to despise himself. It was at this point that he began to idolize Karr, who was everything honorable that Bob was not. It was also then, between the stars and far from watchful authorities, that Bob stopped dosing up, dropped into slowtime, and began making a twisted penance for his sins—by shoving Karr's passengers out the airlock. Day after subjective day, week after subjective week, Bob's toil continued.

One day, some time after their chat in the dreamchamber, Karr surprised Bob by appearing on Wendworm Way, still as a statue, but with the concerted look of a man who has places to be and things to do.

Grinning, Bob poked Karr in the chest.

"Hey Lindal, you got a drop of *fugue* on your ghimpsuit." Karr did not look down as the joke demanded, but Bob flicked him under the nose anyway. Then he went back for another body, chuckling all the way.

Fourteen trips later Bob got bored.

Bob laid his present burden across Karr's arms and shoulders. The ghimpsuit fibers tightened up like muscles to compensate for the extra load. Bob knew that Karr's own muscles were of little use in fuguetime. Even in the relatively low gravity caused by the fugueship's deceleration, Karr could not support his own weight without the ghimpsuit. The suit even exercised his muscles with electrical charges so they would not atrophy in low gravity. It was an amazing piece of technology all right. Except for showers, Bob never saw Karr without one on.

Bob was only two times slower than realtime, so he didn't need a ghimpsuit to move around. Bob could talk with his own vocal cords and everything. Sure the ghimpsuit fabric also protected against foodyeast contamination, but it was hot and sweaty.

Bob smirked. It was kind of funny the lengths his naïve buddy went to decontaminate, when he, Bob, had missed several decontaminations and it hadn't affected him in the least. In fact, it had increased his mental capacity; it was only after missing the decontaminations that Bob got the fabulous connection between airlocks, the backstabbers in the dreamchamber, and what he could do with them in combination. Yes, that was when it all started to make sense.

Still smirking, Bob examined Karr's face. Bob had come upon Karr during a blink, so Karr's eyes were closed. With thumb and forefinger, Bob rolled one of Karr's eyelids open. The pupil did not register Bob. Of course not. He Bob, Avenging Angel, was far too fast for his slow friend. He let the eyelid go and it eased back down. Bob felt a fleeting pang of guilt, but it soon passed. Life on the fugueship was boring and Bob needed a bit of humor once in a while, even if he was the only one laughing.

Bob succumbed to another mischievous impulse, suddenly pursing his lips and blowing air up Karr's nose. Karr still did not move. Bob held Karr's eyelids open. Bob leaned in. Bob licked Karr's eyeballs. Giggles shook Bob's withered body. Afterward Karr was as unmoving as usual, no wincing, no flinching.

"You are such a good sport, buddy," Bob said. He tousled Karr's hair, picked up the dreamer, and continued with his angry task.

When Bob passed Karr on the way back, his friend was frozen in the act of rubbing his eyes. Bob giggled again. He just couldn't stay angry, not with a guy like Karr around to keep him amused.

Once out of his quarters, Karr never stopped moving, never stopped to tend the new wounds Bob had caused to his beloved ship, although it almost killed Karr to pass them by. Dreadful minutes elapsed. Karr knew Bob was messing with him. Karr's senses did register the unwanted intimacies, even if he could not see the perpetrator, but Karr bit his lip and pressed on, shirking off fits of burning in his eyes or sudden moist sensations in his ears. When a pair of his underwear appeared over his face like a deranged mask, he simply tossed them off. Nothing stopped Karr's inexorable progression of one foot ahead of another.

Karr turned onto Airlock Alley.

Now came the tough part of his plan. Karr had one shot at stopping Bob. If Karr didn't get it right the first time, there would be no second chance. A stiff weight in Karr's thigh pocket reassured him that the manual *qi* stick was still where he had put it. All the physical elements were falling into place. Now if Bob would just take the bait, and if Karr could only survive the upcoming mental ordeal. . . .

Bob shoved the last dreamer into space long before Karr made it to the airlock. Bob slept (in Karr's bed), masturbated (wearing Karr's underwear), then spent several frustrating hours shooting needles into various parts of *Long Reach*. The fugueship wasn't doing what Bob wanted. The more needles he shot, the less result he got. Bob had a temper tantrum, slashing and stabbing *Long Reach* until the ship shook with pain around him. That would teach the stupid beast. Panting, Bob sat down and congratulated himself into a better mood. After all he had a lot to be proud of; all the backstabbers were gone. All of his problems were solved.

All except one.

There was one more body to heave out the airlock: Karr's. Karr was a really great guy; Bob loved Karr, but Karr was misinformed. Karr gave his loyalty to the wrong people. Just look what Karr went through for *them*: the endless workload, the fuguing up, the decontaminations. Bob had to admit that no matter how much he liked his buddy, Karr was not on his side. When they reached Evermore, Karr would turn Bob in to the authorities. That was certain. It tore Bob's heart out to think it, but his buddy had to go. Bob procrastinated a few hours, but the prospect of killing Karr only grew more intimidating, so he reloaded his stolen Gattler and set off to find Karr.

Karr had made it all the way to the "malfunctioning" airlock when Bob caught up with him. Karr's motionless body was poised halfway through the open inner iris-portal.

What was his friend up to? Bob stepped around Karr and entered the lock to get a better look.

Karr's eyes were almost closed, or just opening, and showed only the merest of slits. In one hand Karr gripped what looked like a long, thin ice pick. In the other was the mindercard, held up for Bob to read. Bob didn't want to read the message. It probably said something really nice and that would make killing Karr all that much harder. But Bob was so starved for conversation that he couldn't resist leaning in for a peek.

Bob read aloud, *"I'm sorry, Bob; but I have to kill you now."*

Bob couldn't believe his eyes. Surely his buddy Karr had not written that! Bob double-checked. "You have to kill me now?" That's what the words said, plain as the stars in space. It irked Bob. *"You* have to kill *me* now?" With rising anger Bob realized he had been betrayed, again. First the backstabbers and now his friend.

"What are you going to do, poke me with that hop-stabber?" Bob circled, venting. "You can't kill me. I can kill you, but you can't even think of killing me. You can't even see me!"

To prove his point, Bob pranced like a boxer, jabbing Karr in the ribs with the butt of his stolen Gattler. Ghimpsuit fibers tightened up, absorbing most of the impact.

"Do you like it? You do? Good, because I can do this all day long." Bob jabbed Karr again. "All day long—you traitor! I don't need you anymore. I figured out this Pilot-stuff. I can do it myself!" Bob worked himself into a frenzy. It was okay for Bob to plan to kill Karr. That was just necessity, but for Karr to contemplate killing Bob, that was far different. That meant Karr wasn't Bob's friend and that really hurt. No one ever liked Bob. Everybody dumped on Bob. Bob felt powerless when people dumped on him. "Where do you get off screwing me? After all I did. I kept you alive!"

Bob blustered in front of Karr. Bob should have killed Karr right away, but Bob was a coward. Bob needed an excuse.

"Come on statue-boy, I'll stand still." Bob stopped jumping around. "Take your best shot.

"Come on!

"What's the matter?

"Afraid?"

Bob ranted as minutes ticked by.

"Hurry up you bastard! I'm waiting for you!"

Imperceptibly at first, then ever so slowly, Karr drew back the hand with the ice pick, readying to plunge the steel spike into Bob's heart.

"That's it. Here I am!" Bob challenged.

He waited for the pick to start back down. He would wait until it almost reached his chest, then nail Karr with the Gattler, crucifying him to the walls of his own precious fugueship. Bob was in control and he reveled in it, like a starving man revels in cookies. It never occurred to Bob that he was in danger.

That's when Karr sprung the trap.

To Bob's horror, the pick suddenly plunged down with deadly speed. Bob raised the Gattler to block, but the blow was not aimed for him. Karr's arm sliced past Bob, stabbing the *qi* pick into a critical nerve cluster in the wall.

Karr was not *fugue*-saturated!

Karr winked victoriously. His slow movements had been an evil masquerade to catch Bob off-guard. Bob realized the trick as Karr kicked off of Bob's chest, falling back inside the ship. The inner door irised shut. Bob heard a building, rushing scream behind him, felt tearing wind and biting cold as he was sucked back and pitched out of the growing aperture in the outer airlock door. He clutched at the wrinkled skin, but it was too late. Bob shot free of the lock amid a spray of ice crystals, flash frozen from moist atmosphere hitting the vacuum. Expanding breath ruptured Bob's lungs. Relentless, absolute cold froze Bob's eyeballs open. His last views, as he tumbled further and further away from the airlock, were of the spinning arc of bodies outside, which glittered against eternal night like a string of pearls.

It was a nightmare. A chilling, breathless nightmare that ended, not with a bang or a flash, but with a frozen-solid fading into nothingness, never to awaken. Just like all the others he had killed.

*   *   *

Karr reclined on a seven-yard-wide dome of cerebral cortex in
the brainroom, idly stroking warm pillows of tissue that puffed up
around him like a great feather bed. He stared up, unfocused eyes
not seeing the faintly glowing dome of cartilage overhead or the
blinking of human control consoles around the edge of the pear-
shaped room. It was this place that Karr liked best out of all the
places in the ship and it was in that strange position that Karr felt
the strongest bond between fugueship and Pilot. It calmed him.
And he needed to be calm, because the tiny human and the great
ship were in a lot of trouble.

It all centered around time.

Realtime. Slowtime. Fuguetime. How it slipped away, no matter what the subjective speed. How much had been wasted. How
much Karr desperately needed. How terribly little was left.

Karr was in slowtime. He had not dosed up on *fugue* after eject-
ing Bob from the ship, just as he had not dosed up after noticing
Bob take a disinfectant shower in his quarters. Karr had understood then that he could not fight Bob in the minutes and hours of
fuguetime, only in the seconds. And those were too few. But Karr
knew that if he got to Bob's speed, he had a chance. Karr had
pressed the purifier hoses into his nose and even opened the spigot,
just in case Bob was watching, but unseen in the palm of his hand
he held the hoses crimped so that no fluid made the journey
through his head. By the time Karr left his quarters he was dropping out of fuguetime. Soon he was suffering the agonies of withdrawal from one *fugue* state to another. By the time Karr met Bob
at the airlock, they were moving at the same speed. That had been
the really hard part. It took every ounce of concentration Karr
could muster, but he waited, holding himself immobile—difficult
even in the low gravity and with the ghimpsuit's aid—praying that
his opportunity would come before Bob caught on to the ruse.

The extermination had gone off like clockwork. Karr had won.
Bob had lost.

Sort of.

Accusing voices rang in Karr's head.

Protect the ship. Keep the ship alive. It was his duty. His foremost duty, excluding all others. *He must not fail.* Instructors had

hammered that into Karr at the Pilot Academy. *His primary concern must always be for the ship. Karr came second. Cargo, a distant third. Outside concerns, which did not affect the ship, did not even register as problems.* The instructors had gotten their point across. Horrible though the loss of thousands of human lives was, Karr was more terrified by *Long Reach*'s intensifying sickness. *A Pilot is nothing without his ship. If need be, a Pilot must lay down his life to save his ship.* Without fugueships humanity was trapped in the gravity wells of far flung star systems. Without fugueships there was no Colonization, no Destiny. There were only three of the cherished creatures left in human space. Soon there might be only two.

Karr's fugueship was dying.

Karr could barely bring himself to think the ugly thought. But the facts could not be avoided.

Fact: Bob had gone berserk with Gattler and *qi* needles. Hardly an organ, *qi* meridian or bone in the fugueship had gone untouched. Karr had hunted for and removed many of the needles that Bob had implanted with such callous abandon, but *Long Reach*'s condition continued to worsen.

Fact: Bob had damaged the navigation-lure in a crude attempt to change course. The remotes in the brainroom would take weeks to fix, weeks Karr did not have.

Fact: Bob had opened *Long Reach*'s aft engine orifices at right angles to its proper trajectory, which sent the titanic ship skewing off course.

Result: although Karr had closed the aft orifices and restored the proper flow of fuel from storage bladders into the fusion furnace, there was no chance of getting back on course for Evermore.

Fugueship trajectories built up from day after day, year after year of constant thrust. Before turnover from acceleration to braking, a trajectory change of four degrees was possible. After turnover, trajectory could not safely be altered more than two degrees. Bob, in his desperation to avoid judgment on Evermore, had opened up the reserve hydrogen bladders and attempted a course change exceeding thirty-five degrees. The mad maneuver was doomed to fail, except that *Long Reach* was now three degrees off course, sick, and plunging into deep space like an express elevator to hell. Karr had only enough reserve fuel to correct course one degree and still be able to brake when *Long Reach* dropped below ramscoop speed.

And, perhaps worse than all these physical difficulties, was Bob's final gift to Karr: the realization that it was all Karr's fault. Although rarely at the forefront of his mind, Karr was proud of being a Pilot. And not just a good Pilot, but the best Pilot. Together Karr and *Long Reach* had seeded more colony worlds faster and more efficiently than any other fugueship-Pilot combination. But now it was obvious that Karr was not holding up his end of the partnership.

He was a bad Pilot.

A good Pilot would have paid attention to the levels of disinfectant fluid and antifungal pills in his quarters. A good Pilot would have discovered Bob long ago and *Long Reach* would not be dying. It didn't matter to Karr that no one, not even his drill instructors, would have faulted him for ignoring a billion to one long shot. All Karr had was his duty. The precious moments of Karr's life, which others spent building the memories that make up a lifetime, Karr had spent in the fugueship, alone. Karr did not exist in the real world. There were no friends, lovers, family; they were dead or had never existed at all. What did Karr's life mean if *Long Reach* died?

Nothing. That's what.

It was worse than if he had never been born at all.

Karr closed his eyes and pressed further back into his bed of warm brain. He had to concentrate. Bob had shaken his universe, but Karr must not think of Bob. Karr had to solve this deadly puzzle and save his ship, before time ran out.

PART TWO

COLLISIONS

IV

Enclave of the Body Pure
Planet New Ascension
Seventeen years later.

It was a hopeful evening. The motion of the ground was a soothing wide roll, almost imperceptible. Jorjorra mounds sighed and divided, sighed and divided, piling up content and calm, like melons, and warm breezes caressed clouds of petals down from blooming sailtrees. The darkness, usually full of fear and misgiving, seemed that night to wrap the ring-island and its inhabitants in sheltering arms.

A heavy duty crawler lumbered through this unaccustomed serenity, an overgrown scarab, but with six immense studded wheels instead of insect legs. Electric motors whined as it rolled along a rutted track. A one-man cab, its doors long since removed for ease of use, perched at the front of the vehicle's flat deck. Inside, a teenage-looking Jenette Tesla worked the control levers, her lithe body taut on the seat. Keen blue eyes peered past bobbed hair—which was a light gray, almost white, blonde, marking her as a second generation colonist—and she wore a one-piece daysuit the color of scorched sand. Beside her on the engine cowling sat the predatory silhouette of a Khafra, its dagger teeth glinting in pale dashboard light.

"Rickety-brick-house," said the massive alien.

Unable to feel hopeful that night, Jenette focused on the task at hand. "Rikit-a-brikhauss. No. Rikit—EE—brikhauss," she repeated.

Yellow starlights cascaded down flashbuds on the alien's bullet head. Jenette had said it right.

"That's what I would say," said Jenette. "Then what do you say?"

"Don't-touch-my-mustache."

"Arrou, will you please be serious," Jenette chided. "Your language is hard enough already."

"Easier this way," Arrou asserted. "Easy to remember funny rhyme." He looked down devilishly at her. "Don't-touch-my-mustache."

Jenette sighed and made a valiant attempt to wrap her lips around the alien words. "Din-tixss-ymisstash—"

"Don't-TOUCH-my-mustache," Arrou corrected, body pulsing with the Khafra light-language equivalent. *Flash, pop, sparkle, pop.*

Jenette was limited to the verbal version, and her vocal cords sounded nowhere near as windy and hollow as a Khafra's, but she tried. "Din-TIXSS-ymisstash."

Again, Arrou's head glittered.

Arrou was Jenette's bonded domestic of five years. Large and covered in black armor plate, Arrou had a stunted right forepaw from an injury when human Guards kidnapped him from the wild.

The crawler lumbered over a recently fallen tree; scavenger moss was already wriggling greedily over the windfall. Jenette turned onto a lane paved with roadwort tubers, which glowed golden yellow in the crawler's headlamps. She had been driving clockwise along the ring-island, now she steered into the residential area of the Enclave, inward from its bastion-like perimeter walls. The crawler's hollow wheels rattled on the faux-cobblestone surface.

"Oh great," Jenette grumbled, shifting the vehicle into its low power range. Colonists, unaccustomed to the feeling of well-being that night, had come out of their domiciles to stroll stiffly down the road with their domestics. All of them were moving in the same direction as Jenette, blocking the road. It was impossible to drive faster than a slow amble. "I should shut down. We could walk faster."

Arrou cocked his head, contented waves of green fading from his flashbuds. "Leave crawler?"

"Yes, you lazy Khafra, leave the crawler."

"But crawler good." It was a quirk that domestic Khafra could run a string of human words together in rhyme or play-song, but could only speak simple sentences in regular conversation. "Crawler fast."

"It's not that fast," Jenette snapped as the foot traffic increased. They passed a team of domestics repairing a pothole in the road-wort. The aliens doused damaged tubers with silvery seawater from backpack tanks and then injected immune venom through their long teeth. In response, the tubers grew with visible speed, dividing and swelling like cells reproducing in a petri dish. The hole would be filled in under an hour. Jenette didn't care. Rapid plant growth was commonplace on New Ascension, unlike the traffic. Frustrated, she let go of the drive levers and fidgeted as the crawler idled along.

"Practice more words?" Arrou offered.

"No. My brain hurts."

Jenette steered the crawler around a large group of colonists. She was just about to shoot them a reproachful glare when she suddenly focused instead on two figures farther up the road. "Look," she hissed to Arrou. "Halifax and Luca. Did we get them yet?"

"Not yet," said Arrou.

The crawler crept up behind two humans with appearances in stark contrast to one another. The first was a short, blocky man who filled a simple olive-drab uniform with muscle. His leathery hands and face were scarred from seventeen years fighting the Feral Wars. The other human was a slim dark woman with handmade resin jewelry adorning Consul robes. They stepped aside for the crawler to pass and their domestics did the same.

Jenette stopped beside them, apprehension stiffening her back. "Colonel Halifax, Consul Luca," she said with forced cheer. "Care for a lift?"

"Don't tempt me, young lady," Taureg Halifax said in a coarse bass. "Got to keep these bones of mine moving or they'll seize up."

Consul Prahara Luca shook her head politely. She was one of the lucky few who still responded to hormone inhibitors at the age of twenty-nine and she still had the soft, healthy skin of a preadolescent. Colonel Taureg Halifax, on the other hand, was old. Jenette was both fascinated and repelled by the furrows scoring his brow and the wrinkles bunching at the corners of his eyes, nose, and mouth. Halifax was at least forty, maybe forty-five. Jenette tried to imagine being that old, how it would feel to move around in all that worn-out flesh, but it was hard. There were only three ancients like Halifax left on New Ascension. The majority of New Ascension colonists, like those blocking the road, appeared adolescent by outworld standards. Jenette was reminded that the hormone inhibitors, which kept them immature and turned all their hair the omnipresent blond-gray, had stopped working for her two years ago. Now, at the age of twenty-three, Jenette's body was blossoming into the deadly curves of an outworlder at the age of fifteen. She hoped to live as long as Halifax, but it was not likely.

Arrou sparkled staccato bursts of light at the domestics paired with the soldier and consul. Halifax's domestic, Patton, sparkled back. Luca's looked the other way.

Halifax squinted good-naturedly. "Damn flashers never get tired of that, do they?"

"Not as far as I know," Jenette said, careful not to react to the wink Halifax shot her way. "See you in Chamber."

Halifax groaned. "Don't remind me."

Jenette drove away, whispering to Arrou. "Did they get it?"

Jenette was referring to the domestics, not the humans. Out of the three thousand human colonists on the island, only Jenette knew more than a few words of Khafra language, but the lightcode had been too fast for even her to follow.

"Got it," Arrou confirmed.

"You explained that I want to set the plan in motion?"

"Yes, explained."

"And you explained about sending the envoy and how important it is for them to pass the message on to their humans?"

"Urr, yes, yes." The alien rolled his bulbous eyes. "Explained many times."

"All right, sorry," Jenette said, apologetic, but also relieved. "I know I'm on edge. You know how important this is. Anyway, you're doing good work. Great work. Keep it up."

Jenette twisted her head around. By the look of the colonists behind them, Arrou's secret communications had gone unnoticed yet again; certainly Luca had not suspected anything.

Jenette edged the crawler further up the road. It was still crowded and very slow going. "We should walk."

"Not do pickup?" Arrou asked.

Jenette's spirits sagged once more and her nose crinkled as it often did when she was in thought. The pickup. It was the reason Jenette had requisitioned the heavy vehicle in the first place and she wasn't looking forward to the task.

Jenette maneuvered between the colonists on the road and their dwellings. The spun ceramite structures were yellowed with age, but well cared for and nestled cozily in domestic-tended creepers, vines, and hedges; domestics carefully controlled the rapid growth of all plant life on the ring-island, including food crops, roadwort, and even the island itself. Buildings not made of outworld materials were constructed with sheets of domestic-grown fiber laminates, which gave the Enclave a distinctly organic, frayed look.

Many of the dwellings were empty that night, those who normally hid within being outside and headed for a cottage at the far end of the tree-lined lane. Colonists stood alone or in groups around the cottage, bathed in warm light pouring from its windows. Heads were bowed, fists stacked reverently over hearts. Without thinking, Jenette made the same gesture, and then cursed under her breath. *Insidious conditioning.* Conform or be absorbed.

She drove around to the rear of the house, out of sight, shut down the crawler's drives, and climbed down to the ground. Arrou hopped off the generator cowl and followed her up to the back door, his stunted forepaw not slowing him down at all.

Jenette knocked. Claws clattered inside. Arrou flashed and light flashed back from behind frosted glass.

"Hello Arrou," said a voice. A domestic slid the squat door open. "Hello, Jenette."

"Hi, Rusty," said Jenette.

The aliens flashed some more. Arrou streamed out the secret code patterns. *Poppata-pop-flash-sparkle.* Rusty responded just as fast.

A big, full-grown man with an honest, weary face appeared and bent low under the door. "Subconsul Tesla." Burke Hedren was in charge of Enclave Agriculture. His callused hands shook Jenette's warmly. "It's good to see you."

"It's good to see you too. How is the miracle coming?" Jenette asked.

"Fine," Burke answered with a backward glance into the cottage. Through a distant bedroom door, Jenette caught the briefest glance of a sleeping, pregnant woman. "Mother and all four babies." Burke grinned. "At least that's what Dr. Marsh said at the last hyperscan. I just wish the little beggars would hurry up. Everyone wants it to happen soon." Burke waved his hands toward the crowd out front. "And I guess not just me and Panya." Burke sighed. It was not like the large man to worry, but there were bags under his eyes.

"I could ask the gawkers to give you some space," Jenette offered.

"Naw, it's good for morale. Besides, Panya kind of likes the attention."

Jenette *just bet* Panya liked it, but bit her lip out of consideration for Burke. Not because he was a full-grown man instead of a hormone gelding, but because he was a nice guy who, for no reason Jenette could fathom, loved his wife, Panya.

Always polite, Burke stepped aside. "Please, come in."

"Can't," said Jenette. "Official business."

Burke's gaze darted to a shed out back. His face fell. "I almost forgot."

We all feel the guilt, Jenette thought. No one escaped it. That's why the first pregnancy in ten years was such an event. It was a hopeful sign.

"I'll help," Burke said simply.

They walked silently to the shed, part ceramite and part domestic-woven hedge walls. Jenette guessed its original intent was to house livestock, but no indigenous domesticated animals liked to live indoors and no outworld livestock had survived the Scourge.

Lying on a bench inside was the latest victim of Scourge.

Wrapped in a plain fiber shroud lay Burke's domestic, Trum. Creamy folds outlined a hardened Khafra body. Arrou helped Burke and Rusty carry the cold parcel. With the greatest respect, they laid it on the back of the crawler.

Jenette had watched similar scenes a thousand times. The shroud was crude, but lovingly stitched by Burke himself. Unexpected to Jenette were the bulges on Trum's bullet shaped face. Burke had placed two coins over Trum's eyes. *Ship metal coins. To buy his way into heaven.* It was strictly forbidden. On an ocean planet, the destruction of any kind of metal was unthinkable. Not only that, but her father's policies condemned any sort of burial ceremony for nonhumans, so that the colonists would not become *attached.* Most colonists went along with the heartless edict because of their pathological need to deny how they survived on the suffering of others, but not Burke. Jenette marveled at his defiant gesture.

The big man stood by the body. There were traces of blue-black stains on his neck, Jenette noticed. Stains that would not scrub off. And there were gouges on his arms.

"Rough Sacrament?" she observed.

Burke nodded, clutching the fabric of the shroud, not wanting to let go. "The restraints broke. Wasn't his fault."

Jenette nodded. "Of course it wasn't. . . ."

Silence for a while, and then:

"Why do you do this?" Burke asked. "I couldn't."

Jenette shrugged.

Burke persisted. "The dead ones aren't even part of your job."

Jenette shrugged again. "I drop them off. I pick them up. It's not a big deal." That was a lie. The truth was that Jenette made herself do it, no matter how hard it got. The problem would not get any better if she looked the other way.

Burke's lip quivered. "Good-bye, Trum."

Jenette studied the sky, embarrassed by the big man's grief.

When the tailgate closed, she looked back. "Come by the nursery tomorrow and pick up another domestic."

Burke was confused. "But you already gave me a . . . new friend for Rusty."

"Not for you, for Panya."

Burke was more confused. "But Panya doesn't need another domestic. Tengen's only on his first Sacrament."

"Don't argue," Jenette scolded. "This guy's the pick of the last raid. It won't hurt anyone if he doesn't enter the cycle for a while."

"Feral strong," Arrou agreed. "Bright light."

Burke began to see what Jenette was up to. "If he's so strong, there must be higher-ups in line."

"Screw the higher-ups. I don't see them pregnant." A lot of risk went along with having children on New Ascension. "Panya needs this Feral more than anyone else. His immune rating is very high. First Sacrament should be twice as strong as normal. Panya gets him."

Overcome with emotion, the big man scrubbed an arm over his eyes. "We owe you so much. I don't know how we'll ever repay you."

"You'll repay the whole Enclave with those babies."

"Panya and I were afraid to even try before you helped——"

"I don't want to hear it," Jenette cut in.

"But it's important," Burke persisted. His voice lowered and his hands clamped around Jenette's thin arms. "I want you to know *I'm going.*"

"Burke," Jenette hissed, "not here!" She looked around. Fortunately, no one could see them.

"I want you to know that," he insisted. "I'm going with the envoy."

"No you're not," Jenette insisted back. "Panya's not going and you're not going either. You're going to be a father any time now. End of discussion."

A importunate voice from the house cut further argument short. "Burke? Burke?" it called. "Where are you? I need you."

"Coming," Burke called. Then to Jenette, "Whatever you decide. You can count on me." He hurried into the house. Rusty followed.

Shortly, Panya Hedren came out of the house wearing Burke's sloppy big boots. She was a rare quantity on New Ascension, just like her husband. Panya was a fully matured woman, even though she was the same age as Jenette. Womanly curves filled out Panya's short nightgown. Her bosom protruded, ripe and full. Her hips swayed, seductive and hypnotic. Lately, everything swayed and protruded more than normal due to the enormous distention of her pregnant belly. Panya got a lot of attention because of her good-looking body—and the danger that went along with it. Jenette felt distinctly boyish in comparison and Panya never let her forget it.

"Panya," Jenette said, "should you be out like this?"

Panya tossed her hair haughtily. "I never felt better, Jinny."

Jinny. Jenette gritted her teeth.

"Here," said Panya, "this is yours."

She handed Jenette a little black book. It was a stimpaper collection of Jenette's private prose—erotic prose. Jenette never intended it for public scrutiny. But, as dangerous as pregnancy was for females on New Ascension, the fluctuating testosterone levels associated with sexual activity were even more dangerous for males. Any change in the level of the hormone could trigger the onset of Scourge, and that knowledge often had a stifling effect on the male libido. In a concession to the greater needs of the Enclave, Jenette had loaned the book to Panya when she and Burke initially had trouble conceiving.

Panya's lip curled, ever so slightly. "I found it . . . innocent."

Jenette fumed at the jibe. Panya had conceived within days of borrowing Jenette's book. The *innocent* material must have had some effect.

"I made some notes," Panya continued, "to race it up a bit. Of course there's no way *you* could have known, but that kind of stuff is what really gets a man going."

The self-inflated, nose-in-the-air bitch had written in Jenette's book. Jenette wanted to strangle Panya. The more Jenette bent over backward to help Panya, the worse Panya behaved in return.

Jenette did not understand it, but she reminded herself that Panya's arrogance was the very reason why she had risked a pregnancy in the face of such deadly odds. She simply did not believe she could die. Jenette, and every other New Ascension colonist, envied her that.

Jenette bit her lip. "Thanks."

Panya preened. "Thought I'd give you some pointers, for the future."

Tengen, Panya's present domestic, had followed her out. He exchanged strobing signals with Arrou.

Panya shielded her eyes. "Stop that! It gives me a headache." Tengen obediently went dark. "Burke told me about the new domestic. He'll be flashing day and night," Panya complained. "I'll dust off the prod."

"He won't need the prod," Jenette said quickly.

"I always use a little prod at first," Panya intimated. "Lets them know who's boss." Her eyes skirted Trum's body on the crawler. Jenette didn't notice any sign of emotion.

Two more Sacraments would find Tengen wrapped in such a shroud. The new domestic would then advance to go through Sacrament with Panya. The cycle of exploitation would continue.

With Jenette aiding and abetting.

Panya winced sourly. She clutched her abdomen.

"Are you all right?" asked Jenette.

"Oh, fine, fine," Panya said suddenly sweating, but trying to keep a proud face. She glanced at the cottage. "I better get back. Just in case I need to use the personal, for the twelfth time today." With an affected wave of her wrist, she waddled hurriedly off. "Bye."

"Bye." Jenette climbed into the crawler, generally disgusted with recent events. "Come on, Arrou. We're going."

Arrou hopped up to his place on the cowling. Jenette powered up and cranked the drive levers hard over. The crawler pivoted, right wheels going forward, left wheels backward, and then lurched into forward motion. But Jenette heard a telltale *clink* and stopped. Reaching back, she examined Trum's shroud. The coins had fallen together because of the vehicle's jostling.

Jenette adjusted the cloth so that the coins did not show and drove away.

The crawler idled. The fork to the left led toward the inner edge of the ring-island and the incinerator. The fork to the right led to the political center of the Enclave, the great hall, and someone Jenette had skillfully avoided for weeks.

Her father.

A confrontation was coming that Jenette longed to avoid. She had hoped that the triumph of Panya's imminent births would lessen the mounting anxiety, but it had not. Rather, the meeting with Burke and Panya had crystallized Jenette's convictions— convictions that were diametrically opposed to those of her father.

The confrontation, of course, would center around Scourge.

Everything in Jenette's life revolved around that deadly pathogen. No plant or animal on New Ascension escaped its clutches, and she was no different. Every living thing on the planet was infested. And, eventually—short of accidental death, conflict, or suicide—every living thing on the planet would die from it. The Scourge was diabolical in its evolution, able to shift its own genetic code as needed to infest plants, animals, even nonindigenous humans. It could lie dormant for years, preferring to attack after its host had reproduced, almost as if it knew that a pathogen that drove its host to extinction would soon be extinct itself. The Scourge was why everyone took hormone inhibitors, to forestall the dangerous condition of puberty and the reproductive readiness that went with it. The Scourge was why the men around Jenette feared sex and the women pregnancy. It was a terrible burden to the whole Enclave. Jenette didn't think of it as a mindless microorganism, but as a malignant force, twisting her life.

Even the Khafra, the only life forms to strike an evolutionary bargain with the Scourge, did not escape its final victory. Feral Khafra bonded into pairs who exchanged immune venom at yearly intervals and thus ensured each other's survival; they lived healthy lives, but they all also died at forty years of age, without exception. Her father had discovered that cycle and struck a vile bargain of his own to keep the Enclave humans alive: a repulsive ritual called Sacrament. In Sacrament, humans took immune venom from force-bonded domestics. Because the humans gave nothing in return, the domestics succumbed to Scourge shortly after their third Sacrament. The colonists did their best to forget the yearly nightmare, but it was Jenette's job to place young Ferals—kidnapped from the wild because domestic Ferals did not reproduce—with human colonists to begin drastically shortened lives. So Jenette could not forget. And with each inevitable fatality it got harder and harder to carry out the assignments and pickups.

Arrou shifted, impatient for the crawler to move. "Sad?"

Jenette looked at Trum. "Yes. Burke and Panya will miss him."

Arrou's alien head bobbed, a gorget of flesh swaying under his chin. "Arrou miss too."

Trum's death reminded Jenette that she would soon be missing Arrou. They had gone through the terrible Sacrament twice already, the first time when she entered puberty at twenty-one, and the second time last year. The third time was due even as they sat in the crawler. It would kill Arrou. And the thought of losing him made Jenette very sad.

"Tears," Arrou said.

"I'm okay."

"No." Arrou was looking up at the night sky. *"Tears."*

Jenette followed his pointing muzzle. "A shooting star . . ." she gasped.

A tiny fireball burned its way across the heavens, tail streaming far behind. It seemed to hang, not flashing across the sky as it should have, but taking languorous minutes to pass overhead and disappear to the southwest. Jenette was no astronomer, but that seemed far too long a time. Also, she noted, the crawler's compass was acting up, slowly turning in lock step with the shooting star's passage and then whipping back to true magnetic south when the red plume finally disappeared beyond the horizon.

"Sign," Arrou pronounced cryptically. "Burning Heart comes."

Jenette did not believe in signs, however strange, but she knew it was time to make a decision. Each of the many pickups she had made was a dry run for Arrou's death. At first it had been two years away, then one year, then months and weeks, and now that it loomed like the executioner's ax Jenette knew she could bear it no longer. She steered down the right fork in the road.

"Where going?" Arrou asked.

"To talk to my father."

"Oh . . . talk about Arrou?"

Jenette put on a brave face. "Yes."

"Good. Ask if Arrou can drive crawler?"

Jenette sniffed. "You are so weird."

V

Aliens are raising my daughter, she and all the children born in the early years. An entire orphaned generation. And Jenette is an orphan too, but not because of the Scourge. My hands have done the deed. The Enclave demands every waking moment of my time. What will happen to these sons and daughters of our dream? I am an old man in a world of children and I fear the changing of the guard that must come.

—from the private journals of Olin Tesla

The great hall was a calculated, ostentatious display, even in the dark. Jenette's boots and Arrou's claws clattered on the shipmetal decking and echoed high in shipmetal arches; reflections of their very different bodies smeared across burnished shipmetal walls. The great hall was tooled out of a giant seed-colony container that had been strapped to the back of *Kismet,* the fugueship that had brought humans to New Ascension. It was their link to humanity's destiny and it was also the single greatest concentration of metal on a resource-poor planet. Portions were cannibalized as necessity demanded, but Jenette's father always made sure to loot unseen sections first. That way all who entered the great hall knew this was the Enclave's focus of power.

Jenette tensed more with each step toward the imposing double doors at the end of the hall. Arrou walked lightly, uneasy on the slick deck. They passed other grand doors leading to the grand dining hall, the records vault, the library.

Jenette jumped when the library doors groaned open.

"How's my fiancée?" a voice greeted. The shadow of a man

spilled across the hallway. No, Jenette corrected, not a man—a *hormone gelding.*

"I am not your fiancée, Bragg," Jenette responded dryly.

"Tell that to your father. In his mind it's a done deal." A too-handsome, too-young figure appeared in the doorway. Bragg was twenty-six, but would pass for fourteen on any other colonized world. He looked laughable leaning cockily against the doorjamb. "Why do you fight it? You can't win."

Jenette grinned. "Because I don't like you."

Bragg was undaunted. "What's that got to do with it? Didn't you hear? They made me head of the VF. You're the daughter of the Prime Consul. Together we could own this world."

Head of the VF had never been an important Enclave position. The Volunteer Forces encompassed policing, fire control, and any other emergency services that Halifax's overwhelmed Guards could not. In the past, leadership of the VF had always been handed from one Consul member to another, an expected civic duty, however inconvenient. But Bragg had changed all that, turning it into an influential position by the sheer force of his ambition—and he was not even a full Consul, but a Subconsul like Jenette. Unfortunately, Bragg's moral backbone was sorely lacking. Power was all that counted, a philosophy that Jenette despised, but she knew how to get rid of him. Jenette moved closer, well within the unspoken boundaries of his personal space.

Bragg froze, eyes darting over her body suspiciously. "What are you doing?"

"I was thinking." Jenette put her arms around his shoulders. "If you're my fiancée, then I should give you a kiss." She leaned in, lips parting seductively.

Panicked, Bragg broke free. "What are you trying to do, kill me?" You'll get my testosterone going!" He backed down the hall in terror that a fluctuation of his hormone levels would awaken the Scourge sleeping in his tissues. "You're out of control, Jenette. Your body's swelling out of control and it's affecting your mind."

"I'm not *swelling,"* Jenette shot back. "I'm growing into a woman. It's a natural part of life."

Bragg wasn't listening. "Look, I'm taking double doses of inhibitor," he prattled. "I'm connected. Maybe we can set you up and fix that, that—" he gestured at her chest, "—or at least stop it."

Jenette pressed what little cleavage she had together under her zipped-to-the-neck daysuit. "Breasts, Bragg. Women have these. *Men* know what to do with them."

Beads of sweat broke out on Bragg's immature face. "I've got to get out of here." He turned and quick-marched out the front doors, no doubt to take more illicit hormone pills.

Arrou, who had seemed oblivious to the sexual innuendo, stopped preening a glowbud on his haunch and rumbled in his chest. "Grr-hruuu. Funny."

Jenette didn't see the humor. Bragg's retreat gave her no sense of victory; he was the least of her troubles. She and Arrou continued toward the Chamber of the Body Pure. When they reached the grand doors, Jenette drew a measured breath. *Remember, be concise. Don't lose sight of your argument. And don't let him bully you around.*

Her father's bad-tempered domestic, Toby, lay to one side of the doors. Toby was the only domestic bigger than Arrou. Toby snarled. Arrou did not flash the secret signals to him.

Jenette reached for the entry cord, but before her fingers even touched the braided fibers, and before she was quite prepared, a remote latch *clicked*. The heavy doors swung open on silent hinges, revealing a circular chamber as imposing as the hallway was ostentatious. Jenette wanted to run. Fortunately, Arrou picked that moment to speak up.

"Break legs," he hissed.

"Thanks," said Jenette, some measure of courage returning. Holding her head high, she stepped through the portal.

Arrou remained behind. Nonhumans were not allowed in the Chamber of the Body Pure.

Jenette marched through a ring of desks. Each was constructed of spun ceramite with rich green fiberplast glazing. High-backed chairs behind the desks were matching in color, cut from hard wood, and highly uncomfortable on purpose; her father liked everyone alert and on edge. Engraved upon the Chamber's metal floor was a stylized spiral of galaxy arms, inset jewels mapping human worlds, mysterious old Earth at the center and the Zone of Interdiction around it. Jenette's desk was to her right in the four o'clock position. She toyed with the idea of checking it for official correspondence, but abandoned that charade. Those who came to the Chamber of the Body Pure after session invariably came to see the man in the raised desk at the twelve o'clock position. The seat of government was his private office.

The sign on that desk said, simply: Tesla.

No one mistook whom it referred to. When colonists said Tesla they did not mean J. Tesla, who was Jenette or Subconsul Tesla, and they did not mean H. Tesla, who was Helena or the deceased Prime Lady. They meant Olin Tesla, Prime Consul, the democratically elected leader of the New Ascension Enclave for the last twenty-three years. Those years had been good to him, his tall, brutish body becoming leaner—although no less strong and imposing—his icy eyes becoming sharper and wiser. When colonists looked at him they saw the man who had single-mindedly, and almost single-handedly, lead their colony back from the brink of extinction.

All Jenette saw was the overbearing tyrant who made her life a living hell.

She stopped before his raised desk, unsure of the next move.

Without looking up from his paperwork, Tesla stacked his fists over his heart. "The Body must be Pure."

Jenette went through the motions of stacking her own fists over her heart. "The Body must be Pure."

"Jenette," Tesla said, still not looking up. "Glad you could finally spare a minute. Come up and greet your father properly."

Jenette obediently stepped up onto the platform, walked around the desk, and gave her father a peck on the cheek. Order of dominance established, Tesla jogged a sheaf of stimpaper and slipped it into a folder. Jenette noticed another folder beside the first, with her name on it. No doubt it contained a litany of her recent transgressions. Ammunition to be pulled out and used against her.

"I don't have the monthly domestic assignment report," Tesla observed, picking that folder up.

"It's done—" Jenette began.

Tesla cut her off. "Then where is it? I should have it. The same goes for your evaluation of Ferals gathered in the last raid." Jenette opened her mouth to explain, but Tesla raised a finger, again cutting her off. "Never mind. I'm not interested in excuses. Just get me the reports. Oh, and . . ." Tesla used the finger to tap through several screens on a desktop mindercard. "Another problem: sixteen messages from Consul Trurl regarding the behavior of the new domestic you assigned. Get him off my back, would you?"

Jenette stewed a few heartbeats before responding. "Is that all you have to say, father? A reprimand because Consul Trurl is too lazy to train his own domestic?"

It was just typical.

"Trurl never votes against us," Tesla reminded sternly.

"And he never will," Jenette objected, "but I don't have the time to baby-sit him. In case you haven't noticed, we're just about to have the first births on this colony in ten years. Orchestrating that, in addition to my other duties, has taken every waking minute of my life for the last nine months. None of the other subconsuls put in that kind of effort. How about some credit?"

"You are a Tesla," the Prime Consul scolded. "I expect you to work harder and do better than the other subconsuls."

"And so that's why you second guess and subvert every decision I make?"

"I do no such thing."

"You do!" Jenette felt herself sliding down the slippery slope from reason to emotion. *This was not the battle she had come to fight.* But it was too late to put on the brakes. "I held those reports back on purpose. In fact, if you really want to know, I falsified them and I've been falsifying them for a whole year. You never would have let me place triple-A-rated domestics with the Hedrens. You would have played favorites."

"I do not play favorites," Tesla objected. "The assignments would have been made based on what is best for the Enclave. And I will not be spoken to in that tone, young lady."

"And I won't be patronized! If you don't like my performance, why don't you fire me and find someone else to do your dirty work? In fact, don't bother. I quit!"

"Don't be childish."

"Why not? You treat me like a child. To you I look fifteen, so you treat me like I'm fifteen. But I'm not! I'm twenty-three years old!" Jenette felt the flush of blood to her face. Why did it always have to be like this with her father? Why was conflict so inevitable? "The pills you made me take make me look like this, but that's not my fault. I'm an adult and I wish you would treat me like one. I'm not your little girl anymore!"

For some reason, Tesla looked sad. "No, I guess you're not, but we are a lot alike, aren't we?"

"We're not alike at all."

Tesla grunted. His weathered hands pulled a document from the folder with Jenette's name on it. He shoved it at her. "Here."

Jenette looked at, but did not take the official seeming piece of stimpaper. "What's that?" she asked suspiciously.

"What you wanted," her father replied, going back to his paperwork. "Your credit. You may not be performing to your full potential, but you are performing above average. Stimulating birth rate by manipulation of Feral placement was a smart idea. Wish I had thought of it myself," he conceded. "In any case, the punishment for smart ideas is more responsibility. I've decided you are ready. As of this date you are now the full Consul in charge of population expansion, in addition to your present duties. I've already informed the Body." Tesla shoved the document into Jenette's stunned hands. "The appointment is by edict. They can't object and you can't refuse."

Jenette's head swam with sudden, unexpected happiness. She could not believe it. Her father was actually rewarding her for a job well done? Nothing like this had ever happened before.

"And you can't quit," Tesla added, with the trace of a smile.

All thought of quitting was gone from Jenette's mind. *Promotion to full Consul. Wow.* "I don't know what to say," she stammered.

"Say nothing," Tesla said bruskly. "You earned it. You got it. Now just one more thing: you rescheduled your Sacrament. Why?"

Jenette's happy bubble burst.

"You thought I wouldn't find out?" Tesla probed when she did not reply. "I know everything that happens on this colony. I knew about the Hedren pregnancy despite your false reports, but I gave you some rope. I hoped you wouldn't use it to make a noose around your own neck." Tesla skewered Jenette with a frown. "I'm waiting for an explanation."

Jenette sighed. "As if you really wanted to know."

"Try me."

"All right," Jenette said, ordering her thoughts. This was the battle she had come to fight. She would never be able to muster the courage again, so she might as well have at it. In a calm, measured voice she began, "Sacrament is wrong, father. It's wrong to keep domestics as slaves. It's wrong to kidnap them from their parents and use them in Sacrament. It's institutionalized genocide and every citizen of this Enclave knows it. They bury their heads in the sand, but they can't ignore it. It's murder. In my opinion, if we continue to practice Sacrament, our colony will morally decay. It's got to stop."

There, she had said it.

Tesla's face twitched, but he did not fly into a rage. He put down his stimpaper stylus. "Domestics can't be *murdered,*" he said in an even tone. "They are a resource. They can only be *utilized.*"

"They are not a resource," Jenette disagreed. "Khafra are a sentient species. They think and feel. They have their own language and they have even learned to speak ours."

"Monkeys were taught to speak thousands of years ago on Earth," Tesla insisted. "That doesn't make them sentient. Are their thoughts productive? Do they write books? Do they make machines and colonize the stars? No."

"Khafra are not monkeys. It's wrong to kill them for our own selfish reasons."

"Survival," Tesla explained, "is inherently selfish. It is our most basic, selfish right. The Body of humanity has survived from savanna to continent, from planet to planet for millennia precisely because it is selfish. It is our duty to survive. The Body was seeded on this world to survive, no matter what the cost."

Jenette did not buy it. "Spin it any way you want. Sacrament is still wrong."

Tesla rubbed his eyes in frustration. "Why does everything have to be a crisis with you?"

"Because if it isn't a crisis, you ignore it!" Jenette said resentfully.

"We have to be strong, Jenette. You and I have to sacrifice for the good of the weak. I know you don't believe it, but I'm trying to keep us all alive. This road you're going down, it's a dangerous path. I've seen it first hand. I've allowed it to occur in the past and it always ends in heartache. Why don't you learn from my mistakes? Abide by the laws against becoming *attached*. They are there for a reason: because it hurts. That's exactly why you are avoiding Sacrament right now, because it hurts."

"Because it's wrong," Jenette corrected.

Tesla's temper finally began to rise. "Sometimes we have to make decisions that hurt. Sometimes we make a stand and suffer small pains to avoid greater ones."

Jenette crossed her arms defiantly. "I am making a stand. I didn't reschedule my Sacrament. I canceled it. I'm not going again. It's an abomination."

A dozen angry expressions played on Tesla's face. "You complain that I don't treat you like an adult, that I don't trust you with responsibility? What kind of responsibility is this?"

"The Enclave can't go on like this," Jenette said fiercely. "I have a plan—"

"I don't want to hear it," Tesla roared, furiously. "I have my own plans."

"The supply of domestics is running out. Halifax and I can't keep up with the demand. We must seek help to find a cure—"

"Silence!" Tesla pounded his desk. "I have been patient, but suicide is not an option! Not for you, not for anyone in this Enclave! This is the real world, not your childish fantasy. In the real world adults don't get to do what they *want*. They do what they *must*. If you weren't so selfish you'd see that this colony needs you alive, you'd see that I'm grooming you to lead this world when I'm gone!"

A water mug crashed to the floor. Father and daughter glared at each other.

"I don't want to lead," Jenette spat, refusing to break down and cry in front of her father. "I don't want anything to do with you or your power or your Sacrament. They make me sick."

Muscles flexed up the side of Tesla's head and he spoke through clenched teeth. "I'm sorry you feel that way." He hammered through the entries in his mindercard. "You are due . . . no, you are a week *overdue* for Sacrament. I waited for you to do the right thing and you made a fool out of me. That ends now. Tomorrow you go to Sacrament, either like an adult, or kicking and screaming, but you will go to Sacrament before the meeting of the Body tomorrow night. Do we understand each other?"

Jenette did not argue. What was the point? Battle lines were drawn and they were on opposite sides.

"I understand."

"Good. You and I will talk tomorrow, when you are in a more civil mood."

Jenette contemplated the coins in her hand, heat from the open incinerator warming her face.

Flames licked at Trum's shroud.

"Must be more," Arrou said.

Jenette nodded, catching the philosophical inflection.

Arrou asked, "What father say?"

"We're in trouble," Jenette answered. "We have to go to Sacrament."

"Urrr," Arrou rumbled thoughtfully. "Jenette needs Sacrament."

"Arrou, you'll die."

Arrou shrugged innocently. "Everything dies."

The alien's seeming indifference exasperated Jenette. "Do you want to die now?"

"No."

"Do you want to die tomorrow?"

"No."

"I didn't think so." Jenette clenched the coins until they bit into her palms. It had been foolish to confront her father. His response was preordained right from the start, but she had gone anyway, with childish hopes of—what? Conciliation? Compromise? What a joke! She hated how stupid she had been. Why couldn't she just write her father off, once and for all? Why did she have to keep trying? And why did it have to hurt so much? No matter, she told herself, her plans were already in motion. In a way, Tesla's ultimatum made it easier for Jenette, by forcing her resolve.

Jenette had seen too much death during three years as Subconsul in charge of the Enclave's domestics. Too many had died because of her decisions. Suffering might be the law of the jungle, but she was a sentient being, not a beast. Sentient beings could choose not to kill. Standing there before the flames, Jenette made a pledge that not a single additional domestic would die at her hands, starting with Arrou. She would not go to Sacrament tomorrow; Arrou would not die.

No matter what the cost.

Jenette threw the coins into the flames with Trum's body. When the cremation was over, she gathered the ashes into a jar and left with Arrou.

The incinerator was in an out of the way part of the island, surrounded by agricultural plots and hidden in a thicket of trees. Behind it was a secluded glade where no one came anymore. It was empty, as usual. A lot of flowers grew in and around the stripped hulks of crawlers and skimmers destroyed in the Feral Wars. There were even a few mysterious flitters, which Jenette had never seen fly. Nothing remained of the machines but inert composite-fiber hulls and skeletons. Everything useful had been stripped long ago.

The glade had always been a graveyard of sorts, but now it served double duty.

Arrou dug dirt away from the torpedo-shaped belly of an old, upturned skimmer. His paws opened a battered hatch, revealing a cache of makeshift urns within the hollow hulk. Jenette placed Trum's urn with the others, wrapped it in rags and wedged it in tight so that violent movement of the island during a storm would not shatter and spill the solemn contents. Then she cried, somehow still able to find tears even though she had placed hundreds of similar jars in the clandestine tomb.

As Jenette wept, a change came over the glade. What had looked like rocks or moss-covered vehicles magically transformed into dozens of Khafra gathered in the graveyard, sitting upright and still, like tombstones. They had been in the *empty* glade all along, of course, hidden by their ghostly chameleon camouflage. Their bullet heads bowed in silence; blood red spots flared from flashbuds on their foreheads, chests, and paws. Trum's urn in place, Arrou closed the skimmer hatch, reburied it, and glowed with the same alien stigmata.

After a while Jenette spoke. "Arrou, go keep watch." Arrou padded away. She looked upon the aliens gathered around.

Jenette's hopes hung on these ghostly beings.

These were the domestics Arrou had signaled with secret light-code messages earlier that day. Years ago, Jenette had taken the time to learn their language and in doing so she had learned a precious secret: domestics knew everything that happened on the Enclave. With the exception of the Chamber of the Body, domestics were everywhere and saw everything, every argument, discussion, and decision, no matter how small. Nothing escaped them.

During three years as Subconsul, Jenette had first tapped into that unplumbed pool of knowledge and then put it to use, using it to find other colonists who believed as she did, that Sacrament must end. To her surprise, it was not a small number. Many were scientists, disillusioned by twenty years of fruitless struggle to find a cure for Scourge, but most were just ordinary colonists who feared the tenuous balance between survival and disaster, and longed for a better way. None of these people could meet in person, but they could safely conspire through domestics gathering together for other purposes—a forbidden funeral, for instance. Any domestics taking part would be punished if discovered, but it was unlikely that authorities would suspect a more secret, underlying reason for the breach of Enclave law.

Tonight Jenette would put her conspiracy to the test.

"How do you feel?" asked Burke's domestic, Rusty.

Jenette stood, heart racing. "I feel, yellow," she said, carefully

choosing the Khafra mood color for excitement. But she could
have chosen gray, the color of uncertainty, or orange, for apprehension.

"Yellow, Jenette feels yellow," murmured the ghost army.

"My father made me a full Consul," she added ironically.

The domestics rippled gentle turquoise against the deep green
glade. "Good. Good. Full Consul good." They trusted her. They respected her.

"You all understood my question?" Jenette asked, referring to
the content of Arrou's surreptitious flashing that day.

"Question asked," they domestics replied. "And understood."

"Then what is the answer? Who supports peace with the
Ferals?"

The glade lit up with the colors of unanimity. "Peace good. No
more Sacrament. Humans and Ferals fight Scourge together," the
domestics said.

Jenette held her breath. Of course the domestics supported
peace, their lives depended on it. Now the critical question, the
reason they were all there. "And which humans will join in the
envoy to go and make peace with the Ferals?"

The glade went dark. Not a flicker or a glimmer.

Only Rusty raised his head. "Burke goes."

Jenette shook her head, not feeling very *yellow* anymore.
"Burke cannot go." Jenette would not risk the father of the only
children on the planet, even if they were as yet unborn. She
searched the glade for any further glint of support. The darkness
was eloquent. "No one else will go?" Jenette said in disbelief "Not
one more human supports our cause?"

Reluctant tones were heavy on the glade and a voice called
from the back. "Not want to tell. Not want Jenette *blue*," it said,
using the human color metaphor.

"Not want Jenette blue," the others concurred.

"Never mind what color I am!" Jenette said. "Tell me what your
humans said."

And so the domestics told her, one by one, not meeting her eyes
and hating the words they spoke. "Kora supports Jenette, but cannot go . . . want Onos to go, but Onos not go . . . Prebecca sup-

ports, but not husband. . . ." Jenette's heart sank as the bad news went on.

She walked among them, hunting out a specific Khafra. "What about Dr. Yll?" she asked.

"Wants peace," his domestic offered half-heartedly.

"But will he go . . . ?"

"Will not." The domestic hung her head in shame. Jenette hung her head, too. Dr. Yll was the leader of New Ascension's scientists. If he would not join, then none of them would.

"Jenette blue," Rusty bemoaned and the glade went blue like a lonely midnight sky. It was hybrid domestic–human behavior; blue was the Feral color of serenity.

Anxious to please, Colonel Halifax's domestic spoke up. "Halifax will go, if Body votes."

Jenette touched his head gently in passing. "The Body will never take the risk, Patton. That's why we need a secret envoy to take a peace offer to the Ferals." Jenette felt certain that Ferals, as sentient beings, must want peace. And if she could get a promise from them to cease hostilities, then she could force the Body to vote against her father. Sacrament would end. The constant fighting would stop and things could really begin to change. That was what the whole clandestine domestic–human conspiracy was supposed to be about.

She stood dejectedly beside a decaying hulk. "What's wrong with us?"

"Domestics support Jenette," Rusty consoled, the others flashing agreement.

"No," said Jenette, tapping her chest. "What's wrong with us *humans?*"

There was no answer for a long time, but then a domestic said, "Humans fear."

"Safe to do nothing," added another.

Jenette shook her head in disgust.

A shy domestic named Bronte spoke up. "Bigelow says yes."

There, at last, was a ray of hope. Dr. Clarence Bigelow was a black sheep among New Ascension's scientists, but he was also smart and persuasive.

"Why didn't you say so before?" Jenette asked.

"Not want Bigelow to go," Bronte protested.

"It's your life at stake," Jenette emphasized. "Don't you want to stop the Sacrament?"

Conflicting colors played across Bigelow's domestic. "Yes, but not want humans to die," the alien reasoned. "Ferals demand humans stop Sacrament *before* making peace. That means humans die."

"Not if the Ferals help us find a cure for Scourge," Jenette countered.

"But can Jenette *guarantee* Ferals have cure?" Bronte persisted.

"No," Jenette admitted. "I can't."

Jenette believed Ferals had the knowledge, but she could not guarantee it. And that, she knew, was the reason her conspirators had deserted her. To stop Sacrament before having a cure for Scourge was to throw dice with death and hope you didn't crap out; her fellow humans were not willing to commit suicide for a cause, no matter how noble.

Jenette understood. She did not want anyone to commit suicide.

Jenette believed that the Sacrament must end or all human life would die out on New Ascension. Humans and Ferals had once existed peacefully. In the initial months after planetfall, before her father invented Sacrament and the Feral Wars broke out, colonists had begun to trade and share knowledge with the Ferals. That Feral knowledge of indigenous plant life had led human scientists directly to the discovery of the highly successful hormone inhibitors. But then had come two decades of war. In that time the scientists had still not discovered a cure for Scourge—and Jenette did not think they ever would without a greater understanding of the world around them. They simply did not have the ability to acquire such knowledge, not when no human could leave the battlements surrounding their tiny island without armed escort. Ferals, on the other hand, had been on New Ascension, watching and observing, perhaps recording knowledge, for a very long time. . . .

Without Feral help, it seemed clear to Jenette that humans would never find a cure for Scourge. They would continue to follow the same awful path of Sacrament. Inevitably a day would come when there were no more Feral litters to raid from the local area. Domestics would die and not be replaced and then humans would die, succumbing to Scourge one by one until there were no humans left on New Ascension.

But with Feral knowledge and human science combined, who could say how rapidly a cure for Scourge might be discovered?

Unfortunately, Jenette had no idea how her conspiracy, now reduced to a conspiracy of one, was going to accomplish these goals. It was a bitter disappointment.

"Go home," she said to the assembled domestics. "You have done your best."

By ones, twos, and threes, domestics flashed good-byes and filed out, vanishing into the darkness as magically as they had appeared. There was no question of the domestics forming an envoy. No domestic would leave his bonded human. Jenette didn't even stop Bigelow's domestic as the alien passed her by. She needed fifty volunteers; one, two, or three made no difference.

Jenette did stop Burke's domestic, however. Rusty had been taken from the wild at an older age than most of the other domestics. Pointing toward the world beyond the edge of the ring-island, Jenette asked, "What's it like out there, Rusty? Is there some sort of religious or cultural hierarchy among the Ferals?"

"Hierarchy?" Rusty repeated.

"Who runs things? How do Ferals know who's in charge?"

Rusty considered. "How *Jenette* know who's in charge?"

"Yes."

"Find light," Rusty said without hesitation. "Go to light. Most light rules."

"That's not very helpful."

The alien shrugged fatalistically. "Rusty knows. Rusty dummy."

"You're not a dummy. Don't say that."

He sat patiently as Jenette pondered. "More questions?"

"Yes," said Jenette. "What would happen to you out there? What would happen to you in Feral territory alone?"

"Alone?" Rusty said, puzzled. "Never leave Burke."

"I know you wouldn't," Jenette said, "but what if you did. Try to imagine it."

"Hard."

"What if you didn't have a human, if Burke was dead, and you were out there. Would the Ferals take you in?"

"Oh," said Rusty, suddenly sad at the thought of Burke being dead, but he tried his best to answer. Unfocused eyes searched back in time; to when he was very young and before humans kidnapped him from his native world. His colors became brighter, like the young domestics Jenette took care of in the nursery. His voice, when he spoke, sounded like those young domestics, too, "Pact not kill Pact."

"What's a Pact?" Jenette asked. "Is that what Ferals call themselves?"

"Maybe," Rusty said, the youthful glow vanishing. "Not remember."

"All right." Jenette scratched his head. "Thanks."

Rusty disappeared and, with a last look at Trum's tomb, Jenette left the glade too.

Whatever happened now, Jenette knew she was on her own.

Jenette walked around the front of the incinerator shed. Arrou was keeping watch from the driver's seat of the crawler. He hopped down and sat beside Jenette as she sat disconsolately on a stump.

"Meeting go bad?"

Jenette nodded.

What was she going to do now? She had not forgotten her pledge. No more domestics would die at her hands; Arrou must not die. But everything was turning against her. Her father, her conspirators, even the loyal domestic underground could not help. It all seemed so hopeless.

Jenette would have wept, but she was all cried out.

Arrou's eyes got big and his mouth pooched up sadly over his teeth. "Want back scratch?" he said after a while, paws shifting hopefully under him.

Jenette laughed sadly. "Not right now."

What was she going to do? With or without the help of her fellow humans, the Sacrament must be stopped.

After another while Arrou said, "Look."

For the second time that night, a shooting star streaked across the sky. It burned past the stars even slower than the first one had, in exactly the same direction and exactly the same path the first one had taken across the sky. What were the odds of that, Jenette wondered. A billion to one?

Jenette suddenly rose. She did not believe in signs, but if she did not act now, she never would.

"Come on Arrou. Let's go for a ride."

"Ride in crawler?"

"Yes, in the crawler."

"Where go?" he asked as they climbed up.

That was a good question. Jenette considered it as she slipped the vehicle into drive and followed a winding rut toward the mighty bastions which bounded the outer shore of the ring-island. She didn't actually know where the Feral seat of power lay, or even what kind of society they had, but it was out there somewhere and she was going to find it.

Jenette negotiated the crawler up over a mound of resin boulders. To her distress, when the vehicle's nose and headlights swung back down, the beams highlighted four startled Guards in a copse of trees. One of them, as wide as he was tall, staggered and fell across the rutted road. Jenette jammed on the brakes, cursing.

Of all the bad luck.

The other Guards rushed to their fallen comrade. Two were as stupefied as he and not much help. The third, a melancholy Corporal, stood at a wavering attention and barked at them. "Out of the road you Scourge-bait. Get out of the road before we pull shit shift for the rest of our lousy, short lives!"

Jenette relaxed, recognizing the voice, and leaned out of the cab. "It's all right, Corporal Toliver."

"Oh, false alarm," Toliver declared, slouching woozily.

The other Guards attempted, ineffectually, to get themselves into a semblance of order.

Jenette looked around to make sure no other Guards were in the area. There weren't any. And there were no domestics present, either. That was expected. Guards were under strict orders to keep their domestics locked in the military kennels, the theory being that that way Guards would not get too friendly with creatures they had to kill on a regular basis. Of course it did not work out that way, like all the rest of her father's hypocritical rules. The only practical effect was that because Guard domestics did not mix with the regular population of domestics, these Guards knew nothing of Jenette's underground conspiracy. Jenette knew them anyway. She had done them a lot of favors in anticipation of a time when she might need to be on their good side. Like, for instance, at that very moment.

"Jenette!" The three loudest Guards thrust their fists in the air. "Mook, mook, mook!" they roared in greeting.

"Shshsh," hissed Jenette.

The Guards fell shamefaced and silent.

One known as Skutch, an explosives expert, became overly serious. "You don't hate us, do you . . . ? We try not to hurt the little beggars."

"Yes," slurred Liberty, a musclebound female with a crew cut, all wide-eyed and weepy. "We really do. We don't even frag the big ones if we don't have to."

Like all Guards, these four were required to run Deep Recon Missions—a euphemism for kidnapping, as far as Jenette was concerned—into Feral territory to satisfy the Enclave's demand for young Khafra. It was a despicable practice, but they, like Jenette, were just trying to make the best of a bad situation. And, as Liberty had said, they made a particular effort not to hurt the young Ferals or kill their parents.

"Of course I don't hate you," Jenette said.

"Oh, good," said Skutch, greatly relieved.

"We're blasted," the square-built Guard said in an exaggerated whisper.

"Maggot, Maggot, Maggot!" the squad chanted.

"Grubb! It's *Grubb!*" the square-built soldier protested. The others chortled. Quickly forgetting the snub to his family name,

Grubb conspiratorially held up a flask for Jenette to see. "This is popskull."

"Really?" said Jenette, impatient to be gone.

"Yeah," Grubb confirmed. "Want some?"

"No thanks."

"Oh." Grubb considered, drunkenly. "Well, it's an acquired taste."

"Yeah," said Liberty, taking a long swig from the flask. "And we all acquired it!"

"Fuck, fight, hold the light, and carry out the dead!" Skutch chanted.

"Except no fucking," said Toliver.

"De-fin-ate-ly not," Skutch leered. "Fuck, drink, and be merry and tomorrow we *will* die!"

"Speak for yourselves, shitheads," Liberty taunted, good-naturedly.

"Rub it in, bitch!" the men retorted.

Strained laughter.

Jenette noted that one of the Guard's number was absent. "Where's Mok?"

"Standing graveyard duty on Gate Four," Toliver answered. "Stupid bastard."

"Dumb-ass, stupid bastard just about got us on shit detail, too," Liberty interjected.

"Got caught whacking off," Grubb slurred.

"No more monkey-spanking for him," Skutch agreed. "He's wearing the stiffy-detector."

In the uncomfortable silence that followed, Toliver dug a forgotten pill out of a small box and washed it down with more popskull.

"Limp noodle!" Grubb laughed. "Limp noodle pill!"

This time nobody else laughed.

Jenette didn't find it funny either. She put the crawler back in drive, "Bye guys," and applied power to the crawler's wheels.

"I got a limp noodle, too!" Grubb half-laughed, half-cried as Jenette drove away from the painful scene.

Gate Four.

Jenette steered for that remote post. Mok was there—sleeping on duty—but he woke at the sound of the crawler and let Jenette through the gate without asking any questions or recording it in the official log.

The gate ground open and the crawler rumbled down a ramp, out from the protection of the battlements, and splashed into the dangerous open ocean. The vehicle's six hollow wheels buoyed it up. The large studs on the wheels spun like paddle wheels for propulsion.

"Where do you want to go?" Jenette finally asked.

Arrou looked up at the sky, then down at the horizon where the shooting star had disappeared.

"Find Tears."

"Okay, find Tears."

Arrou was referring to the *Tears of the Burning Heart* or some other such Feral fairy tale and did not understand that the meteorite would have long since sunk to the bottom of the ocean by now, but Jenette supposed it was as good a direction as any. Expecting that they would find tears enough wherever they headed, she angled the crawler in the direction Arrou indicated and set it churning off into the night.

VI

*Pilot Academy transcript from visual recording, Planet
    of Industry, 6.17.3508.*
Document status: CLASSIFIED.
File name: Conscription.
> *(Five-year-old Lindal Karr, a soft-looking child,
> cries as black-uniformed men drag him from a
> faceless warren of domicile cubes. He has just
> tested positive for* fugue *resistance. His worker-
> class parents stand in the narrow alley watching.
> His sorrow-eyed mother shoes Lindal's five
> siblings back into the cubes.)*

Lindal: I don't want to go! I don't want to go!
*Father (hecto-carbon grime blackens an impassive
    face):* Don't be a crybaby.
*Major Vidun (a short, arrogant man, standing beside a
    windowless security transport):* You're destined for
    great things, Lindal. You're going to be a Pilot.
Lindal: I don't want to be a Pilot! I want to stay home!
> *(He reaches for his mother, but the soldiers hold
> him tight and load him into the transport.)*
> Momma!
Mother: Be a brave boy. Try to make us proud.
> *(Dr. Uttz, a thin old man, meticulously seals Lindal
> into a hermetic sphere. Lindal's weeping muffles.
> The transport doors slide shut.)*
Father: When do we get the money?

*Major Vidun (eyes narrowed with disgust): It's already
    in your account.*

Decades after Bob died, Karr was still fighting the madman's
deadly legacy. *Long Reach* shuddered as it ground against the
abrasive atmosphere of an unknown planet. The super-heating friction caused bitter squalls of wind to moan through the ship's innards. Gravity was askew because of *Long Reach's* rakish angle
relative to the planet below. The cockeyed g-forces pulled Karr toward the corners between walls and ceilings.

Karr scrambled along a fuel-bladder gallery, his adrenaline
pumping. Calling on years of training and experience to stay
level-headed, he carefully adjusted the Gattler to its slowtime setting and shot *qi* needles into the base of each bulging fuel-bladder
sack. Flow ducts swelled in response, like sausages, and carried
fuel out of the storage bladders toward unseen bilge-pores on the
fugueship's external flanks.

Must make one hell of a fireworks display on the planet below,
Karr thought. *The mother of all shooting stars.* Atmospheric friction would ignite the fuel into a long fiery tail. Not exactly standard procedure upon arrival at a planet, but then again this was not
exactly a standard arrival. If Karr did not get rid of the reserve fuel,
the whole ship might soon become a flaming smear across that unknown planet's sky.

It had all begun shortly after Bob's death. Karr had left the
brainroom with a plan to undo Bob's damage. Still aching from the
madman's attack in the dreamchamber, Karr had sidled through
narrowing passages, and then crawled on hands and knees as the
ship's internal spaces pinched together near its bow. Karr was very
close to *Long Reach's* fusion core at that point and it was very hot
as he squirmed toward the ship's forward-most airlock. Karr had
not dosed up on *fugue* yet; he was in slowtime, so he was getting
the most possible use out of each individual realtime second. On
arrival at the airlock, he donned a kilnsuit from a storage locker,
rigged pinch-cleats to his hands and feet, attached a descender rig

to his belt, and cycled through the airlock's standard double iris-portals.

Outside, it took a moment to get oriented. Karr clung to the narrowing shaft of *Long Reach*'s engine pinnacle, which projected down from the ramfunnel maw above, like a handle under a red-hot umbrella. Below Karr, pillars of fire erupted from four nozzles spaced around the tip of the pinnacle and thundered into a bottomless black void lined with stars. It was a daunting view. And the fact that the ship was braking, creating the dizzying sensation of gravity pulling Karr *down* toward that bottomless void didn't help matters. But between those engine nozzles, at the very forward-most point of *Long Reach* was where Karr's objective lay, and so he was going there.

Karr attached a safety line, set the torque on his descender rig, and went down headfirst. The initial hundred feet were easy, but as he neared the huge engine nozzles Karr was careful to set the pinch-cleats extra firmly. A slip at that point would have sent him careening out on the safety line and into one of the pillars of engine thrust. There, even the kilnsuit, with its ceramite tiles specifically designed to operate in extreme heat and pressure, would vaporize. Life support mechanisms labored hard inside the suit as Karr reached the narrowest point between the nozzles. A temperature sensor under his chin read one hundred and thirteen degrees internal. Karr didn't look at the outside reading. It was too scary. *Remember the ship.* He pressed on as fast as prudence allowed and disappeared under the very front of the pinnacle.

Karr's impression of being on the pinnacle's forward end was that of being a bug, clinging to the underside of a round table that had four immense pillars of flame for legs. Internal kilnsuit temperature dropped to ninety-three degrees—not much cooler, but at least he was not boiling in his own sweat. Crawling upside-down—again, like a bug—Karr made his way toward the only two features on the circular prow. The nearer feature was a rust-and-white colored metallic knob, two yards in diameter, which was one protruding end of the superconductor that generated the fugue-ship's ramscoop field. Karr ignored it and headed instead for the upside-down teepee directly in the center of the bow space.

It was, in fact, a tent of sorts. Karr pulled back a flap of its light-impervious material and uncovered a ten foot wide, highly reflective shallow bowl that was recessed into the body of the ship above. A ropy stalk grew down from the center of the bowl and that was capped with a torus of bug-eye receptors: it resembled a radio telescope dish. And that is what it was: a living telescope, *Long Reach*'s eye. Light bounced off the broad dish and focused on the receptor torus where different sensory organs responded to, and analyzed, different segments of the electromagnetic continuum: ultraviolet and visible light, radio frequencies and x-rays, red shifts, Fraunhofer lines, and probably a dozen other things humans hadn't discovered yet.

Left to its own, *Long Reach* would chew over what it saw, somehow pick a star, and go there. However, when humans first captured four adolescent fugueships feeding on Saturn's rings, three thousand years ago, scientists had quickly figured out the purpose of the eye-dish array and devised an easy way to trick the huge creatures into going wherever their would-be human masters wanted them to.

Karr called it the carrot-on-a-stick method of interstellar navigation.

Attached where the poles came to a point, on a remote controllable arm, was a translucent sphere that glowed warm, yellow light: the starlure. The starlure simulated types of starlight that *Long Reach* found irresistible. It was only about eight inches in diameter, but because it was so close and so bright compared to real stars, the fugueship inevitably preferred it and tried to move in the direction of the decoy star. Move the lure one way, and *Long Reach* went that way. Move the lure the other way, and *Long Reach* went that way. The blackout tent eliminated any possible distraction. It was simple and effective.

And thanks to Bob, broken.

Karr leaned in and pressed colored studs on the back of the crystal globe. Different types of starlight strobed in a test pattern. The lure itself was unhurt, but the articulated arm was jammed. *Long Reach* was mindlessly following a misplaced starlure into deep space. Karr knew that the regulation-approved solution for this situation was to fix the mechanism.

Instead, he pushed the mess aside.

Before coming outside, Karr had pored over star charts, searching for a new star to set course for, a star within one degree of *Long Reach*'s present disastrous trajectory, which also had a colony. According to the charts, half a dozen stars beyond Evermore were candidates for colonization, which lessened Karr's anxiety a bit. The human race was obsessed with expansion. If stars *could* be colonized, they *would* be colonized and there was a decent chance that another fugueship had already made a run through that area, planting colonists wherever it could. Unfortunately Karr's charts had been compiled a century ago by long-range observation; the slow speed of interstellar communication deprived him of more recent information about which of those stars now had colonies and which did not. Karr fretted long and hard. Any choice he made was necessarily a stab in the dark and an unlucky choice would find his beloved *Long Reach* trapped orbiting a star barren of planets, without even a gas giant to refuel from. That would be a death sentence.

So Karr removed the blinder fabric completely from the tent poles. He would not choose a destination at all—he would let *Long Reach* choose. Karr had great faith in the beast. It had a certain headstrong simplicity in the way it liked to do things: easily, directly and—quite frequently—correctly. Long ago Karr figured out that the less he fought its instinctual behavior, the better things turned out. And while no one had ever handed over the reigns before, whatever natural methods fugueships used to select a destination had to be better than Karr's wild guess.

He hoped.

For half an hour nothing happened. Karr hung from the cleats and forced himself to be patient. He patted the lumpy hide overhead. "That's all right. Take all the time you need." More time passed. Karr was looking down at the small slice of stars visible between shafts of engine fire and feeling the intense vertigo, when the living reflector dish flexed, then flexed again. It focused on one star, then another and another.

"That's it," Karr encouraged, fascinated. "Now you've got the hang of it."

Long Reach cycled through the candidates, narrowing from many to few. Eventually three patterns repeated. *Long Reach* pondered these for a long while, apparently confused.

"Come on, you can do it." Karr held his breath. Finally *Long Reach* eliminated one of the three. After that it didn't take long to make the cut from two down to one.

The eye focused and held in position.

"Yes!" exclaimed Karr.

He felt a gentle flexing of hide above him and saw a change in engine output. The nozzle orifice on the galactic core side contracted, decreasing that column of thrust, and the opposite orifice widened, increasing proportionally. *Long Reach* was turning. Karr did not let up his death grip on the pinch-cleats, but a small portion of tension relaxed its grip on his muscles. For better or for worse, his ship had made its choice.

The outdated star charts identified *Long Reach*'s selected destination as CG-423, a third-rate yellow sun circled by planets in habitable orbits. It was far beyond Evermore and would lengthen the remaining portion of the mission to seventeen years. Karr checked the radio waves for signs of a colony beacon. There was only static. So far CG-423 didn't sound great, but again he forced himself to be patient. Maybe a colony had recently been seeded there and transmissions just hadn't made it out far enough for Karr to pick them up.

With no further time trouble, Karr went back to his quarters and dosed up on *fugue*. After that, the years ticked off at the subjective rate of one per day. Karr fixed the starlure. He did not turn it on, but he *had* to fix it; broken things drove him crazy. After that he kept busy tending his ailing ship. He had become very attuned to its life rhythms over the centuries and those rhythms were far out of balance. Cycles of creation and destruction, which resorbed old tissues to make room for new ones, were fighting one another, new tissue destroying new tissue, old layering on top of old. Karr had never seen the likes of it. Entire regions were dying.

"We're going to make it. I'll keep you going," he would say, pouring his heart into his work and somehow he did keep the ship going during the seventeen-year detour, which was testimony to his skill as a Pilot, although Karr didn't see that in his self-recriminating mood.

When *Long Reach* slowed to the point that its electromagnetic ramscoop could no longer funnel up interstellar hydrogen and therefore switched to internal reserves, Karr's worries abated a bit. Operating long range interferometers from the brainroom, he identified several Jupiter-mass planets orbiting CG-423. And, CG-423-B, a small planet in the habitable range, showed spectra for nitrogen, oxygen, and methane, good indications of life. No beacon as of yet, but Karr focused on the good news.

Later, when *Long Reach* decelerated into the CG-423 system, Karr was downright relieved. There, nestling eighty-seven million kiloyards close to the warm yellow sun, was a silvery-blue orb flecked with white clouds. CG-423-B was a habitable world. Upon seeing it, no fugueship Pilot could pass by without planting a colony. Karr was certain of that.

Karr scratched the brainroom walls affectionately. "Excellent choice."

It was six realtime months to CG-423-B—twelve fuguetime hours—and they were a roller coaster of hope and disappointment. Karr was prepared to fight the ship's tendency to steer for a gas giant, as it normally did upon entering a new system; feasting upon ring belts and atmosphere, *Long Reach* was able to replenish stores of fuel, carbon, and other heavy elements. However, *Long Reach* surprised Karr by heading straight for the silver-white planet. Karr attributed the peculiar behavior to a symptom of its sickness and spent his time monitoring its condition and looking for signs of a colony.

There was a satellite in orbit around CG-423-B.

And Karr was not talking about any of the planet's four small celestial moons, but a man-made satellite—probably a weather-communication satellite. Karr had set them up for each of the colonies he planted. Another fugueship had been here. Good news. Unfortunately, the satellite did not respond when Karr interrogated it. More urgent levels of communication protocol all failed. Only Karr's own weak signal echoed back. Bad news. The satellite was dead. That meant the colony had lost the capability to service it. The only useful information to be gleaned from the dead satellite was the colony's probable location, which should be on the surface, directly under its geosynchronous position.

The day wore on. *Long Reach* closed on CG-423-B. Further instrument checks, between jaunts to dose up on *fugue* and decontaminate, picked up no signs of human activity. No beacon, no overspill of local transmissions, no ozone holes, no sparkle of light on the night side. Karr was disappointed but not really surprised. The legacy of human expansion to the stars was a legacy of hardship. A large percentage of all seeded colonies failed. There were famine worlds, war worlds, plague worlds, disaster worlds (like Sheldon's World), and a dozen other variations. It looked like CG-423-B was just one more failure among many.

This was not good news for *Long Reach*. In its present condition, Karr doubted his fugueship would survive another interstellar jaunt. With the help of a colony, it would take years of nursing and recuperation before *Long Reach* could refuel and brave the voyage back to Evermore. Without help, it might take decades or not happen at all.

Not long after discovering the dead satellite, Pilot Lindal Karr learned the problem with letting a fugueship set its own course.

The first indications of a problem occurred when he was in the brainroom. Karr felt a rumbling through the seat of his crash couch and a warning light blinked on the nav station, alerting him that *Long Reach* was adjusting trajectory. Perilous data spewed from a viewer. *Long Reach* hadn't set itself on just any old trajectory for CG-423-B, *Long Reach* had set itself on an *impact* trajectory with CG-423-B and was coming in way too fast. Karr would never dare to set such a course. The fugueship had nerve, he admitted, but he was not about to wait around and see if it made another engine burn to safely enter orbit later.

Karr sprang into action, initially trying to slow *Long Reach* down by activating the repaired starlure. He set it to maximum brightness, the idea being to fool the ship into believing that it was too close to a real star and brake harder. Karr also used remotes in the brainroom to move the lure across *Long Reach*'s external eye, but the deviations got bigger and bigger until it was a joke. *Long Reach*, it seemed, couldn't care less. Karr's dour expression grew more dour as none of the other simple options worked either.

In the blink of an eye, things had gone from not so good to disastrous. Karr was on a collision course with the only habitable planet within twenty light-years and in severe time trouble. He rebuked himself for not having enough foresight. If he had stopped dosing on *fugue* earlier, he could have reacted more effectively to the ship's errant behavior, but it was routine procedure to stay fugued-up until just before making safe orbit and Karr had followed that routine. So he was moving too slow to stop *Long Reach*. Karr needed to drop out of fuguetime before they plowed into CG-423-B and he needed to do it yesterday.

VII

Pilot Academy transcript, planet Solara, 10.21.3526.
Document status: CLASSIFIED.
File: Consequences 342.

> *(Subject Lindal Karr, aged twelve standard years,*
> *squares his shoulders and refuses to cry. Major*
> *Vidun stands facing Lindal, looking stern in the*
> *blank white room with rounded corners. Tall, thin*
> *Dr. Uttz stands compliantly behind Vidun.)*

Vidun: As punishment for allowing touch-contact with
> Dr. Uttz, you will study in solitary for the next six
> months. Lessons will be taken through indirect
> voice communication only.

> *(Lindal's cheeks redden, but he does not break.)*

Lindal: Yes, sir.

Vidun: If you apply yourself, study your qi harder,
> perhaps the term of punishment can be shortened
> by a month.

Lindal: Thank you, sir.

Vidun: Dismissed. Go wash your face.

> *(A hole appears in the wall. Lindal exits though it.*
> *Dr. Uttz shakes his head. Vidun is not apologetic.)*

Vidun: It is your own fault.

Dr. Uttz: It was a simple touch on the shoulder, no
> more. He did so well on the tests.

Vidun: You know the rules. Trainees are not permitted
> tactile human contact. This facilitates a bond
> forming between Pilot and fugueship.

Dr. Uttz: It is harsh.

*Vidun (irritated): Why state the obvious? Do you wish
    to undermine my judgment? Do you wish my
    position? I will gladly step aside.*

*Dr. Uttz: No, and no. But I worry. He has had no other
    contact for seven years.*

*Vidun: As you know, that is the regimen. We must instill
    a predisposition to shun human contact and bond
    with his ship. If he bonds with his ship he will
    naturally want to keep it alive—at all costs.*

*Dr. Uttz: But I worry. Such isolation can lead to
    abhorrent sociological behavior.*

Vidun: You are the expert. Should we be worried?

*Dr. Uttz (sighs): I suppose not. He has a great sense of
    responsibility. I suspect it is rooted in the belief
    that his parents sold him because he was unworthy.
    Each failure and hardship only strengthens his
    resolve to prove them wrong.*

*Vidun: Good. Mark my words, that boy will be the
    greatest Pilot humanity has ever seen.*

Dr. Uttz: If we don't break him first.

Far too late *Long Reach* altered course, making several destructive
braking orbits through CG-423-B's atmosphere. Unfortunately, by
the time Karr had endured deep-*fugue* withdrawal and could clam-
ber along the perilously tilted ceilings and walls in slowtime,
Long Reach was plunging into the planet's gravity well. Karr succeeded in dumping the reserve fuel, but he didn't have much time
left, maybe one orbit, maybe less, and then *Long Reach* would
break up.

Karr scaled gourds of suede-like tissue past his quarters and
back into the brainroom. He touched the cortex in passing. It felt
feverish.

"Hang in there." Karr strapped into the crash couch, which was
halfway up the wall because of *Long Reach*'s weird angle relative
to the planet below.

The human instrument panels painted a grim picture. Nav readouts were particularly harsh: there was no chance of stabilizing orbit and little chance of a soft landing. Karr should have run for the escape gig right then, but he refused to entertain such thoughts and again tried to correct *Long Reach*'s trajectory, but none of the standard controls had any effect. Karr tried harsher measures, activating a network of remotes that administered painful electric shocks to the ship's nervous system. He preferred *qi* needles hand placed in exact pressure points because they caused less trauma, but there was no time. Karr applied current, intending to open deceleration nozzles and control *Long Reach*'s headlong plunge.

"Brake, *brake,*" he urged through gritted teeth. Electrodes crackled, some right in the brainroom, but nothing happened. Karr increased power to maximum and repeated. Whiffs of scorched fat filled the air, but *Long Reach* stubbornly refused to obey its helm.

"Do what I say," Karr implored. "Please do what I say."

Vital seconds ticked off. Control panels went dead as their corresponding external sensors burned off in the heat of atmospheric friction, but Karr would not admit defeat. Grabbing his Gattler, he unstrapped and slid down to *Long Reach*'s brain. A twist of the selector rotated barrel three into position. Karr aimed the tool at the crenellated dome of gray matter.

Karr bit his lip. "Sorry. This is going to hurt."

It was the last thing Karr could think of. Jerks of his trigger finger shot sonic pulses deep into the fugueship's brain. Unlike human brains, which felt no pain, fugueship's brains were extremely sensitive. *Long Reach* moaned with each experimental shot. Karr could hardly bear it—*he* was hurting his ship—but he kept at the barbaric stimulation until finally locating a target neural cluster.

Engine thrum suddenly reverberated throughout the ship. Karr crashed into the foreword bulkhead as *Long Reach* finally opened its braking nozzles at full power. Karr was so happy, he hardly felt the impact. Climbing back up the wall to the crash couch, Karr made attitude corrections that he believed would increase the chances of a soft landing, but by that time all of the external sensors were burned off. Karr was flying blind with only his gut and inner ear to guide him, and those could be deceptive. A few minutes later, even blind flying came to an end; the controls gave out altogether.

Karr pounded the dash in frustration.

Why couldn't he stop his ship?

Karr felt a dizzy pull down and to the right. *Long Reach* was picking up a foreboding spin. Soon it would start tumbling and that would be the end. Karr gripped the controls, determined to ride *Long Reach* through the gates of hell if he had to, but in his rush to work the helm he had forgotten to strap in. A sudden tilt of the ship ripped his hands free and flung him across the brainroom. Karr got back up, fighting lurch after lurch and unable to regain the control seat.

It was as if *Long Reach* was telling Karr to get out.

"I won't!" Karr bellowed over the growing rumble. "Do you hear me? I won't leave! You can't make me!"

But it could make him. The lurching flung Karr around help-lessly. He could not get back to the helm and even if he did, *Long Reach* would not respond. There was nothing he could do. Nothing. It was a terrible, stark revelation for a Pilot. Like it or not, duty or not, feelings or not, it was time to abandon ship.

Long Reach was burning up.

Karr raced through the dreamchamber, grief tearing him apart. Wendworm Way had collapsed and the space between the inner and outer hulls was now the quickest way aft. Somewhere the hull was breached. Air howled around the kilnsuit Karr had scrambled into. Dream-capsule lids clattered in a gale spawned by decom-pression. Karr picked up Wendworm Way farther aft where it was not blocked, but where the walls had the alarming tendency to con-strict with each spasm of *Long Reach*'s pain, jostling Karr merci-lessly before he arrived under a metal hatch. A sign read: ESCAPE GIG. Karr wasted no time undogging the locking wheel, climbing up into a small, metal airlock, and opening the inner hatch.

Karr expected a view of the gig's interior, cockpit, seats, and overhead storage bins. What he actually saw through the hatch was a snapshot from hades, a gut-wrenching exterior view of *Long Reach* breaking apart. A blizzard of plasma-hot sparks showered over his fugueship. Flaming spirals of hide peeled off and streamed behind it like red-hot ribbons.

And the escape gig was gone.

Karr stood in a hatchway to nowhere, looking dumbfounded out of a gutted half-shell. The gig's other half and innards were missing. Strong winds tried to suck Karr out the opening as a massive fissure ripped open across *Long Reach*'s hull, splitting thick hide apart like a self-destructing zipper and leaving a raw, bleeding canyon behind. Shreds of hide exploded outward as the fault rushed at Karr.

"Shit," said Karr.

He slammed the outer hatch, spun the locking wheel, and then, punching an override code to open the inner hatch without waiting for recompression, dove back into *Long Reach*. A titanic concussion hit, smashing away the remains of the escape gig and the entire airlock, leaving Karr in a bloody foxhole, clinging to a large vein for dear life—and with an even better view of the destruction outside.

It was lucky for Karr that the gig had been moored aft. The turbulent eddies rolling across *Long Reach*'s stern were nothing compared to the pressure wave he saw spraying out from the fugueship's midsection bulge. Those mach four winds would have cut him in half.

Karr needed a new plan.

Salvation, it turned out, was a mere fifty yards from his foxhole, in the form of an ungainly craft with oversized thrusters at the corners of its wide cargo platform, four large robotic grapple arms folded underneath, and a chunky cab that seemed attached to its leading edge as a sloppy afterthought. That decidedly nonaerodynamic vessel was *Long Reach*'s heavy lifter, intended to ferry giant seed-colony containers from orbit to planet surface. It was not designed for high speed atmospheric descents and already showed signs of damage, but it was now Karr's only way off.

Problem: it was impossible to get to.

Karr could barely hold on in his foxhole. Walking or crawling in the intense winds was not feasible, even in the brief lulls when spiral eddies canceled out the force of the wind. Karr contemplated a desperate jump through one such a lull, using the suit's thrusters to propel him to the heavy lifter, but decided that he was only desperate, not suicidal. He would much rather stay with his ship than experience a long, drawn out plunge to his death from one hundred thousand feet.

The process of disintegration intensified. More strips of hide peeled off into the maelstrom as Karr tried to think. One of the strips missed the heavy lifter by mere feet, but the gouge it left behind gave Karr an idea.

Making a note of the geography outside the fugueship, Karr rigged pinch-cleats and crawled deeper inside. Gripping already traumatized surfaces with the spiked cleats, Karr was able to squirm through the sub-hide anatomy. His initial path through ligaments and around a grouping of girder-rib end flanges was a dead end. He backtracked, disoriented, then tried several other fruitless routes, before finally pressing through an intertwining of arteries and subdermal fat and coming out in one of the newly ripped gouges on *Long Reach*'s hull.

Success: the heavy lifter was right above.

Ten feet to the hatch: now Karr would risk a jump. Studying the pattern of eddies rolling down at him, Karr prepared a short safety line with a carabiner on the end. He did not attach it to the fugueship—there were no anchor points on the burned, bleeding mass anyway. Instead, he anticipated the next lull in the blizzard of sparks.

Steady, steady—now!

Karr thumbed the suit's thruster controls and rocketed out of the fissure. Glowing embers showered his helmet and he slammed into the heavy lifter, snapping the carabiner onto a handhold beside the hatch. The eddy passed. Kilnsuit plates locked as the extreme pressure returned. Karr dangled on the end of the line, joints stiff and smacking into the lifter hull. Crack, whack! Then another eddy washed over. The suit loosened. Karr pulled himself around on the line and manhandled the latch, his own muscles and the ghimpsuit fibers straining to the limit. Finally, the seal broke and the hatch grumbled open. Karr dragged himself out of the buffeting winds, plopped into the cockpit, and resealed the hatch behind him.

Karr's lungs wanted to rest and his heart wanted to stay with *Long Reach* until the last possible moment, but every second the lifter spent docked was a second in dire jeopardy. Karr flipped system switches two at a time while recanting the preflight check so as not to mess up. "Engine run-ups number one, two, three, four." Click, click, click, click. "Cowl fields engaged and locked open." Snap. Klack. "Throttle mixtures to rich." Zwik. "Thrusters buffering to full. D.O.I. throughput at seventy-five percent, eighty. . . ."

Through the canopy's transparent ceramite tiles, Karr saw a wide swath of fugueship hull separate from the ship and skid toward him.

The D.O.I. gauge wound up. "Ninety, ninety-five . . . Come on, you piece of junk!"

The strip of fugueship hull tumbled, flattening everything in its path.

"One hundred! Punching!" Karr jammed the throttle levers forward and hammered the emergency release catch. Explosive bolts severed mooring clamps and Karr braced for a three-g rush, but the lifter was not the high performance escape gig. It wallowed up slowly. Karr shoved the throttle levers harder, but they were already full, open. The lifter wallowed only slightly faster. And here came the fracture, like four tons of slow motion bullwhip. Karr gritted his teeth.

Wham! Disintegrating fugueship slammed into the lifter. An ominous *crack* resounded as the heavy vehicle tumbled away from *Long Reach* Visibility dropped to nothing as plasma sparks blotted out every window, then cleared again as the lifter passed through the blazing wake, revealing the whole of the fugueship.

Karr's stomach leapt into his mouth. *Long Reach* was unraveling like a burning onion, riding down on four spears of braking fire. And he could do absolutely nothing to help it. It was Karr's worst nightmare come true. He felt the fiery plasma burning *Long Reach* as if it were his own flesh. He felt each strip of hide peeling away like chunks tearing from his heart.

Karr concentrated on the frenzied activity of flying the heavy lifter. If he did not, he would surely be overcome by emotion. And then he would die, because the lifter had taken damage during launch and was still taking damage from its headlong descent. Karr fought to stop its tumble, but each time equilibrium neared a new *crack* or *groan* resounded and the oscillations grew worse again.

Alternating views of stars, fugueship, stars, and planet whizzed around. A picture of the world below built up in Karr's mind between horror-stricken glimpses of *Long Reach*. CG-423-B was a ball of silvery-blue, unbroken except by clouds. There was no land. Where was it, Karr wondered. Due to the extreme rate of failure, colonies were no longer seeded under water.

Trying to anticipate the gyrations of the heavy lifter occupied Karr down past eighty thousand feet, then sixty thousand. The damaged lifter responded to its helm with a delay between input and response. Karr figured out that he could not react, but must instead anticipate what the vehicle would do a full two seconds later, because *reacting* only added to the errant oscillations and sent the heavy craft spiraling more quickly toward an uncontrollable spin.

Below, the globe swelled to fill Karr's view and there were finally spots of land. The surface of the ocean was dotted with tiny ring-shaped islands, the circles seeming almost too perfect to be natural.

And all the while *Long Reach* continued to drift away, a ball of fire plunging through thin stratospheric clouds. Karr's companion of so many years, the only living creature he had been allowed to care about, was dying.

Down, down they plunged, thirty thousand feet, twenty thousand feet, both ships piercing the planet's terminator. Day turned into night.

It gave Karr no comfort that he had done a better job than he thought during those brief moments when *Long Reach* had responded to its braking controls; both ships were going down in the general area below the weather satellite, where the colony would have been planted. Karr blinked watering eyes as *Long Reach* disappeared, a soft red glow behind thicker clouds at the horizon.

Now it was just Karr and the heavy lifter.

Buffeting increased in the denser, low altitude air. Time for final descent. Saving himself hardly seemed to matter in the depths of Karr's anguish, but Karr rattled through the landing procedure even though he could barely read the instruments. "Everything seems fine," he said in a wavering voice.

Pieces of the lifter began to break off.

"Encountering a bit of turbulence. We've done our checks. Leveling off for final approach." There was no hope of a vertical landing on one of the small islands, but Karr could ditch in the water—if he got the lifter down below one hundred and fifty knots. He checked the airspeed: four hundred knots. Karr turned up the cowl fields.

"Damp it down. Damp it way down," Karr recited. "Bleeding speed. Three ninety, three fifty-five. . . ."

Altitude dropped to under a thousand feet. Surface details resolved. Individual waves tossed on the surface of the ocean. The lifter whooshed over an island covered in spindly trees, their puffball tops tossing in the vehicle's wake.

"Three hundred, two eighty. Slow lifter, slow."

Karr felt the world reaching up to swat him. The lifter was coming in way too fast and the physics were unforgiving. Below one fifty the lifter would hold together, above that speed the hull would experience catastrophic failure.

Whoop, whoop! Abort! warned a klaxon.

"Two seventy."

Karr wasn't going to make one fifty.

"Come on lifter, slow, slow."

Here came the water, rushing up with frightening speed.

Whoop, whoop! Abort!

Karr grabbed a handle above his head and yanked down with all his might. Solid rocket cells ignited, flashing hot under his seat. Ceramite windows shattered overhead and Karr lost consciousness as he shot out of the cockpit into the bittersweet air of an alien world.

VIII

Overesteem a leader and the people become powerless,
Overvalue possessions and the needy become thieves,
Overcling to life and the living become assassins.

—Feral aphorism

The four of them spoke in Khafra light-code:

<<Tesla does it tonight.>>

<<Tonight? No, no.>>

<<Yes, yes.>>

<<But tonight big celebration.>>

<<Especially tonight. Fit pattern. Make Sacrament, call Body to celebration, make big surprise.>>

<<What kind of surprise?>>

<<Not know. Bad surprise.>>

<<Urr, maybe you right. Too bad. So beautiful . . . >>

The dining hall was beautiful. More beautiful—as far as the domestics were concerned—than any other place in the Enclave. Golden rays shone down from clouds of floating glowbeads. Gold light, the color of *happiness*. It filled the grand room. It shone on intriguing, lonely things the humans called *art* and *statues*. It shone on the long white-clothed table, the sparkling see-through glasses, the gleaming metal and ceramic eating things. It shone on the feast plant, around which the table was built; it made the stunted branches, steaming waxy seedpods, and leathery leaves seem almost beautiful. Almost. And the light shone down on a wooden floor so glossy that, reflected in it, the domestics could see themselves and the forty humans that were gathered in their fine Consular robes and glittering badges and pins.

<<So beautiful,>> Tengen, one of the youngest domestics, repeated.

Rusty, the oldest of them, sighed. <<Yes, and so dangerous.>>

Patton looked around the assembled humans. <<Pearl Harbor, 0755 hours, Sunday morning,>> he flashed soberly.

<<What harbor?>> Tengen asked Rusty, confused. <<What-day morning?>>

Rusty looked at Patton, also confused.

<<Never mind,>> said Spike, Consul Trurl's new domestic. <<Patton always talk funny. Maybe Patton and Rusty too paranoid—>>

Spike didn't get the chance to finish his sentence, because at that moment every bullet-shaped head in the dining hall cocked toward the entry doors. The humans, as usual, paid little attention.

Tesla flung the doors open.

Webs, a young Subconsul, snapped to attention. "Prime Consul Olin Tesla," she quickly announced.

Tesla nodded briskly in the silence that followed, his gaze scouring human face after human face.

<<Tries to find friends?>> Tengen wondered at the behavior unfamiliar to him.

<<Tries to surprise enemies,>> corrected Patton, who had seen it many times before.

But Jenette's domestic underground had warned their humans with inconspicuous bumps on their legs or scratches on their feet. Everyone involved had time to put on their secret-hiding faces. The Prime Consul learned nothing from his abrupt, late entrance. Looking disgruntled, he moved to the head of the long table. The other humans followed him to their places. Toby, Tesla's domestic, lead the way, using his large size to intimidate the other domestics.

<<Out of way. Move. Rrrrrrr.>>

The other domestics hurried to clear a path—even Patton, who particularly disliked Toby.

<<Two minutes alone in dark room,>> Patton grumbled. <<That all Patton needs.>>

<<Guard words!>> Rusty cautioned, carefully flashing with glowbuds on a side of his body that Toby could not see. Up until then, the domestics had been using the advantage of light-code to converse intimately even though they were scattered around the large room; now they had to be careful. As soon as he could, Rusty also made sure all the other domestics got the warning.

The humans remained standing around the table. When the shuffling and adjusting subsided, Tesla bowed his head and stacked his fists over his heart. All the humans did the same.

Webs spoke again in a formal voice, "Strong is the Body, pure of thought and action."

"Pure is the Body, strong against temptation," Tesla and the others responded.

"As it was on Evermore," Webs continued.

"Never shall it be in the New Ascension," the others solemnly finished.

Tesla sat. The forty Consuls and Subconsuls did the same, Webs with some relief that she had not messed up the invocation. The domestics recognized this as their cue and the small army of quadrupeds disappeared out alcove holes around the dining hall walls. They reappeared moments later bearing an array of foods that humans considered succulent: alemani-hopper forelegs with suckers stripped and replaced with sprigs of pepper-thistle, the beheaded body of a pugg coated in orange sweet-goo, something called a faux-chicken which was cut into thin strips and served over tuber skins.

<<Weird food,>> said a domestic named Crash.

<<Ruined by burning,>> Patton snorted as he placed a dish before Colonel Halifax.

<<Not burned, *cooked*,>> corrected Bronte, a domestic who had somehow picked up an appreciation for human tastes and was therefore in charge of the feast preparations.

Tengen's muzzle curled as he took a dish to Panya Hedren. <<Why eat *plants?* Yuck.>>

Bronte glared at Tengen. <<Plants healthy, build strong bones.>>

Tengen might have said more, but at the last moment realized he was within Panya's field of view and wisely decided not to flash in her presence.

Having placed the dishes, the domestics backed away from the table.

The humans inhaled the sumptuous odors, or licked their lips, but none made a move for the food.

"Please," said Tesla, nodding stiffly, "eat."

They waited as he took the first mouthful, then followed suit. As they ate, Tesla made an effort to set them at ease with conversation and by showing a lot of teeth—something humans did when they were happy, but something Tesla rarely did. As far as the domestics could tell, this did not seem to have the desired effect. However, since Tesla was the most powerful among them, the humans laughed when he laughed and looked concerned when he looked concerned, and did not speak what they really thought, as was proper in human society. But the mood did lighten, slowly, and what did it was not Tesla's stiff attempt to play host, but the glasses and glasses of droobleberry-ferment. After a time, spots of conversation began to break out here and there. Some humans even laughed.

<<Good to see humans happy,>> flashed Crash as he served his human, Dr. Deena Marsh, who, along with Burke and Panya, was near the end of the table opposite Tesla.

<<Yes, good,>> Rusty agreed as Burke told a peculiar human-reproductive story about an agricultural specialist's female progeny and a roving vendor of manufactured items.

" —so he says, *I don't care if you do it with her anymore, just don't use my hairy ass as a score board!*" Burke guffawed and elbowed Panya, who turned a lovely shade of pink (one of the few colors humans could produce on their skins).

"Oh Burke! Don't be crude," she said, unable to a repress a grin.

Some of the nearby humans laughed. Some did not; in particular, those who were more inclined to be concerned with rules and proper appearances remained stony-faced. Also, those humans on hormone inhibitors seemed uneasy with the content of the story.

"Indeed, well . . ." the human sitting at the end of the table opposite Tesla smiled nervously. Dr. Pondur Yll was old like Tesla, but where Tesla had become leaner and harder, Yll had become more wrinkled and infirm; where Tesla's hair was short-cropped and still grew over most of his head, Yll's was long and gathered like a tail, but thin. Yll seemed anxious to find another subject. "And how are you feeling, Madam Hedren?"

All eyes turned Panya's way. "Couldn't be better," she replied, basking in her newfound celebrity. She patted her ripe belly. "And the quads couldn't be better. Oooh!" Panya squealed, feeling an internal kick. "I think they're getting impatient."

"We've been blessed," Burke said happily.

"Thanks to Dr. Yll," Tesla said, honing in on the dialogue from his end of the table. The Prime Consul held up his glass. "A toast to Dr. Yll and his wonderful fertility drugs."

Yll seemed even more nervous at that toast than Burke's off-color story, but he drank as the rest of the table drank.

Burke Hedren held up his own glass and said, a little too loudly, "And to Jenette!"

Panya sniffed and rolled her eyes.

"To Jenette Tesla," Jenette's supposed fiancé, Bragg, chimed in from his seat near Tesla.

"To Jenette Tesla," Colonel Halifax, also seated near Tesla, agreed.

Some of the Consuls flinched guiltily and the Prime Consul frowned at the mention of Jenette's name—his eyes darted to her empty seat—but everyone drank.

The meal proceeded. The domestics gathered up empty droobleberry-ferment flasks.

<<Why they look funny?>> Tengen asked of Rusty.

<<They who?>>

Tengen nodded at Tesla, Yll, and Halifax. <<Look like skins not fit right.>>

<<Hrrr. They old.>>

<<Oh.>>

Tesla, Yll, and Halifax were the only remaining *ancients*. Tesla and Yll had changed over the years. Halifax's stalky frame and leathery, scarred complexion never seemed to change from year to year—except to become more scarred.

<<Very old,>> Rusty added.

<<How many years?>>

Rusty's muzzle screwed up as he tried to think. <<Urrr. More than four-times-four-times-four.>>

Tengen did the math on his four-thumbed paws.

<<Oh, that *old*. How long most other humans' allotted years?>>

Rusty considered. <<Not definite. Between four-times-four and four-times-four plus four-and-half-four.>>

Tengen counted on his thumbs again. His colors took on alarmed hues. <<That not long!>>

<<No,>> agreed Rusty, also alarmed by the inevitable thought of the end of his human's allotted years.

As Rusty and Tengen exited through the alcoves with empty flasks, Bronte entered.

Going to the long table, she moved methodically up and down each side, attending the feastplant. A seedpod steamed before each seated human. These she sniffed for correct temperature, drawing air over baleen-like nasal furrows in the roof of her mouth. Then, using her long teeth, she injected a tiny amount of immune venom to stimulate the chemical reactions within. Rust spots started to appear on the tightly wrapped leaves. Only when Bronte was satisfied with all the seedpods did she withdraw and allow the next course to be served.

Rusty and Tengen returned to the hall with more flasks of droobleberry ferment. Tengen's worried coloring had diminished, but not his penchant for questions.

<<How come they so old and others not?>> Tengen asked, again in reference to the *ancients*.

Rusty wobbled his head, the equivalent of a human shrug. <<Ancients are immune to Scourge. Scientists study them lots, study their blood lots, but nobody knows why.>>

<<How come—?>> Tengen began.

<<Tengen,>> Rusty interrupted distractedly. <<More how-comes later. Okay? Rusty answer then. Yes?>>

<<Yes,>> Tengen agreed sheepishly.

Rusty kept an eye on Tesla, who was showing a lot of smiley

tceth at the amount of ferment that they were serving. Rusty didn't think that was a good sign.

The feast proceeded. Course upon course of fine food made its way from kitchens hidden behind the alcove exits to the table. Then came the main course. All dishes were removed and wide platters placed under the now brick-red seedpods. At a signal from Bronte, each domestic lined up along the table and simultaneously injected a bit more venom into the waxy stalks behind the pods. Even the most wary Consuls were enraptured as the seedpods unwound like flowers. Puffs of aromatic steam unveiled clusters of red nodules. Translucent sauce dripped onto the platters. This was the pièce de résistance, grown to order while the humans supped.

The humans attacked the nodules with long, narrow forks.

"Is this not superb?" asked a plump man three chairs down on Tesla's right. The man's face pinched with ecstasy as he chewed a morsel. "I find it quite superb."

Tesla responded cautiously, "A simpler diet suits me better, Dr. Bigelow." Tesla obviously did not like Consul Dr. Clarence Bigelow. Bigelow bulged from a Consul uniform big enough for any three other colonists, but Tesla always acted deferential; as Bronte was constantly telling the other domestics, Bigelow was very smart and his position as chief physicist in charge of the Enclave's energy production made him an important human in the Chamber of the Body.

"I applaud it," said Bigelow; he shot a smile in Bronte's direction. "I applaud this entire affair."

Tesla looked disgruntled, but said nothing.

Bigelow continued. "The problem with this colony—" Bigelow always said *colony* and not *Enclave,* which seemed to annoy Tesla further, "—is that no one has any sense of style." Bigelow flourished a hand festooned with metal rings. "This hand-to-mouth existence rubs it out of us. It's not good for the soul. I ask you, Prime Consul, why did we come to this planet if not for passion and vision?" Bigelow was one of the last few dozen or so humans who had come from off-planet, and whose ages now ranged from twenty-four to twenty-nine. They had arrived by fugueship, precious berths that might have been filled by breeding-age colonists allotted to young children in order to secure the participation of parents deemed absolutely necessary for the survival of the colony. Initially considered a waste, these juvenile colonists had turned out to be a blessing now that all the other adults were dead. Bigelow and his kind comprised most of the members of the Chamber of the Body.

Another delicacy disappeared into Bigelow's cavernous mouth. Fat lips sucked pudgy fingers. "I for one will not go quietly, into mediocrity but *rage, rage against the dying of the light.*"

Tesla grunted, unable to disagree with the sentiment, and ventured to taste the feastplant.

<<Look, look!>> Rusty flickered in furtive tones. <<More pattern!>>

<<What? Where?>> asked the younger domestics.

<<Tesla eats only one bite.>>

<<So?>>

<<Look other Tesla plates. Only one bite of each.>>

<<True, true.>>

<<That mean Tesla's stomach nervous. Tesla stomach only nervous when Tesla have big surprise.>>

<<Maybe coincidence?>>

<<No. Look.>>

Toby had also noticed Tesla's dislike of the food and, anxious to please lest he feel his master's wrath, hurried over to Bronte. <<Bring Tesla good food!>> he demanded.

<<Bronte does bring good food,>> the smaller domestic flashed, offended.

<<Bring *special* good food,>> Toby growled.

Bronte relented, scurrying off submissively. She returned a few minutes later with a covered dish, which Toby snatched from her and placed before the Prime Consul. Tesla eyed it suspiciously, but lifted the lid, revealing a plate of boiled flat-grains with no salt. When no other humans were looking, Tesla patted Toby on the head.

"Good boy, Toby."

Tesla ate his flat grains. Toby flushed violet from the praise, then

turned to the other domestics who were standing around watching.
<<Serve more droobleberry! More!>>

The domestics scurried back to their places around the table.

<<Rusty right, Rusty right,>> they conceded after seeing the
plate of flat-grains. <<Tesla has bad surprise. What do now?>>

A group of humans burst into raucous laughter.

<<Not serve any more ferment,>> Patton said forcefully.

Many foolish humans were intoxicated, and even some of the
scientists. Intoxicated humans did not fare well against Tesla's sur-
prises.

<<Is okay,>> flashed Rusty.

<<Okay? Not possible,>> Patton contradicted.

<<Is, is,>> Rusty insisted. <<When Rusty and Tengen refill
flasks, Rusty adds water to ferment.>>

<<Rrrg. But humans still acting silly.>>

<<Humans drank too much before.>>

<<So what do, what do?>> the others asked.

Rusty shook and jerked his head, and then spit a bunch of red
spheroids from pouches in his throat into a forepaw. He took one
and handed the rest off. <<Take one, pass others along.>>

<<Firehead seeds!>> flashed Crash. <<That makes headaches!>>

<<Shshsh!>> cautioned Rusty. <<Also takes away intoxica-
tion.>>

As they refilled the humans' drinks, the domestics palmed
firehead seeds into the droobleberry spirits along with the regular
garnishes. Only Consul Trurl noticed. "Hey, where's my red berry"
he complained, slurring his words. "Don't I get a red berry, too?"
The domestics gave him one before he could make a fuss, but they
would have preferred to leave Trurl drunk. Trurl always said what
Tesla wanted him to say, and did what Tesla wanted him to do.

Dessert followed the main course. Then more servings of spirits. Tesla continued to show smiley teeth. The evening drew to a
close. Thinking the end was near, even the most paranoid of the humans began to relax.

That's when Tesla drew an official stimpaper from the breast
pocket in his daysuit.

<<Oh, oh,>> said Rusty.

"Before you go," Tesla began, "there is a small matter that requires the attention of the Body."

"What's up?" Consul Trurl drunkenly quipped. "Going to declare war?"

There were a few sniggers.

"In a manner of speaking," Tesla continued. "It has become necessary to call up the Reserves."

A gasp swept along the table. Many Consuls went white. "The Reserves! Now? Impossible!"

"It is possible," said Tesla, "and absolutely essential."

"H-how many?" asked Consul Prahara Luca, the head of Administration.

"As many as are necessary," Tesla replied.

Luca nervously reached for a water goblet, but did not push the issue. Administration always sided with Tesla; many of Luca's people owed their positions to his influence. The buzz around the table increased. None of the humans wanted to see the Reserves called. There were few enough humans to fill posts as it was; the tasks of those left would be made that much harder. And then there was the fear of imminent conflict that went along with calling the Reserves.

"On what grounds?" asked Dr. Bigelow, who had not consumed as much droobleberry spirits as the others.

"On the grounds that this Enclave stands at a crossroads. It must expand or perish." Tesla spoke slowly and forcefully to let his words sink in. "This tiny island's resources are stretched to the limit. There is no room to grow."

No humans argued with that. It was true.

"The sink-hole at the center of our island continues to expand," Tesla went on, "Usable land decreases. Raw materials are nonexistent. Production is stymied. Hydroponics works around the clock and conventional agriculture is capped at current harvest levels for fear of draining too much water from deep-root reservoirs and irreparably damaging the very ground we live on. All because of lack of space. And despite our best efforts," Tesla looked, not unkindly, at Burke Hedren, "all attempts to increase that space have failed."

Burke nodded grimly. "The Wart is a total loss."

The domestics glowed sympathetically.

It had been Burke's idea to attempt grafting a smaller ring-island onto the Enclave. Humans and domestics had worked night and day to splice water-carrying roots to keep it alive, but the only result was a dry skrag, dissolving month by month outside the battlements near Gate Three.

"Of course, we've been dealing with these problems for years," said Onos, head of Construction.

"That's right," Tesla agreed. "There is a more serious problem, however. Our practice of *reconning* nearby Feral islands to maintain domestic population is at an end. Colonel Halifax and his brave Guards have stripped every island within twenty kiloyards."

All eyes turned to Halifax. "We can't keep it up," he admitted. "Deep recon sorties range farther and farther into Feral Territory to find fewer and fewer litters. Ferals fight hard. Casualties are high."

Halifax's words had a chilling effect on the Consuls. The old warrior had a reputation for brutal honesty.

"And so what do you propose, Prime Consul?" Bragg asked in rehearsed sort of way.

Tesla stood up.

The domestics, listening as intently as the humans, went dim with anticipation and trepidation.

<<Here it comes,>> warned Rusty.

"We must widen our defensive perimeter to encompass not just this island, but new islands with room for expansion. We must open up new sources for domestics—and we must do it now. Our present stock will be depleted by year's end. Within two years none will be left alive to participate in Sacrament."

The domestics went from dim to somber blue.

They didn't need to be told what that meant: their humans would die. They would die, too, but not one of the quadrupeds was worried about that. Nothing was more important than the lives of their humans. It was only due to Jenette's tireless efforts that they believed their own lives were important at all and that they now could understand how Tesla's plan would mean more fighting between humans and Ferals. More kits would be taken from the wild. And concerted attack by humans on Ferals would short-circuit Jenette's plans for peace and the hopes of getting Feral help to find a cure for Scourge.

No, Jenette would not like Tesla's plan.

<<What to do, what to do?>>

<<Must do something!>>

<<But what?>>

<<Not know. This bad surprise. Not think this far ahead.>>

<<Maybe humans know what to do?>>

<<Humans drunk!>>

<<Maybe firehead seeds work soon?>>

A few of the scientists were rubbing their temples, but they still seemed unfocused. Only Bigelow attempted to stir up dissent.

"Colonel Halifax," he asked casually, "how many troops would you require to implement such a plan?"

Halifax considered. "High three figures, ballpark."

There were gasps, even from Tesla's supporters. Such a number would be over a third of the Enclave's human population.

"Surely," Dr. Bigelow pressed, "you are not in favor of widening the conflict between humans and Ferals?"

Halifax chose his words carefully. "What I am in favor of is not important. I am a servant of the Body. Widening the conflict is a decision of the Body, and I—and my Guardsmen—will do whatever the Body requires." Having stated his position, Halifax met the eyes of both Bigelow and Tesla unflinchingly. "It does mean more risk. Ferals constantly change tactics. Recently they started throwing things. Last week they brought down a skimmer."

Several scientists around Yll muttered amongst themselves. Tesla was quick to interject.

"Concerns, Doctor?"

Yll twitched nervously. "Only that, um, if you call the Reserves, it will be difficult to research a cure for the Scourge with a depleted staff."

Tesla smiled reassuringly. "You told me yourself that Science is close to a major breakthrough."

Yll looked around his colleagues for support, but, being good scientists and therefore bad politicians, they were of no help. "Actually, Prime Consul, what I said was that recent attempts to humanize plant antibodies have yielded promising results, however we cannot put a definitive time frame on—"

Tesla cut the old biochemist off with the wave of a hand. "The Body Pure will prevail. All we need is more time and more domestics and Science will find a solution."

<<Yll not confident like Tesla.>>

<<Yll have hard job. Cure hard to find.>>

<<Rrrr.>>

<<And Yll have no friends same age to help. All scientist humans, Yll trained them. All think like him. Nobody thinks different. Not good for thinking new things.>>

<<True, true.>>

Human reaction to Tesla's confidence in Yll varied around the table. A vaccine for Scourge had been elusive for twenty-three years. Few but the most optimistic humans believed Science would succeed anytime soon, which made Tesla's next argument even stronger.

"In the meantime," the Prime Consul emphasized, "this Enclave must survive."

He paused to find each face around the table, stabbing each with the force of his resolve. "Some of you have questions. About the *expenditure* of domestics. About Sacrament. Some of you are concerned. You are saddened. This is natural. I, too, am concerned, and saddened. And I am open to any reasonable alternate course of action. But until one is found, I feel we must proceed with what we can do now." Many Consuls nodded or grunted assent at that sentiment, including many of Jenette's friends. "As is my right as Prime Consul, I call the Body to account, now.

The assembled humans were too shocked to know what to say or do. Tesla took the official stimpaper and a stylus, and handed them to the first person on his left, Subconsul Bragg.

"You will vote yea or nay," said Tesla, "as is your will."

Bragg scribbled enthusiastically and passed the paper to the Consul next to him.

Rusty shook his head despondently. <<Clever, clever.>>

<<Urrkurrkurrk,>> agreed Patton, looking at the arrangement of the seating. <<Tesla friends vote first.>>

Bragg of the VF, Roddi and Yorn in Operations, Trurl in Maintenance, Withor in Logistics, Logars and Mats in Fabrication, Luca, Ulf and Hedda in Administration, and a dozen other Tesla supporters would put their signatures on the paper before the first dissenter in Science or Medicine even touched it.

<<Many *yeas*.>>

<<Much pressure.>>

It would be hard for Jenette's friends to choose nay in such a public vote. They would side with Tesla.

<<Why humans always pick Tesla?>> Patton grumbled. <<Humans hate Tesla.>>

<<Lesser of evils,>> sighed Rusty.

<<Patton tired of lesser of evils.>>

<<Rusty too. Nothing changes.>>

<<Maybe time to pick greater of evils.>>

Tengen flashed nervously. <<Rusty and Patton talking funny.>>

<<Urrr. Tengen right. Rusty old. One Sacrament left.>>

<<Patton old too. And not know what to do.>>

<<What Jenette say to do?>> Tengen asked.

<<Not say.>> Patton answered. <<Jenette gone.>>

<<Gone where?>>

<<Nobody knows.>>

Suddenly Rusty flashed brightly and head-butted Patton and Tengen.

<<That it! That it! *Nobody knows!* Genius!>>

Tengen clattered his teeth. <<Genius? How—?>>

But Rusty was making his way up the table to Bronte. They flashed secretly together, then Bronte moved up beside Dr. Bigelow. Bigelow, who was looking rather glum, leaned down and listened as she whispered in his ear.

Bigelow's human expression lightened. He stood, abruptly, and waved his hands, theatrically.

"Stop the vote! Cease and desist this breach of Enclave law!"

Human hands froze over the stimpaper. Even Tesla blinked at the force of Bigelow's words.

Colonel Halifax turned red. "Dr. Bigelow, you forget yourself.

The Body cannot be prevented from calling itself to account. I myself am sworn to protect any fair and legal vote!"

"But this vote is impossible!"

"Impossible?" Tesla said, finding his voice. "It is my right!"

Dozens of voices suddenly tried to out shout each other, but Dr.
Bigelow eventually shouted the loudest. "It is the Prime Consul's
right to call the Body to account—but it is also impossible! Consul
Tesla is not present!"

"*I'm* Consul Tesla!" the Prime Consul said indignantly. Bigelow
stood his ground.

"No, Consul *Jenette* Tesla is not present." He looked at Tesla but
his words were aimed for the other humans. "Jenette Tesla was
made full Consul. We all received notice of the Prime Consul's
edict yesterday."

"It is not necessary to have her present," Tesla said through
clenched teeth.

"Only—" Bigelow raised a dainty finger, "—if there is unani-
mous consent from the rest of the Body. And I, for one, would like
to hear what Consul Jenette Tesla has to say on this matter."

The domestics looked around the table. They had never seen so
much human skin displaying so much beautiful red.

<<Will humans submit?>>

<<Or riot?>>

<<Not know!>>

Suddenly Burke Hedren spoke up. "I would too!"

"Yes, and so would we!" proclaimed several scientists.

Dr. Yll nodded nervously.

"Where is Jenette anyway?" Panya, who was a special guest of
the Body and held no vote, asked.

"Nobody knows," Bigelow said, pointedly shrugging.

"I thought I saw her leaving the perimeter in a crawler last
night," said Alphonse Jeej, a geeky Subconsul in Administration.

"Really?" asked Bragg, confused. "Alone?"

"That's what I saw," said Jeej.

<<Urrr!>> wondered Rusty. <<How Jeej know when domestics
not know?>>

Crash answered. <<Other humans not like Jeej. He sad. He

like walk battlements alone at night. Not even take his domestic with him.>>

<<At least Tesla surprised too,>> Tengen pointed out.

Tesla was looking pale and worried.

Sensing victory, Bigelow pressed his attack. "What *is* Consul Jenette doing outside the perimeter in a crawler? Or doesn't the Prime Consul know?"

All eyes, human and nonhuman alike, turned to the head of the table. The Prime Consul was supposed to know everything that occurred in the Enclave, anything less was a sign of weakness. But Tesla was not about to admit to weakness. He quickly recovered.

"She is on an official Consular mission, at my request," he said, standing firm, blazing eyes daring anyone to question his explanation.

<<Tesla mad.>>

<<Jenette in big trouble now.>>

<<Jenette in big trouble already.>>

Angry comments began to pass between the two opposing groups of humans. Tempers flared.

Dr. Yll spoke up. "I propose we postpone the vote," he said in a placating manner, "until Jenette returns."

"I second that motion," Bigelow said immediately.

"She won't be back for a day or two," Tesla said nervously.

"That is quite all right," said Yll, relieved. "We will wait."

Pandemonium broke out among the humans. Tesla's hand went to his stomach.

<<Tesla failed!>> exclaimed Crash.

<<Underestimated Jenette's influence,>> said Patton.

<<Tesla bad looser,>> Rusty cautioned. <<Not make same mistake twice.>>

Tesla leaned to his left.

"Bragg," the domestics heard Tesla hiss in the bedlam. "Have my skimmer ready in fifteen minutes."

IX

*It was a good batch to choose from, raised by her own
hand since she now runs the domestic nursery. Every
one of the kits was eager to be chosen by her. But what
does she pick? A healthy specimen? No. The one with
the clubbed foot! True he is large, but the choice of this
crippled Arrou can amount to no good. My daughter's
soft heart will be the end of her.*

              —from the private journals of Olin Tesla

Jenette's crawler bobbed in a skirt of ever-growing tube-and-
bladder kelp that spread out from the shore of unexplored Feral
Island 716, damping lively little waves which played on the
open ocean. New Ascension's sun baked down on the crawler's
rear deck, where Arrou had captured a buzzer unlucky enough to
land beside him. The sun also shone on a rakishly tilted driver's
cab and Jenette's legs, which stuck out from the generator compartment underneath.

Arrou pawed his fist-sized captive, idly frustrating its attempts
to escape. "New buzzer," he said, plopping a paw across its path.
"Pretty colors."

Jenette muttered under the cab. "Yeah, that's great. New
buzzer, pretty colors. What about Ferals?"

Arrou looked up at the nearby island, an overgrown profusion
of rich greens with a few tall trees towering over the canopy.
Strange calls hooted behind the dense foliage and distinctly pungent land breeze, almost fetid in comparison to the fresh air of the
open ocean, wafted over the crawler, but there was no sign of life
along the shoreline. "No Ferals." Arrou leaned back over the

buzzer and whipped his long tongue across its glittering carapace. "Ugh! Stings!" It was coated in acidic glaze. The buzzer reared up, hissing, and lunged at Arrou's paw, but he was too quick. All it got between its impressive mandibles were deck splinters. "Good teeth," Arrou said appreciatively.

A greasy but delicate hand shot out from under the cab. "Give me the big one," Jenette said.

Using his lame paw to block the buzzer's escape, Arrou grabbed a grippy and handed it to Jenette. Her hand disappeared, but reappeared shaking vigorously. "No, no, the other big one!"

Arrou sighed and rummaged through a small toolkit with both forepaws. He handed Jenette another grippy as the crafty buzzer made a break for it. Arrou tried to corral it with a hind leg, but it beetled over the edge of the deck and plopped out of sight.

Again, Jenette's hand disappeared. There was more muttering, then, "Ouch!" and *klink, plink, splash.* Jenette squirmed back, hitting her head on the overhanging cab. Sitting beside Arrou, she rubbed both skinned knuckles and bruised head in frustration.

"Told you so," said Arrou.

Jenette scowled at him.

"Told you. Not inertializer. Powerpak dead. Now inertializer broke *and* powerpak dead."

Jenette scowled harder.

"And buzzer gone," Arrou added. He pursed his teeth into a cone: a sign of consternation.

Jenette wished for the grippy back so that she could throttle him with it, but all she said was, "Arrou, hush."

The alien leaned over the edge of the vehicle and Jenette heard him slurping. She thought he was fishing for the buzzer, but when he pulled back up he took her hand and spat stinging brine on her skinned knuckles.

"Ow." Jenette tried to pull away, but Arrou would not let go.

"Make better." Arrou spat more silvery water to ensure that the wound was clean, then released her.

"Thank you," she begrudged.

Arrou slobbered the last traces of ill-tasting water over the side. "Jenette welcome."

They sat for a while in the sunlight. Jenette's hand began to feel better.

"What now?" asked Arrou.

"We've got to find Ferals," Jenette replied, rising and grabbing hold of the cab, heaved it back down over the generator compartment and locked it into position. She climbed on top. Shading her eyes, she surveyed their predicament. As Arrou had said, the island appeared devoid of Ferals. Jenette turned a full circle. Many more emerald islands dotted the expanse of mirror ocean, and even a few skrag islands, withered and dry. She and Arrou had circled around many of them, but had seen neither hide nor hair of his wild brethren.

"Where *are* they?" Jenette said.

"Hiding," said Arrou.

Jenette nodded. "Can't blame them for mistrusting humans in vehicles." That was how the raiding parties came. The fact that they used much faster skimmers and not slow, lumbering crawlers might not make much difference to a wary enemy. She looked at nearby FI-716 again. It was overgrown in comparison to the Enclave, but the island was healthy otherwise, with no apparent dead spots, fissures, or cracks that indicated that there must be Ferals present and tending it. "We've got to get over there."

"Leave crawler?"

"We won't find any Ferals in a broken crawler, will we? Won't find your *Tears* or your *Burning Heart,* either."

"Urrr," Arrou grunted, disappointed.

"We have to make contact and if we don't do it at this island, we've got to find a way to keep going without the crawler." FI-716 was a big one, several kiloyards wide, but if there was no Feral population it was of no use.

Arrou scratched his jaw, thinking. "Make paddleboards?"

Jenette lit up. "You can do that?" A paddleboard was a shallow boat big enough for one person to lie face down on and paddle with arms and legs. Jenette had heard that Ferals used them to travel from ring-island to ring-island, but she had never seen one.

"Yes," said Arrou, "on island."

Jenette looked askance at the fifteen-yard stretch between crawler and shore. "Of course, we're not on the island."

"Arrou go, with cable," he offered, pointing to the winch on the vehicle's front. It was dead without the generator, just like the six separate wheel drivers, but the cable could still be used to pull the crawler ashore by hand. The trick was getting across in the first place. The water was not safe and Jenette doubted the kelp skirts would hold her up, never mind Arrou. Their constantly curling, sprouting tendrils might even impede progress.

"It's dangerous," she observed.

"Go fast."

"Un-hunh." Jenette was skeptical, but hung over the front of the cab, unlocked the winch, and retrieved a hook-ended cable. Arrou stepped onto the cowling and she looped it over one of his muscular shoulders and under the other. "Ready?"

Arrou bunched his powerful back legs, butt wiggling in anticipation. "Ready."

Jenette slapped his wide back. "Go! Go fast!"

Arrou sprang forward, shoving the crawler deck down in the water and bounding a good five yards before splashing onto the weeds. He began to sink straight away, but did not slow, his sure footed claws grasping the thickest bunches of kelp. Jenette marveled at the display of athletic prowess; sheer speed kept Arrou from submerging. The winch whined, the crawler bobbing up and down as cable paid out.

"Go, go!" Jenette encouraged, catching a flurry of motion out the corner of one eye. Zigzags of water splashed up a few dozen yards from the crawler, like the motion of fish fighting on hooks.

Arrou missed a step with his clubbed paw. That leg sank up to his chest.

"Don't stop!"

Arrou struggled to pick himself up, but the unanticipated weight of the cable held him down. His mighty legs flailed in the water, half crawling, half swimming in the grasping ropes of kelp. More flurries of water appeared, drawn by the motion. They closed on Arrou with alarming speed.

"Faster, Arrou!" Jenette yelled. "Faster!"

The underwater disturbances converged on Arrou as he neared the shore. Jenette closed her eyes, afraid to look.

"Raaak!" Arrou howled. Jenette peeked.

Arrou lay on the embankment at the edge of the island, kicking a mottled, red torpedo shape: a sharkworm. Its jaws were sunk into Arrou's leg. His bullet head twisted back, lips retracting from teeth, and he sliced the yard-long predator in half, yanking the still-biting head off his leg and crushing it between strong, radial jaws.

"Are you all right?" Jenette called.

"Think so," Arrou gasped, wolfing down the large chunks of sharkworm which would later be ground in his gizzard. "Head taste good," he added, catching his breath and shaking off strands of wriggling tube-and-bladder weed. He gave a test yank on the cable. The crawler twisted in the kelp skirts, but swung back when he let go. "Wheels stuck."

Jenette reached into the cab and unlocked the hubs. Now the large wheels could spin freely. Arrou turned and, leaning on the cable like a tug-of-war contestant, disappeared into the lush jungle. Under his power the crawler ambled over the weeds and butted against the island. Jenette gathered the few useful items from the vehicle's cab, locked it down as best she could, and hopped ashore.

Arrou reappeared, picked up the other half of the sharkworm, and held the raw thing up as Jenette tied the cable to a tree. "Want some?" he asked, huffing hot, fishy breath at her.

Jenette's nose crinkled. "You caught it. You eat it." She checked the sharkworm bite on his leg. It had barely penetrated the thick hide, but, along with the broken crawler, it was an inauspicious beginning to their quest. What else could go wrong, she wondered? The jungle glistened darkly, its decomposing-plant smell much stronger up close. "Come on, let's make some boats."

Deeper and deeper they traveled into the island. And more and more Jenette realized how little she knew of the world they lived on and how frightening it all appeared. It was very different from the Enclave, which was all trimmed and cultivated, the unwanted eradicated and the foul-smelling replaced with the fragrant. Myriad plants grew under the canopy of FI-716 and the occasional shaft of sun filtering down through the jungle canopy did not ease Jenette's wary and dismayed eyes. She searched for familiar things, because there were no dangerous plants or animals within the Enclave's perimeter walls, but familiar things were few and far between and highly-outnumbered by the unfamiliar. The plants were most obvious, thick menacing bushes with oily blossoms and unpleasant bouquets, or brightly-hued creepers strangling haunted tree trunks. But there were unfamiliar sounds as well, sounds of moving things that tickled blonde hairs on the back of her neck and whispered nasty hints in her ears about what lay in wait for the foolish and unwary. *Jenette remembered creepy tales Colonel Halifax had told her when she was very young.* Even those things Jenette did recognize, like the ever-present brainturf (after the first ripe *squish* she tried to walk on roots or resin nodules instead), seemed larger and more menacing to her anxious senses. There were many dark holes underfoot from which creatures could spring from and neither she nor Arrou had so much as a big stick to defend themselves with.

After a tense couple of hours foraging, they had seen no sign of Ferals and Jenette had lost track of the direction from which they'd come. The sun was to the north, she reasoned, but ring-islands had a habit of slowly spinning, so that didn't mean much. And Arrou, in his quest for paddleboard material, was leading them into thicker and thicker growth.

"What are you looking for?" Jenette asked.

"Sailtrees."

"We've been walking all afternoon in search of sailtrees?" Jenette asked impatiently. "There are sailtrees all over. Look, there's one. And there's another, and another."

Arrou scrutinized every tall tree she pointed at, but dismissed them with a sniff and a toss of his head. "Not right." He slunk into denser growth.

Jenette didn't like the look of the thickening foliage. So far it had been convenient to let Arrou lead, but even if Ferals lived there, maybe it was rash to plunge ahead in hopes of finding them.

Maybe they wouldn't like being bothered so close to home. She
liked the idea of making paddleboards closer to the shore. "Do
you know what you are doing?"

Arrou gave a curious shrug. "How hard can be?"

Jenette stiffened. "Haven't you made paddleboards before?"

"No."

"But you've seen it done, right?"

"Yes."

"Oh, good." Jenette was relieved. "So what's the problem?
What's taking so long?"

"Find bodybags."

"Sailtrees don't drop bodybags for another six months,"
Jenette reminded him.

"Urrrkurrrkurrrk," Arrou rumbled, suddenly thoughtful.

"Even I know that."

"Forgot. Documentary not say."

"Documentary not say? You saw paddleboards being made in
a human recording? You didn't learn from Ferals?"

Arrou tilted his head and looked hurt. "How?"

Jenette instantly regretted her previous words. Of course Arrou
had not learned from Ferals. He had been captured when just a kit
and hadn't seen a wild Khafra since. The reason they were tramp-
ing through untamed jungle in search of Ferals, who had every
reason to kill them on sight, was to put an end to that very practice.

"Well," Jenette considered, gazing at the trees around them,
their leaves sagging in the heavy, still air, "maybe a green bodybag will work."

Arrou brightened, literally, at that suggestion and they spent
the next while looking for sprouting bodybags. There were buds
on high branches and some were quite big, even out of season.
Jenette saw that with a little luck they might find one big enough
for her or Arrou, but just about the time that Arrou spotted a likely
looking bulge behind a collapsed sail leaf, Jenette began to fret
once more. The afternoon had become hot and oppressive, so that
only the scuffling or peeping of New Ascension's most energetic
creatures was heard. But now it became dead silent. Arrou went

stiff, head outstretched on his neck, jagged breath drawing air past the nasal plates in the roof of his mouth.

"What is it?" Jenette whispered.

"Not know," Arrou whispered back. "Smells like pink."

"Smells like *pink?* What's that supposed to mean?"

"Trouble. Funny smells."

"Feral smells?"

"Not know. Wind weak." Arrou's ear pits, small depressions at the crest of his head, flared wider. "Rrrr," he rumbled. "Something coming."

Jenette's heart raced. "Is it Ferals?" she pressed.

"Maybe," Arrou conceded, "but other somethings come, too." He turned away, presumably in the direction of the shore. "Go back."

Jenette had a similar impulse to flee, but resisted it. "No. No, we stay."

"Ferals not safe," Arrou protested. "Jenette alone. Jenette unarmed."

"That's why you're here," she admonished, "to protect me. Besides, this is what we came here for and I'm not going to run away without even trying to make contact."

Arrou didn't like it. He shuffled from side to side, his back emitting a warning display as the distant rustling of foliage grew loud enough for Jenette to hear. It amplified rapidly, crashing and snapping with a certain frenzied rhythm.

In her mind Jenette ran over the Khafra words Arrou had taught her. *Rikit-ee-brikhauss.* She hoped she would get them right. "You might have to help translate."

"Urrr."

Suddenly a panicked bleating, like a child yelling through a hose, resonated and the greenery burst apart. An olive-furred creature with long legs and a body made up of three melon-sized spheres crashed into view, tube mouth yowling. It leapt sideways to avoid Arrou, its yowl Dopplering lower in tone as it careened past Jenette.

Arrou shot her a look, longing to go.

Jenette was getting pretty panicky herself. More creatures

crashed through the foliage around them. A few she recognized: mlums, forfaraws, and wompets. Most she did not, like the small hairless ones with long tails and hopping gates, or the larger ones with thick, bristled bodies and forward stabbing tusks in massive jaws. For a place that had appeared deserted minutes before, the numbers were phenomenal.

"Can't let a few herbivores scare us off," Jenette said, trying to sound brave.

"Not afraid of herbivores," Arrou huffed. "Ferals *hunting* herbivores. Hunters not want talk. Hunters want kill."

Two of the bristly creatures bowled Jenette over. She scrambled back up, shaken. Maybe Arrou had a point. Maybe Ferals hot with blood lust would not be in a diplomatic frame of mind. Maybe it would be prudent to wait until after their hunt. "Okay, let's get out of here."

Arrou instantly bounded off with the flow of animals and Jenette followed, but if he was hoping for safety in the numbers of the stampede, it was not to be. Jenette could not run as fast as the four-footed prey creatures. Arrou had to check up and wait for his human companion and they were quickly left behind as another noise grew to their rear, not a panicked desperate noise this time, but a measured one, spreading out on all sides.

"Hurry," Arrou exhorted, leaping ahead.

Jenette began to recall Colonel Halifax's stories in more detail, she remembered how he had earned all those ugly red scars in Feral ambushes, and how he had told her that Khafra in the wild grew larger and more ferocious than domestics. Arrou was big enough already. She tried not to think of a bigger creature with bigger claws, longer teeth, and thicker armor.

Jenette ran faster. She and Arrou plunged through pools of light and shadow, leaves whipping their faces, slick molds greasing their steps.

"Owwurr," Arrou cried as they crashed through a stand of hitchhiker brush. Cashew-shaped burrs clung to Jenette's clothes. Arrou's velvety snout bled from a dozen tiny scrapes.

The noises behind accelerated.

Arrou raced back from scouting the path ahead. "Dead end, dead end," he said and bounded off in a different direction.

There was motion behind the curtains of leaves now, shimmering smears of green on green, like heat waves on water. Jenette's legs complained; gasps of air burned her throat and she fell further and further behind.

Arrou paused to wait.

"Keep going!" she ordered. "Get away!"

Arrou stubbornly refused to move. "Impossible."

Jenette stumbled up to him, expecting Ferals to burst out of the foliage any instant. Arrou hunched his shoulders and bared his teeth, prepared to go down fighting. His back shimmered defiant waves of orange.

This was not the peaceful encounter Jenette wanted.

"Hide!" she cried.

"Okay."

Like turning off a switch, Arrou's defiant markings vanished and his thousands of glowbuds became a perfect imitation of the mottled forest around them.

He disappeared.

"You'll have to teach me that sometime," Jenette said, as exposed as ever. Looking around wildly, she dove under a fallen log by the foot of an enormous moss heap. *Whoof!* Arrou dropped his four hundred pounds on top of her as a flurry of feet rumbled up.

This would be the end of her little crusade, Jenette realized. Surely the Ferals would see her, and if not they would certainly smell her. Would the Ferals rip them apart all at once as a pack, or bit by bit in revenge for all the misery Jenette's species had inflicted upon them? Jenette's heartbeat pounded in her head. Primal fear blotted out the higher functions of her brain. She waited for the characteristic howl that Arrou made when he trapped a small animal.

The ground shook, but no chorus of victory howls arose. Instead, the log slammed down onto Arrou and her as an unknown prey animal vaulted off of it and fled, a gangly, pinkish smudge as seen through the corner of Jenette's eyes. The hunters stampeded past. When the vibrations ceased and Jenette could bear Arrou's weight no more, she shoved at his knobby flank.

"Get off," she gasped.

He rolled off and they looked around. The jungle was empty again. Leaves were trampled and branches broken, but the hammering of feet receded and there was no sign of Ferals to be seen.

Jenette didn't believe it. The Ferals had passed them by.

"What was that all about?"

Arrou shook his head and sniffed. "Funny smell," he said, perplexed. "Funny, flowery smell."

X

It is a demanding life. Full of bittersweet accomplishment and distant, rare glory. Many times it is harsh. Always it is lonely. But it is the only life we know. And there isn't anything any of us wouldn't do to prolong it a month, a day, a few sweet seconds more.

—anonymous Pilot

Karr ran through the jungle, emotions numbed by the loss of his fugueship, body fatigued from too many hours without sleep. The ghimpsuit had kept Karr's muscles in good condition during *Long Reach*'s last ill-fated mission, but there were limits to his stamina. He could not run for more than a few more minutes. The bloodthirsty life-forms on his tail, however, showed no signs of weakening. Their rustle of pursuit was dangerously near and drawing nearer by the second. Karr had to do something—and fast—with the limited resources at hand: ghimpsuit, light Pilot's boots, and Gattler. He had nothing else, and the Gattler was growing heavier with every step. The creatures had cut Karr off from the rest of his equipment when he ventured inland searching for water and food.

Deciding to use the Gattler before he couldn't carry it any longer, Karr spun its selector knob. Barrel six whirred into position and he stopped and turned, squeezing the trigger. Mountains of aqueous sterilizing foam gushed out like suds from a mad washing machine, swamping a wide swath of jungle to a height well above his own head. Karr heard several gratifying *slurshes* as the creatures slid into it, followed by howls of displeasure as the stinging foam got into eyes, mouths and noses—assuming they had those. They thrashed in blinding, slippery confusion.

The voice of fear counseled Karr to select a different barrel and riddle the foam with *qi* needles, or better yet, use a cutting beam to fry the creatures, but he turned and ran. Downed on an alien planet and surrounded by hostile life-forms, every Pilot knew better than to stand and fight. Karr had played these scenarios in survival training. It didn't matter that the Gattler could be used as a weapon. The creatures had the advantage. It was their turf. They knew it better than Karr and they outnumbered him. Even with rocks and teeth to his needles and cutting beams, all they had to do was swarm him. In a game of attrition wherein Karr had only one of himself to lose, Karr lost. *Keep moving. Keep hiding. Stay alive from one moment to the next and try to get away. If they don't get you in the first forty-eight hours, you will probably make it.*

So Karr fled, half-running, half-falling over the constantly rippling ground. CG-423-B harrowed him with sensual stimulation unlike anything on the interior of his lost ship. Harsh, unidentifiable sounds hammered his ears. Varied odors wafted in atmosphere lacking the chemical scent of air scrubbers. And the sights were nerve-wracking! *What was that thing?* Karr wondered at gourd shapes strangling the base of a tall tree. They resembled a drill corporal back at the Academy, bulbous nose and all. Below that proboscis, a squirmy thing struggled in a plant mouth lined with teeth. There were rainbow bubbles, blowing from viscous fluid that stretched over irregular hoops of liana. Yards long, the bubbles undulated in the lazy breeze above Karr, floating many paces before popping. They were beautiful—but what were the fine fibers that fell on him? They smelled like spun sugar. Karr brushed them off. Mounds of puff sacks underfoot shot stinging needles.

Ouch. Don't rub. Let the swelling go down by itself. The creatures closed in again, grumpier—and presumably cleaner—than before. Karr summoned his last reserves of energy and sprinted around a stand of velvety leaves. The crowded foliage parted like a curtain, revealing a doughnut-hole lagoon in the middle of the island. One hundred yards of calm water mirrored the stately trees around it. The shore was rotting, slowly submerging unlucky plants and bushes as the lagoon grew wider.

Karr followed the decaying shoreline counterclockwise until an ill-placed inlet blocked further flight. To his left, the ground sloped down to a narrow peninsula with a tree on its sinking end. To his right, the way he wanted to go, the sounds of pursuit were growing louder and louder.

Karr was trapped.

He ran down the slope onto the dead-end peninsula, stopping short of the tree, which resembled the mast and sails of an ancient Terran sailing ship. Because of the rotting shoreline, its roots were submerged and it leaned at a precarious angle.

Rustle, rustle.

Karr spun. The aliens broke out of the jungle into view— or rather, Karr deduced their positions by the parting swaths of greenery and shadows on the ground. The deadly creatures were impossible to see directly because of highly effective camouflage, ever-changing on their skins. Karr counted eight shadows, noting that they appeared to move in pairs. Those shadow pairs stopped midway down the peninsula to size up the situation.

"Rachikatikachiktik," went the disembodied voices, like coins churning in cogs. Patches of color smeared clear air.

"Rakachikutuktuk," said the blur over the biggest shadow.

"Krikadrishtix," its partner clattered. Karr heard suspicious sniffing.

Was it speech or just animal sounds? It sure sounded like communication to Karr.

The shimmering pack of aliens spread out across the narrow wedge of land. Karr backed up, splashing ankle deep into the water. It felt chilly in contrast to the hot air and reminded Karr that he had nowhere to go. The aliens certainly thought he was trapped, because they dropped their camouflage and displayed synchronized waves of black and yellow as they prowled forward.

"That's far enough," Karr barked, vocal chords gravelly from lack of use. He twisted the Gattler's selector and fired a burst of *qi* needles. They were not designed as darts and only flew straight a few yards before tumbling and bouncing off the ground or spinning harmlessly into the creatures. It was a pretty sad display. The Gattler's barrels spun again. This time Karr fired globs of adhesive froth. The aliens were able to dodge these, but they got the point:

the Gattler was a weapon. They halted when Karr pointed it at them.

"Urrrrrr," growled the one that had sniffed suspiciously. It poked a patch of adhesive with a stick. The glue held; the stick broke off.

Tool use, thought Karr, intelligent behavior. Were these fierce aliens the reason he had not found a colony on this planet? Had they wiped the humans out? Karr kept backing up until he banged into the roots of the sinking tree.

Climb or swim?

The creatures edged closer.

"Look," he warned, selecting the cutting beam. "Don't make me hurt you. . . ."

The suspicious creature clattered its nasty teeth. "Rikurrkur-rkurrk."

"I don't want to hurt you," Karr continued, "but I will if I have to." He menaced them with the Gattler. The threat was largely a bluff. Karr didn't think he could get them all before they pounced on him. He just wanted them to back off.

The aliens did not back off, but they did stop at the edge of the water, eyeing it distrustfully, which gave Karr pause. *Observe indigenous species. They know the local hazards.* If they don't want to wade, Karr concluded, I don't want to swim. So he turned and, letting the Gattler dangle from its shoulder strap, clawed up the tree, fingers finding purchase on its wrinkled bark. Before the creatures knew it, he was five stories up, standing on a branch that protruded over the inlet. Karr hugged the main trunk as it swayed back and forth, exaggerating the gentle motion of the ground below.

The aliens watched with hungry eyes.

Karr was reluctant to venture onto the branch, but he did not know how long the water would hold them back, so he straddled the downward-sloping limb and—not looking down—shimmied out toward the tip. Thankfully, the branch was strong and did not bend under his weight. Karr made good progress until one of the sail-like leaves got in the way. It grew down from the limb above, its lower end anchored by curly creepers wrapped around Karr's branch.

No problem.

Getting a firm grip on the Gattler again, Karr used its cutting beam, set narrow, to sever the creepers. The aliens paced restlessly, "richikaticking" and "rackattakatakking" their distress at Karr's actions.

Karr inched forward as each creeper broke. The sail leaf fluttered and snapped as the last anchor parted, whipping Karr about the head and back as he shimmied past. At its thinner end, the branch sagged uncomfortably under his weight. Karr looked down. The tree's motion described dizzy circles over aliens and inlet, swinging in a loop over to the far side and back on around. If Karr could nerve himself to leap at just the right moment, he would land on the opposite side. However, in spite of the tree's lean and the downward slope of the branch, he was still quite high. The water would feel very hard from that height. Hitting the ground would certainly kill him.

Up till that point, Karr's decisions had been based on flight, but now he needed a plan. Unfortunately, leaping from trees had not been part of survival training. *Don't panic. Breathe. In, out. In, out. Focus.* . . . It was a puzzle. He just had to think of it as a puzzle. He needed to get down, but could not jump, climb, or raise the ground. Therefore—a few more breaths stripped away obvious impossibilities—the only option was to lower the tree. That determined, everything else just fell into place.

While the tree continued its giddy motion, Karr sat up and, carefully lifting first one leg and then the other over the branch, faced back toward the tree's trunk. He flopped back onto his belly, picked a low-power setting and fired a cutting beam at the base of the tree. Steam rose from the moist bark and then smoke. Karr kept the cutting force moving across the trunk so that things would happen slowly.

The creatures, upset at his leaf cutting, were incensed at this new offense. They growled and gnashed their teeth. When flame appeared around the cutting beam and the tree shuddered, they let loose a chorus of outrage.

The dominant creature backed up to make a jump at the tree. The suspicious one tried to hold it back, but snarls exchanged and the dominant splashed across to the trunk. It yowled on contact with the super-heated bark, but dug in and climbed. The others, spurred on by its success, followed on after another. Only the dominant's counterpart held back, distrustful.

Karr held to his target with the cutting beam and was rewarded by a sudden lurch of the tree. Its angle of lean increased, every branch and leaf swaying as the base weakened. Karr's plan was working. Another minute or two of slow descent would deposit him safely on the other side of the inlet. But the aliens were clawing up at him too fast.

Again, Karr could have turned up the power and simply fried the creatures, but the bizarre geography of the confrontation worked in his favor. As the leading creature prowled out onto the branch, opposing pairs of digits on each paw gripping like vises, Karr changed barrels and aiming point. Jerks of the trigger spewed globs of adhesive froth and this time the aliens could not dodge. The lead alien stepped into a glob. Karr was satisfied to see it stuck; several hours and a whole lot of skin would be missing before it tore free. Before they knew it the others were stuck too, splattered by Karr as they bounded onto the branch. They thrashed, but that only made them more stuck.

Now the suspicious alien climbed the tree. It stayed on the glue-free trunk, tearing up the bark in frustration and not venturing out onto the sticky limb.

The branch shook violently, ominous creaks resonating through the wood. Karr shook with it. He worried how much load it could handle, guessing that the seven trapped aliens weighed at least three thousand pounds. As it turned out, the branch was not what Karr needed to worry about.

Crack!

Wood shattered below. A shuddering groan rose from the base of the tree to the tip of its bole as rotting roots crumbled. The tree toppled faster than planned, flexing and spinning, and falling in a different direction than planned. Karr hung in the air for an awful second, facing straight down, then plummeted with the tree as island and water rushed up. The force flung him into the inlet. The aliens were not so lucky. Held by the molecular glue, two were crushed where the tree hammered into the opposite side of the inlet. The others were pulled into the water.

Karr came up spitting bitter brine as the last, suspicious creature raced along the branch, risking imprisonment on the sticky globules to get to the others. They thrashed harder, filling the air with submerged wailing. The lone alien artfully avoided entrapment, sinking claws into its brethren, trying to rip them free. It paid particular attention to the large dominant, its partner, but the glue was designed to hold fugueship wounds sutured shut against the stress of high g-forces. The glue held. It was already an awful sight. And, as Karr averted his eyes and stroked for land, it got worse. The water around the drowning creatures erupted like a thousand tiny explosions. Torpedo-shaped worms attacked the helpless creatures, shredding the water pink.

Karr gripped the far shore. The roots and fronds were slippery and he fell back into the murky under-surface world. The water near the tree was a froth of bubbles and blood. Karr kicked hard, breaking the surface again and stabbing the Gattler spear-like at the bank. It stuck and he kicked his legs up, rolling to safety. Spitting and choking, he looked back.

The lone alien was a blur of talons and teeth, slashing the ravenous torpedoes to pieces, uncaring of its own wounds; but for every enemy slain, two more attacked for a mouthful. In no time the submerged aliens were stripped to the bone.

The survivor raised its head—the glowbuds on one half of its body suddenly blanking out—and let out a mournful cry.

Howwurrrraouuuu!

It was the sound of loss, the sound of a being losing the most important thing in its world, and it pierced Karr to his emotional core, because if there had been a sound he could make to sum up the feelings of a Pilot losing his fugueship, that howl was it. The carnage he had inadvertently caused sickened Karr. He did not like to kill. And if not for his arrival on CG-423-B, those aliens would still be alive. Man-eating they might be, but Karr had not wished them such a grisly end.

The keening died down, absorbed by the foliage of the ring-island, and the survivor turned its head at Karr. It bounded across the tree bridge with vengeance firing its chameleon skin. Karr rose to his knees, yanking the Gattler out of the bank, but had no chance of firing before the creature was on him. Karr braced the stock on the ground and aimed the barrels at its chest. They glanced off the alien's thick breastplates and dug bloody furrows up the side of its neck and head.

The beast snarled in pain and backhanded Karr into a pile of hardened resin globules at the base of a fractured tree. The Gattler tumbled out of reach and before Karr could react, the monster was on top of him, pinning him under its suffocating weight, stabbing him with its raging eyes. Angry breath huffed on Karr's face.

One deliberate pull of the alien's talons shredded the ghimp-suit from Karr's chest. Karr struggled helplessly as the beast flexed its teeth inward, then pointed them outward again, head swinging down. The many blades straddled Karr's neck, squeezing effortlessly—each seemed to be rooted in its own separate mandible, Karr couldn't help noticing. And all the while the creature never broke its malevolent eye contact.

Know who kills you, said those bottomless, black eyes. *Know your death.*

Karr stopped struggling. If he was to die before those eyes, it must be as a Pilot and not a coward.

The teeth tightened and cut. Karr felt cool air on his neck as the alien sucked up trickles of blood. Karr felt its tongue press against his throat as it swallowed heavily.

"Get it over with," Karr gasped.

But the alien unexpectedly pulled back, its streamlined face cramping into what could only be described as a grimace. It retched.

"Achkt," it spat, utter shock in its eyes. *"Gaack."* It sprang back, sniffing Karr in dismay. Then, gagging, it bounded across the fallen tree, up the peninsula, and out of sight into the jungle.

Karr collapsed, confounded, panting, holding his neck—and thanking his lucky stars for the unforeseen blessing of tasting really, really bad.

XI

The fugueship is a kiss, a musky kiss on her nude skin, a kiss sweet with fugue and pungent like an outworld spice.

That's how it is in her dream.

Kissing-lip doorways draw her deeper, wrap her in their moist forgetfulness. The kiss steals away what was Before. The kiss is Sanctuary. The kiss takes her away from the danger of her world.

Soon it will take her to secret places.

Naked and nameless, geldings line the love-passages, heads bowed, embarrassed hands over limp nothings. In the past they have taunted her. They have punished her with their bitter nothings. They have tried to tell her that it is she who is inadequate, and not them. But she knows better. She has read. Beyond her world, there are no geldings.

She ignores them.

The kiss is on her. The kiss will show them what to do with a real woman.

Curves on curves, caress on caress. Steamy tongue-shapes lure her to the center of the ship. To the ruby womb. She feels the heat of it in her nipples and throat.

He is standing there.

In white.

And he knows what he wants: her.

Fingers interlock. Naked, charged flesh presses against muscles under crisp pressed fabric. Hot breath on face. Then contact. Firm lips on hers, touching. Not flinching. Lingering. Tasting. Darting in and out. Savoring.

This is the kiss for her.
And all the geldings can do is watch.
She feels the heat. She is the heat. Wet heat. He is
the heat. Hard heat. He moves, she moans. She parts
the white uniform, hungry for what she needs. She
grabs. He shoves her legs apart.
They are connected.
Willowy legs over thrusting buttocks. She arrives
where the kiss will take her. To the secret place. She
arrives. Such feeling! She almost faints. She takes his
gift. And arrives. And arrives. And arrives . . .

—from the black book of J. Tesla

Impossible!

A naked man, who Jenette had never seen before, motored by
the shore on a strange craft, which she had also never seen before.

Jenette and Arrou were hiding under droobleberry bushes at the
edge of FI-716, disconsolate after their first abortive Feral encounter and trying to figure out what to do next. Hiking through
dense jungle in search of Ferals would only get them killed. Jenette
needed a different, safer way to locate Ferals.

Those problems were forgotten at the sight of the naked man.

The encounter had begun with a peculiar hum. Arrou heard it
first, the prickling of his ear pits alerting Jenette to possible trouble. Then she heard it herself.

"What is it?" she whispered.

"Machine."

Jenette at first assumed the noise was a deep colony patrol, sent
by her father to bring her back. And, although the idea of being
whisked away from the dangerous island appealed to a certain part
of her, Jenette resolved to hide from the vessel. However, the noise
did not really sound like a crawler or any other kind of Enclave vehicle. Jenette pushed aside her fear, and several bunches of swollen
mauve berries, and found herself staring out from the island at a
wholly improbable boat.

The vessel's general appearance was that of a wreck. Torn composite fibers and bent metal fringed a shallow, flat rectangle, fif-

teen yards wide and thirty long. Massive charred cowlings, fat at the bottom and tapered on top, sat at the four corners. Jenette guessed some sort of propulsion units were concealed within. There was a shattered cockpit at the front and a pile of junk in the center, and the whole thing was leaking so badly that an ankle-deep lake sloshed inside the shallow sidewalls.

But more important than the craft itself was the man. Jenette knew every one of the Enclave's three thousand human colonists on sight—and he wasn't one of them.

Hence, the impossibility.

"We don't have anything like that, do we?" Jenette asked rhetorically.

"We *should,*" Arrou said, enraptured by the strange vehicle. "Big engines."

The craft quickly passed out of sight. Jenette scrambled forward and leaned over the bank as the vessel disappeared around a bend of the shoreline.

Arrou fidgeted. "What do?"

Jenette sputtered, still in shock from the sight. "Don't let him get away!"

The words hardly left her lips before Arrou bounded off through the bush. Jenette followed as best she could.

Karr rummaged through a heap of salvage on deck, flipping over what was left of the ejection couch and digging into a survival kit attached to it. He unzipped a small packet and poked it inside out. On contact with air, the fabric expanded into a wet simulacrum of a Pilot uniform, which Karr needed now that the vicious alien had destroyed his ghimpsuit. Already Karr was feeling the heat of the yellow sun above and he didn't want to get burned. He waited impatiently as the memory-cloth cured, his brows drawing into an unhappy glower at the remembrance of the last two days.

Karr had awoken on the morning of day one, bobbing in CG-423-B's strange chrome sea, suspended by a survival raft that had inflated out from compartments on the back of his kilnsuit. Torpid waves rolled from horizon to horizon with no sign of land, lifter, or fugueship in sight. The warm water surrounding him reminded him of being enfolded in *Long Reach*'s brain, and for a while, as it dawned on him that his magnificent ship was gone, he did nothing but despair. The creature that for so long had been his sole companion, the very reason for his existence, was dead.

And what good was a Pilot without a ship?

Karr would gladly have given his life for *Long Reach* to live, but of course there was no bartering with Fate. No matter that he felt his life was over. No matter that he had trained all his life, believing his choice a noble task, forsaking any human contact, family, friends—forsaking time itself as the centuries stole away. No matter that he had roots nowhere and that it would have been better if his kilnsuit had cracked on ejection so that he could drown at the bottom of the silvery ocean. None of that sacrifice brought his fugueship back from the dead. That was the terrible truth. His helmet began to fog.

Lindal Karr, who had not wept at the loss of several thousand units of human cargo, who had not shed a tear for twenty million lost souls on Sheldon's World, took his helmet off and wept at the loss of his ship.

And his tears became flower petals . . .

Or so it seemed.

Wherever his tears fell on the quick-silver waves, clouds of rich indigo birthed into the air, swarms of insects fluttering up, twirling on tissue-paper wings, out of control, joining and mating for a few stolen minutes of life and then, spent, snowing back onto the waves like flower petals. The cycle repeated over and over, sometimes near Karr, sometimes in a chain reaction that swept far away, the ocean surface stippling as if from invisible rain, chasing itself before a wind of fairy-like procreation and death. Such was the pace of life on that alien planet, but Karr neither counted the endless cycles nor marveled at the fragile beauty. He remained unmoving, inward-locked in misery.

Many fluttering life cycles passed.

Eventually, Karr's ingrained determination did kick in. His sense of duty was just too strong to give up; even though his ship was gone, he must go on. *Long Reach* would have wanted it that way. Somewhere in that great, dumb brain it had feelings for its tiny symbiont. Karr was sure of that. Furthermore, Karr remembered as he rose increment by increment out of the pit of his sorrow, that it was his duty to locate *Long Reach*'s crash sight, record what he saw, and try to transmit an account of the events and his actions for dispersion throughout human-colonized space. Maybe other Pilots could learn from Karr's misfortune and save their ships where he had failed. Only after that would he be free to wallow in sorrow.

Until then, he was still a Pilot.

So, Karr heaved himself into the survival raft and paddled along a trail of floating wreckage. In time it led him to the heavy lifter. It was submerged on a free-drifting reef of snarled green hoses and wire like corals, fifteen yards under the surface. Over the rest of that day, Karr made several descents in the kilnsuit, eventually reactivating the orbiter's engines and bringing the wreck to the surface. Karr patched it together as best he could. The Gattler's molecular glue worked very well to bond the larger broken hull sections, but evidently he hadn't found all the tiny cracks because the hull still leaked. Water immediately began to accumulate on deck. He decided he could live with it. The faster he got the vehicle flying, the faster he could head southwest, the direction in which *Long Reach* had disappeared.

That had been the first day. He fell asleep that night watching a peculiar red glow on the southwestern horizon.

Which brought him back to the present.

So far this second day had not gone as productively as the first. The probability that Karr was the only human within twenty light-years was increasing. Karr reasoned that no primate-descended colonist could have watched his fiery plummet from the heavens without swinging by to take a look, but the skies were decidedly clear of flying machines and the ocean devoid of ships. He had to face the fact that he was alone; there might not even be a colony beacon from which to transmit his report. And the planet's bloodthirsty inhabitants would be of no help to Karr. They made the simplest tasks of searching for food and water next to impossible; he had been lucky to escape his first interspecies encounter with his life.

It was at this sorry point in his rumination that Karr heard a voice.

Karr hung the curing Pilot's uniform on the ejector couch and walked to the shoreward side of the lifter. The sound repeated, seeming muffled, weak, and vaguely human. Karr listened skeptically. It was probably those aliens, trying to lure him back for a second round of Capture Lunch. Having already ascribed them a certain degree of intelligence, Karr wasn't going to fall for any of their tricks.

Still, it sure sounded like a human voice.

Karr went to the cockpit, the top of which had torn off during ejection, and leaned in to adjust the throttles. They were the only method of steering the lifter at that point. The landward thrusters were set at a lower power level than the ocean side thrusters, so the large hull chugged along, veering with the gentle curve of the coast. Karr used a fingernail to pry up the stub of a thrust lever. The ocean side thrusters thrummed a little faster and the lifer nosed in toward the ring-island, pushing through a skirt of floating kelp and on under the shadow of overhanging jungle growth.

Karr returned to the landward side.

The repeating voice sounded like a call for attention. No. A warning. Which didn't make any sense to Karr. Even if the aliens could imitate humans, why would they make warning sounds? Karr was just about to go back to the cockpit and make another throttle adjustment when he saw movement in the greenery some distance behind the lifter. He could not be sure what it was, but the warning sound was coming from that direction, too.

Thwump, went a heavy noise behind him.

Karr whirled and came face to face with another of the alien predators. He could not be sure if it was the same one as before, since it was silhouetted against the glare of open ocean behind it. Apparently, it had misjudged its leap from the overhanging jungle growth and missed Karr, but it was still far too close for comfort. Karr lunged for the ejector couch, and the Gattler leaning against it.

"Urrrkurrrkurrrk." The alien rumbled, hesitating.

But when it saw Karr grasp the multi-barreled tool, it sprang, easily swiping Karr's legs out from under him. Karr splashed into the water on deck, rolling and swinging the Gattler to bear. He snapped the selector knob to full-power cutting beam as the alien pounced on top of him.

"Stop!" shrieked a distinctly human voice. "Stop!"

From his horizontal position, Karr saw a lithe, human figure darting along the shoreline, but he was too concentrated on saving his life to give it much attention. He jammed the Gattler against the alien's chest, intending to vaporize its midsection.

An amber colored lump suddenly arched through the air and hit Karr between his eyes.

"Ah!"

Karr flinched and the beast smacked the Gattler out of his hands. It pursed its teeth into a cone. Karr reached up and gripped the soft underside of its neck before it could jab the ivory daggers through his heart.

"Khaaaghk!" squawked the alien.

Karr's human hands lacked the strength to strangle the creature. He let go one hand and groped into a survival kit beside him. His fingers darted into a pocket and pulled out a serrated knife, which he slashed at the creature.

The blade glanced off its thick hide.

More resin lumps pelted down, thrown by the unknown human—a young girl. She wasn't a very good shot; most of the lumps hit Karr and not the beast.

"Stop! Stop!" she screamed. "Don't hurt him!"

Karr wished the girl would take more drastic action. Such a vicious creature would not respond to threats, and the rocks she threw were hurting him more than it.

As if to prove that point, the creature grabbed Karr's knife arm and hammered Karr's knuckles painfully against the ejector couch. Karr lost his grip on the knife—and then almost lost his grip on its neck as the lifter slammed into the shore. Engine thrust pushed the craft up the slope at an angle. Vegetation ripped and snapped. Water sloshed around the hull and the creature lurched down on Karr, squashing all the air from his lungs. Pain stabbing through his chest, Karr tried to reach the Gattler again.

The girl followed as the lifter skipped along shore. She threw more misaimed lumps.

"Ow!" Karr gasped. "Ow! Ow! Stop throwing rocks!"

The girl sprang onto the lifter.

"Take it!" Karr yelled, nodding frantically at the Gattler. "Grab it and shoot! Shoot!"

The girl darted across the bucking deck, grabbing the Gattler as instructed. She fumbled for a second before locating and crooking a dainty finger over the trigger—but then she aimed the barrels squarely at Karr's head!

"Careful with that!" Karr exclaimed.

"Stop fighting!" the girl warned, looking Karr straight in the eye. Her aim did not veer from the center of his forehead.

Karr froze.

"Arrou," the girl continued, slowly and vigilantly, "now you stop fighting, too."

"Ghuukk," the beast choked, but to Karr's surprise, it eased up its grip on him. Cautiously, Karr did the same.

"Are you okay?" the girl asked the alien.

"Okay," it replied, rubbing its neck. It growled at Karr. "Not nice."

"It talks," Karr blurted stupidly.

"Of course *he* talks," the girl snapped. "Why did you attack him? He wasn't going to hurt you!"

The Gattler's business end continued to waver over Karr's forehead. Karr decided he had better do something before the girl accidentally vaporized his head. But what? Pilot–flatlander encounters were Karr's least competent, and least liked, area of expertise. He wracked his brain for an appropriate section of Academy procedure. *In hostile situations seek to keep discourse calm. Endeavor to diffuse volatile encounters by placating individuals armed with life-threatening devices.*

Karr attempted to follow that procedure.

"I'm sorry, young lady. Please understand, a pack of these things just tried to kill me—"

"Don't call me *young lady!*" the girl said angrily. "Nobody calls me that, not even an outworlder!"

Karr realized that his first impression of the female was incorrect. Although she had appeared quite young from a distance, up close was a different, contradictory story. She couldn't weigh more than one hundred pounds soaking wet, her build being sprightly and only just beginning to flesh out, as if she were fourteen or fifteen, but there was a mature ease to her movements and her icy blue eyes burned into his with none of the shyness of puberty.

"I'm twenty-three standard years old," she said indignantly. "How old are you?"

Karr thought it a strange question, but her response to his answer, "Thirty-four," was even stranger. She gave Karr a once over, as if seeing him for the first time, abruptly lowered the Gattler and backed off.

She slapped the creature on its flank. "Arrou, get off him. Get off."

Arrou got off. The alien's great weight eased up and Karr felt needles of circulation returning to his extremities. He stood up, flexing his hands and stomping his feet, but then the young-looking woman's face went pink and a cool breeze reminded Karr about his lack of clothing. Slapping hands over modest regions, he splashed across the deck to the limited cover of the cockpit.

Krunch! The lifter glanced off the island yet again. Karr took a moment to adjust the throttles. The hull veered out to sea. Then, looking back, he pointed at the crash couch and asked, tentatively, "Would you pass me that uniform, please?"

Jenette picked up the garment, her cheeks flushing hotly. The outworlder was so *different* from New Ascension men—and certainly not a gelding, that was for sure.

"Could you just throw it from there?" he requested as she neared the cockpit.

Jenette obliged, mesmerized. The outworlder was not a pimply-faced adolescent or a weather-wrinkled geriatric, but thirty-four. Thirty-four! That was *middle-aged* by New Ascension standards. Jenette had read about that condition in books, but had never seen it first hand.

The still-curing uniform stuck together, resisting the outworlder's attempts to put it on. Jenette knew she should look away, but her eyes were tempted as he squirmed into it. Arms slipped into sleeves. Pant legs stretched as long limbs pressed into them.

The fabric slid over a nicely toned butt.

Technician's hands sealed a fiberweld-strip up the front and pulled on boots, which Jenette also tossed upon request. Finally, he climbed out of the cockpit—killing the engines as he did so—and stood, looking quite ill at ease, but also quite dashing in the white uniform.

Nobody moved. Nobody said anything.

He tried, ineffectually, to smooth a shock of unruly hair. "Sorry about the misunderstanding," he ventured, eyes darting at Arrou.

"Rrrrr," Arrou growled, sniffing him. "Smell like flowers."

Jenette drew a sharp breath—jasmine!—and abruptly remembered the significance of the smell of jasmine and a white uniform. She took a step closer. There were gold shooting stars on the outworlder's collar and gold bars at his cuffs.

"You're a Pilot!"

"Yes," the outworlder said nervously, adding, "I crashed here yesterday."

The word "Pilot" hit Jenette like a tidal wave. It was a word steeped in Enclave history, spoken with reverence verging on the religious. She unconsciously stacked her fists over her heart. "If you're a Pilot," she said as the implications caught up with her, "then you came in a fugueship. You can take us off this planet!" For a brief instant Jenette imagined a wonderful new future on a different world, without Sacrament and Scourge: no more fear of growing old, no more slavery, no more war. . . .

But the Pilot held up a hand. "I *crashed*," he repeated.

Jenette looked around the wrecked vessel, suddenly realizing that it was not a boat, but the remains of a spacecraft of some kind. "Can't you call another one down from orbit?" she asked.

The Pilot's face, already grave, became graver. "You don't understand. I'm not talking about this heap." He stole a look to the southwest. "I crashed my fugueship."

Those words caused him pain, Jenette saw.

But she barely knew what to think, never mind say. The hope

of evacuation had been euphoric, and short, which was disappointing, but the reality of a Pilot on New Ascension, that changed everything. Her father's plans. The Body's plans. Her plans. . . . A Pilot was a wild card. Jenette quickly decided that until she knew how he fit unto the grand scheme of things, she must be careful of what she said. Still, she could not help sympathizing with the strange man. He knew nothing of the maelstrom that he had fallen into, nothing of Sacrament and Scourge and, like her, he was stranded in a hostile environment not of his own choosing.

She extended her hand. "I'm Subconsul—er, Consul—Jenette Tesla, and that's Arrou."

The Pilot stared at her outstretched hand, his own hovering undecidedly between the two of them.

"*I* don't bite," Jenette joked.

Slowly, tentatively, his fingertips drew closer to hers. She shivered involuntarily as their palms touched, then slipped together, and Jenette was pleasantly surprised by a firm clasp. He did not flinch like a gelding.

"Fugueship Pilot Lindal Karr," he said.

"Welcome to New Ascension."

Karr rolled the words over his tongue. "New Ascension." He pulled his hand back.

Jenette couldn't read his expression. Was the dour set of the Pilot's mouth a wry grin or a grimace? Was he relieved, distressed, happy? She couldn't tell.

"Is your colony near?" Karr asked.

"No," Jenette said quickly.

"Yes," Arrou blurted at the same time.

Karr frowned.

"No and yes," Jenette hurried to find an explanation that served her purposes, without outright lying. "But we can't go there. Our crawler is broken."

Unconsciously, she glanced northeast, back toward the Enclave.

Karr caught the look. His frown deepened. "It seems we are at cross purposes."

Jenette cursed herself for such a stupid mistake. Now the Pilot

would demand to be taken to the Enclave. "Not cross purposes,"
she said, trying to smooth things over, "no, a miscommunication . . . that's all."

Karr stiffened. "No miscommunication. Your attempt to deceive
is clear. I am trained to spot such flatlander behavior patterns."

"No," Jenette protested, "that's not—"

Karr cut her off. Clearly uncomfortable with how their dialogue
was unfolding, his words came out stiffly and formally. "Let us be
direct with one another. My objective lies in the direction opposite
your colony. I cannot transport you there. If you wish I will deposit
you on a nearby island, but considering the violent nature of indigenous species, that does not seem wise. You may accompany
me, if you desist in attempts to manipulate, and I will attempt to
return you to your colony after my objectives are complete. But I
warn you, that may be some time from now. I regret speaking so
harshly, but that is the situation."

Karr stood defiant, expecting protest.

Jenette could hardly restrain her joy. She forced herself to look
suitably chastised. "I'm sorry. Of course we will be glad to go with
you and help you any way we can."

Karr relaxed a little.

"How far southwest is your goal?" Jenette asked sweetly.

"I don't know," Karr admitted. "Perhaps days."

Again Jenette was overjoyed. The farther they got from the Enclave, the better! "And time is of the essence, I suppose?"

"Exactly," said Karr.

Jenette scrutinized the water-filled lifter. "It looks as though
we'll be lucky to still be floating by night fall."

"It is not as bad as it looks," Karr said, becoming a bit more an-
imated. "I could get it flying with a few critical parts." He pointed
at the cockpit. "The controls are shot."

"What kind of controls do you need?" Jenette asked noncha-
lantly.

"Just about anything. All colony equipment is standardized."
Karr went to the pile of junk in the center of the deck and rummaged through it. He pulled out a device with a strange array of
servo arms on one end. They scissored crab-like when he twisted

the main shaft. "The right tools wouldn't hurt, either. This is all that's left of the emergency repair kit," he said disgustedly.

Arrou trotted over and sniffed the tool. "Not good."

"You're telling me," said Karr, still nervous around the large alien. He waved an arm where the cockpit canopy used to be. "It's designed to adjust a nav system that fell off at ten thousand feet."

Jenette had an idea. Her mind traced pathways of cause and effect and then, with an internal decision made, she innocently said, "We have tools and parts back at our crawler."

Arrou shot her a wary look. "No nine-sixteenths grippy," he rumbled suspiciously.

"We can make do with an adjustable grippy," Karr said. He did not pick up on the sudden tension between Jenette and the alien.

"Great," she said lightly. "Why don't we take a cruise around to the other side of this island?"

Before Arrou could object, Karr leaned into the cockpit. The two rear engines thrummed to life and the lifter arched around in search of spare parts.

"Rrrrr," Arrou growled from the deck of the lifter. "Not hurt crawler."

The six-wheeled vehicle was moored alongside the heavy lifter. Both vehicles floated within fifty yards of the Feral island. Karr lay in the crawler cab, where he had begun unfastening parts from its dash. At the menacing rumble from Arrou, he looked at Jenette, who was on the crawler with him.

"Don't worry about him," she reassured. "He'll get over it."

Karr was not convinced and kept one eye on the alien as he resumed disassembling the dash. He grabbed hold of a module, working his fingers under the edges. It was stuck.

"Pull."

Jenette grasped a braid of microfiber relays.

Arrou twitched, distressed. "Fibers break."

The fibers were stronger than Arrou thought. Jenette yanked and, with a screech of wedged plastic, the module came free, still connected to the relays. But it was too much for Arrou. He sprang onto the crawler, grabbed the module from Jenette, and held it protectively. He barred his teeth at Karr. "Not hurt crawler!"

Feeling angry alien breath for the third time that day, Karr squirmed back against the control levers.

"Arrou!" Jenette scolded.

"Pilot hurts crawler!" Arrou accused.

"He's not going to hurt it," Jenette reasoned, "just borrow a few parts. I'm sure he can put them back later."

Arrou looked at the tangle of microfibers, considered, then leaned over Karr, looking very menacing. "Put back *now.*"

Jenette was mortified. "Arrou! That's not very nice! You apologize."

"No."

"Arrou!"

"Not hurt crawler."

Jenette apologized to Karr. "I'm sorry. He's not usually like this. Arrou, get back on the heavy lifter this instant."

Arrou would not budge. He stood between the two humans, clutching the module to his breast and ready to stop Karr from further pillage. Karr felt intimidated, but to his surprise, he also sympathized with the alien; after all, protective feelings for a vessel were something he could understand. Karr sat up.

"Grrrrr."

Karr moved his hands away from any crawler components. "Arrou," he said to the alien, "you like the crawler a lot; I can tell."

"Like a lot," Arrou confirmed.

"Why?"

"Crawler fast."

"I see. How fast?"

Arrou responded proudly. "Twenty-five knots."

"Twenty-five knots?" Karr reflected. "And what sort of propulsion system does it have?"

"AstroFlow electric. Six hundred horsepower. Twenty-six thousand pounds tow."

Karr looked at Jenette. "Is that correct?"

"If he says so." Jenette shrugged. "He knows more about that stuff than me."

Karr returned his attention to Arrou. "See those big thrusters?" he said, pointing to the corners of the heavy lifter. "They can boost sixty million pounds to high orbit. And you want to talk about fast? An undamaged heavy lifter can do five hundred knots in atmospheric flight, and this one can probably still do one hundred."

"Five hundred knots," Arrou repeated, taken off guard. "That fast."

"Exactly," said Karr. "And we can go that fast, but to do it we need to use parts from the crawler."

Arrou was not ready to give up yet, however. "Want to drive crawler," he emphasized.

"Arrou," Jenette interjected. "You know that's impossible."

"Forbidden," Arrou said stubbornly, "not impossible."

Jenette threw her hands in the air. "I don't make the rules. This crawler is Enclave property and Enclave rules say domestics don't drive crawlers."

It looked like another impasse, but Karr had a simple solution. "Arrou, I'm in command of the heavy lifter. I make the rules. What if I teach you how to drive it?"

"*Fly* it?" Arrou corrected.

"Yes, fly," Karr confirmed.

"Really?"

"Really. And we can take the crawler too. There's plenty of room on deck. Good plan?"

"Urrrkurrrkurrrk," the alien rumbled, looking between the two vehicles. "Promise?"

"Cross my heart and hope to die."

Jenette flinched—nobody said that on New Ascension—but she was impressed with how Karr handled Arrou, like an equal and not an underling. "Well Arrou, what do you say?"

Arrou's gaze settled on the lifter, his answer coming in the form of a dreamy, glazed expression and hushed words. "Five hundred knots . . . !"

XII

"Failure shapes us: no one ever learned by trial-and-success. Every tear shed and every drop of blood spilled hammers us on the anvil of our flaws. But do not be misled! Do not idolize failure. Mere failure does not ensure wisdom, just as mere survival does not ensure strength. Many fail and are found wanting, pervaded by weakness. We must drive out the weakness in our minds and turn our failures into weapons. Only then will we attain the Body Pure."

—*from the speeches of Olin Tesla*

The remainder of that afternoon was deceptively uneventful. Slow-motion streams of bubble-seeds floated downwind over the water. Frequently the rainbow-on-glass balloons popped over the heavy lifter, raining moist spore strands down on everyone's heads. It was all very beautiful, and quite lost on Pilot Lindal Karr, consumed as he was with the sense of time slipping away and the desire to locate the remains of his ship.

Karr made steady progress getting the lifter back in flyable condition. To show Arrou his good faith, they first winched the crawler on deck, where Karr strapped it down, and then finished stripping components. For his part, Arrou watched Karr like a hawk, flinching or groaning as each piece came out, but not interfering, for which Karr was thankful, if uneasy. Even once the stripping was accomplished, the large alien insisted on following Karr around and breathing down his neck, but somehow Karr began the task of reconstructing the heavy lifter's controls. It was a challenge. The heavy lifter had been refitted at Sheldon's World, which

meant that its technology was twenty-seven standard years old.
The crawler was from New Ascension's original seed-colony
equipment, which, based on its manufacture date, made it nearly
one hundred years old. So, while the basic design of all colony
equipment was standardized, it was still a challenge to make the
two sets of components work together. Karr quickly realized that
it would never be possible to get the lifter cockpit back to its original condition. The best he could hope for was a workable jury-rig
system that would allow him to fly at low altitudes and speeds, and
that's what he set out to make.

After an uneasy period of alien shadowing human, Karr and
Arrou arrived at an unspoken truce. Karr was careful to show the
Khafra exactly what he was doing with the crawler parts and Arrou
assisted—which was mostly helpful—by holding the units and replacement lengths of microfiber in position as Karr swapped good
modules for bad. Karr even drew on the alien's knowledge of the
crawler when confronted by components he did not recognize. The
new control system began to take shape, all in accordance with a
blueprint in Karr's head. And, as a small bonus, the activity kept
Karr from thinking about his ship.

Jenette did her best to bail water out of the leaky craft. It was
tedious, but she attacked the problem with single-minded fury, as
if every drip of water in the hull was a personal affront. She tried
several stratagems, including scooping with her hands and bailing
with small receptacles.

"That's not necessary," Karr said at one point.

"Those are my crawler parts going into your lifter," Jenette
replied. "I've got an investment in keeping this thing afloat."

Karr shrugged. At least it gave her something to do with her
abundant energy. Already Karr saw that Jenette had the determination of humans twice her size. She eventually settled on using a
wide chunk of fiberplast to set up sloshing patterns and sweep
waves of fluid over the lifter's shallow sidewalls.

By the time a setting sun pressed onto the horizon, the lifter had
not yet sunk and its control systems had been completely re-
worked.

"Making progress?" Jenette asked.

Karr nodded, double-checking his circuitry.

Enthusiastic paisley patterns course down Arrou's limbs. "Arrou fly now?"

"First we test," Karr cautioned. "Then you fly."

Arrou's spirits dampened, but not by much. "What wait for?"

Satisfied that they had done the best job possible under the circumstances, Karr climbed into the cockpit and sat on a pile of cases that Arrou had put there to replace the missing ejector couch. The dash was a jumble of dead instruments and bolted-on crawler components. Karr flipped them on, tensing as they glowed to life. Each thruster purred in turn. *One, two, three, four.*

"Excellent," Karr said to Arrou. "We did it."

Yellow stars sparkled on the alien's head, a pattern Karr hoped indicated happy agreement. He looked at Jenette. There was no place to strap her in. "Hold on to the back of the cockpit," he advised. "I'll take it slow."

Feeling fluttery in her stomach—this would be the first flight of a New Ascension native in two decades, and her first flight ever—Jenette knelt and grasped an exposed strut. Arrou crouched beside her, claws gripping metal and ceramite.

Karr took hold of the new collective-throttle lever, which had been the crawler's power range selector, and pulled. It was much easier than trying to move four broken-off sliders at the same time. The engines ramped up smoothly. Silver water frothed under the cowlings.

"Three, two, one, *liftoff!*"

Water vaporized and strands of bladder weed sprayed out as the reborn lifter rose into the air. Karr hovered at ten feet, letting cataracts of water drain from a thousand tiny fissures. The hull creaked, but did not break apart. Karr eased the lifter upward. Soon they were floating higher than the tallest trees, with a stunning view of the emerald ring-island below. The ocean stretched in all directions, its silvery waves burnished copper near the setting sun. Shadows stretched long from islands scattered around the horizon.

"Howoooo!" cheered Arrou.

Jenette's knuckles tightened on the cockpit strut.

"Now we'll attempt forward flight," Karr said.

Arrou's head bobbed in agreement. "Five hundred knots!"

Karr pushed the yoke forward. The heavy lifter nosed down as invisible thrust vectored aft and he pulled up on the collective throttle to keep from losing altitude. The lifter transitioned to forward flight.

"Five hundred knots, five hundred knots!" Arrou chanted.

Karr kept the airspeed well below that, but the wind still whipped at them with exhilarating force.

"Free, freeee!" crowed the alien.

Karr looked back at Jenette. "How are you doing?"

"I'm fine," she said, feeling the heady rush like Arrou, but also keenly aware of how exposed they were on the flying slab.

"High good," Arrou observed. "See lots."

Jenette looked below. Arrou was correct. The view was superb. They were over open ocean and heading away from Feral Island 716—which distracted her from her misgivings about altitude and speed. "How about a closer look at that island?" she asked Karr.

Karr obligingly turned the yoke toward it. The lifter banked around. Soon they were humming above golden cotton-ball tree-tops. The landscape reminded Karr of whimsical children's book illustrations.

Jenette caught a glimmer of light in a clearing and tapped Karr's shoulder. "Over there," she pointed. Seconds later, the lifter buzzed over a group of very surprised creatures.

"Ferals!" Jenette exclaimed.

It was a settlement of some sort, with several dozen startled inhabitants looking up at the flying machine. Jenette was overjoyed. Gone was the chaos of rampant jungle. Fast-growing plants had been tended into leafy, humpbacked shelters and there were stockpiles of dried sharkworms and tubers. Stands of meat-fruit trees grew in rows with hedge barricades to keep out wild animals. It was exactly what Jenette was looking for. Settlement meant social structure, social structure meant organized leadership, and organized leadership meant an authority that she could approach.

The Ferals quickly recovered their wits, kicking on their camouflage and blending into dusky shadows.

"Veering off," Karr announced.

"No, go back," said Jenette. "Circle around."

"I don't like it," said Karr, with a nervous glance at Arrou. "Those things are smart. Who knows what kind of projectile weaponry they've developed."

"None as far as I know," Jenette argued. "Besides, we're a hundred feet up!"

"Another reason to be cautious," said Karr. "We should set down and give all systems a once over."

"Please," Jenette pleaded. "I need to get a fix on that location. It's important."

"Very well," Karr said reluctantly.

Of course Jenette didn't tell Karr that she intended to contact those Ferals as soon as they set down. "Arrou, remember that spot."

"Okay," Arrou said as they swung around.

The clearing was empty on the second pass, but Jenette was pleased to see Arrou look for landmarks and choose a distinct square pattern of sailtrees, which poked above the jungle canopy nearby.

Karr was not so pleased. Aside from his distrust of Ferals, the lifter was not responding to his liking. Karr tapped the left rubber pedal, which should have activated a thrust correction and brought the tail around, but instead there was a strange vibration.

"Aborting," Karr declared, using the control yoke to bank for the ocean. No more than two seconds had elapsed when there was a loud crack and a shower of blue-white sparks erupted from the left front thruster.

The lifter pitched down at that corner.

Jenette yelped and lost her grip. She tumbled through the sparks and slammed into the thruster cowling along with an avalanche of Karr's salvage. The crawler shifted in its restraining cables, further imbalancing the load. The deck pitched steeper. Arrou's claws skittered on the hull and he fell onto Jenette.

"Get off!" Jenette yelled, unable to move.

"Trying!" Arrou clawed for grip on the slippery ceramite.

The heavy lifter was losing altitude, a trail of sparks blowing out behind it. Karr worked furiously, shutting down the malfunctioning thruster, which put the flying craft in a tight, downward spiral.

"Brace yourselves!" Karr warned. "We're going down!" Karr did his best to clear the island. Tree pompoms whipped at the lifter, snagging on its leading edge and exploding into blinding sprays of leaf matter. The flying slab shot out over open ocean, losing altitude and splashing down. The hull slid thirty yards, water spraying up in the sideways light of sunset, before coming to a stop. Karr, and the boxes under his butt, hammered forward into the dash. Arrou fell into the water.

Bruised and aching, Karr staggered out of the cockpit and threw a line overboard. Arrou was already stroking back, a flurry of sharkworm splashes honing in on him. He closed both forepaws on the cable and heaved himself over the sidewall.

"Not hurt," the alien sputtered.

Karr then helped Jenette free of the wreckage. "That was exciting," she said, brushing herself off.

"Too exciting," Karr agreed distractedly. He broke off and followed a trail of soot across the deck, then pulled up a strand of charred microfiber.

"Braid shorted out," Arrou panted.

Karr's voice was full of self-reproach. "I must have spliced it badly. This was my fault."

"Don't beat yourself up," Jenette said, already thinking about the Feral encampment. "You couldn't know this would happen and we all agreed to go up."

"It's not about *agreeing*," Karr spat. "It's about choosing and consequences. I'm a Pilot. If my choices lead to personal injury and the inability to locate my ship, that's gross dereliction of Duty. I cannot allow that to happen."

"Point taken," Jenette allowed; not wanting to get into an argument over it. "Don't let it happen again," she added, which seemed to mollify Karr.

"Flying fun," said Arrou.

"Hush," said Jenette.

The sun, swollen into a wide orange ember on the horizon, disappeared before they could speak again and an unwanted howl called attention to the fact that they had come to rest scant yards from Feral Island 716.

Howrrraaaaaaaooooooouuuuu!

The single cry ululated from the depths of darkening green jungle. Another voice took up the call, and then another and another. Arrou went stiff, sniffing and listening.

"Ferals?" asked Karr.

"Many Ferals," replied Arrou.

Karr frowned. "They must have followed us down."

"Are they close?" asked Jenette.

"Wind funny. Not know." Arrou abruptly leaped the five yards between lifter and shore. "Back soon."

"Arrou, get back here," Jenette demanded.

But Arrou bounded off into the foliage. "High good," he called, "see lots."

"Where is he?" Jenette hissed, straining to see in the lowering light.

"There." Karr pointed to a shooting-star palm fifty feet in from the shore. Its trunk quivered, and then Arrou climbed into view, rimmed by the fading glow of sunset. "Third tree on the left, above the deep red leaves."

"This is stupid," Jenette cursed. She wanted her next encounter with Ferals to be on her terms, not theirs.

Karr called out Arrou's actions. "He's looking around. Checking for trouble. . . ."

"I see him."

"He's coming back down," Karr continued, but the four-legged shape suddenly stopped and turned the same color as the leaves of the trees. "He just went invisible . . . ?"

"Bad news," Jenette decided.

The shoreline seconded her opinion. The foliage was alive with the sounds of unseen movement. Karr picked up the Gattler and pulled Jenette behind the crawler as, rapidly, the unseen menace became ominously visible. *As far as the eye could see, stretching beyond the island's curve in either direction, the twilight shore was lined with Ferals.*

*   *   *

Ferals stacked up, two and three deep, along the shore. Karr waited for an attack, bracing the Gattler on the hood of the crawler. The Ferals saw them clearly, a mere spring away, but for some reason held off a final rush. They stood, staring, with unnerving, unblinking eyes, skins perfectly matching the deepening indigo sky.

"Why don't they attack?" Karr whispered.

"They are not inherently violent," Jenette hissed. "Maybe it's some sort of greeting ritual."

Karr did not lower the Gattler. The last *greeting ritual* he had participated in consisted of snarling and chasing.

For a while, the Ferals made no noise. The forest made no noise. Not even buzzers or peepers dared break the eerie quiet.

Then, a peculiar thing happened.

One by one the horde of Ferals bowed down on their forelegs, facing their chameleon backs outward from the island. Like a spectator wave sweeping across a stadium, they blacked out, discernible only as blacker shadows against dark jungle. Except for the gentle roll of the island on water, the scene was motionless. The minutes drew on. No one and nothing stirred.

"Creepy," said Karr.

Karr's predisposition to assume the worst about Ferals annoyed Jenette. "I told you," she insisted, "they are not inherently violent."

When ten minutes elapsed with no immediate attack, Karr's attention switched from the Ferals to the inoperative thruster. "I'm going to fix that," he decided, shoving the Gattler into Jenette's petite hands. "You hold them off."

"Forget it," Jenette objected. Whatever the Ferals were doing, they were calm and she was not about to jeopardize that by brandishing a weapon. It was perfect. She had intended to search out the Ferals from the encampment—instead they had come to her.

"They respect a show of force," Karr insisted. "I know that much. Here. Hold it like this."

"Don't tell me what to do," said Jenette. "I know how to hold a gun and I know how to shoot—but I'm still not taking it."

Karr saw that further argument was futile. Laying the Gattler in plain sight on the crawler, he squirmed into the cab and, trying not to make too much noise, fumbled in the toolkit. Then he felt under the dash for more microfibers. "How's Arrou?" he asked, finger-tips closing around a braided strand.

"They haven't spotted him yet," Jenette responded. "I think he snuck back into the treetop." She wished he was beside her, both for his protection and knowledge. She reviewed her vocabulary of Khafra words, preparing to speak. It was a big gamble and she wanted to get it right. No one knew how Ferals would react to a human speaking their own language.

Karr sighed after crimping a few strands. Night fell fast on New Ascension and the cab interior was pitch black. Strangely, though, he could see Jenette's face above him, mouthing silent words in a faint red glow. "Where's that light coming from?"

"The horizon . . . that way," Jenette pointed, her mouth going slack.

Karr recalled the aura he had seen on the previous night. "Southwest?"

"Yes," Jenette mumbled. "I guess."

"So it's not colony lights."

"No. That's the other way. Oh, my. . . ."

From the floor of the cab, Karr saw a spray of light across Jenette's features. Glistening rainbow reflections frolicked in her eyes.

"What is it?"

All Jenette could say was, "Wow."

Karr sat up.

The Ferals were glowing. Hundreds of motionless bodies lit up the shoreline with a dance of ghostly colors, shimmering will-o-the-wisps. Karr stared, entranced. "What is it?" he asked again.

"Don't know," Jenette muttered. "Never seen anything like it."

The luminescent phenomenon was not restricted to FI-716. Karr saw that wherever island silhouettes loomed on the ocean, firefly dots of alien light blinked in the night. It was beautiful in an eerie, elegant way—so beautiful that Karr forgot about the mi-crofibers in his sweaty hands. As he watched, the ground-bound aurora began to build in intensity. Ferals near the lifter absorbed one another's patterns, each adding its own splash of color as the radiance bled from one alien to the next. A sameness spread along the shore, and the more *same* the light became, the more powerful it became. Yet, it was not bland, safe sameness, but the sameness of an avalanche, of many differences reveling in a rush down a mountainside. The light sang, intoxicating. Karr felt as though he was being swept along in the light, riding the front of the radiant avalanche, following it around crests and valleys of darkness. . . .

To a single Feral.

A lone Feral with the glowbuds on half its body darkened—and a gouge on its neck like that left by the barrels of a Gattler. Karr recognized his enemy from that afternoon, the suspicious Feral who had fought Karr to the point of defeat and then inexplicably left after tasting Karr's blood. That Feral was the leader of the light.

That Feral raged.

Despite half the Feral's glowbuds being blackened out, his rage was a sight to behold. Irresistible. When he raged, the whole island raged. When he challenged, the whole island challenged with him. His sorrow and anger drove the others on. What Karr had felt in the alien's desolate howl that afternoon now filled Karr's vision, bathing his body in that emotion. It was like the sorrow of centuries lost to loneliness. It was like the bittersweet splendor of centuries given to Duty in a fugueship.

Karr was frozen in place as, across dark ocean waters, other Ferals on other islands rallied behind other emotion-filled leaders, building radiant arsenals of their own and then unleashing them. Broadsides of light smeared over the waves. Salvoes of radiance exchanged under the night's star-dotted dome.

XIII

*It is easy to dodge the teeth of an enemy, but difficult to
avoid the claws of a friend.*

—*Feral aphorism*

Arrou clenched his eyes. He must not look.

But he wanted to look, so very much. The lights spoke to him.
They called to him, caressed him. They enticed him with memory
feelings of warmth and belonging. Feelings from a long time ago,
before Jenette, before humans.

No! He must not look. Must not participate. He was on a mission
and must stay secret.

But the lights made patterns on his eyes, even when tightly
shut. He burrowed his head under fibrous leaves atop the tree. Still
the bright light shone through.

Join us, it said. *We are the Radiance. Come to the Radiance.* . . .

Arrou's breath came in short gulps. The smell of palm flowers
in the tree's top smelled sour compared to the sweet glow of the
Radiance. Each moment apart from its light was torture. Without
realizing it, Arrou's blending colors had gone dark and his back
raised up like the bowing Ferals below. He trembled like a leaf before
a storm—he must not give in!

But he could not help it.

Be the Radiance. . . .

Arrou's eyes opened. He saw the Radiance. Shivers swept along
his glowbuds as he lit up, adding his spark to the splendor. And the
Radiance saw him too. It brought Arrou to its soft, warm bosom.

And for the first time in his memory, Arrou was *home*.

*   *   *

The islands battled into alliances of brilliance, attacking and counterattacking, conquering and surrendering. Very bright were the islands arrayed against FI-716, but Karr saw that it would not be beaten. For, no matter the spectacle united against it, Karr's enemy played the light with unstoppable strength of feeling. His enemy's longing enflamed the longing of his radiant allies; his misery consoled their misery and his loss eased their loss. Soon, all the points of light, all the visible ring-islands, were enveloped in a single, synchronous radiance, following that single Feral's will. The radiance throbbed lighter and brighter until it reached a unified peak and held, proclaiming its existence to the heavens.

Pain and pleasure. Sorrow and love. Hope and desolation. These things Karr experienced stronger than he had ever experienced before, stronger than he had ever thought possible. It was just light, after all, but so strong, so, so . . . so much more than just light. Karr found himself wishing that he could light up his blank skin and glow in synchrony with the aliens, no matter how painful the double-edged feelings might be, wanting never to let them go. Never, ever. Jenette felt it, too, as well as the numb void that followed, like a blind man seeing for the first time, and then returning to blindness.

Slowly, the light faded.

"I feel . . . invisible," said Jenette.

Moving as if in a trance, vision smudged with afterimages, Karr dropped out of the crawler and solemnly began swapping good microfiber relays for bad.

The Ferals on shore began to shift.

Jenette looked for Arrou. He had been in his tree the whole time. She remembered now that he had flashed with all the rest, unable to resist the magic and blessed with the means to respond in kind. His energetic colors had been out of sync, like a human child tooting a kazoo to Mozart. Now that the light show was over, Ferals prowled at the base of his tree. They could have climbed it as easily as Arrou had, but made no aggressive moves. The Ferals did not even look in his direction.

The Khafra opposite the heavy lifter were a different story.

There was no question of their focus on the humans. In arching backs and colors steeped in hatred, Jenette recognized their mood. She looked at the Gattler, wondering if Karr was right, but refused to pick it up. Weapons were the way of her father.

She must follow her own path.

"Just a few more seconds," Karr said. Ferals bunched up on shore, pressing to get closer to the humans as he merged microfibers into the left front thruster control conduit. He snapped the last connector into place. Double-checking the strands, and paying no attention to Jenette, Karr hurried back to the cockpit, flipping switches and pushing buttons to power up. All four engines spun up to a gentle hum.

"Prepare for launch," Karr said with satisfaction.

"No," Jenette said from behind him, the strange tone of her voice staying his hands on the controls. Karr turned, intending to protest, but fell silent.

Jenette was standing in a precarious position on the lifter's landward sidewalk where any sudden use of the engines would topple her into predator infested waters. She extended her arms, palms outstretched to the Ferals.

"What are you doing?" Karr hissed.

"Rikit-ee-brikhauss," Jenette said, her voice cracking.

"Rickety brick what?" Karr said, confused. "Get down from there. You'll make those things mad!"

The Ferals were just as shocked at Jenette's behavior as Karr was. They stopped in their tracks and tilted their heads in surprise.

"*Please* get down from there," Karr urged.

Jenette ignored him, counting on her vulnerable position to prevent him from taking off. She repeated the Khafra words, stronger, "Rikit-ee-brikhauss." *Light be upon you.*

The Ferals angled their ear pits toward her, straining to hear. Their eyes pressed fully forward from their skulls, as if straining to see in the dark (which could not be right, Jenette knew, since Khafra had extremely good night vision).

Leaving the engines running, Karr darted behind the crawler and retrieved the Gattler.

"Rikit-ee-brikhauss!" Jenette said as loud as she could.

This time several of the aliens responded, bodies flashing with light language, *flash, pop, sparkle, pop.* "Din-tixss-ymisstash," they vocalized, hesitantly. *Shadows away.* But they clearly were reacting without thinking. Some even held four-thumbed paws over shocked mouths as the words tumbled out. Other Khafra rumbled threateningly, distrustful of the human using their language. They, Jenette saw, wanted to kill her more than ever.

But at least she had their attention.

<<This one brings peace,>> Jenette said in words she had rehearsed with Arrou many times. <<This one brings peace from human colony. Who speaks for Khafra?>>

The Ferals stared at her, uncomprehending. Jenette had said the words right, she knew, but the expected response did not materialize. She struggled to find alternate words. <<Humans and Khafra must . . . stop conflict. Want peace for humans and Khafra. Do Khafra understand?>>

The Ferals were trying to understand her. They repeated some of her words, as if struggling with a foreign language and not their own, and they flashed at her, *pop pop flash crackle,* trying to communicate.

<<Not . . . *flare, glare* . . . understand.>>

<<Peace,>> Jenette repeated. <<Stop fighting. No war. No dying.>>

The Ferals were more confused by her last comment. <<No dying?>> They began to growl.

<<No dying from humans—*because* of humans,>> Jenette added, quickly realizing that she had made some kind of mistake. <<No more fighting. No more Sacrament.>>

Again, there were confused looks. But the Ferals had picked up the word Sacrament. They barraged her with light-code questions.

Flare, flash, poppata, sparkle?

Sparkle (blue), sparkle (green)?

Jenette could not follow the rapid-fire light words, never mind answer, but at least it was a positive sign. If she could keep them talking and not attacking, she reasoned, then there was hope.

Shuffling broke out in the Feral ranks. Those on the shoreline parted as a large Khafra worked his way to the front. Powerful muscles bunched and stretched under tight packed glowbuds, those on one half of his body were pitch black and those on the other dazzling bright.

"That's the one that tried to kill me," Karr warned from behind the crawler.

Karr's enemy snarled to its brethren. <<Lies . . . lies.>> Jenette caught a torrent of unfamiliar words and angry flashing. <<Blank-one lies . . . turn away!>>

Ferals began to avert their eyes from Jenette.

<<No!>> she begged. <<Listen, please! This one comes in peace!>>

The leader raked his mighty hind claws through ghutzu root. <<Blank-ones kill,>> he challenged. <<Blank-ones . . . twist truth. Heed Tlalok! Blank-ones make no Pact . . . kill mothers . . . steal young.>> The leader glowed like an angry neon sign. The hatred was clear, and growing, infecting the Ferals around him.

<<Yes,>> Jenette began, <<but, but . . .>> the right words failed her, <<humans might change . . . humans might stop.>>

<<Never!>> raged the leader.

The Ferals crowded forward on the shore. Jenette was losing them.

"*Thhssss.*" The leader hissed through his teeth, muscles coiling. <<Blank-ones never stop. Tlalok knows . . . but Pact can stop blank-ones!>>

<<Stop . . . blank-ones,>> the mass of Ferals flashed like angry embers. <<Stop blank-ones . . . Stop blank-ones . . .>>

Jenette knew the warning signs. She was no longer in control. Talking was over. And she had placed herself in a very vulnerable position. Suddenly she was afraid.

"Back away from the edge," Karr said in a low, forceful voice. He had stood up behind the crawler, Gattler raised obviously and threateningly into firing position. His right forefinger twitched and the multitool's barrels whirled. "Don't make any sudden moves. I'll cover you."

Jenette did as Karr said, stepping down on the deck and edging back toward him. She made it halfway before the Feral leader, suddenly hunched back, like a spring coiling to launch. The others mimicked him. "Get down!" Karr yelled.

Jenette half dove, half fell to the deck as a wave of Ferals sprang at her. A stream of brown liquid hissed over her head, striking the foremost Ferals. They tumbled back, sticking to their island and howling in frustration. But more and more Ferals pushed forward to leap— always in pairs. And in pairs, Karr hosed them with molecular glue, pair after pair, after pair. Beep, warned the Gattler; the adhesive cartridge was half empty. Karr kept firing, sweeping the stream of adhesive from side to side, and none of the Ferals made it on board.

Beep, beep, beep.

The brown stream stopped. *Pfitzle.*

Karr was out of adhesive. He switched the Gattler to antiseptic froth and foamed the shore, but the Ferals were beyond being stopped by stinging bubbles and a second wave of the aliens lunged forward.

"Back off!" Karr barked in the deepest voice he could muster. He had no more non-lethal options. He aimed the Gattler from side to side, trying to look as menacing as possible.

Pairs of Ferals sprung through the air at the heavy lifter, teeth cones splayed.

Karr's Pilot instincts kicked in. He snapped the selector knob. Chrome barrels spun, set for cutting beam, medium power, narrow distribution.

"Get into the cockpit," Karr yelled at Jenette as he pulled the trigger. "And stay down!"

An invisible beam stabbed out from the Gattler. Karr shot surgically, searing off extremities, trying to wound rather than kill, but his noble intentions backfired. Wounded Ferals fell screaming into silvery water and were torn apart by a feeding frenzy of sharkworms. Those on shore redoubled their efforts to board the lifter.

Karr selected a wide cutting beam dispersion as another wave of Ferals launched into the air. He pulled the trigger. The first to land on deck exploded into steaming vapor, but still the Ferals did not stop. They leapt, unafraid of the danger, focused only on getting at their human enemies. Jenette scrambled on hands and knees, through a rain of flash-cooked remains, and into the cock-pit as the slaughter accelerated. More and more Ferals made it across the water before the cutting beam got them. Smoldering skeletons piled up on deck. Karr could not sweep the Gattler fast enough to incinerate them all. Each wave got further and further inboard before exploding into heated mist.

"Grab the steering yoke and pull up on the throttle!" Karr yelled at Jenette.

"Grab the what and pull the what?" Jenette yelled back. "I don't know how to work this thing!"

"Hold the center stick and pull up on the left hand lever!" Karr gasped out between shots.

Jenette looked around at the foreign controls, her hands tentatively hovering around the throttle lever and steering yoke.

"Now!" Karr yelled. "Do it!"

Jenette grabbed and yanked.

The lifter surged out of the water as if a bomb had detonated under its hull. It lunged up through the building cloud of crimson vapor to a height of twenty feet, but Jenette had trouble holding the controls steady and the vehicle faltered, lurching from side to side.

Ferals sprung from the shore to the platform, clawing over the sidewalls and scrambling across blood-slick decking. One jumped at Jenette, talons extended to slash her head off. Karr fired. Five hundred pounds of dead weight slammed the outside of the cock-pit and tumbled down into ocean water.

"Get us higher!" Karr ordered.

Jenette manhandled the controls as best she could. "Fly," she exhorted the lifter through clenched teeth. "Fly, fly, fly!"

The heavy lifter rose erratically. Adrenaline pumping, Karr washed the Ferals on deck with the cutting beam. A last surviving Feral sprang at him. Karr held the trigger down as it charged and bowled into him. By the time they both tumbled to the deck, most of the alien was missing.

The lifter labored to treetop level.

Karr pulled through the center of the smoking, spasming corpse and scrambled over to the orbiter's sidewall. Below, Ferals were doing everything in their power to get to the lifter, clawing on top of one another, even climbing and leaping from treetops in a vain attempt to get airborne.

Karr couldn't help but respect their uncompromising ferocity.

A different moving form caught his attention. Arrou was leaping from treetop to swaying treetop in an effort to get closer to the flying platform.

"Wait, wait!" he called.

But the lifter was sliding sideways out to sea. Karr ran to the cockpit. "Shove over." Jenette squeezed aside. "Now give me the yoke." The lifter bucked once as Karr leaned in beside her to take the thrust lever, and then again as Jenette hopped out and he climbed in behind the yoke. Karr quickly stabilized the sideslip and banked back toward the ring-island.

"What are you doing?" Jenette suddenly asked.

Karr nodded to Arrou's tree. "Going back for him."

Jenette's nose crinkled, her thoughts in chaos. Her attempts to contact Ferals had failed disastrously, causing the very death and carnage she had sought to stop. She looked down at Arrou. Ferals were frothing at the mouth trying to get at the out-of-reach heavy lifter. But they ignored Arrou. Jenette made a decision. It wasn't how she had planned it—she had not planned it at all—and it added to her feeling of sickly distress, but Jenette suddenly knew what must be done.

"We can't stop," she said to Karr. "Get us out of here."

Karr wasn't sure he had heard right. "Abandon him?"

"He'll be all right," Jenette said in a cold voice.

"Recovery is possible," Karr insisted. "I can maneuver right up to the tree."

"That's not the point. It's better this way."

Karr circled the shooting-star palm, unsure what to do. "But they'll rip him apart."

Arrou waited anxiously, preparing to leap.

"Are they ripping him apart now? Look! They aren't hurting him!"

Karr looked. The Ferals could easily have climbed Arrou's tree, but those around the base merely mulled around—unlike the snarling pack that jumped and gnashed at the air trying to get at the lifter.

"See?" said Jenette.

Karr hesitated. "This doesn't feel right."

"You have to trust me," Jenette said, becoming more desperate. She had to convince Karr before she lost her own weak resolve. She had to do what was right no matter how much it hurt. "Please! You're an outworlder and you don't know what's going on. I do. This is for the best."

Karr could not make a rational decision without facts. It all boiled down to gut instinct—and there were tears pooling in Jenette's eyes. Apparently she had not made her decision lightly.

Without further argument, Karr turned the lifter and accelerated away from the island.

Arrou's face fell, shocked and confused.

Karr looked back once to see the tiny figure waving frantically. Neither he nor Jenette saw Arrou jumping to the last tree on the edge of the island, nor did they see him sit quietly and hang his head, but both Karr and Jenette—who, overcome by emotion and the recent bloodshed, doubled over, wracked by dry heaves— heard the mournful howl rise into the night as Arrou realized they had left him behind and were not coming back.

XIV

Life or death is not important. The cycle of life and death, that is the core of Pact. Death gives time for life to grow in. Life gives itself for death to feast on. One does not exist without the other.

—*Feral aphorism*

Imprisoned by the sticky substance, Tlalok watched the blank-ones flee into the night. Many Pact had fallen to their barbarism, as it had been for so many nights and seasons before. Tlalok looked down. Water frothed where voracious mouths feasted on his dead brethren.

Their flashbuds had flared and dimmed as their lives were spent without fulfilling Pact.

Tragedy.

Their brilliance faded without being passed on. The Red Mouths would overflow before Balance was struck again. So many bondmates sundered. Many would pay so that others might live. Tlalok would offer himself up when the time came, but for now he lived. In pain. And the pain where the male blank-one gouged his face earlier that day was nothing compared to the pain of Tlalok's loss.

Tlalok thrashed at his bonds.

Members of the pack hurried into the jungle and returned a few minutes later with hungry grubs, placing them on the sticky goo. They then ladled ocean water over and dripped immune venom onto the wriggling masses. The worms grew, relentlessly doubling and tripling in number and consuming the sticky bonds with insa-

tiable hunger. Tlalok directed the grubs to be used on others before
himself. Unfortunately, the grubs could not eat fast enough to save
all. Some Pact had already lost their brilliance; the blank-one's
substance had sealed off their breath.

"Harouuuuuuu," howled a sadness above.

Tlalok tried to shut it out, as he tried to shut out his own sadness. The male blank-one had killed Tlalok's bondmate, extinguished her light by felling the wind-grabber tree into hungry
waters. There had been no time to find grubs then . . . Lleeala had
been the radiance of Tlalok's life, the radiance of their pack. Always they had followed her, and fought with her and lived with her
as she shone, but now she was gone and there were lonely shades
in Tlalok's heart.

Tlalok was half-blank. The glowbuds on his right side blacked
out in the instinctive Pact way of mourning.

Why had he not killed the male blank-one when he had the
chance, Tlalok wondered. Why did that blank-one taste like Pact?
How could the impossible be true? And how could the blank-one
have tasted so strongly of Pact—with the intensity of not just one,
but *many* individual Khafra? Knowing that it was some kind of
blank-one trick had not helped Tlalok overcome it. The blank-one
had tasted of Pact—and Pact did not kill Pact.

Freed pack members began applying grubs to Tlalok's sticky
bonds.

Tlalok's sorrow at Lleeala's passing was such that if members
of the pack had not gathered around him and loaned him their
light, he might have surrendered to the blackness in despair, losing
his light to sorrow without fulfilling Pact. After sorrow had come
rage. Tlalok had shone that rage in the Clash of Radiance and it
had united the pack under his Radiance—and the packs of neighbor islands, too. All now followed Tlalok. All were bonded by the
unexpected Clash of Radiance.

How could there be a Clash without four moons swollen to full-
ness in the night sky? It did not fit the Balance. The Four Messengers carried small Radiances from the world of light into the world
of night, just as shadows carried small darknesses from the world

of night into the world of light, to keep the Balance. Without the Messengers there could be no Clash.

And yet there had been.

Tears had fallen. The birth of the Burning Heart glowed on the edge of the world . . .

"Harouuuuuuu," wailed the no-pact in the tree.

Tlalok was not the only one with a hole in his heart.

Pact circled around the no-pact's tree. They were unsettled by the sadness, but they did not look. They must not corrupt their Radiance. It was the way.

"Harr-harrouuuuuu!" the no-pact keened.

The female blank-one, who came with the no-pact, had almost corrupted Tlalok's pack with her twisted words. *Peace between blank-ones and Pact.* Of course it was a trick, a vile deception to play on their hopes and longings. Tlalok had never seen a blank-one trying to communicate that way before. So why now? To catch Pact off guard, that was why! To inflict further blank-one atrocities upon them. It had almost worked, only the female blank-one was not speaking the true Pact speech, but the loathsome pidgin speech used by enslaved no-pacts. Tlalok's pack members did not know it—and the female blank-one could not use the light-speech, which made up most of true Pact conversation. So Tlalok's pack had been slow to understand what she said. A little more time and they would have fallen for her corruption, but fortunately Tlalok did understand the pidgin no-pact speech and was able to silence the blank-one female before it was too late.

"Harr-harrouuuuuu! Harr-harrouuuuuu!"

When the hungry grubs finished their work, freeing Tlalok, he joined his pack at the base of the no-pact's tree.

<<Quiet!>> Tlalok flashed angrily.

"Left behind, left behind . . ."

Bile washed Tlalok's long tongue. He felt sorrow for the no-pact and Tlalok could not bear any more sorrow. More suffering would drive him to an extreme act. A severe thing. And he did not want to do it. It would be out of Balance.

<<Silence!>> Tlalok blazed.

The no-pact's sadness recalled too many memories that Tlalok needed to shut off, not because the memories were sad, but because they were happy . . .

The place of new Radiance was thick with the breath of Pact. Their light warmed the enclosing petal walls of the giant blossom. Females moaned with the pain of creation. They lay in a ring around the Red Mouth at the center of the giant flower that enclosed them. Males like Tlalok knelt behind their bondmates, to give comfort, while mid-mates hovered in preparation for the wonder to come. The rest of the pack lined the curving, pink walls: the old, the young bonded pairs who had missed this cycle. None were excluded from the miracle of coming Pact.

Behind each expectant pair were the soon-to-be grandsires and grandmares, knowing that this would be the time for them to fulfill Pact. Only Lleeala's parents glowed behind Tlalok. His had been slain by blank-ones, of course.

As the time neared and female cries grew louder, the pack pulsed in time to their rhythms and the rhythms of the mid-mates. The flower chamber was bright. There must be no shadow, yet. Lleeala cried loudly and dug her claws into Tlalok. Her sleek body shuddered. Tlalok held her tighter as the contractions grew, like those of all the females, rising to excruciating ecstasy and then falling. Many times the unified cycle of pain and brilliance filled the blossom.

And then there were new voices, vulnerable new cries in the light.

Lleeala's mid-mate beamed, holding Tlalok's legacy for the pack to see, as the other mid-mates held other miracles for the pack to see. Four tiny nursling, miniature Tlaloks and Lleealas, skin still blank, squalled in the cold world outside their mother. Four, the sacred number of Pact. Lleeala had done well. Tlalok's heart, so long closed off, and even longer pried at by Lleeala, flooded open at that moment. He wanted to keep the nurslings safe and warm, to keep them from the cold that he, Tlalok, had felt.

Tlalok snipped the umbilicals with his teeth.

Lleeala was dim with fatigue. Her mother and father, full grandmates now, crowded near to share the moment. This was the time all pack member's lives lead to: the completion of Pact. Not all the grandmates were so lucky, some must wait for the next cycle. Lleeala's parents nuzzled the nurslings, and then Lleeala, radiating colors of farewell, but they were not sad. This was how Balance was maintained. It was right.

They blessed daughter and bondmate (they had treated Tlalok as a son, never holding his past against him). Then, each taking two nurslings, they did as other grandmates around the interior of the flower and advanced to the Red Mouth, the center of the blossom, the heart of their island. Not all who advanced were grandmates by blood, some were Pact whose daughters were dead by accident or blank-ones, who stood surrogate for females whose parents were dead by accident or blank-ones. All would be worked out. All would be Balanced in the end. Pact must endure.

Lleeala's sire and mare laid the nurslings at the flower's blatantly sexual stamen and pistils, which were symbolic of Pact, of the cycle binding Radiance and life to Shadow and death.

All Pact dimmed. Now was the time for shadow, when the old gave the secret of life to the young. On their flashbuds, grandmates performed accounts of their allotted years to the blank newborns, their successes, failures, loves, and perserverances. As the essences of the grandmates' lives crescendoed, they bent over the nurslings, ever so carefully nipping tender throat flesh with deadly teeth, and injecting their special essence of life, half into each nursling. The grandmates' drained their bodies of immune venom, which they had received from their grandmates before them, and which they had mingled with that of their bondmates year after allotted year. That essence now passed to the new generation, who would pass it to the next in an unending, expanding cycle.

The nurslings began to sparkle as the Radiance of the grandmates faded. The old generation slumped, falling in on the Red Mouth, cold as ash, the new generation glowing like embers. Midmates advanced, slitting swollen sacks between the grandmates' hind legs, and dipped claws into the writhing darkness within. This contagion they smeared into the nursling's mouths.

The die was cast. The pack flickered approval, for the transfer of immune venom, the essence of life, was not the greatest gift that night. Rather, it was the gift of death that blessed the newborns. While the blank-ones did not know the hour of their endings and spent their lives in constant fear of it, Pact knew their exact allotment of time and were comforted. One hundred and sixty seasons. Every Pact knew his passing appeased the Balance. Every death had meaning. The shadow—that which the blank-ones called Scourge—was now growing within the nurslings. It would nurture their lives. No sickness would afflict them; no plague would strike them down, no madness twist their hearts, until the preordained moment it took them.

This was the Pact. The bargain they all made.

Guaranteed life for guaranteed death. It was good. Barring accidental injury, or death at the hands of blank-ones, the nurslings would grow into adults, fight jealously for Balance, bond into pairs, make Pact, and continue the cycle until their time was up and it was their turn to pay a debt to the Balance with the husks of their bodies and the Radiance of their souls.

Three nights hence, the husks of the grandmates would be gone, dissolved by Scourge into the Red Mouth.

It had been Tlalok's greatest hope to end his days with just such meaning, but that was not to be. Further years saw more tragedy than he had yet known. His nurslings were killed by blank-ones, Lleeala taken from him, and his world thrown into the chaos of the Burning Heart.

And so Tlalok was driven to an extreme act. As long as the no-pact existed, it reminded Tlalok of his loss. Tlalok would find no peace. He must do the forbidden thing.

Tlalok spoke up at the tree. <<No-pact, how are you called?>> Tlalok's pack murmured displeasure.

<<What does the no-pact call itself?>> Tlalok repeated.

<<Name Arrou.>>

Tlalok squinted up at the tree. This Arrou was barely old enough to be considered a young adult, perhaps four and four, perhaps less. He must have been taken by blank-ones at a very early age, for he spoke only the pidgin no-pact words. Tlalok spoke simply so that the no-pact would understand.

<<Come down, Arrou.>>

More displeasure from the pack, but Tlalok darkened them with a crest of warning along his back. <<I am Tlalok, Radiance of this pack. Come down, Arrou. Face fate on four legs.>>

<<Come up,>> Arrou said, mouth blades clattering defiantly.

Such words from a no-pact. Tlalok admired the boldness, but it would not do in front of the others. Tlalok bowed before the tree and said, <<No fear, Arrou.>>

Pack members fluttered iridescent disbelief. Tlalok offered Radiance to the no-pact! <<No, no,>> they protested. <<Balance will shift. Not the way. No-pact is not worthy!>>

<<Who forgets too soon!>> rumbled Tlalok, his words bathing himself in shame even as he spoke them. <<Tlalok was once no-pact! Is then Tlalok not worthy?>>

The pack glowed submissively. <<Tlalok is worthy. Tlalok is Pact now. Arrou is no-pact.>>

Tlalok looked back at Arrou, alone in his tree. It was not the way, but it had been Lleeala's way, all those years ago when Tlalok was no-pact, grieving, suicidal over the loss of his fallen blank-one, as always happened when Bonds were broken, Pact or blank-one. Lleeala had succored Tlalok, given him a new reason to live. Arrou was Tlalok's past and his grief. Tlalok knew he must face that grief. He must cleanse this no-pact with it, so that he might cleanse himself.

He must be merciful and show the no-pact the error of his ways. Lleeala would have wished it that way and Tlalok would abide by her memory, because otherwise her life would truly have meant nothing. This was the path of Balance.

Tlalok reddened out the dissenting flickers in his pack and then they bowed, too. Arrou descended warily. The others made a clearing around the tree and he dropped into it, distrusting and unspeaking.

No-pacts did not know the way, Tlalok remembered. They were taken young. Stolen from Radiance. Orphaned by blank-one avarice. Fettered and stunted by blank-one oppression. Bonded by hideous obscenity to blank-ones. Enslaved and doomed to die without Pact, but made dependent on the very monsters who would kill them.

And now cast off like garbage.

At the whim of those same blank-ones. They had no heart, no shame. The no-pact would die. He did not know the way. Did not know the light. Could not shine the Clash of Radiance. No, his survival was impossible. He could not even feed himself when the island went dormant. This no-pact Arrou knew nothing of these things. The blank-one's gift of abandonment was not freedom. Without belonging and knowing, it was a sentence of unfulfilled death as surely as was enslavement at their hands.

What arrogant cruelty.

<<Must go, must follow,>> Arrou moaned.

Truly, it would be easy to despise this stunted one—as it was easy for Tlalok to despise himself. <<Arrou, does Arrou seek freedom?>>

<<No.>>

<<Good.>> Tlalok said after a pause. He had asked the wrong question for the right reason. <<That is not the way. Come make Pact. Bond with and serve Balance.>>

<<Arrou Pact with Jenette.>>

Tlalok's pack murmured dissent at the blasphemy.

<<There is no Pact with blank-ones,>> Tlalok warned.

<<Must go,>> Arrou flashed adamantly. <<Must find Jenette. Karr take. Must follow.>>

Jenette. That was a female blank-one name, Tlalok remembered. That would be the name of the one who had tried to speak with his pack. And *Karr,* that had to be the name of the male blank-one, the one who had taken the life of his beloved Lleeala. Tlalok rose from his bowed position to full height, which was much larger than Arrou, and rumbled, <<Blank-ones dance against death, not with it!>>

<<Not all humans bad,>> Arrou protested.

Tlalok balked at the hated word. <<All *blank-ones* steal life from Pact to live.>>

Arrou nodded sadly, blank-one fashion. <<Arrou knows.>>

<<Jenette steals life from Arrou to live.>>

Arrou nodded again.

Tlalok hoped that he was making progress. He pursed alternating teeth in the age old gesture of unity—or conspiracy. <<No-pact and blank-ones: same heart,>> he accused.

<<No,>> Arrou argued. <<Domestics want life. Domestics want peace with Ferals. But domestics want humans live, too.>>

"Urrrr!" More hated words. Domestics! Ferals! More blank-one lies. <<Doesn't Arrou want to live?>>

Arrou looked down. <<Not matter.>>

But Tlalok would not let Arrou off that easily. <<Does matter! Doesn't Arrou want the light?>> he persisted. <<Doesn't Arrou want the Radiance?>>

Arrou closed his eyes, shivering. Ghostly remembrances of the Clash of Radiance peeked from his glowbuds. <<Yes. . .>>

<<Then choose! Make Pact, or be blank-one slave. Choose.>>

<<No choice,>> Arrou said, shaking his muzzle.

The pack shifted, ill at ease.

Leaning closer, Tlalok whispered, in the vile human tongue. "Arrou, Tlalok can help you. Tlalok knows you. Tlalok was once no-pact, a . . . *domestic.*" The despicable word seared his tongue, but he had to get through to Arrou. "Tlalok was just like you."

"Then Tlalok knows," Arrou said, meeting his gaze. "Choice made. Long ago."

Tlalok chuffed in frustration. This was the true horror of the blank-ones. With freedom in his teeth, Arrou chose to run back to his fetters. Arrou was powerless to do otherwise because he was force bonded to the blank-one female. The female would have to die—as Tlalok's blank-one had accidentally died—or Arrou would always spurn Tlalok's offer. And even if the blank-one female did die, then it would still not be over. With shame, Tlalok remembered his sorrow at the death of his blank-one. Tlalok remembered the suicidal mourning, the desire to wink out his Radiance, one glowbud at a time, until none remained and the shadow world took him. Only Lleeala had saved Tlalok from such a passing.

It was of no use. Tlalok was wasting his heartbeats. Tlalok had known it all along, but he had hoped. . . .

Tlalok turned away, dismissive.

The rest of his pack followed his lead and headed for the jungle.

<<Wait!>> called Arrou.

Tlalok stopped. <<What, no-pact?>>

<<Arrou thanks Tlalok.>>

Tlalok became grim. <<No-pact cannot give thanks. No Pact, no value. No value, no thanks. No gift. Only taking.>> Tlalok sighed at the waste. <<And the blank-ones keep taking from Arrou.>>

Tlalok looked up at the sky. Soon the Burning Heart would be upon them. There would be many more Clashes of Radiance and many more Tears, and all because of the blank-ones.

<<Blank-ones must die, Arrou,>> Tlalok warned. <<Do not follow them.>>

And with that, his pack pulled paddleboards and larger boats from the undergrowth and, using the thrashings of a bush-peeper entwined in a vine ball to distract sharkworms, they paddled off to the southwest, away from the island that they had tried to tend and defend for so many years, toward the distant glow on the horizon.

XV

*Pilot Academy transcript from visual recording, planet
   Solara, 6.17.3533.*
Document status: CLASSIFIED.
File: Consecration.

   *(Lindal Karr, aged nineteen subjective years,
   marches up the aisle of the High Solaran Assembly
   Hall, Station 1, in geosynchronous orbit. Academy
   staff fill the low gravity seats on his right, Solaran
   planetary officials those on his left. Realistic
   effigies of his father and mother from the Planet of
   Industry sit in the front row. He spares them no
   glance; his duty precludes self-pity. Live-broadcast
   pickups follow his steps up to a broad stage.
   Lightning-troops in black and silver flank a robed
   figure in crimson and gold. Karr stops before the
   figure, his back to the assembly. A hush falls over
   the hall.)*

High Praetor: Citizen Solarans, this day we gather to
   confirm a new Pilot on the path of High Duty and
   Destiny, and to affirm our personal dedication to
   the Spread of Humanity, as manifest in the
   candidate before us. (Places his hand on Karr's
   shoulder.) The candidate is ready?

Karr: Yes.

High Praetor: Then repeat after me. I, Lindal Karr. . . .

Karr: I, Lindal Karr. . . .

> *High Praetor: Being of sound will and focused*
>   *mind. . . .*
> *Karr: Being of sound will and focused mind . . . do*
>   *solemnly swear . . . to execute my Duty . . . to*
>   *safeguard my fugueship . . . without question or*
>   *reservation . . . to the fullest of my abilities . . . and*
>   *obeying no other authority other than Duty . . .*
>   *forsaking all other concerns, personal,*
>   *professional, or moral. . . .*
> *High Praetor: As long as you both shall live.*
> *Karr: As long as we both shall live.*
>   *(A golden lanyard hangs over Karr's shoulder. A*
>   *tiny, dingy sphere—a miniature representation of*
>   *the Planet of Industry—dangles from the end. The*
>   *High Praetor severs the cord with a ceremonial*
>   *dagger and seals the miniature world in a tiny box.*
>   *He gives it to Karr, a symbol of what is lost and*
>   *what is gained.)*
> *High Praetor: So it is spoken, so it shall be done.*
>   *(At a motion from the Praetor, Major Vidun and Dr.*
>   *Uttz flank Karr. They pin shooting-star badges to*
>   *his epaulets.) Pilot Lindal Karr, having graduated*
>   *the Pilot Academy at Solara with high honors, I*
>   *present to you the fugueship—Long Reach!*
>   *(A panel slides back revealing the void outside.*
>   *Long Reach hangs above Solara's tan and gray*
>   *continents. Karr steps up to the window. From this*
>   *moment on he belongs only to the ship. He has left*
>   *the sphere of human concern behind. The*
>   *fugueship is his ticket out and he cannot wait to*
>   *leave.)*

The lifter flew through a blanket of still, hot fog. The only clue to the orbiter's motion was the scrolling of *things* across the ocean below—things Karr did not want to look at.

"Does this planet have sea serpents?" he asked.

"No," Jenette said from her perch back on the crawler, where she had been brooding all morning. "No animal forms larger than Khafra."

Karr slowed the lifter as a sinuous shape appeared out of the mist ahead, floating in the mirror-like water. It was a few yards thick, charred and knobbly on one side and fleshy pink on the other. *They were nearing the location where his ship must have impacted.* A lump grew in Karr's throat and he sped up again.

The smothering humidity stuck Karr's uniform to his neck, but that wasn't the only unpleasant atmosphere that morning. A sharp smack resounded behind Karr as Jenette drove a petite fist into the palm of a petite hand, yet again. It wasn't hard for Karr to guess what she was sulking about.

"It's your own fault," he observed.

"I gave him his freedom," Jenette retorted.

Karr tried to focus on his memory of Arrou waving pathetically for them to come back, and not the fleshy shapes in the water. "He didn't seem very happy about it."

"Well, at least he'll be alive, won't he?"

"I don't understand."

"Of course not," Jenette sneered. "You're an outworlder. How could you understand?"

The lifter passed over another long strip of flesh.

"What's eating you anyway?" Karr complained. "You made a choice. Live with it."

"What's *eating* me?" Jenette repeated. "That's funny. Wouldn't you like to know—Mr. Blood and Guts?"

"I acted as required," Karr said, with an accusing look back. "The actions of certain individuals forced my hand."

"Your hand seemed happy enough pulling the trigger on your fancy gun."

"You would rather have been torn limb from limb?"

"That's not the point and you know it."

"In the future, leave me out of any misguided, suicidal plans that you might come up with, okay?"

Jenette's expression soured even further and she tugged guiltily at the fastenings to her boots. Then she pounded her fists, again. "This planet is such a hellhole!"

Karr didn't understand the woman at all. The New Ascension climate was well within tolerable norms, if a bit warm, and the colors of the local sky and flora were pleasing, unlike some of the nerve-jangling worlds he had seen. Ferals aside, it seemed like a nice place for habitation. "I would have planted a colony here," he decided.

"And you would have been in error," Jenette retorted, "because that's how the original Pilots and colonists thought and they were all wrong. They didn't know anything about Scourge and not in their wildest nightmares did they even imagine Sacrament—but now we know and it's too late to change our minds, too late for us and too late for the Khafra!"

Jenette had been tight-lipped all morning, so her tirade caught Karr's attention, and one word in particular stood out. Just the way she said it sent chills down Karr's neck. Scourge. Visions of dead planets popped into his head: war worlds, famine worlds, disaster worlds, ghost worlds. Karr and *Long Reach* had planted them all—and then listened to the pathetic transmissions pleading for evac. Evac that could not come. With a sinking feeling, Karr realized where he was.

"This is a plague world. . . ."

Jenette would not meet his eyes, which was all the answer he needed, but she vindictively filled him in on all the details.

"Scourge. *Chorea vermiculorum.* It's a living pathogen, microscopic worms." She shivered. "There is a different substrain for every living thing on this planet: plants, animals, sea creatures, even us. Our scientists think the strain that attacks humans is a mutation of the strain found in Khafra. And it's the reason why there are no sea serpents, by the way; no creature larger than Khafra has evolved biological strategies to deal with Scourge." Jenette outlined how Ferals formed into pair bonds to exchange immune venom and how humans had short-circuited that relationship to extend their own survival.

"Pathogens, microscopic worms," Karr repeated. "How do I get off this planet?"

"That's what I've been asking myself for twenty-three years!"

Jenette's teenage body slumped, defeatedly. "But you don't have to worry. You're a Pilot."

"What's that got to do with it?"

"Scourge doesn't like *fugue*," Jenette explained. "No one died in the first six months after planetfall. Until then we still had traces of *fugue* in our bodies from transit."

It made awful sense to Karr. *Fugue* was an extremely potent immune substance. Scourge would probably still infect Karr, but *fugue* would suspend its life functions before it could do him any harm. And, thanks to his Pilot's regimen of dosing up, Karr had thousands of times more *fugue* in his bloodstream than any ex-dreamer colonists. More than enough to last a lifetime, he guessed. "So you and Arrou were due for your, what did you call it, Sacrament?"

Jenette nodded, looking very sad. "He's my best friend. I couldn't let him die. That's why I tried to speak to the Ferals last night. I wanted to find a way to make peace between humans and Ferals, to stop the fighting and work together to find a cure. I don't expect you to understand, but that's why it happened. We're desperate here and that was my desperate attempt at a solution." Jenette sniffled. "You're right, it was all my fault. I'm really sorry how it worked out." Guilt-ridden, she stared into the fog. "As you saw, it was an abysmal failure. They didn't want to talk peace. And I hardly blame them, after all the Ferals humans have killed. Why would they want to talk to me?"

Karr sighed, beginning to grasp the reasons behind the fiery woman's actions. "I don't think the Ferals understood. Did you note how their light patterns change when they talk?

"Of course."

"Is it language?"

"Yes," Jenette said, a bit defensively. "Khafra language has two components, verbal and visual."

"Then I don't follow," said Karr. "Seems like trying to communicate with the verbal components only is like trying to write a message but leaving out every second word."

Jenette considered. "I never thought of it that way. I always assumed the two aspects of Khafra language overlapped enough so that one part could be understood without the other. But I guess I was wrong." She smiled sadly. "I don't suppose you can make me grow flashbuds or turn me into a Feral?"

Karr couldn't laugh. "I'm a Pilot, not a magician."

They continued flying in silence. Karr wished the oppressive fog would close in entirely so that he would not have to watch the ominous shapes in the water below.

The paddleboard was tippy on the wide ocean rollers, but every stroke brought Arrou closer to Jenette and that was all that mattered. He murmured a rhyme she had taught him, to keep time.

"Fatty Feral, puff, puff, puffs,
"Fatty eats, he snuff, snuff, snuffs,
"Fatty hunts, he roar, roar, roars,
"Fatty sleeps, he snore, snore, snores."

Arrou had been very upset when Jenette left in the heavy lifter. It had been hard for him to think. He had wanted to jump into the water thick with sharkworms and swim after her. Crazy thoughts. Luckily, Tlalok had been there. Tlalok made Arrou think about many important things. Ending Sacrament was important. The coming of the Burning Heart was important. Tlalok's offer was important—it had been very hard to turn down: the wonderful Radiance, to live a long time. . . . Arrou shook the memory out of his head. It was no use to fill your heart with wishes you couldn't have.

Jenette was most important.

And Karr was important, too, Arrou determined in an afterthought, because Karr had taken Jenette away from him. Jenette would never leave unless Karr made her. That was clear to Arrou. He would do anything for Jenette, and he knew Jenette felt the same way. Jenette had taken him and cared for him when he was small and none of the other humans wanted a domestic with a broken paw, and when he had been the last one in the lonely domestic nursery, she had snuck him into her room where he hid under the covers. Later, where her father found out and punished her, Jenette had slept in the nursery with Arrou, both of them curled in the straw, safe and snug. Now Jenette was risking her life to propose peace with the Ferals and try to end Sacrament. Arrou knew it was because of him, even though Jenette thought she kept that a secret.

It was unthinkable that Jenette would leave Arrou.

It had to be Karr's fault.

Too bad. Arrou was just beginning to like Karr and he might still have given Karr the benefit of the doubt, but Jenette always told Arrou that humans who broke their promises were bad and Karr had definitely promised to teach Arrou to fly—and had *not*—which made Karr bad and made Arrou doubly angry with him.

Urrr.

Too many bad thoughts. Arrou lost his paddling rhythm.

Dark thoughts were not typical for Arrou, and he didn't like them. There was always something to be dark about, he knew. It was better to be happy, even if you had to work at it. So he concentrated on paddling and getting rid of the bad thoughts.

Fortunately, the paddleboard itself made Arrou feel better. Arrou had made it all by himself and he was quite pleased with it. The boards Arrou saw Tlalok's Ferals use had not been made out of bodybag pods like in the human documentary. They were made out of layered sailtree leaves. After a little trial and error, Arrou had succeeded in pressing two living leaves together and stimulating their growth with his immune venom. Injections at key spots cause them to bind together. More venom injected at the stems caused the leaves to harden as he pressed against them, forming a shallow boat in the shape of his body. By dawn Arrou had snipped the cured hull free (careful not to damage the living tree it came off of) and trimmed the edges with his teeth. By mid-morning he had a working paddleboard.

It took a few hours to get the handle of paddling, but a little after noon, and with the help of the rhyme, Arrou was going quite fast. He got bored with the first four lines of the rhyme soon, so he experimented making up new ones.

"Fatty wants, he try, try, tries,

"Fatty dreams, he sigh, sigh, sighs,

"Fatty weeps, he cry, cry, cries,

"Fatty fights, he die, die, dies."

Arrou didn't like that batch of lines. They were too dark. And they didn't all end in sounds. The rules were that the lines had to end in sounds, but it was hard for Arrou to think of better rhymes because human words were hard to rhyme. In the end he settled for timing his strokes by humming the rhythm without words.

Time passed. The cool water felt good on his legs and prevented him from overheating in the glare of the sun.

He would make a better board next time, Arrou decided. For instance, the Feral boards had funny knots where paddler's legs hung over the edge. Arrou had not understood what these were for until he paddled for a few hours and rubbed his thick skin raw against the edge of the board. Also, he had used the wrong side of the leaf on the bottom. The smooth side should go down, so that it was slipperier in the water, never mind that the fuzzy side would make him hot. And it would be good to figure out how to make the sharkworm lures. Arrou cold not get the peepers to hold still long enough to mold a cage around them. Three got away before he gave up and took a running leap off the shore, paddling like mad to get away from the dangerous waters near the island. Fortunately he had not tipped over, because he didn't think he could get back on the tippy board if he did.

More time passed. It was exhilarating paddling up the face of waves and racing down their other sides. The movement of ocean rollers in the direction opposite his line of travel added a great sensation of speed. Arrou was tranquil for quite a while, but then he started to think about the speed difference between his paddleboard and the heavy lifter. If Karr flew for eight hours at just twenty knots, then Arrou would have to paddle all day and all night long to keep the same distance between them. If Karr went faster, or Arrou stopped paddling . . . more bad thoughts.

He worried about Jenette.

The world outside the Enclave walls was dangerous. Arrou didn't know much about that world; Jenette knew less than he; and Karr—well, Karr didn't know a thing. That was why Karr lost his clothes and almost got killed by Tlalok. If Karr had forced Jenette to leave without Arrou, who knew what stupid thing Karr would do next? Arrou hoped to find the humans soon, before the Burning Heart made everything crazy.

Arrou had few memories from before Jenette, but he remembered a nighttime feeling, big, soft, and warm (he guessed this was his mother), and he remembered a gentle voice cooing to him and his siblings about the Burning Heart of Night. The others in that pleasant memory were all dead now, and Arrou did not recall the exact words spoken, but he remembered . . . *the Burning Heart brings change. Big things happened when the night wept—big hurts that make people wise. Or dead.*

Arrou paddled harder, spurred on by the belief that he, Arrou, could somehow keep Jenette from harm if he could just find her.

About then, when the sun was highest in the sky, things got complicated. Arrou heard a whining noise, far away but crystal clear in the way that sounds can be when they travel long distances over water. It came to his ears in spurts, intermittently as his paddleboard dipped into wave valleys then rose on wave crests. Arrou's first thought was of Tlalok and the Ferals. They were on the ocean, but they should have been ahead of Arrou. Had he somehow passed them by without knowing it?

Arrou spun his board, trying to stay on the wave crests as long as possible, and tried to keep his ear pits focused on that sound. Over the course of several minutes, the sound swept back and forth, from north to south and back again.

It was searching.

Arrou recognized the sound as it got closer. It was not Ferals. It was a colony vehicle. And not the one that Arrou had ridden in recently, but a fast one. It was probably a skimmer. In spite of his love of speed, Arrou did not like the skimmer's turbine whine. *It was a bad memory. Human raiders used skimmers to collect young Ferals.*

So Arrou did not know how to feel when he saw a fast moving speck on the horizon. Of course it was humans, but what humans? And what would they do? Arrou knew that humans in skimmers killed Ferals on sight and few humans could tell a domestic from a Feral, especially if the domestic was in a handmade Feral boat, like Arrou was.

It was not a good situation. Definitely not.

XVI

*"An adequate solution applied vigorously is better than
a perfect solution applied half-heartedly."*

—*from the speeches of Olin Tesla*

The speck continued to sweep the horizon, an ivory plume of water
billowing up behind it. It moved out of view each time before coming back, larger than before. Arrou focused his vision on it as much
as possible. The speck widened into an oval and, as the distance between Arrou and it diminished, stubby wings sprouting from its
sides became visible. It was definitely a skimmer. Skimmers did not
plow through the water like boats or lumber on top of it like
crawlers, but floated a couple yards above the waves, cushioned on
a pillow of air trapped under the stubby wings. Raised at the rear of
the craft, in an oversized cylindrical cowling, Arrou recognized the
PanaTech G-14 B turbine that gave it power: 1500 bhp, 1100 lbs
torque, max speed when mounted in skimmer 175 knots.

But, Arrou reminded himself, those things were not important
just then.

Should Arrou try to meet it or should he try to hide? Maybe he
could use the rollers to keep from being seen. He could certainly
imitate the color of the ocean, but if he did that and they saw him
anyway, then he would really look like a running Feral.

Arrou decided hiding was not the thing to do.

Next time the skimmer came by, he turned into an oncoming
swell and, as his board slid diagonally up to the crest, sat up and
waved with his good foreleg. Initially the skimmer looked like it
would pass by, but it banked at the last moment and then circled in

wide arcs around Arrou. He watched a human stand up at the controls.

The human had a pulse-rifle.

The long weapon foreshortened, pointing Arrou's way. Arrou hoped the human was looking through the far-sight tube to check him out, and not aiming.

The skimmer circled again.

The human's arm rose and jerked the weapon back in an all too obvious arming motion. The human would have a perfect shot the next time by.

"Urrrk-urrrk-urrrk," Arrou worried. What to do? What to do? Everything died, but this would be a silly way to die, killed by humans of his own side. In a flash of desperation, Arrou waived both forelegs in the air, pointing and calling attention to his lame right one. The skimmer circled around. The human did not lower the weapon. Arrou waved harder and almost capsized the paddleboard.

Eventually the human sat back at the controls and the skimmer turned in, its rooster tail spraying sideways and diminishing as it slowed. The hull glided lower, hydroplaned on the vertical ends of its short wings, and then sunk into the water, pushing a large bow wave which fanned out and almost swamped Arrou's tiny boat. The skimmer engine whined down to idle as it drifted within hail.

Now Arrou saw that it wasn't just any old skimmer, but the fastest one, so he was not surprised when Olin Tesla stood up into view.

"Arrou!" Tesla demanded, not at all pleased. "What are you doing out here? Where's Jenette?"

"Ferals attacked. Separated," Arrou answered. "Arrou follows Jenette."

Tesla grunted. "That's what I thought. The homing device went dead yesterday."

"Home device?"

"Homing device," Tesla corrected. "Every Enclave vehicle has a transponder." He looked around the empty ocean for any sign of Jenette. "It's like a big smell that you can sniff from far away—oh, never mind."

Arrou understood enough to know that a *transponder* was a device in the crawler that he hadn't known about before, and that Karr had probably accidentally disabled it when they borrowed parts from the crawler. Arrou also understood that Tesla was talking down to him.

The skimmer drifted closer. Arrou grabbed its wing, to keep it from crunching into his fragile leaf boat and he noticed with displeasure that Toby sat on the seat beside Tesla.

<<Arrou look stupid,>> the larger Khafra hissed in Domestic dialect. <<Stupid in stupid boat.>>

Tesla ignored Toby. "Is Jenette all right?"

"All right, last night," said Arrou.

"Good." Tesla actually looked concerned, which surprised Arrou. Tesla usually looked and acted angry, but true to form, Tesla's next words sounded gruff again. "Get in."

Arrou hesitated.

"I said get in."

Arrou did not want to go with Tesla. Tesla was not nice. Tesla made him and Jenette do bad things. Also, Arrou was proud of his little boat, no matter what Toby said, and he did not want to leave it behind. Things got lonely when they were left behind.

Tesla misread Arrou's hesitancy. Shaking his head, he attempted to speak in a softer tone (which seemed to Arrou a bit like a pit-lurker trying to talk sweet around all its many, many sharp teeth). "You're not in trouble, Arrou. I know you only did what Jenette told you to. You won't be punished."

Arrou let Tesla be confused. Jenette always told Arrou not to tell Tesla the truth. So Arrou gave up and tried to step carefully onto the skimmer, but his paddleboard wobbled and filled with water anyway.

He watched it sink.

Toby read his colors and gloated. <<Ruuharrr. Stupid boat gone.>>

Arrou did not return the growl. Toby was bigger and not very nice, either. Toby thought he was better than Arrou because Tesla was his human. Toby was a bully. Arrou wished he could wipe the smug colors off Toby's back.

Tesla did it for him. "Toby, get in the back."

Toby turned a humiliated brown. "Toby in back?"

"That's right. Out of the front seat. Let Arrou sit there."

"But . . . Toby not bad today."

"It's not about bad."

"Toby's place in front. Arrou go in back."

"Toby," Tesla warned. "Don't make this hard." Arrou noted a dangerous change of tone in the human's voice. Toby did not.

"Toby want sit in front," Toby protested submissively.

Tesla matter of factly grabbed a triangular, palm-sized device from his belt. Arrou recognized the device instantly. So did Toby. The large domestic half-jumped out of his skin scrambling to get into the back, but not before Tesla touched it between Toby's eyes with a *bzat!* Toby yowled in terror, falling into the rear compartment, teeth chattering convulsively from the effects of *the prod.* Jenette had once told Arrou that it was actually an *amaurotic prod,* in an effort to lessen his fear of the device; it temporarily short-circuited the neural connections between eyes and brain, she had explained. But those explanations did not lessen Arrou's sickly horror of the device which domestics called *the blinder.* Nothing could be more terrifying to a Khafra than to be forever without light. Butt pressed against the rear bulkhead, Toby's claws clattered on the deck. He tried to back away from the awful darkness—like a mlum with a bag over its head. Tesla methodically replaced the prod at his belt. Arrou felt sorry for Toby, bully or not. Tesla casually held Toby's head to keep him from injuring himself while the blindness lasted. Toby whimpered. Then, eyes clearing, Toby snapped at Arrou.

<<Get you, get you!>> Toby hissed.

Oblivious to the conflict, Tesla demanded, "Arrou, you sit there. You know where Jenette went."

Arrou climbed off the wing into the front seat.

Tesla revved the skimmer. The turbine built up speed. The hull hydroplaned, whipping salty mist onto the windscreen and Arrou's nose, and then lifted off the water to a height of two yards.

"Which way did she go?" asked Tesla.

Arrou obediently pointed southwest and Tesla steered in that direction. Arrou didn't offer any information about Karr, the Burning

Heart, or anything else. The less Arrou said, the less chance Tesla would get mad at him. For the rest of the trip, Arrou did what he was told and thought bad thoughts about Tesla, for which he felt very guilty.

The fog had taken on a suffocating yellow tinge. Visibility was up to a hundred yards, but Karr wished it was not. Big chunks of disintegrated flesh littered the ocean under the heavy lifter and their origin was clear. Karr was looking at the remains of his fugueship. They smelled like burned meat, even from twenty feet up, and they grew thicker in the water the farther the lifter penetrated into the fog. Karr did his best to keep his emotions in check.

Focus. Focus on the mission. You are a Pilot, damn it.

"Is it always this hot?" Karr asked, raising his voice over a rumble that had been building ahead of them for the last few kiloyards. Both he and Jenette were drenched in sweat.

"Can be," Jenette replied, "but this yellow fog is not normal. Hey, what's that?" She pointed ahead to several patches of flickering red and orange in the mist, ghostly candles with dark smudges above.

Karr did not want to know.

Jenette's dainty nostrils flared. "Smells like burning hair."

Karr rode out a lurch of his stomach and forced himself to alter course and fly close by one of the patches. It resolved out of the fog into a smoldering clump of organic growth, half the size of the lifter. Sickly smoke rose off of it into the air, but to Karr's relief it was not a piece of *Long Reach*.

"It's a fragment of ring-island," Jenette decided. "I don't see any surface growth at all, no brainturf, no trees, but that dark stuff is ghutzu."

Like a scene from Hades, the debris grew denser as the lifter proceeded. The ring-island fragments progressed from smoldering to burning and came in all shapes from head-sized bits to sections poking skyward like the sterns of sinking ships. One large serpentine form, easily as big as three or four Terran blue whales placed end to end, Jenette said was the shattered island's keelroot. She said that they always floated to the surface when a ring-island broke up.

Karr steered the lifter through pillars of lazily rising smoke.

"Ouch," said Jenette, blinking rapidly and scrubbing her face as clouds of sooty flakes stung their eyes.

Glints of metal and plastic bobbed in the debris field, amid much, much more fugueship tissue. It coated the oily water, like the leavings of an unsavory butcher shop.

Jenette whistled at the destruction.

Karr suddenly felt very cold in the tropical heat. The stinking remains confronted Karr with the awful end *Long Reach* had suffered. The burning wasteland was a graveyard.

Jenette shot Karr a glance. "You didn't expect to find your ship alive . . . did you?"

"No, no," Karr said a bit too quickly.

As he had a thousand times in the last two days, he checked the cockpit compass. It read the same as it had for the last two days: the lifter was pointing southwest. "Does that look right to you?"

Jenette craned her head up, trying to place the position of the obscured sun. "Near as I can tell. Why?"

"A living fugueship has an electromagnetic field large enough to cause false readings on a compass."

"Ah." Jenette remembered how the crawler's compass had acted up when a certain shooting star had passed over the Enclave. "So if your ship was alive, you would expect the compass needle to point straight at it, as if it were the north pole . . . ?"

"Or the south pole," Karr said darkly. "At least it went with a bang and not a whimper," he added, too softly to be heard over the growing rumble.

"I wonder why sharkworms haven't eaten the remains?" Jenette wondered indelicately. "There was a ring-island here. There should be sharkworms."

Karr shrugged, trying to muster the cool professionalism that he expected from himself, but it was elusive.

Jenette touched his arm. He jumped. "Are you okay?"

"I'm fine," Karr lied.

"You look gray."

Karr changed the subject. "It's louder here." The rumble was becoming louder, but it did not emanate from the burning fragments.

The sound resonated full and huge, seemingly from just out of sight ahead of the lifter. "Like a big waterfall or a forest fire," Karr observed.

Jenette did not understand either concept. The debris field thinned as Karr explained them. Jenette countered that New Ascension had no waterfalls or forest fires. "There is no water above sea level, except that stored in plants, so no waterfalls, but the idea sounds very beautiful," she yelled, trying to imagine the concept. "And as for forest fires, natural fire is rare. It rains a lot here and the plant life tends to be quite moist, so it takes a lot to set it on fire—although," she allowed, "I guess a fugueship exploding would be pretty hot."

"Hydrogen fuel burns at forty seven hundred degrees," Karr said, becoming more and more pallid, "and it fuses into helium in the fusion core a whole lot hotter than that."

Jenette stared at the smoldering fragments of ring-island. "These tiny fires couldn't be the cause of the glow we saw on the horizon last night, could they?"

Karr shook his head somberly.

The temperature in the fog rose rapidly as they proceeded. The yellow tinge became a yellow radiance ahead of the lifter, which grew in intensity until it rivaled the sun above. They were very near the source of the mysterious phenomenon.

"Are you sure you want to see this?" Jenette asked, leaning close for Karr to hear.

Karr's expression tightened. "Yes."

The rumble had become a roar. They squinted as the fog became painfully bright. The enveloping water vapor abruptly parted, leaving them face to face with a breath-stealing panorama. Fog surrounded a sunny, clear circle of ocean that in turn centered around four columns of yellow-white fire, the cause of the fog's yellow tinge. The pillars of fire extended from sea level high into the heavens, leaving sharp after-images on the awed observers' eyes. Below the pillars was an iceberg-sized mass of . . . raw meat?

Jenette didn't know what to make of it. "It's big. What is it?"

Karr's face fell in utter, ashen disbelief. "It's . . . it's my fugueship!"

XVII

*Pact, guard your actions! Do not unleash great evil to
perform small good! Great is that arrogance. Great is
that guilt. Purge hearts of this selfishness or the
Balance will swing.*

—*Feral warning*

Even from five hundred yards the heat was scorching. Karr raised
an arm to shield his face. There, bobbing face down in the ocean
with its stern humped above the surface and its engine fires thundering into the sky, was Karr's ship. Somehow, *Long Reach* had
landed without tearing into a million pieces. Karr was overwhelmed. Tears of relief mingled with the sweat pouring off his
face.

Alive. His ship was alive!

"So that's a fugueship," Jenette yelled, awestruck. She had
never seen one of the legendary creatures before. It was like turning a corner and unexpectedly coming face to face with a dragon
or unicorn. A fugueship had seeded New Ascension twenty-three
years ago, so this one before her was a tangible link to her past as
well as the intangible worlds beyond New Ascension's sky. Its
sheer physical presence was astounding. The tiny part of the
fugueship above the waves was huge, a thousand times bigger than
the largest creatures on New Ascension. The sheer force of its engines enlivened the water with marching rings of vibration; the
rows became beads where conflicting sources of the turbulence
overlapped and made moiré patterns. Jenette gulped air smelling

of jasmine even as a prickling in the back of her mind warned that something was amiss. "It doesn't look like the pictures I've seen."

It didn't look like a fugueship to Fugueship Pilot Lindal Karr, either. The portion above the waterline did not swell out from the stern to make the grub shape he knew so well, but was slimmer. The four engine orifices opened, not from knotty bulges set directly on the hull, but from the ends of tall, living columns. And the ship's surface was not wart-infested and knobbly like toad skin, but a glassy crimson. Furthermore, there was no sign of charring as there should have been after such a catastrophic landing— and where was the magnetic field? The compass was still rock steady, accurately reading southwest, which should have been impossible so close to a fugueship; fugueships could not turn their ramfields off.

Karr needed to board and investigate.

But he dared not fly any closer to *Long Reach* for fear of searing himself and Jenette to a crisp. His attention returned to the controls in the cockpit. In the light of that day's dawn Karr had set down temporarily. He had cleared the deck of the previous night's carnage, plugged most of the remaining cracks in the hull, and made additional repairs to the flight controls. He had rigged additional circuitry—sort of a rudimentary autopilot—which now allowed the lifter to be flown with simple inputs to the steering yoke and made it capable of executing simple operations like hovering. So Karr could now set the heavy lifter to hover two yards above the waves. He did so, then pointed at the collective throttle lever. "watch that," he said in Jenette's ear. "If the lifter starts to sink, pull up. You can handle that, right?"

Jenette looked at the controls skeptically.

Oblivious, Karr climbed out of the cockpit and rummaged through his gear, retrieving a small outboard thruster from the survival raft and a reflective blanket. That he tossed to Jenette, motioning that she should put it over her head to block the heat.

Karr pulled on the segments of his kilnsuit.

Wearing the blanket like a shawl, Jenette joined him. "Where do you think you're going?" she demanded.

Karr tipped his head at the blast furnace that was *Long Reach*. "To shut that off," he yelled.

"You'll be burned to a crisp!" Jenette objected.

Karr patted his ceramite suit. "Not in this."

Jenette looked even more skeptically between the kilnsuit and the fugueship. "This can't be safe. Let it burn out."

Karr locked his glove seals, shaking his head. "It won't burn out. The ship eats hydrogen and it's face down in an ocean of food." *Long Reach* could split water molecules into hydrogen and oxygen atoms indefinitely. "And it's my Duty," Karr added, before Jenette could object again. "It needs me."

Jenette acquiesced, returning to the cockpit, but she didn't like it.

Karr locked his helmet into place. The suit's life-support system activated, circulating cool air over his sweaty skin. Karr looped the Gattler over a shoulder, grabbed the thruster unit, and, with a final thumbs up to Jenette, stepped over the side.

Karr splashed under the surface and then bobbed up like a cork. Holding the thruster unit ahead of him, he twisted its handgrips. Thrumming, it pulled him through the oscillating water. The marching waves of interference grew as he neared *Long Reach*. Karr felt the vibration through his helmet. Readouts under his chin showed the external temperature rising, but still well under the suit's limits. Karr actually felt cooler inside the suit that he had outside of it.

Shortly, the small thruster bumped into *Long Reach*. Karr climbed onto the towering hull and wiped water droplets from his helmet. What he saw weakened his knees.

Long Reach was one gigantic, raw wound. Atmospheric friction had stripped its outer hide away—in fact the entire outer hull was gone, which accounted for the ship's thinner profile. *Long Reach* had survived planetfall at the expense of sloughing off half its mass. The scope of its trauma was horrifying. Exposed muscles pulsed and writhed under Karr's boots.

"I'm sorry," he whispered, as a parent might upon finding a badly burned child. Karr's vaunted Pilot training was obviously lacking. Never once had a lecture or manual explained what to do when half a fugueship's body was burned off. He had no idea how *Long Reach* was still alive or, more importantly, how to keep it alive.

Karr took deep breaths of reconstituted air. Panic wouldn't help *Long Reach*. And it didn't really need the missing parts of its body anymore, he rationalized. The outer hull largely contained storage cells and bladders for fuel and other materials needed to cross interstellar space. All vital life processes occurred within the smaller inner hull and, in a way, that made Karr's task easier, since he was closer to the internal locations where a few judicious *qi* manipulations would shut down the engines. After that he could begin the healing process in earnest.

That was, if he could get in.

Karr did not recognize the new external topography. There were no landmarks on the bleeding mass of ship. His best guess placed him in the neighborhood Wendworm Way, where it used to cross from the outer hull to the inner hull, but a slow walk around the circumference of gently bobbing stern revealed no passageways or iris-portals leading inside. The stern towered six stories above Karr. Fusion fire pillars speared thousands of yards into the sky above that, but there was no entrance anywhere on the steep slope. Below the water, where *Long Reach*'s slimmer profile disappeared into foreboding silvery darkness, was the only hope.

So without a second thought about the risk, Karr waved to Jenette and allowed himself to fall forward into the water. Huddled under the blanket in the cockpit, Jenette waved back.

The thruster unit pulled Karr's buoyant suit down. The sensation of descent was a lot like being weightless, a warm pressure all around, resisting Karr's movements, not like the giddy, fear-of-plummeting sensation of zero gravity. Karr panned a headlamp back and forth along the descending curve of the fugueship, eventually focusing on a depression which looked, in the deepening gloom, like an iris-portal. It turned out to be collapsed and impassable. Karr continued down and around. External pressure rose as he descended. A gauge read two atmospheres at twenty yards, then three at thirty, which was still nothing compared to what the kilnsuit was designed to withstand, but then he was only a tiny way down the four-kiloyard-long hull. Karr had to grip the thruster firmly to keep from slipping and bobbing back to the surface like a bubble.

As he inspected another collapsed portal, he began to worry that all the entrances to the ship would be blocked, but a glance back at the surface saved the day. What looked like squirming pools of liquid mercury jiggled under overhangs all around *Long Reach*'s hull. Karr floated back up to one. It was actually a bubble of air trapped in an unsealed opening; because the opening faced down, the air was unable to escape. Looking through the flexing, fish-eye refraction, Karr saw a passage that snaked into the ship. Perfect. He killed the thruster unit and burst up inside.

Karr was back in his ship.

But the inside, which should have been a cocoon of familiarity and safety, was not. It was dark, the man-made lighting systems having failed. Karr was forced to use the helmet's less than efficient spotbeams for illumination. And the passages Karr climbed through were distorted, squeezed and twisted by the pressure of atmosphere and water on a creature evolved to live in zero gravity. So Karr could not figure out where he was. Walls seeped blood, in spasms as *Long Reach* reacted to its pain. Water leaked in everywhere. Karr splashed though pools of brine. Tiny creatures, sucked in with the ocean water, floated in *fugue*-coma, hairy yellow foodyeast already feasting on their belly-up bodies. As Karr pressed deeper, trying to find a landmark of any kind, lakes of viscous blood replaced seawater, coating his kilnsuit in congealing, ropy strands, making it difficult to see and note the windings of his path.

Twist left, crawl right, open sphincter, climb up, press on.

It was a nightmare. Believing *Long Reach* dead in a quick, catastrophic impact had been hard enough, but Karr was confronted with his ship alive and suffering now—suffering that his own ineptitude had lead to. He recited from training manuals to reduce his emotions to a manageable level. *Concentrate on the big picture. Isolate the ship from additional trauma. Triage tasks to maximize the results of treatment.* Right then, that meant closing the engine orifices and damping down the fusion furnace to minimum, thereby decreasing the chance of the hull shifting and also lessening the tremendous heat and danger outside.

One small mercy: the volume of the inner hull was much less than that of the outer hull. Karr eventually recognized a series of gigantic vertebra. They paralleled a ceramite pipeline, three yards across, which ran vertically through the ship. Karr followed the vertebrae, climbing down using bone spurs for footholds and looking for an entry duct. After a short descent, he discovered that the paralleling pipeline was broken in half, shattered from the force of the crash impact. Inside, the ceramite of *Long Reach*'s superconductor core was visible, a striated column of rust and white, plated in platinum and then wrapped in insulating ceramite. Grown in zero gravity, the crystals of the superconductor structure were perfectly aligned to the massive current that coursed through *Long Reach* to generate an electromagnetic ramfield. The break in the superconductor explained why *Long Reach* was not affecting compasses. The circuit was broken and couldn't generate a ramfield anymore.

Climbing down a dozen more yards, Karr put the superconductor out of his mind and located a suitable entry to the vertebrae. A fine cutting beam broke a milky membrane sealing an entry duct, and then *qi* needles calmed the spasms of a narrow crawlway. Karr squirmed through like a worm and entered the spinal foramen, a triangular conduit formed by the gentle curve of the vertebrae on one side and the processes of shorter bone spurs opposite.

The beam of Karr's helmet lamps glistened on strands of nerve fiber that filled the conduit: *Long Reach*'s spinal column. Three days ago, Karr would not have considered entering this delicate area for fear of crippling the ship. Today, he set to work inserting *qi* needles with the Gattler. Lying on his back with his arms outstretched into the spinal conduit and his body confined in the entry duct, Karr aimed for fatty junctures where nerve strands split off to different parts of the ship. Calm the sympathetic systems. *Bwap, bwap.* Simple. Stimulate the parasympathetic systems. Equally simple. *Bwap, bwap.* Now the risky shot. *Thwok!* A long non-resorting needle to block a nerve cluster and anesthetize the aft sections of the hull before attempting to damp down the engines.

If it worked Karr's task would be a whole lot easier. He waited for an adverse reaction. Nothing. "Hang with me," he muttered to the ship while visualizing a picture of the best meridians for the next needles.

A trickle of seawater dribbled down the entry duct, slithering past Karr's shoulders and cascading into the spinal conduit. The whole ship shuddered and the narrow duct clamped down on Karr, shoving the interlocking plates of his kilnsuit together. *Long Reach*, it appeared, did not like seawater in its nerve canal—at all. For a few nervous seconds Karr was immobilized by the ship's tremendous muscular power, but then the duct relaxed again.

Karr held his ground. "Sorry. Just a little more." He hurried the *qi* injections, but another spasm followed, stronger than the first, and a third was more violent still. Each spasm held longer, severely decreasing the slack time in between. Karr should have left right then, but persevered until muscle pressure made work impossible. The kilnsuit creaked ominously and his helmet made the sound of sand grinding on sand.

Using only his fingers and wrists, Karr twisted the Gattler around to point back at the entry duct. It was difficult to keep his gloved forefinger on the trigger in that position, but he managed to fire a ring of *qi* needles around the duct. Pressure eased off enough for him to squirm back half a yard, but then clamped back down. Karr repeated the process several times. He kept squirming as the ship kept lurching. Finally, he inched far enough back to slip out into a rising pool of blood and water. *Splash.*

Karr swiped his helmet clean as best he could. All the connecting tubes and cavities around him were convulsing. It might settle down if he waited, but it might worsen, and if it got much worse, there wouldn't be any safe place for Karr inside the fugueship. With only half his job accomplished—anesthetizing the engines from the spinal conduit—Karr decided to flee and finish the job from outside.

Long Reach had other ideas. Each time Karr attempted to take a passage, it slammed the passage shut with crushing force. It was as if the ship didn't want to let him leave. "I have to go, just for a little while," Karr promised, trying a different route, "but I'll be back."

Slam!

Sheets of muscle hammered down on him.

Karr tried to pull back, but the outboard thruster caught on a tendon. The kilnsuit withstood the force; the thruster was crushed to bits.

Spurred on by the fear of losing the Gattler in a similar fashion, Karr fired *qi* needles like never before. *Bappata-babada-bap!* A complete ring around the passage. Advance and repeat. *Bappata-babada-bap!* Karr ignored the ammunition and propellant counters. *Bappata-babada-bap! Bappata-babada-bap!* If they reached zero he was dead anyway. His rhythm built up. Karr jogged back along the steps of his mental map. Straight out, climb up—oops, duck back, *wham!*—shoot again, crawl left, twist right.

Bappata-babada-bap! Bappata-babada-bap!

Beep, the Gattler warned. Low ammunition.

Bappata-babada-bap! Bappata-babada-bap! Bappata-babada-bap! Bappata-babada-bap!

Click. Empty.

Karr had made it to one of the few fuel-bladder galleries within the *Long Reach*'s inner hull. He scrambled down the gallery, which was large enough that even when compressed there was still room for Karr to move safely, but he was forced to halt at a sledge-hammering muscle group at the far end. By Karr's calculations, he was less than twenty yards from an opening that would lead to the freedom of open water. All he needed was a few more needles.

So near and yet so far.

Karr ransacked crates in the netting between fuel bladders, but came up empty-handed and confused: ancient statues, priceless paintings, masterpieces of jewelry and art looted from Sheldon's World. Useless, useless, useless.

"Goddamnit!" The bastards from Sheldon's World had screwed him again. Karr hurled a solid gold statue at a fuel bladder in frustration. It bounced off the skin, making a hollow sound—and a strange, man-made flap fluttered open.

Karr splashed over and looked through the opening. His helmet lamp illuminated a treasure trove inside. Heaped around a simple bedmat, amid piles of garbage and dirty clothes, were cases of *qi* needles, propellant, adhesive, other Gattler munitions, the jewel-studded sphere of a spare starlure, an empty *fugue* purifier, and many other pilfered items.

Bob. It was Bob's hideout.

This was how Bob evaded detection for so long. The interior walls of the bladder were artfully braced so that they appeared to be swollen full from the outside. Karr must have passed by a hundred times and not seen the hideout.

Long Reach lurched.

Karr decided to berate himself later, shimmied into the hideout, and reloaded the Gattler as fast as he could. Empty metal spheres hit the floor as new ones snapped into position and then Karr fastened as many extra loads as possible onto the kilnsuit's attachment clips.

A scrap of stimpaper caught his eye.

For my buddy, Karr, it read.

The paper was attached to a data cube. Karr wanted to kill Bob all over again, or at least throw the cube away like he had the statue, but he couldn't—what if the message contained information that would help Karr in his struggle to rescue and repair *Long Reach?* Karr angrily stuffed the cube in a suit pouch and turned to leave. As an afterthought Karr stopped, reached under a heap of trash, and grabbed the spare starlure. Discarding one precious Gattler reload, he clipped the sphere onto the kilnsuit and exited.

Karr careened down the pitching gallery and used the refilled Gattler to shoot his way out. Minutes later, he dropped into the ocean and let his suit's buoyancy pull him past the convulsing leviathan to the surface.

Karr crawled out of the water back onto the hull. It shuddered and shook. Jenette waved frantically for Karr to return, but he ignored her and scaled the raw surface. Halfway up, he stole a glance back. Jenette was a small huddled figure on the lifter. Further behind, small fires winked in the encircling fog bank.

Above Karr, great beams of thrust shifted dangerously against the sky. Why were the stern engine nozzles open, he wondered. If anything, *Long Reach*'s bow nozzles should have been open, as Karr had left them when he abandoned ship. Like so much of what Karr saw, it did not make sense.

Karr pulled his way to the top. Like the rest of the ship, the stern looked very different from how Karr remembered it. In the very center was a striated column of superconductor, which before had been only a knob barely protruding from surrounding hide. Now it was ten yards high. Karr felt an unsettling electrical buzz, even over the engine rumble. It was the superconductor's *I've got a hell of a lot of electrical charge on me* warning; he must not touch it in his dripping wet kilnsuit, because that would make a circuit with the hull and then there would be a *flow,* and flow of that magnitude was bad. Arrayed around the superconductor were four wide pillars with engine exhaust spewing from nozzles on top. They were also ten yards high: the thickness of the missing outer hull at that point.

Karr swallowed hard. A whole new set of muscles was exposed and therefore an unknown set of *qi* points. Karr circled the engine nozzles, trying to deduce the *qi* meridians. A layer of flexor muscles lay over a layer of extensor muscles. Good. Karr wanted the flexors. A shot in the correct location would constrict all four nozzles and shut off the thrust. That in turn would cause *Long Reach* to dampen its internal fire. Closer inspection showed Karr that these muscles were not so different from the outer hull muscles he was familiar with. Encouraged, he set the Gattler for long, permanent needles; Karr wanted the orifices to shut and stay shut.

That should be the spot. Karr aimed at a point nearly centered amidst the four engine nozzles. *Unless he was badly miscalculating the new meridian . . . no.* The point was tricky to locate, but Karr was right.

He shot.

The living pistons contracted under his boots, pulling unseen plates of heat-resistant bone across the nozzles and the pillars of engine thrust constricted. However, unlike the external muscles Karr was used to, which responded slowly and predictably, the inner-hull groups reacted vigorously, clamping down in a fraction of the anticipated time. The thrust nozzles sagged. The fiery columns of exhaust sagged with them, like the petals of a titanic, wilting flower.

Unbalanced thrust began to tip *Long Reach* over. A mass of bubbles exploded to the ocean surface from below, presumably from one of the many openings Karr had seen. Escaping air meant water was rushing into the hull, further complicating matters.

Long Reach began to sink, rolling ponderously, twisting downward, its oily hull disappearing under vibrating water.

Alarmed, Karr dropped to hands and knees and grabbed the head of the *qi* needle, but his gloves were slick and he could not get it out. Karr struggled with locking rings on his wrists, intending to pull his gloves off and grab the needle with bare flesh. However, his hands were saved from hideous burns by a convulsion, which suddenly rippled every muscle on the ship from the surface of the waves all the way up to its top.

Karr lost his balance and his grip and tumbled down the side. Arms and legs skipped off slippery surfaces. The kilnsuit froze, plates locking up at each impact. The ocean surface rushed at him, frothing and bubbling as it pulled *Long Reach* under. Karr bounced the last stretch and splashed hard into the water, holding the Gattler for dear life, bubbles whirling around his helmet. It was hard to tell which way was up. Karr was spun and jostled in the turmoil near the descending fugueship hull. He had to get away or be sucked down with it, but his outboard thruster was gone and he could not swim in the bulky suit. The end over end motion was making him sick. With few other options, Karr activated the kilnsuit's maneuvering thrusters, punching them at full power. Uncontrolled thrust yanked his arms and legs to the end of their sockets; Karr broke through the boiling surface, feet flipping into the air. He cartwheeled right over before landing head up and bobbing on the turbulent surface.

Long Reach's stern was half gone. The pillars of engine thrust were diminishing in size and force, and sagging down at the ocean surface. One of the petals was sagging right down at Karr! He would be incinerated. Karr thumbed the thrusters again. This time the backpack kicked him in the small of his back, and he plowed across frothing water like a rag doll skipping behind a speedboat. Karr crossed the space between fugueship and heavy lifter before he knew it. The hovering craft loomed up fast. Ten yards, three yards, one yard. Karr killed the thrusters and reached up. No good! He needed longer arms. Either that or he should have thought to extend one of the lifter's robotic grappling arms before he set out, because he couldn't reach any part of the orbiter.

Jenette solved the problem for him. The lifter suddenly splashed down, nearly crushing Karr. He bounced down off the hull, briefly sinking underwater, but then bobbing back up and grabbing hands that reached down at him. Thrusters pushed; both humans pulled as hard as they could, together managing to heave Karr over the lifter's shallow sidewalls.

Karr rolled to his feet, muscles complaining. He lumbered for the cockpit while unlocking and removing his helmet.

"Got to get out of here!" Jenette yelled, pointing up at a column of fire that was sagging their way. It was far thinner than last time Karr had looked, almost sealed off in fact, but would still do great harm to the heavy lifter and its occupants.

Karr clambered into the cockpit and worked the controls, raising the lifter off of the water and side slipping neatly between two of the wilting columns. Fiery exhaust hit the water with a great hiss as *Long Reach* disappeared from view, but the conflagration was not extinguished. The boiling bubbles increased a hundredfold as seawater rushed over the exposed superconductor end. Hellfire glowed underwater as the fugueship sank. As the heavy lifter's engines spooled up, the force of gasses bubbling up from below became so strong that Karr felt a strong updraft buffeting the hull. Curlicues of fire appeared here and there, erupting high into the air like miniature solar flares.

The lifter engines reached full pressure. Karr hauled up on the throttle and twisted the steering yoke hard over. "Take cover!" The lifter rose, turning tail and accelerating away.

Jenette crouched under her reflective blanket as the ocean surface burst open under them, a gout of flame hammering skyward. Unlike *Long Reach*'s fusion exhaust, this fire was not confined to four narrow columns, but expanded on contact with the atmosphere—a wall of fugueship vengeance roaring into the sky, swelling wider and wider and eating up everything in its path. A wave of stifling heat hit the lifter.

Karr was already at maximum power. All he could do was angle the lifter to surf the pressure wave that expanded in front of the thundering inferno. The encircling fog bank was blown away in an instant. Smoldering island fragments were swept up and vaporized. The fire on the lifter's tail grew brighter and brighter, gaining; the dashboard in front of Karr glowed red beside the shadow of his head. He tipped the lifter's stern up, hoping to shield himself and Jenette with the hull.

The fury washed over them. Fire swamped the lifter on all sides. Only a tiny patch of blue sky remained ahead, as if they were looking up from the bottom of a deep flaming well. Fingers of the flame licked over the lifter's sidewalls. Jenette screamed as, for one horrible moment, the dot of blue sky was gone. Unrelenting heat sucked the air out of their lungs and seared Karr's exposed head. He clenched his eyes shut as the tremendous force tried to flip the lifter over; even closed, the insides of his eyelids were white hot.

"Sonofabitch!" he swore, fighting the controls.

And then the inside of his eyelids dimmed. He could breathe again. Cool air rushed across Karr's face and he opened his eyes. The lifter had shot out of the wall of fire, singed, but unhurt. Jenette peeked out from under her blanket.

"We're alive?" she asked, incredulous.

Karr was afraid to look back, but he leveled the hull anyway.

A new column of flame burned in place of *Long Reach*'s comparatively tiny exhausts. Kiloyards wide at sea level, the firestorm reached thousands of feet into the daytime sky, disappearing into clouds turned luminescent by its brilliance.

The ocean was on fire.

"My God," Karr whispered, "What have I done?"

XVIII

The proto-man lies before her. She removes his generic gray clothes. She opens the lock on his head, removes and places his boy-mind in a jar by the headboard, twisting the lid up tight. It must not get out. It is the boy-brain that holds the man-body back. The body alone is enough. Masculine, like a rocking-hross, like one she had as a child. A toy.

For her to play with.

She explores the man-body as she once explored the rocking-hross, feeling every smooth flank, every firm curve. It does not move. It might be dead. Except for the heat. She shivers at the diabolical thrill.

Suddenly her clothes are off, like a young girl that doesn't know any better. The woman straddles the man-toy as the girl once straddled the rocking-hross. But girl play is far from her thoughts. She leans forward. Her breasts touch it. Her nipples harden. Unfettered by the boy-brain, the man-body rises to the occasion, and hardens, as the rocking-hross seat was hard.

As she sat on the rocking-hross, she sits on it.

And rides. She and the man-toy. How they rock, how they buck. She does not seek end to the game, it sneaks up on her, as the end of girl-games snuck up on her. She's it. Home free. Rubber and glue, bounces off her and sticks to youuuuu. . . .

The girl is gone.

The woman dresses.

But she takes care of her man-toy. Cleans it. Feeds it. Clothes it in white, the color of true love. And hopes one day to find a man-brain to put in its empty head.

—from the black book of J. Tesla

Jenette worried about Karr. His face and neck were red and blistering, his short dark hair singed into tight curls and, more disconcertingly, he did not pay attention to his flying or to her, but stared backward at the inferno like a hole-wompet hypnotized by Khafra hunting patterns.

"But . . . how?" he mumbled to no one in particular.

Except for her fingertips, which had protruded out from under the protective blanket and now throbbed painfully, Jenette was unhurt. She stepped into Karr's line of sight. "Do you have a medipak?"

Karr wasn't listening. He leaned to look around her. "How . . . ? Water doesn't burn."

Jenette gently grabbed his shoulders and forced him to look at her. "New Ascension to Lindal Karr. Do you have a medipak?"

"It doesn't burn, you know," Karr emphasized. "It's a very stable molecule."

"I'm sure it is. Where's the medipak?"

Jenette's patience ran thin. She was about to yell at Karr when his hands went to his face. "What have I done?" he groaned. Bits of his face flesh sloughed away where he touched it. He didn't feel it.

Jenette realized Karr was in shock. "Stop the lifter," she commanded with as much authority in her voice as she could muster. "Put us down. Now."

Like a robot in need of a recharge, Karr slowly turned to face forward and lowered the throttle. The lifter floated down. Jenette tensed, but her fear was misplaced; dazed though he was, Karr brought them down with only a small bump on hitting the water.

"Turn everything off," Jenette said, "and stay put."

Karr methodically switched power off. The thrusters wound down.

Jenette hurried back through the salvage littering the deck. Recent events had scattered it, but she easily located and focused on the ejector couch and the survival raft; they were the most likely places to discover emergency supplies. The couch was a disappointment, so she turned to the raft, unzipping its conical awning. The interior was damp. The awning was designed to condense moisture on its inner surface; fresh water dribbled down gutters into catch pouches around the bottom. Jenette crawled in, arms and legs squeaking against rubbery surfaces, sucked a quick drink from a flexible hose as her eyes adjusted to the dim light, and then grabbed a case emblazoned with a red cross.

Karr was still staring at the firestorm when she returned, but at least he acknowledged her existence. "Burn packs inside," he mumbled, seeing the case. "Open pack, load beads, spray . . . spray. . . ." Karr lost his train of thought.

"I can read," Jenette said, nose crinkling as she dutifully followed instructions on a sealed packet, first cleansing her own hands with sterile cream, then removing strips of hanging flesh from Karr's face. Next, beads of medical dressing went into a pump applicator and she sprayed the resulting foam onto Karr's wounds.

Jenette regarded her handiwork. Karr's head was a pink cake, iced with white frosting.

He reached for the medipak. "Now the powerbuds," he mumbled on, "to activate the healing. One on each side, for a current flow."

Jenette snatched the medipak away. "Sit still and close your eyes, firebug. I can handle it."

She immediately regretted her choice of words, because Karr did shut up, but he also resumed staring at the conflagration behind them. She pushed two pinheads out of a blister pack and inserted them into the icing on Karr's head. They ignited on contact. Jenette felt a cool tingling expand from the powerbuds, turning the white dressing into transparent goo, like melted wax.

"Ahh," Karr sighed.

Jenette smeared the dressing around, the sting easing from her own burned fingers as she worked. "These are good," she commented, reading the package. *Remodels first and second degree burns in minutes*, it bragged. *Allow longer for third degree burns, checking frequently.* Jenette stood watch to make sure the powerbuds did not slip, leaving her fingers in contact so that they could also heal. Not only did the medicinal current calm the throbbing of her burns, but there was a certain thrill in touching an adult male this way—a sweet stolen thrill. With the exception of the ancients, all post-pubescent males that she came into physical contact with inevitably fled in terror, so this was a novel sensation. After about five minutes, the redness on Karr's face began to fade.

The goo around his mouth parted. "Current flow," he repeated. Then two more breaks formed in the goo and his eyes popped open. "Electrolysis!"

"Excuse me?" said Jenette, puzzled.

"Electrolysis," Karr repeated. "The splitting of water into hydrogen and oxygen by electric current. The superconductor is broken."

"What superconductor?" Jenette said, more puzzled than before.

"The one *Long Reach* uses to generate its ramfield—oops, *used*," Karr corrected. Jenette watched thought processes on his gooey face. "The superconductor is broken into an anode and a cathode," he explained, "like the poles on a powerpak. Current could not move when *Long Reach* was floating . . . but now that both poles are underwater—salt water, with all those electrolytes—" the goo-head blinked, "—all that energy is flowing between the poles, electrolyzing the ocean water into hydrogen and oxygen. That's what's burning. Not the ocean."

"It's electrolyzing a *lot* of water," Jenette said, looking back. Two kiloyards distant, the flames still blotted out a huge portion of the sky.

"Fugueship fusion produces an exceptional quantity of power," Karr admitted glumly. "Which equates to a lot of fire." He moaned. "It's all my fault. How am I ever going to put it out?"

"Calm down," Jenette ordered. "You screwed up. But if your ship is alive now, it will still be alive tomorrow. In fact, as long as that fire's burning we know it's still alive. Right? Otherwise no electrolysis, no fuel and the fire goes out. We have to get to a safe place, rethink, and come back with a plan, but first you have to shut up and heal."

"Right," Karr said, grasping onto Jenette's logic. The flame meant *Long Reach* was alive. "You're right."

New Ascension's sun lowered behind the pillar of flame. The lifter drifted in lazy circles, alternating their views of evening sky and hypnotic, fiery horizon. Karr sunk into quiet self-recrimination. Up close, Jenette again noted how Karr smelled like flowers. Even the sheets of his sloughed-off skin smelled like burned flowers.

Some time later Jenette removed Karr's dressing. Both his burns and her burns were healed to the point where the skin looked healthy, if a little tender, and would continue to heal on its own. Karr stripped out of the kilnsuit. Then he powered the lifter back up and flew away from the burning horizon.

It was with a lump in her throat that Jenette realized the direction Karr had chosen: northeast. Back toward the Enclave. When Karr wasn't looking, Jenette sealed a hermetic bag, where she had put his burned skin for later disposal, and stuffed it into a pocket.

Hours later, with the column of flame still visible even though its base had sunk far below the horizon, Karr and Jenette were treated to a second Clash of Radiance. It was even more impressive than the first, because there were more islands grouped on the water below and many more points of Feral light. There were even Ferals on the ocean in small craft. The patterns danced from island to island like wildfire. From their high vantage, Karr and Jenette saw designs radiate from competing bright spots in curling fractal patterns. It seemed to the humans that those patterns were different from the previous night, as if influenced in some way by the column of flame and its forest fire glow. Rainbow shockwaves enveloped all the points of light on the horizon and, as the rite drew to a close, those waves centered around a single angry spot of light on the water.

Despite the beauty of the display, Jenette felt a chill. What did it all mean?

Karr kept flying after it was over, wanting to keep moving, but after another hour his head began to nod from fatigue.

"I've got to stop," Karr decided, his head snapping erect.

"Good idea," Jenette agreed. It was the third time Karr had momentarily lost consciousness.

The ideal spot to land for the night would have been on a ring-island, but they didn't dare risk another encounter with Ferals, so

Karr flew until they found a wide expanse of open ocean and put the heavy lifter down.

"Someone better keep watch," Karr said, heaving himself out of the cockpit. "If the Ferals spot us. . . ."

"I'll go first," Jenette volunteered. "I slept last night."

Karr pushed a couple of empty storage crates together for a bed, spread the survival blanket on them, and wadded up the remains of his old ghimpsuit for a pillow, but before he lay down, he detached an object from his kilnsuit and unwrapped it. "Here," he yawned, offering the object to Jenette. "This is for you."

"What is it?" she asked, looking at, but not taking the lumpy sphere.

"It's a starlure," Karr explained. "It might help with your communication problem."

Before Jenette could say anything more, Karr connected the starlure to a powerpak and tapped its colored studs. The sphere lit up like a galaxy of stars, spraying the lifter with fairy like ballroom lights. "Try?" Karr asked, reoffering it to her.

Jenette took the globe, tentatively tapping the studs with her small hands. It repeated whatever sequence she made, long pulses, short flashes, rapid patterns, sparkling strobes, and in any color of the rainbow. "Din-tixss-ymisstash," she whispered, tapping.

Flash, pop, sparkle, pop, went the starlure.

Jenette's mouth hung open.

Karr smiled wearily. "I thought you might like it."

Jenette cradled the precious sphere. "This is worth all the metal on New Ascension. I can talk to Ferals with this. But . . . I thought you didn't approve of my attempt to talk to Ferals?"

Karr shook his head. "I didn't understand. I was in error." He plumped his makeshift pillow and lay down. "It's a noble cause and I'll do whatever I can to help."

"You will?"

"After I save my ship." Karr curled up and pulled the blanket over himself. "Wake me in a few hours." It wasn't long before his breath came slow and deep, the lullaby motion of rollers sweeping across the ocean and the lapping of water against the hull rocking him fast asleep. Jenette resisted the urge to play with the starlure for fear of attracting unwanted Feral attention, but she held it close.

Hours passed. Jenette kept watch sitting on the crawler or standing quietly with Karr in view. There was little noise other than the wind and wave, not even the sounds of hoppers or violin bugs, which filled any night on a ring-island. Between periodic scans of the lonely horizon, Jenette found her attention drifting to Karr. His arrival was already affecting the course of New Ascension history. For better or for worse, she could not predict which. Although the burning ocean was certainly not for better—but the starlure was a promising sign.

Time flowed.

She found more and more of her attention focused on Karr. Sleep, she noticed, softened the perpetually dour expression on his face. Why did that inconsequential observation seem so important to her? She couldn't say. But Pilot Lindal Karr was different, and not just because he was a grown man, although that *was* alluring. No, Karr was also fresh. Karr was new. He was mysterious and a bit dangerous. And that was somehow exciting, which appealed to the woman-child who wrote naïve erotic prose in a little black book. And he was honorable. That was clear in the actions he took to save his ship, however doomed those actions might be.

All of this Jenette felt rather than thought. Her thoughts were scarier, because looking at a man in such a way was a sure sign of the changes taking place in her body. The hormone inhibitors had failed her. She was turning into a woman—and little girls on New Ascension did not live happily ever after when they turned into women.

At least Arrou would live.

The night glowed red.

Jenette had no clear memory of when she first heard the whine building behind the *shshsh-shshsh* of the elements, but at some point her trance was broken by the recognition of a sound: man-made skimmers. How many she could not tell.

What were skimmers doing so far beyond the defensive perimeter? The answer popped into Jenette's head: they were look-ing for her; that was the only reason skimmers would venture so deep into Feral territory. With that answer came personal responsibility and concern. It could be Toliver or Skutch or Grubb in the skimmers, and they were headed toward the area that she and Karr had just overflown, where the water was thick with Ferals. Remembering Halifax's warnings that Ferals had recently brought down a skimmer, Jenette stepped over to the crawler and pulled a flare pistol from the cab.

She had to warn them.

Jenette broke the pistol open, plugged a flare into its breach, and flipped the safety off. Pistol outstretched at the sky, finger wrapping around the trigger, she scanned the ocean. Where were they?

Crimson light glinted off a sleek shape. A rooster tail crept across the water far to the south, like a shimmering veil, a single skimmer jumping into sharp delineation as it passed in front of the red horizon.

A single skimmer.

Jenette's blood ran cold. Her finger hesitated on the trigger. Only one man had the arrogance to fly a lone skimmer outside the Enclave's perimeter and risk such a valuable machine. Halifax would not allow it. He would send several skimmers armed to the teeth. And only one man had the power to override Colonel Halifax in such a matter.

Jenette's father.

An ugly little thought slithered into her mind. If she did nothing, the Ferals would bring the skimmer down and all her problems would be over. She didn't have to do anything, just hesitate. No one would know. Karr was asleep. And even if the Enclave somehow found out, she could say the flare didn't work. It was old, just like everything else from offworld. Her hand wavered. *Put it back in the crawler,* the ugly thought teased. With her father gone, life would be so much easier.

And so . . . empty. No chance for her to prove herself. No chance for her and her father to ever understand one other. In spite of everything, he was the only father she had. If only things could be better between them. . . .

Jenette jerked her arm up and squeezed.

Pfish, the flare sputtered, and then *whoosh!* Up, up, a climbing green star, sizzling into the night on a trail of fading smoke.

The skimmer's rooster tail diminished as it slowed and turned back.

Still wrapped in the emergency blanket, Karr got up and rubbed sleep from bleary eyes. "What's wrong?"

"We've got company." Jenette pointed to the skimmer. "Enclave company."

Karr tossed the blanket and ran his fingers nervously through his hair.

Jenette wanted to flee as the skimmer hydroplaned toward them. The coming confrontation would not be pretty. Maturing body or not, she felt very much like a little girl about to get a spanking.

The skimmer nosed down beside the lifter. As predicted, there was only one human inside, but there were two domestics.

Tesla's voice resonated across the water. "Lose something, young lady?"

The alien seated beside Tesla flashed a happy yellow.

"Jenette, Jenette," Arrou yipped.

"Arrou," Jenette sighed, conflicted in her heart. It was good to see him, even though it meant her flight from the Enclave had been a total failure. She had not even ensured Arrou's life, and her father would see to it that she never got another chance. That was for sure.

Shifting attention to Karr, Arrou suddenly growled.

Toby growled, too.

"Quiet, both of you," Tesla commanded, climbing onto a stubby wing as the skimmer bumped into the heavy lifter. "Stay."

Tesla ignored the hand Jenette offered and hopped onto the lifter with surprising agility for a man of his years. Jenette resolved to be brave, not wanting to appear weak in front of Karr.

"Father, I—"

Tesla silenced her with an upheld hand, his glance saying *I'll deal with you later.* But as he looked from the stolen crawler, around the heavy lifter, and finally stopped on the man in the white uniform, his characteristic scouring expression faltered.

"You, you are a . . . Pilot?"

Standing stiffly, Karr gave the formal greeting. "Lindal Karr, Fugueship *Long Reach*."

"And . . ." Tesla wet his ropy lips, "and you are not from *Evermore?*"

Karr thought the question strange, but answered. "No, born on Planet of Industry, trained at Pilot Academy on Solara. Last stop was Sheldon's World."

Tesla reached out abortively, as if to touch and verify, but quickly withdrew, staking his fists over his heart and bowing his head. "The Body Pure."

Jenette expected a lot of reactions from her father, rage and retribution among them, but not the unguarded expression she saw when his head came back up. The overpowering aspect of Olin Tesla at that moment was awe, relief and awe.

"I have waited a generation for this day," said Tesla, gruff voice cracking. "I have prayed every night for twenty years. Blessed be the Body Pure. We are saved."

Thoroughly confused, Karr shook Tesla's hand.

XIX

Those who shine their own light cast their own shadows.

—*Feral warning*

The ring-island was caught upon the great pillar of Radiance, pulled in by wind rushing along the waves to feed the enormous fire, and then swept up, its Pact guardians mesmerized by the glorious light, until it was too late. Tlalok watched the Radiance pull the heavy island out of the water. The power was unthinkable. The island bent up as spears of brilliance tore it apart, flash vaporizing gouts of runoff water, incinerating the rising, exploding chunks, obliterating generations of careful tending in the space of heartbeats. The great Radiance silenced the cries of tiny Khafra forms, falling, cascading from the dying island, or swept up from paddleboards on the surface. One heartbeat, there were hundreds-of-fours of tiny dots; the next, nothing but ash.

The Radiance was false.

At first, after the second unexpected Clash of Radiance, Tlalok's pack had flocked to the great wonder: a shaft of Radiance as wide as five islands, stabbing from the underworld up through the sky into the stars. A direct connection between Radiance and Shadow. The fulcrum of the Balance. The great Radiance called them like moths to a flame. They idolized it. And they had swarmed in, riding the islands-that-moved. One of those precious islands was gone now, destroyed by the terrible Radiance. Fours upon fours of innocents perished.

Something was wrong. The Burning Heart had come, as foretold by the Tears in the sky. But it was false.

How could it be that the Radiance was false?

It was beyond Tlalok's imagining. Radiance that was false. No Pact had seen such a thing. Radiance was truth. Radiance was life. Radiance held the secret knowledge. And yet there it was. False Radiance. Tlalok strove to make sense of it. The False Radiance was like fire, which was rare, but which Pact knew. Fire's colors cleansed the corrupt so that new truth might take root. But the False Radiance did not cleanse corruption. It was corruption. It destroyed the healthy, stealing innocent life, telling great untruths and leaving nothing but ruin in its wake.

Tlalok flashed warnings to his pack, calling them back, but his brilliance was nothing before the great corrupt light. His command took a long time to ripple forward. Tlalok entered the water himself, to get that much closer, to try to rescue as many as he could, but many more Pact were incinerated before his warning reached the forward ranks. More still passed after receiving his command, without fulfilling Pact, paddling furiously to escape, but unable to resist the mighty updraft, snuffed out like embers rising from flame.

Tlalok lay in the water a long time after they withdrew to safety, striving to find his own inner Radiance again, but he and the others were blank with shock.

How could Radiance be false? How? How!

And then word came. A blank-one dressed in white had been seen. When he came on a flying machine, the sky was clear. When he left, the False Radiance was eating the world.

And then Tlalok's fury was a hue to behold.

It was Karr, the blank-one temporarily forgotten because of the corrupt light. Tlalok knew it as certainly as he was alive. It was the blank-one Karr who had killed Lleeala, who had made Tlalok half-blank with mourning.

Karr had awakened a shadow in Tlalok's heart.

A shadow from before Lleeala. A shadow Lleeala had shooed away. Now this shadow wrapped around Tlalok's heart once more. Tlalok had come thinking to find the wonder of the Burning Heart

and reap justice upon the blank-one Karr, but instead found False
Radiance. The blank-one Karr had made the Burning Heart bad.
He and all the other blank-ones had warped the world, with their
enslaving and truth-twisting and death-cheating with the Pact of
others. They had bent the world so much that there was now bad
light.

And Tlalok knew what he must do.

*The blank-ones must be eradicated, before the False Radiance
destroyed the world.*

Tlalok had the means to do it. Tlalok's grief on the first Clash
of Radiance had grown his pack to hundreds-of-fours. His passion
on the second night grew it to thousands-of-fours, even after all
who died in the False Radiance. And it would grow still more. For
until the bad light went away, there would be Clashes of Radiance
for many nights to come. By the time Tlalok returned to blank-one
territory, his force would be many more thousands-of-fours strong.

Tlalok knew where the blank-ones were weak and he knew
how to strike them down. He knew because of his shame, because
he had been a blank-one slave, because they had taken him and
raped him with their Sacrament and put their shadow around his
heart. They had created him, and he would be their undoing.
Lleeala would not approve, Tlalok knew. He would beg her forgiveness in the great nothingness after Pact. But for now he would
keep her cherished memory locked away and use his shadow to
fight for the Balance. For if there cold be False Radiance, then
there could be True Shadow.

Yes.

Tlalok would go where the blank-ones lived and he would
show them what his True Shadow could do. He would hunt them
down and kill them. And he would save the blank-one Karr for
last. And when Karr had paid the price for all the Pact slain by the
False Radiance, only then would Lleeala's memory be freed.

It would not be pretty.

No, by the shadow in Tlalok's heart, it would not be pretty.

PART THREE:

THE BLANK-ONES

XX

Fugueship Kismet. 4609 A.D.

*Olin Tesla and Pondur Yll stand over a porthole in
the ship's fugue-free chambers. The round glass looks
down on a silver-blue planet dotted with minuscule,
viridian rings. The diminutive Yll is reserved. Tesla,
brawny and stern, is troubled.*

*"Decide," says the older of two men in white behind
them. Bondir Malda, Senior Pilot of Kismet, is wrinkled
like fruit left in the sun too long.*

*Tesla's mouth presses tight. "If we decline, will we
be allowed to seed the next planet?"*

*Malda sucks his long teeth. "Refusal of seeding
places dreamers at the end of the queue, as you well
know."*

*"Maybe they'll get lucky," the younger man in white
says offhandedly. Handsome in a hollow sort of way,
Rookie Pilot Talaylan wears his uniform like a peacock
flaunts its feathers.*

*Malda scowls at the thoughtless comment. "The
other candidate systems this tour are not promising,
Pilot Talaylan. In a best case scenario, one of the other
dreamer groups might agree to absorb Representative
Tesla's surplus population."*

*Surplus population. Tesla flinches. It is not a good
option. He and his people will lose control of their own
destiny, and forever be at the mercy of some less pure
ideology. Like the one they left.*

*Malda continues in his aging parchment voice.
"Worst case, refusal of seeding will find two thousand*

dreamers disembarked back on Evermore, ousted in favor of more daring individuals."

The old Pilot's words are spoken without sympathy—or malice—but Tesla feels the pressure of seeding regulations like a knife to his jugular. He stares hard at the planet below. *"What do you think, Pondur?"*

Dr. Yll recounts his findings cautiously. *"I think . . . CG-423-B has a magnetosphere larger than necessary to shield against radiation. Gravity is close enough to one g as to be irrelevant. Atmosphere: textbook nitrogen, oxygen. Weather: temperate to tropical all year round due to minimal axial tilt. The biosphere teems with diverse life-forms, including a possibly sentient species, and conserved DNA from the cross-section of specimens I collected approaches ninety-nine percent Terran. We breathe what they breathe and eat what they eat. And what they eat grows wild and plentiful for the taking. CG-423-B is a biological Elysium."* The scientist motions out the porthole. *"Just look at all that free water."*

Tesla clenches his eyes to clear his thoughts, but an afterimage of the seamless silver orb hangs in his head. *"I don't trust a planet without land."*

"The apparent lack of plate tectonics is peculiar," Yll admits, *"but we can mine the sea floor for metals and fossil fuels, and there is plenty of room to settle on the floating islands. We might eventually be able to link them into artificial subcontinents."*

"So you say go?"

"I say it seems rather encouraging."

"I need a yes or a no."

Yll pulls at the tip of his high-bridged nose.

Tesla presses. *"From your report, this world seems almost perfect. Is there a problem?"*

"There is the matter of disease. . . ."

"What kind of disease?" Tesla immediately asks.

"Actually, an apparent lack thereof. My specimens exhibited very little sign of it, in fact almost none, but it is possible those results were a consequence of rushed methodology. Obviously not a wide enough sampling."

Tesla scoffs. "No disease? Is that possible?"

"Very little disease," Yll re-emphasizes. "The large sentient species, which are most like us in biology despite their four-legged locomotion, exhibits no sign of disease of any kind. It is most peculiar. Dissection and analysis revealed no trace of harmful bacteria, viruses, cancers, or any other form of malady. A few symbiotic bacteria, but that's it. Of course the lower life-forms prey upon one another and their life cycles are rather rapid and short, but if one eliminates parasitism, there seems to be very little disease." Yll's pinched body language becomes more erratic as he futilely attempts to stifle his enthusiasm. "It goes against all my scientific training to make sweeping statements, you know that Olin, but . . . we may have stumbled upon a paradise. We may be on the verge of founding the first colony on a disease-free world!"

"We've got diseases," Tesla remarks, surprised at Yll's outburst.

"I applaud your altruism," Yll says, with building vigor now, "but concern for the native life forms is surely not primary."

"That's not the point," Tesla argues. "If there is no disease down there, what if the bacteria in our sweat kills off every living thing on the planet? We'd starve to death on a dead planet, that's what."

Yll argues back. "The entire biosphere seems to have evolved sharing slightly different mutations of a single super-potent immune system. I doubt they will be affected by our bacteria." The scientist reflects. "It will be interesting to see if we might biofacture a version of their immune defense for ourselves." Yll takes a deep breath, as if coming to a momentous decision, leans closer to Tesla and speaks in a lowered tone. "You wanted me to give you a definitive answer and now I'm giving you one. I say yes."

Tesla clenches his hands over his heart. "I don't know Pondur. The seeding has to be viable for the Body Pure to survive."

"It will be viable. Olin, this is our chance, what we

*all talked about and dreamed about. What you made
happen. This is our chance at the Body Pure. Life
without corrupt air and corrupt bodies. Our minds our
own. A New Ascension for those who have Fallen. Let's
not let it slip away. No one wants to go back . . ."*

The old Pilot steps up to the porthole. "Decide now."

"We need more time," Tesla asks.

"Your chosen scientist has already expended the
allotted weeks."

"But I should have been awakened at the same
time," Tesla protests. "I am the representative of my
dreamers and I did not get a chance to guide Dr. Yll's
investigation."

"You were removed from dream capsules at the same
time," Malda says. "We cannot be expected to allow for
exceptionally slow rates of fugue withdrawal."

Tesla reaches out a conciliatory hand. "Please—"

Malda jerks back. "Do not presume to touch me!
Decide now or risk return to your . . ." he searches for
the right word, "cosmopolitan homeworld."

Tesla growls at the thought. CG-667-A. Better known
as Evermore. Summer on that green sphere brings
flowering plants that fill the air with pollens that rival
the most potent narcotics discovered by man. The
planet's entire population is forced to migrate from
southern to northern hemispheres and back again each
year to stay in relatively unpolluted, winter
environments. And even so, a huge proportion of the
population is incapacitated at any one time, the
narcotics polluting their bodies and minds.

"They have lost the way," Tesla says disparagingly.

"Morals have evolved on Evermore," Talaylan
objects. The apprentice Pilot, like Tesla and his
dreamers, is also a native of Evermore. Tesla regards
Talaylan as an incompetent and he suspects Malda
does, too; he suspects the mummified-looking senior
Pilot would do anything to be rid of the young
interloper, so that he could stay with his precious ship
and not be forced into retirement, but Tesla does not
know how to use this knowledge to his advantage.

*"Society thrives on Evermore," Talaylan laments
haughtily. "I left it only to serve the greater good."*

*Society thrived on Evermore, because norms of
morality had devolved to suit the planet. It was not the
kind of society Olin Tesla wanted any part of.*

*Tesla realizes the choice is made. This is where his
Fallen people shall make their New Ascension; this is
where they will strive to attain the Body Pure.*

"Wake my wife first," he requests.

*Malda inclines his head, seeming almost sympathetic
for a heartbeat; his loose neck skin sways. "A wise
choice. I respect your dream, and it might have been
lost. The seeding begins."*

*Tesla's gut tightens. In a few months the new colony
will be established. Kismet will leave the system. There
is no turning back.*

The island fortress grew on the horizon, proud, challenging the
surrounding seascape with a brown band of walls and guard towers. Trimmed and orderly plant life peeked over its battlements in
a defiant affront to the profusion of leaf and tree which overflowed
from every Feral island. Trees within the fortress grew in rows.
Sunlight glinted from prefab rooftops, also planted in rows.

Karr was reminded of a prison island on Solara.

"Bear right," said Jenette.

Karr steered the heavy lifter where she pointed, closing the
final stretch to the large island, slowing, setting down a few dozen
yards from the island and then coasting through a waterway
cleared of tube-and-bladder kelp to an immense gate in the defensive walls. He cut the engines as the hull nudged against a broad
corrugated ramp. The fortifications loomed above, five stories
high. Constructed from layered composite fibers, they flexed with
the faint motion of the large island. Heavy mount pulse-cannons
bristled from evenly spaced towers.

There was no sign of activity, no people on the battlements, no
vessels on the water, no sound of activity behind the walls.

"Is it always this quiet?" Karr asked.

Jenette looked around warily. "No." Why were the gates closed, she wondered. They were customarily open during daylight hours. Where were the fishing craft, which cleared Enclave waters of sharkworms and provided food for the domestic population?

Two soldiers appeared from a small door beside the large gates. They jogged down and moored the lifter to the ramp. To Karr's eye they appeared over-young, recruits fresh out of boot camp, but their movements were practiced, precise, and formal. They snapped to attention as Jenette stepped off the lifter.

"Consul Tesla," they greeted, careful not to eyeball her—and especially careful not to eyeball Karr as he stepped onto the ramp behind her.

"Where's my father?" Jenette asked suspiciously.

Olin Tesla was nowhere to be seen. He had been acting strangely ever since first meeting Karr. That night of their meeting, Tesla had listened to Karr's synopsis of his arrival, never interrupting. All the time the uncharacteristic awe and relief was plain on his face. When Karr was unable to stay awake any longer, Tesla had returned to his skimmer without saying a word to Jenette. She spent the night sleepless. The few yards of water between the two vehicles might as well have been an ocean. The next day, Tesla led off before she could speak to him. He and Karr played a slowly paced game of tag across the ocean, the lifter capable of traveling much faster, but forced to stop more and more frequently as the engines began to overheat. When they stopped for the night near FI-716, Jenette again tried to speak to her father, but he was back to his domineering old self, extolling the virtues of the New Ascension Enclave, painting a heroic picture of their struggle to bring civilization to a barbarous world, and conversing with Jenette just enough so as not to arouse suspicion in Karr. Tesla didn't actually need words to show his displeasure with her, accusing eyes or averted shoulders did that quite effectively. Tesla slept in the skimmer again and took off the next morning, racing ahead at full speed to attend to "pressing Enclave matters," and instructing Jenette to meet him at the main gate. Tesla kept Arrou on the skimmer the whole time, an unspoken hostage to Jenette's compliance.

"You are requested to proceed through the gates," one of the Guards said, in tight-lipped response to Jenette's query. Jenette started toward the small door the Guards had appeared from. "By your leave, Consul," the same Guard interrupted, gesturing to the main gate itself. A mighty *boom* resounded behind the walls and the huge doors rumbled open, just wide enough for two people to pass through.

Karr shot a questioning glance at Jenette. She shrugged and shook her head and led on up the ramp. Karr followed, not knowing what to expect as they passed through the imposing vertical opening. Inside was a short alley ringed with high walls and with another set of double doors on its opposite side. The Prime Consul waited for them on the back of a low-slung crawler, which had official seals on the doors and flags on the engine cowl and polished metal railings on the rear deck. An honor squad of six Guards stood double file ahead of it. Two more stood at either side of carpeted boarding steps at its rear.

Jenette cringed at the sight.

She and Karr climbed on. Tesla motioned for them to stand in the place of honor behind the cab.

Karr felt like a bug in a web.

"Ostentatious displays are not absolutely necessary," he muttered, beginning to fear where events were heading.

"Nonsense," said Tesla. "You are a Pilot and must be treated with ceremony befitting your rank."

Karr looked up. Battlements ringed the high walls, well positioned to rain down death on uninvited guests. Again, he was reminded of a prison.

Tesla stood at Karr's right, Jenette on the left. The rear Guards folded the steps, locked a railing into place and fell into line with those out front.

Tesla rapped on the cab. "Drive on."

Another *boom* resounded. The inner gates grumbled open. The crawler lurched across the threshold, honor guard preceding in perfect lock step.

Karr did not know what to expect. He had seen many strange colonies on many strange planets, but none of those other worlds quite prepared him for New Ascension's human colony and its combination of the mundane and surreal. A cobblestoned avenue, the color of twenty-four-carat gold, stretched inland from the gates; it was lined with rows of shooting-star palms and scattered human structures, weathered prefab units rubbing shoulders with constructs of local material, whose component materials looked plant-like and were frayed at the edges. At the far end, Karr caught the unmistakable metal sheen of a seed-colony container, high and wide compared to the buildings clustered densely around it. His overall impression of the colony was of ivory and khaki cubes set in a profusion of sensuous greens. Golden cobblestone arteries snaked off the main avenue into tiled agricultural plots, which Karr could have seen on a dozen other worlds, but these fields teemed with working domestics, as did the rest of the colony. On Karr's left, they tended orchards of mysterious, squid-like bushes. In the distance on his right, they carried heavy head-sized polyps to and from a grouping of military buildings. Everywhere else they worked at a profusion of tasks both pedestrian and peculiar. And, last but not least on the scale of surreal, was the view of the whole landscape rolling with the big island's lurid, gentle motion upon the ocean. The Enclave was a sight to see.

And nowhere near as weird as the gathering horde of human faces.

Hundreds of heads turned toward the crawler. Mouths hung open. Silent. Not cheering, not welcoming, like the crowds of other worlds. Enraptured colonists stared, unblinking, eyes locked, focused in religious fervor.

A murmur swept down the street. *"The man in white . . . A Pilot . . . Can it be?"*

The crowd parted as the crawler inched forward.

"The Body . . . the Body Pure. . . ."

The crowd was young, eerily young. Some were tall like adults, but all were too thin. Males were gangly and awkward, females sprightly like gymnasts. Their adolescent faces gaped at Karr, changed by the alien forces of New Ascension. Jenette had warned Karr about hormone inhibitors, but it was startling to see the effects en masse. It was a colony of proto-humans, not quite teenagers, not quite adults, looking ghostly with their gray-white hair and simple earthen-colored coveralls. Here and there were young adults, men and women hardly older than Jenette, but who were world-weary where youthful optimism should have reigned. More rare still were those nearing their thirties, worn beyond their years, glowering at Karr bitterly but unable to turn away. Tesla was the only truly old face. And there were no children.

"Welcome to your new home," said Tesla.

Karr gulped, wanting to flee from the hollow faces. He had nothing in common with them, a Pilot, born and bred to solitary life between the stars, bound to duty, to sacrifice, to self-reliance. These were victims. Unmoving. Needy. They didn't even look human. What did they want from him?

The gates boomed shut behind Karr. Cell doors, locking.

The horde pressed closer as the crawler inched on, their strange stillness holding, for now. Halfway down the street, where buildings crowded closer to the golden pavement, a colonist suddenly dove at the crawler, his arm thrusting in over the crawler deck, fingers brushing Karr's boot before he tumbled off. Karr looked back as the young man picked himself up, waving his hand triumphantly.

"I touched him! I touched him!"

The man *licked* his hand.

Like a pebble starting an avalanche, the zombie crowd began to move. Outstretched hands pressed in, straining to reach Karr. And they found their voices, calling for his attention.

"Me, pick me, touch me . . . please!"

"Father . . ." Jenette warned, worried by the crowd's behavior. They began to push and shove. Hundreds of hands tried to get closer to Karr.

"Out of my way! The Pilot! I must touch the Pilot! No, me!"

The crawler jerked to a halt, its path jammed. Karr clutched the deck railing, feeling the same uneasy dread as when crazy Bob had danced around him like a high-speed gnat. Looking back anxiously for orders, the honor guard tried to hold the colonists off.

"Stand clear!" Tesla thundered. The colonists bunched up momentarily. "I bring you a Pilot and this is how you shame me, how you shame the Enclave? How dare you!"

Karr saw that the colonists were beyond words, immobile for a few split seconds like a frozen wave, but indignant, swelling stronger in anticipation of its final crash on shore. Fear motivated them—the same fear that told Karr to run. He felt that. Fear about to explode.

Tesla motioned the Guards to arm their rifles.

"No," Karr said suddenly. There were too few soldiers; all they could do was trigger the explosion. And Karr had seen enough riots to know he didn't want to be at the center of one. Because he was a Pilot, he was bad with crowds; because he was a Pilot, he must now take action. "It's all right. It's okay."

Before Tesla could stop him, and before he lost his nerve, Karr slipped over the railing onto the crawler's engine cowl and reached out to the frightening mob. The wave of humanity broke then, a surf of hands rushed up onto him. Warm hands, sweaty hands, cold clammy fingers, callused palms, soft palms. So many, so close. The sticky intimacy threatened to overwhelm Karr.

"Easy! Easy!" roared Tesla.

Karr focused on single faces in the ghoulish crowd. There was need and terror. There was shock and wonder. On the right were faces full of longing and there on the left were hopeful ones. Karr reached from side to side; there were the disbelieving and the eager. Obsessed and desperate swept by as the crawler began to move again, as well as angry and jealous. Karr saw adulation and felt tears against his palms. These people looked strange, but they had human emotions.

And there, at least, Karr saw common ground. A place he could cling to and not be completely overwhelmed by his fear.

The crawler made the slow journey up the street. More people poured onto the cobblestones from buildings and alleys. Jenette and Tesla watched nervously, hoping the tenuous balance would hold.

XXI

4609 A.D.

New Ascension colony at Elysium island. Three months after seeding.

Olin Tesla's blood-engorged face stares down at Dr. Ponder Yll. Yll fears. Tesla's meaty hands clutch the collar of Yll's pristine labjumper, shaking the smaller, slender man. Tesla's wintry blue eyes are shot with red.

"Please Olin!" Yll squeaks. "Control yourself!"

"Control myself?" Tesla rages. "It's too late for control! We're all dying, you stupid sonofabitch!" Tesla's grip tightens.

"Olin, please!"

"It's all your fault, Yll! "

Yll gasps, thin appendages clawing at Tesla's overpowering limbs. "Olin, you're choking me."

Tesla shoves Yll away. The smaller man slumps against a counter as the big man angrily sweeps a rack of test tubes and glass piping to the floor. Crash!

"You told me there was no disease on this planet!" Tesla pitches a beaker into a wall. The purple fluid of another failed vaccine trickles down sterile surfaces.

"Very little disease," Yll squeaks.

"Eleven hundred dead and you banter words?" Tesla turns a darker shade of red. More beakers shatter against walls and floor.

Yll cringes. The dream is dying. Olin's dream, Yll's dream, the colony's dream. To live the Body Pure, free of corrupting intoxicants, masters of their own bodies and minds—but the human colonists have exchanged the narcotic vapors of Evermore for another, less forgiving contagion.

The New Ascension of Fallen to the Body Pure may not happen now.

Three months ago, Kismet *off-loaded two thousand dreamers, fifty percent men and fifty percent women. This day barely half that number survives. Five hundred women, those who were pregnant in transit, gave birth, as planned, two weeks ago. Today they are all dead. Six hundred of the colony's nine hundred sexually active men are also dead.*

"I'll . . . I'll ask Pilot Malda for a dustoff," Yll stammers as Tesla trashes more beakers full of failed science. "I'll reason with him, beg him, whatever it takes—"

"There isn't going to be any dustoff," Tesla spits. "Didn't you hear? Pilot Malda has just declared this planet a Plague World. Interdicted. No contact. We stay. We stay and we live or we stay and we die, but nobody's going to help us. Do you understand? Nobody!"

Yll flinches, understanding all too well.

A lot more dying is to come.

A second wave of prescheduled pregnancies was set in motion before the first mothers began to die, before the awful discovery that the human population was infected with a pestilence the likes of which had never been seen on a human-settled world. Too late came the knowledge that what Yll at first believed to be a shared planetary super-immune system, was actually a deadly pathogen; there appeared to be no other disease on New Ascension because that pathogen was territorial and aggressive, allowing no other organism to harm one of its hosts before it eventually decided to consume that host. Too late came the knowledge that this pestilence—the Scourge, as Olin has named it—is triggered by the very basic biological function that New Ascension's human colony depends on for survival: procreation.

The lab is in shambles. Yll cowers, unable to escape Olin's abhorrent physical violence.

"We must talk about the third wave of pregnancies," Yll blurts, a desperate act of courage for the frail man.

Tesla stomps over. *"Third wave? There will be no third wave! "*

"There must be," the scientist yells from the floor, *"if you want this colony to survive!"* Like a cornered rat, Yll does not back down as Tesla looms over him. *"So far there have been five hundred births to eleven hundred deaths. I have discontinued gestation-acceleration in the hopes of decreasing second-wave mortality, but I hereby serve notice that if another four hundred of us die, there will be too few breeding adults to maintain a healthy genetic cross-section—and another four hundred are certain to die. Our first generation gene pool is doomed. Our only hope now is to birth a sufficiently large second generation gene pool. Allowing for child mortality, accidental death, and other unforeseen decreases in stock size, I estimate that three thousand infants would be a safe number."*

"Three thousand?" Tesla repeats, dumbfounded. *"Who is going to raise three thousand orphans when their parents are all dead?"*

The scientist breathes rapidly. *"I don't know, I don't know. But without a third wave consisting of at least fifteen hundred more infants this colony will inbreed and perish. I know that as certainly as anything I've ever known."*

Yll's words freeze Tesla in place.

"There will not be many women left alive after the second wave of pre-planned pregnancies," Yll continues, *"so for the third we need to consider multiple births, massive doses of fertility drugs, ex-vivo ovum splitting—and we also need to consider using the frozen zygotes from Evermore."*

Now it is Tesla's turn to flinch. To use prefertilized eggs, taken randomly from morally degenerate Evermorites and implant them in brave, pure-hearted New Ascension women—one month ago, such an abomination was unthinkable, but now?

> *Olin shudders. "Who is going to convince our*
> *women to commit suicide for your plan, Yll? Who?"*
> *The little man stiffens, perhaps taking spiteful*
> *revenge for the indignity perpetrated on him by the*
> *Prime Consul.*
> *"Why you will, Olin. You will."*

The next few days were frustrating ones for Karr. His time was split between two equally repellent tasks.

The first was being Dr. Yll's guinea pig, spending hours on end having blood drawn, being biopsied, poked, prodded, and generally made uncomfortable by all manner of sharp and pointed instruments. The pretext for the torture was to provide Enclave scientists with badly needed samples of *fugue* to analyze in hopes that it would help them biofacture a cure for, or at least a vaccine against, Scourge. For humanitarian reasons, Karr could hardly refuse such aid, but as days added up, Yll wielded his implements more and more greedily.

Karr wondered what they were doing with so much blood and tissue.

The second task was equally repellent, if not more so. Tesla insisted on personally introducing Karr to each and every one of the Enclave's three thousand proto-humans—and on having Karr touch them. Except for sleep, and Yll's butchery, that's what occupied Karr's every waking moment. Meeting after meeting, lunch after lunch, function after function blurred by. Following the incident at the main gates, Tesla was careful to keep the groups small, but Karr could not enjoy the procession of ghostly faces. His overpowering impression of the colonists was one of having stumbled into a mortuary and having surprised the corpses swaying to a silent, zombie waltz; that somehow it was only his gaze which kept the colonists alive and that if he turned away they would all fall back into tiny, over-young graves.

Three girls shrieked as Subconsul Bragg herded Karr from a crawler into a cluster of hydroponic domes for his next session of greet-and-grope. Volunteer Forces, green and red armbands distinguishing them from regular colonists, held the girls at bay. Karr was of half a mind to bite the bullet and go over to the girls. Maybe then they would stop following him around. But the unmitigated hero worship was off-putting, and besides, they were not high enough up on Tesla's list to be permitted access to *the Pilot* yet.

It was all political maneuvering.

As a Pilot, Karr was used to being at the beck and call of local leaders during his stints planetside. It took great concerted efforts on the part of fringe worlds like Solara or Evermore to outfit a fugueship: constructing the enormous seed-colony containers and stocking them with the vast quantities of equipment and materials necessary to start a new world, selecting and training thousands of new dreamers, and many other labor intensive tasks. The decades necessary for these exploits put great strain on populations of below one hundred million. So, when a fugueship finally arrived for refitting, it was a big planetary event. Parades and celebrations inevitably focused on the Pilot. The wheels must be kept turning. It was part of Karr's job description, a part he learned to tolerate, just barely.

So at first Karr did Tesla's bidding, but after days of playing figurehead, anxiety reared its ugly head. There was a major difference between those other times and being on New Ascension. Then, Karr had been killing time between missions. Now, Karr had an urgent need to rescue *Long Reach* from the bottom of New Ascension's ocean. That meant somehow extinguishing the mountain of fire over top of it, a task Karr could not do alone. He had to get help and every hour that elapsed was an hour wasted, an hour in which his anxiety mounted.

Upon entering the interlinked domes, Karr spotted Tesla buttering up a group of influential colonists. Karr attempted to push his way through the crowd to get to the Prime Consul, but as had happened every other time, Bragg conveniently stepped in the way.

Teeth, smiling teeth. "May I be of assistance?"

"I must speak with the Prime Consul."

"The Prime Consul has asked me to tell you that he will be unable to speak freely until later."

"When later? Tonight?"

Slippery smooth was this Bragg. "As soon as the furor over your arrival dies down. I'm sure you understand?"

Karr was not good with people, so each time Bragg adroitly maneuvered him away from Tesla. Karr was silent, but his apprehension and annoyance grew.

Bragg disappeared before Karr could protest further.

More faces swirled around Karr. More hands thrust at Karr. Shake, shake, smile like an idiot . . . blank reverent face after blank reverent face. *They sniffed their fingers after touching him or surreptitiously rubbed his sweat onto their faces.*

Karr's skin crawled.

Occasionally, the gapers spoke. "I'm Panya Hedren," said a haughty woman. She stood out, not only because of her attitude, but also because of her obviously adult, very pregnant body. Karr found himself comforted by the familiarity of her full, womanly figure. He checked his stare before it became rude, but not before Panya flirted back at him with her eyes. Baring her midriff, she thrust her pregnant belly out. "Kisses for luck?"

"Yes, of course," said Karr, bending stiffly at the waist and pecking her ripe abdomen.

"Now three more," Panya said before Karr could stand back up. "That was for Kayli. Now for Shona and Soren and Gall."

Karr gave her three more pecks.

"You're so kind." Panya beamed, turning to a giant of a man beside her, also a full-grown adult. "This is Burke, my husband." Burke had arms as big around as Karr's legs. Karr hoped Burke had not noticed the flirty eyes Panya had made in Karr's direction. Panya suddenly bubbled over. "Oh! There's the Prime Consul!" She flittered off to get into an influential orbit—with no impediment from Bragg, Karr noticed sourly.

Burke remained, giving Karr a stern appraisal. Karr prepared for trouble as Burke leaned close. Would he break Karr in half, or request a kiss of his own? Karr did not relish the options.

"Jenette says hello," Burke said in a low voice.

Karr perked up. "Jenette?" he whispered back. "Where is she? Why haven't I seen her?"

"You are out of bounds," Burke said, with a significant jerk of his honest face at Tesla.

"I must speak to her—" Karr started to hiss.

Burke silenced him with a headshake as other colonists moved around them. "Be patient. Your goals are hers. She is working on them."

A commotion broke out in an adjoining dome.

Burke took the opportunity to slip away. "Be nice to Jenette," he said in parting, "or I'll have to break your arms."

What the hell did that mean, Karr wondered.

The commotion spilled in on the official gathering as the girls from outside rushed in through a back entrance. "There he is!" screamed the youngest looking. Bragg and his VF police tackled the first two, but the third screamer zigzagged between invited guests and before Karr knew what happened, body tackled him. He fell backward. She rubbed her twelve-year-old's body against his, grabbing his face and thrusting her tongue into his mouth. Karr tried to push her off, but thin legs wrapped around him like a vise. Her boyish pelvis rubbed against his crotch.

"I want you!" she breathed in his ear. "I want your babies!"

Colonists rushed to help, swamping in on Karr like an evil tide, too many and too close.

"Young lady! Control yourself!" Karr heard Tesla yelling from somewhere. Strong arms pulled the struggling girl off Karr. More clutching hands pulled him to his feet, brushing and cloying at his uniform.

"Are you hurt?" Tesla asked, his concerned face looming before Karr.

Karr's own voice sounded far away in his ears. "I'm fine," he panted, but it was a lie. The weight of people pressing in was too much for a fugueship Pilot. A circuit in Karr's brain snapped. Ingrained anthropophobia drowned his rational mind in a flood of panic.

Karr needed out. Now.

Suddenly his legs were carrying him through the agricultural domes, leaping over rows of bulgy vegetables, running out into a yellow-paved alley between the domes and a three-story hospital complex.

What sort of hospital had bars on the windows, his panic-stricken mind wondered.

Tesla, the VF police, and a horde of domestics swarmed out behind him. Karr looked frantically for somewhere, anywhere, to get away; he could not out run the quadrupeds. He fixated on a potential haven. Darting past two very surprised domestics, Karr ran through a restroom door and slammed it behind him.

Karr jammed the latch locked and leaned against the door, hyperventilating in his odd refuge. Organic looking toilet stalls, sinks, and urinals were built amid the spidering legs of a tree. Karr staggered over to a sink, jabbing and twisting until he figured out how to activate a timer bulb, and splashed water on his face.

There was pounding on the door. Karr ignored it.

He felt dirty, violated. He tasted the crazed girl's tongue in his mouth and smelled every one of a hundred repulsive handshakes on his fingers. Karr rinsed his mouth for a long time, then switched to hot water and washed his hands for even longer. The mirror fogged over. The stream of water described lazy circles around the drain as the island swayed.

Gradually, the pounding of blood through Karr's ears decreased.

"Pilot Karr!" came a muffled voice. "It's Consul Tesla. Please open the door."

"Just a moment," Karr gasped. "I need a personal moment." He turned on the other spigots to drown out further questions and kept washing. When his irrational mind finally admitted that further scrubbing would do no good, Karr straightened up and stood with dripping hands, looking for an evaporator, towel, or anything at all to dry off with.

Kla-tik, went a valve behind him. *Foosh!* Karr jumped as water rushed from tree pod reservoirs above him down through overhead piping and into a closed toilet stall.

Suddenly the empty bathroom was crowded.

An obese man, three times larger than Karr, stepped out of the stall hiking up his daysuit, and drew a basin of water. Everything about him was plump: the pudgy fingers dipping in water, the piggy eyes peeking out from fat-crowded eyelids, the full lips pursed in mirth at some secret joke. It all jiggled when he moved.

Karr watched the man suspiciously.

The man made a show of plucking a wide leaf from the living ceiling and delicately drying between his fingers. Remembering his own wet hands, Karr copied him.

"My name is Dr. Clarence Bigelow," the fat man said, conspicuously tossing the leaf into a compost hopper, "and you, sir, are a person I simply have to know."

Karr froze.

"And I don't want to touch you, either," Bigelow added.

Karr relaxed a bit.

"I don't believe any of that *residual fugue* nonsense, not a bit of it."

"Residual *fugue?*" Karr managed.

"Certain non-cognoscenti, an unfortunately profuse portion of our population it seems, believe that *fugue* oozes off Pilots and that if they touch you they can prolong their lives by a few miserable days. That goes in there," Bigelow reminded.

Karr tossed his wet leaf into the hopper.

Bigelow straightened his immaculate daysuit and picked lint from crossed lightning bolt patches on his shoulders. "Do you know about Scourge?"

"Yes, a bit."

"Well, we worry entirely too much about Scourge around here. It gives us a rather . . . skewed outlook."

"I noticed," Karr said, stealing a glance at the door.

Whether he noticed Karr's displeasure or not, Bigelow kept right on talking. "I have heard of your exploits."

"You have?" said Karr.

"Certainly," said Bigelow, "They are quite impressive. Let me be the first to congratulate you on setting our ocean ablaze."

"The ocean is not actually burning," Karr said defensively.

"Of course not," Bigelow replied. "Your fugueship is electrolyzing salt water into oxidizer and fuel. Nevertheless, a conflagration several kiloyards wide and who knows how tall, that's big, that's *style!*"

"It was unintentional," Karr assured. "I need to put it out to save what's left of my ship."

"Not to mention the ecosystem of our poor planet," said Bigelow. "Consider what just one small meteorite or a volcano can do to an atmosphere, and those are limited in duration, relatively. I wonder what is more stylish, boiling in greenhouse heat, or freezing from a premature ice age? I am exaggerating, you understand—by no means am I a planetologist—but you follow my drift?"

"Perfectly." Karr's imagination filled with images of devastating electrical storms, changing air and water currents, seas of dead ocean creatures, and clouds of moisture blocking out New Ascension's sun and either suffocating or freezing the tropical planet, both of which left a dark hulk in space. Karr slumped against the sink.

The outside door rattled again. "Pilot Karr?" Tesla called. "Are you sick? Do you need a doctor?"

"I am all right," Karr called back, not wanting to go back outside yet. He felt secure in the organic restroom. It reminded him of *Long Reach*.

"Let us know if you need anything."

"I'll tell Dr. Bigelow if I do."

"Bigelow?" the muffled voice said with a tinge of consternation. "Dr. Bigelow is in there?"

"Yes, Prime Consul," Bigelow announced, grooming his eyebrows with a flick of dampened thumbs. "Attending to important Enclave matters."

Tesla became silent.

"Philistine," Bigelow muttered. Presently he extended a pinkie finger and traced three lines on the fogged mirror. "Let us examine your problem. Since I am in charge of the Enclave's power supply, I know a certain amount about these things." The lines on the mirror joined into a triangle. Bigelow labeled its sides *fuel, oxygen,* and *ignition.* "This is the combustion triangle. All three sides are necessary to sustain a fire, from a humble candle right on up to an inferno of your size. Remove one and the fire expires. Fuel is your best bet. See?" A Rubenesque hand covered one side of the triangle, "Without fuel there can be no combustion, even with oxygen and a source of ignition present. Likewise for the other two sides of the triangle. Ignition and fuel produce nothing if oxygen is removed from the equation. Oxygen and fuel cannot burn without a source of ignition. In the case of your fire, can we stop the supply of fuel?"

"I think so," Karr said, "but only if I can get inside my ship, and that can only happen if the fire is already out."

Bigelow shook his head. "In that case, that's not a useful strategy. Perhaps you can remove the source of ignition?"

"The engine orifices are already shut," said Karr. "The fire itself is the source of ignition."

"Self perpetuating. I see." Bigelow's face pooched up with displeasure. "A nasty pickle then. Removing the oxygen, which is in the air we breathe as well as being produced in copious amounts by your ship, might prove difficult."

"Unless you just happen to have the largest fire hose in the universe lying around," Karr said without much mirth.

"Alas, no," Bigelow replied, thinking, "but . . . there just might be a workable substitute. I'm imagining a big, stylish *poof!*" With a flourish of his hand, Bigelow suddenly rubbed out the *oxygen* side of the triangle. "No more fire."

"An explosion?" Karr asked, following the scientist's train of thought.

"Correct. One of sufficient size would consume oxygen in the local area with extreme efficiency. Provided that the engine orifices of your ship are truly shut," Bigelow cautioned, "and provided that there is not so much as a lightning strike or a spark of static electricity to set it off again, it could work. But, even if the flames are extinguished, your ship will still be producing hydrogen and oxygen. That is a very unstable situation."

"Agreed. But with the fire out I could drop down in my kilnsuit, enter *Long Reach*, and block the flow of current to the broken superconductor."

"Is that possible?" Bigelow asked. "No one has ever dissected a fugueship—fascinating creatures by the way—but I understood that they produce current as long as their fusion processes continue to function and that shutting those processes off is very likely a death sentence."

"It is," said Karr, "but maybe I can disconnect the superconductor from the supply of current without shutting the fusion furnace down." Karr's face lengthened as he considered the bloody, risky task.

The door rattled again. "Pilot Karr, please hurry. We are late for your next function."

"Do you have a large stockpile of explosives on this island?" Karr asked hurriedly.

"No," said Bigelow.

"Can you manufacture explosives?"

"No," Bigelow said again. "At least not in the magnitude you require, but," a faraway look shone in Bigelow's beady eyes. "But I just might know of something that would suit our purposes."

XXII

*Antisocial behavior must be carefully balanced in the
training of a Pilot. Too much and the Pilot loses all
commitment to humanity; no sociopath cares whether a
cargo of dreamers is alive or dead at journey's end. Too
little antisocial behavior and the Pilot will form
dangerous bonds when exposed to societies outside his
ship, no matter how short the exposure, and then the
safety of such a Pilot's fugueship will be at risk.*

—*Major A. Vidun,
founder, Pilot Academy*

"Coffin Island?" Jenette repeated, incredulous. She had wanted
news of Karr during the days of forced separation, but not this
kind. "Karr's going to Coffin Island? In the Dead Zone? Now?"

"Soon," said Byussart, the domestic in charge of a certain
toilet-tree. "Loading lifter now. Ready before dawn."

"But why?" Jenette fretted, rising from her small desk. She
paced between the cages in the Khafra nursery; a paltry few Feral
kits slept curled in the straw.

"Not sure, not sure," said Byussart. "Wants *big bomb*. Toilet
door thick. Hard to hear," he added when Jenette scowled.

The news was not to her liking. The sudden disappearance of
Karr would seriously affect tomorrow night's vote in the Chamber
of the Body. Now that she was back, her father was trying to ram
through his proposal for expanding the Enclave perimeter and se-
curing new supplies of Feral kits for use in Sacrament. He was
using Karr to help lock down support; who would vote against a
Prime Consul who controlled access to a Pilot? However her fa-

ther's plan had a flaw in it, a flaw Jenette intended to exploit, and she was using every surreptitious Khafra connection she had to influence the coming vote, but she needed Tesla to keep flaunting Karr around the Enclave. Otherwise Jenette's maneuvering would fail and Tesla would steamroll over all opposition once and for all.

Karr must not go to Coffin Island.

A message would have to be sent to Karr, but Jenette didn't think Byussart could pull it off by himself. Byussart was full of good intentions, but he did not know Karr and Karr did not know him. Arrou was the logical choice to send, but he was out in the Enclave at that moment, relaying critical information to Jenette's supporters through their domestics. Besides, Arrou—believing Karr responsible for abandoning him on FI-716—was not on speaking terms with him. Jenette tried to set Arrou straight on the matter, but other issues had gotten in the way. Harsh words were exchanged.

"Forget it," Jenette had ordered.

"No," Arrou said, indignant. "Worried about Jenette. Soon Jenette sick."

"No Sacrament. Just put it out of your peanut brain."

"Jenette die."

"Arrou die," she had returned, angrily mimicking his pidgin speech. "You can't make a clear decision on this. You think you want to commit suicide for me, but it's not true. You don't have to. I force-bonded you. Your genetic instincts are overriding rational thought."

Arrou did not back down. "Have to, want to: not matter. Better Jenette live. Arrou not want live without Jenette. What happen if Jenette die? Tesla makes Arrou bond with other human Arrou not care about! Arrou then forced to Sacrament anyway!"

Jenette could not respond. It was one of the longer, hottest sentences Arrou had ever said to her. And he was right. He had then stalked off to relay her messages to the domestic underground. She did not expect him back soon.

Jenette would have to speak to Karr herself.

Jenette cursed under her breath, locking fingers in a chain link cage and shaking. Feral kits raised frightened eyes. She stopped,

embarrassed by her selfish display. "Sssssh," she soothed. "I'm
sorry. Go back to sleep." Slowly, the kits curled back up.

Byussart thought hard. "Bronte knows more."

"Why? Was she there?"

"No. Outside with Byussart, waiting for Bigelow. But maybe
she hears more."

"Where is she?"

"Not here. Hiding."

Jenette was not surprised. Bigelow's domestic, Bronte, was shy,
verging on cowardly—as she had been the night of the secret
meeting in the glade.

"Does my father know about this?" Jenette asked.

"Not yet. Domestics *never* tell Toby."

"Good." Jenette scratched Byussart behind his ear pits. "You
did a good job."

Byussart, who didn't get much attention from his human,
glowed happily. "Thought Jenette want know."

"You were right."

Jenette grabbed a flashlight, doused the lights in the nursery,
and hurried out the door.

Jenette crept across the island, moving from cover to cover with
the help of Byussart and a few other friendly domestics. They
scouted around corners and up streets to make sure the coast was
clear, blending into night-darkened plant life whenever humans
were present. Jenette kept to hiding spots at those times, waiting
for the all clear signal. At one point, Bragg and a squad of VF police drove by in a crawler. She held her breath and her position, but
the unpleasant gelding did not see her.

Pop (red), pop (white), pop (red), Byussart flashed when it was
safe to move.

Jenette and the domestics skirted around the most heavily pop-
ulated areas of the island and through the pathetically few buildings of the Enclave's manufacturing sector. Tiny glowstrips
glimmered inside silent, empty warehouses. She followed the domestics through fields of New Ascension polyp-grains, the stalks
rippling and rolling with the motion of the island. Jenette skulked

on past the incinerator, toward the sinkhole at the center of the Enclave, which was not a perfect doughnut-hole lake like those found
in wild ring-islands. Thanks to concerted human and domestic efforts to keep the space healthy and usable, it more closely resembled a series of swamps and pools. Jenette found the heavy lifter
floating in one. Karr was not present, but the deck was heaped high
with bulging sacks and nets.

"Keep watch," Jenette whispered.

Byussart and the other domestics slunk away to take up guard
positions. Jenette crept across a short gangplank onto the outworld
vessel. A quick examination of the sacks revealed a collection
of pilfered food and mechanical items. There was even a self-
contained water desalination unit. Karr had enough supplies to last
a month.

Khafra light staccatoed across a field. <<Pilot comes.>>

Jenette heard Karr before she saw him, pulling huge loops of
industrial strapping that clattered behind him. How he had made it
back without discovery, she didn't know. She stood up from behind a heap of meat-fruit melons, ready for confrontation.

"Pilot Karr."

Karr just about jumped out of his skin, but his face lit up when
he saw who it was. "Consul, am I ever glad to see you."

"You are?" Jenette said.

"Yes," said Karr. "You're just about the only friendly face
around here."

Jenette felt suddenly disarmed. For a moment all she could
think of was his grimly handsome face, its dour mouth almost bent
into a smile, its gray eyes staring into hers for a too-long heartbeat.
She realized, to her surprise, that she was glad to see him, too. But
there was important business at hand. Her euphoria soon fizzled.

"What are you doing?" she demanded as he pulled the strapping across the gangplank and piled it on deck.

"Bugging out," Karr replied.

"To Coffin Island?"

"Yes. Why ask if you knew?"

"You can't go."

"Why not?" Karr asked. "I fixed the last of the leaks in the hull, and the overheating thruster, too."

"Let me rephrase that: I can't let you go."

Karr's grin slipped away. "You don't have the authority to stop me. No one on this planet has the authority to stop me. Check your Colony Charter if you don't believe it."

Jenette was sure that Karr had the rules on his side, but she did not care. "Why would you possibly want to go to Coffin Island?"

Karr counted off on his fingers. "One, to find a stockpile of abandoned C-55 core-boring warheads. Two, to retrieve said warheads. Three, to bring them back for Dr. Bigelow to fashion into a large explosive device."

"A big bomb."

"Exactly." Karr explained his plan to snuff out the fire over his fugueship. "It will require a yield of forty to fifty kilotons. It's a standard technique to extinguish fossil-fuel fires on other planets."

"Setting off a fifty kiloton explosion is *standard technique?*"

"Well, on a much smaller scale, but the principal is the same."

Jenette shook her head. "This is nuts."

"It is perfectly sane," Karr said, launching into a detailed explanation of his plan. "Dr. Bigelow reminded me that the explosive blast from a C-55 is extremely direction specific. I should have remembered myself." Pilots were required to be familiar with all the types and numbers of munitions seeded with a colony. "They are used to bore thermal mines deep into colony planet cores. Spaced properly across the surface, they are a great way to raise a planet's temperature from sub-habitable ranges. Of course, New Ascension is tropical already and does not have that problem, so they were never used." Jenette glared as Karr rambled. He cleared his throat uncomfortably and spoke faster. "In any case, Dr. Bigelow assures me that he can turn the unused stockpile into a single, large shaped-charge, which will funnel most of the blast up and away from *Long Reach*. Also, force follows the path of least resistance, so it will naturally tend to explode up through the air as opposed to down into the water. If the detonation was submerged, that would be a different story. That would probably kill half the aquatic life on the planet," Karr laughed nervously at his hyperbole. "But we'll detonate in the air. *Long Reach* being a couple hundred feet under the surface, trauma from the blast should be minimal."

Jenette threw her hands up, exasperated. "How did you get out of your quarters without being seen? Where did you get all this stuff?"

"I climbed through a back window while the guards were sniffing my dirty clothes," Karr sneered, "and as for this equipment, your father dragged me from one end of this island to the other. He even gave me a map." Karr unfolded a sheet of stimpaper from his pocket. "I noted where things were."

"And then you stole them?"

"Again, I refer you to your Colony Charter," Karr said defensively. "This colony is required to render assistance to any and all fugueships and their Pilots—on demand. I repeatedly asked your father for assistance, and he was not forthcoming."

"Forget my father! Think about how crazy this is, going into Feral territory, trying to find Coffin Island, alone!"

"I like working alone. I'm trained to work alone. Me, myself, and I are very productive that way. No one gets in our way. Besides, crowds give me the creeps." Karr couldn't repress a shudder at that thought.

Jenette put a consoling hand on his shoulder. "Please, be reasonable," she said.

Karr stiffened and stepped back. "Reasonable? Don't you know I'm a *Pilot?* Pilots aren't allowed to be reasonable! My Duty is to my ship—and that's it! *Long Reach* might live a few weeks under the water or just a few days and I can't let a bunch of sweat-licking zombie colonists get in the way. However unreasonable you think it is, I have to take matters into my own hands!"

Hurt by the zombie remark, Jenette lashed out. "This is beyond unreasonable. It's outright foolishness!"

"If it is foolishness, then you should not talk."

"What do you mean?" Jenette sputtered.

Karr's eyes narrowed. "That crawler you were in when we met—you stole that, didn't you? You had no permission to be outside this colony and your father was searching to bring you back when he found us, wasn't he?"

"Maybe . . . maybe that's right," Jenette admitted reluctantly. "Maybe if we hadn't met up on FI-716 at the right moment I'd be in some Feral's gizzard right now, but that's exactly why you shouldn't go. It's dangerous out there."

"Duty takes precedence over personal safety," Karr said rigidly. "Pilot's Regs: chapter one, section one, top of the page in bold type."

They stood silent for a while, the small space between them feeling like a million light-years to Jenette. Eventually, Karr broke the standoff.

"Why are you trying to talk me out of this?" he asked. "It's obvious there's no love lost between you and your father. You hate his guts."

"I love my father," Jenette said weakly.

Karr dug around in his loot. "Here, you forgot this." He held up the starlure. "Come with me. I'll make an exception to my working alone rule. You can even bring Arrou. He's useful. We can make a swing by a Feral island after we pick up the C-55s."

"It's not as simple as that."

Karr handed Jenette the starlure. "It is to me."

Jenette stared down at the crystal globe, entranced by what it represented: peace, freedom, life. She wanted to tell Karr that she really wanted to go with him, that he didn't know how much she would love to get back on the heavy lifter and fly fast and far away from the Enclave, forgetting about Scourge and Sacrament, everything. But what she said was, "I can't. There's a very important vote in the Chamber of the Body tomorrow night and a lot of people are counting on me to be there, people that I care about. I know you've been having a hard time here. I know we look like a bunch of mutants to you, licking your sweat and smelling your laundry, but this is my world. I was born here and I have to live here—you do too, by the way. I want it to be better, for humans and Khafra, not the way it is now. That means being here tomorrow night."

Jenette pleaded with Karr. "Give me twenty-four hours, just twenty-four hours. It's really important that you play the heroic figurehead for just one more day. After tomorrow night, things will be different. You'll be able to mount a proper expedition with full Enclave support, take any equipment you want—not just stolen junk—and you'll be able to pick any personnel you want to go along."

"I don't want any personnel to go along," Karr objected.

"Not even Dr. Bigelow?" Jenette challenged. "The man you want to build your big bomb? He couldn't possibly be of any use recovering your warheads, could he? Hmmm? Or hadn't you thought of that?"

"Yes, but I assumed he is too valuable to your colony to be permitted to go on a dangerous mission."

"Normally," Jenette allowed, "but not after tomorrow night. After tomorrow night, I'll be able to put together a party of people with the skills and expertise that can really save *Long Reach*— because that's what it's going to take, not a wild gamble like this. Right?"

Karr didn't say anything and Jenette couldn't read his shadowed expression.

"Right?"

"I guess," Karr finally said.

Jenette smiled in the dark. "Thank you, I'll . . . make it up—"

Karr held up his hands, all business. "Twenty-four hours. Not a second longer."

Jenette's heart sank at his cold tone, but there was little else she could do. She looked around the lifter and then at a thicket of dumbbell-shaped bushes. "Better hide this stuff over there." Karr nodded. Jenette continued. "Byussart and his friends will help. I can't be here. I'm under strict orders to avoid any contact with you." If her father found out, Jenette would be slapped under immediate house arrest, and therefore cut off from her underground communication network. And she couldn't let that happen, or the vote in the Chamber the next night would be a horrible disaster.

XXIII

4610 A.D.

New Ascension colony on Elysium island.

Eighteen months after seeding.

8:31 P.M.

Olin Tesla stands in the shower with his clothes on.
He holds his wife Helena in his arms, helping her to
stand, letting the water pour down on the two of them,
hoping that the enveloping warmth will somehow
reinvigorate her, and willing her with every fiber of his
being to hang on just a little longer. She was always a
slim woman, but where before she felt firm and alive in
his arms, now she is gaunt. How she has lasted this
long, Olin does not know.

She has refused the Sacrament.

He can feel her slipping away, heartbeat by
heartbeat. He clutches her tighter.

"I should never have let you talk to those Ferals,"
he chokes, trying to be strong for her and not break
down. "I should have made you take Sacrament."

Ever so faintly, Helena smiles. He has never been
able to make her do anything she did not want to do.

"I love you, Olin."

"I love you, too, Helena."

She leans her head against his chest. He kisses her
forehead. "No one is going to refuse Sacrament, ever
again," he weeps. "Never again."

"You must always do what you think is right," she
says, without anger or sarcasm, only the honesty and
conviction Olin has always respected her for.

And then she is slack weight.

*Olin's legs go weak. He slumps down the tiled wall
into a corner, still holding her, the water pouring down
as he weeps.*
   In another room, baby Jenette cries.

Arrou huddled on the roof of the great hall, peeking through a skylight down info the forbidden Chamber of the Body and carefully
keeping his glowbuds as dark as he could in the starless night.
Wind blew, roaring through Enclave trees as the vote proceeded
around the ring of desks below. Arrou could not hear through the
transparent ceramite, even with his acute Khafra senses. He
wished Patton had come onto the roof with him; Patton had very
good hearing and could probably listen to the humans even
through the skylight. But Patton would not break the rules and go
onto the roof without direct orders from Halifax. So Arrou puzzled
it out on his own. Gradually, he figured out how the humans were
voting from other signs they gave. *Ayes* were strong faced, upright,
united like forfaraws. *Nays* were defiant, like cornered pleens,
shifting in their seats. Arrou counted, ignoring the Subconsul
vote, which did not matter except in case of a tie.

So much work he and Jenette had done! Eating little and sleeping less, Arrou had passed the secret messages until his glowbuds
ached. But would the humans listen to the message their domestics
relayed? Hearing was the humans' most important means of communication, but they were not good listeners. So far, the vote was
eighteen ayes and four nays. Not good.

They needed fourteen nays.

Arrou scratched. A *good-boy* collar was locked around his neck.
Good-boy in the sense that if he wasn't one, Arrou would feel the
prod built into the fiberplast ring. Tesla had put it on him because
there was a transponder inside. It was an effective leash. For
Jenette, not Arrou. If Arrou's transponder left the Enclave, Tesla
knew Jenette had escaped again (and Arrou would get a sudden, en-
during jolt of blindness).

The vote went from the most senior Consul, Tesla, down
through the ranks. Nineteen ayes, seven nays. Better. It did not
sound better, but for important votes the humans had a funny way

of counting. Tesla needed two out of every three Consuls to win. That meant that if fourteen out of the forty voted nay, he lost, and Jenette's friends won. And the newer Consuls coming up were on Jenette's side.

Nay, nay, nay, nay.

Very good!

But then: *aye, aye, aye—nay—aye, aye, aye, aye!*

"Urrkurrkurrk!" Arrou exclaimed, slapping paws over his head to blot out instinctual flashes of consternation and almost sliding down the slope off the roof. His claws scraped on metal. After regaining his grip, he held still, hoping no one had seen or heard.

The proceeding was heating up. Few heard, much less cared about a faint scraping on the roof when the vote was so close. Twelve nays. Twenty-six ayes. One vote was left, then Jenette's. The fate of the Enclave hung on those two votes. Bigelow feigned indifference, but compulsively spun the rings on his fingers. Burke Hedren was firm, nodding with all his might, as if he could force the outcome by sheer force of wanting. Yll sat perfectly still; having already voted against the Prime Consul he felt distinctly panicky.

Webs, the Subconsul of the Tally, called the next vote. "Consul Alphonse Jeej."

Jenette turned to the man next to her. Jeej was slightly older, but still on hormone inhibitors. Long limbs and limp hair attached to a pear-shaped body.

"Abstain," Jeej said immediately.

The Chamber grumbled with disapproval. It was not a strictly acceptable vote. Webs looked around nervously, but since there was no protest, she called the next name.

"Consul Jenette Tesla."

All eyes turned to Jenette.

Tesla did not *expect* her to vote with him, but he hoped. Father and daughter did not see eye to eye, he knew, but Jenette was intelligent. Being a Tesla, she was headstrong (Tesla felt a surge of pride at that). Surely she had learned from the folly of her recent flight. Surely she saw that rash action had lead to nothing—except failure and the need to be rescued. Perhaps she would finally stop fighting him and they would work together. Tesla's stomach burbled nervously. *Jenette looked so much like her mother, another woman he had never been able to control.* After returning to the Enclave, Tesla had been careful not to lord Jenette's failure over her. He had not confined her to quarters; in fact, he had not punished her at all except to put the tracking collar on Arrou and warn her away from the Pilot. In his mind, Tesla had made every effort to treat her with respect, like an adult, as she demanded. Maybe she would see that and meet him halfway.

Jenette rose and voted, "Nay."

Tesla glowered. The count was now twenty-six in favor and thirteen opposed. No clear victory for either side. But the battle was not over yet; Tesla was not the only one disappointed with the vote and he expected an objection.

"Protest Consul Jeej's abstention!" Dr. Bigelow suddenly said.
Perfect.

Tesla fixed the full might of his gaze on Jeej. He had a lot of experience influencing the weak, young Consul; Tesla had nominated Jeej to a seat in the Chamber because of that very fact. "Agreed. The motion before the Body is too important to allow abstention."

Webs backtracked on her list. "Consul Alphonse Jeej."

Jenette also focused on Jeej, who was staring resolutely at the surface of his desk. She knew little about the Consul just above her in seniority, except that he usually voted with Tesla's majorities, and that he rarely replied to her clandestine messages. But, to keep the pressure up, she had sent Arrou to meet with Jeej's domestic several times.

Jeej's mouth twitched. "Nnnnn," he hummed, indecisive as ever. "Hmmnnnn."

Jenette wanted to reach over and throttle a vote out of Jeej. If she was going to lose, she wanted it over with.

Jeej's shoulders bunched up from the strain. "Nnnnn-nay!" he blurted, to Jenette's intense surprise and relief.

"Yes!" she cheered, giving Jeej an unanticipated hug.

Olin Tesla watched in utter dismay.

Webs double checked the count. "By my tally, the vote on the motion to mobilize Reserves under Prime Consul Olin Tesla's authority is twenty-six in favor, fourteen opposed. Those in favor have not achieved the twenty-seven votes required for a two-thirds majority." Webs voice cracked as she proclaimed, "The motion is denied."

The Chamber of the Body Pure erupted into chaos.

Prime Consul Olin Tesla had never lost an important vote in the history of the Chamber of the Body. His supporters gaped, speechless, or protested loudly. Tesla's opposition was ecstatic. There were back slaps and congratulations all around.

Only Jenette noticed the faint *harooing* and joyous sparkling of light from the skylight above, or heard the yelp and skittering of claws on steel as Arrou lost his grip and tumbled off the roof of the great hall.

Tesla felt the defeat most keenly—like a knife stabbed into his back. For not only had his daughter voted against him, but she had obviously engineered the opposition to his motion. Apart from her initial outburst, she did a good job of hiding it, but the smiles and winks aimed in her direction gave her away. Tesla had failed to appreciate how much influence she held over the Chamber. And, in doing so, he had failed the Enclave. *He should have made the Consuls understand what had to be done, no matter what. That was his sacred trust, the reason destiny had kept him alive so long, to guide the Fallen to the Body Pure. Tesla did not care about himself, but now what would happen to the Dream?*

Bigelow rose from his seat and addressed the disorganized Chamber. "The Body has spoken, and I wish to propose another motion for immediate consideration." A modicum of order returned as the scientist spoke. "You are all aware of the recent arrival of a Pilot among us, but something else has also arrived on our planet, something that is, in many ways, even more wondrous than a Pilot, but which has not been thought much about. What am I talking about? A fugueship!" Bigelow paused a moment. Expressions of sudden understanding swept around the room. "Yes, a fugueship—an unlimited source of *fugue*—and all we have to do to reap its bounty is recover it."

"It's under a mountain of flame," Bragg grumbled.

"Yes it is," Bigelow conceded, "but Pilot Karr has a plan to deal with that, a prodigious plan which if successful—as I deem it will surely be—may change the very course of human history on this planet. Imagine what unrestricted access to a *fugue* supply would mean for this colony."

Jenette relished the turn of events. Bigelow's proposal was her proposal, from the secret communication that Arrou and all the other domestics worked so hard to disseminate. The words were paraphrased, but Jenette recognized them, and there was satisfaction in knowing she had swayed the Chamber. Hers was the inspiration, risk, and initiative. Bigelow winked at her. Burke beamed from his weathered face. They knew.

"What are the specifics of Pilot Karr's plan?" Colonel Halifax asked, guardedly.

Bigelow explained, in his flowery manner of speaking, and with just the proper amount of detail to keep the scientists happy but not lose the rest of the Consuls, Karr's plan to extinguish the fugueship fire with an explosion. "A tremendous, most stylish explosion."

Tesla sat through it all, as if in a fog, trying to figure out where he had failed.

Jenette knew.

Tesla's parading of Karr around the Enclave, intended to strengthen Tesla's position as controller of access to the Pilot, had backfired. Instead, seeing so much of the Pilot had given the Enclave a false sense of security. Given any excuse, of course they would vote Tesla down. He proposed expansion and war. That was hard. Sitting back and feeling safe was easy. Denial of harsh truths was easy. Jenette had learned that the night of Trum's funeral, when all the support she anticipated had evaporated. She had learned from that experience and modified her tactics accordingly. Strong supporters received different clandestine messages than half-hearted ones. She played to strengths or fears, whatever worked the best. That was why swing votes like Jeej had gone in her favor; Jenette was not elated at the underlying reason, but she was also not going to roll over and let her father win.

Bigelow was wrapping up. "Therefore, I propose a motion to provide our Pilot with whatever manpower he requires, drawn from a pool of *volunteers*," he emphasized for the weak-hearted, "as well as any material support he deems necessary to carry out his plan with all haste and utmost priority." Bigelow was in his glory, sensing the general approval. He ended with a flourish of his wrists.

Bragg, who had been stewing for some time, could not contain himself any longer. "This is unbelievable! We have the Body Pure in our hands. We shouldn't let him out of our sight. We don't need the fugueship. We keep the Pilot here and he will be our source of *fugue*. Dr. Yll, you know better than anybody, am I on the wrong track?"

"No," Yll said cautiously. "The Pilot is an excellent source of *fugue*, albeit in limited quantity."

"Limited, but available, here, and now," said Bragg, mutterings of support from a few Consuls encouraging him. "He is our bird in the hand. I think that Dr. Yll's estimates of how much *fugue* can be safely drawn from a Pilot's body are too low. I think they might be doubled, or tripled. Who knows what we can do? Maybe Dr. Yll can come up with a way to pump our blood through the Pilot's body, allowing it to absorb *fugue*, without significant injury to the Pilot himself!"

Hairs prickled on the back of Jenette's neck as many of Tesla's die-hard supporters began to chime in. "Yes, yes, hear him, hear him," or worse, "how much tissue can a human body supply on a monthly basis?"

"Stop!" Tesla boomed, rising to his feet. "I will not stand for this kind of talk!"

Bragg faltered, puzzled. "My apologies, Prime Consul, I only wanted to point out that the Pilot is the answer to all our problems, the guarantee of our survival."

"Our survival as what?" Tesla raged. "Savages? We do not prey upon the Body Pure to attain the Body Pure! Sacrilege!"

Dead silence.

Tesla bowed his head and stacked his fists. Shamed, the others in the Chamber copied his example.

"The Pilot will go," Tesla said quietly. "This is not my choice of a plan, but it is a righteous plan. I hereby sanction an expedition to Coffin Island by edict." The Prime Consul's supporters shifted unhappily. "If you can marshal the spine to vote me down, go ahead, but you might as well elect a new Prime Consul while you are at it, because I will resign!"

Tesla turned from his desk, looking suddenly old and weak, and left the Chamber through a small, back exit.

Jenette was relieved at his intervention, but not very sympathetic. Her father wondered why the Consuls were so quick to consider using Karr for their own survival, when it was he, Olin Tesla, who had invented Sacrament. He was the one who had accustomed them to living off the suffering of another sentient species. How big a jump was it to then substitute a sentient human in place of a sentient alien?

The colonists were stunned by Tesla's departure, especially Bragg. Olin Tesla was their lifeline. They had never known another Prime Consul, and the thought of losing his leadership was far more frightening than the possible loss of the Pilot. No one so much as proposed a vote to challenge Tesla's edict.

Jenette lived in a one room cube in the domicile for unmarried colonists, one of many heaped up like children's blocks among sprawling meat-fruit vineyards. Flat surfaces inside the domicile were piled high with books and Khafra artifacts, every bit of information Jenette could find from before the Feral Wars. The walls were papered with holos of far-off worlds: squat temples in the mountains of Valhalla, triple sunset on Solara, a happy robot bounding through fields of whispering poppies on Chazz. Peaceful places. One day Jenette would add another holo to that gallery: a picture from New Ascension.

Bleep, went the entry chime.

Jenette slid the door open for Dr. Deena Marsh, a handsome young woman with olive skin, curly dark hair pulled back from a gaunt face, and a labjumper sealed to the neck. Marsh was expected. She handed Jenette a stimpaper printout. Jenette scanned the printout's complex graphs and stacks of numbers.

"The sample was positive for *fugue,*" said Marsh. "Hope there's more where it came from."

"There isn't."

"Too bad."

"Yes. Who knows about this test?"

"Me and my shadow," said Marsh. "And I wasn't here. I never saw that report." With a wink, she left.

Jenette closed the door and sat on the edge of an unmade bed. Her head throbbed from the chaos she had unleashed. Arrou lay beside her, dozens of tiny scrapes on his armor from when he fell off the Chamber roof and landed in a bristle bush. His face was full of concern.

"Jenette okay?"

She tossed the printout on the bed. "I'm fine."

"Want back scratch?"

"No, thank you." She rubbed dirt from a scrape on Arrou's back. "What am I going to do with you?" she chided. She had warned him the Chamber roof was dangerous.

"What Arrou do with *you?*" he chided right back.

Knock, knock, knock, went the door.

Jenette got up. What had Marsh forgotten?

Arrou's head dipped low and he turned a somber blue. Jenette though that strange behavior; Arrou liked Marsh. She slid the panel aside.

Her father stood on the balcony. "Jenette," he said, entering.

Jenette stood aside, baffled. Her father never came to visit her. She was always summoned to him.

"Arrou, out," Tesla ordered.

Arrou slunk out, insult patterns washing over his back. Jenette pulled the door shut and cleared a pile of data cubes and clothes from her only chair. These she discreetly dropped on top of Marsh's printout.

Tesla paced the tiny room, looking less the tyrant, but still giving the disorder a wintry once over. He stopped abruptly and, like Marsh, handed Jenette a folded stimpaper.

It was Karr's official request for equipment and personnel—and right at the top of the list was her name. Karr wanted Jenette to head up the New Ascension side of the mission to Coffin Island.

"You're not going," said Tesla.

"But—"

"Show me your neck."

Jenette's mouth became a thin, hard line and she lowered her chin.

"Your glands are tender and swollen," Tesla accused. "Am I wrong?"

Jenette's hand went reflexively to the juncture of her jaw and neck. It did feel swollen, but she knew from close scrutiny in a mirror that her neck still looked normal. *At least there was no movement under the skin yet.* Her hands went clammy at the thought.

She forced her arms down to her sides.

Now Tesla sat on the arm of the chair, arms folded. "No Sacrament. No mission."

"I won't."

Tesla frowned. "I'm going to tell you a secret, Jenette. *Against* isn't good enough. You have to be *for* something in order to succeed. Against is the coward's way. Against is bitterness and failure and a misspent life. That's why I voted for your motion to assist Pilot Karr's mission."

"Dr. Bigelow's motion," Jenette corrected.

"Your motion," Tesla asserted. "Let's get to the point. It took guts to vote me down. And it took guts to take off in the crawler," stern fatherly disapproval met her eye. "But it was stupid."

"Maybe," Jenette begrudged.

The half-concession mollified Tesla a little. His conversation spun onto a different track. "You know what this Enclave needs, Jenette? It needs a new generation that stands by its convictions—not like the simpering toadies I see in the Chamber every day. My convictions took me to the top. Yours will, too."

"I don't want to get to the top."

"So you say. There won't be any choice when the time comes, believe me." Tesla fell quiet a minute, as if reliving distant memory, but soon enough he was back to business. "I've arranged a different domestic for your Sacrament. Not as good as Arrou, but it will keep you alive. You can head up the mission to Coffin Island. We'll take the tracking collar off Arrou. You can even take him and dump him on another Feral island to die of starvation, whatever you like."

Jenette was surprised by her father's concession, but held steadfast. "If it's wrong to kill Arrou, it's wrong to kill any domestic."

"Nothing comes without a price, Jenette. Nobody will fight your crusade if you're dead. Please decide. I'm feeling very tired."

"Decide tonight?"

"Now."

It felt unreal. Her father was talking to her like an equal. She hesitated. "There is another option." Digging into a bedside drawer, Jenette retrieved a medipak filled with the substance that she had told Marsh didn't exist. Unzipping the seal, she offered it to her father.

Tesla took a sniff: jasmine, burned jasmine.

It was the shriveled strips of Karr's burned flesh.

"The Body Pure," Jenette said.

Tesla grimaced. "Haven't you been paying attention? Weren't you in the Chamber tonight?"

"The Body Pure doesn't mean the same thing to us, Father," Jenette confessed. "I subscribe to the principals, but it's not a religion to me."

"More sacrilege," Tesla said numbly. "Where did I go wrong?"

"I didn't choose to come to this planet; I was born here. I'm just doing the best I can."

Jenette pulled out a strip of oily skin. Before her father could react, she popped the stringy strip into her mouth and chewed. She swallowed, clapping a hand over her mouth to keep it down.

"You see, Father," she gagged, "you won after all."

Tesla rose, looking older than ever, and let himself out the door. "Nobody won. I lost a vote and you lost your soul. May the Body forgive you." To Arrou he said, "Don't call a doctor."

"Not call doctor? About what?" the alien asked from the balcony.

"You'll see," the old man said. "She will sleep now and you won't be able to wake her up, but she will be okay."

Arrou padded into the cubical. Tesla shut the door. When she was sure he was gone, Jenette bent over, jabbed her fingers down her throat and vomited into a waste bucket. Then she curled onto fetal position on her bed and prayed that she had been quick enough, that she would not sink into a *fugue*-coma and that she would live long enough to accomplish what had to be done.

PART FOUR:

COFFIN ISLAND

XXIV

It is always the same when They find her, at her weakest, after the Geldings have slunk away, tails—if nothing else useful—between their legs. The Geldings are soft. As They are soft. The Geldings are smooth-faced. As They are smooth-faced. The Geldings are not-men. And They are not-men. They are made of perfume and secrets. They are made of unsatisfaction and fantasy fermented. They are born of lust.

They are the night women, wearing night masks that Geldings never see in the light of day.

"Come," they coo, all curls and tresses, accidentally touching her as they circle. Predatory feminine essences. Fingers accidentally brushing her flushed skin, teasing, promising. The unsatisfaction is on her—They know—the fermented fantasy strong in her blood.

Follow us, They say.

She sees the press of their nakedness and smells their play. They play for her, They entice her.

"Do you want to know?" They tempt. "We will know you like this . . . and this." Tongues trace paths along breasts and necks. "Do you want to touch? We will touch you like this . . . and this."

And then They touch her, knowing the curve of her skin as they know their own. They lick into her ears, knowing where she will flush, as They flush to similar caresses. They want to caress and grab as They desire to be caressed and grabbed. They want to entwine a leg and press, as They want to be entwined and pressed against.

They know she waits for the Kiss, the man-kiss, as

*They have waited. But They wait no more, these women
of night. They find the kiss on each other, groaning,
begging, like cries under a jungle moon.*

They lust.

"We will kiss you where the boys can't."

*They start to kiss her, like soft poetry. And start to
caress her, like slithery love. She feels the unsatisfaction
brewing, the fermented fantasy bubbling. The promise
of release, forbidden, addictive.*

And she flees.

*As always. With her unsatisfaction and fermented
fantasy. Before They've barely started. Hers is not the
way of the night women. Hers is the way of waiting, for
the Kiss. Her longing is the longing for the man in
white, her only strokes the strokes of the pen in this
book . . .*

                                    —*from the black book of J. Tesla*

Tepid drizzle fell over the heavy lifter, intensifying as they flew
through curtains of low, ragged cloud, and then lessening, but
never letting up. Sky and sea blurred together, blue-gray above,
steel gray below. Water ran off orange bubble tents and pooled
around bundles of supplies and stacks of equipment. The back of
the lifter resembled a nomadic campground. A few humans in rain
gear stood on deck. Most took cover inside the tents, while two domestics huddled together off to one side, rain trickling down faces
and dripping off snouts. The aliens were depressed by the lack of
sunlight and resigned to wait it out, but curious ballroom lights,
glowing on the inside of Jenette's tent had caught the attention of
Crash, Dr. Marsh's domestic.

Crash skewed his head sideways, trying to make sense of the
phenomena. The tent sparkled. Crash chattered his teeth. The tent
pulsed. Crash blinked billiard ball eyes. Finally, unable to restrain
himself, Crash lit up his glowbuds. *Flash, pop, sparkle, pop.* "Din-
tixss-ymisstash."

Bronte gave Crash the evil eye. "Who Crash talks to?"

"Tent."

"Tent not talk."

"Tent talk. Look." Crash pointed a talon. "Tent say *come in peace.*"

But Bronte refused to look.

"Arrou in tent," she sniffed indignantly. "Playing trick."

"Arrou not in tent," Crash said, enthralled. "Now tent say *peace between Ferals and domestics.*" His glowbuds tittered in response to the strange oracle. "Oooohhhrrrr, that good. Right?"

Bronte rolled her eyes impatiently. "Crash sucker. Crash stupid. Rain stupid, mission stupid, tent stupid." She sulked, edging away from Crash. "Want home. Want Enclave. Want dry."

Crash didn't argue back, because Bronte was older, smarter, and had more beautiful glowbuds then he, but he didn't take his eyes off the talking tent, either.

Jenette put down the wonderful starlure, her retinas afire with afterimages. With it she could say anything. The next time she spoke to Ferals, there would be no bloodbath. There would be meaningful discourse and that would lead to . . . well, her mind was dizzy with possibilities. But she could not practice forever; there was work to be done, here and now. Reluctantly, she placed the sphere in a high impact case and, carrying a kiss upon her fingertip to the gem-studded crystal, sealed the latches tight.

The particular *beep* of the lifter's autopilot attracted her attention. Unzipping the opaque inner flap of her bubble tent door, Jenette watched Karr hop out of the cockpit and walk to the stern of the flying slab. Water beaded off his uniform and slicked tendrils of hair to his forehead. He leaned down to converse with a shadow under some crates. Jenette couldn't hear what was said, but saw Karr's conciliatory body language. Karr's overtures were met with a distinct *snarl*. The encounter ended. Despondent, the Pilot trudged back through the drizzle to the open cockpit.

Jenette slipped into a rain poncho and donned a floppy waterproof hat. Unzipping the transparent outer tent flap, she scrambled out before too much water rained in, resealed the flap, and wound among crated supplies to where Karr had just been.

She turned to a shadow under the crates. It had initially looked a lot like a domestic, but as she splashed closer it abruptly mimicked the texture of wet deck and shadowy crates, and pretty much disappeared.

"Arrou, come out here so I can talk to you," Jenette said.

No answer.

"Arrou, I know you're in there."

"Not want talk," came a grumpy, disembodied voice.

Jenette leaned down. Only Arrou's flashing teeth were visible. "Is there a problem?"

"Karr problem," the alien said, turning sulky—but visible— colors. "Bad man."

"He is not a bad man. He's a good man."

"Took Jenette. Left Arrou behind. Flew away."

Jenette guiltily remembered the image of Arrou in a shooting-star tree, waving frantically for them to come back. She felt like a sinner at confession. "Arrou, Pilot Karr didn't force me to go with him. I went of my own free will." Arrou did not relent. "Will you please come out of there?"

"No." Arrou crawled deeper under the crates, his bullet head nestled on his forepaws.

"Fine, be that way." Grumbling, Jenette hunched down on all fours and followed him. Tepid water seeped into the fabric of her daysuit; it would be a long time before she could get it dry. "Don't be mad at Karr. It wasn't him that left you. It was me."

"Jenette?" Arrou said. "Not believe. Jenette covering up."

"No, I'm not," Jenette protested. "Remember how we circled around you?"

"Remember," the alien agreed.

"Karr wanted to pick you up. He wanted to fly close to your tree—"

"Not Arrou's tree," Arrou sniped. "Nobody's tree."

"*The* tree," Jenette conceded, not wanting to get sidetracked into a Khafra argument about whose tree was whose, or who tended what. "Karr wanted to pick you up, but I wouldn't let him. I told him to leave you behind. So you see, he had nothing to do with it. It was all my fault."

"Jenette left Arrou?" Arrou said, finally beginning to believe.

His bullet head swiveled around, disconcerted green circles glowing around his eyes and mouth. "Why? Arrou do something bad?"

"No, you didn't do anything bad. I was trying to save you."

"Funny kind of save," Arrou accused.

Jenette attempted to explain herself. "It was the only thing I could think of. I was upset because the Ferals wouldn't listen to me, but I knew they wouldn't hurt you and I knew that we would have to go through Sacrament when we got back to the Enclave."

Arrou thought about that for a while, but it didn't make him any happier. "Arrou never leaves Jenette behind. Left behind worse than Sacrament. Besides," he pointed out, "was no Sacrament at Enclave. Jenette still here. Arrou still here."

"I don't want to talk about that."

Arrou regarded Jenette with stern colors. "Jenette ate *bad* food."

"All right, all right," she hissed, feeling a little sickly just thinking about it. "It wasn't the best of decisions, but I didn't fall into coma."

"Hnrrrph."

"And I did it for you."

"Hnrrrph, hnrrrph." Arrou crawled out of his hideaway.

"Where are you going?"

"To apologize," Arrou said, turning his back and padding shame-colored toward the cockpit.

"He's whacked," Skutch said to Bigelow. The physicist's knuckles gripped the edge of a thruster cowl as the heavy lifter skimmed over the ocean. The Guard grinned. "No question about it: full on nutbar."

"Five hundred knots, five hundred knots!" Arrou chanted from beside Karr in the cockpit.

The day was still gray, but the rain had stopped and all nine humans were on deck. Skutch and Bigelow stood on the port side, where, until the recent rapid acceleration, they had been discussing explosives; potential energy and the catastrophic release thereof.

Jenette overheard their words from the bubble tents, where she and Dr. Marsh kept a firm grip on tie-down cords.

Jenette had crewed the expedition with colonists sharing her views. Bigelow and Skutch, of course. And, on the other side of the lifter, were Corporal Toliver and the rest of his squad. Toliver cleaned his pulse-rifle glumly. Grubb and Liberty cheered at the rush of speed. Mok, off punishment detail thanks to Jenette's string pulling, napped like a true grunt, upon damp bails of supplies, indifferent to wind, cold, and speed. Crash stood at the bow, snout extended to the wind, drinking in sea scents, the standoffish Bronte behind him.

"Yes," Bigelow said, looking nervously at Karr, "you have to concede, the man's got panache."

Karr was not hunched over the cockpit controls, as might have been expected, rather it was Arrou who gripped the steering yoke and throttles with his paws. Karr leaned over the alien's shoulder giving a stream of instructions.

Skutch's grin broadened. "I hear you."

"Hurrakurrk!" Arrou growled in concentration.

"Hurraroooooo!" Crash howled in encouragement.

"Keep the nose up," Karr coached. "That's it. Easy on the stick."

"Rrrraaarrrk," Arrou snapped his teeth in the wind. "Five hundred knots!"

"Thirty-five knots," Karr said firmly. Tapping the appropriate mark on the airspeed indicator, the needle having risen several notches too far. "Back it down."

Arrou reluctantly eased up on the throttle, but without any protection from the headwind, thirty-five knots was still enough to blow tears from Karr's eyes. The ocean whizzed by below, endless whitecaps bucking across the waves. For the comfort of exposed crewmembers, Karr normally kept the airspeed down to fifteen or twenty knots. Just then, however, he wanted Arrou to get the feel of how the lifter reacted at different power ranges. Arrou's enthusiasm for speed and intense concentration made him a natural heavy lifter pilot; the alien was going to be good, as opposed to Karr, who was decent but never really liked the unwieldy craft and had to constantly work at it. Karr even let Arrou try a few simple turns. The only drawback was that Arrou squatted on the rein-stalled crash couch and could not reach the pedals with his hind legs, so he was limited to flying with autopilot assist.

"What's the proper startup sequence?" Karr quizzed.

Arrou recited carefully. "Master switch on. Engine run-ups, one, two, three, four. Cowl fields engaged and locked open. Ur-rrrrr. Throttle flux mixture *rich.*" He tentatively tapped the left side of a knob; Karr nodded. "Thruster buffer needle at yellow line."

"Ninety percent," Karr confirmed. "What else?"

"Urrr . . . autopilot engaged?"

"Yes, what else?"

"Urrkurrkurrk . . . not remember," Arrou admitted sheepishly.

"D.O.I. throughput to one hundred percent." Karr tapped the red line on a gage. "Very important."

"Sorry."

"Don't be sorry," said Karr. "That's pretty good considering I only ran you through it once. Just get it right next time."

Arrou rumbled with determination.

"Take her down," Karr instructed.

Arrou pushed the yoke forward and the lifter descended slowly. When they got below ten yards, water sucked up behind them and flared out like a cloud. The lifter bounced.

"Feel that?" Karr asked.

"Pillows," said Arrou, feeling the spongy response of the controls.

"Yes. Pillows of air trapped under the hull. It's called—"

"Surface effect," Arrou interjected. "Like skimmers."

"That's right," Karr said, appreciatively. Arrou continued to surprise him with his knowledge of machines. "Saves a lot of power to fly like this."

Arrou concentrated on his task. Water scrolled by.

Karr could not help but note that there were a lot of Ferals on the ocean surface, singly or paired in small watercraft. He hadn't seen them at first because of their chameleon camouflage, but he got better at spotting them as the day drew on. There were small

clues: odd shadows on the water, blocked highlights on wave
crests. "Are there always this many Ferals around?" he asked.

"No," said Arrou. "Usually Ferals hide from machines."

At first Karr thought they must be the Ferals that Jenette tried
to talk to with such disastrous effects—Tlalok's Ferals—but the
math didn't add up. Feral Island 716 had been a day's flight west
from the Enclave, and the lifter was now a couple of hundred kiloyards south of the human colony. It didn't make sense that the Ferals below might be Tlalok's Ferals. This must be a different
group—a group that was indifferent to the passage of a human flying machine. If they looked up at all, it was not to gape in wonder
or fear, but merely to take an idle look. Arms and legs kept paddling over the waves, the bows of their tiny vessels all pointing in
the exact same direction.

"They're all headed west," Karr noted.

Arrou looked down. "Yes. Weird."

For some reason, Karr felt a chill.

"He's very cute," Dr. Marsh said as Jenette inspected a minder-
board with Marsh's medical manifests and contingencies.

"The Pilot?" Jenette asked lightly.

"Who else?" Marsh replied.

"I hadn't noticed."

There was a territorial flash in Jenette's eyes.

The doctor quickly added, "That is, if one goes that way."

Jenette looked at Marsh sideways. New Ascension males could
not participate in any sort of sexual activity, not even self pleasure,
for fear of changing their testosterone levels and triggering the
onset of full-blown Scourge. For females, after *growing old* (the
primary trigger for full-blown Scourge in both sexes), the release
of the XS hormones during pregnancy was a primary Scourge trigger in females. However, forty-seventh-century birth control being
highly efficient, there was no biological reason for decreased female sexual activity. Except, of course, for the lack of willing male
participation. Most New Ascension women had very private forms
of release. Jenette wrote erotic prose in her little black book. But

some found *alternate* partners for diversion, which was what Marsh was alluding to.

Liberty strolled by, ears dragging. "Don't believe the brombel-crap, Consul." Liberty put a friendly arm around Marsh. "The doc here would jump him at the drop of a hat. Hell, I'd jump anything good and stiff that didn't run away."

Marsh and Liberty guffawed.

Karr, for some reason, stopped moving in the cockpit. Jenette hoped it was not because he had overheard.

Liberty continued to yuck it up. "We all would. Except, of course," she winked at Jenette, "when it ruffles the boss's glow-buds."

Marsh grinned innocently. "What she said, boss."

"I have no idea what you two are talking about," Jenette said, feeling herself turning red.

Jenette returned Marsh's minder-board, walked forward on the bow, and stood close to Karr.

From that vantage, Jenette also noticed the Ferals on the ocean below. Her instinct was to run back to her tent, grab the starlure, and get Karr to stop so that she could try to communicate with them, but she strangled that impulse. Karr's mission—their mission —was of critical, urgent, pre-emptive importance. After much internal wrestling, Jenette had decided to put off her own agenda until after recovering the C-55 warheads. It wasn't even putting off her own agenda, she had told herself; a rescued fugueship would provide an endless source of *fugue*, eliminating the need for Sacrament as well as the primary reason for her father's objections to peace with the Ferals. Jenette was determined that Karr's mission should succeed as quickly as possible, then she would call in his promise to help her make peace.

"Need anything?" she asked.

"Hunh?" Karr started up from staring at the ocean. "Oh, uh, I need all those Ferals to go away."

Jenette smiled wanly. "Sorry."

A blue-purple cloud sat pregnant in their path. Karr returned his attention to Arrou. "Take us around that squall," he instructed, "then I'll take over."

Arrou made a smooth, wide turn, growling, "Haaaarrraaaa-rrrk!" with infectious exhilaration. Crash, and even Bronte, howled with him.

The sullen day drew on hour after hour. The lifter passed over many more Ferals paddling west. Karr experimented, changing course to try and find the bounds of the armada, but the net of aliens stretched kiloyards in every direction. Their numbers were unsettling. After an hour of zigzagging, Karr admitted defeat and returned to the original heading of due south.

Evening neared, as evidenced by a darkening from gaunt gray to oppressive gray. Not much later, the expedition members ate. Jenette suggested Karr consume the self-heating gutbombs in the cockpit.

"We need to cover as much ground as possible."

"Agreed." Karr kept a watchful eye on the autopilot as he pulled the pins on gumball-sized spheroids, popped them into his mouth, swallowed, and waited. Three seconds later, Karr felt a warm swelling, like a gas bubble, and tasted the aroma of food rushing back up his gullet. "Corporal Toliver," he called back to where the others were sitting on cases and canisters near the bubble tents. "How's our course?"

Toliver put down his mess kit and cross-referenced a mapreader. "Steady on one-eighty magnetic, sir."

"Thanks."

Toliver resumed popping gutbombs.

"This blows," Mok complained, holding a spheroid disgustedly between thumb and forefinger.

Bigelow concurred. "They do lack a certain *je ne sais quoi.*"

"Yeah and they taste like shit, too." Mok rifled through his segmented tray of spheroids. "Hey, which one of you freaks snarked all the desserts?"

Grubb, always hungry, grinned.

"You fuck!" Mok said angrily.

Grubb made kissy-faces.

"Don't make me kick your ass," Mok said angrily.

"Don't make me like it," Grubb taunted.

"You wankers work it out later," Toliver barked. "Some of us want to eat in peace."

"I'm not a wanker! I want to live! *He's* the wanker."

"I want to live too! It's not my fault the pills don't work on me!"

"Shut up, both of you!"

Karr didn't mind the gutbombs. He was used to fugueship rations. A Pilot's first fuguetime meal might be fresh, but the second meal of a tour was already six realtime months old and the third a full year stale. A few fuguetime days—realtime years—later and only the blandest meals remained. Karr had vivid memories of dipping reconstituted crackers into bland pap. The gutbombs weren't that bad, really. Besides, they kept him warm and flying well into the twelfth hour after setting out from the Enclave.

Off to the southwest, sunset pressed a reddish smear against the brooding horizon. Karr tried not to look at it, staring instead at the ocean, but the ocean was alive with color, too—and not from the sunset. Waves of light were radiating from the net of Ferals below, each of them pulsing communication patterns like a giant telegraph web. The patterns carried out to a point behind the sunset.

"What are they saying?" Karr asked.

Jenette puzzled. "It's hard to read. Arrou?"

Arrou's head was already hanging over the side, enraptured by the Feral light patterns.

Jenette rapped his back. "Hello?"

"Words funny," Arrou rumbled. "Not normal Feral speak. Fussy."

"Fussy?" Karr asked.

Jenette shrugged. "It seems to be an older, more elaborate dialect of the Khafra tongue used around the Enclave. I can only make out the slower word-strings."

That lined up with Karr's assumption that the Ferals near the Enclave could not possibly have gotten this far south ahead of the lifter, but it didn't answer the question of who they were, or where they were going. Karr observed the single pattern of light pulses coursing off into the sunset, again and again. "So what are they saying?"

Arrou lifted his head. "Asking question."

Jenette set her mind to translating the repetitive pattern. *"Question/answer: why—"*

"When," Arrou corrected.

"When," Jenette repeated, *"does the Burning Heart blossom/birth/escape? Is that right?"*

"Maybe. Funny, funny words."

"When does the Burning Heart blossom/birth/escape?" Karr repeated, baffled.

Jenette shrugged. "Don't ask me."

"Not know Burning Heart could blossom/birth/escape," Arrou admitted.

The ocean sparkled, Ferals twinkling like so many swimming stars. The patterns were hypnotizing. Karr felt a headache building, tension spreading over his head. Fortunately, a blanket of fog formed over the ocean. Karr gladly pulled up on the throttle. The engines torqued up, climbing one hundred yards and muffling the Ferals under the fog.

Karr set the autopilot as darkness enfolded them. The lifter cruised between cotton-candy hills below and marbled heavens above. Time passed. Guards and scientists retired from the unaccustomed chill in the high air. Arrou curled up on deck. Karr turned up the thermostat on his uniform, which warmed his limbs, but also made him sleepy. He tensed the muscles in his neck to shake off a fit of yawns. Jenette, who was never far away, disappeared into the tents and returned with a steaming mug of reddish-yellow liquid.

"Ghll?" she offered, standing quite close.

Pilots might prefer solitude to crowds, but Karr was still a mortal man and could not help but notice Jenette's proximity. She smelled good. Part of Karr was inclined to enjoy the interaction. Another part, however, that part which was mainly preoccupied with worry and vexation, protested. *She's not twenty-three. No way. Not a day over fifteen. And fifteen will get you twenty—on a prison planet.* But the pleasant sensation of Jenette's proximity did not relent easily . . . after all; except for the very pregnant Panya Hedren, every other New Ascension woman looked twelve. Jenette's every

tiny, apparently fifteen-year-old curve was magnified by comparison. When she brushed against Karr, while handing him the mug, it
felt nice.

*She's just a little girl! Remember the ship. Pilots don't need
entanglements!*

Unsettled, Karr complained at the sour-smelling drink. "This is
not Ghll."

"Of course it's not Ghll," Jenette chided. "Where do you think
we'd get real Ghll? Nothing from off-planet grows here. This is
New Ascension substitute."

"It sure doesn't taste like Ghll."

"Don't be difficult. And don't swallow the floaty bits."

The floaty bits resembled tiny insect legs, either that or large in-
testinal cilia. Karr didn't ask which was the more accurate description. The bitter drink was entirely unpleasant in aroma, unlike
true Solaran Ghll, but it did keep him awake longer.

Misty hours elapsed.

Faint starlight chilled the fog. The sealed bubble tents seemed
far away. Even the hum of thruster engines was lost in the rush of
breeze across the lifter. Jenette hung around, so Karr continued to
be conflicted by his reaction to her presence, but at least she did
not chatter, so he didn't feel pressured to manufacture small talk.

Just about the time Karr decided to search for a spot to set down
for the night, the clouds cleared to Karr's right. There on the horizon, almost blotted out by patches of fog and distance, was a faint
red glow. Karr wondered what it was for a few seconds before another, closer, phenomena drew his attention.

Silent lightning erupted in the fog below.

It reminded Karr of electrical storms as seen from orbit, the
kind that blot out small continents. Countless pinpoints of light
diffused into sheets of iridescence, linking and brightly ringing
around dark, lurking masses which Karr assumed were ring-islands.
It resembled an aurora, only below and not above, and no solar
wind or magnetic field was behind the luminescence.

It was Ferals.

The sheer number daunted Karr. The aliens were far thicker
than those seen before the fog rolled in, more tightly packed at the

edges of islands, more dispersed over the ocean. There wasn't a clear patch of water as far as the eye cold see. If he had been foolish enough to set down, the lifter would have been swarmed.

The Feral radiance continued to build. There seemed to Karr a disturbing tinge to the colors that night. Karr felt as though a tendril of the moldy green light would reach out and swat the lifter out of the sky.

Arrou uncurled, attracted by the display, and looked below.

"Islands moving," he announced as the light battled on, consuming itself. "Fog flows around."

"He's right," Karr whispered. The backlit mist billowed up and over dark ring shapes, like slow motion water over rapids, as the islands left eddies of lazy turbulence in their wakes. "They're still moving west." Karr wondered where all those Ferals were going. The Enclave was north, behind the lifter. Coffin Island lay south, dead ahead.

Karr looked west.

There, far off in the direction the Ferals were heading, shining from beyond the curve of New Ascension's horizon, was the faint red glow he had noticed moments before—the same glow which Karr now identified as being caused by the distant, but thousands of yards high, pillar of flame blazing over his beloved *Long Reach*.

XXV

The next day.

Three military skimmers closed on Feral Island 538. They maintained tight formation. Their fuselages were mottled with silver and gray camouflage to match the mirrored surface of the ocean. Their open cabins bristled with pulse-rifles and Guardsmen. And each skimmer mounted a heavy weapon. The two flanking vehicles bore triple-barrel pulse cannons. The vehicle on point was armed with a pressure-focused flamethrower. Patton rode in that skimmer. Ahead of him, in the bow, were two imposing human figures.

"That's it, sir," said Colonel Halifax, his battered skin twisting into a grimace, "the last reported position of Deep Recon 8, before the transponder went dead." Halifax wore dappled green-and-black battle dress, like all the Guards.

Olin Tesla, a full head taller than his barrel-chested companion, shaded his eyes as the skimmers spiraled in. Tesla made an effort to stand proud as usual, but Patton thought Tesla looked a little slump-shouldered. Patton had noticed that ever since the night of *the vote.*

"Miserable excuse for a ring-island," Tesla observed.

Patton didn't like to agree with the Prime Consul, but he did. FI-538 was on the very edge of the Enclave's zone of control. It was small, less than a kiloyard across, its mop-top of green ragged and overgrown. Fissures spider-webbed a shoreline starved of fresh water. Large chunks of island clung together only by strings of vine and root, looking like they would break free and float away at any instant.

"No self-respecting Feral would be caught dead here," Tesla said pointedly.

Halifax flinched. Patton flinched. Tesla was asking why a recon team had been lost on an island with no Ferals, which was a good question, but it was Tesla's fault that the recon team was out there in the first place. Tesla needed more and more Feral kits for Sacrament. That meant missions farther and farther from the Enclave. And more and more risk. Now that potential for risk had turned into real trouble.

"I take full responsibility," Halifax said stiffly, "for whatever happened."

"Don't fall on your sword, Taureg," Tesla said. "Just explain."

Halifax obliged. "Orders were issued allowing squads to use their own initiative. Feral stocks are too depleted for missions targeted at specific islands. Without the ability to hunt as they see fit, we risk men and vehicles and come up empty-handed. Recon 8 must have seen Ferals."

Tesla grunted. "Did you also give permission for the skimmer teams to split up?"

Halifax shook his head. "No sir. Standard orders: teams of three. They must've taken a chance."

Patton had been present when Halifax ordered three teams out on the previous evening. Recon 8 promptly disappeared. No transponder signal. No response to com signals. No SOS. Recons 7 and 9 had returned, but 8 was now half a day overdue, six valuable men and an irreplaceable skimmer missing. Of course Halifax was going to investigate personally. Halifax always worried about his fellow humans, especially if they were under his command. Patton had seen Halifax risk his life many times to save them. Patton was proud of that. He hoped Halifax would save the humans in Recon 8. And he wished Tesla had not come. Halifax did not need to be worrying about the Prime Consul at a time like this.

"See anything?" Halifax quietly asked Patton.

"See nothing."

Patton had good senses, even compared with other Khafra. Halifax often said Patton could see the wart on a gnat's butt a kiloyard away, and hear it fart at ten, but those heightened senses detected nothing on the shore of FI-538, no signs of life, human, Feral, or otherwise.

The skimmers circled the island at Halifax's signal, engines winding down to a low thrum. An inlet appeared along the ragged coastline. It widened as they neared, revealing itself to be a fissure right through one arc of the ring-island. The jagged passage showed foreboding glimpses of a small lagoon at the island's heart.

More than ever Patton agreed that no Ferals inhabited FI-538. The ring was breached. It would break up during the next big storm. Why had the recon team come here? It made no sense. Patton sniffed the air.

"Smell anything?" Halifax asked.

"Trouble," Patton replied. There was a funny smell. Every flashbud on his body prickled.

Patton was not afraid. Halifax had trained him to know what to expect from trouble and how to react to it. Patton always did what Halifax ordered and never panicked. That was why he was the only domestic allowed on Guard missions. Halifax was proud of that and Patton tried to keep Halifax proud. In a way, trouble was Patton's natural element, but that did not mean Patton always liked what trouble brought.

The skimmers neared the jagged inlet.

"Over there!" a Guard behind Patton cried, pointing. "Smoke!"

An oily tendril smeared skyward from behind shooting-star palms. It was a sure sign of human activity. Ferals used organic chemical reactions for heat and their glowbuds for light. They did not need fire.

The smoke explained the funny smell.

"Look like come from center of island," Patton decided.

Halifax nodded and turned to the skimmer's driver, who was seated at the controls just behind Patton. "Take us in." Then, switching his comset to the open battle channel, Halifax called orders to the skimmers and squads. "All teams prep. Danger close."

The water clattered with full-auto pulse-rifles loading and locking. Quiver-shiv bayonets snapped into place. Halifax drew the arming pin on a nasty looking mauler pistol. Tesla armed his personal, single-shot pulse-rifle. Patton flexed his claws.

The skimmers formed a single line, the command skimmer leading the way into the inlet. There was no room to turn around in the constricted waterway, no retreat. Drivers used one hand to steer and kept the other on the throttles, ready to accelerate rapidly if they had to.

"Don't shoot without visual recognition," Halifax warned the squads. "There may be friendlies down, probably in need of assistance."

The humans swept their weapons across overhanging branches and the attached heavy foliage. The greenery loomed like the walls of a canyon. Lianas, squirming from constant, accelerated growth while in contact with the water, trailed across the surface like questing fingers; one groped onto the command skimmer; Halifax idly scrubbed it free with a bootheel. The inlet narrowed as the skimmers penetrated deeper into the island, but just as the waterway threatened to choke off completely, the jungle fell away and the skimmers glided out into a circle of open water, barely one hundred yards across and surrounded by a thin strip of sinkhole muskeg.

All heads locked onto the source of the oily smoke.

A smoldering hulk lay beached on the far shore. As the skimmers slid across the glassy water, Patton recognized the wreck of a military skimmer, its fuselage charred, slashed open in a hundred places. Frayed layers of composite material showed where one stubby wing had been torn completely off. The capture cage, where Feral kits were held for transport back to the Enclave, lay to one side, a mangled heap.

Patton saw no sign of the recon team and told Halifax so.

The colonel motioned with his pistol, calling on comset. "Second Team, *in.* Everyone else, cover them." As the orders rattled down the chain of command, Halifax spoke in a low voice to Patton. "You go too."

"Go too. Urrr."

"And take a headset."

"Urrr."

Patton pulled on a comset specially rigged for his earpits and muzzle. He hopped onto the command skimmer's right wing and made an easy leap over a ten-foot gap and landed on Second Team's skimmer, which then turned and jetted in to the shore, its prow nosing onto spongy sinkhole muskeg while the other skimmers took up protective positions.

Patton jumped out along with six Guards in skirmish armor. The humans assumed attack formation with Patton on point as they advanced on the hulk. *This was definitely the time to be cautious.* Patton remembered the battle at the ancient Terran city of Troy. Ferals could be hiding in the wrecked skimmer. Patton edged closer, trying to sniff the air, but stinging smoke overpowered the possible odor of Ferals and made his eyes water. When no ambush materialized, Patton closed to examine the wreckage. He checked the mangled capture cage first. It contained no live Feral kits and, mercifully, no dead ones either.

The squad followed Patton.

Jott, Second Team's corporal, rubbed his stinging eyes. "No bad-guy activity, Colonel," he reported by comset. "Lots of burned stuff, but no friendlies."

Hagan, a round-featured private, poked a bayonet through one of many slashes in the skimmer fuselage. "Skimmer's fucked up good."

"Teeth marks in hull," Patton clarified for Halifax. Moving around to the side of the wreck hidden from the shore, his own teeth clattered.

"What is it?" Halifax asked.

"Turbine problems."

Patton picked up a few shards of curved composite material. The shattered edges were torn outward from the inside. "Funny marks on turbine cowling."

Corporal Jott joined Patton. "He's right, Colonel. The turbine blew off from the inside out. The whole nacelle's gone."

Halifax's voice buzzed in their ears. "Assessment. What took them down?"

Corporal Jott looked around. "Looks like the flashers hit them on the water."

"Urrr," Patton concurred, nosing along a furrow that ran from the water's edge up the soft ground to the wreckage. "Crashes onto island. Then melée ensues." There were thousands of tiny, almost invisible claw rips in the surrounding muskeg. "Then skimmer catches fire."

Hagan pulled a badly burned transponder box from the hulk and held it up for those in the other skimmers could see. "At least we know why the transponder cut out."

Patton heard the distinct *clicks* of two comsets cutting out of the circuit. The taller of the two standing figures in the command skimmer tilted its head at the other. Patton aimed his overly sensitive ear pits at them.

The Prime Consul's voice carried faintly over the water. "How the devil did they bring down a skimmer? They're animals for God's sake."

Patton watched Halifax tilt his head, as if not in agreement with his commander in chief.

"Simple thoughts," Tesla lectured in a louder voice. "Not like us. They parrot our words, but that's it. They are incapable of independent thought."

Halifax crossed his arms. "As I reported in the Chamber, Ferals have taken to throwing things at skimmers." He jerked his blocky head at the rear of the command skimmer, and the raised turbine mounted there. "We modified the cowlings with protective gratings, but it looks like they defeated them."

Patton turned from eavesdropping, searched, and picked up a charred screen from near the hulk's exploded turbine cowl. "Blocked with goo," he observed, rubbing the clogged mesh with the opposed pairs of thumbs on his paw.

The comsets *clicked* back onto open channel.

"Corporal Jott, you're sure there are no bodies?" Tesla demanded.

Jott poked inside the hulk with a boot toe. "Yes, Prime Consul. The wreck's pretty much gutted."

"Then strip it," Tesla ordered. "Salvage everything you can. Even a few spare parts are worth recovering."

"As soon—" Halifax's voice interjected, "—as you *secure* the area."

The squad spread out around the wreck.

"Smells like a Kdathic whorehouse in summer," commented Jott.

"All I smell is burning plasteel," said Hagan.

"No, not that." The corporal sniffed. "This smoke smells acrid. There's something else, though. Something . . . rotten."

Patton inhaled deeply, drawing air over the olfactory organs in the roof of his mouth. He smelled it too. And it wasn't the clogged turbine grate (that smelled sweet). He tossed it and, crouching low, followed the faint, foul odor up a small rise. At a hand signal from Jott, Second Team followed. Humans and domestic alike froze as they reached, and looked over, the crest.

"Sweet mother of Scourge," Jott gasped.

"Fuck me for living too long," groaned Hagan.

"Report," Halifax's voice commanded in their headsets. "Corporal Jott, report."

None of the humans in Second Team could find words.

"Patton," Halifax said, "what do you see?"

Patton rumbled quietly into his microphone, searching his memory for an appropriate historical incident that would convey what he saw. "Urrkurrkurrk," he finally decided, "Vlad Tepes at Tirgoviste."

Colonel Halifax's blocky figure turned immediately in the command skimmer and he gestured at its driver. The vehicle whined to life, accelerated forward, and nosed up beside Second Team's skimmer with a soft thump. Halifax hopped out and hurried up to join Patton and the squad. Tesla followed.

"What's going on here . . . ?" Tesla began, his voice falling off when he saw what Halifax and the other speechless Guards saw.

Patton was padding down the far side of the rise into a clearing recently cut from dense jungle. Sap dripped from bitten-off stalks and stumps. A turpentine smell assailed the olfactory organs in his snout, but there was another assailing smell, the rotten one Jott had smelled near the wreckage. A cloying, festering-sickness smell. And it was much stronger.

In the center of the clearing, impaled on six vertical poles, were the members of Deep Recon 8. Narrow poles disappeared between human legs and rammed out of up-thrust human mouths. Clouds of buzzers swarmed hungrily at the fluids oozing from the bodies.

Patton had never seen anything like it. Four men and two women. Naked. Their suffering displayed for all to see in vivid detail.

Halifax, Tesla, and the Guards stumbled down the slope behind Patton, ashen-faced.

"Blessed be the Body Pure," Tesla murmured.

"At least they went fast," Halifax said, attempting to sound calm and controlled.

Keeping a wary eye on surrounding jungle—where any number of Ferals could be hiding, camouflaged, motionless, and undetectable, even to him—Patton looked closer at the impaling poles. They were grown out of a species of plant commonly used by domestics to form hedges or living walls back at the Enclave. The delicate green leaves with serrated edges and purple mottling were easily identifiable, but what jumped out with awful clarity was the realization that the humans of Recon 8 had not been impaled on the poles—*the living skewers had been force-grown through their internal passages.* Shoots pressed out overtaxed nostrils and tear ducts. Green tendrils bulged translucent under fingernails and slithered out ear canals. Vegetable creepers stretched urinary tracts and distended sexual organs, pulling faces into expressions of frozen agony. Halifax was wrong. The squad's passing had been slow. And it had been recent. The telltale bruising of Scourge had not yet begun to appear on the tortured bodies.

In view of the looks of horror on Second Team's faces, Patton decided it would be better to tell Halifax those details later.

Hagan's voice cracked in the heavy silence. "Why did they do that? Ferals never did that before!"

"What does it mean?" another Guard asked fearfully.

"Savages!" Tesla spat, shaking. His pulse-rifle fell to the ends of a shoulder strap as he stacked his fists and pressed them to his lips. *"Blessed be the Body Pure, blessed be the Body Pure. . . ."*

Patton touched the base of a pole. His thumb pads detected bumps where immune venom had been injected to stimulate growth; the Ferals had done a masterful job, growing the torture garden so accurately. Saddened, Patton reached up and touched the human impaled on that pole.

The human blinked.

"Oh shit!" exclaimed Jott.

"They're not dead!" cried Hagan. "Look they're breathing!"

"Corpsman!" Halifax hissed into his comset. "Up here, now!"

A medic jumped ashore from the command skimmer and jogged up the slope.

The impaled humans' chests heaved, ever so slightly, each breath, each blink, each swallow a living torture, a swollen-from-the-inside-out agony. Skin, still warm twitched under Patton's fingers. Bulging eyes, choked by green tendrils between muscle and lid, strained to look down, pleading.

"Khhhhhhhhll mmmhhhhhh," the human gurgled.

Patton tilted his head quizzically.

Halifax stepped closer, trying to hide the horror on his face. He spoke quietly. "What was that, son?"

"Khhllllll mhhheeeeeee."

No one within earshot misunderstood that time.

The corpsman arrived. Behind a mask of detached medical proficiency, he touched, prodded, observed.

"Can we save them?" Halifax asked.

The corpsman shook his head furtively. "Incinerods?"

Halifax nodded, thumbing off his mauler's safety. "Go back to the skimmers, sir," he said to Tesla. "The men need you there."

Patton's color faded as he realized what was about to happen. The recon team could not be saved; they must be put out of their misery. That was why Halifax tried to shoo Tesla away.

The Prime Consul also understood. "No," he said, standing his ground and clutching his pulse-rifle in sweaty palms. "Can't leave, Colonel. Burden of command. No easy outs. Not now, not ever."

The corpsman pulled six thick, palm-sized disks out of his pack and stuck them onto the impaled Guards' abdomens.

Hagan shook his head violently. "No, no. This isn't right. We've got to get them down. We've got to take them back!"

"Do you want to leave them for the *worms,* private?" Corporal Jott barked.

"But they're not dead!" Hagan blubbered on. "They're alive!" He turned to Halifax. "Those aren't just some pieces of meat, sir. Those are our guys!"

"I know, soldier," Halifax said. "I know."

Patton saw that the young, tortured bodies upset Halifax far more than probably most humans or domestics could tell. Halifax knew every one of his humans by name. On the first pole, that was Bryn, son of the best lieutenant Halifax ever had. Then privates Knaefer and Swasin. And there was Knute, who always told stories that made humans laugh. Lastly, Nance, the human with long, shiny hair which still gleamed in the sun despite the fact that the playful spark was gone from her eyes. Patton had seen Halifax train them all personally, giving them every shred of knowledge in his old head, wracking his brains late at night trying to think up better battle drills, better recon formations, anything to keep them alive just one day, one hour longer. Halifax had no mate, so no children of his own, except these Guards.

Hagan persisted, "We got to cut them down and take them back . . ."

A blood-curdling howl cut the Guard's words short. A battle cry of massed Feral voices rose up and gave challenge from the jungle around them. It was as Patton had feared: the enemy had been hiding motionless and invisible all along. He could hear the rumble of many paws in the undergrowth now—many, many paws.

Guards manning heavy weapons swiveled around in the skimmers.

"Trouble in the east grid!"

"Scourge almighty! The whole shore's alive!"

The edge of the circular lagoon shimmered like heat waves over water, thousands and thousands of stampeding heat waves. That's what the humans saw. What Patton saw was a horde of four-legged, Feral-shaped blurs closing in on the humans from all sides.

"Trap! Trap!" Patton howled.

"Set those incinerods!" Halifax barked.

The corpsman flipped safety catches on the thick disks and activated red arming timers.

"Withdraw!" Halifax bellowed, springing into action. As the rest of the humans fell back, he fired well-placed shots at the impaled humans. Flechettes enveloped in kinetic plasma impacted, transferring energy on contact. Heads and chests exploded.

True to his words, Tesla did not run. His pulse-rifle sang out. *Krak! Krak!*

It was all over in five heartbeats. The recon team suffered no more. Incinerods ignited. Concentrated heat shot out, enveloping the lifeless forms. Soon there would be nothing but ashes.

"Heavy weapons fire at will!" Halifax ordered, turning his back on the carnage and running with the other humans.

The heavy gunners needed no encouragement. Pulse-cannons chattered. *Chuk-kuk-kuk-kuk-kuk!* Recoil rocked the skimmers, agitating water around their hulls. Heat-wave silhouettes exploded along the shore like sacks of congealed blood.

It was a drop in the bucket. A tidal wave of Ferals rushed at the torture garden and wrecked skimmer. Running, Patton could see the Feral forms more clearly than the humans, how fast they were moving and how close they were getting, so he knew there was little time to get to the skimmers, but he was careful not to outpace Halifax and Tesla.

Second Team laid cover fire of their own as they skidded back down the swampy ground toward safety. Tesla slipped. Halifax and Patton pulled him up as the Ferals bore down.

The flame-thrower mounted on the command skimmer opened up with a throaty roar, spitting high-pressure gouts of fire. Burning, shrieking arcs of Ferals held the rest of their kind back long enough for the humans to pile into the waiting vehicles. Turbines thrummed as they backed away from shore.

"Head count!" Halifax roared.

"All present and accounted for!" Jott called from Second Team's skimmer.

Halifax slapped his driver on the back. "Hit it!"

Turbines whined. The skimmers turned, spraying rooster-tails of water and accelerating across the donut-hole lagoon.

Patton turned to face the strange grumbling sound behind him.

It was Tesla, eyes looking bloodshot. "I warned them," he said to no one in particular. "I warned them, but they didn't listen. We'll see how they vote *next time."*

The skimmers crossed the lake rapidly.

"Patton," Halifax demanded, pointing at the jagged inlet that had brought them in from the ocean. "What do you see?"

"Lots of Ferals."

The jungle on either side of the inlet crawled with shimmering movement.

"Reload," Halifax ordered the Guardsmen. He swapped out his own mauler clips.

Pulse-cannons hammered as the skimmers slowed to negotiate the waterway in single file. A wash of saltwater spray hit Halifax and Patton as their skimmer fell last in line behind Second Team's skimmer. Drivers swerved around shallows and snags. Individual Guardsmen fired at blurred shapes rushing through the dense foliage along the banks. Focusing on the blurry aliens hurt their human eyes. It was impossible for them to follow such a target for long in the confusion. The flame-thrower had better results igniting huge sections of greenery as the skimmers passed.

Motion overhead caught Patton's eye.

"Look up," he warned. "Look up!"

A pair of sky-colored silhouettes launched from the overhanging canopy. Halifax swung his pistol to bear and blasted, clouds of flechettes hit the silhouettes in mid-jump. Gray Ferals congealed out of nothingness as their glowbuds flared and went dead. The skimmer lurched as limp bodies slammed onto the left wing and splashed into the water. The open ocean was just a couple hundred yards away, but the number of Ferals was chilling. Patton had heard Halifax talking about attacking hordes during the Ferals Wars, but, in all the missions he had accompanied Halifax on, Patton had never seen so many.

"There! There!" Patton pointed at more falling blurs.

Tesla's rifle spat death, but one Feral made it through, landing aft in the skimmer as its bondmate exploded from a well-aimed pulse-rifle shot. The survivor wheeled, half its glowbuds dimming with loss and rage, and it shredded three men, including the driver, before Halifax shot it point-blank in the head. The skimmer fishtailed, skipping over a submerged snag. The flame-thrower operator swung helplessly on the end of her heavy weapon. Guards in the other skimmers ducked to avoid indiscriminate gouts of napalm.

Covered in human and Feral ichor, Tesla flung the dead driver from the controls and took over.

"Shoot the treetops!" Halifax ordered.

Pulse-cannons blasted the jungle canopy, mowing off clouds of leaves and atomizing blood from hidden Ferals. The suicide attacks diminished.

Tesla drove like a madman, following the first two skimmers down the inlet.

"Taking fire!" someone yelled from ahead.

Suddenly, a hail of projectiles enveloped the lead skimmer. Patton looked up. Undaunted by the carnage of human weaponry, shimmering aliens hurled fist-sized objects from the trees, the shore, everywhere.

Patton could barely see the lead skimmer through the barrage. The skimmer's turbine pod, mounted on a raised strut at its rear, began to shake, torquing the vehicle over. It rose up on one wing. The driver tried to recover, but the engine cowl suddenly exploded. Shattered turbine blades sliced through soft human tissue and hard machine hull mercilessly. The remains of the skimmer cartwheeled, flinging hapless Guards into the air. Some landed on shore, their bodies crushed by impact and then torn to pieces by Ferals. Others plummeted into silvery waters. Sharkworms, attracted by all the vibration on the water, feasted upon them.

Unable to stop, Second Team's skimmer plunged into the deadly barrage. All too soon, its turbine began to shake with unbalanced gyroscopic motion.

"Your screens don't work," Tesla shouted at his military commander.

"I don't understand," Halifax yelled back between shots of his pistol. "We tested against objects much larger than those!"

Second Team's skimmer began to heel over like the first, but its driver had the foresight to cut power before catastrophe struck. The vehicle nosed down into the water, slowing drastically and drifting near the dangerous banks of the inlet.

The command skimmer plunged into the hail. Patton ducked his head down as Feral projectiles pummeled his armored back.

Splat! Plort, bloosh, splutz!

Sweet perfume filled the air as reddish spheroids exploded, spewing stringy, orange goo all over.

"It's fruit!" Halifax exclaimed, incredulous. He wiped sticky strands from his face. "Rotten fruit!"

Tesla jerked the command skimmer's throttle shut as he swerved to miss Second Team's drifting skimmer. Second Team was in big trouble. Ferals were stacking up along the shore. Pairs of Patton's wild brethren sprung at the unmoving vehicle despite withering pulse-cannon fire from its defenders. A wounded Feral made it across, decapitating a young woman before her comrades could thrust their bayonets between its armor plates; the quiver-shivs, which sliced through ceramite like butter, neatly sectioned the angry alien.

"Throw a line!" Halifax commanded as Tesla brought them alongside. A guard in the rear of the command skimmer grabbed a coil of filament and hurled one end across. Corporal Jott jumped out onto the immobilized skimmer's near wing, caught the line and secured it to a towing pintle.

Tesla slammed his throttle full open. The command skimmer's turbine roared, but Ferals aimed a barrage of spheroids at it. The thin skins ruptured on impact. Powerful turbine suction instantly drew the fibrous, fruity strands right through its protective screen. The engine pod began to shake as the tough strands jammed in the blades, throwing the turbine off balance.

Halifax's hand stopped Tesla's from cutting the power. The colonel turned to the flame-thrower gunner. "Fire into the turbine!"

"Sir?" said the shocked gunner.

"Do what I say, soldier! Lower pressure and fire directly into the turbine!"

Confused, the woman spun her heavy weapon around on its swivel, adjusted the weapon's fuel focus and shot a diffused, howling stream of napalm at the turbine intake. The fruit fibers were incinerated. The engine pod ceased shaking as balance returned to the spinning blades. The turbine inhaled the flaming fuel and spit it out in a long tail. Clouds of black smoke rose from the overrich exhaust mixture and power dropped due to reduced oxygen supply to the turbine, but it was otherwise unaffected. The towline went taught, pulling Second Team's skimmer away from the Feral-choked bank. Second Team ducked as the napalm exhaust tail arced over their heads with every zigzag of Tesla's hands on his controls.

The skimmers picked up speed. Feral bombardment thickened, but the flame-thrower burned away the sticky fibers long before they reached the vulnerable turbine blades. Scattered Ferals began to throw resin rocks, spiked seedpods, anything to hurt the fleeing humans. Sensing victory, the Guards began to cheer.

A camouflaged paw hooked over the edge of the skimmer behind Halifax.

Nobody saw but Patton. *And now was the time when Patton showed why he was the only domestic allowed on Guard missions. Pact did not kill Pact. As a domestic, Patton might not know those exact words, but it was something all Khafra felt deep down in their bones. Other domestics would have frozen, torn between defending their bonded human and their instincts. At best they would have hesitated.* Patton did not hesitate. As the intruder heaved itself up, drawing its fearsome talons back to swipe Halifax's spine out of his soft human body, Patton charged, hammering Halifax off of his feet. The brunt of the Feral's blow slashed down, gouging deep into Patton's armor. Blood sprayed. Patton yelped.

The Feral froze, its colors jangling in deep-rooted distress—from its own Pact-shall-not-kill-Pact instincts—a second, slashing forcarm froze, poised to attack, above its head. The reaction would only last an instant, Patton knew. The Feral would not attempt to harm him again, but it would soon enough take another swipe at the nearby, prostrate form of Halifax.

The Guards, turning, as if in slow motion, could not fire for fear of hitting Patton.

Lowering his head, Patton butted the Feral in the center of its chest. It fell, again as if in slow motion, backward over the wing. Pulse-rifles cracked. *Kuk! Kuk! Kuk!* Chunks of the Feral's body ripped off, spinning through the air, bouncing off the wing. *Kuk! Kuk! Kuk!* Nothing larger than a jorjorra melon hit the water. None of the humans saw it, nor did Patton consciously see it, but on a base, instinctive level, Patton absorbed the spectacle of each fragment of the Feral flaring and fading to blank in the horrible display of a Khafra life ending without fulfilling Pact.

A Khafra life ended by Patton.

Patton's orb eyes went unfocused. He sat up, suddenly paralyzed. His glowbuds flared a somber blue, and then began to blink out in sequence, from his hind haunches up, spiraling around his thick body, like the unraveling threads of a sweater. His blackening body fell, rigid, into the bottom of the skimmer hull.

Halifax, blood dripping from a gash across his forehead, scrambled over to him.

"Wish we could afford to take more of them on missions," Tesla said as the skimmer cleared the island and the banks of the inlet began to fall away.

Halifax ignored the Prime Consul, cradling Patton's head in his arms. "You did good, Patton," he whispered. "You did good."

Patton's teeth chattered feverishly. "No problem. Skimmers safe?"

"The skimmers are safe," Halifax said gently. "And you saved my life, again."

"Halifax owes Patton," the domestic joked, getting weaker by the moment.

"Big time," the soldier agreed.

As the skimmers raced out to sea, Patton heard the victory yowl of a thousand Feral hunters thundering from behind.

"What see?" Patton asked faintly.

Halifax looked back at FI-538. "Ferals. The shore is lined with blood-red Ferals. What a sight."

Their massed cry resounded across the water, drowning out the whine of the single straining turbine and sending shivers up the spines of the beaten humans in the skimmers. Even in the darkness filling his head, Patton knew what it was, as one fighting creature knows the blood lust of another.

It was a declaration of war.

"It won't stop now," he heard Tesla say self-righteously. The Prime Consul's voice sounded full and determined, no longer drawn and remote from his defeat in the Chamber of the Body. "It won't stop until we kill them all or they kill us all."

Patton lost consciousness.

Halifax tilted Patton's closed eyes toward the brilliant afternoon sun. The domestic would need all the light he could get for the next little while. His scarred, blood-anointed face heavy with the losses that day, the old human murmured, *"Animals incapable of independent thought: two. Humans: nil."*

The blank-one force retreated, decimated. Tlalok's horde throbbed the colors of exultation.

Sweet was the odor of blank-ones on the run.

The forces of Radiance, so long in retreat, had evened the score one small notch. Soon Tlalok's horde would even it more. The blank-ones would return to their slave colony with the tale of what they had witnessed, a tale of *Feral* atrocity. And the blank-ones would be horrified. They would know what it was like to live in terror as all Pact had lived in terror for so many years. If Tlalok's horde had its way, the blank-ones would soon know subjugation and death, too.

Tlalok himself had impaled the blank-one raiders yesterday, growing the impaling poles with his own immune venom as other pack members held the despicable bipeds in place. Tlalok had pinched each sapling around its base, injecting temptations to grow *here* and *here*, *there* and *there*. The immune venom did not force compliance, only entice. There was no master and slave between Pact and plant, only need and want. Where those needs and wants converged, there were results.

In this case, vengeance.

How the raiders screamed when venom-enticed shoots and runners grew through their insides where there was no room to grow! It was shockingly savage, even to a Pact. But Tlalok remembered Lleeala screaming as sharkworms ate her alive, one bloody bite by one bloody bite. And when the blank-ones whimpered for mercy, Tlalok remembered how he had whimpered for mercy as his force-

bonded blank-one inflicted Sacrament upon him so many years
ago. Tlalok returned the same amount of mercy that had been meted
upon him then. None. And when shoots and creepers grew, bulging
out of blank-one mouths, stopping the *hunh, hunh, hunh* of overwhelming, unbearable torment, when the ugly pink faces prayed for
death as the only escape from a haze of misery, Tlalok remembered
the misery of his ten-season-old nurslings, slaughtered in a blank-
one raid gone bad, tiny bodies broken and big-eyed with incompre-
hension at the horrible world that he, Tlalok, had not been able to
protect them from. That memory killed any pity he might have felt
for the blank-one raiders. He did not flinch, he did not falter, he did
not stop.

He would never stop.

But he must pause. The horde could not move night and day.
They must rest and gather their ferocity. After that, nothing could
turn them aside from massive retribution. The horde outnumbered
the blank-ones ten to one. Tlalok champed his teeth selfishly and
clawed at the roots under his feet. Somewhere in the coming strife,
he would find the blank-one Karr. And then . . . and then the pay-
back for unleashing the False Radiance on Tlalok's world would be
good.

For a while Tlalok glowed blood red.

And then he realized what he was doing and dimmed the glowbuds on his right side, to be half-blank in mourning, as so many of
his pack were half-blank. He looked around. None of them seemed
to notice. But none of them had any trouble observing the grieving
ritual, as was proper. As Tlalok turned his back on the receding
blank-one skimmers, he wondered why it was that he struggled to
consciously do what any Pact should do without even thinking.

XXVI

Question: When you look into the radiant sun, what do you see?
Answer: Yourself.
Question: And when you look into the waters of the shadow world, what do you see?
Answer: Yourself.

—Feral riddle

The lifter flew deep into the Dead Zone, deep into the belly of a storm. Rain came down in smothering sheets. It was afternoon, although the dark sky gave no clue. Karr had been flying seventy-two straight hours since leaving the Enclave, unable to land. This was not because of Ferals —they had been left behind long ago— but because the water was too choppy to set down. And the winds were too violent to risk letting Arrou spell him at the controls. Fatigue numbed Karr's muscles, dulling his mind, enticing his eyelids to close over raw eyes, eyes hypnotized by never-ending, swirling droplets of rain. *Just a few minutes of sleep, that's all he needed. A nap. Then he would be all right.* But Jenette wouldn't let him. Neither she nor the rest of the crew would relent. Karr was dimly aware that they were staring at him, but he didn't register their concern and anxiety. *Didn't they have duties to attend?*

"I've decided something," Karr mumbled.

"What?" asked Jenette.

"You can let me sleep now."

Jenette turned to Arrou. "Can we set down?"

The alien looked over the edge of the lifter. Whitecaps tore across waves big enough to swamp the lifter. "Not think so."

"No sleep," Jenette said to Karr, slowly and forcefully. "Now pay attention. Look at the water. Look."

As if he could look at anything else. "Rain, rain, rain," Karr griped.

"No, look at the ocean," Jenette corrected. "See how it's not shiny? See?"

Zombie slow, Karr looked down the side of the cockpit. The water below was dull, like normal oceans on other, normal planets. Only a few marbled streaks of mirror-like surface were mixed in.

"The shiny parts are nutrient rich," Jenette explained, trying to keep his mind engaged. "The dull parts aren't. You can swim in them because nothing lives there. No nutrients: no plankton. No plankton: no sharkworms, no ring-islands, no nothing. Anything that drifts into the Dead Zone is doomed to a slow death."

And where does that leave us? Karr wondered idly.

As he looked down, his weary body leaned along with his lolling head—and unconsciously pulled the control yoke over, too. "Mmmm, I see."

The heavy lifter began to bank.

"Okay, stop looking!" Jenette said with rising alarm.

The wind kicked up, catching the rectangular hull like a sail. The lifter bucked up. Humans and domestics slid and skittered down the steepening, slippery deck. Dr. Marsh yelped as a bubble tent broke its moorings, bowling her over. Toliver and the Guards chased it downwind, barely grabbing the hemisphere before it could flip over the side. Supply crates strained against tie-downs.

"Level off! Level off!" Jenette yelled, hanging onto exposed cockpit struts.

Eventually Karr's sluggish reflexes kicked in. Shuddery muscles pressed the controls and the deck became level once more. Again, he didn't see the worried looks the expedition members shot his way, but an influx of adrenaline momentarily revived him.

"Why . . . ?" Karr gulped, struggling to wake up and correlate Jenette's words with what Bigelow had told him back at the Enclave. "Why pick an island in the Dead Zone to plant the original colony base?"

Breathing heavily, Jenette said, "It was deemed a good choice because there were no Ferals living anywhere near."

"Safer, I guess," Karr mumbled.

"Safe had nothing to do with it." Jenette looked around the lifter. No one had fallen off. "The original colonists bent over backwards to be friendly with Ferals, setting up lines of communication, rudimentary trade, and exchanging knowledge. Humans and Ferals got along well at first."

"Then why move the Enclave?"

"It turned out the reason no Ferals lived on Coffin Island was because it was a bad place to live."

"Because it was in the Dead Zone."

"Right. It seems obvious now, but it wasn't then. They didn't know shiny water was better. And they didn't call it Coffin Island. They called it *Elysium* island." Jenette pursed her lips wryly. "The *Coffin* part came later, after we strained its ecosystem to the limit, drained its reserves of fresh water, and had to move or die. That's when the Feral Wars began."

Karr nodded, but stopped when his head threatened another sleepy loll. "The Ferals saw weakness and attacked?"

"Oh no," said Jenette. "They tried to help, but the Scourge was wiping us out." Her voice lowered into an angry mutter. Karr strained to hear her over the wind. "My father spied out a large inhabited island, took it by force, dubbing it *Golconda*, moved the Enclave there, and promptly enslaved the Feral population to use for Sacrament, which he had just invented. Ferals call it the Great Betrayal. The War Years. Our losses were frightening, Feral loses devastating. We didn't get everything transferred from the Enclave's old location to the new one. We lost all our heavy vehicles, all our flying machines, our manufacturing plants, the larger items in the armory—your C-55s for instance . . ." Jenette trailed off as Karr's eyelids began to droop again.

She sent Arrou back to the tents.

Somewhere deep in the back of his mind, Karr surmised that he was in bad shape, because he heard music in the wind. Hollow, foreboding music, like a distant pipe organ. It couldn't be real.

Arrou returned, legs and claws spread against any unexpected gust of wind or kick of the deck, the cone of his teeth pinched delicately on a steaming mug. Jenette took it and shoved it at Karr, but he turned his nose up at the vile liquid.

"I don't want it." If Karr drank, he would have to urinate again—it seemed that one could not truly own New Ascension pseudo-ghll, just pay rent on it—and that meant forcing his sore muscles to work. That meant *moving*.

"Drink," Jenette ordered, forcing the cup to his mouth.

Karr gulped, burning his palate and choking on bits of chitinous legs. He knocked the mug back, spitting scalding fluid. Jenette lost her grip on the mug and it tumbled over the side, down, down, down . . . *splish,* a tiny spot punched in foaming sea. Under it went, to the serene water below the surface. Karr wanted that serenity. He could rest in serenity like that, wrapped in a womb of primordial water, like *Long Reach* was wrapped in water. Karr was too far gone for the pain in his mouth and lips to revive him. Distant conversation behind him:

"Deena, give him another stimulant."

"I've already given him twice the safe dose. I can't give him any more."

Jenette swore.

"Corporal Toliver! Where's that damn island?"

Leaning against the wind, Toliver jogged over and checked his map-reader. "We're at the right spot on the charts," he apologized.

"Then where is it?" Jenette repeated.

"Islands drift," Arrou reminded.

"He's right," Toliver agreed. "And these charts haven't been updated since the satellite went offline ten years ago. Sorry, Consul."

Jenette cursed again.

For some reason, the exchange amused Karr. Coffin Island, like a piece of driftwood, had floated away, like Karr's mind was floating away, spiraling into dreamy mist, like the spiral search pattern he was trying to fly.

An ethereal organ hummed a lullaby. Sleep. Sleep.

Discontinuity.

Karr's head jerked upright. Jenette was screaming in his ear.

"Pilot Karr, Pilot Karr!" At first Karr's fuzzy reasoning concluded that he had suffered a *fugue*-flashback: an unexpected release of *fugue* from fat cells into his bloodstream, which could and did paralyze Pilots at the most inopportune times. Then Karr thought that the lifter had gone down. That they were drowning. Water choked his eyes and nose, but it was just a thicker deluge of rain, beating against his head as the organ music moaned on. He couldn't see five yards in front of his face.

"Wake up! Wake up!" Jenette cried. "Arrou, help me!"

Unnerved humans and Khafra struggled not to be blown overboard behind them.

Karr felt claws on his shoulders. Shaking him. Fishy breath on his neck. And he remembered that fish lived in the sea. The sleepy. Sleepy. Sea.

Discontinuity.

"Aaaah!" he cried, awaking to a painful cone of teeth biting into his shoulder. A leathery alien hand gripped his, pulling the steering yoke back to center. The lifter rotated out of its dive. And the moaning music vibrated through the hull, his body. *Toccata and fugue in Sea Minor.* Ha ha. There was a crazy thought.

But not so funny were the moaning bones around them.

Karr was flying through the grim reaper's erector set. Above, below, and to either side were what looked, to Karr's deluded mind, like titanic femur and humerus and ulna bones. More, dead ahead. Collision course ahead. Karr yanked the controls hard right. The heavy lifter veered off, banking back through the forest of hollow, petrified bones. Silver-white fossils swayed in the wind, clattering in eerie syncopation. Wind blew over their open ends, playing a horrible pipe organ thrum as the lifter flew back out over water.

The chaotic snapshots merged. A picture built up. Storm and wave battered against an endless curving shore, cliffs made of bones piled on bones towered one hundred feet high. And rising from the undead plateau, highlighted by the flash and rumble of lightning, were skeletal tree trunks, like hoary bristles on an old hog's back, needle fangs biting the sky, arching inland, the landscape of death blurred into darkness by ever more distant curtains of water.

Coffin Island.

Karr knew it with certainty before he heard the gasped exclamations behind him. Lowering the throttle lever, he brought the lifter down, nosing back inshore, weaving in between the curving bone columns. He flew slowly inland, sinking lower and lower. The lifter lurched, scraping against a fossil tree. The bone shattered, toppling into other howling bones. A hail of shards pelted down on the island below.

Karr spotted a break in the vertical bones and aimed the lifter for it, descending and scraping across uneven ground.

"Hold on!" Jenette warned the others.

Karr brought the lifter to a cockeyed halt. Once more, loose gear skittered down the deck. Karr looked around and, with a bleary-eyed "Okay," swiped off the engine switches and collapsed into deep, deep sleep.

XXVII

From the transcripts of Major Vidun's implanted
    personal recorder, planet Solara, 10.29.3531.
Document status: CLASSIFIED.
    (Looking out of place, Dr. Uttz enters a dim bar,
    scans the lethargic crowd and spots Vidun, who
    hunches over an empty slammer rig. Uttz joins the
    military man.)
Vidun (looks up bleary-eyed): Well, if it isn't the good
    doctor. What brings you to my lair?
Dr. Uttz: Fifteen years of daily briefings, rain or
    shine, then today nothing. It gave me pause. When
    heard a rumor you might be found here, I came.
    May I sit?
Vidun: Suit yourself. You won't partake, of course.
Dr. Uttz: In fact, I will.
    (Surprised, Vidun motions to the barkeep, a run-
    down anthrosimalcrum robot, who brings over a
    new slammer rig and refills Vidun's. The Academy
    instructors attach the transfer tubes and patches to
    their necks and absorb the luminous fluid in
    silence. Uttz is the first to empty his rig.)
Dr. Uttz (slumping): Why so melancholy, colleague?
Vidun (brooding): Only a few years left. He's seventeen
    today. In the blink of an eye, he'll be assigned a
    ship and we'll never see him again.
Dr. Uttz: We may not see him, but we will be near for a
    while, in the dreamchamber of his fugueship.

*Vidun (head hangs glumly): It all starts again. Hop
    from planet to planet. Test the populations. Gather
    the candidates. A century or two passes, and then
    we set up another Academy on another world. I'm
    too old for this shit.*
*Dr. Uttz (shrugs): You and I have a few more terms in
    us each.*
    (Vidun leans overly close to Uttz, waxes maudlin.)
Vidun: He hates our guts, doesn't he?
Dr. Uttz: I fear you are correct.
*Vidun (pounds table): Goddamn, whore-mongering,
    mother-fucking shit! Well . . . (laughs suddenly) . . .
    I guess we did our jobs then?*
Dr. Uttz: I suppose we did.
    *(Their bloodshot eyes twinkle. Vidun motions the
    barkeep.)*
Vidun: Two more!

Karr dreamed of *Long Reach.* He dreamed of *flesh,* of being enfolded deep in the warm cocoon of his fugueship, of being caressed and comforted by the velvet folds of its fleshy body. Like
the security of a baby nestling at its mother's bosom. *Flesh.* The
handshake of a friend. *Flesh.* The press of a sleeping lover's embrace . . . all nurturing kinds of contact denied to a Pilot, all except
the flesh of his ship, the only living thing he had ever been allowed
to care about, to belong to. The flesh was his life. The flesh was his
friend. The flesh was home.

Karr awoke.

The flesh was gone. He did not open his eyes. He was alone in
his mind with the strangling feeling of separation, as it had been
every morning that he woke away from *Long Reach.* Every morning it was harder to fight the emotions back. Karr had never been
separated from his ship this long before. He struggled to regain his
wits.

Where was he?

The moaning thrum of Coffin Island was still in Karr's ears, but
the crash of wind and rain were gone. He was in a sleeping bag,

naked (how had he gotten that way?), and the air around him was stuffy. He must also be in a bubble tent. Karr opened his eyes—and jumped. Arrou loomed over him. Four hundred pounds of alien stared down from a squatting position. For a second or two Karr lay flat on his back, smelling hot, swampy breath.

"How long have you been there?" Karr managed.

"Whole time," Arrou said patiently. "Jenette say watch Pilot." The bullet head twisted under the orange tent material. Bulbous eyes lined up with Karr's. "How feel? Still sleepy?"

"No," said Karr. "I feel much better."

Arrou took a short step in the small tent. "Not smart. Fly three days." He nosed into Karr's duffel and then stepped back with a clean, white uniform in his teeth.

"Arrou," Karr said, taking the garment from his preaching student. "I didn't exactly have a choice."

"Always choice. Just not always *good* choice."

"Hmmm," said Karr pulling the uniform on inside the sleeping bag.

"Brace self," Arrou said when Karr finished. Opposing pairs of thumbs on one of the alien's paws unsealed the tent. "Weird place."

The island's moaning grew louder as Karr stepped out into a melancholy, fleshless world. Arrou padded quietly behind.

Pipe organ bones towered against an overcast day. Not real bones, Karr saw in the glum light. The moaning shapes were actually the silvery-white inner boles of New Ascension's queer trees. And the ground was not heaps and stacks of skeletal debris as he had first assumed, but interlocking masses of knobby, bone-like lattice; the normally flexible ring island root material was dead and petrified. Karr's bubble tent sat upon a relatively flat section with tarps folded into padding underneath, as did the other domes, all of which crowded like yellow mushrooms around a rainwater pool at the bottom of a gully. The heavy lifter tilted steeply up one side.

Expectant heads turned Karr's way, but no one spoke.

An uneasy mood hung over the encampment. Toliver's Guards stood alert around the banks above the gully, atop bleached piles of ring-island skeleton, pulse-rifles charged and ready, plates of skirmish armor strapped into position. The domestics, scattered throughout the area, did not flash, but sat dimly like cowled, mourning humans. Bullet heads tilted this way or that at any strange noise. They didn't like the big, dead island. It went against their instinct to keep ring-islands alive. Crash made an abortive bite into a patch of brittle stalks, trying to inject immune venom and stimulate growth, but there was nothing to stimulate; chalky fragments shattered between dagger teeth. The island was stone cold dead, except for the lamenting of fossils in wind, which only exaggerated the somber mood.

Karr joined those at a fire pit. Bigelow handed him a tray of rations.

"Breakfast or lunch?" Karr asked, holding up a gutbomb spheroid.

"Sort of an early dinner," Jenette answered.

"How long was I out?"

"Over twenty hours. It's late afternoon."

That explained why Karr was so stiff. He sat on a plastic crate and swallowed a spheroid. "What did you find out about this place?"

Jenette sat next to him, as usual a little too close for comfort. Karr felt her warm *flesh* through their clothes. "Not much."

"It's hard to search very far on foot," Bigelow explained, with a look at the cockeyed heavy lifter.

"Do we at least know where the C-55s are?" Karr asked, covering his mouth as the gutbomb ignited in his stomach.

The rotund scientist pursed his lips. "We know where they were." Bigelow borrowed Toliver's map-reader and called up an overview of Coffin Island. "They were stored in a munitions bunker right about *here.*" Holding the device for Karr to see, Bigelow touched the island's center (the Enclave's initial island base apparently had no doughnut hole at its center). The spot glowed red. Around it, the map showed homes and industrial buildings and streets and plantations, from one shore to the other. Putting down his ration tin and taking the map-reader, Karr climbed up one side of the gully for a better view.

A maze of silvered skeletal boles encircled the gully. Here and there the horizon was studded with thicker groves.

For the first time since crashing on New Ascension, Karr had relatively firm ground under his feet. Coffin Island did not undulate like a living ring-island. The heaps and furrows of jagged bone only creaked and groaned as the ocean shifted. Pools of runoff water, which had carved ruts in loose heaps of material, rippled faintly at the bottoms of ditches and ravines. But there was no constant rolling and pitching like the surface of a bowl of gelatin, only a gentle, almost imperceptible, swaying. Karr would have appreciated it more if not for the morbid atmosphere which seemed to cling to his skin, like the smell of scorched grass. Coffin Island seemed to beckon to the unwary, eager to leech the life out of anyone foolish enough to challenge it. Karr shook off the feeling and glanced around. No homes, industries, streets, or plantations were visible.

Just bones.

He slid back down the slope, no wiser than before.

"Obviously the problem is that we don't know where we are," Bigelow observed.

"Easily solved," Karr said, turning to his awkwardly tilted orbiter. "Give me a minute to get the thrusters fired up."

Nobody moved.

"What?" Karr asked.

Desires for an alternate mode of transportation were mumbled.

"I'm feeling much better," Karr explained. "There's no need to be concerned. Let's get going, before we lose the daylight."

The others remained skeptical, but at Jenette's urging, the Guards made short work of striking camp. Fifteen minutes later, the expedition was back in the air.

For the benefit of those with a recently acquired fear of flying, Karr kept the heavy lifter low and slow, weaving between upthrust fossils. The island was a maze, even from above. Karr flew a gentle spiral in from shore, attempting to locate any sign of the abandoned colony. Below, tangles of bone material formed ravines and pathways that snaked back upon themselves with no rhyme or reason—and bore no resemblance to Bigelow's map. Dead ends and snags of impassable ivory logs abounded.

Jenette shivered behind the cockpit. Coffin Island was a nightmare that no colonist forgot, no matter how young they had been before the Enclave moved. "Be a good little girl," she whispered, "or we'll send you to *Coffin Island.*" Scourge killed many colonists during the first few years of habitation on Elysium. Every inch farther inland Jenette expected to see human remains mixed in with the jumbled white shapes, a skull or an arm bone protruding out from under crumbled buildings. But there was none. No buildings, no human remains, not so much as a discarded quickfood carton.

They searched. The sun poked a gash in the overcast; lukewarm sweat trickled through Karr's hair despite a clammy breeze. They saw nothing but desolation jumbling away in all directions, heaping slightly higher here or lower there. They did, however, discover that Coffin Island was not as solid as it had felt from the ground. Deep, trench-like fissures scarred the surface every kiloyard or so, like shatter lines on a ceramite plate. Some were deep enough to be filled with water at the bottom. "It's going to break up soon," Jenette commented. "The next big storm, or the next one after that. . . ."

Nothing else stood out as an hour slipped by.

"There was a human colony here?" Karr asked at last. Despite what he'd been told, it didn't seem possible, given the place's current desolation.

Bigelow nodded. "Yes, and most of it was left behind during the evacuation: buildings, large machines, even the colony beacon itself. Not to mention infrastructure like roads and such. All abandoned."

Karr rubbed his jaw quizzically. "So where is it?"

Shoulders shrugged behind him.

"Maybe this is the wrong island, sir," Corporal Toliver offered. "Any island in the Dead Zone could look like this. Maybe this isn't Elysium."

Karr didn't like that possibility at all, considering how long it might take to find another island in the Dead Zone. "Arrou, do you see anything?"

"No."

"Do you smell anything? Oil? Machinery?"

"From up high?"

Bigelow dug into one of the many pockets on his daysuit. "Perhaps this will help." He removed a compact, cylindrical device which sat on the end of a short handgrip. He flicked it on and it spun, lights blinking along the cylinder. "C-55s degrade over time. Over the last two decades there should have been a loss of three to five percent of initial warhead strength. Now that's not much, but when you factor in the size and number of the core-boring warheads, that may be enough radiant energy to detect. . . ." Bigelow turned a full three hundred and sixty degrees, his face fading. "Or not."

At that point Karr abandoned the spiral search pattern and banked inland, closing on a landmark that looked like distant skyscrapers. It proved to be nothing more than densely packed sailtree skeletons, leaning together, snagged and cracked, and threatening to crumble down. There was no sign of human habitation near or in the overlapping bands of shadow underneath. Beyond them the towering skeletons fell away. The lifter flew over a wide clearing. The smooth expanse mounded up in the middle, like the exposed cranium of some huge, buried creature. Karr swooped low. The surface seemed to be made of bony fragments, compacted like sandstone.

Bigelow cross-referenced his instrument and the map-reader. "We're just about dead center over the island."

"Anything on the scanner?" Karr asked.

"Bupkiss, I'm afraid. Unequivocal bupkiss." The lights on the instrument were dim. "But at least we are in the general vicinity of the armory as indicated by the map." Bigelow leaned over the side of the lifter, trying to get a better reading.

"Time to cut our losses," Karr decided. "We'll continue the search elsewhere."

"Are you sure?" Jenette asked. "This place looks like Coffin Island. It feels like Coffin Island and all my instincts tell me this is Coffin Island."

"Mine too," Karr agreed. "But facts aren't proving our instincts correct and a good Pilot doesn't make the facts fit the theory." He applied power and the lifter began to rise. "One more quick sweep on the way out, then we search for another island."

At which point Bigelow said, "Oops."

Karr looked over his shoulder. The scientist was frozen at the sidewall.

"Oops?"

Bigelow was a portrait of embarrassment. "I wholeheartedly beg your pardon."

"Define *oops,*" Karr pressed.

"I dropped the scanner," Bigelow admitted. "I was concerned that the hull was blocking the signal—ceramite is such an excellent insulator—so I leaned over the side and it fell from my grasp. Again, my apologies—"

Karr held up a hand. "Never mind. Where is it?"

"I can see it." Bigelow looked back over the edge and pointed at the center of the clearing. "Right down there."

Karr began to descend, circling, until he spotted the tiny instrument. He maneuvered the heavy lifter beside it. Thruster fields kicked up small vortices of chalky dust as they hovered.

"That's it," Bigelow said enthusiastically and, before anyone could say a word, hopped over the side and down the two yards to retrieve his instrument. "It still works," he declared happily, as the lights spun and bleeped.

Not wanting Bigelow to burst a blood vessel climbing back in, Karr brought the lifter to a perfect four-point landing, the hull level with the smooth ground and nobody's stomach in his or her mouth.

Abruptly there was a *crunch.*

The lifter lurched. Cracks spread out from under the hull as the ground buckled. With an inelegant squawk, Bigelow's head disappeared below the level of the lifter's sidewall. His fingers barely managed to grab hold as a collapsing roar sounded from below. The lifter hung an awful moment and then began to drop. Karr punched the throttle. Ceramite deck slammed up into humans and domestics as a boiling white cloud billowed up from underneath.

One of Bigelow's hands slipped, unable to hold his weight. Bronte lunged, claws skittering across ceramite decking, her teeth biting into Bigelow's daysuit to keep him from falling. Humans staggered to assist her, heaving the scientist inboard as Karr regained control and the deck steadied.

"My goodness," Bigelow panted, plopping down hard onto the deck. "What an adrenaline rush! Thank you one, thank you all." He nodded to his human rescuers while scratching Bronte under the chin.

"What happened?" Jenette asked, scrambling back up beside Karr.

The answer became clear as the dust thinned, revealing a gaping hole where the lifter had touched down. Beyond and below its ragged edge lurked a subterranean cavity, several stories deep and an untold dimension wide. Karr spun the lifter for a better view. He and Jenette caught their breath at the same instant.

There at the bottom, spotlighted in a dusty shaft of light and almost obliterated by recently fallen debris, was the unmistakable gleam of golden, New Ascension roadwort pavement.

XXIX

Radiance is the language of truth, openly spoken and unmistakable, impossible to hide. Untruth cannot survive where many eyes are keen. Sound is the language of secrets, whispered from tongue to ear, where only a few may judge its meaning. Pact use both, as the Balance demands: Radiance for outer truth, sound for inner secret. How then can Pact trust blank-ones, whose only language is the language of secret, which they use for both truth and deception?

—Kthulah, Keeper of Gnosis

Tlalok was a prisoner. Four magnificent Pact hunters led him blindfolded to his reckoning. Strong footfalls drummed the turf around him, their unchanging pace bespeaking measured power, control. Where Tlalok's horde fought with passion and fury, these hunters channeled ferocity into regimentation, focused force. Tlalok was more than a match for any one or two of them, perhaps three, but their sacred number of four (the number of thumbs on a paw) guaranteed his defeat. Yet, it was not threat of physical force that shackled Tlalok that night. Nor did he wear bonds. Nor was it the coarse-fibered hood, filling with his own breath, that held him.

It was the Clash of Radiance which had beaten Tlalok.

Tlalok's horde had been closing inexorably on the blank-one colony, forming a noose and drawing tighter day by day, heartbeat by heartbeat. Each night when sunset brought night, and the red glow from the False Radiance brought another Clash, the number of the horde swelled. This night, Tlalok had expected no different.

Until he lost.

The Clash of Radiance had turned on Tlalok. At the moment when he was ready to unleash his fury on the blank-one colony, an even greater Radiance ambushed Tlalok. Tlalok battled to the limits of his fury. One to one, he might have been victorious, but the numbers of Pact allied with the opposing Radiance were irresistible—so great was their force that the underbellies of low hanging clouds lit up, nearly as bright as day. Tlalok's thousands-of-fours succumbed to thousands-upon-thousands-of-fours. Soul-flaying beauty beat Tlalok. Whispers of its sharp Radiance echoed on Tlalok's captors when they arrived on warboards to take him away. The ecstasy of it teased its way through Tlalok's head even now as he walked—the wondrous, wretched ecstasy of defeat.

Klak, klak, klak. Tlalok's captors champed their teeth rhythmically, guiding his blind steps up from the water's edge, deeper into the mysterious island they had brought him to. *Klak, klak. Turn here. Klak. Now the other way.* Onward they marched, always ascending, two hunters ahead of Tlalok and two behind. *Klik, tik. Go straight.* Up they wound, along broad avenues. No wild island was this, Tlalok decided, feeling finely manicured roadwort cobblestones under his paw pads.

The procession narrowed to a single file, passing over a long tree-root arch. Tlalok's claws knocked bark loose. The ragged bits fell a great distance; he did not hear them hit bottom. So, they were high now. But Tlalok felt no motion. This far above ocean level all islands rolled with the waves. But this one did not. Tlalok shivered at the thought of an island so large.

The hunters resumed their formation around Tlalok. The sound of many paws came to his ears from beyond. Many plates of armor rasped ahead of them, moving aside. Tlalok sensed throngs of Pact assembling to watch the conquered Radiance being brought to be absorbed, just as Tlalok had brought Pact newly joined to his Radiance to be absorbed. But there the similarity ended. Tlalok welcomed those less radiant than he with open arms, and they gladly joined their ferocity to his.

Tlalok never brought them in bondage.

Higher and higher the hunters marched Tlalok. Fog condensed on his flanks, and then as they climbed higher still, fresh breezes evaporated the fog. Tlalok longed for the cool caress of those breezes inside his suffocating hood. His captors had affixed a single dead star-buzzer inside, but its light was weak. Under the hood there was almost complete darkness. To stay calm, Tlalok played every childhood counting game he could think of. He counted blank-ones slain by his own claws, subdividing those into categories by dimension, gender, smell, and ferocity. And that had a tranquilizing effect for a while, but even so, his agitation rose.

After what seemed like eternity, a musical tinkling came to Tlalok's ears, muffled by the chafing hood fabric and the bellows of his own lungs. The texture underpaw changed to groomed hook-turf between splayed tree roots. *Klak, tak. Klik, tik.* Tlalok obeyed, winding through the unseen tree trunks, marching headlong toward whatever fate the Balance had in store for him; he would not give his captors the satisfaction of seeing him flinch.

The ground peaked. The tree maze ended and Tlalok's captors padded down a gentle slope, drawing to a halt at the bottom of a grassy bowl. The chiming sounded all about him there, and Tlalok heard murmuring, followed by a hush. The space felt serene, calm. Tlalok's arrival had been trying, but he began to hope that the indignities were over.

That's when strong paws grabbed the back of his neck.

<<Down!>> commanded his captors, forcing Tlalok prostrate and shoving his face hard into the ground.

The hood was ripped off of Tlalok's head. He drank cool air, blinking hard after the awful dark and endeavoring to gather his bearings with only one eye (the other was mashed into the ground).

Quick impressions—

A grassy glade, at night. Bowl shaped. Encircled by columns of ebony-colored trees. Elegant interlocking branches. Overhead, a vault of glassy leaves, tinkling with every caress of the wind. Starlight filtered through, tinted serene shades of rose and turquoise by the leaves. Pact ringed the sheltered area, orderly both in posture and of glowbud. They displayed patterns unfamiliar to Tlalok, curiously subdued patterns that did not move or change with feeling and intent, but held fast. Some displayed wide patches of red and green, others showed intricate mosaics on flank and limb or concentric rings radiating back from muzzle over torso and haunch. Silver strips ran across the backs and out to the claws of the four hunters holding Tlalok down.

A presence spoke from ahead of Tlalok, just out of sight. Its light and sound-words ricocheted off the glassy leaves above and on back down to Tlalok's upturned ears and eye.

<<This is the savage?>> it asked, with quiet, rooted power. Tlalok immediately recognized the signature of the Radiance that had beaten him.

Four monochromatic light-voices answered the first, their tints and tones brittle like twigs. They spoke no sound-words at all. Tlalok struggled to make out their speech from the reflecting leaves.

<<The savage.>>

<<Savage Radiance.>>

<<From the Fringe.>>

<<Forgotten and forsaken,>> the four voices intoned in sequence.

A pause, as if to size Tlalok up.

The first presence spoke again. <<Does the savage know when the Burning Heart blossoms/births/escapes?>>

Apparently it was addressing Tlalok as *savage*. Tlalok bit back a foul retort. He was defeated. He must abide by the will of the conquering Radiance. That was the way of Pact, no matter how little Tlalok felt like cooperating. He dredged his memories for what he knew of the Burning Heart of Night. They were of no help, but an unbidden image leapt to his mind, the image of falling star-streaks against the night sky, and then of a distant red glow on the horizon. How many nights ago? Tlalok counted on thumbs and claws: four hands of four nights ago.

<<Four upon four?>> Tlalok ventured.

Excited colors swept around the bowl. <<The number of the square . . . the number of the blossom is the number of the square!>>

<<The savage reveals Truth,>> the strong presence announced, <<Truth the Pack of Gnosis did not know.>>

The four monochromatic voices were not so impressed.

<<Truth>>

<<Is the>>

<<Most dangerous weapon>>

<<Of all,>> they warned, again in their peculiar habit of speaking in rotation.

<<And,>> they continued,

<<The savage>>

<<Violates>>

<<The Prophecy!>>

Tlalok heard *clicking,* as of large seeds striking together.

<<The Prophecy,>> the first voice repeated with reverence. <<*What is our progress?*>>

<<Gnosis has moved>>

<<Two stars>>

<<Toward the Burning Heart>>

<<Since last night,>> the brittle voices solemnly informed.

Approving light from the onlookers.

<<And the savage leads his pack *away* from the Burning Heart?>> the first voice considered.

Condemning light from the onlookers.

<<What says the savage to this Truth?>> the dominant voice asked.

Tlalok lost his patience. <<The *savage,*>> he snarled from his prostrate position, <<speaks only with Pact face to face and on four legs, not as from master to slave—as blank-ones do!>>

A gasp from the onlookers.

<<Challenging!>>

<<Accusing!>>

<<The savage confronts>>

<<Those who confront it!>> the four voices exclaimed.

Tlalok heard more clicking.

<<And the savage is full>>

<<Of fury>>

<<And far, far>>

<<Out of Balance!>>

Tlalok was not shamed. <<It is the Pack of Gnosis that is out of Balance, not Tlalok!>>

<<Outrageous!>>

<<Intolerable—>> the four began in uncharacteristic unison.

But the single voice interrupted. <<Again, the savage reveals Truth.>>

<<But—>>

Another interruption. <<Gnosis must protect Prophecy, Gnosis must also abide by what is Just. *It is decided.*>>

Onlooking Pact sparkled in surprise, then fell dim.

The four monochromatic voices did not argue further, but flashed a sustained white light. When they spoke again it was with the solemn rhythm of an often repeated ritual.

<<Four upon four?>> they asked themselves.

<<No,>> they answered themselves back. <<Four of itself.>>

Again they lit the glade with white light. Stillness followed, broken only by a harsh *thwak, thwak, thwak, thwak,* which Tlalok could not identify. Then more stillness.

Eventually the original presence found its voice. <<Release the savage.>>

Claws and weight lifted from Tlalok's neck and limbs. The four hunters retreated two paces.

<<Rise>> commanded the single voice.

Tlalok rose to his legs, pleased but defiant, head bobbing on neck to confirms his initial impression of the bowl from his new upright vantage. Beyond ebony trees, the tops of fog banks billowed under starlight. *How high was this place?* The onwatching Pact stood within those trees, eminently sophisticated in their still patterns; a gathering of court, Tlalok decided, advisors, witnesses, trusted seconds. A space, then the four hunters encircling Tlalok. And then, directly ahead . . .

What were they?

Four ascetic Pact squatted by the corners of a simple, wooden platform, their glowbuds darkened except for single blue dots between their eyes. Tlalok growled involuntarily at the mental discipline required to stay in such condition, teetering on the boundary between life and death. Also, their earpits were bound over with cloth to mute out the deceptive language of sound. Each of these Pact monks clutched a long rod, held upright in forepaws, butt end planted on the turf. Strings of black and white beads hung from the rods, cascading down onto the ground.

<<We are>>

<<The Judges>>

<<We judge>>

<<The Balance,>> they announced, using a minimum number of glowbuds to carry their words.

Between the Judges, in the center of the square platform, sat a Pact of no less interest to Tlalok. It seemed to be of an extreme age, as evidenced by sun-faded armor. Tlalok sensed it was near the end of its allotted years, but it did not give the impression of infirmity. Its limbs were thin, but in the way strong muscle is bereft of fat. Its movements were slow, but with the measured intent that comes from deep understanding. This compelling old Pact now lifted itself onto all four feet.

<<Kthulah, Keeper of the Roots of Wisdom, Radiance of the Pack of Gnosis, greets Pact face to face and on four feet.>>

Since Tlalok was already standing, he inclined his snout. <<Tlalok, avenger of Pact, bane of blank-ones, greets Kthulah.>>

The Judges thumbed their beads, counting individual black and white spheroids from one loop to another as Tlalok spoke. *Click, clack.*

Kthulah squinted at Tlalok. <<Avenger?>>

<<Purger of blank-ones,>> Tlalok responded.

Click, went the Judge's beads.

<<Fighter for Radiance,>> Tlalok added defiantly.

Click, tik.

<<And Balance leveler.>>

The Judges strobed disapproval.

<<The savage>>

<<Seeks to Balance the world>>

<<But cannot Balance>>

<<The head upon its shoulders!>>

Kthulah admonished hid prisoner. <<True Balance comes from

within. Seek not a rigid scale, Tlalok. Seek inner Balance, while the scales swing to and fro.>>

Tlalok snorted at such a ridiculous thought.

Tik, tik, tika, tik went white and black beads (mostly black).

<<Prophecy violator!>> the Judges accused.

Because he did not know what they were talking about, Tlalok snorted again.

Kthulah scrutinized Tlalok. <<Tlalok does not know the Prophecy.>> The old Pact nodded to the Judges. <<Speak the Prophecy.>>

The ascetic Khafra glared sanctimoniously at Tlalok, but obediently bowed their muzzles and fell into ceremonious rhythms.

<<In the time of Many Sorrows>>

<<Shall fall the Tears.>>

<<And the Tears shall bring>>

<<The Burning Heart of Night,>> the Judges intoned.

<<Every kit knows that much,>> Tlalok said defensively.

The Judges glowered more sternly, but continued.

<<Out of ignorance, Radiance>>

<<Out of arrogance, Death>>

<<Out of repentance, Pact>>

<<Out of Balance . . . Gamut.>>

Their words flashed brighter and quicker.

<<Radiance,>>

<<The Burning Heart shall consume! >>

<<The imBalanced,>>

<<The Burning Heart shall devour!>>

Now the assembled Pact joined the Judges with their own radiant voices.

<<Gather the Balanced>>

<<To the Burning Heart>>

<<Gather to the altar of Radiance>>

<<And preserve a piece of the light.>>

Suddenly Tlalok grasped what they meant—Burning Heart, altar of Radiance—they were talking about a column of fire, bursting out of the ocean and stabbing up at the stars themselves!

<<The False Radiance!>> he exclaimed. <<The Burning Heart is the False Radiance!>>

<<False Radiance?>> the Judges shrieked. Beads jangled out of carefully ordered positions. *Clatter!*

<<Radiance>>

<<Cannot>>

<<Be>>

<<False!>>

Tlalok hurried to explain. <<Tlalok thought so, too. But Tlalok has seen the False Radiance with his own eyes. Tlalok realizes now that is what the Pack of Gnosis calls the Burning Heart. Tlalok was at the Burning Heart. The great Radiance speaks not Truth. It speaks Corruption. Do not go to it! Many of Tlalok's pack perished listening to its false meaning!>>

Tlalok looked around the bowl. No one understood. Not a single sympathetic face. Not even Kthulah, who had treated Tlalok with some respect.

The Judges hurried to reorder their beads, refiguring Tlalok's tally. Many black beads added up. These they tied off into sub-loops—too many sub-loops. The Judges raised and pointed their rods at Tlalok.

<<The imBalancer>>

<<Must>>

<<Be>>

<<Balanced!>>

Agreement glittered through the glade.

<<Those who defile>>

<<Radiance>>

<<Must see Radiance>>

<<No more!>> the Judges decreed.

Tlalok could hardly believe the words, but the intent was clear. His guards turned inward, lips folding back from teeth, shoulders hunching, ready to spring. *They meant to blind him.* And they called Tlalok a savage! Tlalok remembered the airless, cavernous darkness of the hood and readied for a fighting leap. Pact did not kill Pact, but perhaps Tlalok might blind one or two of the miserable Judges before the hunters overcame him.

*   *   *

<<Wait!>> commanded Kthulah, staying the imminent blood-shed. <<Tlalok has violated Prophecy, imBalancing the Balanced. But even the imBalanced must have a say.>> Kthulah turned to Tlalok. <<What does Tlalok say?>>

Tlalok wanted to prepare well thought out, irrefutable words, but arguments flashed off of him, fueled, as so much of his existence, by fury. <<Blank-ones upset the Balance long ago, not Tlalok!>> he raged. <<That is what Tlalok says. Where Tlalok lives, under blank-one shadows, Balance is hard-won. Talk does not make Balance. Beads do not make Balance. *Action* makes Balance.>>

The Judges counted more beads.

Kthulah sighed. <<Action upsets the peace.>>

<<Peace?>> Tlalok sputtered. <<What peace?>>

Kthulah explained, patiently. <<Four upon four of years there has been peace between blank-ones and Pact.>>

<<There has?>> Tlalok flashed, dumbstruck that Kthulah could say such a thing.

Every Pact—Judges, onlookers, guards—glowed in agreement with Kthulah.

Tlalok flashed angrily. <<Tlalok has not seen this peace! Tlalok has seen fighting. Tlalok has seen suffering and servitude. Tlalok has seen bondmates and kits killed by blank-ones without fulfilling Pact. That is what Tlalok has seen. No peace. Only spilling blank-one blood can level the Balance now.>>

<<The wise Pact,>> the Judges lectured,

<<Retreats>>

<<From unwinnable>>

<<Battles.>>

Tlalok snarled. <<Retreat is for cowards.>>

The onlooking Pact shifted uneasily.

<<Retreat,>> Kthulah explained evenly, <<keeps the Pack of Gnosis safe from suffering and servitude, keeps safe bondmates and kits from blank-ones. There is Balance. There is peace.>>

<<False Balance, false peace!>> Tlalok argued. <<The Pack of Gnosis retreats while Tlalok's pack cries and bleeds! The Pack of

Gnosis leeches off the bravery of others. Tlalok thinks the Pack of Gnosis is afraid to fight, afraid of blank-ones!>>

Glowbuds prickled in ire along the crest of Kthulah's shoulders. <<The Pack of Gnosis is not afraid. The Pack of Gnosis can kill blank-ones any time it chooses.>>

<<Tlalok does not believe it.>>

Tlalok began to see colors of shame on Kthulah and the assembled Pact.

<<The Pack of Gnosis battled many years,>> the old Pact sighed. <<Too great were the losses. Kthulah had to think of the Roots. Kthulah had to think of the Prophecy. Much good has come from retreat, but . . .>> Kthulah looked up at the stained glass leaves, his wizened features pained. <<Kthulah has regrets, too.>>

The Judges thumbed beads in agitation now, reordering some of their count.

<<Kthulah regrets that some stayed in the Fringe when most retreated. Kthulah regrets that many who stayed were the fiercest and the bravest—as Kthulah now sees Tlalok is fierce and brave, as Kthulah once thought he was. . . . Now Kthulah sees the savagery he has created.>> Kthulah looked from one Judge to another. <<What says the tally now?>>

More agitated thumbing of beads. Many spheroids changed places as the monks tied off loops of white. Consternation crossed their glowbuds. Tlalok was surprised how much care they devoted to each swapping of white for black—considering how strongly they had pressed earlier for his blinding. Their claws stopped moving. Bead clatter ceased. The Judges blinked numbly.

<<The tally,>> they admitted,
<<Is even.>>
<<Kthulah must decide>>
<<The fate of the savage.>>

Kthulah pondered long and hard, shifting from one uncomfortable position to another on the wooden platform, as if a different vantage would make his decision easier, but none of the positions made a difference. Finally, solemnly, he spoke, <<Kthulah must live with the savages he makes. *It is decided.*>>

<<It is decided,>> the Judges echoed, reverently loosening the

knots of Tlalok's tally and shaking the white and black beads back to starting positions. They sat back, shining together the white light that Tlalok had seen before.

<<Four upon four?>> they asked themselves.

<<No! Four upon four upon four!>> they decided, turning on Kthulah. They raised their rods high overhead and, one at a time, swung powerful blows down on Kthulah's back. *Thwak, thwak, thwak, thwak.* Tlalok saw that it hurt, even through Kthulah's plated hide. Kthulah's glowbuds welled up angrily, but only the merest hint of pain twisted his face. After a count of sixty-four the Judges reverted to rest positions, heads bowed, paws clasped on staves held upright before them.

<<Decision>>

<<Is punished.>>

<<The Balance>>

<<Is conserved.>>

Kthulah noted the horror on Tlalok's face. <<Do not be distraught, savage Tlalok,>> Kthulah said weakly. <<Watch and grow wise. A leader must, above all, keep within Balance. Power corrupts. But a leader must use power. It is a contradiction.>> Kthulah wiped spittle from his ancient lips. <<By definition, a desirable leader must not desire to wield power, lest that leader become imBalanced and corrupt. Such a leader is ineffective. But those who do desire to wield power are necessarily unfit to lead. Therefore,>> Kthulah pointed to the Judges, <<Kthulah must be purified of desire after each decision or become intoxicated with power. Only this way can Balance be maintained.>>

Tlalok was aghast.

<<The savage of Kthulah's making does not comprehend,>> Kthulah observed to himself. <<But he will.>>

<<What,>> asked the Judges,

<<Will Kthulah do>>

<<With his>>

<<Savage?>>

Kthulah did not hesitate. <<Many things upset the Balance, which, in time, right themselves.>>

<<Kthulah>>

<<Will grant>>
<<The savage>>
<<Time?>>

Kthulah bowed to Tlalok. <<Go now Tlalok, with your pack of fierce and brave, and kill those blank-ones who must be killed—as perhaps Kthulah should have killed many seasons ago.>>

XXVIII

Earlier that same night.

Karr rode a rescue cage down the shaft of dusty light. The Guard squad dropped past him, rappelling with speed and military precision down thin filament cables. Human and Khafra heads peered at them from the jagged opening above.

"Watch the speed on that cage," Toliver's voice buzzed in Karr's headset.

Karr's cage, already descending slowly, slowed even more.

Karr was quite capable of rappelling down the cables and had said so, but the Guards insisted on reconnoitering the bottom first. Karr chewed his cheek impatiently as the Guards touched down. Coaxial searchbeams stabbed out from pulse-rifles into the surrounding darkness, sweeping shadows around the bright patch below.

"No threat," Toliver declared shortly.

A winch whined from above and Karr's cage picked up speed as the Guards spread out. The floor was concave under their searchbeams, gently rising as they moved out from center. Karr's cage clattered onto a heap of recently fallen rubble.

"That's good," Karr transmitted. The cable stopped unreeling. Gattler in hand, he hopped out and slid down the scree to a patch of yellow cobblestones. "Looks like the stuff you colonists make roads out of." Karr crouched and ran his fingers over the nodules. "And it's growing in a hexagonal pattern, like it does back at your Enclave."

"Doesn't mean anything," Jenette transmitted. "That's how it grows naturally."

Karr moved out of the patch of light, which was formed by spotlights shining through the opening above. He kicked away shell-like shards, which covered most of the floor. "Does it also grow naturally in long roadways five yards wide?"

"No."

Karr followed the upward slope of pavement, flanked by Guards alert for any sign of trouble. More interesting sights appeared as his eyes adjusted to the gloom. They were in a cavern, a squat bubble one hundred yards across. The tangled-root floor bent up into walls and all the way around, curving into the ceiling. As they neared those walls, the Guards' searchbeams began to pick out haunted shapes.

Karr whistled.

"No way . . ." Liberty whispered in her husky way, mouth hanging open. "Ah shit."

The com-channel came alive with voices.

"What is it?" Jenette asked.

"Is anyone injured?" Marsh piped in at the same time. "We can't see your lights anymore."

"Negative," Toliver reported. "No casualties. We are uninjured."

Searchbeams flicked over rectangular shapes, collapsed like houses of cards and half-buried in the walls and floor of the cavity. Karr recognized the material immediately: ceramite, that ever-present building block of humankind in space. Empty windows stared back from man-made ceramite panels like blind eyes, doorways rimmed in ceramite gaped like tormented mouths.

"Nice job dropping that scanner, Dr. Bigelow," said Karr.

"Oh yes?" came the scientist's transmitted voice. "Really?"

"Really. You found the missing colony."

The rescue cage shuttled up and down, first bringing humans, then reluctant domestics, who did not like the idea of *underground* at all. Bronte had to be pulled from the rescue cage.

"No, no," Bronte whimpered, claws digging in. "Too dark, too dark."

Crash, when it was his turn, was no more eager. "Underground bad. Too dark."

"That's what you have glowbuds for," Dr. Marsh chided. The young doctor pulled on Crash's backpack straps, to no avail. "Now come on out."

Crash shook his low slung head. "Unh-uuhh."

In the end no human or humans could move the resisting alien—the harder they pulled, the harder Crash dug in—and only a fishy-smelling cookie eventually enticed him out. Arrou came down last, his spherical eyes peering uncertainly into the great, dim space.

"Don't even think about it," Jenette hissed as he opened his mouth to object. "You are far too smart for that."

"Urrr?" the alien rumbled, with a distinct *who me?* expression.

"Yes, you. Out."

Against his better judgment, Arrou began to slink out of the cage, but he stopped halfway, rethinking. His head tipped hopefully.

"Cookie?"

Jenette planted her fists on her hips. "Out!"

Arrou and Jenette joined those huddling on the yellow pavement. Arrou, Crash, and Bronte sniffed around, their four-legged forms lit up like green-white specters among the lonely structures.

"Nothing?" Karr asked Bigelow, who was turning slowly, scanning with his detecting device.

"No," the scientist admitted.

At which point Skutch stepped up and pulled out a detector of his own, a small rod with lines of lights along its long axis. "This one keys on atmospheric traces of explosives, as opposed to radiant energy. Setting to C-55 now." Skutch gave the rod a twist and watched. Karr waited hopefully, Bigelow leaned over the explosive expert's shoulder to watch. The device failed to react. Skutch shrugged and pressed a test stud, which caused the rod to light up and bleep. "The instrument is reading correctly," he decided. "There just isn't anything to detect."

"Same here," Bigelow sighed.

Skutch clipped his detector onto the barrel of his pulse-rifle.

Karr followed the yellow roadway through scattered ruins. The others fanned out, both repelled and attracted to the foreboding structures, and staying close to their domestics. Khafra glowbuds couldn't match searchbeams for range, but they provided good illumination a full three hundred and sixty degrees around them, and they were far better than the civilian issue flashlights that the unarmed humans carried.

Jenette peeked into a doorway. The interior was dark and musty. Arrou poked his nose in too, bringing his light with him. The door itself was nowhere in evidence, perhaps buried in the overgrown ghutzu roots which covered all of the floor and most of the back wall of the room, like blown sand. There was no sign of the building's contents, or what purpose it had served. It was small, like all the structures in the cavity, and neither it nor any of the others looked very important to Jenette.

She turned to a clatter behind her. Crash, laden with medical supplies, had tripped over a fallen wall panel.

Edgy, Bronte looked down her muzzle at him. "Fumblefoot."

"Snooty-tootie," Crash retorted, just as nervous. He slipped again as he tried to get up.

Bronte extended a paw. "Lickslobber."

"Smooch-butt," said Crash, accepting the help.

"Arrou," Karr called from where the yellow road dead-ended into a curving wall, "can you give me a light?"

Arrou trotted over and glowed.

Karr examined the surface. It appeared smooth from the distance, but was actually composed of interwoven roots, dead and hardened like everything else on Coffin Island. Arrou pawed at it. Little came free, even under his strong talons.

Jenette and the others came up behind Karr and stood quietly in the eerie cavity, waiting for his next move.

Karr retreated ten paces from the wall, raised the Gattler and thumbed its selector knob to a cutting beam, low power, wide dispersion. Chrome barrels and ammunition globes spun. He pulled the trigger. A cutting beam thrummed, searing a hole two yards across and five deep. Karr walked the beam forward. The Guards kept pace, shining searchbeams into the deepening tunnel. A hot wind roared back at them, driving shattered bits of root into every-one's faces. Ten feet, twenty feet, the borehole grew deeper. Karr crouched, entering the new passage, but didn't stop cutting until the first ragged signs of a breakthrough.

The Guards eyed the Gattler with respect as Karr released the trigger.

"AB-5 Ruger?" Toliver asked.

"AB-8 Colt & Krupp," Karr replied.

"The latest model?" asked Grubb.

"As of thirty-seven years ago," said Karr, preoccupied with peering through the break. Of course he had the latest model; he was a Pilot. Every time Karr put in at a major world, decades had elapsed during which technology advanced; *Long Reach* got refit-ted, and Karr got new equipment.

"What's her beam capacity?" asked Toliver.

"At full power, there's enough charge to burn through five yards of solid granite a second."

Toliver nodded appreciatively, no doubt thinking of bloodier applications for the medical tool.

"That's almost as good as one of these babies," Skutch said, patting a series of grenade-sized explosives that hung from his belt. "C-23 proportional charges. They're designed around a prin-cipal similar to the C-55 core-boring warhead, but on a smaller, friendlier scale. And they're fully adjustable, from blowing up a few Ferals, right on up to cutting through twenty yards of rein-forced plasteel."

Karr looked up. "What about sixty feet of root overburden?" he asked.

"Not a problem," Skutch said, catching Karr's train of thought. "You find the warheads and I'll blast a hole down to them, without so much as putting a scratch on their casings."

"Perhaps your proportional charges will be useful," Karr al-lowed.

Skutch grinned. "In a pinch they're pretty good for fishing, too. No hook or net required. Just lob one in the water and, *BOOM*, take your pick from what floats up."

"The New Ascension lure," Liberty quipped.

Karr lost interest in the banter and started to break out of the tunnel, but the Guards stepped in the way.

"Is this really necessary?" Karr hissed to Jenette as they insisted on preceding him.

"Yes," said Jenette.

"This is why I prefer to work alone," Karr protested. "A fully-trained Pilot needs no chaperoning."

Jenette sighed. "Just let them do their job, okay?"

Weapons ready, the Guards kicked through the last bits of root at the passage end. Musty air wafted from the opening as they scrambled out of the borehole into a cavern with a lower ceiling, but which was wider than the first. At the okay from Toliver, Karr crawled out and followed the yellow road as it emerged from the wall and lead on into a crowded ghost town. Larger and more numerous structures occupied that second cavity, some disappearing into the ghutzu root like sinking ships. Most were in various states of collapse, their innards strewn across the ground. All sorts of human items were visible under an ivy-like tangle of dead roots, which covered everything like snow on a trash heap.

They ambled through the wreckage.

The New Ascension natives swallowed or fidgeted, but said nothing.

Karr tried not to let what he saw bother him, as was proper for a Pilot, but the Coffin Island ghost town was a textbook example of a failed colony. Pilot Lindal Karr had not seeded it, but given a slightly different set of random events he easily might have. The dreamers ferried in *Long Reach* had always been numbers to Karr; execute the mission, get the job done. If one or two percent of dreamers died in transit, that was within tolerable limits. If a couple of colonies failed out of each six or seven seeded, that was unfortunate necessity. The greater destiny of humanity lay in the stars. Only the big numbers counted. Here, however, personal possessions spilled from residence blocks: holos of families, inscribed jewelry, toys, souvenirs from planets Karr didn't recognize. Evidence of individual hopes and aspirations. Evidence of broken dreams. And numbers weren't supposed to have dreams.

It was an unsettling sight, even for a Pilot.

The roadwort path was twisted by whatever process had sunk it into the island. Other roads crossed it at odd intervals, disappearing into narrow alleys or blocked altogether where structures had collapsed down on them.

"Just, um, call out if you see a landmark," Bigelow said, trying to make sense of their position on the map-reader in his left hand while also keeping an eye on the detector in his right hand.

The gaping windows and hungry doors seemed endless. The humans poked into ruins as they went, but found no useful information. After some time, Arrou began to lag behind. Jenette dropped back to him as he stood, head cocked, focusing his earpits behind the party.

"What is it?" she asked.

"Urrkurrkurrk. Not sure. Tapping noise?"

Jenette tried to listen in the intimidating gloom, but her human ears were not sensitive enough. "I don't hear anything."

"Gone now," Arrou admitted.

They hurried to catch up. The expedition pressed deeper into the second cavern, Arrou still straining to hear behind them. After a few tight twists of the road, he froze at the intersection of a descending side street. Annoyed polka-dot patterns bristled on his back.

"Rrrrrrrr," he grumbled. "Tapping. Like noise in engine. Teases, then hides. Sneaky." His head turned, as if tracking the sound. His patterns cycled angrily. "Rrrrrr. Not like."

Again Jenette tried to listen. "I still don't hear—"

Then Jenette heard it, a dry scraping noise echoed up from below. *Kekitekitekitek.*

"Rrrrrrrr!"

"Arrou, wait!" Jenette hissed as the alien suddenly bounded down the slope. His glowing form disappeared behind a distant building as Karr and the others came over. "I couldn't stop him," she explained. "He just ran off."

A distant yelp sounded.

Moments later, Arrou came tearing around the rubble and back up the hill. "Big bug, big bug!" Chaotic orange and blue slashes strobed across his glowbuds. "Big bug!"

"Calm down," Jenette said as he made it to the top.

"Big bug!" Arrou plopped down on his haunches and held his forepaws a yard apart to show scale. "Many legs. Big teeth. *Raaagh!*" He pantomimed chomping mandibles with his talons, then held up a forepaw. "Bit Arrou."

Arrou's wrist was swollen.

At first there had been nervous chuckles at Arrou's story—New Ascension had many different species of large buzzers and most were harmless—but now those died off and Dr. Marsh was suddenly digging through medikits strapped to Crash's back. New Ascension neurotoxins worked *very* fast.

"Worms in me, worms in me," Arrou fretted.

"Calm down. It's all right," Jenette repeated. Feral Khafra were highly resistant to neurotoxin, thanks to their yearly exchange of immune venom with bondmates, but domestics were not—and they knew it. She wrapped an arm around his hulking, shaking shoulders. "It's going to be all right. There are no worms in you." *There were worms in her, but not in Arrou.* Gulping, Jenette concentrated on calming her friend. "Dr. Marsh will take care of the poison."

Marsh grasped Arrou's forearm and turned it under a flashlight. "Hold still. No signs of trauma to the inner skin. Slight abrasions of the lateral armor, probably bite marks. No creeping necrosis. Slight swelling." She bent Arrou's wrist. "Pain?"

"No. Numb."

"I said hold still," Marsh admonished.

"Can't stop," Arrou said with worried eyes as his limb twitched. "Not doing."

"Interesting," Marsh hummed. "Involuntary nerve stimulation. Haven't observed that before." She considered the rest of Arrou. "You're a big one aren't you?" Marsh pulled a handful of transparent pouches out of her supplies. Each had two compartments, one filled with red fluid and one filled with green. They came in several different sizes. "Three hundred and fifty pounds?" she estimated.

"Four ten," said Jenette.

Marsh selected the largest pouch.

"Biomorphic fungi," she explained to Karr. "Another failed cure for Scourge, but it eats neurotoxin at a phenomenal rate." She gave the pouch a sharp shake. The barrier between the red and green fluids burst. "Just mix in catalyst and apply." Marsh removed a protective sheet from one side and applied the exposed sticky back to Arrou's forearm. "Osmosis does the rest.

"Now stay still," she warned Arrou. "This'll hit you pretty fast. You may feel warm, but that's normal. Tell me if you feel any constriction—tightness—in your chest."

Everyone took a break in the oppressive silence, sitting next to or leaning against one of the many vine-covered walls.

"That was not smart," Jenette said, "running off and getting bit by a strange buzzer."

Arrou hung his head apologetically. "Not see. Buzzer comes out of hole in wall."

After that remark the expedition members continued to wait, but they stood up and clustered together. The walls were riddled with many dark holes.

Searchbeams lanced through an archway. Guards, and then the rest of the expedition members, followed the tactical lights into a long forgotten storage yard. The soldiers' eyes scanned nests of holes around the bottom of perimeter walls and under rows of chemical tanks.

The place was in shambles.

Dry particulate matter spilled onto the floor from broken pipes. Three kinds of impressions showed in the loose material: one set of Khafra paws running in, a set of Khafra paws bounding out, and many skittering lines of tiny imprints—some even over Arrou's tracks.

Arrou pointed. "Saw buzzer at back."

The Guards split up and took separate aisles between the towering tanks, working to the rear as Arrou indicated. The Searchbeams grew smaller, sweeping back and forth or jabbing into holes and crevices.

"Don't see anything," Toliver's voice came over the comsets.

"Something hungry chewed through this ceramite," Skutch observed from the far end.

"Yeah," Toliver acknowledged, "but judging from the size of these prints, it was small."

Jenette turned to Arrou, who had no comset to listen to the conversation with. "Where's the big bug?"

"Not know," Arrou admitted, his head sweeping around suspiciously. "Was here. Big bug. *Raaaaagh*." Again he pantomimed large mandibles biting, as if that would bring the creature into the open.

"Did you catch that?" Jenette asked into her headset.

"Yes," Toliver answered. "We'll stay vigilant, but there's nothing here now."

Karr and the non-military expedition members advanced.

"Hey," called Liberty from a couple aisles over. "I found bones."

"This damn island is nothing but bones," Jenette grumbled.

"Yes ma'am," Liberty agreed, "but this is a *skeleton*."

Humans and domestics converged on a narrow, dim aisle. Jenette ran her fingers over many rents in the chemical tanks to either side; always there were four conspicuous gashes in parallel, like those made by Khafra claws. And there were also telltale spider-web ripples on the tank walls nearby those gashes.

"Pulse-rifle hits?" Karr wondered.

Jenette nodded morbidly.

"Look at this," Liberty said as they arrived. She brushed debris off a half-buried ribcage. Bits of desiccated flesh held the bones together.

Dr. Marsh joined Liberty at the remains. Together they pried at a bullet-shaped skull. It came free, with another strange skull impaled on the teeth of its many radial jaws. Cancerous nodules contorted the second skull like knots on a sickly tree.

"Homo sapiens," Marsh announced.

Karr squinted at the repulsive object. "That?"

Marsh held the specimen next to Karr's head for comparison. "You see, it's the right size."

"I don't get it," Karr said. "How can that be human?"

"That's what Scourge does to bones," Jenette said quietly.

"Ugh," said Bigelow, hastening away from the grisly sight.

"Oh, this is nothing," Marsh said, examining the remains with clinical detachment. "What it does to living tissue is far more severe."

Jenette's hand instinctively went to the glands in her neck. She began to sweat in the cool underground air.

Many more bones were mixed together in the dust. They painted a picture. One quadruped and one biped skeleton were locked together, still in combat. The quadruped's teeth had pierced the biped's skull, and a large blast hole—presumably caused by a pulse-rifle—ripped through the quadruped's ribs.

Bigelow, who had no stomach for such unpleasantries, walked down an aisle hoping to get a C-55 reading with his detector. As he neared the far end of the yard, he abruptly stopped and straightened in the dark.

"That's not funny," he said, an indignant hand going to his buttocks.

"What not funny?" asked Bronte, who had gone ahead to where Guardsman Skutch stood in an archway at the rear of the yard.

Bigelow turned around. There was no one in sight, no practical joker, no mischievous domestic—nothing that could explain the distinct sensation that someone had just pinched him on the butt.

"Problems?" asked Skutch.

"Never mind," said Bigelow, hurrying to join the Guard. "My mind is beginning to play tricks on me."

"Go figure," said Skutch, rolling his eyes at the glum surroundings.

They exited the storage yard.

Behind them in the shadows, a deeper shadow moved.

"Nice skin," it hissed.

XXX

Action causes more trouble than thought.

—the private journals of Olin Tesla

"Check it out," said Skutch.

"Oooh," said Bigelow.

Karr followed the voices out into a back alley. A narrow strip of roadwort bent sharply down, pulled by the weight of a sinking dome, which was the cause of the exclamations. The structure glittered like mother-of-pearl under Skutch's searchbeam. As the rest of the colonists followed Karr, they, too, stared at the rosy pearl.

"What is it?" asked Jenette.

"N253-G pleasure-drome," Karr answered.

"A pleasure-drome?" Liberty asked, puzzled.

"Standard colony issue," said Karr. As a Pilot had he off-loaded one with every colony seeded—disassembled of course, but he recognized the parts.

The locals shared looks of confusion.

"A *relaxation* center," Jenette finally said, remembering that her father disapproved of the impure connotations of the structure's common name.

"A meditation mosque, a brain brothel," Karr said, rattling off a few slang terms from other planets. "A twitch palace."

"A *pleasure-drome,*" Bigelow said with glassy eyes, "by any other name would smell as sweet." He crept forward and caressed the burnished half sphere. "Now this is stylish."

"More than stylish," said Karr. "It's a landmark."

"Oh, yes, of course," the large man said, pulling out his map-reader. Everyone crowded around. "We're here." He pointed out the pleasure-drome, offset a few blocks from Coffin Island's center on the old map. "But we still don't know where the bunker is."

Karr looked around. They were at the lowest point of the cavern, where its floor seemed to have been pulled down by the pleasure-drome. Root matter nearby was stretched and cracked by the weight of the large structure. "It's sinking," he decided.

Jenette followed his train of thought. "It looks like the larger, denser structures are sinking faster than the smaller, lighter ones."

"Mmmm," said Bigelow, gazing again at the wondrous pleasure-drome. "And a munitions bunker would be particularly heavy. Much heavier by volume than a pleasure-drome, certainly."

Karr looked at the map-reader, cross-referenced the armory's last mapped position in relation to the pleasure-drome, aimed the Gattler at a forty-five degree angle down, and began to bore a descending tunnel into Coffin Island.

Karr bored a series of tunnels down through consecutive caverns until one came out on level ground. Then, the explorers searched for the elusive bunker. The deeper they burrowed, the larger the structures became and the more morbid the caverns became. Soot charred many crumpled buildings. Some of the prefab sections were shattered, as if blown out from the inside. Pulse-rifle hits were peppered across walls.

Scourge-twisted skeletons littered the ruins. Jenette tried not to look at the reminders of her own probable demise, but that proved impossible. Instead, she tried to focus on the other things around her and not the mutilations caused by the pathogen inside her own body. Many of the skeletons were still clothed. Man-made fabrics had not decayed after nearly two decades. However, she could not find a single garment without ragged slashes and accompanying pools of red-brown stain. Broken pulse-rifles, mauler pistols, quiver-shivs bayonets, and other improvised weaponry lay amidst the bones. And for every human skeleton there were many Khafra skeletons.

The Ferals had attacked ferociously after the Great Betrayal.

Karr kept the Gattler thrumming, burning through a series of de-

scending cavities and a lot of ghutzu root without locating another
landmark. Bigelow periodically scanned for signs of the warheads,
but came up empty; either they were not degrading (impossible, he
said), blocked from his sensors by too much root mass, or gone;
Skutch's scanner also read nothing. Headway was slow and made
even slower by Corporal Toliver's insistence on double-checking
every step Karr wished to make. Although the soldiers were rapid
and efficient, Karr railed at the wasted time. The Guards picked up
on his impatience and tried to hurry, but that only increased everyone's tension.

"You are not very good at working with other people," Jenette
scolded quietly.

"Why would I be?" Karr asked in all seriousness. *"Teamwork*
and *trust* are four letter words to a Pilot."

"You are seriously messed up," Jenette said.

"I suppose I am," Karr agreed. After that he gritted his teeth and
tried, not very successfully, to accommodate his overprotective ret-
inue.

Not very much later, Karr felt the resistance of the ghutzu burning under the cutting beam slacken, but instead of the expected
usual draft of musty air wafting out of the new tunnel, a torrent of
water geysered back at the humans and domestics. The stream was
relatively small, but powerful, and knocked several unprepared humans off their feet. Karr himself slipped back into Arrou, who dug
in with all the claws on all four of his paws. Leaning against the
alien, Karr grasped the Gattler's now-slippery selector knob and
twisted. Chrome barrels whirled and he sprayed surgical adhesive
into the breach. In no time at all the flow of water was staunched.
There were no injuries, only wet clothes, but the incident effectively served to reignite the group's fears about tunneling so far
down into the dead island.

"Must have cut into one of those crevices we saw on the surface," Karr remarked, as the water slowly seeped away.

"Or the ocean," Mok mumbled nervously as the expedition
members scrambled to their feet.

"Stuff it, Mok," Toliver ordered.

Skutch dipped a finger into a puddle of the water and tasted it. He frowned. "Not the ocean. Not salty. Just collected rain water."

"Yeah," said Mok, "but when's it going to *get* salty? We're a long way down. We'll be underwater soon. And what happens if that—" Mok gestured furtively at Karr's Gattler, "—cuts through to the ocean? No glue shooter is going to stop the weight of the ocean from pouring in and drowning us!"

"I said stuff it!" Toliver snapped at Mok, but the damage was done. Humans and domestics, who were not warm to the idea of being underground in the first place, began looking around as if the walls of the passage might crush in on them at any moment.

Karr tried to picture the pattern of crevices on the surface in relation to where the lifter had set down. As far as he could remember they had been at least half a kiloyard distant in any direction, so if he was breaking through into a crevice, he was wandering too far afield from the last recorded location of the munitions bunker. When Karr resumed tunneling with the Gattler, he kept the pattern to a tight spiral, twisting ever deeper toward the island's center. Karr was fairly confident they would not breach through into any more pockets of water, but the others were not so sure and for a while nobody spoke much.

Eventually, Karr burned through a section of ceramite into the upper end of a different sort of cavity. Unlike the previous convex caverns, this space was rectangular and the floor sloped down at a very steep angle.

Karr and the Guards hopped down from the entry hole.

Menacing shapes rose up from the sloping floor and loomed overhead, sporting appendages tipped with pincers and claws and vise-like mouths. Oily blood seeped from metal-wrapped cables. The humans edged down the incline between the large shapes. Arrou and the domestics skittered down the hard, slick surface, claws finding no purchase.

Jenette slipped and slid down the slope, thudding with a woof against a giant shape. Arrou hurried down to her and helped her to her feet. She was dirty and dusty but none the worse for the wear.

"I know where we are," she declared suddenly, shining her

flashlight up at a multi-armed giant, whose arms seemed poised to
snatch her up. "This is the robotic factory!"

Searchbeams zigzagged over machined surfaces. Arrou nosed
curiously, if suspiciously, around dusty control panels and power
conduits. The looming shapes were assembly robots, set in lines or
clusters and bearing all manner of appendages from huge lifting
claws down to tiny dexterous arms with even tinier pincers like for-
ceps and microwelders designed for precision work. Roots, grown
in from the building's broken windows, clogged joints and hy-
draulic hoses, but the factory was largely intact.

"What we wouldn't give to get this back to the Enclave," Jenette
wondered, all their other troubles temporarily forgotten. "No more
shortages. No more patching and repatching broken equipment."

"*New* things," agreed Marsh dreamily.

As they slid down from one shadowy titan to the next, Jenette
sidled up to Karr. "Could your heavy lifter transport this factory?"

"Most likely," Karr admitted, skidding to the bottom where the
angled floor made a v-shape meeting a wall. Two large sliding
doors hung askew on tracks in the tilted wall. "Assuming the pieces
could somehow be brought to the surface."

"That's a process that *will* need to be figured out," Jenette said.
"Any deeper than this and we'll need a submarine to recover the
C-55s."

"I know," Karr fretted. He had been hoping to find the munitions
bunker at a relatively shallow depth, use Skutch's explosives to
blow off the overburden and then simply hoist the core-boring warheads out with the heavy lifter, but that plan didn't seem very plau-
sible anymore.

Karr dropped through a crack between the sliding doors and
found himself in a small cavity. In its center lay a wrecked robotic
crane.

A shrill *bleeping* sounded from the factory behind him.

"Hey," said Skutch. "My detector's going nuts."

"That's funny," said Bigelow. "Mine reads zero."

Karr edged forward, squeezing around the crane to get a look at
the back of the small space, and came face to face with a very large
plasteel door, set in a reinforced plasteel wall, and with a large

locking wheel in the center. An increasingly fast-paced bleeping alerted Karr to the fact that Skutch and the others had squeezed up behind him.

"Jackpot!" said the explosives expert.

"Tell me what you see!" Bigelow called from behind them. "These factory doors are too tightly closed for me to pass through."

Karr described the scene.

"That certainly sounds like the munitions bunker," Bigelow called back. "I wonder why I'm not getting any readings on my scanner?"

Despite the conflicting readings on the two sensors, Karr began to feel excited. He and the Guards spun the locking wheel and were able to heave the door open a few feet before it jammed on over-hanging ghutzu growth. Searchbeams stabbed in, glancing off of upright torpedo shapes in a dark, cube-shaped room. Skutch went in alone for a closer examination. He clicked off his screaming detector as he neared one of the torpedo forms.

"Yup, these are C-55s all right. Looks like three, six, nine . . . at least twenty-four." Skutch whistled. "That's enough to bore a thermal mine straight through the planet's core and out the other side *and* snuff out the fire over your ship." Karr sensed that the Guard might be exaggerating a little, but was too pleased at that moment to care much, that is, until the tone of Skutch's voice changed. "Oh . . . never mind." For some reason, the Guard then leaned into one of the teardrop shapes and pushed.

Karr, and everyone around him, tensed as the baby whale-sized munition toppled with a loud clang, but no explosion followed, only a puff of dust rose into the air.

Hutch motioned them in.

Karr and the others entered. The combined light of searchbeams and Khafra illuminated a disappointing scene. The bunker was filled with C-55s and a host of smaller explosive devices, with all manner of differing shapes and intended purposes, but they might as well have been stuffed animals for all the use they could now serve.

Skutch pointed to the end of the toppled C-55. "Warhead's missing," he said, indicating where the bomb's tip should have been. "The propulsion system is intact, but there is no bam-bam."

As quickly as Karr's hopes had been raised, they were dashed. Further scrutiny revealed that all the warheads, detonators, and explosive charges had been removed from all of the munitions in the armory. Anything that could explode, engulf, or ignite had been removed, hollowed out, or chewed to pieces.

"Big bugs," said Arrou.

"Big bugs that can lock and unlock blast doors," Dr. Marsh observed nervously.

"Something has gone to great lengths to disarm this stockpile," Jenette agreed. She turned to Karr. "What do we do now?"

"I don't know," Karr admitted glumly. "Are there other bunkers?"

Skutch shook his head. "There were, but they were evacuated. And, anyway, this was the only stockpile of C55s."

Karr kicked angrily at a pile of chewed-up explosive matter. "Are we agreed that the warheads are not present?"

Skutch looked around, nodding. "Yes."

"Then we will just have to keep searching, and find them, even if we have to disintegrate this island foot by cubic foot."

None of the others seemed happy at that prospect, but they did not get a chance to protest, because at that moment, Dr. Bigelow's voice echoed down from the robotic factory.

"That's not funny!"

"Who's he talking to?" asked Guardsman Grubb.

No one knew. Jenette did a quick head count. Aside from Bigelow, everyone else was in the bunker.

"I have had enough of this. I demand to know who—oh shit!"

Bigelow screamed. The sound then trailed away into the distance.

"Dr. Bigelow's in trouble!" said Jenette.

All at once, there was a mad rush out of the bunker, around the wrecked crane, and back to the factory doors. Too many people tried to shove through the narrow crack. Jenette only just managed to poke her head through and look around. Two shadowy *things* were dragging Dr. Bigelow away, scuttling deeper into the darkness at one edge of the inclined factory floor. One of the things was human-pink, like Karr, one human-tan, like Marsh. But no human Jenette had ever seen moved that way, first upright, then on all fours, then upright again.

"Something's got him!" she yelled to the others.

"Clear the door, Consul!" Toliver barked. "Move through!"

Jenette squirmed into the factory, but Guards and domestics blocked up the narrow crack in their haste to pass through behind her.

"Get out of the way!" Toliver ordered, to no effect.

"Must go! Must chase!" the panicked voice of Bronte moaned from behind the corporal.

The confusion continued. Seconds dragged by, seeming like hours.

"EVERYBODY DOWN!" a voice suddenly yelled.

Jenette heard the clatter of weapons and bodies hitting the deck and then, abruptly, a two-yard circle of factory door began to glow bright red beside Jenette. The ceramite sucked up a prodigious amount of heat being thrown at it. Finally, it vaporized, revealing a bunch of humans and domestics crouched on the ground, and Karr standing upright behind them, grim faced, with the Gattler in his hands. An instant later domestics sprang up from the ground and through the hole. Toliver and the Guards followed the aliens. Marsh and Karr came last.

The mob rushed along the angled factory floor. Bronte tried to bound ahead, her fear of the underground forgotten in her concern for Bigelow, but for once the quadrupeds were at a disadvantage. Rubbery soled human boots gripped the slick surface better than claws. Crash repeatedly skittered down into the v-shape where the sloping floor met the wall.

Guardsman Mok scrambled up a flow of roots that cascaded around a robot base. His searchbeam slashed across towering machines but did not locate the kidnapped scientist. "I don't see him!"

Liberty climbed up beside Mok, her weapon also slashing from side to side. "Dr. Bigelow! Dr. Bigelow!" she called on the comset. "Do you know where you are?"

There were a few words, cut short by static, and then silence.

"Must find! Must save!" Bronte moaned.

"Quiet, everyone!" Toliver ordered. Bigelow's cries echoed chaotically in the otherwise silent factory. The humans were confused.

Except for Jenette. "Arrou" she asked, "which way?"

Arrou's earpits swiveled, then locked. The other domestics, calmed by his capable demeanor, did the same, then they sprinted off, following Arrou as he leapt from one robot base to another. They dove through a hole chewed in the far factory wall and raced out into a series of interlocking caverns.

Bigelow's cries were louder there.

"That way!" Jenette said, coming out of the factory as the domestics took off, finding plenty of purchase for their claws in the rough ghutzu.

"Go, go, go!" yelled Toliver.

The pursuit wound through a series of bubble-shaped grottos, Bigelow's abductors always managing to stay one turn ahead and out of sight. Domestics careened around a corner where two grottos met. By the time the humans caught up, the aliens were clustered at the far end. Bronte was poking her head into a tower of steel lattice that slanted down out of the grotto's ceiling and stabbed further down into its floor.

"Colony beacon support strut," Karr announced before any of the colonists could ask what it was. There would be three other struts buried somewhere in the roots and, presumably, a parabolic dish three hundred yards in diameter, which they were designed to support.

"Bigelow, Bigelow!" Bronte called as the domestics bolted down a shaft formed by the three inner sides of the beacon strut.

The humans arrived and looked in. Above, overgrown roots blocked the inside of the strut. Below, the shaft descended as far as searchbeams could penetrate into the rotting bowels of Coffin Island. A few faint human cries echoed up from below the domestics, who were still visible in the Guard's searchbeams, climbing down spider-like by digging in with their talons.

After a second or two, the human cries stopped.

The Guards immediately started to rig themselves to a line.

"I'm not staying up here," Jenette said, as Toliver suggested the Guards continue pursuit alone. "Not with *things* coming out of the walls and grabbing people."

"Me neither," said Marsh.

"All right," Toliver acquiesced. "Clip on." He attached a descender rig to the each of their belts and set the tension to high. "If it gets too hairy for you, just clamp down on this hand brake and stay put."

Karr attached his own descender rig, quietly and efficiently. Toliver checked and found nothing wrong with his setup.

When everybody was secured to the line, the descent began. Guards went first, walking down the walls face down and with weapons ready. Karr went next, Pilot-style, headfirst with legs wrapped around the line for extra control. Jenette and Marsh came last, sitting in their harness rigs and letting the descender gullies slowly let them down.

The inside of the beacon strut, which should have been straight, was warped by the overwhelming pressure of island growth pressing in on it. The faint glow of the domestics below disappeared as it twisted.

"What's that? Water?" Mok asked from below Karr, where the sides of the shaft had begun to glisten. "Hey, water's leaking in. Guys, water's leaking in."

"Heard you the first time," Toliver said from the bottom of the line.

Skutch swiped a wet patch with his forefinger and then licked his finger.

"Is it salty?" Mok asked.

Skutch frowned.

Coffin Island creaked and groaned eerily around them, presumably due to the distant motion of the ocean putting stress on brittle ghutzu fibers. Mok shivered. "I'm a soldier, not a sharkworm."

"Ah, get some gusto in your shorts," Liberty chided. "We volunteered. There's no backing out now."

"Who said anything about backing out?" Mok retorted, suddenly defensive. "Not me."

Mok kept quiet after that, even when a patch of irregular shadows on the walls proved to be head-sized holes, chewed in the fibrous material by some unknown creature or creatures, but his eyes goggled wide.

Some distance later, Dr. Marsh cleared her throat and whispered. "Jenette?"

"Yes, Deena?" Jenette whispered back.

"I've been thinking about our theory that these colony structures are sinking. I don't believe they are."

"No?" said Jenette, a bit relieved to have conversation to take her mind off the harrowing descent. "They certainly *seem* to be sinking."

"No," said Marsh, clamping her brake hard after letting herself slide too fast. "I have studied ring-island biology, and I suspect that we are making a mistake by assuming that ecological processes are the cause of the apparent sinking around us. Heavy objects do sink on ring-islands, but not to this extreme extent, maybe a few feet per year, but that is due largely to the growth of new island over the objects in question as old island growth sinks. Forgetting about the fact that this island is supposedly dead and should not have been growing at all, seventeen years of normal ring-island subduction could account for perhaps a one hundred to one hundred and fifty foot depth for extremely massive objects."

"We are clearly lower than that now," said Jenette.

"Exactly," said Marsh. "Also, the cavities we have been encountering do not line up with what we know of ring-island growth. There are typically small cavities underground, two to five yards in diameter, but nothing big enough to accommodate buildings and streets. The entire subterranean structure of this island seems to have been compromised."

"So what are you saying, Deena?"

"What I'm saying is that some force or selection of forces has drastically altered the growth pattern of this island, and I, for one, would like to know what those forces are."

"Don't wish too hard," Jenette said as she adjusted her own descender rig speed. "I'm not sure we really want to know."

The light of the three domestics reappeared below, silencing further discourse on the subject. The aliens were stopped at a level patch where the shaft bent at right angles to itself, both leveling off and narrowing to a tight horizontal crack. Dr. Bigelow was nowhere to be seen, but one of the glowing quadrupeds, Arrou, was holding a blinking object. Toliver halted a few feet above their heads. The object turned out to be Bigelow's detector. The Guards handed it up the chain of humans to Jenette.

"Can anybody read this?" she asked.

The lights on the scanner were blipping, but Jenette could not tell if that indicated the presence of nearby warheads, or if that was just the instrument's normal negative readout.

"Any one of us can set it to read the charge level in our pulse-rifles," Liberty said in reference to herself and the other Guards, "but that's it."

"Better than nothing," said Jenette. She handed Karr the scanner. He handed it to Liberty, who hooked it onto her belt.

Toliver slipped off the line to the ground, then dropped to his belly near the horizontal fissure.

"You think Dr. Bigelow got through that crack?" Jenette called skeptically from above.

Toliver shrugged. "I don't see any other way he could have exited this shaft, Consul."

"Point taken."

Squirming on his chest, Toliver entered the tight fissure. Bronte, and then the Guards followed, Grubb and Mok hanging back to bring up the rear after Karr, Arrou, Jenette, Crash, and Marsh.

The fissure was six to eight feet wide, but no more than eighteen inches high and required a determined effort to maneuver through, pulling with hands and scrambling with feet—and all the while feeling the immense weight of Coffin Island surrounding and pressing down in the near dark. Light beams flickered off sweating faces.

"In the dictionary—" Skutch grunted, breathing out to pass through a particularly tight spot, "—right next to *claustrophobia*, I bet there's a picture of this place."

A few yards in, Karr noticed that the surface pressing down on his back had transformed from abrasive fiber strands to something slick, damp, and pliable. As the Guards inched on, Karr managed to roll over. Beside him, Arrou looked up and gasped.

"Aaaahhrr!"

"What's wrong?" Jenette asked from behind them.

"Ghosts!" Arrou exclaimed.

Skulls leered down at Karr and the alien. Tightly packed, Scourge-crippled human bones pressed down on a transparent barrier filled with murky blue fluid. Preserved flesh clung to hundreds of cadavers and skeletons, the great mass of which faded into gloom above as the fluid devoured Arrou's glowbud light.

Jenette crawled up between Karr and the Khafra, and turned over herself. "Arrou, there are no such things as ghosts—ugh!" Jenette immediately tried to flatten out and not touch the clammy membrane. The skeleton of a baby stared hollowly down at her. She clenched her eyes and did not move.

"What is this?" Karr asked.

Jenette shivered, saying, "Body dump," as if that explained it all.

"I don't understand."

Forcing herself to open her eyes, Jenette explained further. "From when there were too many Scourge deaths to bury colonists individually, and before the invention of reusable incinerods." *Jenette shivered. She remembered rumors of strange experiments perpetrated on dead human bodies in an effort to understand Scourge better. . . .*

Gathering her courage, Jenette wriggled for the far side of the fissure. Karr and Arrou kept pace. The humans worried that the alien's armor plates would rip the membrane, but it held.

They came out of the crack on a cliff-like ledge where the shaft reopened and took a sharp plunge back downward. The body dump now pressed in on the shaft from the sides of the support strut structure as well as the ceiling. Skulls wore silent screams like victims drowning under ice, testament to their final horror.

No one wanted to spend much time there.

"Hey stragglers," Toliver muttered into his comset. "You coming through or what?"

"Just about, sir," buzzed Mok's voice. "Grubb and Dr. Marsh are coming through now—whoa . . . !"

A strange noise carried over the comsets: *Kekitekitekitek.*

"What's that?" said Jenette.

"Sonofabitch!" came Mok's voice.

Thok, thok! Pulse-rifle concussions thumped.

"Mok? Report!" Toliver dropped down to the crack, but he couldn't see through. "Mok? Mok . . . ? Grubb, fill me in!"

"Can't see!" Grubb replied. "I'm in the squeeze."

Kekitek, kekitekitek.

More shots resounded. *Thok! Thok! Thoka-thoka-thok!* Then the noise died down.

"Whooo-hoooo!" buzzed a jubilant voice. "Look at 'em run!"

"Mok, report!"

"I'll do better than that, sir. I'll show you."

"This better be good," Toliver muttered to himself as they waited for Mok to come through.

Shortly, the fissure lit up with wavering searchbeam light. "Make way, make way! Man on a mission!" Mok wriggled out and stood up. He opened a thigh pocket and, carefully, pulled out a plum-sized object. "Hey Arrou, is this your *big bug?*" Mok held a diminutive creature between thumb and forefinger. Legs and mandibles twitched helplessly under a helmet-shaped carapace. Mok feigned fright. "Ooooh, aaaaah."

"That not big bug," Arrou grumbled.

"There were thousands of these," Mok reported to Toliver, "but a few well-placed blasts frightened them off."

Faces leaned in for a closer look at the helpless creature.

Mok grinned at his triumph. "They're kind of cute, don't you think?" He winked at Arrou. Arrou rumbled grumpily. Mok gloated. But then, abruptly—

Snak!

"Aaaaagh!" Mok yowled as the suddenly not so helpless creature twisted its tree-pruner mandibles around and snipped off his right forefinger. "Ah fuck! Ow! Owwww!" Mok flailed his hand. The buzzer fell away with its ill-gotten prize firmly in its teeth and skittered for the narrow fissure. Blood fountained from Mok's stump. "It's got my finger! It's got my fucking finger! Don't let it get away!"

Dr. Marsh grabbed for the Guard's hand.

Grubb dove after the tiny thief.

"No!" Karr yelled, too late.

Grubb's pulse-rifle, which was slung over his shoulder and sticking point up, ripped into the body-dump membrane. With appalling speed, the small puncture widened into a huge gash. A tidal wave of cadavers and blue embalming fluid vomited out, engulfing the hapless humans and Khafra on the ledge.

Karr was swept down the chasm, spinning end over end in the noxious brew. He clung to the Gattler for dear life as the flood scraped him against tower girders and roots, pummeling him with clammy bones and body parts. Impacts came without warning in the dark. Karr couldn't see or feel anyone else. He couldn't breathe. Ten seconds elapsed. Twenty seconds. Forty seconds. Karr had not been able to take a deep breath before the flood hit him. His lungs burned from stale air.

Just as Karr's instinct to breathe was about to force him to gulp a lungful of blue death, the torrent passed out of the bottom of the beacon tower. Karr broke the surface and gulped fetid air, uncaring of its flavor. For a spinning instant he heard screaming—Mok? Marsh? And he saw a glowing Khafra head rise above the flood— Arrou? The faint glowbud light illuminated scattered images: an inverted teardrop cavern, an extremely large root running down through the center, steaming pits ringing that thick trunk at the narrow bottom of the hollow.

The torrent swept Karr down into one of the pits. He jammed the Gattler into its smooth lip and was rewarded with a precarious hold, but then a Khafra body slammed into him. The Gattler slipped free and the torrent sucked Karr down a long, subterranean tube. Twisting. Falling. Half-breathing, half-drowning. In the dark. Karr felt the torrent speed up. His stomach heaved as the fluid flung him down a cataract and then pressed him through a jam of cadavers around the inside of a tight curve.

And then, as quickly as the flood had hit, Karr was left behind, tumbling over a heap of fetid corpses, alone and gasping for air, his head hitting too hard against the floor. He fell unconscious in a black passage deep under Coffin Island.

XXXI

Man is great, Man is good,
Let us thank him for our food.

—In-human prayer

Consciousness returned to Karr. Stiffness in his joints hinted that he had been out for a while. Stench in his nostrils compelled him to move. In the pitch black, he rolled off a pile of slippery corpses and leaned against the side of what seemed to be an organic sewer pipe. Groping about, he located the Gattler. The device had no searchbeam or flashlight; Karr made a mental note to report the design flaw to its manufacturers, if he ever got the chance. He tipped the device down and heard fluid drain from its many barrels.

"Hello?" he said quietly into the darkness.

Only a distant gurgling answered.

Karr strained with his other senses in the dark. The tunnel was small and round; outstretched arms touched all sides. Karr noted that while the fetid air seemed smothering and hot, the walls were cool. He felt disoriented, as if the entire tunnel was swaying gently. He decided that his inner ear was still spinning from the trip down and sat still for a minute or two, but the sensation did not go away.

"Hello?" he called again, louder. "This is Pilot Karr. Jenette? Arrou? Anybody?"

No response. And he couldn't just sit still. They had come to Coffin Island to gather enough munitions to make an explosive device yielding forty to fifty kilotons. That, he admitted, might be a bit difficult, considering recent developments. But that was his mission, and he must attempt to fulfill it, even if he had no idea how that could now occur.

A muffled buzz arose from his left.

Karr tensed, finger on the Gattler's trigger. He thumbed the selector to check that the cutting beam was still activated. But nothing attacked. Slowly, Karr crawled toward the sound. Lumps of flesh slipped out from under his hands and feet. After a few feet, the buzzing seemed to be below him, and sounded halfway familiar. Karr wormed his left hand into a heap of body parts. Cold and soft . . . cold and soft . . . warm and firm. Karr's fingertips closed around a thin object and pulled it free. It buzzed. Karr jumped, then cursed himself for a fool and squeezed dry foamies on each end of the flexible loop in his hands and pulled it over his head.

Mok's disembodied voice buzzed over the comset. "—my leg's broke!"

"Thank piss you're still alive," Liberty's gruff female voice complained.

"And my finger's gone," Mok moaned. "My finger's gone, my leg's broke, and I can't feel my arm."

"Fuck your fucking finger," Liberty exploded. "You dumb shit, it's always the same, fuckup, fuckup, fuckup. Squad on punishment detail. Squad on graveyard watch. Squad on KP. Now this!"

"It wasn't my fault," Mok whined. "Grubb broke the body dump open."

"Fuckwit," said Liberty. "I've had it with your stupid, pud-pounding crap!"

The com channel squawked with arguing Guard voices.

"Liberty, do you talk to your mother with that mouth?" Jenette's unmistakable soprano cut in.

"Not anymore—she's dead," Liberty at first quipped. Eventually, she regained her composure. "Sorry, Consul."

"Whatever," said Jenette. "Just everybody pipe down. Pipe down." The radio chatter subsided. "Where's our doctor?"

Marsh obligingly broke into the circuit. "Mok, how's the leg? Is the skin pierced by bone?"

A brief pause as Mok examined his leg. "Oww. Shit. I don't think so."

"So it's not bleeding?"

"No, just broken."

"At least it's not a compound fracture. Do you have a venom kit for your arm?"

"No," Mok said in a worried tone. "Dr. Marsh, I can't feel my arm. The poison's moving up my arm and it's twitching all by itself."

"Wrap something around the stump. And don't move. Hold your arm below your heart. You don't want to pump the toxins through your system faster than you have to. Try to keep your heart rate low."

"Keep my heart rate low?" Mok said with rising panic. "How the fuck am I supposed to do *that?*"

"Just stay calm. *Calm.*"

Mok moaned.

"Mok, do you have any idea where you are?" Jenette demanded.

"No."

"All right," Jenette paused. Karr had a distinct mental image of her nose crinkled up in thought. "Stay put. We'll find you. Deena, are you hurt and where are you?"

"I'm with Skutch. Neither of us are injured."

"Liberty?"

"Up to my ass in cadavers and bitchy as hell."

"I'll take that as an *uninjured.*"

"Did I mention alone and lost in the dark?"

"That makes two of us," Jenette's voice buzzed. Further conversation revealed that Liberty's searchbeam was broken. Everyone else, except for Skutch, had lost their light sources in the flood. "What about our domestics?"

Crash was with Marsh and Skutch. No one knew where Arrou and Bronte were.

"Where's the Corporal?" Skutch asked. "Why isn't he on comset?"

"Toliver? Corporal Toliver?" There was no response to Jenette's query. "And where's our Pilot?"

Karr spoke up, "I'm okay."

"Pilot Lindal Karr . . . ? Anybody see Lindal Karr?"

"I'm okay," Karr repeated.

Liberty sighed angrily. "Great. We lost the fucking Pilot."

Karr realized that he was not getting through to them. As he had done for so many fuguetime years, Karr unconsciously reached to adjust a voice emulator at his throat. Of course, there was no voice emulator at his throat. It and the pitch adjusters for his ears had gone missing when he crashed into New Ascension's ocean. Rethinking his predicament, Karr examined his headset in the dark. The microphone tip was broken off. The comset could receive, but not transmit.

Disembodied voices bantered for a while in his ears. Then a *bleeping* sounded over the channel.

"Crap," said Liberty, "Dr. Bigelow's scanner is flipping out."

"Must be the warheads," said Skutch.

"*Now* we find them," Karr sighed to no one in the dark as the comset voices talked on.

"Please don't say that they are farther *down*," Jenette said.

"I don't think so," said Liberty. "The scanner freaks out stronger when I aim it upward."

"Fine," said Jenette. "That's as good a start as any. We'll backtrack, following the scanner signal. Eventually these passages must link back together."

"What about me?" asked Mok. "I can't move. You can't leave me down here."

"Nobody's leaving anyone," Jenette reassured. "Which of you Guards has rank after Corporal Toliver?"

Liberty's reluctant voice responded. "Guess that would be me. Does that mean I have to smarten up and act like a big girl?"

"That would be helpful," Jenette said. "Okay, this is the plan. Mok, you keep talking—off circuit. If we hear a voice around us, we'll follow it. If we haven't found you by the time we regroup, we'll come back down together and do a systematic search. Liberty, any objections or suggestions?"

"No ma'am. Sounds like a good course of action."

Mok didn't like it and kept moaning to that effect.

As the others started to move, Karr began to creep back up in his own pitch-black tube, his right hand holding the Gattler and his left outstretched to the wall. The going was tough, the passage still slick from the recent torrent of embalming fluid. Karr didn't know what his boots would land on from one step to the next and he fell into cold ooze several times before getting the hang of walking in the slippery stuff.

"Warmer, warmer," Liberty's radio voice huffed in regard to the scanner. "Every light is blinking. They've got to be around here ... I'm turning a corner ... Sure is hot in here ... I see a light ahead, red, throbbing like a beating heart." Brief silence as the Guard closed on the unknown phenomena. "This is weird," Liberty hissed. "I see a body. Dr. Bigelow? Bronte?" Slow foot-steps sounded in Karr's earpiece as Liberty called out. "Please be alive. Please move ... oh ... *oh* ... fuckshitpiss." Karr's comset squawked with rapid, heavy breathing and running, fleeing foot-falls. "Shit-shit-shit-shit!"

Sounds of a struggle ensued. A rising shriek. The transmission cut out.

"Liberty!" Jenette called. "Respond!"

"The buzzers got her," Mok moaned when Liberty did not an-swer back.

"The little things that bit off your finger?" Skutch's voice scoffed. "Liberty'd eat those alive."

"Guess so," Mok admitted nervously. "But what else could it be?"

"Possibly something bigger," said Jenette. "Possibly much big-ger, like Arrou said, creeping around down here in the dark, where we can't see it, just waiting for fools like us to —"

Mok's voice raised half an octave. "Okay, okay, Consul! Please, no more descriptions. I get the idea!"

Skutch's voice broke in at that point.

"Hey, Marsh," he asked quietly, "would you say that's a 'throb-bing red heartbeat' up there?"

Dr. Marsh gulped, a gravelly sound. "Yes, I think I would."

Karr strained to see any sign of a red glow in the dark ahead of him, but saw nothing.

"What do you say we turn around?" Skutch suggested in a hushed voice.

"Works for me."

"Consul, we're going to retreat and try another way up."

"Do it," buzzed Jenette.

Karr heard boots splashing in a hollow tube.

"What's *that?*" asked Marsh's voice. "You hear that, Skutchie, that tapping . . . ?"

Kekitekitek.

"I hear it, but I don't want to hear it."

"It's getting louder."

"Look, over there! What's down there?"

"Bad smell," came Crash's alien voice from the background. "Bad, bad smell."

Jenette's voice overrode the circuit. "Maybe you guys should go a different way."

"Copy that, Consul," Skutch agreed. "We're scramming. Down that way, you two. On the double." More sounds of boots splashing, then, *"Dr. Marsh, get down!"*

Again, chaos broke out on the open channel. Male, female, and alien screams overlapped, cut short by the dead *click, click* of microphones overloading and cutting out. Karr felt pulse-rifle shockwaves in delayed synchrony with the clicks; the encounter was not far away. Karr jogged forward, careening through the pitch dark, eerily giddy from the swaying in his inner ear. He slipped and fell, scrambling back up on all fours and spitting chemical syrup as the disembodied combat rattled in his broken comset. There was a loud—*BWAMPH!*—much louder than the pulse-rifle concussions and then the sounds of combat ended, as Liberty's encounter had, leaving only a faint skittering sound before the transmission stopped altogether.

"Liberty? Skutchie?" Jenette called in the dead airspace. "Crash? Crash, pick up a comset if you can hear this. . . ."

Karr stumbled onward and upward. A patch of dark gray appeared and expanded in the blackness ahead. Before he knew it, the tunnel suddenly ended. Karr fell a few feet in the dark. When he scrambled to his knees, he found he was in a transparent pod too small to stand up in.

And he was underwater.

The tunnels he had been running through were not tunnels at all, but tubes in the ocean under Coffin Island. Contrary to its skeletal surface, and what Jenette had told Karr of its biology, the ring-island's underside was alive. A long, thick root protruded down from the island—sort of a natural keel or sea anchor, Karr guessed—and from that keel root hung a forest of interlocking tubes. The effect was similar to that of tendrils hanging under a jelly-fish, each swaying sickeningly in the ocean currents. Karr was shocked at the sheer mass of the living structure; it must have comprised a large proportion of Coffin Island's total weight, for the keelroot and tendrils loomed all around his tiny blister and disappeared into the icy depths of Dead Zone ocean far below.

Each individual tendril ended in a bulbous bladder, like the one Karr was in. On the other side of its waxy walls, schools of hideous, luminescent marine vertebrates darted around in the tangle, feeding on each other and basking in an evil, red glow.

Vermilion illumination shone down from above Karr, where a cancerous knot bulged in Coffin Island's keelroot. The bulge glowed, a baneful underwater sun. Many of the interlocking tendrils anchored to that point, like twisting leprous feelers. The light pulsed, first racing, then lagging, like a faltering heartbeat, and as it did so, the ugly water creatures reacted, swimming frenziedly or laying deathly still. What could cause the underside of a dead island to grow in such a strange manner, Karr had no idea, but just from their limited description, Karr concluded the glowing, cancerous knot had to be the "throbbing red light" that Liberty, Marsh, and Skutch had commented on.

Grim transmissions continued in Karr's ears.

"Come on guys," Jenette's voice buzzed. "Give me a sign. Grunt if you can't speak."

"I'm still here," said Mok.

"And me," Karr said to himself.

Karr scanned the swaying tubes for sign of Khafra lights or searchbeams. None were visible, but there was no question in his mind that the others had met with trouble near the writhing red bulge. He, and perhaps the unlucky Mok, must have been washed the farthest down in the flood.

Karr doubled back, once more in the dark, listening and feeling for any indication as to how he had gotten lost. The first clue was the clatter his boots made on the down-sloping floor; the torrent of cadavers had not passed this way. The second clue was when his footfalls began to *splat* and *squish* in body parts once more. Karr backtracked to the division between the wet and the dry and felt for openings. At first his fingertips only met with firm tube wall, but then he reached upward. Ceiling, ceiling, nothing. Standing on tiptoes, Karr felt a slime-ringed hole where the torrent had poured down. He tried to grab the edge and climb up, but it was too slick. His feet got no purchase on the rounded walls, either.

Kekitekitek, Karr heard in his earpieces, and then Jenette's whispers, "Oh, hell."

"It's the buzzers!" Mok panicked. "Don't let them get you, Consul! Run!"

Now Karr heard Jenette's rapid breathing and footfalls in the comset.

Karr tossed the Gattler up, then stepped aside as it fell in the dark, tossed it up, stepped aside as it fell. Then it didn't fall. The tool lay across the opening overhead. Karr jumped, grabbing the metal barrels, and chinned himself up. Chunks of unseen matter dislodged and splattered his cheeks, but he was able to hook a leg over the lip and rolled onto the steep upper surface. Without pausing to humor his protesting muscles, Karr began to ascend, jabbing the Gattler barrels down hard into the slope for extra grip. Karr's heart pounded against his ribs as Jenette's breath sawed in his ears.

"Arrou, where are you?" came a whisper that sounded like a lost little girl.

Karr reached the top of the incline and felt two tubes splitting off. The slick trail wormed left, but warm air flowed out of the opening to the right—warm air that might be coming from the glowing bulge. Karr jogged right. The tunnel wound back and forth, like a snake tied in knots. Other passages opened under his fingertips, but Karr kept to the ones exuding warm air.

Kekekitek—kekekitek, the evil noise rattled in his headset.

"Run! Run!" Mok's voice encouraged. "Don't let them get you!"

"Quit making so much noise!" Jenette panted.

Kekitekitekitek.

In the heat of the moment, Karr could not discern if the tapping was on the comset or right beside him. He whipped the headset down onto his neck.

Kekitekitekitek.

It was close. Scraping and splashing echoed from ahead in the smothering dark. "Jenette," Karr hissed. "Jenette?"

Mok's voice rang staticky around Karr's neck. "I hear them! Oh man, they're coming this way!"

"Mok, please," Jenette buzzed. "I can't hear myself think!"

It was hard for Karr to tell if the thrumming sound was coming from ahead or behind. Deciding it was probably coming from ahead, he fell to one knee and switched the Gattler from cutting beam to adhesive froth; a cutting beam might slice the tube walls open and let in the sea. His forefinger fidgeted on the trigger as the cacophony drew closer. *Friend of foe? Friend or foe?* Adrenaline accelerated Karr's thoughts: he must not shoot without knowing if it was Jenette. A wild spray of surgical adhesive could easily suffocate her.

"I don't deserve to go like this!" Mok wailed. "I'm a lazy coward, but I don't deserve to go like this!"

Scraping and splashing echoed from ahead of Karr in the smothering dark. *Running human footsteps?* In desperation Karr yelled, "Consul! If it's you call out—or I'll shoot!"

"Don't shoot!" yelled a female voice very close by.

Karr's finger froze on the Gattler's trigger. A split second later, the footfalls pounded across his path from right to left. And then the thrumming, drumming noise went past like a mag-lev freight train. *KEKITEKITEKITEK.* Karr fired. The Gattler chugged against his shoulder. A boiling-shellfish screeching filled the tube as the adhesive hit unseen creatures. Seconds dragged by. The tube reverberated with chattering legs and shrieking mouthparts. Grad-

ually, the noisy torrent diminished. Karr imagined layers of blind
crawling things building up, wave after wave becoming trapped in
the adhesive froth until the horde could not move over the carapaces of suffocating hive mates.

Beep, warned the Gattler. The ammunition load was half empty.

Karr let loose the trigger and held his breath, expecting a wave
of creatures to swamp over him. In his imagination he already felt
the crawling of bug-like feet, paralyzing venom running in his
veins, and mandibles snipping him apart.

"Fuck-shit-they-got-me!" Mok's screams blared from Karr's
headset. Karr pulled it back over his ears as the Guard, confused,
relieved and angry all at the same time, spoke again. "Oh crap!
Don't ever sneak up on me like that! Give me some light, dumbshit."

"Dumbshit," a strange voice echoed over the channel.

"Don't give me any fucking lip. I'm not in the mood."

Karr's own paranoid vision of death had not come true. The
skittering near him had diminished. And he hoped that he had
helped lessen the number of creatures pursuing Jenette. Mok, however, was not so lucky. A terror play sounded over the comset.

"Fucking lip, fucking lip."

"This isn't funny, jerkwad. I gave you an order." A pregnant
pause. "What the hell is wrong with you? Uagghh! What's wrong
with your skin?"

"Good skin. Jerkwad."

Tinny screams rang in Karr's headset. "Oh shit! Shit! Aaaaaaar-
rrrrgh—"

Static.

XXXII

They shall the Body Pure value above all others,
Those who love Loyalty and Truth before all else.

—*from the speeches of Olin Tesla*

The quarters of Colonel Taureg Halifax glowed like the heart of a yellow-white star. Every available area of ceiling, walls, and floor was plastered in adhesive glowstrips. Wearing black-green blast goggles, Halifax withdrew another strip from a case stashed in a corner. He affixed the strip to a clear spot by the room's only door, and turned the narrow band on. Sweat poured over skin-weld sutures that held Halifax's gashed forehead shut. It was very hot in the room. Alone, the glowstrips produced very little heat, but in such concentration they raised the ambient temperature far in excess of human comfort levels.

Halifax reached into the case for another strip.

"Damn."

The case was empty, as were the others Halifax rapidly dug through.

Patton lay on Halifax's military style cot, which had been moved into the center of the square room. A transparent ceramite sheet substituted for a mattress; glowstrips attached to the floor shone up through the plastiwire mesh on the bottom of the cot. Patton was a dark silhouette, getting darker by the minute. The domestic's coat of somber blue glowbuds was winking out one by one. Only a few spots atop his head still showed color.

And hour, maybe two, and there would be none glowing at all.

Halifax sought out every drawer, compartment, and crevice in the room looking for more glowstrips.

Patton shifted on the cot, groaning faintly. "Not stay, not stay."

Halifax continued to search.

"Reserves," Patton mumbled louder. "Halifax not stay. Call Reserves."

"Reserves units are deploying for duty as we speak," Halifax said, keeping his voice even despite the fact that all the stash spaces in which he normally stockpiled glowstrips were empty. "Here I am required; here I stay."

Patton grew agitated in his fever. "Defend Enclave. Ferals attack. Patton knows. Ferals will attack."

Halifax hurried back to the cot, picked up an already activated glowstrip and held it in front of himself so that his body did not cast any shadow onto Patton. Normally, Khafra reacted to bright light by brightening their own glowbuds in return. Many times before, Halifax had played on this instinctual behavior to trick Patton into glowing brighter and stronger. This time the trick wasn't working. Patton's glowbuds continued to wink out.

Halifax cursed. He needed a new plan. "Listen up, soldier. It's time for a report." Patton made no response. "Are you listening?" Halifax demanded.

"Listening," Patton mumbled.

"That's better. This is your briefing. Recon patrols have detected a large force of Ferals approaching our zone of control. At 0700 I placed all Enclave forces on alert. Defenses are being manned. The situation is urgent, but stable."

Patton groaned, his muzzle twisting, mirroring his inner conflict. The alien buried his already closed eyes under a forearm. "Halifax must not worry about Patton. Halifax must defend Enclave."

A couple more glowbuds winked out.

Halifax pulled Patton's light-blocking forelimb off of his eyes—no mean feat, since even a weakened Khafra was far stronger than a human. "It wasn't your fault! You didn't kill that Feral. We humans killed it, with pulse-rifles!"

"Cheating words!" The alien's forepaws pantomimed abortive jabs in the air. "Patton *pushed.*"

The alien convulsed under Halifax.

It all stemmed from the conflict at FI-538. Pact shall not kill Pact. Halifax was not aware of the details of that instinctive injunction, but he was all too familiar with the consequence of breaking it: a slow, suicidal winking out of glowbuds. In the past Halifax had always been able to bring Patton back from the brink of his alien mortality. But then in the past Patton had not taken action that caused the demise of another Khafra; Patton had caused plenty of wounds, but never a fatality. It didn't matter that Patton's action had saved Halifax's life, nor that Patton's actions had only indirectly lead to the death of the Feral. The Feral had flared its death glow and gone dark; a Radiant life had been taken. To Patton's Khafra instincts, a Radiant life must be paid in return.

Halifax did his best to subdue his thrashing domestic. "Easy, easy! No more cheating words! I promise. Just open your eyes! That's a direct order! Open your eyes!"

Patton attempted to comply. His eyes squinted open, briefly.

For that instant one or two glowbuds on his head flickered brighter.

Halifax thought fast. "Right. Okay. Time for a verbal exercise, a test to make sure you remember your training. Are you ready?"

Patton rumbled weakly. Halifax proceeded.

"Question one: when were the most mechanized fighting vehicles ever used in combat?"

At first Patton only grumbled, but then his teeth clattered and one eye opened slightly and scanned numerous maps and military diagrams plastered on the walls under the many glowstrips. The alien's gaze fixed on a Terran map of Eurasia with a red line running down from the Arctic Ocean to the Black Sea.

"Battle of Kursk. 1943?"

"Correct. Bonus question: why did the assaulting forces fail?"

"Spies. Defenders expected attack."

"Good. Another one," Halifax continued. "On what planet did the forces of Kut Al Imra fall after one hundred years of Bloodstone Wars?"

Patton struggled and peeked at the wall maps again. Normally Halifax would have been against such cheating, but at that moment the old soldier couldn't have been happier. Patton was forced to look a long time before he found the right map; Halifax had specifically chosen a diagram mostly obscured by glowstrips to base the question on.

"Planet Paradise?"

"Correct again."

A few of Patton's glowbuds actually flared back to life.

Halifax was encouraged.

A comset buzzed. "Command for Halifax."

Frowning, Halifax touched his earpiece. "Go for Halifax."

"Colonel," an efficient voice said. "The large Feral force is moving again. Long range patrols four and six report skirmishes."

"Instruct them to fall back, as per orders. No direct engagement. Delaying tactics only."

"Yes sir, delaying tactics only. And sir . . . ?"

"What is it?" Halifax asked impatiently.

"Sir, the Prime Consul is declaring Marshal Law and he requests your presence in the war room. He says he has formulated a plan to take the battle to the Ferals."

Halifax was troubled by Tesla's invocation of Marshal Law, but he was not surprised that the Prime Consul had a plan—although he did not at that moment see a necessity to take the conflict to the Ferals when the Ferals were bringing it to their doorstep very nicely all by themselves. "Thank you. Tell the Prime Consul I will attend as soon as possible."

"Yes, sir."

The comset went quiet.

Halifax refocused his attention on Patton. "This is the situation. We can't stay here forever. There's work to do. But I'm not leaving without you, so that means you've got to pull out of this."

"Never give up," Patton agreed, a little more energetically than before.

"That's more like it," Halifax said. "Cite six examples of commanders who achieved improbable victories through inspired use of tactics."

"Alexander at Issus . . . Napoleon at Austerlitz . . . Kolomgombara at Joolloolabad . . ." Patton recited, searching, finding the right maps, and answering as more and more glowbuds reignited along his armor plate.

XXXIII

If a Pact has done an evil act,
And is afraid lest it become known,
Then there is still a portion of goodness
In that Pact's evil.

Such a Pact
May yet be Balanced,
And must be shown
Compassion.

But if a Pact
Has done a good deed,
And is eager that the deed
Be proclaimed to all the world.

Then this Pact must be treated
With harshest reprimand,
For only misfortune
Can flow from such unBalanced intent.

—the Judges of Gnosis

Karr retreated from the sticky roadblock and took the first side passage with an upward slope. Thus began a dizzying series of explorations and backtracking in the darkness. A normal human would have been lost after the first few switchbacks, but, calling on his fugueship experience, Karr was able to map the convoluted pathways in his head. Right, right, left. Left, right, left. Reverse if necessary and try a different track. So it went, always choosing upward, warmer tubes in favor of downward, cooler ones, occasionally splashing through trails of bitter, pungent embalming fluid. The entire time, a distant droning grew.

Kekitekitekitekitekitekitekitek. . . .

Karr's path turned sharply upward. The droning became thunder. *BRAKA-BRAKA-BRAKA-BRAKA.* Ten paces above Karr, the tunnel ended. Erratic beams of vermilion swept into the passage from an open space beyond.

Karr crept up and looked out onto a bizarre sight.

Jenette's boots slipped off a hard object.

Her arms flailed, but she did not fall. Reaching down, she retrieved a machined item. In response to her fingers on its stock, a searing beam of light stabbed out from the object. Jenette's eyes clamped shut and she could see nothing for several minutes.

"Pulse-rifle," she whispered to herself. "Probably Skutch's."

It was comforting to hold the weapon in her hands, and to have a source of light. The only downside was that Jenette could not imagine a Guard abandoning it except under the most dire circumstances. Jenette remembered that she herself was lucky to be alive. Whatever had been following her had been on her heels when she passed Karr in the dark. After he fired something from the Gattler, there had been the terrible screeching and the unsettling, snipping-grinding noises, but his actions had bought her time. Jenette had fled into the darkness with the distinct impression that whatever was following her had turned back to feast upon its entrapped brethren.

When her eyes finally adjusted to the brilliant searchbeam, Jenette saw where pulse-rifle hits had cracked the tube walls around her. Cold, salty water was trickling in. Jenette wasn't surprised. She had already pieced the strange swaying motion of the passage together with what she knew of ring-island growth and concluded that she was in a passage surrounded by water; there was only so far *down* you could go before the solid portion of a floating island ended. Jenette advanced a few paces and stopped to pick up a medikit. It was Marsh's. It was covered in blood, red and copious, unlike the anemic fluid one would expect from a buzzer, no matter

how big it might be. The red liquid instead resembled the blood of
a large warm-blooded creature. A hollow feeling in her belly,
Jenette clipped the kit to her belt and flashed the searchbeam at the
floor of the passage.

Crimson smears trailed up the tunnel.

Jenette followed the bloody trail. The incessant rattling, like
gravel on glass, increased in volume as Jenette climbed.
Kekitekitekitekitekitekitek. . . . Jenette shut off the searchbeam as a
flashing red opening appeared around a bend. The red pulsing was
quite strong, shooting up from below and bleeding through the
walls of the tunnel like light through fiber optics. What Jenette
could see of herself was thrown into sharp silhouette. She crept
over to the opening and looked down. The thrumming increased to
a din.

The view made Jenette's skin crawl.

The opening looked down on a roughly spherical chamber about
one hundred yards across. It was pockmarked by scattered tube entrances like the one she looked out of and lined with countless, toe-
curling buzzers—and not tiny buzzers like the one which bit off
Mok's finger, either, but giant albino mutants every inch as big as
Arrou had described. Helmet-shaped and over three feet across,
Jenette saw organs and fluid pumping under translucent carapaces.
Segmented legs, mandibles, and blind, staring eyes protruded from
bellies lined with hairy gills. Thousands of the creatures crowded
the inner surfaces of the spherical chamber, clinging to vertical and
inverted surfaces as easily as they sat upon the more upright surfaces.

In the center of the chamber, supported by root buttresses that
splayed from the walls of the sphere, hung a massive machine. It
was twenty yards long and consisted of two metal cones whose
apexes joined in the middle like a huge hourglass. The object was
not level, so one of the cones was tilted higher than the other.
Jenette squinted. It was hard to see the machine because of a fluctuating forcefield, which began a few feet from its surface. Rays of
the forcefield spread out and traveled down root webs, glowing in
the walls like hot coals, or coalesced into beams of high-tech fire
and swept across the open chamber onto the malignant buzzers,

stimulating them to quiver and pound the roots and walls with their many moving mouthparts. Waves of motion rushed around the spherical chamber, producing a combined thunder that Jenette felt as much as heard.

BRAKA-BRAKA-BRAKA-BRAKA-BRAKA.

As the visual centers of Jenette's brain adjusted to the parting and unparting of the forcefield across the machine, she was able to discern more clearly what was on its surface. She clapped a hand to her mouth.

A male form lay inverted; its head gnawed open. It took Jenette a moment to recognize Corporal Toliver. Bronte hung from the lower half of the machine, eviscerated, glowbuds awfully dull. Dr. Bigelow faced out from the black-pearl metal, eyes bulging in terror, but not blinking. His corpulent, naked bulk quivered with uncontrollable neuro-venom tremors. Crash convulsed not far from Bigelow. A human, female hip—Jenette could not say if it was Liberty's or Dr. Marsh's—protruded from behind the upper cone of the reactor, lying as if on an autopsy table.

And that was not the worst of it.

Frightful shapes moved in the carnage, age-withered and hideous, clambering crab-like into view from the back side of the double-coned machine. Sickly flesh, too long in the subterranean chamber of horrors and mottled with scabs and rashes, hung loose from skeletal bodies. Dagger teeth, rotted and grown overly long from lack of use, jutted out of cracked lips. With a gasp of horror, Jenette recognized the creatures as Ferals—the most hideous Ferals she had ever seen. And even more disturbing than how they looked was what they wore: human-skin garments. Baby pink skin stretched over one creature's malnutrition-softened armor plate. Rich sienna skin wrapped around the emaciated arms and legs of another. Their hideous garments came in as many hues as humans came in. Human flesh masks were pulled over skeletal alien heads in a grotesque mockery of human form. So adorned, these vile Khafra swayed in time to the buzzer drumming.

BRAKA-BRAKA, BRAKA-BRAKA.

More buzzers entered the spherical cavity and marched through the sea of hammering carapaces. Most carried writhing white mag-

gots the size of human infants. One swarm, however, lead by another human-skinned Khafra, bore Mok's body up a winding root
to the large machine. Still another swarm carried Mok's head. The
scuttling buzzers bore their prizes to the metal and affixed them
there with ropy strands exuded from mandibles.

It was to Jenette's credit that at no point then or in the trying
minutes that followed did she allow herself to buckle over and
vomit.

Arrou pulled Grubb's body very, very slowly, his glowbuds imitating the glowing coal color of the spherical chamber, just in case
the buzzers weren't as blind as they looked.

BRAKA-BRAKA-BRAKA-BRAKA.

Arrou was far below Jenette, near a path of embalming fluid that
glistened from a tunnel opening above him all the way down the
curving wall of the chamber and disappeared into another tube
opening below the hourglass-shaped machine. Grubb lay at Arrou's
feet, unconscious. The human was wounded, but not yet poisoned,
so he did not twitch. The blue flood had disgorged the two of them
in the dangerous space some time ago and ever since then Arrou
had been creeping, dragging Grubb down toward the nearest tunnel
exit.

It was tricky, tricky.

Arrou saw from the awful evidence on the large, hourglass-
shaped thing—Arrou guessed it was a human machine of some
kind—what would happen if he made a mistake. He wished he
could rescue the others, too, but he did not know how to get past the
horrible Ferals. They made Arrou sick just to look at them. They did
terrible things to his friends. They did horrible things to themselves.
They had gouged out their own eyes! Under the terrible human skin
masks, Arrou saw scars slashed through vacant eye sockets. *To be
blind, forever away from light, forever trapped in darkness, and to
have done it on purpose . . . Urrrrr!* It was horrible to think about.
Arrou tried not to look at them as he tugged Grubb toward safety.

Where was Jenette? Where was Karr?

Arrou's heart leapt when he spotted two human figures peeking
in from separate tube hole entrances. On Arrou's left, about halfway

up the sphere, was a male human dressed in white. Of course that
was Pilot Karr. High and to Arrou's right was a thin female human
with short, gray-blonde hair. That had to be Jenette. Arrou was overjoyed that Jenette lived and wanted to bound over to her, but that
would get Grubb killed, and maybe himself, so he could not.

He had to be smart.

And he had to make the humans smart, too. The horrible Ferals
could not see. The buzzers could not see either, or hear or feel very
well with all their pounding, but Arrou knew that would not last forever. If Jenette or Karr moved when the buzzers were quiet, the
buzzers would sense the vibrations and attack. That was why Arrou
had not been noticed or captured; he knew the buzzers' weakness.
Arrou had to warn Jenette and Karr. Deciding to take a risk, Arrou
let his camouflage fade and flashed at Jenette.

<<Not move (exclamation flash), not move (exclamation
flash).>> Arrou clenched his talons in frustration as Jenette did not
respond. <<Not move (exclamation flash), not move (exclamation
flash).>>

Finally, Jenette looked Arrou's way.

<<Humans must not move!>> Arrou warned, using the most
distressed hues he could think of to carry his words. <<Not move
when bugs quiet! Only move when bugs loud! Jenette understand?
Understand move only when bugs loud?>> Arrou worried. Jenette
should have easily known what he was saying, but there was still
no response. <<Jenette *see* Arrou . . . ?>> he asked.

Nothing happened immediately, then Arrou rejoiced to see a
searchbeam flash in Jenette's hands. Too bad it was inadequate for
communication. Jenette could not form any words with the single
intensity, single color, beam. A one second flash, which was either
the first part of the Khafra word *concentrate* or the end of the word
droobleberry, blinked at Arrou.

Arrou stopped dragging Grubb as the buzzers went into one of
their quiet, motionless phases. A buzzing null-field swept over
Arrou and he had a hard time keeping still as its tingling numbness
engulfed him. It made him want to urinate. Of course he could not;
that would attract the buzzers' attention. Two seconds later the field
was gone. The buzzers resumed twitching and drumming, but

Arrou, confused, did not resume moving. What to do? What to do? How to communicate with Jenette? Then it hit him. <<One flash equals no. Two flash equals yes,>> he blinked. <<Understand?>>

Jenette blinked the searchbeam twice.

Arrou was so relieved that he just about fell over. <<Jenette hurt? Jenette hurt?>> he asked.

Jenette blinked once.

<<Good, good, good, good, good,>> Arrou flashed, reiterating, <<Buzzers feel moving. Not see. Not hear. Only feel vibrations. Move when buzzers loud. Stop when quiet.>>

Jenette blinked twice.

<<Good, good. Tell Pilot Karr. Karr need to know too.>> Arrou said as he resumed dragging Grubb.

Above Arrou, the albino buzzer's finished sticking maggots and humans to the big machine. As they did, each subservient buzzer received a deep kiss from an ancient Feral female, who sat like a gargoyle atop the machine in her cloak of human skin. Mandibles and tongues swapped immune venom and the buzzers crabbed away with their reward.

Below the ancient female Arrou saw—and smelled, *ugh!*—maggots that had been on the reactor for a long time: striated sacks of nacreous tissue, swollen by venom and heat. It was a revolting sensory barrage, even to a Khafra like Arrou, who liked strong smells.

I'm food, Bigelow thought hazily. He was obviously placed on the warm metal, along with the gelatinous grubs, to ripen in the heat. Bigelow supposed, with his venom-impaired thought processes, that the disgusting Ferals would eat him at some point when he became appropriately tasty.

And I'm affixed to a null-fusion reactor. Groggy or not, Clarence Bigelow knew that. It was not just any null-fusion reactor either, but the New Ascension colony's primary null-fusion reactor. Its smaller cousin, which Bigelow worked on all the time back at the Enclave, was merely a backup reactor. This much larger, much more efficient and powerful null-fusion device had unfortunately been abandoned in the evacuation of Coffin Island. It seemed in good shape, Bigelow decided, considering it had not been serviced in two decades. Of course the null-field was sorely out of tune. He wondered numbly if the erratic vermilion pulsations and beams were responsible for the dead island's unexpected, mutated growth patterns. He decided that seemed probable and that he must argue the matter out with Dr. Marsh—if he lived long enough to do so.

The buzzer pounding stopped.

The ancient Feral female, barely more than a skeleton, had shuffled over to a service hatch on the reactor casing, opened it, and used her stained teeth to adjust something inside. The pulsing of the null-field changed slightly. Bigelow did not understand the purpose, but the buzzers somehow detected the change in the null-field and fell silent.

Another of the loathsome Ferals, whose human cloak was ragged and filthy, slunk down to Mok's body and decapitated head. The creature moved, as all the nasty Ferals did, in the gap between the reactor hull and the erratic null-field, which began about three feet out from the metal. To Bigelow's surprise, the creature spoke, in a sniveling voice, and its words were human.

"Ruined," it mourned, looking at Mok. The ragged Feral crept down and fondled Bigelow's abundant flesh. "Good skin," it cooed, nipping the scientist's arm skin to test its resilience. Bigelow did not feel the pinch on his arm, nor did he feel any of the rest of his body; he was too pumped full of buzzer venom.

"Supple," said the ragged Feral. It reached out for another pinch. As its claws hovered over his eyes, Bigelow wondered if this maybe this wasn't the moment to take up deity worship and to pray very hard.

"No!" snarled the old female, her voice sounding like poison boiling in a vat. She was a strange sight. Her eyes did not flash; her glowbuds did not glow.

"This one's turn," whined the ragged Feral. "This one's skin."

"Wait for the Null. Null makes man bigger."

"Big enough now. This one must hide," the ragged Feral protested, fondling its tattered pink cloak.

The ancient female rattled her claws on the reactor. "Blaspheme! Do duty first! The Null gives all. The Null must be safe."

The ragged Feral scuttled back submissively. It twisted around to Crash's quivering form. It caressed Crash's snout with its arthritic digits. "Must hide, must hide," the fetid creature sniveled, and then abruptly jabbed one of Crash's eyes out with a talon. Crash convulsed. A dull moan rose from Crash's chest as the ragged Feral ate its disgusting prize.

"The Null is safe," the ragged Feral proclaimed.

Fortunately for Crash, injuries on the other side of his head made it look like his other eye was already missing. Bigelow, however, could see that the swollen, bruised flesh actually concealed an intact eye—not that he had any intention of enlightening the blind monsters to their mistake.

"The Null is safe, the Null is safe," they chanted.

The old female reached into the open service hatch and made another adjustment to the null-field. The rhythm of its pulsing changed. In response, the buzzers began to thrum in a fairly quiet pattern: *kekitekitek, silence, kekitekitek, silence.*

The old female sat up on her haunches, her movements both oddly reverent, jerking and bug-like at the same time.

"Is man good?" she asked.

"Man is good," the uglies reverently replied.

A three-legged Feral snatched the tongue out of Mok's severed head and ate it. "Man *very* good."

The elder female was outraged. "Blaspheme! Wait for the Null!"

"The Null, the Null," the others gibbered.

"Sorry, sorry," whined the cripple.

"The Null helps us hide!" ranted the female. "We must hide from Balance!"

"Balance is unfair. Balance lets humans live," the others chanted.

"But who are we?"

The loathsome creatures called out their names. "In-charles, in-mary, in-john, in-delilah. . . ."

"In-robert," said the ragged one.

"In-joan," the ancient female said, holding her arms as if beseeching unseen heavens. "Are we not human?"

As one, the unsavory beasts tugged at their human-skin cloaks. "We are *in-human.*"

"We are in-human!" in-joan confirmed. "The Balance is fooled. We live!"

The in-humans made fists of their forepaws, stacked them under bowed, bullet heads and intoned, in obvious and chilling imitation of a gesture Bigelow had seen ever since he was a little boy, "The Skin must be Pure. The Skin must be Pure!"

The thrumming of the buzzers grew, filling the subaquatic chamber with hypnotic vibration.

Jenette just about jumped out of her skin when a hand clamped down on her shoulder. Whirling around, she came face to face with Skutch. The Guard's hair was singed, his face was blackened, and Jenette noticed that a C-23 proportional charge was missing from his belt.

Jenette's shoulders sagged with relief, but she held up a hand for Skutch to wait while she finished speaking into her comset.

"Did you copy that, Pilot Karr? The buzzers are motion sensitive. Move or talk only when they make noise. Otherwise hold still."

A white-suited figure in a distant tube entrance gave her a thumbs-up. "Okay, that's good. I see and confirm your signal." Leaning close to Skutch's ear, Jenette explained that Karr could receive but not transmit.

Skutch touched a melted headset hanging from his own neck. "That's one notch better than me."

He and Jenette stared down at their comrades on the reactor.

"Can we fight our way to them?" Jenette asked. Skutch looked skeptically at the horde of twitching carapaces. Jenette's nose crinkled in consternation. "That's what I thought. But we have to do *something.*"

"And fast," Skutch agreed, pointing.

Jenette looked in the direction indicated, down, past the reactor, to the bottom of the spherical chamber. Water was bubbling up from below. It was only a small pool, but it hadn't been there when Jenette first arrived. Turning back to Skutch, Jenette noticed that the Guard's legs were wet and wondered if his missing C-23 had anything to do with the water pouring in below.

"Wasn't me," Skutch said, throwing his hands up to protest his innocence. "Must've been a stray pulse-rifle shot."

Jenette looked askance at the Guard's singed hair, but decided to let the issue lie. "Any ideas how we rescue our people and get out alive?"

Skutch grinned and tapped the C-23s on his belt. "I've got an idea that involves these."

Jenette gritted her teeth. "Should I be scared?"

"Maybe," said Skutch. "But tell me what's *not* scary down here."

Jenette did not respond because the buzzers had become silent, but Skutch had a point. And the number one scary thing was directly below: the pool at the bottom of the chamber. It continued to rise, increment by inexorable increment. A lot of medical advances had been made in the last few millennia, but none of them allowed non-biofactured humans to breathe underwater, which was what the humans and domestics on the reactor were going to have to do all too soon.

The buzzers resumed thrumming.

"Hello, hello . . . ?" a soft voice buzzed in Jenette's ear.

"Clarence?" Jenette whispered back. "Clarence Bigelow? You're okay? Skutch, Bigelow's okay!"

"Okay," Bigelow hissed into his headset, "is a relative term . . ." He strained against the glue holding his neck and glanced at the in-humans atop the reactor. They squatted motionless, heads bowed in some sort of trance. " . . . but my paralysis has lessened, due in most probability to my great body mass diluting the buzzer venom. I can now move my lips."

Bigelow flexed his face, trying to work out the swollen numbness. As he did so, his eye was drawn to motion halfway up the wall of the spherical chamber. "Ah," he grunted, "rescue is at hand."

"Rescue?" Jenette squawked on the comset. High above, Bigelow saw her tiny head swing around and look in the direction that he was looking in. "Ah, frig."

XXXIV

If a Pilot wants a task done right, he should do it himself.

—*Pilot Academy Manual, v1.03*

Karr was moving through the sea of buzzer carapaces. Jenette's voice came as a low, tense sound in his headset earpiece.

"Pilot Karr . . . what are you doing?"

Careful not to make any vibrations that the buzzers would pick up, Karr gave her a thumbs-up.

"What do you mean *thumbs-up?*" her voice hissed. "This is not a thumbs-up moment. This is definitely a thumbs-down moment. The situation is bad enough as it is. Let's not do anything hasty. We need to work together to come up with a strategy. Do you copy that?"

Karr made another thumbs-up and kept moving.

The comset relayed a frustrated groan, but Karr was not about to retreat. He could see the water rising at the bottom of the chamber just as well as Jenette. Prospects for finding and recovering the C-55 warheads were not good as things stood, but they would certainly be worse if the humans trapped on the reactor became submerged; even Pilot Lindal Karr with his instincts to work alone could see that, and he did not have time to wait for Jenette to call a committee meeting and mull over the options. The water level was rising too fast for that: three feet in the last five minutes alone.

Action was called for, therefore Karr would take action.

He moved down the side of the cavity, only when the buzzers were thrumming, as Jenette had warned and as he had seen Arrou do with Guardsman Grubb. As far as Karr could deduce, the translucent creatures had entered a sort of sleeping state, vibrating, then holding still, vibrating, then holding still. He edged down the curving wall, then froze, edged down further, then froze. The most difficulty lay in not losing his footing and sliding down the steep incline.

Karr's objective was a nearby root buttress that spanned the space between a curving chamber wall and the null-fusion reactor. Soon he was at the near end of the buttress. That was the easy part. Now he must get across. Not only did he have to keep his balance so as not to topple off the log-like support and fall into a horde of buzzers below, but he had to avoid the buzzers perched on the buttress itself. Karr had to somehow get around them, without running or jumping or touching them.

The buzzers did not seem to care for *up* and *down*. Many clung to the bottom or sides of the buttress. These Karr edged past fairly easily. It was unnerving to see their vestigial, blind eyes staring right at him, apparently waiting for him to get close enough to pounce upon. Karr attempted to concentrate on other things, like their quivering feelers and leg parts. He mustn't step on any of those or it was game over.

Karr made it to within six feet of the reactor without incident. Bigelow was straight ahead on the lower cone of the reactor. The machine's lower end was to Karr's left. The *in-humans* were on the upper cone to his right. They had not detected his presence and so were not a problem, yet. What was an immediate problem were two large buzzers, on top of the buttress where it abutted the reactor casing. They were directly in Karr's way and there was no way around them. Karr craned his neck around, checking to see if any other support buttresses were close enough to be helpful. A buttress overhead looked like it might be close enough to grab and use to swing over the buzzers. Karr tentatively reached up.

"For goodness sake, don't jump or do anything that makes a big vibration," Jenette's voice cautioned in his ear. Bigelow apparently did not want Karr to jump either, because the scientist's eyes widened and he shook his head in tight, little, imploring shakes.

Karr cursed them as naysayers; what did they expect him to do, *fly* over the buzzers?

Just then Bigelow made a sucking sound—and spat.

A gob of saliva splattered on the buzzer nearest to Karr. It jerked, spinning in Bigelow's direction, feelers questing for the source of the bombardment, and bumped into the second buzzer. Mandibles flared and the creatures hissed at each other. Karr was hopeful they might change positions on the buttress, but after a short, grumpy conflict, they settled in exactly the same positions as before.

Bigelow shrugged ever so slightly, as if to apologize for the lack of results, but his actions had given Karr an idea. Creeping as close as he dared, Karr reached over the near buzzer, raised the Gattler high into the air—and brought its butt end down as hard as he could onto the far buzzer's carapace.

Wham!

The fight was on! The two buzzers woke up, the far one thinking that the near one had assaulted it. The far buzzer attacked. The near one defended itself. Legs squirmed, mandibles scraped off chitin, venom sprayed as the albino creatures scrapped, spiraling around the buttress in an effort to gain a superior combat position. Karr crossed his fingers and remained immobile, even when they battered into him. When the battle finally subsided, the buzzers were in different positions, still on top of the buttress, but each tilted a little to one side. When, after a relatively long time, Karr was sure that they had reentered their state of torpor, he zigzagged through them and on over to the reactor.

Bigelow's eyes glistened hopefully as Karr approached, but Karr did not move to the large man's immediate rescue. The scientist's expression fell as Karr sidled to an access hatch near the butt end of the reactor casing. Unfastening the latches at each corner, Karr cautiously pulled on the hatch.

It squeaked.

Sweat beaded on Bigelow's face. The scientist stole a look up at the in-humans, but they remained in their trance and did not react.

Incrementally, when the buzzers vibrated, Karr tugged the hatch fully open.

*   *   *

Skutch shook his head. "Got to admit, he's got gusto in his shorts."

Down below Jenette and the Guard, Karr was reaching into the access hatch and fiddling with the reactor's innards.

A low murmur sounded in Jenette's comset.

"Interesting," said Bigelow. "I believe I have deduced our Pilot's plan. And, if he is attempting what I think he's attempting, it may just work." The scientist sounded only partly convinced. His speech became slow and heavily emphasized. *"However, he must keep in mind to close the bleeders back down as soon as the bulk of energy in each null-field sector is purged."*

Jenette cringed as Karr made yet another thumbs-up, this one aimed at Bigelow.

Karr turned back to working inside the access hatch. Shortly thereafter, Jenette noticed a change in the pulsations of the null-field. The erratic beams slowed and appeared to draw back toward the reactor. The buzzer horde stopped thrumming in rhythm and began shifting agitatedly, and the ghastly in-humans tilted their hooded heads up from their trance as the field thickened and brightened in a patch just above them.

And then—*FKOOOOOOM!*

The section where null-field energy had been swelling exploded, a blinding geyser shooting out from the reactor in an incinerating funnel, spreading across the ceiling of the spherical chamber. This was no faint, tickling forcefield, but a crackling bludgeon that shattered hundreds of buzzer carapaces, leaving a gooey, steaming mess before vanishing as suddenly as it had erupted.

"Impressive," said Skutch.

"Maybe," Jenette allowed, begrudgingly. She appreciated Karr's results, but she was not going to celebrate until everyone was safely back on the surface and onboard the heavy lifter.

Another section of swelling null-field exploded. Another section of buzzers was squashed to bits.

FKOOOOOOM!

"The Null is hurt, the Null is hurt!" the in-humans shrieked, crabbing helter-skelter across the reactor casing.

Karr ignored them and kept to his task of purging the null-field sectors. Open a bleeder, allow energy to coalesce and disperse—*FKOOOOOOM!*—close the bleeder before reactor feeds overloaded. Repeat.

FKOOOOOOM! FKOOOOOOM!

The reactor shook with each discharge. A smile appeared on Dr. Bigelow's face and stretched wider with each blinding jolt. Buzzers were dying by the gross. Karr was careful not to purge any sectors that might discharge near Arrou and Grubb. The buzzers surrounding the human and the domestic twitched, like automatons in need of orders. Those near patches of crushed carapaces scuttled around and feasted on the remains of their kindred.

FKOOOOOOM! FKOOOOOOM! FKOOOOOOM! Karr figured he could destroy most of the buzzers by purging the sixteen null-field sectors that didn't bear on Arrou and Grubb. Already two-thirds of the creatures were dead. After dealing with the buzzers, Karr would turn his attention to the in-humans.

"What do? What do?" shrieked the in-human named in-robert.

"Keep the Null safe!" in-joan shrieked back. "The Null must be safe!" The old female scrambled for the open access hatch near her. Reaching in with her teeth, she began meddling with the controls. Instantly, Karr's purging process went awry. The null-field changed intensity and color, dropping from fire orange to a bloodier shade of red.

The reactor began to make a dull, winding-up noise.

"Oh, oh," said Bigelow, no longer grinning. He looked at Karr. "Overload."

In-human heads swiveled in the direction of Bigelow's voice. "Unsafe! Skins unsafe on the Null!"

Karr's hands flew over valves and breakers within his access hatch, in an effort to keep the purging process under control, but just as he got one sector back under control, the ancient female made another interfering adjustment of her own. Karr's limited knowledge of null-fields was stretched to the limit; he did not know the correct counter measures. Field sectors that had been building up fizzled. Others, already purged, began to re-coalesce.

Two of the in-humans, the females in-mary and in-delilah, scuttled down to Bigelow. They shrieked, flexing their blade-sharp teeth near Bigelow's throat, "Bad skin, bad skin! Must make the Null safe!"

"Stop, stop!" wailed in-robert, hurrying down to block them. "In-robert's skin! Not hurt!"

The in-human creatures snarled and spat at one another as null-field sectors began going off at random. *FKOOOOOOM! FKOOOOOOM!* The reactor shook in its web of root buttresses. The sector over Karr's head discharged. The access hatch slammed down on his wrists.

"Aaaah!" he howled.

"More skins! Free skins hurting the Null," in-joan cried in alarm.

In-mary and in-delilah forgot their conflict with in-robert and turned, cocking their earpits in Karr's direction. In-robert placed himself between Karr and Bigelow and snarled, fiercely defending his prize. In-mary and in-delilah lunged. Karr yanked his hands free and jerked the Gattler to bear, squeezing its trigger. *Splat! Foosh!* Foaming adhesive streamed onto the attacking in-humans, plastering them to the reactor. They screeched in outrage, legs flailing helplessly.

A null sector began to swell dangerously over Arrou and Grubb.

"Arrou, run!" Karr yelled, scrambling to reopen the access hatch and cursing the need to make noise and allow the in-humans to hone in on him. "Run!"

Arrou had been making slow progress dragging Grubb. The two were almost home free, only a few paces from a tunnel opening, but the errant null-field sector swelled bright and discharged. *FKOOOOOOM!* The powerful emission hammered down onto the curving chamber wall, obliterating Arrou from Karr's sight.

Two feet closer and the discharge would have crushed Arrou as flat as the many buzzers, whose ruptured inner organ fluids he could now smell because they were splattered all over him. Buzzers near Arrou swarmed past him to gorge on the vile meat.

Arrou froze. The next coalescing null-sector was on the other side of the reactor. All he had to do was be smart a few more moments. He would wait until the buzzers passed by, then grab up Grubb and run for the nearby tube opening.

The human's arm flopped over. He began to wake up.

Buzzers swiveled in Arrou's direction, feelers questing for the source of the vibration. Arrou tried to hold Grubb immobile and not move himself, but that was too difficult to pull off. The Guard's head lolled and he moaned.

That was all the buzzers needed. A wriggling albino horde converged on poor Grubb, sinking mandibles into his flesh and injecting venom. They dragged him out of Arrou's grasp.

"Harruuuurk!" Arrou roared in consternation.

In-joan, hearing the sound, shrieked from atop the reactor, even more agitated than before. "Feral! Feral! Skins *and* Ferals attacking the Null!"

Buzzers sprang at Arrou, trying to entrap him in their waxy spittle. He leapt about, desperate to avoid the scissoring fangs and reluctant to abandon Grubb, but it was merely a matter of time until he would become trapped himself.

Splat! Ploosh!

Gobs of adhesive arched down from Karr's Gattler, tumbling in decidedly non-aerodynamic fashion between the root buttresses and plopping with wet heaviness among Arrou's buzzing attackers.

"Go, go!" yelled Karr.

Trapped buzzers chittered, yanking at the adhesive froth. Waves of cannibalistic hunger imploded around Karr's hits. It was the break Arrou needed, but he was still reluctant to flee without Grubb.

"Go Arrou," yelled a commanding female voice from above. "Go! Get out of there!"

So ordered by Jenette, Arrou finally turned and bounded through gaps in the buzzer horde, bowling them over or shredding through their delicate undersides with his strong talons. Those he wounded also became fodder for the horde.

*   *   *

Karr kept firing until he saw Arrou disappear into the tube mouth. Then, twisting about, he blasted another in-human—the crippled one—as it sprang at him. The blind monstrosity toppled off the reactor casing, cartwheeling down through the air before sticking to a root buttress below.

The reactor continued to make its ominous winding-up sound.

"The red breaker! Hit the red breaker!" Bigelow shouted.

Karr wrenched the access hatch open, slammed his right hand down on the only red switch in sight and was gratified by an immediate lowering in pitch of the overloading sound.

"Bad skin, bad skin!"

One of the male in-humans bowled into Karr. Karr jammed the Gattler tip into its mouth and fired a stream of adhesive down the creature's throat, but Karr lost his footing and tumbled backward into open space as the choking in-human's talons dug into his uniform. *Wham!* They glanced off a root buttress. *Wham-wham! Krik!* The in-human's talons went slack and its neck lolled at an unnatural angle. *Splash!* Karr hit bottom, in the deepening pool of water, his breath knocked out of him.

Buzzers spun to attack, attracted by the strong vibration.

Gasping, needles of pain squeezing his ribs, Karr staggered out of the water. He stumbled for a tube opening, spraying a wide semi-circle of adhesive behind him. A wave of buzzers hit the goo. It wasn't much of a reprieve—a second wave of bugs poured over the first—but it was enough for Karr to stagger into a passage opening and plunge down a red-glowing tube. All too soon, buzzer feet echoed in the passage behind him.

Karr peered into side passages but they mostly turned downward, and those downturned routes were filling up with water. Finally Karr found a tunnel that ascended. He began to scale the confined space. Unfortunately, he was forced to retreat fast when the clatter of another buzzer horde began to rumble louder and louder from above. Karr slipped back down to the original tube and ran on, his feet hammering, making strong vibrations for the buzzers to follow. Their chattering grew louder. Dark helmet shapes poured around glowing corners behind him. More seriously, the source of the flooding water became apparent. Ahead and below

Karr seawater thundered in where pulse-rifle hits had breached tube walls. Probably one of the Guards had put up a fight nearby, but Karr did not have time to search for clues to who it had been. He was trapped. He whipped around, frantic for any possible escape in the dim light.

The buzzer horde neared.

Karr's only option was a narrow tube going straight down. Knowing he didn't stand a chance against so many buzzers, Karr jumped in. He tried to slow his descent by spreading his legs, but the slick sides gave no grip. As the buzzers blotted out the light overhead, Karr plummeted down into the dark. The shaft squeezed tighter. Karr drew rapid breaths, expecting to splash into icy water at any instant.

Abruptly Karr hit bottom. The Gattler cracked painfully into his already hurting ribs. He was in another transparent blister, but there was no time to gawk at the undersea view. Karr wriggled onto his back and raised the multitool. A many-legged avalanche poured down at him. Karr ringed the tube with adhesive, but the sheer weight of creatures kept the mass moving, tearing off limbs and heads of those entrapped out front.

Beep, beep, beep, warned the Gattler. Low ammunition.

Karr fired in small, sparing bursts as the horde pressed down. Seven yards. Three yards. Any second he expected the Gattler to run dry. One yard. The mass slowed. Dead buzzers smeared along the sticky walls, living ones pressing through the center. Finally, Karr held the trigger down, spraying from side to side across the entire leading edge of the mass.

Pfisht. The Gattler ran dry.

Karr flinched as a fountain of scissoring claws and mandibles pressed into the blister and ground to a halt mere inches from his vulnerable human flesh. Slowly the moving parts stuck to one another and froze hanging over Karr's head. Milky buzzer blood dripped down on him.

Arrou bounded down a tube, his mind full of unfamiliar emotion, a burning-in-his-gizzard emotion that made the sounds of his own legs and claws underneath him seem remote and the roaring clatter of pursing buzzers seem almost quiet. He clamped his ring of teeth on the unknown feeling.

Hatred.

Arrou was familiar with a whole array of emotions common to domestics. He *loved* Jenette, *disliked* Tesla, and *feared* Sacrament, but outright malice he had never known. Slow to anger and forgiving by nature, Arrou nonetheless felt acidic hatred for the in-human Ferals. And for Arrou the most awful, angry thing about them was that they were not *Ferals* at all. The in-humans knew too much. They spoke human language. They knew human religious gestures and how to do things to a null-fusion reactor. No Feral knew those things. No, the in-humans were not Ferals.

The in-humans were *domestics*.

Domestics just like Arrou. But unlike Arrou, they broke the sacred human-domestic bond. They killed humans.

Arrou wanted to kill them.

Arrou hunted to eat, and he would kill to defend himself and the humans he cared about, but this was different. Arrou wanted to kill the in-humans, not to eat or save lives, but because they were *wrong*. He did not know if his Khafra instincts would let him kill another Khafra, but he very much wanted to try.

First, however, Arrou had to survive. He was better at running and evading than his biped friends. On four legs Arrou ran and climbed faster than the poisonous buzzers and his glowbuds provided good illumination. Initially he made good progress away from the reactor chamber, but the buzzers knew the winding passages better than he did. He heard them catching up, trying to get around in front of him through parallel tunnels, and every time he backtracked from a wrong turn or dead end, they got closer.

Arrou rounded a turn and clawed to a halt, barely avoiding a fall into a deep pit. There was no backtracking this time; the buzzers were too near. Trapped in the dead end, Arrou knew he had to think of something smart. He wracked his brain for a clever way to beat the horde, but the only thing that came to his mind was a stupid trick that he remembered from when he was a kit playing hide-and-go-seek around the Enclave nursery. Still, it was the only idea he had. Arrou turned around and ran head on at the rumble of pursuit, back up the tube to a break in the smooth surface. It was no more than an irregular niche in the ceiling, but it would have to do. Stretching up, Arrou sunk his foreclaws into the tunnel fiber. He pulled his body up, his stunted right paw complaining, sunk his teeth in for extra grip, and finally heaved his hind legs up to find purchase with his rear claws. Hanging upside down like a night creature, he then let go his bad paw and fished through a collection of Grubb's equipment, which was looped over his back. Pulse-rifle: no good. Ammunition belt: no good. Medikit: good, but not for this. Canteen. Canteen?

"Urrkurrkurrk."

Arrou did not want to use the canteen. In hide-and-go-seek the object was customarily a resin rock and the target a leafy bush some distance away. But the nearing echoes forced his choice. Twisting the cap off the plastic gourd, Arrou gulped down the precious fresh water, and then hung motionless. For his trick to work, he must not make any movement that the bugs could feel, not until the last moment.

Kekitekitek—kekitekitek—KEKITEKITEK!

Arrou felt a rush of air, prelude to a mass of bitter smelling carapaces. Just before the awful legs and teeth were on him, he coiled his free foreleg and heaved the canteen. It bounced down the tube, making all sorts of vibrations in the process. Arrou felt the rumble of buzzer feet on the tube wall, then saw the many-legged terrors. Irrationally he dimmed his glowbuds. The buzzers passed underneath, slimy carapaces glancing off of him. They followed the offensive canteen vibration as it careened into the pit. Arrou, hanging motionless, both sets of double thumbs on his free hand crossed, did not exist as far as the buzzers' senses were concerned. For a long, long minute, they clattered under him and then they were gone.

Arrou's stupid trick had worked. He could barely restrain a yowl of relief. Good thing he did though, because as he began to let himself down, he abruptly jerked himself tight against the tunnel ceiling.

Sounds of a very different sort of threat were approaching.

XXXV

Tesla's nightmares are his torment.

It is always the same. Tesla is back on Coffin Island, back when it was still called Elysium. Fireballs rise from explosions. Colony buildings burn. Screams of wounded and dying echo in the night as the Ferals close in. Ferals have overrun the island in retaliation for Tesla's attack on and occupation of Golconda island, the new home of the Enclave. Soon they will spot the hovering jump-lifter platform (a scaled down version of the heavy lifters used by Pilots) and Tesla will be forced to give the order to flee.

Again and again Tesla relives the same part of the dream, the part where the jump-lifter is overflowing with refugees. No one else will fit. There will be no rescue for the distant crying wounded. Below, faithful domestics struggle to attach jump-lifter lines to the colony's main null-fusion reactor, but the small lifter cannot carry the refugees and the heavy machine at the same time.

Tesla orders the cables cut. "Retreat."

Six loyal alien faces fall as the flying platform starts to leave. "Wait, wait!" they cry, running along underneath. "Throw down ladder! Ladder!"

Tesla's own domestic, Blacky, is among the stranded. "Master, master! Not leave! Please, please!" But there is no room on deck.

"Stay and guard the null-fusion reactor," Tesla says, trying to diffuse the situation before the human refugees become agitated. "We will come back. Keep the null-fusion reactor safe until then."

*"Keep the null safe, keep the null safe," the
domestics repeat, obediently running back to the
hourglass-shaped reactor.*

*In the dream Blacky looks back, his bullet-shaped
face perfectly clear, despite the fact that the jump-lifter
is racing away.*

"Tesla be safe, too," he says. "Come back soon."

*Tesla turns away. There is no going back. Elysium is
lost. There is no hope. And even if there was, the dream
always ends the same way. Fire erupts on deck, from
some colonist's improvised weaponry. A thruster engine
explodes. The deck tilts. Refugees slide into ocean
waters, Tesla amongst them, as the flying machine
crashes. Tesla paddles furiously to keep his head above
the waves. Choking heads disappear one by one as they
pray for rescue. . . .*

*And then Tesla wakes up. And remembers it was all
too real. So many years ago, and still so vivid. A
sleepless night or two elapses before he once again
locks the memory out of his mind.*

"Smell sweet, smell sweet by Null," whined a voice.

"Smell skin-in-white," said a cracked, ancient voice. "Smell
jasmine. Smell . . . Pilot."

The voices drew closer.

"Pilot? Fugueship Pilot?"

The click of overgrown claws stopped directly below Arrou. It
was the in-humans. They didn't notice him. Apparently the buzzer
guts, which were splattered on his hide, masked his scent from the
vile Khafra. Arrou didn't really care. He would just as soon drop
down and tear out their throats, but Jenette had told Arrou many
times that it was smart to be sneaky and listen. So he did that.

"Real Pilot," said the voice of the ancient female. "In-joan remembers smell from long time back, when in-joan was evil, when
in-joan was friends with skins."

"Real Pilot," in-robert burbled excitedly. "Must catch."

"Yes. Because what do Pilots bring? More humans! Must catch.
Must stop."

"Good, good. And then?"

The older voice dripped evil. "Then, do what in-humans do to humans. . . ."

"Take skin?"

"Take skin."

The other gasped. "In-robert becomes in-*pilot?*"

Arrou heard a smack in the dark.

"In-joan becomes in-pilot. In-robert becomes in-bigelow."

Obsequious whining. "In-bigelow, in-bigelow. That what in-robert means. Good, good."

The abominations scuttled off down the tunnel.

Arrou let himself down. He needed to talk to Jenette, to find out where she was and what he could do to help. A way to do that popped into Arrou's head. It was not allowed, but then the pulse-rifle and ammunition on Arrou's back were also not allowed, and neither was throwing away a canteen. Arrou fumbled Grubb's headset up under his jaws (the only way he could get the human-scaled device onto his head), positioned the tiny speakers near his earpits and flipped on the power switch.

Water gushed into the tube from a breach somewhere out of sight above.

"*That's* your plan?" Jenette yelled at Skutch as they fought the current. "That's definitely *scary*."

Skutch attempted to brace himself against the slippery passage wall and not be swept away. "Scary is a matter of perspective," he yelled back. "Did I mention I can't swim? Besides," he gulped, "it should work. You saw the fissures on the surface, and you've seen skrags after a storm. That's what usually happens."

"It's the *usually* part that bothers me."

"I hear you," Skutch said with a fatalistic grin. "It's your call, Consul."

"I just wish we had less drastic options!" Jenette complained.

"We do," said Skutch. "We can do nothing and hope for a miracle. Or we can abandon our guys and head for the surface ourselves."

"Those are both out."

"Agreed. Which leaves the third option. . . ."

Jenette shook her head angrily. "I'm going to strangle Pilot Karr." Jenette hated having her hand forced. If not for Karr's rash course of action, they might have remained hidden from the buzzers and in-humans for quite a while. That, at least, would have allowed them time to talk and think—and hopefully come up with a fourth, less drastic plan of attack: Jenette had had no alternative but to order Arrou to flee when Karr's plan went awry. Swarms of buzzers had immediately chased her and Skutch deep into the tendril tubes under Coffin Island. The creatures would not pursue them into the gushing water, but that was a temporary and very questionable reprieve; at any moment the torrent might sweep them away to drown in darkness. "What about the heavy lifter?" she asked Skutch. "If we lose the heavy lifter, we're as good as dead!"

Skutch grimaced, as if to say *no plan is perfect.*

More water surged into the passage. Skutch lost his footing. Jenette grabbed one of his epaulets as the current threatened to sweep him away and for several frantic seconds she felt as though her arm would be torn from its socket, but Skutch did regain his footing.

Jenette realized her comset was squawking at her. She adjusted dislodged earpieces. A throaty voice resonated from the speakers.

"Lose heavy lifter?" the voice protested. "Not good, not good. Must save heavy lifter!"

"Arrou!" Jenette exclaimed. "You got away from the buzzers?"

"Yes, got away."

"That's great! I didn't expect to hear you on comset."

Arrou's voice tensed. "Urrr. Sorry. Know comset out of bounds, but can not think of better idea."

"No, no, it's all right," Jenette said hastily. "You did good." Desperate inspiration came upon her. "Arrou, how long have you been listening?"

"Hear Jenette talk about losing heavy lifter."

"Well, maybe we won't lose it after all. Can you fly the heavy lifter all by yourself? Without Pilot Karr to help you, I mean?"

There was a pause. "Think so. What have to do?"

"Power up. Lift off and fly straight and level. You can do that?"

"Urrr. Think so."

Jenette looked around her. The flow of water showed no sign of lessening, and she had no reason to believe it would. It was decision time. "All right Arrou, here's the plan. . . ."

The malevolent jellyfish, which was the underwater side of Coffin Island, glowed through the transparent blister. Karr was trapped, alone, sealed off from fresh air and with only the blister's waxy walls separating him from the deep, frigid ocean. A sticky tongue of buzzers protruded down at him from the plugged entrance, leaving barely enough room for Karr to lie on his back. The air grew warmer and warmer from his breath while icy water dripped into the blister; probably, Karr considered, the tube above was flooded and only the mass of dead buzzers kept that water from drowning him. To top all those unpleasantries off, he had lost his comset during his flight from the reactor chamber.

Karr was completely cut off, completely alone with his thoughts, and in that time he pondered his recent actions. He had done exactly what Jenette had warned against; he had made the situation worse. It had seemed the proper course of action at the time. Certainly Karr's actions abided by all of his Pilot Academy training. Nevertheless, it began to creep into his mind that maybe he should have worked in concert with Jenette and the Guards, that maybe together they might have contrived a better result than the circumstance in which he presently found himself.

Karr shivered.

It was just so hard to trust other people. Karr's experiences on other planets had not exactly shown him that *trusting* was a prudent course of action—sometimes experience had shown trusting to be shockingly dangerous. There was no question that Karr trusted Jenette more than any other human in the last few centuries, but unfortunately that had not been enough to override his ingrained paranoias.

Well, he was going to pay for his sins now.

Freezing water seeped through Karr's collar and down the small of his back. He turned up his uniform's fabric thermostat.

The water would remain at a tolerable temperature for as long as the oxygen in the blister held out.

The walls of the beacon support strut were still moist with blue fluid as Arrou clambered up. Clawing up out of the tube tendrils had been hard: getting lost, hiding from marauding buzzers. Now that he had evaded the hordes, he moved quicker, pulling himself ever upward, talons digging into the gnarly roots, but his head swam with concern over Jenette's last transmitted instructions:

"Power up, fly at least a kiloyard off shore, then hover. Don't land, don't come back, don't do anything. Just hover and wait. Got that?"

"Power up, fly, hover," Arrou had repeated. "But what about Jenette? Arrou wants to rescue Jenette!"

"Never mind me. Do what I say and keep hovering until I contact you on comset. Okay?"

"But—"

"No buts. The only way to rescue me is to do what I say. Okay?"

"Urrr . . . okay."

"Good. We'll give you as much time as we can, but that might not be very long, so get going!"

It had taken hours for the expedition members to penetrate Coffin Island down to the robotic factory and, despite not having to bore the tunnels through rock-hard ghutzu, Arrou knew that he could not retrace that path as quickly as Jenette needed. Jenette and Skutch were going to do something. Jenette had refused to tell Arrou what that something was before the intervening mass of Coffin Island grew large enough to block comset transmissions, but Arrou knew it was dangerous. Arrou could tell by the tone of her voice.

Shoulders heaving, Arrou hoisted himself onto the ledge where the body dump had exploded and washed humans and domestics down into the tubes and tendrils below. Plastic membrane hung in tatters. Fetid, slimy caverns opened above Arrou where the cadavers had been packed so tight. Arrou desperately needed rest, but he pressed on into the narrow horizontal fissure, which lead to where the beacon shaft continued upward.

Whoops!

Arrou froze, halfway through the fissure. He saw movement on the far side, faintly illuminated by his own glowbuds. A section of the shaft-wall flapped open and two sets of sickly Khafra legs stepped into view. Arrou instantly recognized the ancient in-joan and her ragged companion, in-robert. Fortunately in-robert was not light-footed and made lots of noise, which prevented the in-humans from hearing Arrou before he saw them.

"Pilot goes up?" in-robert asked, his blind-eyed skull turning up the shaft. "Think Pilot goes up?"

"Yes," hissed in-joan, creeping upward on joints that seemed to be hinged all wrong.

"But buzzers followed sound *down* tube. Found canteen in pit."

"Sounds tricky. Buzzers stupid." A thousand wrinkles contracted on the female's muzzle. "Maybe not Pilot that goes down. Maybe Feral goes down, but Pilot goes up. Remember, was sneaky Feral near Null, protecting humans."

"Yes. In-robert remembers." The wretch began to shiver. "Maybe . . . maybe Null not safe. In-robert wants to go back and make sure Null is safe."

"Null will be safe when in-joan is in Pilot's skin," in-joan gurgled evilly.

Moving like arthritic crabs, the in-humans climbed the beacon tower. Arrou carefully wriggled out of the fissure. On his left, a half-closed flap of ghutzu covered a tunnel chewed into the depths of the island. It swung slowly closed, blending seamlessly into the tower wall. Arrou guessed the in-humans had probably dragged Dr. Bigelow through that secret passage when they kidnapped him for his skin; it probably connected to the tube tunnels below and served as a quicker way to the surface from the reactor chamber. Arrou wished he had known about it before.

Letting the in-humans climb to the limit of his hearing, Arrou followed, climbing and stopping as they climbed and stopped, so that if the two nasties heard anything, they would think it an echo of their own noisy progress. At the top of the tower, Arrou peeked into the interlocking grottos near the robotic factory. The in-humans were paused at the joining of two bubble caverns. In-robert started for the factory, but in-joan turned aside.

"No," she said, ambling toward a swooping wall. Arrou wondered at her peculiar gait on level ground: four steps on four legs, as all Khafra walked, but then awkwardly rising up and taking four rapid, unbalanced steps on hind legs. It took a few repetitions for Arrou to figure it out: the in-human was imitating bipedal human locomotion. Reaching the wall, in-joan's leprous forearms grabbed a broken ceramite slab and toppled it, revealing another secret hole. "Short way," she announced.

The ragged in-robert scuttled over in the same strange two-footed, four-footed gate and sniffed the hole. "Aaahh. In-joan sneaky," he gloated.

Both creatures disappeared into the hole. When Arrou felt it was safe, he crept over to the opening and looked up. A buzzer-chewed tunnel climbed almost straight up into the darkness. He could still hear the in-humans' movements and chatter.

"Short path good," said one.

"Beat Pilot to top," snickered the other.

Trusting the in-humans' superior knowledge of the island, Arrou decided to follow. He ascended rapidly behind them, hampered only by the occasional avalanche of loose material. Once he slipped when a section of roots crumbled under his hind feet, sending a slide rushing into the darkness below. Arrou skidded down, digging in with forearms and pressing his armored back into the roots behind him. Sheer upper-body strength stopped his fall. He held on, wondering what the in-humans had heard.

Arrou heard a smack and a yelp. "Climb quiet!" snarled the old female.

"In-robert does climb quiet," the feeble one protested.

"Quiet like sick Null," in-joan snarled again.

Another smack, another yelp.

Arrou caught his breath and continued up. The buzzer tunnel branched off at points and smells came out of those alternate paths: smells like machinery, smells like mildew, smells Arrou could not identify. He stayed to the path behind the in-humans as it snaked upward, occasionally leveling, sometimes steepening, and eventually becoming a precipitous vertical pipe. At one point he heard in-robert inexplicably chanting, "Made Null safe, made Null safe." Almost immediately, the tunnel became less steep. Arrou was forced to squeeze around a jumble of shiny cones, which had been crammed into the tight passage. Arrou guessed right away that they were the missing C-55 warheads; they had threads that looked like a perfect fit for the torpedo shaped casings in the munitions bunker. And he saw the meaning of in-robert's words: the metal cones were chewed open, their innards strewn about. The in-humans had made the warheads useless to keep their Null-God safe. Pilot Karr would not be happy, but Arrou could not stay and mourn for broken warheads. Mindful of Jenette's warning to hurry, he kept on climbing after the in-humans. The tunnel snaked erratically for some distance more and then twisted back to a gentle upward slope.

A short time later, Arrou saw the two cancerous in-humans. Less than ten paces ahead, they were stopped in a snug, den-like chamber. Arrou watched their sickly necks crane out a hole at the far end.

"This one smells sunlight," said in-robert.

"Ugllugllugh," in-joan burbled, shrinking at the very mention of such a terrible, infectious word as *sunlight*.

In-robert's reaction was different. "This one misses the light," he whined. "Misses the colors."

In-robert flinched when he realized what he had said, expecting the female to strike him, but instead her voice was sweet, as one might speak to a kit or demented elder.

"Do humans live by light? Do humans live by colors?" she asked.

"Yes," in-robert answered.

"No!" shrieked in-joan. "Humans live *in* the light and *in* colors, not *by* light and *by* colors. Humans are *blank*." In-joan walloped her weaker companion where his pink human skin cloak stretched over his head.

Arrou crept closer as they argued.

"How do humans live?" in-joan demanded.

"With mouth and ears?" in-robert replied meekly.

"With mouth and ears," in-joan agreed. "Humans live with mouth and ears. We must live with mouth and ears." To emphasize the point, she scraped her claws across her empty eye sockets. "We must be blank."

Arrou froze as the two fell into silence, but he was near enough to see beyond the den. Outside lay a low-ceilinged cavern, filled with root-smothered colony buildings. It was lit by the faint light of Arrou's glowbuds streaming out of the den. Even in that dim light, he recognized the second underground chamber where he had been bitten by the large buzzers.

"Hear wind," said in-robert. "Smell burned roots."

In-joan opened her mouth and drew air over her olfactory membranes. "New human hole to surface. Close. Below us." Her breath rattled in her emaciated chest. "Go no further. Pilot will come. Lay trap here."

A new human hole. Below the den. Now Arrou knew exactly where he was. That *new hole* was the first one Karr bored with the Gattler, it lead to the cavern with the cracked roof and the winch lift to the surface—and the heavy lifter. All he had to do was get past the wretched in-humans and he was home free.

With no time to waste, Arrou coiled and sprang, leaping higher and farther than a human could from such a crouched start. Unfortunately, his back brushed the roof of the small den as he arched toward the exit hole. The keen-eared in-humans heard the grind of armor plate against ceiling.

"Feral!" in-robert shrieked and cowered.

The ancient female, however, rolled and slashed at the noise with nasty accuracy. Leprous forearms raked across Arrou's unarmored underside, gouging deep, then clung to Arrou's hind legs, but the feeble creature was half of Arrou's size and could not hold his mass back. They tumbled out of the den, falling, locked together, down the cavern wall, and smashed into a crumbled building. Ceramite sections collapsed on top of the combatants, Arrou taking the brunt of the impact. His head swam from the concussion, and in those heartbeats of dizziness the in-human attacked with unforeseen ferocity. Teeth sunk into Arrou's armor plate. Talons gouged at his vulnerable eyes.

"Die Feral! Null foe!"

Arrou lashed out ineffectually. The vile smelling in-human was virtually wrapped around him. Arrou felt its horribly smooth human hide sliding against him, felt in-joan's talons cutting cool incisions in his flesh, which would hurt like crazy as soon as his head stopped spinning. In desperation, Arrou leapt straight up—dragging the clinging creature with him—and then let his four hundred pounds crush down on her. The in-human's bones snapped like brittle sticks. She howled, crippled, but was still able to thrust out her neck and scissor her cone of teeth on Arrou's neck. Arrou felt death slicing down on his jugular. Another second and his blood would spray upon moldy roots, but eons of Khafra fighting instincts had been activated. He drew his massive hindquarters up and let loose, raking with his rear talons, disemboweling his opponent with a sound like air escaping a greasy bladder.

The loathsome female expired.

XXXVI

Good intentions are no substitute for good outcomes.

—*Reflections of a Fugueship Pilot,*
Lindal Karr

It was a new location, a new critical juncture where a tube tendril met Coffin Island's keelroot, but it looked the same as all the others to Jenette. Salt water gushed down from above and it was dark, except for the light from the searchbeam Skutch held in his teeth. Skutch's head was half submerged. He worked, choking, to place a proportional charge into the clasp of a piton. Jenette held his legs against the torrent.

"Don't let go!" Skutch warned, gulping a lungful of air and disappearing beneath the water. He placed the C-23 in position, then used the butt of his pulse-rifle to hammer its attached piton into the fibrous wall. Finally, making sure the charge was secure, he set its detonator receiver to *armed*.

Skutch curled around and broke the surface, sucking in air. "That takes care of the main charges," he gasped as Jenette helped him up. "Now we lay the last three in a pattern designed to set the chain reaction off."

"That means we go up?" Jenette asked hopefully. They were below the level of the reactor chamber at that point and the tendril tunnels were flooding with alarming speed and force.

Skutch nodded. Jenette turned and began scaling an ascending tubeway.

Arrou staggered to his feet, bleeding from a dozen stabs and gashes, numbly looking at his kill. His head still spun, but, his

blood lust, spawned of rage against the vile in-human, was desert-
ing him. He had killed it. But that did not feel as good as he
thought it would. His guts heaved and he suddenly feared he would
loose his bowels like a scared kit. He clenched every muscle in his
body, head hanging, gulping sickly breaths. His glowbuds wavered
a dull purple—but they did not turn blue and begin to wink out in
the typical instinctive Khafra reaction to having taken the life of
another Khafra. The in-human's fetid, deformed remains, covered
in the tanned human hide, partly concealed from Arrou's brain
what had just happened. Most importantly, in-joan's glowbuds,
covered in scar tissue, had been incapable of flaring and fading to
blank, as any normal Khafra's glowbuds would if it died without
fulfilling Pact; they had not made the death flash, which would
trigger a suicidal reaction in Arrou. A living Khafra was a radiant
thing; a Khafra whose glowbuds did not glow was a dead Khafra.

As far as Arrou's instincts were concerned, in-joan had been
dead all along.

None of which made Arrou feel any better about what he had
done. There was, however, no opportunity for regrets or wound
licking. The remaining in-human abruptly let out a wail like the
cry of a domestic losing its human, or the howl of a Feral mourning its bondmate, and charged out of the hidden den, bowling into
Arrou from behind.

"Killer! Murderer!" it shrieked, clawing and biting like a possessed buzz saw. If its strength had equaled one tenth of its resolve,
it surely would have killed Arrou, but in-robert was even weaker
than the ancient female. Arrou easily flipped the wretch onto the
ground, slamming it into pipes and broken walls, at which point it
lost its stomach for face-to-face confrontation and curled up in a
feeble attempt to shield itself with its sickly, limp armor.

"Not kill! Not kill!" the in-human whimpered pathetically.
"Bad Feral, bad!"

Arrou shoved a hind foot onto the in-human's neck, ready to
tear unhealthy sinews from unhealthy vertebrae. "Not Feral!" he
huffed angrily. "*Domestic*."

"Not true, not true . . . not domestic." In-robert looked up with his blind face, first in disbelief, and then, gradually, in accusation. "Not right. If you domestic, you serve humans."

"Arrou serves humans!"

In-robert's empty eyes narrowed. "Then you bad domestic. Good domestics serve humans. Good domestics serve *all* humans. Not serve just *some* humans." The wretch adjusted his human skin mask. "In-robert is human. You must serve in-robert, too."

The sick logic almost made sense to Arrou's swirling head. Almost.

Arrou growled. "Not human—*in-human*. Sick, abomination." Arrou tore off in-robert's offensive, pink cloak and flung it into the darkness.

"No! In-robert's skin! In-robert must hide!" The ragged Khafra wept, a miserable, burbling sound. "No skin, no hide, no safe anywhere . . . Null not safe. In-robert fails, fails. . . ."

And then Arrou surprised himself. He stayed his claws on in-robert's neck.

Arrou felt unexpected pity for the pathetic, self-blinded wretch; pity for all the years passed in dank tunnels away from the light, eating heat-festered maggots and worse, with no hope to end its suffering. *Away from the light.* Arrou shuddered. Could he have survived away from radiance for so long? He did not think so.

Arrou was torn. Did the squalid creature deserve mercy after what it had done to his friends? Definitely not. Did it deserve to die for what it had done? Probably yes. But Arrou decided he did not like the taste of this game of vengeance. Hunting to eat was fun. Killing for hate was not. Perhaps . . . perhaps the game of mercy would taste better.

Arrou turned his back on in-robert and started to leave.

The in-human instantly screeched and leapt. "Join us, join us!" In-robert landed on Arrou's back, gouging at Arrou's face, trying to dig out Arrou's eyeballs, as in-robert had done to poor Crash. Arrou blinked his eyes down into his skull and clenched his brows with all his might. Prickly talons dug into his eyelids, trying to pry them open and slice tender tissue underneath.

"Rraaaagghhhhh!" roared Arrou. "In-human not bother Arrou anymore!"

With one sweep of a forearm, Arrou backhanded in-robert fifteen feet through the air into a gutted crawler. Once more the dank air resounded with whimpering. The in-human did not move. Satisfied that he would not be attacked anymore, Arrou turned away again and headed toward the surface.

Water frothed up the ascending tube. It rose to their knees, their thighs, their waists. Skutch held a remote detonator in his hands.

"Now?"

"Wait," said Jenette.

Ahead of them, the tube opened onto the reactor chamber. In the middle of the spherical cavity, at the same level as Jenette and Skutch, water lapped at the lower end of the null-fusion reactor.

The water rose to Jenette's chest.

"Now?"

"Wait."

"We've got to do it."

"We've got to give Arrou as much time as possible."

Skutch fidgeted.

The water rose to their necks. Skutch raised the detonator above his head to keep it dry.

"Now?"

Jenette looked out at the reactor again. The water was up over Dr. Bigelow's feet. She adjusted her comset. "Get ready, Clarence. This is going to happen fast."

"Do it," the scientist's voice crackled bravely on the circuit.

Skutch flipped the detonator's safety latch off and thrust the exposed red button at Jenette.

"Fire in the hole?"

With one last look at her friend on the reactor, Jenette clutched the detonator in Skutch's hands.

"Fire in the hole," she agreed, jamming the firing toggle down hard.

Hellfire erupted in the water around Karr. A series of timed explosions flashed around the keelroot's immense girth. *Whuf, whuf, whuf*—a quiet beat—*whuf, whuf, whuf, whuf, whuf!* Pockets of ex-

plosive gas swelled, hollow balloons in the water, then rapidly collapsed back upon themselves. Expanding, roaring shockwaves
blurred the deep water, hammering into Karr's fragile blister. The
turbulence buffeted him inside the translucent tendril, slamming
him violently into the hardened tongue of buzzers and molecular
glue; Karr choked on the water splashing around with him. For
a brief moment, there came darkness and relative quiet, but then a
wrenching groan built and resounded through the water, a
sound like heavy steel plates being torn. As Karr's eyes readjusted
to the dull glow emanating from the reactor-chamber bulge, he saw
the keel root moving not too far above him. Damaged fibers
snapped and tore in a widening gash where the explosions had just
gone off. He felt the vast mass dropping, taking him with it.

Coffin Island shuddered. The safety cage swung in and out of a
shaft of daylight and newly disturbed dust. A distant winch complained, rewinding cable as fast as it could, the backup winch atop
the cage adding its meager power to the effort, but that was not fast
enough for Arrou. *Jenette had done the dangerous thing!* Arrou's
pairs of opposed thumbs gripped the braided filament above the
cage and he began pulling his bulk up the moving cable, forepaw
over forepaw, hind leg over hind leg. Suddenly sunlight—glorious
sunlight!—bathed every glowbud on his body and he burst out of
the jagged hole at the top of the underground cavity and into fresh
air. Arrou let go of the line just before it passed through a pulley
rig on the tripod over the hole and let momentum fling his four
hundred pounds safely away from the subterranean world.

Arrou hit the chalky ground running. The island vibrated violently under his feet. The pulley rig teetered and collapsed, but the
cable kept reeling in. Arrou followed the tumbling, sliding, scraping tripod legs as the winch drew them back to the heavy lifter at
the edge of the clearing. Arrou came in fast, skidding on loose
bone material, slamming into the vehicle's sidewall, and then
springing onto the deck. He scrambled into the cockpit and sat his
butt down on the human crash couch.

Blinking dust out of his eyes, Arrou focused on what Karr had
taught him. His alien digits moved methodically over the dash.

The big red toggle flipped up. *Master switch on.* All the lights flickered alive. Now he pushed the four sliders to the top of their tracks. *Engine run-ups one, two, three, and four.* Powerful thrusters purred to life at each corner of the lifter—even as the sounds of cracking, shattering ghutzu root joined the rising moan of pipe-organ bones towering overhead.

Large cracks and fissures formed on the underwater side of Coffin Island: The keelroot swayed on a last, tenuous connection that strained and frayed like a steel cable unbraiding under too heavy a load, and Karr swayed with it. Severed from the glowing null-fusion chamber, stalks below the rent faded from vermilion to gray, like cooling cinders, their fiber-optic connection broken. They intertwined with tendrils still connected and glowing, but even those were growing dim. The underwater sun was dying. The lower half of the reactor bulge was dark, where it was filling with water, and no longer radiating the red light.

It was a plan, Karr told himself as his blister was buffeted and battered by other tendrils and blisters. The explosions were of human origin, that was for sure. The placement around the keelroot, the perfectly timed pace of the detonations, all of it indicated a course of action with purpose. Whether it was Jenette's plan, or Skutch's plan, or some combination of the two, Karr presumed that it was calculated to extricate the human and Khafra members of their expedition from the current adverse situation.

However, something had gone wrong.

The explosions had been intended to detach the keelroot from Coffin Island. That was clear, even if Karr did not understand why. But the keelroot was not completely separated. One of the charges must have misfired; probably that had been the dead beat in the series of thundering explosions. Whatever the plan's originator had intended to occur was not occurring and, to make matters worse, geysers of air were bubbling from every ruptured tendril. The underwater tunnel system was losing its life-sustaining atmosphere, fast.

Karr twisted so that he was facing the tear in the keelroot. He knew what he must do. *He must Trust.* No matter what his training had taught him. No matter that Jenette and the others were flat-

landers and he was a Pilot. His own machinations had not succeeded. He must cooperate. He must add his contribution to the efforts of the others. He must put himself at the service of their
intelligence and intent. He must silence the protestations in his
head. Or, very obviously, all would be lost.

It was not easy.

Trust. *No.*

Trust! *No!*

TRUST! TRUST! TRUST!

Karr jammed the tip of the Gattler against the transparent blister wall, the only barrier between him and countless tons of crushing, smothering water. He turned the selector. A barrel spun into
firing position. Karr thumbed a power knob to maximum intensity.
And then Karr began to hyperventilate. That was crucial for what
he was about to attempt, he knew; he must fool his body into thinking it did not need to breathe. As his head began to spin from hyperventilating, he watched for the right moment. The blister
swayed, bucked, jerked sideways, and then held still for a critical
split second. In that instant Karr aimed through the fish-eye walls
and squeezed the trigger.

TRUST!

The multitool thrummed, expending all of its remaining charge
in one monstrous shot. It kicked hard into Karr's shoulder. A huge
cutting beam lanced out from the barrel, blasting the blister wide
open. A snake of flash-vaporized steam bubbles rose from the
beam's path through the water, frying underwater fish-things on
contact; the bubbles slid around tube stalks, which scorched,
cracking and curling up like salted slugs. The beam itself expanded
as it shot out, until, as it reached the severed portion of keelroot, it
was a few dozen feet wide. The beam incinerated the last tenuous
connections.

Simultaneously, deep ocean pressure hammered into Karr's
blister, flushing him out into the deep. The awful cold set his
human muscles into seizure and Karr clenched his jaw to keep
from inhaling the liquid death. The keelroot plummeted, dragging
its attached network of tendrils down with a watery roar.

The loss of counter-balancing weight sent a series of shock-waves through the main mass of Coffin Island.

The lifter deck tilted sickeningly out of level. Looking up, Arrou saw that the horizon was all wrong. It was jagged, far too near, and rising up out of the water. Looking down, he saw that the island was breaking up, along the lines of the fissures that he and the humans had seen from the air. Mountain-sized chunks began to roll over, slowly but inexorably and with a deafening rumble, sections of ocean water becoming visible between the gaps. The part of island under the lifter steepened rapidly. The lifter slid down, crashing through skeletal trees and starting avalanches of fossil fragments. The tumbling scree picked up speed and plunged beneath frothing ocean waves. Rivers of white shard also streamed down at Arrou from above, raining over the lifter as the rakish angle of the ground increased.

"Must fly, must fly!" Arrou rumbled, tapping claws impatiently against the dash. The small readout was at the yellow line. *Thrusters buffered.* But the big readout was not at the red line yet. *D.O.I. throughput rising.*

The lifter fishtailed, plummeting, and then lodged amid a stand of petrified stumps. A score of yards below, angry seawater churned. Above, vast chunks of ghutzu root shattered free of the island section; Arrou heard the debris rumbling down its backside. Free of such a large amount of weight, the island section surged to vertical, hanging in the air for a giddy second at the peak of its arc, and then, with the ponderous motion of extreme mass, continued flipping right on over. The heavy lifter went with it, Arrou clinging to the controls. A shadow draped across alien and orbiter as the island fragment blocked off the afternoon sun.

All Arrou could see was imminent impact with the water below. The big readout on the dash was still not at the red line, but he yanked on the throttle anyway. Stuttering force pulsed out from the thrusters, leveling the deck from its vertical orientation and accelerating it into a dive away from the island fragment. Arrou pulled back hard on the steering yoke. The lifter responded at the last possible instant, pulling out of the dive and skimming along the surface. Orange lights blinked across the dash, the Khafra color for apprehension; Arrou guessed the human meaning was the same or worse, but he needed no urging to be apprehensive. Island fragments, rolling ominously, loomed in all directions around the lifter. And the one casting its shadow over the flying machine was coming down at Arrou like a gargantuan fly swatter.

The reactor chamber tumbled around Bigelow. Now he was right side up, now he was inverted. Buzzers cascaded like rocks in a polisher. Bigelow smelled bile on his lips. He heard gurgling, muffled screams from nearby in-humans, drowning underwater where Pilot Karr had glued them to the reactor casing. Bigelow felt no pity, not after what the wretched creatures had done to Toliver and Mok. Bigelow hoped the in-humans suffered, as they had made his beloved Bronte suffer. He wished them a painful, drawn-out cessation of life functions. The creatures clad in human skin thrashed, and he savored it. Perhaps later he would be ashamed of his emotions. At that moment he was not.

Water flooded the chamber from a dozen tubeways, adding their energy together to create a frightening maelstrom. At one point, Bigelow saw Jenette thrashing to keep her head above water. Currents grabbed her and sucked her out a random tubeway, presumably to an untimely fate.

Bigelow would meet that same fate, of course. His obese body would have floated quite nicely, the scientist reflected; maybe he would have floated face up and not have drowned. Alas, he would never know, not affixed to the reactor as he was. Whenever his half of the double-coned reactor went under, so would Dr. Clarence Bigelow. He wondered how it would feel to breathe water. It was said to be quite euphoric after the first wet gulp, after the panic was gone. The problem with that was that his panic was not gone. In fact, it was rising higher and higher as the water rose higher and higher. Bigelow doubted he would be able to manage any composure at all, never mind be calm enough to enjoy the euphoria.

Karr breathed out and out and out as Coffin Island self-destructed. Long after his lungs would normally have been empty he felt an aching expansion in his chest and that feeling grew as he bobbed upward.

Most humans would have panicked and perished instantaneously in the frigid, smothering deeps, but Pilot Lindal Karr figured he had at least a thirty percent chance of survival, maybe better. Pilot Academy had versed him well in the problems of staying alive at pressures higher or lower than preferable for an unshielded human being. Perversely, while the rest of his frail body struggled to survive, his mind was suddenly filled with the overbearing, haranguing voice of Major Vidun:

"You will now practice the Emergency Escape Ascent. As opposed to earlier training in the simulator, there is no room for error in the Tank. Failure to observe proper technique will result in drowning. You are too valuable to be allowed to perish. We will recover and revive all trainees who expire during training, but the predeath experience is extremely unpleasant, so I suggest you listen up and try to avoid it! The Emergency Escape Ascent is a centuries-old technique for exiting a heavy lifter, escape gig, or any other vehicle that has crashed or become disabled at depths of up to two hundred feet under water. The principles are simple to grasp: get out and rise up. The practice is not so easy and not without its dangers."

Tube stalks thrashed in the water around Karr as he rose. Severed ends spewed bubbles. Glistening balloons of air escaped and darted past Karr, racing for the surface. Buzzers also tumbled out; their inflexible carapaces were unable to cope with the sudden pressure changes and cracked, squirting inky viscera into the sea. Ropy entrails clouded the water and slithered off Karr as he kicked in the same direction as the rising bubbles.

Vidun lectured on in Karr's head:

"Low on the scale of danger is the risk of getting the bends. Since you will not have descended into the water using a highly pressurized air source, or spent long amounts of time in the deep water pressures, which would allow nitrogen to build up in your tissues, your risk of getting the bends is less than ten percent. More likely is the risk of hypothermia. Pilots wearing non-regulation gear will almost certainly die from the shock of deep water temperatures—another good reason to stay in uniform. Pilots in uni-

form will find the fabric kicks into emergency heating mode on contact with water. You will experience moderate discomfort, but you will survive."

Moderate discomfort? Karr thought numbly. Had Vidun actually practiced what he preached? From the instant the eight-and-a-half atmospheres of deadly cold ocean hammered in around Karr, icy daggers seemed to pierce his body, sapping the heat from his very bones. The discomfort was higher than *moderate,* that was for sure.

"As in any sort of compression or decompression event, the micro-capsules implanted in your lungs will release a one-minute charge of pressurized air. As you rise up through the deep water, this air will expand as the external water pressure decreases around your body. You must not hold your breath. You must instead constantly exhale or expanding air will rupture lungs. A ho-ho-ho pattern of exhalations is recommended."

On and on the ascent continued. Karr guessed his entry into the ocean had occurred at a depth of about two hundred feet. Objectively, his rise from that depth should take only two or three minutes, but subjectively, each agonizing second seemed endless.

"Don't forget to have your carpules recharged if you survive."

The water temperature suddenly changed around Karr.

"That's good. You just passed through the thermocline, the boundary between deep, painfully frigid water and the merely horribly cold water above it. That means you are at least halfway."

Light began to grow above Karr, rippling down from between the rolling island fragments. It was beautiful in a deadly sort of way. The air in Karr's lungs ceased expanding and began to feel hot. Karr's thought processes began to feel sludgy.

He was losing his patience with the phantom lecturer.

"Are you paying attention, Pilot-trainee Karr?" Vidun's voice demanded. *"The greatest danger of the Emergency Escape Ascent is the risk of shallow water blackout. As the air from your carpules runs out, and the oxygen stored in your cells is depleted, the carbon dioxide trigger, a part of your natural breathing processes, will be screaming for your brain to breathe."*

Shallow water blackout. Carbon dioxide trigger. Mumbo-jumbo! All Karr knew was that every cell in his body was on fire.

"As you rise within twenty-five to thirty feet of the surface, the need to breathe may become so great that you may pass out. Then you will breathe. Then you will die. You must focus. You must not lose consciousness. Too much has been invested in you. It is your duty to humanity to stay alive."

Fuck off, Vidun!

Karr would pass out and breathe water if he goddamn wanted to! At least the pain would end! The more Karr thought about it, the more he liked the idea.

And then he saw Jenette.

The slowly rotating central section of Coffin Island was directly above Karr. Jenette had recently been spit out of a broken tube tendril and pinned in a tangle of ghutzu roots. Her short hair rippled as she struggled to free herself from of the trap. Air bubbles broke from her nose. Karr kicked feebly toward her. He contacted the bottom of the island. Somehow, he pointed the Gattler at the roots holding her and fired. A feeble line of steam erupted from the multitool's tip as the dregs of its charge sputtered through the water, but it weakened the roots enough for Jenette to break free.

Karr's vision tunneled in. He no longer had control of his limbs. He floated helpless. Now he would breathe.

But hands clapped over his mouth and nose, and suddenly he was being pulled along the island's underside. Jenette's slender limbs kicked, propelling, dragging him frantically from root to root, headed for the light that he could just barely see now, as if from the bottom of a deep well. Too bad it was so far away. . . .

He and Jenette erupted onto the surface, spitting salty water, and gasping deliciously fresh air. Jenette thrashed to keep them afloat. Slowly, the island rolled up underneath them. The cool air seemed tropical after the deep water. A gorgeous sun beat down on their shivering bodies. Karr collapsed on a tangle of green weed.

Jenette rolled over, choking, grabbing Karr's collar. "Are you alive?" she demanded. "Say something!"

"I'm alive," Karr groaned.

"Good!" Jenette said angrily. "You fucking self-centered bastard!" The fiery blonde waif slugged Karr in the gut.

XXXVII

It is hard to escape the eternal cycle of suffering.
It can be far harder to escape the delicate snares of
pleasure.

— *Kthulah of Gnosis*

Tlalok and the female circled while the island burned around them. Sailtrees smoldered like spent torches. Gusts of cinder and spark twisted high into the night sky. Glowing trails of red destruction wormed inland wherever the blank-one forces had penetrated the island, and fire circled its shore, marking the passage of skimmers with flamethrowers. The blank-ones had tried to kill Tlalok; they had very nearly succeeded.

Tlalok and the female were aware of none of this. They circled one way and then the other in the secluded glade, their eyes locked upon one another, their bodies slowly drawing closer.

It had started with that night's Clash of Radiance. In spite of Tlalok's immense Khafra force, the blank-ones had mounted a daring, preemptive strike, darting with their skimmers through many islands crammed to overflowing with Pact, following the radiating patterns of light to the center, to Tlalok. Their intent had been clear: cut off the head of the attacking monster army and it would wither and die. It had been a clever gamble. The blank-ones knew they could not fight Tlalok's entire horde, therefore they had engaged only a small portion of it, using their vehicles to cordon off the island from reinforcement. Only fanatical defense from those on the island had beaten the blank-ones back.

The female had been part of that defense. She appeared in the

chaos, at the darkest point of the battle, using her prehensile teeth
to snip the head off a blank-one who was aiming a pulse-rifle at
Tlalok. She was not large, but also not fragile. She was sleek and
fast, with deep, melancholy eyes. And she was a deadly hunter.
She fought not with brute force, like Tlalok, but with surgical precision, using no more and no less force than necessary to dispatch
her foes. When the last blank-one fell, she and Tlalok found themselves alone in the glade, panting, staring, smelling . . .

In the distance beyond the glade was the aftermath of battle.
Khafra, silhouetted by flames, nursed their wounded, or hurried to
douse patches of fire or inject immune venom to stimulate the island to heal and regenerate. Hot winds carried the smell of blood
and cinder and *victory*. The horde had taken the best the blank-
ones could dish out and driven them back—and no one believed
the blank-ones could withstand what the horde would now unleash
upon them. That knowledge was like a narcotic. Every Pact tasted
it. In many it triggered strong emotions. In some, like Tlalok and
the female, it triggered deep-seated instinctual behavior.

Tlalok and the female spiraled ever closer to one another, first
their blank, grieving flanks facing inward, then their brilliant, radiant sides.

In some dim part of Tlalok's mind, he regretted. Ghosts of
Lleeala haunted him. He saw her echoes everywhere, in the proud
arch of the strange female's neck, or the shades of compassion in
her fierce radiance. No two sunrises had passed with Tlalok apart
from Lleeala since the day she opened her heart to him. He remembered her eyes sparkling with mirth as he bumbled at learning
the ways of Pact life. He remembered the heat of her breath and
the softness of her muzzle. He remembered her shaking with grief
after the blank-one murder of their nurslings and he remembered
holding her tight because Lleeala, his savior and Radiance of their
pack, needed comfort from Tlalok the Shamed. These things were
precious to Tlalok. He did not want to let them go.

But they were letting him go. The biological compulsion drew
him closer to the new female. Instincts were cleansing his heart of
grief, whether he liked it or not. It was the way of Balance, the way
of Pact, the way of survival. A new beginning. If one alone would

die, then two alone must be bonded together. The immune venom must be exchanged. Pact must be preserved. The cycle of things must continue. Tlalok might regret, but Tlalok must not resist, not against these things he and Lleeala believed so strongly in. Balance and Pact allowed no endless grieving. Besides, Tlalok knew, Lleeala would not want Tlalok to resist, to be alone. She would have approved of the brave female with the sad eyes.

<<What is your name?>> Tlalok asked, as if in a trance.

<<Kitrika.>>

<<I am Tlalok.>>

<<Kitrika knows,>> the female said with a quick gulp. Tlalok caught shimmerings on her glowbuds that showed she was both hopefully excited and a bit intimidated.

They touched, blank side to blank side.

Luminescent patches erupted. Glowbuds twinkled like opening flowers and spiraling galaxies, crossing from male to female and female to male, where they contacted at shoulder, hip, and muzzle, growing more intricate and synchronous with each breath and heartbeat. They began to fill each other's blank sides with light. Tlalok's filled Kitrika. Kitrika's filled Tlalok. They surrendered to it. It was good. It was right.

But then why did Tlalok feel the sinking feeling in his loins, the tightening around his heart?

Suddenly Tlalok convulsed. His glowbuds strobed, freezing the motion of his flailings into many brief tableaus of pain. Kitrika at first recoiled from the sickening light, but then drew her eye orbs back deep into her skull and crept forward. She grabbed Tlalok gently, but firmly, and held on. Some time passed before his convulsions eased.

<<It is all right,>> Kitrika cooed. <<It is going to be all right.>>

Eventually Tlalok clattered his teeth. <<It will not.>>

Kitrika flinched. She looked away in shame.

<<No,>> Tlalok said. He reached out and clasped his paw around hers. <<Not Kitrika's fault. Kitrika is worthy of Pact.>>

Kitrika was reassured, but still confused. <<But then what is wrong? Tlalok is . . . *already bonded?*>>

<<Tlalok has no bondmate,>> he reaffirmed. <<Tlalok swears this.>>

<<What then?>>

<<Tlalok does not know,>> he said, gathering his breath. He attempted to rise to his feet, but failed. <<Something had gone wrong with Tlalok's Pact. Tlalok does not know what it is, but Tlalok feels it, deep inside.>> Kitrika hurried to slide a shoulder under Tlalok and helped raise him to his feet. <<What happens now?>>

<<First, Kitrika must go.>> Tlalok looked around. <<Tlalok has shamed Kitrika, but no one has yet seen.>>

<<Do not be foolish,>> Kitrika said sternly. <<No one shames Kitrika but Kitrika. But Kitrika will surely be shamed if she abandons Tlalok in his time of need.>>

Kitrika glowed with determination. Again Tlalok saw ghosts of Lleeala; these ones told him there was no point arguing against a female with such a set to her radiance. So he did not. Tlalok gathered his strength and composure. Kitrika waited until he was ready, and then accompanied him out of the glade toward the cinders and flame.

PART FIVE:

DANCE OF THE
LITTLE WORMS

XXXVIII

She imagines Feral lovemaking as she lies on the cold surface. She imagines a year's bottled passion, brewing, building, like magma doming up under bedrock, then releasing in a single glorious night of union. She imagines tenderness. Orgasms of radiance.

No restraints, no muzzles, no blindfolds.

Those are Sacrament.

Tables side by side. Medical spotlights glare in a sterile operating room. A figure in hooded surgical greens inserts the needles, runs IVs from human veins into those of a domestic. A litany of pseudo-religion spills from the hooded figure's mouth. The Body Pure. The Body Pure. Blessed be the Body Pure. The domestic makes no sound, tries to be brave.

Her mind wants to flee, but every cell in her body thirsts, giddy for the nectar that will keep her alive.

The hooded figure activates the transfusion. Milky ochre flows in the tubes from the domestic to her. Machines pump worthless plasma back into the alien. A faint salt and blood smell burns in her sinuses.

Now the domestic whimpers. It hurts. And there can be no anesthetic. That would taint the transfusion. It will hurt the domestic a lot more as the process nears its end. But that is not the worst thing about Sacrament.

The worst thing about Sacrament is how much she loves it.

When the immune venom hits her blood, it hurts for a while. A horrible burning, as if each and every one of her cells is on fire. And she is glad of this, for while there is pain, she feels less ashamed, less guilty. At least

she is suffering for her sins. But once enough of it
circulates in her veins, it turns off switches in her brain.
Her conscience disappears. Boundaries crumble. And
the euphoria hits. Glorious, self-preserving, self-
centered bliss. She cannot stop now, no matter how the
domestic wails.

And it wails.

(In her state she wishes to think of the quadruped
only as "it." Not as "him." Not as "friend.")

She cares not.

Sight and sound accelerate the rush. How much
horror-pleasure time elapses, she cannot gauge. She
wants it to go on forever, to draw every last succulent
drop of immune venom. No matter the consequences.

But the hooded figure stops the flow.

The golden sense of well being trickles away. She
rails. Threatens. Begs. Despicably. But the hooded
figure will not reopen the flow. And she cannot. She,
like the domestic, is also strapped to her table.

Doesn't the figure understand? Doesn't it know how
badly she needs the Sacrament to go on?

Against her will, she ramps down.

Of course the figure knows. All the colonists know.
This is the way they survive. Some, this knowledge
breaks. Others, it makes hard. How long, she wonders,
can it go on?

When is enough too much?

Her mother believed that never was too much. Her
mother let herself die to prove her conviction. Sometimes,
the woman on the Sacrament table wishes her mother
had taken her with her. And sometimes, like now, the
woman hates her mother for abandoning her to face the
misery alone.

Now, the hooded figure injects the domestic with a
sedative.

It is a mercy that the domestic will not remember. It
is her punishment that she can never forget, even as she
lapses into post Sacrament coma.

—a confession, in the
black book of J. Tesla

Jenette did not feel well. She shambled across a patchwork of base camp tarps and bedrolls, only half aware of her surroundings. *She must stay upwind of the smell or it would surely drive her mad.* Crinkling her nostrils as tightly closed as possible, she bent over Guardsman Grubb and checked the biosentry on his neck. His skin was ashen, but the buzzer-venom paralysis had subsided and the indicators all blinked green. Probably, Jenette tried to reason, those were good signs.

It was so hard to think straight.

Ten yards beyond the base camp tarpaulins, an incinerod did its grim work. Black smoke rose from a humanoid body bag, which combusted under the squat disk's intense heat. A scorched patch beside that body bag evidenced the remains of a previous humanoid cremation and a third body bag lay on the other side, as yet untouched, the features of a quadruped outlined by the shrinktight plastic. *It was that quadruped form which Jenette tried desperately to ignore.* The bags contained, or had contained, Mok and Toliver. The last contained Bronte. *Immune venom had spilled on the body bag's hermetic seal. Jenette could smell it, even from upwind. And she wanted it. Craved it. With every cell in her body.*

Far beyond the base camp, the shortened remnant of Coffin Island's keelroot lay flaccid across a belly-up landscape of slouching tubules and mounds of slime. The heavy lifter labored up out of a ragged hole in the reactor-chamber bulge, its extended robotic arms appearing next, then the null-fusion reactor, held tight in grappling claws. Tendrils of ghutzu fought against the heavy lifter, drawing tight between the reactor and their unseen anchor points. Karr, a tiny figure standing on the double-coned machine, waved frantically as the roots snapped and lashed up at him. Thruster hum decreased as Arrou lowered power in the cockpit.

Jenette moved from one prone form to another, checking for progress. Crash slept, a clean dressing covering his missing eye. Liberty was much the same as Grubb, but passing in and out of consciousness.

"You did it. You got us out," Liberty mumbled to Jenette. "For a woman, you got king-sized gnards."

Jenette's mouth twitched: not a smile, not a grimace.

"That's a compliment," the Guard added, and then promptly dozed off.

Bigelow was faring pretty well, physically. Most of the buzzer-venom was out of his system. Emotionally, however, that was another story. His eyes flitted over to Bronte's body bag as Jenette removed a spent osmosis pack from his arm. Sorrow contorted his pudgy features and Bigelow quickly averted his eyes, looking into the distance.

Pilot Karr shot clinging ghutzu roots off of the null-fusion reactor as Arrou hovered. Karr was not a good shot with a pulse-rifle. He expended quite a few charges to sever each of the organic restraints.

"It will make a superb explosion," Bigelow murmured as the last tendril broke free and the heavy lifter began rising with its prize once again. "A trifle too strong for our purposes, perhaps, but an excellent substitute for the missing C-55s."

"Oh?" Jenette said, not really paying attention.

"Indeed," the scientist continued, happy for any distraction from the death around them. "An overloading null-fusion reaction converts a phenomenal amount of matter to energy in an extremely short period time. The sequence in which the null-fields drop will be critical in shaping the escaping energies and extinguishing the fire over Pilot Karr's fugueship. I will have to confer with Guardsman Skutch." Bigelow craned his neck up off his bedroll. "How is he?"

Jenette turned to the explosives expert, who slept fitfully, covered in sweat. "The biosentries think he's going to live," Jenette answered, no less remote.

"Excellent," Bigelow said, trying to sound chipper, but his sadness over Bronte showed as he closed his red-rimmed eyes.

Jenette continued her rounds of the patients on the tarps. *I should be more sympathetic,* she berated herself. *I must concentrate.* But to Jenette's displeasure, she found that her apparently random movements around the base camp had drawn her to the edge of the tarps that was nearest to the incinerod and body bags. *The* body bag.

Jenette shook her head in denial. *"No."*

Dr. Marsh lay nearby. Eyes that had been slitted and watching Jenette for some time fluttered open. Dry lips parted.

"Ask Bigelow. He won't object."

"What?"

"I said, 'Dr. Bigelow won't object'."

Jenette brushed sweat from her forehead. "I don't know what you're talking about."

"Don't waste your breath," Marsh croaked. "You can't even fool yourself. You're not going to fool me: you look like shit."

"I told you, I don't know—"

Marsh abruptly levered her head and shoulders up. Her arm shot out and grasped Jenette's chin. Fingers probed swollen glands under her jaw. "As I thought," the doctor pronounced. "Feeling giddy?"

"Maybe a little."

"Chills. Hot flashes?"

"Not yet," Jenette lied. Marsh glared and felt Jenette's forehead. "Well, some," Jenette admitted.

Marsh moved her fingers down Jenette's neck and, frowning, took a pulse.

Jenette gulped, suddenly fearful. *"Second stage?"*

Marsh nodded.

Jenette tried to hide her reaction, but her arms and head hung with the weight of the revelation. It was the Scourge. No more denying it now. The pathogen followed no exact timetable, instead it progressed through stages that could take months, weeks, or only days. The host's immune defenses and stress levels played a critical role in the progression. The opportunistic parasite was always alert to exploit weakness and escalate to its next growth cycle. Jenette's last few days had been particularly stressful; if that kept up, she worried how quickly she would progress through the remaining stages.

Unless, unless. . . .

Jenette tore her eyes away from Crash's body bag.

"I shouldn't be getting sick. I'm not pregnant."

Marsh withdrew her hands, cold and sober. "You know very well that refusing Sacrament leaves you defenseless, you will get sick whether you are pregnant or not. Again I say, ask Dr. Bigelow." Marsh rolled over to get the scientist's attention, but found the large man already staring in their direction.

"It's all right with me," he said solemnly.

Jenette clenched her eyes. "But it's not all right with me."

"Why not?" Marsh asked.

"How can you ask that? Bronte's dead, Deena, dead. Don't you care?"

"I care. That is not relevant. All the combined knowledge of colonized space can't change *dead*. What *is* relevant is that you are alive and we want to keep you that way. Isn't that right, Dr. Bigelow?"

Bigelow nodded, eyes glistening.

Jenette gritted her teeth. *She wanted to give in.*

Marsh eased back on her bedroll. "Think of it as a transplant—like how we'll replace Crash's missing eye."

"That's not the same thing."

"Yes it is. In fact, since Bronte is already dead—since we are not killing her with Sacrament—it's no different than implanting biofactured cells into your eyes to cure myopia or inoculating your teeth against dental caries bacteria, or any of a dozen other routine procedures that I have done for you in the past."

"Deena, stop, please."

A few seconds passed. Bigelow marshaled his grief. "Jenette," he said, "you got us into this. We believe in the cause, and we believe in you and that means you have to live, otherwise—" Bigelow waved an arm to encompass the wounded, Coffin Island, the body bags, "—otherwise all this was for nothing."

Marsh piped up again. "That's right. Don't get me wrong, we're all in this together—but you are the one with the vision." Marsh chose her next words carefully. "Some of us have seen *the worms* too many times, and it isn't nice. I don't know how Dr. Bigelow feels, but some of us don't want to end up that way—we've vowed to never end up that way. We're not evil people. We'll do anything for the cause, except commit suicide. We're not as strong as you. So when it comes right down to it, we'll keep on going to Sacrament and domestics will keep on dying unless you find a solution."

Confession over, Marsh closed her eyes.

Jenette found herself staring down at Bronte's shrinktight cocoon. Somehow, she had moved over to it. *The smell of immune venom was overwhelming.* A few feet to the right, the incinerod had charred Mok's remains to ash.

"Who's going to carry the torch if not *for* Jenette Tesla?" Marsh asked, eyes still shut.

What should she do? What?

The fate of every human and domestic on New Ascension hinged on what Jenette chose. The options were horribly simple: compromise her principles and have a chance to find a solution to Scourge and Sacrament, or stand firm to those principles and die. This, she realized, must have been how the whole travesty of Sacrament started, with her father making a series of pragmatic decisions to stay alive, convinced that he was making the high moral choice every step of the way.

As Jenette agonized, the heavy lifter floated slowly closer, the heavy reactor skimming a few yards above the ground, then sinking as Arrou let the thrusters idle down. An uncomfortable flatulence sounded as the reactor compressed heaps of slime, forcing bubbles of trapped air through the grim goo. The lifter's robotic grappling arms disengaged and folded under the lifter's belly. Then the orbiter itself landed.

Jenette forced her hands off of the body bag.

Every fiber in her body protested, crying out with craving. Craving!

Jenette picked up the incinerod. Shook off the ash.

"There won't be a torch to carry if I give in," Jenette said, as much for herself as for Marsh and Bigelow.

Flip, flip, twist. She reset the burn cycle. Click.

Get up now. Steady. Don't look back.

The incinerod began its task yet again as Jenette turned and, stumbling, fled into the lurid landscape.

XXXIX

Pilot Academy transcript, 10.21.3530.
Subject: Lindal Karr, aged sixteen years.
Document status: CLASSIFIED.
   (Vidun and Uttz march down a sterile looking
   corridor.)
Vidun: Why haven't you examined the surveillance
   recordings?
Dr. Uttz: I am no voyeur, sir. If you desire information, I
   suggest you examine them yourself.
Vidun: I suggest you attend to your duty, Doctor. Pilot
   candidates must procreate.
Dr. Uttz (annoyed): We are using all possible methods
   to breed candidate Karr. We have extracted every
   drop of semen that he's produced since becoming
   pubescent. We've artificially inseminated
   thousands of women. We've isolated DNA
   sequences, which we suspect code for fugue
   immunity, and spliced them into human zygotes.
   Nothing works. None of the resulting children
   exhibit fugue-immunity. Obviously, whatever makes
   Lindal Karr a Pilot is not reflected in his sperm
   cells.
Vidun: What about cloning? Why aren't we cloning him?
Dr. Uttz: We are, but I must warn you, it is a widely
   held misconception that clones are identical copies
   of the original individual. This is simply not the
   case. Whatever makes Lindal Karr a Pilot is not

merely reflected in his sperm cells. Random factors effect both cloned and normal human zygotes, in utero and after birth. Exposure to chemical and biological influences as well as radiation may cause DNA mutations outside the germ cells. I believe that a whole series of unlikely cellular mutations have combined in Lindal Karr to produce fugue-immunity. *The chance of recreating such random mutations in a clone is practically nil.*

Vidun: *I refuse to admit defeat, Doctor. The stakes are too high. It may be that there is something we don't know about old-fashioned intercourse that is part of the equation.*

Dr. Uttz: *Unlikely.*

Vidun: *Unlikely or not, we will try. We must push him harder.*

Dr. Uttz: *You push too hard. Some things cannot be pushed. They wither under too much pressure.*

Vidun: *Bullshit. Too much thinking: that's his problem. It's not good for a man to get locked up inside his own head. He gets to questioning every action. Fear takes over. Moral paralysis follows. That is why we train to focus on action.*

Dr. Uttz: *We also train our candidates to avoid human contact. It is a measure of our very success that he has difficulty with intimate behavior.*

Vidun (rubs his temples): *He does like girls doesn't he? That would be just our luck; we finally find a Pilot and he's gay.*

Dr. Uttz (sternly): *Not that that would have any effect upon artificial insemination, cloning, gene splicing—or his ability to perform his duties as a Pilot.*

Vidun: *No, not of course not, but it would be problematic as far as reproduction is concerned.*

Uttz: *Would it? I wonder. In any case, trainee Karr is heterosexual. He simply does not like the girls you*

> *send. If you insist upon pursuing this course of*
> *action, I suggest eliminating prostitutes from your*
> *selection pool.*
>
> Vidun: *Prostitutes! These women have undergone the*
> *highest scrutiny. Only the most intelligent, most*
> *well-bred, physically attractive candidates are*
> *chosen.*
>
> Dr. Uttz: *They give their favors in exchange for*
> *personal profit, for the not inconsiderable prestige*
> *and riches that ensue should they be lucky enough*
> *to bear a future Pilot. They have no feelings for*
> *Lindal and he knows it. That is the core of the*
> *problem.*
>
> Vidun: *He must be bred before he ships out. (pause)*
> *Can you give him something for it?*
>
> Dr. Uttz: *A pill to cure him of his conscience? I think*
> *not.*
>
> Vidun: *No, no. Calm down, Doctor. I am only*
> *suggesting a shot to get his blood, you know,*
> *flowing.*
>
> Dr. Uttz: *I suggest you consider the tried and true*
> *method of exposing him to a wide selection of*
> *females his own age and letting nature take its*
> *course. That is how normal people do it.*
>
> Vidun: *Oh, no. No, no, no. Normal people fall in love.*
> *Normal people become attached and don't want to*
> *leave their families behind. Normal people don't*
> *become fugueship Pilots.*

Karr spotted Jenette at the edge of the fractured island section. She sat at the rim of newly-formed cliffs, atop an arch of drying tube root, hugging her knees girlishly, her face buried in her arms. Karr wound through the limp-noodle topography and climbed the arch. The slight young woman did not react as he sat down beside her. Karr waited patiently, inspecting the root surface. It was dying in the sunlight, like all the other underwater life forms which had been stranded by the break up and roll over of the once large island. Bark-like flakes sloughed off under Karr's fingers and fluttered down into ocean far below.

Without raising her head, Jenette eventually spoke. "Pilot Karr?"

"Yes."

"I'm sorry I hit you."

Karr unconsciously rubbed his solar plexus. Jenette might be small, but she had given him a good bruise. "That's all right. I think I deserved it. My self-preoccupied Pilot training led me to believe that purging the null-field sectors was a sound strategy. In fact, I only succeeded in getting us into more trouble than we were already in. You and the others got us out. Obviously I should have trusted you. Obviously I was wrong."

"You were what?" Jenette asked, surprised.

"Wrong?"

Jenette's head lifted. Here eyes were rimmed red. Unfocused, confused thought processes were clearly visible in the movement of her face. "Why can't I hate you, Lindal Karr? It would make things so much easier."

Karr did not know what to say. He fumbled for a different course of dialogue. "That's, um, a wonderful view you've found here. . . ."

A rare New Ascension sight spread out before them: a blue-green sea, with no silver sheen anywhere to be seen. Foam frothed against the remaining fragments of Coffin Island, which floated around the island Jenette and Karr watched from. In the distance storm clouds billowed up from the horizon. *Cumulontmbus* clouds, Karr remembered from some deep crevice of his mind. Towers of fluff boiled up into the atmosphere, meeting New Ascension's jet stream and smearing downwind into enormous, anvil-shaped thunderheads in a blue, blue sky.

Jenette was not looking at the vista, but at Karr. Her nostrils flared, she took a deep breath, and then buried her head in her arms once more and shook.

"What's wrong?"

"Nothing."

Even Karr with his limited interpersonal skills could see that was not true. "Well . . . the thing is, I just had an encounter with a four-legged friend of yours. After we recovered the reactor, he trotted off to find you, happy as a Pilot in *fugue*, but he came back looking like a grumpy light-festival tree."

Jenette clutched her knees tighter.

"I'm no expert," Karr ventured, "but I'd say he's pretty upset."

"So?"

"So, he claims you yelled at him and told him to go away. He says that you were angry, but that he didn't do anything wrong, and that you said he smelled bad."

"He needs a bath," Jenette snapped. *Arrou smelled of immune venom.*

Misunderstanding her comment, Karr whiffed his own armpits. "Guess I'm pretty ripe, too," he said apologetically.

"Oh, no," Jenette objected. Her chest expanded as, without looking up, she drew another deep breath. "You smell *good*."

Karr considered. Their recent underwater ordeal had washed away most of Coffin Island's nasty filth. In fact Jenette looked relatively clean, her blonde-gray hair showing no trace of embalming-fluid stain. She wore a suit of mottled green-and-black battledress (probably one of Liberty's); it hung loose on her smaller frame, but it was neat. Karr, on the other hand, had just spent a sweaty day prying the null-fusion reactor free from the keelroot's clutches. Karr stank; so he questioned Jenette's pronouncement that he smelled nice. He also noted that she looked even paler than usual.

"It's the Scourge," Karr decided, "isn't it?"

"Dr. Marsh has a big mouth."

"Dr. Marsh didn't say a thing."

The pain in Jenette's cramped posture reminded Karr of *fugue* withdrawal, which he had endured so many times.

"If there's any way I can help, any way at all. . . ."

Jenette turned her frosty eyes on Karr.

"Do you think I'm pretty?" she asked suddenly.

"Um . . . " said Karr.

"Do you think I'm pretty?" she repeated.

Karr was struck by how pretty Jenette looked just then, teary-eyed, ill-fitting daysuit, and all. It made no rational sense, but that was how he felt. "Yes, very pretty," he admitted quietly. "But I don't see how that affects—"

Jenette abruptly clasped the back of Karr's neck and drew him to her lips. She was tender and soft. He smelled the incense of her breath, felt the delicate intimacy. It was a surprise. And it was nice.

He allowed the contact to continue. He even began to participate.

But the encounter changed. Soft became tense. Tender became urgent. Caressing hands gripped tighter, holding his head to her hungry mouth. She was probing, devouring. Feasting.

The girl-woman seemed to be sucking at his very soul.

Karr broke her grip and pushed her away. Jenette fell back in shock and then turned away in shame. Again, she shook. Not weeping, but shuddering as hints of color flushed her ghostly skin. She swooned and nearly fell off the root arch, but Karr quickly grabbed her. He steadied her, utterly confused. He had no experience with Scourge. Should he run back to camp and get Dr. Marsh, who was hardly in a state to make the trek back, or try to carry Jenette to base camp? Just as Karr was testing to see if Jenette was light enough to convey such a distance, her eyes fluttered open.

"I'm sorry," Jenette said, feeling despicable. *She had compromised after all. She had been utterly wicked. And yet . . . the immune venom cravings were already abating, the fog rapidly lifting from her mind as the traces of* fugue *in Karr's kiss worked into her body. She had bought time at the cost of her honor.* "Please don't hate me."

Karr wiped his mouth, more confused than ever. "I don't hate you."

Jenette smiled sadly. "You should."

"No . . ." said Karr, trying to figure out his own mixed-up feelings. He had enjoyed the kiss, just not the way it ended. "No, I shouldn't. I kind of liked what just happened. It was just a little too fast. I don't exactly have a lot of experience with . . . this sort of stuff. Pilots are solitary creatures, you know. And, uh, I know intellectually that you are twenty-three standard years old, but you don't look a day over fifteen by off-world standards."

Jenette shook her head. What could she tell him? Until that day she had feared every change her body made towards adulthood. Now she fervently, irrationally, wished that she had never taken hormone inhibitors at all. Frustration laced her voice. "I can't change the way I look! If I looked my true age I'd be dead!"

"I don't want you to change the way you look," Karr hurried to explain. "There's nothing wrong with looking young. When you're thirty-five and look twenty-five, you'll be the envy of every off-world woman, believe me. It's just that right now you look out-of-bounds young—underage, off limits upon pain of imprisonment, banishment, loss of rank, or marriage-at-the-barrel-of-a-splatter-pattern-projectile-weapon *young*."

Jenette resigned herself to that explanation.

Karr groped for a consoling thought.

"It must be rough, being born—" Karr almost said *on a Plague World*, but caught himself at the last instant and said, instead, "—here. Scourge and Feral wars and hormone inhibitors. Destiny can be a harsh master."

Jenette snorted. "I don't believe in destiny, other that that which I make for myself."

"No? No greater meaning? No purpose for existence? How do you keep your sanity?"

Jenette's forehead crinkled philosophically. "One day," she said with a nod of her chin at the spectacular skyscape, "I plan to be a cloud."

Karr didn't understand.

Jenette waxed poetic. "One day, when I'm dead and gone, all the water in my body will be free. The molecules of water will evaporate from my mortal shell, float into the air and join clouds high above all these earthly troubles." Jenette pointed at a wispy streak high in the stratosphere. "Little bits of me will bask in eternal sunlight. Young humans and Khafra will lie on their backs and stare up at me. I'll be a treasure ship, or a mushroom, or a faraway island castle. Scourge won't mean anything to me then. I'll be a tiny, content part of the larger cycle of life."

For some reason, Karr, was reminded of his relationship with *Long Reach*. "And you won't be lonely?"

"No. The way I see it, every cloud up there was part of some-body alive at one time or another. I'll have good company." Jenette didn't speak for a while. "Sometimes I'll have to be rain, but I can put up with that. I'll float and rain and then evaporate back into clouds, over and over. Maybe I won't know it's me anymore, but I'll be a part of it. Leave the worrying to someone else."

"I like it," Karr declared.

"Yeah?"

"Yeah. Count me in."

"Okay then." Jenette smiled. "It's decided."

They sat quiet for a while then, not touching, but feeling very close as souls billowed and raced across the afternoon sky.

Karr kept Jenette safe when she slipped into a brief *fugue* coma. He said nothing about it afterwards and the two of them returned to base. An hour later the camp was packed up and the heavy lifter hovering with Karr at the controls. Grapple arms flexed down and plucked the null-fusion reactor from its slimy bed.

No one noticed a cancerous shape that clawed to the surface from a deep gouge in the island, sniffing and listening, head cocked intently. Nor did anyone notice as it ducked out of sight and fronds wriggled from mole-like movement underneath the is-land's sloppy surface, or as a creature clad in anthropoid skin scrambled up in the blind spot under the lifter's hull. Thruster en-gines throbbed. The lifter's bow dipped. And soon the flying slab was no more than a speck, accelerating away from the foul-smelling shores of Coffin Island, with the even smaller speck of a four-legged in-human clinging, inverted, to the precious Null which had given meaning to its wretched life for so very, very long.

XL

Two days later.

Ferals were thick on the ocean, in paddleboards and other grown-to-order craft. Arrou was on shift at the heavy lifter controls, Karr and Jenette standing just behind the cockpit, and they all saw the vast net of Ferals. There were so many that Arrou could actually smell them, even from fifteen yards up and traveling twenty-five knots per hour.

Jenette found the display captivating. The Ferals appeared to be following some sort of overall plan. Scores and scores of legs and paws paddled in perfect rhythm. Each and every bow of each and every vessel pointed in the same direction—the very same direction the heavy lifter was heading.

It was a development Karr did not relish. Where *were* all those aliens going? They hardly looked up as the lifter's rectangular shadow passed over them. What could be so all-consuming that these Ferals paid such little heed to a flying machine from another planet? The sooner the Ferals were specks in the distance behind them, the happier Karr would be.

"Arrou " he ordered, "accelerate to thirty knots."

"Urrr, accelerating."

Arrou pulled the throttle up a bit and pushed the steering yoke forward a bit further. The lifter's nose dipped slightly and the breeze caused by its passage through the air rushed slightly faster, but the increased speed brought Karr no greater sense of security. Rather, even more Ferals on paddleboards scrolled into view from beyond the horizon ahead—and a cluster of islands came into view with them. Karr squinted distrustfully at the green blobs.

They seemed to be spaced very evenly across the water.

Jenette observed that the green silhouettes appeared different from those she saw regularly around the Enclave. As the lifter drew closer, checkered patterns of lush jungle foliage and lighter, cleared plots became visible on the backs of the ring-islands. Furthermore, the islands were not *ring-islands* at all, but solid, healthy disks without a characteristic sinkhole at the center. Jenette began to get excited. She almost squealed aloud in delight as she spied large dome structures peeking out from stands of trees and clusters of smaller domes gathered where several open plots joined together.

"Give them a wide berth," Karr said to Arrou.

"No, please," Jenette said, a hopeful sparkle in her eyes. "I'd like to see what's down there."

Karr acquiesced, against his better judgment. "All right. Hold your course, Arrou, but keep us well above the tallest trees."

"Hold course, keep vertical clearance, urrr."

The lifter swooped up over the first emerald isle, giving a beautiful top-down view. The open spaces were clearly agricultural plots: viridian squares with neat pink furrows or khaki patches with light green hedges, some even contained herds of animals.

"Look, look!" Jenette pointed. "Domesticated forfaraws! And villages! And roads!"

Beaten mulch pathways linked the fields and domes. Golden roadwort connected clusters of domes to other clusters of domes. And there were Ferals everywhere, not like the abandoned-looking Feral Islands near the Enclave. Ferals worked the fields. Ferals carried baskets full of fruits and tubers along the paths. Ferals tended groups of kits that played in pools of standing water or raced in and out of the domed huts. Some of the adults even seemed to be teaching classes of kits. Jenette could hardly believe her luck.

At that moment, a collective gasp rose from the other expedition members, who were peering over the side of the heavy lifter.

Orderly lines of sailtrees soared above the island below. Swarms of Ferals clung to the noble white trunks, injecting immune venom into bud and branch, stimulating the trees to keep every single sail-shaped leaf fully unfurled and spread before the wind.

"They're *sailing,*" Karr exclaimed.

The island was indeed pressing through ocean rollers, the foaming swells breaking across its prow-like forward shore as it moved by power of the wind.

"In formation," Arrou added as the lifter cleared the first island.

At least two dozen more islands stretched across the ocean ahead, each green mound keeping perfect place in a multi-tiered formation, holding pace with the web of Ferals on paddleboards and progressing slowly, inexorably to the northwest.

"I knew it! I knew it! I knew it!" Jenette said, unable to contain her excitement any longer. "I mean," she babbled giddily, "I didn't really know they could do that. We've always known Ferals could influence the drift of their islands by stimulating sailtree growth, which is why Enclave recon teams carry flamethrowers and regularly torch sailtrees on nearby islands, to stop the islands from drifting out of range and depriving us of a supply of domestics . . . not that I would have minded." The torrent of words expended, a smile split Jenette's face and the lithe young woman dashed aft, leaned into her bubble tent and extracted the starlure from its high-impact case. Safety strap over her neck, powerpak belt cinched around her waist, she returned to the bow cradling the crystalline sphere.

Hairs rose on the back of Karr's neck.

Connecting a wireless trans-tap from the powerpak belt to a receptacle on the lure, Jenette noted Karr's reaction. "If you didn't want me to use it, you shouldn't have given it to me in the first place."

"Remember what happened last time," Karr warned, clearly wanting to say a lot more than that. "That's a lot of Ferals down there."

"A lot of well-organized, highly sophisticated Ferals," said Jenette.

"They don't look all that sophisticated to me," Karr argued weakly. "Just a few agriculturalists, and non-technological ones at that."

"Don't quibble," said Jenette. "I agreed to put my agenda on hold until we recovered the C-55s from Coffin Island. Now you didn't get them, but you got a much bigger null-fusion reactor to blow up, so it's your turn to live up to your promise and help me."

Karr opened his mouth to retort, but nothing came out. Defeated, he turned to Arrou. "Throttle down, way down." The thrusters dropped in pitch. The lifter's speed decreased to a crawl. "That's good. Keep station with their pace, no faster, no slower."

Jenette smiled a *thank you* at Karr and stepped to an easily seen vantage on the lifter's leading edge, the starlure held in her outstretched arms.

Shaking his head in disapproval, Karr knelt, wrapped his arms around Jenette's legs, and held on tight.

Jenette's fingers played on starlure studs. Wheeling shafts of starlight—G class yellow and F class white, M class scarlet and O class purple—the spectral radiances of Capella, Solara, Betelgeuse, and all the hues in between shone down on the unsuspecting Ferals.

<<Light be upon you.>>

Feral heads suddenly swiveled upward. Cones of teeth gaped. Eye orbs blinked into skulls and popped back out in disbelief.

Had she done it right, Jenette wondered. She repeated, choosing bolder color combinations.

<<Light be upon you.>>

<<Shadows away.>> The Ferals responded instinctively, then abruptly went blank, as a human might clap a hand over its mouth, for several shocked heartbeats. An eruption of rapid-fire light code ensued, only snippets of which Jenette could make out. <<Starlight/communion . . . The blank-one speaks with starlight . . . Impossible! Blank-ones are *blank* . . . ! But starlight is not blank . . . How can starlight be blank?>>

Dissension swirled on the waves below the lifter. *Flicker, flash, flare.* Ferals stopped paddling, or missed their strokes and capsized their tippy craft. The ocean became an artist's palette, with areas of conflicting Feral opinion as blobs of color upon it, intertwining, mixing, slowly melding into a reddish-purple consensus. <<Kthulah must know!>> the Ferals decreed.

Without further delay, a message telegraphed from under the

lifter was relayed across the backs of ever more distant Ferals, disappearing beyond the western horizon. <<A blank-one speaks with starlight, a blank-one speaks with starlight,>> it repeated, like a fading echo. <<A blank-one speaks with starlight. . . .>>

Not very much later, a response rippled back from that same unseen location, presumably, Jenette reasoned, from the "Kthulah" the Ferals had mentioned.

<<A blank-one speaks with starlight?>> it asked, in bold, strong colors.

<<Truth,>> the Ferals relayed back.

A longer pause, as if that distant presence was thinking. Finally, it asked, <<What does the blank-one say?>>

The Ferals looked up, dutifully repeating the message at Jenette. <<Kthulah asks what not-blank blank-one says.>>

Jenette carefully tapped the starlure studs, her pulse pounding. <<This one *(flare green to yellow)* seeks *(glow silver)* peace *(flash white)* between blank-ones *(fade to no color)* and Pact *(staccato rainbow)*.>>

The Ferals relayed her message. An equally colorful reply rippled back.

<<There can be no peace *between* blank-ones and Pact until peace exists *within* blank-ones and Pact.>>

It took a moment to decipher the reproach in the message, but Jenette was not discouraged. <<This one seeks peace *within* blank-ones and Pact as well as peace *between* blank-ones and Pact.>>

<<Killing is the way between blank-ones and Pact,>> flashed the message from Kthulah.

<<Time to find another way. No fighting. Cooperating.>>

Jenette's limited exposure to the dialect of these sophisticated Ferals began to catch up with her. It was one thing to guess the meaning of an entire phrase, inferring intent from the whole, quite another to improvise a conversation together piece by piece. <<Sharing . . .>> What was the light code for *knowledge?* <<. . . all truth. No matter what . . .>> Species? Race? <<. . . no matter how many legs, two or four.>>

The Kthulah presence responded, <<Blank-one or Pact, how many legs matters not to the Balance. Two might learn from four,

four might learn from two. Wisdom begets wisdom, trust begets trust. If there is trust.>>

<<Exactly, there must be trust!>>

<<But where does it begin?>>

<<Here!>>

There was a long pause. <<Perhaps.>>

Shivers ran up Jenette's spine. *It was a start.* She hurried to keep the dialogue going. <<This one has not seen so many wise Pact together. Where do so many come from?>>

<<So many Pact come from five-fours of days before the dawn.>>

Twenty days east, Jenette inferred.

<<And where are so many Pact going?>>

Kthulah's relayed words took on reverent hues. <<So many Pact seek the Burning Heart of Night.>>

Below on the water, Ferals instinctively turned to the northeast, a direction Jenette had a hunch about.

<<The fire glow beyond the curve of the world?>> she asked.

<<Kthulah affirms.>>

"They're headed for your ship," Jenette said to Karr. "Or the fire over it, to be more specific. I think it's some kind of religious pilgrimage."

Karr grumbled a few less than enthusiastic words as another message cascaded toward Jenette.

<<And where is the not-blank blank-one going?>> Kthulah asked.

<<The same place as many Pact,>> Jenette answered.

<<The blank-one seeks the Burning Heart of Night?>>

Unable to explain the complicated concept of a submerged fugueship under a burning pillar of hydrogen fuel, Jenette took the easy way out.

<<Yes.>>

As one, every Feral in sight *gasped* vivid orange, warning colors.

Whoops, thought Jenette. What had she said?

<<Blank-one seeks the Burning Heart of Night in sky-flyer?>> Kthulah asked, more specifically.

<<Yes,>> Jenette answered, trying to choose nonthreatening hues.

Silence. Seemingly endless.

"What's happening?" Karr asked.

"I think I messed up," Jenette said, stepping back from the lifter's forward rim.

Ferals on the water took on edgier colors and began to fidget.

"Maybe we should move along," Karr suggested, ever the paranoid.

Jenette hung her head and stared angrily at the starlure. In her excitement she had not been as cautious as she should have been, and that was stupid. She would never let her guard down with members of her own species; what had possessed her to make such a foolish mistake in a dialogue with a society of unknown Ferals? Jenette felt the frustration hot and moist at the corners of her eyes and she gritted her teeth.

Karr let go of Jenette's legs. "Arrou, ease us on out of here."

"Easing."

"Oh, wait!" Jenette blurted as another light code message headed their way.

<<Blank-one?>>

<<Yes?>> Jenette hurried to flash.

<<Sky-flyer will arrive at the Burning Heart before Pact?>>

<<Sky-flyer arrives at Burning Heart in one day.>> On the water, another orange gasp.

<<Blank-one?>>

<<Yes?>>

<<Kthulah wants to go on sky-flyer, too.>>

Karr was adamant. "No. No. Unequivocally, unthinkably: no. Arrou, get us out of here. And don't fly over any more islands, either."

Engine thrum and headwind picked up.

"But this is the chance of a lifetime!" Jenette pleaded. "This could be the beginning of a whole new era in human–Feral interaction!"

"Interaction from a distance is one thing," Karr countered, "but a bunch of bloodthirsty Ferals on board the lifter, with us? Too risky."

"One is not a bunch, and you don't know he's bloodthirsty!"

"I don't know he's not bloodthirsty!"

Jenette looked big eyes at Karr and spoke as sweetly as she could. "Please? This is really, really important. There has to be a compromise."

"Pilots don't compromise."

"And Pilots are wrong sometimes," Jenette said, just as sweetly. *"Aren't they?"*

Karr cursed and rubbed his temples, feeling suddenly, excessively guilty. "That is not fair. I'm not the one who wants to take chances this time. This time it's you. And besides, saving my ship could very well benefit human–Feral relations, because human colonists will no longer require immune venom and Sacrament if they have a ready source of *fugue* from *Long Reach.*"

"That's long-term. This is now," Jenette countered. "What did you say about *trusting* me more?"

The argument bounced back and forth for a while, and so it was not entirely surprising that Karr and Jenette did not at first notice the phenomena on the water below. In a slow ripple, spreading out from the west, every Feral on the ocean began to mimic the exact hue of the sky. So close was the color match that the ocean appeared to be a giant, platinum sieve, punched with holes wherever there were Ferals—a silver sieve with turquoise sky shining up from below, as well as down from above.

What Karr noticed first was a disagreement between his inner ear's perception of level and the angle of the deck under his feet.

"Are we drifting?" he asked. "Arrou, check your drift."

Arrou's head was tilted at a peculiar angle to the left.

"Are we in a bank?" said Karr. "I think we're in a bank."

In fact Arrou's whole body was canted subtly to the left and was thereby pulling the steering yoke off center, so the heavy lifter was slowly banking left.

"Check your attitude. Arrou? Arrou?"

"Ooooooooooooooooh," said the alien.

Karr followed Arrou's glassy stare down to the ocean. The sky-colored Ferals were blinking on and off in swirling, hypnotic patterns. The effect was not so strong directly below the lifter, but as distance and perspective packed the Ferals closer together near the horizon, the patterns became quite intense.

"What *is* that?" Jenette shrugged.

Karr rapped on Arrou's leathery back. "Arrou? Pilot to Arrou, we need to make a course correction. Hey! Is anybody in there?"

"Arrou—in—here," the alien responded, zombie-like. "Arrou—follow—sky—holes."

The Feral patterns were a giant whirlpool of dots swirling in the same westerly direction that Arrou was leaning.

"Go to auto-pilot," Karr ordered. "I'm taking control."

"No," Arrou said simply, and, as Karr began to climb into the tiny cockpit behind him, he swatted Karr with a foreleg. It was a casual swat, but one with the force of a four-hundred-pound creature behind it. Karr sailed through the air sideways, hitting the lifter's side rail in the vicinity of the right front thruster cowl.

Karr made an internal note not to try that again. A few inches further and he would have taken the long plunge overboard. "You might help," he gasped at Jenette as he staggered back behind the cockpit.

"I might," Jenette remarked, "*if* I thought there was a problem."

At which point Karr realized he would not prevail in that situation. Short of severing control system microfibers from the individual thrusters, so that the heavy lifter would go into safety glide-down and sink into the horde of Ferals, there was nothing he could do to alter Arrou's course.

The *sky holes* were growing more psychedelic by the minute. "I don't get it," he complained. "It's not affecting us. Why is it affecting him?"

"Khafra are extremely sensitive to certain phenomena involving vision," Jenette said loftily. "Remember his reaction to the Feral light display on the night we first met."

"But that was night, with bright, bright lights. This is broad daylight and a bunch of dumb, blue spots on the water."

"Perhaps you should take it up with him," Jenette suggested, in reference to Arrou. "Reason it out."

"Preeeetttty," Arrou cooed, as to confirm how useless that course of action would prove.

"This is just wonderful," Karr grumbled.

The heavy lifter flew into the midst of a vast Feral fleet. If the islands on the periphery had been destroyers and frigates, then these islands were cruisers and battleships. Karr counted ten islands bigger than the Enclave colony island and more were appearing as Arrou took the lifter deeper into the formation, following the sky holes, which now cycled like landing lights at a spaceport.

"Wow," said Jenette.

On a flat ocean planet, where nothing was taller than a sailtree, it was a shock to see the island at the end of the *landing lights*. To Jenette it seemed to be a fabled off-world mountain, towering many times higher than the tallest sailtree. To Karr—who had seen many mountains on his own homeworld and others—the island's silhouette resembled the spiraling end of an enormous seashell, its landforms twisting up out of the water hundreds of feet into the air.

It was a city. A burgeoning Feral metropolis.

Tier upon tier of squat violet domes and spindly indigo minarets competed for space on the slopes of the great cone. Countless Ferals walked four-legged across impossibly thin archspans and swarmed along boulevards of roadwort cobblestones and crowded open-air markets and floating docks, which jutted out in profusion from the city's waterfront. Large double and triple hulled vessels with spider-leg outriggers and sails that fanned out like peacock tails, unloaded goods from surrounding islands. Offshore, other vessels waited in turn for a berth and still others plied the waters between islands, deftly maneuvering through the ever-present communication net of Ferals on paddleboards, to acquire cargo from other islands of the fleet.

Karr imagined landing and all those Ferals swarming aboard the heavy lifter. He imagined tearing, limb from limb, and he wasn't the one doing the tearing. Karr began pounding on Arrou's back. "Stop! Stop! Bank away!" But Arrou followed the pattern of lights, which had been picked up by the inhabitants of the Feral city, and no amount of yelling could prevent Arrou from following the concentric circles up the rising slopes to the island's summit. There he hovered over a ring of ebony colored trees.

Stained glass leaves irised open below the lifter, revealing a grassy glade. At the center, four ascetic Ferals with bandages around their ears and staves in their forepaws sat at the corners of a wooden platform. The entrancing pattern of sky holes ended at a wise-looking Feral who sat in the center of that wooden platform. The wise Feral raised its forepaws and brought the entire display to an abrupt halt.

Sparkle, sparkle, sparkle, flashed the old Khafra.

Karr wished for a weapon. As if reading his mind, Liberty, Skutch, and Grubb cocked their pulse-rifles—*cha-chik!*

"Hold your fire!" Jenette said, waving them to hide the weapons. Fingers eased off triggers, and the Guards backed out of sight, but they did not put the rifles down.

Sparkle, sparkle, sparkle, the old Feral repeated.

Jenette held up the starlure. *Flash, flash, flash.*

Sparkle, sparkle?

Flash, flash.

Sparkle, sparkle, sparkle?

Flash, flash, flash.

The old Feral bowed. The four ascetics did the same.

Jenette turned to Karr, barely concealing her glee. "That is Kthulah, the leader of all these Ferals. He wants to go with us. He proposes a truce between us and he also proposes an exchange of hostages to guarantee the truce."

"Hostages?" said Karr.

"Yes," Jenette said happily. "He will ride upon the heavy lifter to the Burning Heart of Night; and one of us will stay behind here, on the island of Gnosis."

"And who's going to do that?"

"Why, me, of course."

Karr didn't say anything further. The situation was bizarre beyond belief. Up on the lifter it was obvious Jenette had made up her mind to stay and would not be swayed from her rash choice. While below, in rhythms of four hits to a cycle, the ascetic Ferals were beating the old Feral with their bead-laden staves.

XLI

Flash (red), flash (green-blue-purple)?
Flare (dark), glare (dark).
Sparkle (scarlet), flash-flare (viridian-azure-mauve)?
Flare, glare (dark-dark).
Glow, fluoresce (silver-gold), flash (yellow), flicker-
flash (gold)?
Flare (light), glare (dark)!

—*answer to the meaning of life*
in an untranslatable Feral light poem

The grotto was dark. Water dripped, echoing. Root pillars towered high into the blackness overhead, veins thick and gray, dotted with gray bud-growths, cankered by bulging gray knots. The four ascetic Judges lead Jenette between the pillars, staff beads rustling and guided by only the faint light of the single, blue glowbuds which shone in the center of their foreheads. Jenette followed, moisture cool caressing on her face, her boots occasionally splashing through underground streamlets.

At a spot, the Judges stopped short.

<<Why have you brought me here?>> Jenette asked with the starlure. The spot seemed no different from any other point in the grotto.

<<Because this,>> the Judges chanted one at a time,

<<Is where>>

<<The blank-one>>

<<Needs to be.>>

Jenette flashed, <<The blank-one does not understand. Where is the knowledge?>> Part of the bargain struck between Kthulah and Jenette was that while Kthulah accompanied Karr, she would be free to delve into ancient Feral lore. <<We are searching for it now? Yes?>>

<<No,>> the Judges said in uncharacteristic unison, bullet heads bobbing in disapproval and fingering beads on their staves from one dangling loop to another.

<<Pact search not>>

<<For that>>

<<Which is>>

<<Not lost.>>

They turned to a wide, aged pillar beside them and nipped a vein bulging at its base. Jenette fully expected a hidden passage to open or a cache of scrolls and tablets to be revealed. What did Feral writing look like, she wondered?

Phosphorescence appeared.

Will-o'-the-wisps flittered up the pillar, inside the intricate trace work of its gray veins, to clusters of the gray bud-growths. Suddenly the pillar was somber no more, but unfolding with radiance. The flow of immune venom had ignited phosphorescent blooms in carefully timed sequences.

And the sequences formed *words*.

<<*Filthy are manure worms, yet manure worms transform into flutterbys,*>> the root pillar gleamed. <<*Not lustrous are decayed grasses, yet dry pods in decayed grasses transform into pearl berries. Roots here remember knowledge filthy and lustrous both. . . .*>>

"It's an archive!" Jenette exclaimed. "A radiant, organic archive!"

The words shimmered on, reflecting across echelons of the gray pillars, each one a volume, lovingly preserved and added to by generations of scholarly Ferals—each a cache of Feral answers awaiting Jenette's questions.

<<*It is for the Seeker and Rememberer,*>> the root concluded, <<*to transform both luster and filth into Knowing.*>>

<<Behold>>

<<The>>

<<Roots>>

<<Of wisdom,>> the Judges said as the blossoms reverted to somnolence.

<<Seek>>

<<And truth>>

<<Shall be>>

<<Found.>>

XLII

"As we approach the moment of total victory, that is when we are most vulnerable."

—*from the speeches of Olin Tesla*

The lifter auto-hovered ten yards up and two kiloyards out. Karr, who was already sweating from the radiant heat, Kthulah, who was watched closely by armed Guardsmen, and the other expedition crew stood at a siderail, staring in abject shock toward *Long Reach*.

Karr's mouth fell slowly open.

Kthulah flashed, faint with dismay.

Arrou translated, <<Burning Heart not right, not right with Prophecy.>>

Not one, but five pillars of flame thrust up out of the ocean, stabbing high into blue sky, the wide main column of flame that Karr was already familiar with and four smaller columns, rotating lazily around it.

Everything had to be rethought.

In tow behind the lifter, connected by a grapple anchor and thirty yards of high-g orbital filament, floated a skrag island. Guardsmen Skutch had used proportional charges to excavate a pit in its center. Karr's plan had been to place the null-fusion reactor in that pit. Bigelow and Skutch would then prepare the reactor for its explosive demise. Finally, the makeshift floating platform was to have been towed as close to the shaft of fire as possible and cut loose with as much forward momentum as possible. The heavy lifter would withdraw and, just before the rooty mass was sucked into the column of flame, the reactor would be detonated. The fire would be snuffed out. Hopefully there would then have been a few minutes without lightning or sparks in which Karr could fly in to ground zero, drop into the ocean, and descend into *Long Reach*. Once there he would stop the flow of fusion energy through its damaged superconductor. Electrolysis of ocean water would stop. Problem solved.

Only that wasn't going to work now.

The unpiloted skrag mass stood too great a chance of running afoul of one of the smaller, rotating flame pillars before it reached the large central pillar. And since the null-field nodes would be programmed to drop in a very specific order, it was imperative that the skrag the reactor rested on not be tilted or tumbled, as such a collision would surely cause. Such a mishap could potentially channel the force of the explosion down at Karr's ship under the water instead of diverting the force harmlessly up into the air.

Besides which . . . something else was bothering Karr.

"How can there be five?" he wondered numbly. *Long Reach* had only one superconductor, with only one cathode and one anode to create the volatile hydrogen–oxygen mixture—which accounted only for the main conflagration. Something baffling and deeply disturbing was occurring on his ship.

Kthulah scintillated, equally confused.

Arrou translated. <<Kthulah say should be only four.>>

"Four?" Karr asked. "There should be only *one.*"

<<Kthulah say Prophecy demand sacred number of *four.*>>

Karr shook his head slowly. "I don't put much stock in prophecies, Arrou. Too many people invest too much hope and time waiting for mumbo-jumbo which doesn't ever come true."

Arrou and Kthulah flashed. The old alien turned on Karr, wrinkled muzzle skin furrowing.

"Kthulah say Karr not understand. Kthulah not waiting for Prophecy to *come true*. Kthulah waiting for Prophecy to come true *again.*"

Karr turned to the old Khafra. "This?" Karr pointed at the five fires. "This has happened before?"

"Kthulah says yes. Long time ago. Three times."

Karr shut up as Kthulah told a story. . . .

*   *   *

Arrou translated:

Long, long before. Before Pact. Before Burning Heart. When world was cold and dark. Many things grew, plants, foodbeasts. Many different kinds of things. Khafra lived forever. Never old, never dying. Khafra lived Balanced.

But Khafra sad.

Why? Because Khafra are blank!

(Like humans.)

Long this before-time lasts, like bad dream. Always in shadow. Always hiding, always fearing. Never ending, never seeing. Always night and never day. Khafra not even can wish for better, because Khafra not even now there is "better" to wish for.

(Urrr. Scary story.)

Long time passes.

Then, one time, Khafra see Tears. Long, red Tears fall from sky. And big light blossoms in night. Burning Heart of Night. Now Khafra see what is better than dark. Radiance. Burning Heart births Radiances (four) into dark world. Suddenly there is day. Khafra worship Burning Heart. And when Burning Heart escapes with three Radiances, one Radiance stays. This Burning Heart's first gift to Khafra:

Present of Radiance.

Present to Balanced Khafra, suffering-long Khafra. Present goes into Khafra. Now Khafra are not blank.

Khafra shine in dark like bright day. Khafra not scared anymore.

Another long time passes. Always in light and never dark. Always living and never dying. Too long a time! Khafra forget suffering. Remember only selves, think of and love only selves. Want only pleasure. Tears fall again. Burning Heart blossoms again. But selfish Khafra ignore it. Not Balanced.

(Stupid, stupid.)

Burning Heart births four Radiances and escapes with four Radiances. Leaves present for imBalanced Khafra:

Present of Death.

Now Khafra get old. Khafra die. Big sickness comes. Light gets weak, night gets long. Now Khafra remember dark, remember afraid. Many things die fast: plants, foodbeasts, slitherers, and buzzers. Many things not live ever again. Extinct. Only animals that birth fast survive. Or trees that birth very slow. Khafra almost go extinct.

So Khafra are sorry for being bad, sorry for being imBalanced. Promise to be different next time Tears fall. Promise very hard. Ferals use knowledge of plants to try to stay alive. Barely stay alive. But suffering keeps memories good. Next time when Tears fall and Burning Heart of Night blossoms, Khafra go. When Burning Heart births four radiances, Khafra gather. Keep to good, keep to Balance. And when Burning Heart escapes with Radiances, Khafra save one piece, keep one Radiance. So Burning Heart leaves present for Balanced Khafra:

Present of Pact.

Pact keeps Khafra never sick, always healthy. Khafra not immortal. Khafra live forty years, then die. That is Pact. But Pact keeps Radiance strong. Night and day Balanced. Birth and death Balanced. All not happy, but all not sad. Khafra live satisfied, for long, long time.

The Roots of Wisdom spoke to Jenette, the Judges stimulating vein after vein on the columns, like turning pages in a musty tome. The amount of ancient lore overwhelmed Jenette at first, but gradually, methodically, Jenette began to sift the intermingled mythology and superstition from history and fact.

The Burning Heart of Night—It all kept coming back to that.

The more Jenette searched for an understanding of the Feral life cycle for any sort of clue that could help human scientists in the quest for a cure to Scourge, the more the root-archives lead her back to the Burning Heart of Night, and the more the imagery of the root tomes rekindled images Jenette had seen with her own eyes. The descriptions of Tears falling from the sky—shooting stars circling the night sky, once, twice, before falling into the ocean—were exactly as Jenette had seen them fall the night she fled the Enclave with Arrou. And the descriptions of the Burning Heart itself, of its towering pillars of Radiance, were like the pil-

lar of hydrogen fire over Karr's ship. Eventually, the roots foretold, the Burning Heart would change from one large Radiance, to
four smaller Radiances, which did not line up with what Jenette
had seen herself, but other than that it was the same. She could not
conclude otherwise. Karr's fugueship *was* the Burning Heart of
Night, that crucial event which so much of Feral society and even
biology, pivoted around. And that was not all. Jenette soon came
to another shocking conclusion . . .

Fugueships had been to New Ascension before!

Not just once, but at least three times. The Roots of Wisdom revealed many crucial facts which Jenette began to work together to
form a timeline of Feral life cycles and runaway planetary biology,
of the coming of Scourge and immune venom, of fugueship immune systems and infinitesimal interstellar stowaways. Each time
Fugueships had come to New Ascension, drastic change to the
planetary ecology accompanied them.

Ferals had no glowbuds. Then a fugueship came and Ferals
suddenly had flashbuds.

Ferals did not die, or at least lived a very long time. Then suddenly a fugueship came and Ferals got sick and died.

Ferals were dying out as a species. Then suddenly a fugueship
came and Ferals had Pact.

Jenette's conversion of base-four Feral dates had the instances
occurring over a span of ten thousand years—far more rapidly than
evolution could account for such biological upheaval. There was
only one deduction Jenette could make:

Fugueships were infecting New Ascension.

Somehow, foreign bio-matter was surviving the rigors of interstellar space, the fugueship's vigorous immune defenses, and the
fiery planetfall into New Ascension's oceans. The odds were long,
but then Jenette reasoned it would only take one microscopic par-
ticle finding its way to a living, New Ascension host. Growth and
change would transpire exponentially from there as the foreign in-
vaders worked their way through the local biology.

Gifts the Feral mythology named the infections.

First infection: foreign bio-matter plus Ferals equals glowbuds.
No plausibility problems there. Even contemporary Khafra kits

had to be exposed to immune venom essence before their hair follicles transformed into glowing nodules.

Second infection: foreign bio-matter introduces a pathogen that kills large numbers of plant and animal species on a planetary scale. Those species with high reproductive output adapted better to the unstable new ecology. Slow reproducing Ferals cling to life with all their knowledge of healing and plant chemistry.

Third infection: foreign bio-matter—Jenette suspected the fugueships themselves this time, and not just a malignant hitchhiker—introduces immune venom to Feral biology. Immune venom was a substance closely related to *fugue*, as Jenette knew from Dr. Yll's researches. It balanced Feral life cycles once more.

<<Out of ignorance, Radiance>>

<<Out of arrogance, Death>>

<<Out of repentance, Pact>>

<<Out of Balance . . . Gamut,>> said the Judges.

<<Gamut?>> Jenette asked. <<What does that mean, Gamut?>>

<<The Judges do not know.>>

<<It is the fourth Gift>>

<<Of the Burning Heart of Night>>

<<According to Prophecy.>>

The fugueships brought light. The fugueships brought Scourge. The fugueships brought a cure for Scourge. It was that cure and the healing plant chemistry, with which the Ferals had clung to life before Pact and immune venom, that interested Jenette. Whatever the fourth Gift of gamut was going to be, it did not concern Jenette at that point.

The Judges activated more roots at her request, Glittering lore lead her deeper and deeper into the library grotto. . . .

(Hrurrff? More story? Urrr, okay. Arrou translate more.)

Pact live satisfied. Long, long time. But then come blank-ones. Blank-ones not Balanced. Blank-ones make world not Balanced. Some Pact are Balanced. But some not. Many sorrows. Tears fall. Burning Heart comes, Burning Heart blossoms. Pack of Gnosis comes to save piece of Radiance. But Burning Heart is imBalanced. Five and not four!

Arrou stopped translating.

<<How will Kthulah's pack save piece of Radiance this time?>>

<<Prophecy says a Pact will come who knows.>>

<<When does that Pact come?>>

Flame pillars reflected in Kthulah's distressed, spherical eyes. <<Kthulah does not know. The Roots of Wisdom do not know. Kthulah is afraid . . .>>

The old alien said no more. Arrou turned to Karr. The human stood motionless, head craned back and arms shrouded around his head.

"I've been so stupid," Karr said, voice shuddering and cracking.

"What wrong, what wrong?" Arrou asked, pressing around front of Karr, muzzle long with concern.

Tears of joy streamed down Karr's face. *It suddenly all made sense: why* Long Reach *had been sick, why it had chosen this world to come to when he gave it free reign, why it had refused all of his efforts to put it into orbit, why it had crashed and why it was now submerged under the ocean of this alien world.* Words choked from Karr's mouth.

"It's a miracle. My ship, Arrou. It's *spawning.*"

XLIII

Opposites give birth. In adversity the noble Pact seeks wisdom from ignorance, beauty from filth, hope from despair.

—*Feral wisdom*

Jenette lay at the foot of the root pillar, the grotto silent but for the hush of stifled sobbing, the Judges withdrawn a distance in the gloom, uncomprehending, but respectful.

<<Seek>>

<<And truth>>

<<Shall be>>

<<Found,>> they glimmered amongst themselves.

<<But beware>>

<<What truth>>

<<Is>>

<<Sought.>>

The pillar Jenette lay before was young and narrow in comparison to the wide, ancient roots around it. Its knowledge had been encrypted within the scope of a single Feral generation, a generation that had seen the arrival, and taken part in the first interactions with humans from beyond the stars; a generation that had recorded everything it saw and heard of what those humans did and said openly—and even some of what they tried to keep secret.

XLIV

Before making peace with blank-ones, first prepare for war.

—*Tlalok*

Four Feral hunters hastened Jenette down the roadwort avenue, snapping at her heels.

<<What>>

<<Decision>>

<<Has>>

<<Been made?>> the Judges asked, hurrying along behind, their beads in disarray.

<<The blank-one>>

<<Has violated>>

<<No>>

<<Pact law.>>

The hunters replied gruffly, <<Kthulah commands.>>

Down the mountain island the golden cobblestones wound, from the entrance to the Roots of Wisdom grotto, toward the waterfront. Throngs of Pact parted, staring at the peculiar procession.

Jenette passed wondrous sights with indifference. There were huts smelling of spice and displaying bowls heaped with medicinal herbs, roots, and ground up animal bones. There were markets teeming with the firework flash of bartering Khafra, filled with the produce of outlying islands: grains and seeds, tiny caged animals with pink feet, piles of nut paste and tree pitch, heaps of salt, and a thousand forms of hollowed gourds that varied in size from little jugs to great water urns. There were orchards where the hypnotic swaying of branches extruded and wove resin fibers into fabric, fabric that Ferals used to bind wounds because it inhibited infection and then dissolved when the healing process was complete. There were fermentaries where curdled marsh ooze was pressed into bread that tasted of cheese. There were open-air sick bowers run by white-pawed Feral healers from whom Jenette could have learned, and nurseries full of bouncy Feral kits that Jenette could have played with. Another time the Feral guards would have had to bind her limbs and physically drag her away from such sights.

Not that day.

Jenette bore the ignoble treatment of the hunters with a resignation that comes from having answers to questions that were better left unasked. She moved like an automaton, placing one foot in front of another, her arms wrapped protectively around the star-lure.

At sea level, the press of domes and minarets parted and Jenette saw the heavy lifter hovering over a finger-shaped quay, the null-fusion reactor still clutched underneath in its cargo arms. Jenette's guards maneuvered her straight for the quay and up to the foot of a gangway purposely grown for boarding the flying machine. Humans stood formally at the edge of the square deck; domestics squatted near, equally stiff. The Guards clustered at the top of the gangway, pulse-rifles pointed at Kthulah, who squatted like the domestics.

The Feral hunters prodded Jenette up the curving span.

Just as confused as Jenette, the Judges flashed secretly,

<<Farewell, blank-one.>>

<<Remember the wisdom of the roots.>>

<<And choose well>>

<<The paths it takes you.>>

The span leveled near the top. The hunters held Jenette back with six paces to go.

Karr whispered something to Arrou. Arrou sparkled. Kthulah flashed back, seething crimsons and oranges. Jenette grimaced at the words. Arrou flinched, but dutifully translated for Karr.

"Kthulah say, burn in darkness, get off fecal-worms, larval puss-maggot—"

Karr sighed and held up a hand to stop the translation. "Tell him we are not going to use the reactor, not now that we know my ship is spawning. We're on his side."

"Kthulah say Karr not on Kthulah's side," Arrou translated. "Not on Pact side. Kthulah not trust words from mouth of Radiance-killer."

"But we're not going to do that anymore."

Kthulah snapped his teeth at Karr.

"Kthulah say Kthulah must go and take punishment for deciding to trust blank-ones."

Karr sighed again. At a nod of his head, Liberty and the Guards let Kthulah go. The old Feral rose to all fours and padded, glowering, onto the gangway. Jenette's Feral guards gave her a shove. She stumbled, passing Kthulah midway, and fell onto the lifter near Karr's feet.

Joining his brethren, Kthulah turned. <<Leave now. Do not return to Gnosis. Do not return to the Burning Heart. Pact will attack. Kthulah warns. Go now. Pact give blank-ones sixty-four heartbeats, then truce is rescinded.>>

In unison, the crowd of assembled Ferals began to blink on and off, counting down heartbeats. Karr gave Jenette an arm up, then waked calmly to the cockpit.

Jenette followed, displeased, but making no comment.

"Our mission has changed," Karr announced, adjusting himself before the flight controls. As the lifter disengaged from the gangway, Karr's mouth bent into a guilty grin. *"We're going to witness the birth of four baby fugueships!"*

"Don't get too excited," Jenette cautioned. "We have to go back to the Enclave first."

"Back to the Enclave? But the spawning could occur at any moment."

"The gestation period is two hundred and fifty-six days," Jenette said matter-of-factly. "Four days after the Tears fall, the Burning Heart *blossoms.* Four times four, times four, times four days later, the Burning Heart *births.* Your ship sank and ignited twenty days ago. Therefore there are two hundred and thirty-six days to go. Therefore we have time to return to the Enclave—and I need to return right away."

"You extracted this information from Feral texts?"

"Yes, and I believe them to be accurate."

"Fine," said Karr, taking only a little time to think it over. "I trust you."

Jenette smiled stiffly.

With a last look at the Ferals, who were counting down to a renewed state of hostilities, Karr pulled up on the throttle and the lifter soared high into the sky on a heading for the human colony.

No one was able to make comset contact with the Enclave; no one had been able to since leaving Coffin Island. Karr and Arrou flew shifts of four hours on, four hours off; that night, after a switch of hands for paws at the helm, Arrou trotted to the left-hand edge of the deck and looked down.

"Urft."

Arrou's earpits opened and his head tilted, orb eyes narrowing. He gripped the sidewall, then his head and shoulders disappeared from view entirely.

"Hrrr-rrrrffft."

Dr. Bigelow, whose nights had been melancholic and sleepless since Coffin Island, craned his head up from his bedroll. "Problem?"

Arrou's head bobbed back up, teeth clattering. "Reactor door open."

"An open hatch, on my reactor?" Bigelow levered himself to his feet and trundled over to join Arrou. "How could that happen?"

Bigelow looked down. Arrou looked down.

"Where?"

Arrou pointed. "There."

"I discern no open hatch."

"Urrr . . . was open."

"I hauled myself out of a cozy bed for 'was open'?"

"Heard scraping," Arrou insisted. "Saw with own eyes. Vrrrrrph—look, look!"

Bigelow squinted in the moonlight. The reactor was a dark

hourglass shape against the glimmer of moonlit waves. He retrieved a searchbeam and swept the gunmetal reactor casing.

"There, there!" said Arrou.

Bigelow moved the beam where Arrou indicated. "Well, what do you know? It's not exactly open, but it's not exactly closed, either."

"Was open before."

Stringy green fronds were jammed in a hatch preventing it from locking fully shut. Only Arrou could have seen it without the searchbeam.

"However did that happen?" Bigelow wondered.

"Arrou want to know, too."

Bigelow considered. "In any event, we can't leave it like that. The Enclave could use a second reactor and I intend to keep this one functional." He unfastened a cargo hook from the sidewall, extending its telescoping segments. "Lend a paw, please."

Human and alien maneuvered the long pole down and hooked the seaweed. A flip of the pole tossed the hairy mass back down into the ocean and a broadside smack closed the hatch with the distinct clunk and click of latches locking.

"That ought to do it," Bigelow said as they pulled the pole back onboard, collapsed it, and re-stowed it on the sidewall.

Bigelow snapped off the searchbeam and returned to his bedroll, his melancholy, and his insomnia. Neither Karr nor Jenette took notice of the incident; each was wrapped tight in their own concerns. But Arrou remained where he was for some time, looking down suspiciously at the reactor and the hatch that wasn't open anymore.

The Enclave island and the Feral island were rammed together, edges overlapping; other smaller islands drifted nearby, apparently abandoned. The impact had crushed a portion of the Enclave's battlements near a cluster of hydroponic domes. Feral bodies littered the breach. Pulse-cannon gouges smoldered like fissures to the underworld. Fires burned from wrecked crawlers and windowless buildings, bathing the grisly scene in flickering crimson.

It was eleven hours after Jenette had been summarily ejected from Gnosis.

Karr spiraled the heavy lifter through funnels of oily-smelling smoke, warily closing on the battleground. He flicked on the lifter's landing lights; four broad beams shimed down from the corners of its hull. His human passengers looked down in silent distress. The domestics moaned deep in their barrel chests.

Within the colony walls, human and alien corpses lay where they had fallen. Feral dead outnumbered human dead many times over. Tall parasitic grasses had sprung up all over the island, attracted by those carcasses, overgrowing and inundating fields, streets, and alleys with an eerie flood of shoulder-high fronds.

"Polyp-grass," Dr. Marsh observed.

The other colonists shivered.

Jenette pointed to a wide boulevard which led to the cylindrical Chamber of the Body Pure. "Set down over there."

Karr didn't like the idea of setting down in the high fronds and said so. Liberty and the Guards swept the area with searchbeams, the tight bright beams illuminating details of the carnage. No Ferals were visible, but Karr still didn't like it.

Jenette glowered. "Just get us down. I don't care where—"

"Look!" interrupted Skutch. "Searchbeams! On the crawler barns."

Lights shot up from a warehouse roof. Narrow beams waggled frantically in thick smoke. Karr flew closer. Colonists waved and shouted from the roof. Karr's passengers waved and shouted back. More colonists showed themselves, crowding surrounding roofs and alleys. All of them gestured for Karr to land.

"This roof won't take the weight of the reactor," Karr said, sizing up the area, "and the streets are too narrow to set down. I'll drop you off, then hover until you can get back to me with a report on where it's safe to land."

Jenette nodded.

The lifter sank, its edge contacting the edge of the garage roof. Karr held the flying platform steady as Jenette and the others hurried off, eager for news of friends and family.

*   *   *

Colonel Halifax, Subconsul Bragg, and a score of battle-bruised colonists rushed to meet Jenette on the roof. Halifax opened his mouth to speak, but Bragg interrupted.

"Where's the *fugue*?" Bragg demanded. "We need the *fugue* right away." Dirty battlefoam dressings swathed Bragg's left arm. Many of the Guards and Reserves bore wounds as well.

The flicker of disappointment on Jenette's brow was enough of an answer for Halifax, but Bragg and the others were not so observant. Their hopeful faces fixated on the heavy lifter and those same faces fell when Karr flew up and away from the roof.

"Where's he going?" Bragg shouted, stirring the colonists up.

"Steady," Halifax growled. The Guards in the crowd wavered and held, but the less disciplined Reserves (many of whom wore the red-and-green armband of Bragg's Volunteer Forces) rushed the roof edge with Bragg.

"The Body Pure! Stop! Come back!"

"Order, order!" Halifax barked. "Form up in squads!" The Reservists might have rallied, if Bragg had not been adding to the hysteria. Halifax's voice lowered in disgust. "Someone should code red that bastard."

Jenette looked around. The roof top vantage gave a clear, unambiguous view of the colony's desperate position.

"Where's my father, Colonel?"

At that point, the stalwart soldier frowned.

Karr auto-hovered at a safe height for a minute or two, collecting items from his small equipment stockpile: extra charge nodules for the Gattler, a tool whose handle looked like it would make a good club, even the data cube that Karr had recovered from Mad Bob's hideout in *Long Reach*. Anything that looked like it could possibly be useful went into his pockets or snapped onto belt loops in preparation for the time when he must land on the battle-torn island below. Then Karr flew slow circles over the Enclave, observing as he waited for word from Jenette.

Human and Feral forces had fought to a standoff. Humans held a small triangular area bounded by the crawler garage, the armory, and the Great Hall. Ferals occupied the rest of the island. Karr could see them, hiding in the polyp grass; sometimes they reflexively flared white when the lifter's landing lights passed over them. Karr suspected there were several thousands of the aliens within the Enclave's breached defenses. A no-man's land—the exact width of a pulse-rifle shot—separated the two opposing forces. The humans were in a bad way, but the Ferals did not seem to have the ability to finish them off.

Karr saw the reason why.

A pair of Ferals attempted to sneak across the contested area. A fusillade of pulse-rifle fire erupted from its human defenders. The Ferals stopped and took cover, but did not retreat. What drove the Ferals back was a wide line of domestics, lead by a single, bold domestic, who left the cover of human barricades and paced slowly, unwaveringly, straight for the Ferals. Unwilling to fight their domesticated brethren, the Ferals retreated. At a signal from their leader, another domestic, the domestic line halted and then, without breaking formation, marched slowly backward to the human barricades.

Stalemate.

Karr continued overflying the crawler garage. Each time he looked for Jenette, but she did not reappear. The circuits began to add up. Karr began to feel uneasy. In their haste to disembark from the lifter, the colonists had not left him a comset. What was going on down there? After quite some time, a few searchbeams stabbed up to attract his attention. Karr flew closer. A press of colonists shouted and gesticulated at him. Karr leaned over the edge of the cockpit.

"Over there! Put the reactor down over there!" they shouted, pointing to a wide street that ringed the Great Hall.

"Where's Consul Jenette?" Karr shouted back.

The response was hard for Karr to make out, something about an emergency briefing with Colonel Halifax and that they, the crowd, would take Karr to Jenette as soon as he set down. It was a less than perfect scenario as far as Karr was concerned, but then the situation at the Enclave was far from perfect. Karr followed the crowd to a space where they had flattened the polyp grasses down into a makeshift landing pad. With a last look around for Ferals, Karr let the lifter sink; he felt a solid jolt as the null-fusion reactor touched ground. Karr worked the grapple remotes. The hull bobbed upward as the robotic arms released their weighty burden.

"Now set down!" the crowd shouted. "That's it! Over here!"

Karr hovered over to a second flattened patch of polyp grass and was just easing down on the throttle, everything seeming okay, when the crowd became agitated, like a disturbed buzzer nest. A man came running out of an alley, screaming and waving madly at Karr. "No! Don't do it! Get away!" A scuffle broke out. Crude wooden clubs appeared in the hands of individuals in the crowd, which seemed peculiar, but then the colonists turned and beat the protesting man into unconsciousness—which seemed absolutely bizarre.

Karr reapplied power to the thrusters. Unfortunately, his reaction was a split second too late.

Zing, clak!

A grappling line shot up and hooked the lifter. Zing, zing, zing! Clakety, clak, clak! A dozen more lines hooked around engine cowlings, cargo arms, and sidewalls. Karr ducked as a self-guided rocket whooshed around the cockpit, looping a noose of filament around Karr and cinching him tight in place. Karr yanked the throttle. Colonists holding the lines soared off the ground. Bunches of other colonists grabbed hold of the lines, but the orbiter easily pulled them all into the air. Karr jerked the power, hoping to dislodge the attackers. A few fell, but most hung on tenaciously, some even activated climbing winches and reeled themselves upward. One industrious group spooled out more line, dropping to the ground, and anchored the line around a sailtree. Now Karr gunned the engines to full force. The lifter swung to the limit of the tether, bowing the sailtree over with brute force. The high tensile cable shuddered. Tree roots tore up from the ground, clinging, clinging— and then gave out all at once. Freed of restraint, the heavy lifter shot sideways over the island, colonists dangling from the grapple lines, the uprooted tree trunk caroming behind, crushing ceramite structures and flesh-and-blood bipeds with uncaring abandon.

Karr almost regained control of the lifter at the edge of the structures that marked the boundary of no-man's land, but another swarm of colonists charged out from a cluster of water treatment spheroids, each carrying shoulder mounted launchers. Pif, pif, piffff. Glittering braids of thread arched up and exploded. Fap! Charged strands showered down on deck, contacting the micro-fiber relays that ran from cockpit to thrusters. Sparks crackled. White-hot current jumped. Karr clung to the stick and throttle as the engines sputtered and went into safety glide-down. The heavy lifter twirled out over no-man's land, altitude dropping. The rear of the deck hit first, crushing polyp fronds, the aft thrusters gouging deep scars into the island; colonists bounced like rag dolls, losing hold of their lines and falling limp. Engine thrust tapered out, leaving Karr with no control whatsoever.

Karr prayed that the lifter would just skate through the polyp field, bouncing and tearing up the parasitic grasses and dissipating energy. Perhaps the orbiter could then come to a stop relatively un-hurt—and hopefully not in Feral territory. But the hull pitched side-ways as it passed over a small rise in the ground. The right front corner dug in, causing the lifter to flip end over end and, as ill luck would have it, smash down on the only hard object in the open area, a bunker-like hexagonal structure. The lifter's ceramite hull broke into several sections upon impact with the unforgiving plasteel for-mation. Karr's forward section ground to an abrupt, violent halt, up-side-down and with its leading edge in a shallow depression. Only the engine cowlings saved Karr from being crushed flat. He hung upside down from the cockpit, entrapped by the grapple lines, his head swimming from the impact, and the sound of pulse-rifle shots cracking in his ears. Before he could collect his wits and sever the imprisoning grapple line filaments, colonists swarmed the lifter.

"Get him! Hold him, hold him!"

White-haired, pasty-skinned preadolescents—too many to fight, even if Karr hadn't been dazed—grabbed and clutched. They cut his bindings, stripped the Gattler, club tool, recharge containers, and any other potential weapon from Karr's possession, and man-handled him out from under the lifter.

"The Body Pure! The Body Pure!"

The mob hoisted Karr into the air like a trophy and, firing pulse-rifles to cover their retreat, swept him across no-man's land and back behind the buildings within human-held territory.

XLV

"It is not the unconquerable soul of man, nor the complexity of his tools, but the white-knuckle fear of death that insures his survival."

—from the speeches of Olin Tesla

Jenette entered the room expecting a fight. What awaited her was closer to a funeral.

The gutted records room was at the back of the Great Hall. It made a poor infirmary, but then the hospital had been overrun by Ferals, and furthermore, the room's occupant had refused to be evacuated from the Enclave's seat of government. Olin Tesla lay on a couch at the rear of the narrow space. Dusty outlines revealed where boxes and shelves had been removed to make room for him. The air smelled of stimpaper, dust, and sterile spray. Medical devices provided the only illumination: biosentries blinked along Tesla's form, powerbeads glowed in battle dressings, hoses pumped in luminescent fluids under green surgical sheets and drew other, darker fluids out and away.

Jenette drew the door shut behind her. Click.

The wounded Prime Consul strained, unsuccessfully, to turn his head. "Who's there?"

"It's me," Jenette answered in a small voice. She did not want to go any further into the room. She did not want to see what she would see if she moved closer. She leaned against the door for support. *Don't forget, he brought this on himself. He brought this on all of us.*

"Jenette," Tesla said, hope flaring in his weak voice. "I knew you would come. Your mission, was it a success?"

"No," Jenette admitted. Her father sagged visibly. "Sorry."

"Don't be sorry," he said. "Succeed or fail, but don't be sorry as long as you did your best."

Jenette flinched. Was that compassion from her father? She did not want it. *Not with what she had festering in her gut. Soon it would explode. Soon, but not just yet. . . .* For now Jenette was still intimidated by what she saw. "Colonel Halifax says you saved a squad of Reserves," she said, her voice sounding distant in her own head. "He says you fought off two Ferals with your bare hands."

"With a knife. I didn't fare so well."

"Halifax says you won."

"Halifax has a strange definition of *winning*."

As if to punctuate the irony of that word, a fit of choking overcame the Prime Consul. Thick fluid appeared at the corners of his mouth. The drawn-out sounds left the room feeling empty.

Jenette's hands began to shake. She clenched them behind her back and forced herself to walk to her father's side. His Feral opponents had not surrendered their lives easily. Her father's head was a broken mess, his extremities slashed in a dozen places, his abdomen gored open. Surgical foam covered the wounds, inset organ-sims buzzed frantically to stem internal damage, but they could not hide the severity of his condition.

Jenette's father, Olin Tesla—the berator, accuser, and cold remote rock around which so much of her existence revolved—was dying. So many times she had wished death upon him, and now here he was, just as she had wanted, the planetary pathogen consuming from within what his attackers had not incapacitated from without. Conflicting emotions made Jenette queasy. Elation. Guilt. Fear.

Time was running out.

And Jenette desperately needed more time. Time to yell and scream. Time to hold her father accountable for his transgressions. Time to demand explanations and receive answers. *How had he made such callous decisions? What could he have been thinking?*

*Didn't he see how badly those decisions hurt the colony? Didn't he
see how badly he had hurt her? Fathers were supposed to make
things better, not worse! Weren't they?* Jenette wanted to know.
And, deep down, maybe she wanted something else, too. Maybe
she needed to find an intangible *something* which had been lost in
all the anger and expectation and rebellion, whatever it was that fathers and daughters were supposed to have but which she and her
father had never found. If only she knew what to say . . .

Her father's hands, thin and swollen-jointed, fumbled with a
froog, a golden-pink fruit with spiky skin and succulent insides.
He was too weak. His nails scratched the thick rind, freeing a few
sweet vapors, but were not able to break through. They fell still in
frustration.

Before Jenette knew what she was doing, she picked up the
froog. Her own youthful hands made short work of peeling the
spheroid and splitting the internal nodules into bite-sized clumps.
Her father strained to eat them. Jenette put a hand under his neck
to hold his head erect. The physical contact seemed electric to her,
in a chilling sort of way. His body, so long robust, was shrunken
and bony. She felt tremors of his pain as he slowly chewed and
swallowed.

"Your mother used to peel *froogs* for me when we gathered
flutterbys," her father ventured after consuming a few nodules.

The comment took Jenette by surprise. Her father never talked
about *her.* "You and Mother gathered flutterbys?"

"Back at Elysium." Tesla's expression became nostalgic as he
thought back. "Clouds of color in the air. Your mother liked the
blue-blue ones best."

Jenette imagined her parents stealing away for a quiet afternoon
on the open ocean, misting fresh-water on the wave crests to sim-
ulate rain and then angling hand-tossed nets to capture the clouds
of damsel wings which sprang up to court, mate, and die in the
course of their absurdly short life cycles.

"Some things you can't forget," her father continued. "You can
put them away for a while, but they always come back. Even if you
don't want them to."

"Don't you want to remember her?"

Wistful eyes said yes, but Tesla's words were full of self-reproach. "Now is now. Then is then. Living in the past is good for nothing."

To Jenette, who had no memory of her mother, the idyllic image sounded nice. Jenette remembered her father taking her flutterby hunting once, the two of them simply spending time together, not talking and far from the demands of the Enclave. She had liked it, but after a while he had grown sad. They stopped suddenly and he had never taken her again. Until that moment in the records room, Jenette had thought that it was because he did not want to go with her, but now she saw otherwise.

"You still miss her."

Tesla stopped eating. His neck, still cradled in Jenette's hand, bowed foreword and shook. It took a moment for her to realize he was weeping.

"You have her face, her nose, her chin," he said, without looking up. "I see her every time I look at you."

"Is that . . . good?"

A bony hand sought out one of Jenette's and clasped it tightly. This was a father she had never seen before, a father who showed emotion, a father who tried to communicate on a real, honest level. Jenette did not know how to react. All at once, the confrontation she had come for came out of her—but not in anger, in utter childlike disbelief.

"Why, father? *Why?*"

Tesla looked up with watery, uncomprehending eyes. "Why what?"

"I've been to a Feral city," Jenette said miserably. "To a place where they record history chemically in glowing roots. One of the roots told the history of humans coming to this world. It recorded everything those humans did when they came to this planet. I read it."

Tesla's face pinched, as if he knew what was coming.

"We could have made Pact!" Jenette wailed, verbalizing the awful revelation for the first time since reading the Roots of Wisdom with the Judges. "It said so in the Feral texts. Pact is not specific to Feral physiology. It's a substance they pass on to their

children—and twenty years ago, when we were all born, there were childless Ferals willing to pass their Pact on to human children. *But you didn't let them!* None of this had to happen! All the fighting, all the suffering, all the dying. . . ." Jenette choked up. The scope of the atrocity was too much to comprehend. Every year of Sacrament, the Feral Wars, every human or Khafra who was dead outside the Great Hall at that very moment, it all stemmed from the same incomprehensible decision. Jenette's head pounded so hard she thought it would explode. "Why? Why?!"

Her father's voice rasped quietly. "Evermore. If you could understand Evermore . . . but you can't."

"How bad could it have been?" Jenette railed. "Nobody on Evermore died just because they grew up!"

Tesla struggled to explain. "Our bodies lived, but our souls did not. Do you know how much you hate Sacrament? That is how much we hated Evermore. It was so beautiful, the white rolling hills, the rift valleys, the everblue forests, but . . . the sound of an evening breeze would chill our hearts. Narcotic pollens came on those breezes. They would come and our minds would numb and our bodies would do things that should not be done. Sick things. Immoral things." Tesla clenched his eyes. "And as if that that was not bad enough, humans on Evermore began to forget what was right and what was wrong, even when the winds did not blow. Whatever abomination occurred, they were not to blame. *It was the breeze. The winds made them do it.*" Tesla's nostrils flared as if he could still smell those malevolent pollars. "But some of us woke each morning, remembering and knowing. We dreamed in the daylight what we could not dream at night. We dreamed to live our lives in control of our minds and souls, in bodies pure from the corruption of Evermore. We left to seek that Body Pure. That was what we wanted for ourselves and for our children. That is what I wanted for you."

"I can't believe you wanted things to turn out this way," Jenette said, unable to reconcile her father's wishes with the harsh reality of New Ascension. "Sacrament is not the Body Pure. It controls our minds and bodies as much as the narcotic winds of Evermore. It's just the same."

"No," Tesla wheezed. "We choose. That is different. If we do not choose Sacrament, it does not choose us. And it is not permanent. Making Pact would have been permanent, no more hope for a cure to eventually set us free. No more hope of the Body Pure, ever."

Jenette did not accept her father's reasoning. "No sickness, no disease, life in perfect health until you die—maybe Pact *is* the Body Pure, father. Did you ever think of that?"

Intravenous tubes rattled as he shook his head. "We came from Evermore to find our humanity, not to give it up. Besides, only infants can make Pact—or did your Feral friends not tell you that?"

"They did," Jenette allowed.

"You see, we did what we had to do."

"I do not see."

"Well, perhaps the best we can do, you and I, is to agree to disagree."

Jenette nodded; at least that was something. A fit of coughing overcame Tesla, and then his hand gripped hers harder.

"Jenette, it is time for you to take my place."

"Father, please, I don't want to talk about that."

Tesla persisted. "But it is time to talk about it. Someone needs to make the hard decisions for the Enclave when I am gone—and that person is you. You are ready for it. I can see that." Jenette opened her mouth to protest. "Shhh, please, let me finish. You say you don't want to lead, every time we talk you say that, but your actions show me otherwise. They show me what a great leader you will make. Stop fighting it. Accept your fate. Accept your responsibility."

"If it means accepting Sacrament, then you know what my answer is."

Tesla frowned. "It means accepting responsibility for always doing what you think is right, always. You make the hard decisions no one else will make. And you must be responsible for every single human in this Enclave, not just those you like or happen to agree with. You must be responsible for the lives of those you disagree with as well as those who are your allies. No matter what they do, you are their keeper. You may guide, cajole, manipulate,

threaten and punish—but you may never abandon. Never. That is
the sacred trust. You are the only one who can do it. Say yes and
let an old man die in peace."

Her father's icy eyes seemed bluer at that moment than they
had every been before and Jenette wanted to honor his last wish
more than anything, but . . . to keep every human in the Enclave
alive without condoning Sacrament. It was impossible.

"Father, I will do everything I possibly can, everything within
my power, everything I can think of, but . . ."

"There are no *buts*. There is complete acceptance, or not. Anything in between is only failure."

Jenette hung her head. "Then the answer is no."

Tesla let go of her hand, the color fading from his eyes. "Then,
I need a favor," he said, doing a bad job of trying to hide his disappointment.

"What?"

"Find Toby. He was wounded. He may be in a temporary infirmary in the Guard barracks. Bring him here."

"Bring Toby here? But if he's wounded . . . ?"

"Someone must make the hard decisions," Tesla said wearily.
"If you are not ready for that burden yet, then it must be me. I must
live."

Abruptly it hit Jenette, why her father needed Toby. "Final
Sacrament!" she gasped. She could hardly comprehend it; after
feeling closer to her father than at any other time in her adult memory, after reaching a level of understanding, if not acceptance, how
could he ask her to participate in such an atrocity? Final Sacrament
was a vile procedure where a mortally wounded human extracted
all of a domestic's remaining immune venom in a desperate bid to
stay alive. It never worked—at best it prolonged the human's life
by hours or, rarely, days—but it always killed the domestic. In
Jenette's opinion, only the most depraved humans engaged in
Final Sacrament and, for all his obvious flaws, she had never
counted her father among their number. "I can't believe you'd ask
me to do that!" she said, in horror.

Because she would not allow herself to cry in front of her father, she turned and headed for the door.

"Jenette wait!" her father groaned. "Someone must make the hard decisions! Someone must make the hard decisions or we are all lost!"

Jenette fled. The door slammed shut behind her.

There were noises, outside. Inside, it was safe. It was dark, inside. Inside the Null. In-robert knew that. No one could see him, and that was good because he wanted to stay hidden. He mustn't be found. If he was found he would be taken away from the Null. And then how would he keep it safe?

But. . . .

Something was different. After days of floating and flying, there had been a big bump. And then noise from lots of skins and Ferals outside, yelling and shooting. (In-robert remembered shooting from long, long ago, before he had discovered his *purpose.*)

Maybe the Null was not safe.

He had to find out! He squirmed about in the tight space until he felt the hatch below him. He fished a claw into the latch mechanism. *Snikt.* The hatch released. He held it from falling fully open as sounds poured in.

He heard the roaring of angry skins in the distance. Closer, he heard Feral footfalls in tall grass. Then he heard strident Feral voices.

"Arrou, Arrou!"

"Rusty! What wrong?"

"Trouble, trouble. Bragg humans doing bad things. Bad, bad things. Where Jenette?"

"In Great Hall, with Tesla. Come. Arrou take you."

Great Hall. Tesla. Those were things in-robert recognized. They were things important enough to make him leave his hiding spot. Without a second thought, he let the hatch swing down, and scuttled off, following the sound of Arrou's and Rusty's passage through the high polyp fronds.

Jenette leaned against the wall outside her father's sick room, head bowed and with a hand covering her wet face. Arrou and Rusty barreled around a distant corner and clawed to a stop. Their heads swung, searching the narrow service corridor, and then fixated on her.

"Jenette, Jenette!" Arrou called. "Must go, must go!"

Jenette swiped tears from her eyes. "What's wrong?" she asked, numbly.

"Eating him, eating him!" Rusty cried when she did not immediately follow him and Arrou.

Jenette looked up, her eyes sharpening with sudden concern. "Eating someone? Eating who?"

"The Pilot!" said Rusty. "Jenette and Arrou come quick! Come quick!"

The mob swept Karr through prefabricated colony structures.

"The Body Pure! The Body Pure!"

Karr's feet never touched the ground. Hands gripping painfully tight held him above a torrent of white-haired heads. Mob sweat stank in Karr's nostrils and mob fury roared in his ears. Occasionally voices challenged the mob from beyond the periphery of his vision; all Karr could see was the night sky and the tops of walls and roofs that bounded the winding streets and alleys. Sometimes scuffles followed the protests, but none lasted long. The mob's greater numbers always won out.

"The lab!" shrieked Subconsul Bragg. "Over to the lab!"

The mob turned. Karr's starry view narrowed and then disappeared, as the sky above him was replaced by a narrow ceiling with a line of stark bright glowstrips running up its middle. The mob jostled tighter under Karr, carrying him up a staircase into a second-story room. The gripping hands shoved him down onto a cold, flat surface. Straps cinched tight about his wrists, ankles, waist, and neck. Then the mob parted. The juveniles retreated to a doorway, revealing an antiseptic room. Karr lay on a shiny plasteel table. Intrusive-looking apparatus hovered over him on whirring, machine-controlled arms.

A man in lab whites adjusted an overhead light.

Karr squinted against the glare. "Where am? Who are you?"

In stark contrast to the rest of the colonists, the man was old, quite old. He spoke in a nasal voice. "I am Dr. Ponder Yll and this is, not strictly speaking, my lab." Yll's shoulders hunched apologetically. "Actually this is the domestic vivisection operatory. *My* lab has fallen to into Feral clutches. Twenty years of work," he mourned, "gone." Dejected, Yll selected a mediprobe from a nearby tray of instruments.

Upon the lab walls were charts detailing the proper procedure for dissecting a Khafra. And there was a blood-draining groove running around the edge of the table that Karr was strapped upon. He tried to remain calm. "Dr. Yll, there has apparently been some sort of misunderstanding. I am Pilot Lindal Karr of the fugueship *Long Reach*."

"Your identity is known to me."

"Then I request that you allow me to speak with Consul Jenette Tesla."

Yll looked pained. "That will not be possible. I am deeply sorry." Yll pressed the mediprobe against Karr's neck. It hissed. Karr felt cold seeping into the muscles around his throat and suddenly his vocal cords would not work.

"Ghaghkt!" Karr protested.

Yll patted a consoling hand upon Karr's shoulder. "It will be better this way, believe me."

Yll's fingers swapped the mediprobe for surgical cutters and he began to snip off pieces of Karr's uniform. Karr gurgled ineffectually as his arms and torso were exposed. Yll then picked up a syringe-like instrument. It had a small opening at one end and a mechanical plunger at the other. Karr did not like the look of it.

"Gugh whagh?"

"Indeed," Yll said, his brows pinching regretfully. "Anesthetic is contraindicated for this procedure, but I will endeavor to make the experience as painless as possible." Yll tested the plunger. A ring of tiny blades whirled out of, and then retreated back into, the instrument's open end.

Karr squirmed in the restraints.

"Struggling will only increase the level of discomfort," Yll warned. He placed the device against Karr's arm. Cha-chick! The blades bit a half-inch divot out of Karr's flesh.

"Unngh!" he moaned.

The instrument emitted a pureeing whine. A diode on its tip blinked red. With a sneer of distaste, Yll placed the instrument against his own forearm and depressed the plunger again.

"Oh, yessssss."

The sneer disappeared as Yll's eyes rolled into the back of his head. His wrinkles drew into an idiot's grin. "Yesss, that is quite acceptable." The instrument left a purple welt. Yll did not care. Yll's countenance was fully transformed from apologetic and reluctant to euphoric. "Quite acceptable," he said happily. "More than consistent with expectations."

Colonists in the doorway began to lick their lips.

With a giddy spring in his step, Yll joined them at the entrance and opened a crate filled to overflowing with the same flesh-extracting instruments as he had just used on Karr. He passed them out. A queue of colonists formed. Sunken-eyed juveniles with pasty complexions stepped up to the vivisection table one by one. Karr noted that many of them were wounded and looked even worse than they normally did. They stacked their fists, each in turn bowing their heads. "Blessed be the Body Pure," they chanted, holding the syringes like holy icons. One by one, they removed sterile wrappers and applied the instruments to Karr's exposed skin.

Cha-chik. Whir. Hiss.

Eyes rolled and the colonists filed giddily back out the door as others pressed in to take their place in line. The gouges in Karr's arm did not bleed, but they hurt like hell.

Cha-chik. Whir. Hiss. Cha-chik. Whir. Hiss.

"Ergh! Aagh!"

Karr's arm soon took on the cratered look of a moon peppered by asteroids.

"Make neat incisions," Yll giggled from the doorway. "There are many in line."

More and more colonists filed in. Karr wracked his brain, trying to remember what the Enclave's population was. Two thousand? Three thousand? He did not think a human being could live long with the outer half inch of its body mass removed.

Karr thrashed harder.

Yll turned heavy-lidded eyes on Karr. "Please attempt to conserve your dignity." The old doctor-abruptly swayed. "Oh my. I seem to have miscalculated the onset of *fugue* coma . . ."

Suddenly, in the midst of all the pain, the peculiar scene made sense to Karr. They were extracting *fugue* from his tissues and injecting it into theirs to save themselves from Scourge. The giddy expressions, Yll's increasing stupor and lack of balance were all textbook responses to a high dose of *fugue*. Any moment now, Karr calculated, the next reaction would set in.

Yll collapsed to the floor.

A brief silence followed. The sound of many voices arguing in the streets outside entered through the lab's only window, but neither that nor Yll's comatose form stopped the progression of colonists. They merely grabbed their own syringes from the crate and the line, if anything, moved even faster.

"Blessed be the Body Pure. Blessed be the Body Pure."

The ghoulish faces paid no attention to Karr's discomfort. Cha-chik, cha-chik, cha-chik, cha-chik. Only the arrival of Panya Hedren diverted the single-minded progression in and out of the lab. Looking as though her pregnant belly would burst at any instant, Panya carefully retrieved a syringe from the crate on the floor and waddled over to Karr.

"Oh the poor, poor Pilot," she cooed, removing her instrument's sterile wrapper. "He looks so pathetic."

The colonists giggled nervously. Karr stared daggers at Panya. Derogatory words from a dozen different colony worlds popped into his head; none of them seemed strong enough to express how much Karr hated her at that instant.

Panya smirked. "A kiss for good luck," she said, bending and pressing her lips onto his. Karr tried to bite her, but his teeth suddenly clicked onto a hard object. He froze, confused. Panya winked and tongued the object firmly into his mouth. Then she stood back up and made a show of using her syringe. The device clicked and whirred, and she rolled her eyes, but the blades never actually touched Karr's flesh and therefore did not inject anything into her own.

Lips held firmly shut, Karr probed the object in his mouth. It was an inch long cylinder with one tapered end and a conspicuous bump halfway along its length. Karr pressed the bump with his tongue. Immediately, a spot within his mouth began to burn. Karr clicked the activator bump again, but not before a painful blister formed inside one cheek.

It was a beam cutter of some kind!

Before Karr could smile a confused thank you to Panya, she turned away. Reaching the doorway she abruptly clutched her distended belly, let out a theatrical moan and collapsed blocking the stairs.

Karr needed no prodding. As distracted colonists clustered around Panya, he maneuvered the beam cutter between his teeth. Crooking his head, he pointed the emitter end at the wrist restraint that the colonists could not see from the doorway. The beam was invisible, and weak, but Karr was able to correct his aim by observing the welts that bubbled up on his skin. The pain was hardly noticeable compared to the throbbing of his cratered arm. The restraint began to smolder. Karr prayed no one would notice the burning smell.

"Oh, oh!" Panya groaned right on cue. "It's time! It's time! Find a doctor!"

Ten seconds, twenty seconds. *Snikt.* The fibers parted. Karr fumbled one handed to free his other wrist, then released his neck and waist straps, but when he sat up and unbuckled his ankles, the colonists looked up from Panya.

"The Body Pure escapes! Stop him!"

Karr hit the floor running and dove out the open second story window onto a rooftop. He spit the beam cutter into his hands, then ran to the roof's edge. The clamor of many voices washed up from below. Two factions of colonists were facing off below: the mob surrounding the vivisection building, all of whom wore green-and-red armbands, and the Guardsmen who in turn surrounded the mob. Colonel Halifax and Jenette stood toe to toe with Subconsul Bragg.

"By the authority of the Prime Consul," Halifax ordered, "I order you to put down your weapons."

"The Prime Consul is on his deathbed!" Bragg shot back. "There is no authority here except the will of the Body!"

Halifax protested something about an orderly transfer of power, but the roaring crowd drowned him out. Jenette waved her arms in an attempt to calm them.

"Stop! Think! Is this what you want? Anarchy? Humans fighting humans, humans *eating* humans? What's wrong with you people?"

The mob, in no mood to be lectured, roared its disapproval.

Bragg's boyish face appeared. "You don't get it, do you Consul Jenette Tesla? Do you think we *want* to do these things? Do you think we *enjoy* doing these things? We don't! But we want to live! While you've been gallivanting around the planet, we've been fighting for our homes and dying of Scourge! Look at us; we're all wounded. We can feel the worms growing inside us, but we can't even make Final Sacrament, because Halifax stole our domestics to man the battle lines!"

"I didn't have anything to do with that," Halifax responded angrily. "They volunteered."

"It's your fucking domestic that's turned ours against us."

Halifax clenched his jaw. "It's those *fucking* domestics that are keeping your sorry asses alive."

"Wrong!" Bragg said pointing up at the vivisection lab, where he believed Karr still lay. "It's *fugue* and only *fugue* that's going to keep us alive! His life for ours, it's a good trade!"

"It's murder!" Jenette accused.

The mob roared louder and pushed forward. Halifax's Guards shifted sweaty palms on pulse-rifles (Karr noted Liberty, Skutch, and Grubb front and center beside Jenette), but Karr didn't get to watch the confrontation unfold. Boots scraped behind him. Colonists were clambering out the lab window, their ravenous eyes fixed upon him.

XLVI

CHOREA VERMICULORUM, Latin (dance of the little worms), *scientific name for deadly xenoparasite commonly known as Scourge, which was responsible for nearly wiping out the colony seeded at New Ascension [4609 A.D.].*

—*New Encyclopedia Galactica,*
34th edition

Karr ran around the lab to the back of the roof. There was no way down and, even if there had been, the narrow alley separating the vivisection building from its nearest neighbor was crammed with frenzied colonists.

"There he is! Grab him, grab him!" pursuing voices cried from behind Karr on the roof.

With no alternative, Karr backed up, took a running start, and jumped. He sailed across a ten-foot gap, falling down hard onto a darkened roof across the alley, but quickly gathered his legs under him. A colonist leapt after Karr, bloodlust in his eyes. He, however, fell short of landing on the neighboring roof and ended up hanging from its edge by his fingertips. The mob cheered and shouted encouragement as the colonist scrambled to climb up. Karr stomped fingers until the crazed pseudo-juvenile fell into the mob below.

"He's getting away!" colonists on the lab roof shrieked in alarm.

Karr fled across the dark roof as the clamor increased below. He bruised his shins on shadowy condensers and scraped his arms on half-seen cooling fins as the sound of opposing colonists' voices merged into a violent din. Weapons fire cracked as Karr scampered around a series of pipes, jumped up, and then pulled hand over hand along a cable to the next darkened structure. Across its roof he went. Smoke billowed from broken skylights, choking his breath. At the far end, he clambered down a ladder and dropped the last few feet into an alley.

Karr's arm throbbed. He ignored the pain and ran out into the street. The glow from burning structures and vehicles shone brighter at ground level. In one direction, the parasitic grasses grew thick and high. In the other, those fronds had been trampled down. Karr saw colonists fighting one another in that direction. Pulse-rifle reports echoed off plasteel and ceramite.

Karr turned and walked at a measured pace toward the untrampled grass fronds, hoping to avoid notice, but after only a few steps, a hue and cry arose. "There, in the white! There!" Cursing his beloved uniform, Karr charged into the disturbing sea of grass. Bulb-headed stalks enveloped Karr, battering his face. Cloying, mildewy, malodorous fronds impeded his speed. He could see no further than an arm's length ahead. And there were *things* in the deep grass. Karr stepped on them all too frequently; they were both squishy and brittle at the same time. Karr tried not to think what they might be as he ran pell-mell down the street.

Tesla lay in the records room alone. The pain of his wounds was overwhelming, fogging his mind. He struggled to differentiate between reality and hallucination . . .

The door opens again.

Once more Tesla strains to look, but he cannot see who it is and there is no other sound.

"Jenette?" he calls. "Jenette?"

The faint tik-tik of four multi-clawed legs sounds on the hard floor. Through the fog of his pain, Tesla hears them move tentatively closer.

"Toby? Is that you?"

The footfalls stop halfway across the room.

"Toby," Tesla says harshly. "Come here."

But the only response is a suspicious sniffing. Teeth chatter indecisively. Finally, a hushed voice speaks. It is not Toby.

"Master?"

The sound triggers a flood of bad memories. Tesla remembers a battle-torn Coffin Island. He is on an overloaded jump-lifter. Below are the domestics that must be left behind, their forlorn faces upturned—one in particular locks eyes with Tesla.

"Blacky?" *he says aloud into the room.*

"No," *says the voice from the past. It sounds irritated and confused.* "Not Blacky."

Again the voice triggers bad memories. "Come closer," *Tesla croaks weakly.* "Come."

The four-legged shape shuffles nearer. The room is dim and Tesla's vision is blurred from his injuries. He cannot identify the domestic, but the voice is the voice from his nightmares. It must be Blacky. Only, why does the hunched form look pink? Tesla reaches out a shaky hand. At first the domestic flinches away. Then, with renewed sniffing, it allows contact. Tesla feels a warm muzzle under his palm—and then he feels the instinctive nose-butt that the domestic from Tesla's memories always gave to a scratching hand.

"Blacky, it is you."

"No," *the voice denies.* "Blacky is dead."

"Dead? But you are Blacky."

"No. In-humans killed him."

"In-humans . . . ?" *Tesla wonders if he is dreaming. He can feel all the needles and hoses connected to his body. Are the anti-pain drugs affecting his mind? It seems so real—the breath, for instance, huffing on his hand, becoming more rapid and agitated.* "Be a good boy," *Tesla says, feeling ill at ease with the hallucination.* "Be a good boy, Blacky."

"Blacky was a good boy!" *the voice snivels.* "Master says guard the Null. Blacky guarded the Null. Master says keep the Null safe. Blacky kept the Null safe. Master says he will come back. But master never comes back. Why?"

Tesla knows he has no worthy answer. Blacky was courage, loyalty, and honesty embodied. Blacky was one of the hard decisions.

"Why master never comes back?" *the domestic asks again.*

"You would never understand," *Tesla says.*

There is silence, and then anger. "Understand master lies. Un-

derstand only Ferals come. Ferals try to kill Blacky, Ferals and in-humans." Tesla feels the domestic push closer still. He feels its breath on his neck. Tesla's feeble hand and arm, still in contact with the familiar muzzle, stiffen apprehensively. "In-humans get Blacky first," the voice whines and accuses. "In-humans take Blacky away from the light. In-humans take the light away from Blacky!"

Now the alien head bows under Tesla's fingers, allowing Tesla's fingers to slip up along its bullet-shaped skull. Tesla feels an awful coldness as his fingertips drop into empty eye sockets.

"Because master does not come back," the voice snarls.

Tesla withdraws his hand from the horror he has created.

The Khafra looms over Tesla. "Master is bad. Very, very bad. Master says he is good. But master does bad. Master says he does bad to do good. But only bad happens."

"No," Tesla protests, "the Body will be Pure. It must. . . ."

Tesla feels paws pressing down on his chest, talon tips pressing painfully into his solar plexus.

"Now what must Blacky do?" the menacing voice half growls, half weeps. "Blacky tries to do good, but only bad happens. Blacky tries to be good, but Blacky only becomes evil." The voice rises in tone and des-peration. "Blacky must be like master!" the specter decides, voice cracking from the strain of seventeen years of torture. "Blacky must not do good! Blacky must be like master! Blacky must do bad to do good! That is what Blacky must do! Then maybe good will happen to Blacky!"

All at once the talons pressing in the center of Tesla's chest gouge down, ripping skin, tearing and breaking cartilage, bur-rowing down, pressing aside fat and muscle and finally grasping the pulsing red organ so revealed. It tries to beat in Blacky's tight-ening grip, tries to pump blood. Tesla feels unbearable pain. His head swirls. Oblivion closes in. And suddenly he has a vision that it is not Blacky who is squeezing the life from his heart, but a much younger, idealized version of himself, before disillusionment, be-fore all the choices that have brought his feeble body to this deso-late end—before the hard decisions have come full circle.

The old man's heart exploded.

The alien's head hung low.

"Blacky is dead, " it said.

*   *   *

The sound of many pursuing feet drowned the sound of Karr's own passage through the polyp fronds. Karr fled as fast as he could, but no matter how he twisted between prefab domes or around blocky storehouses, he could not avoid leaving a trail of trampled stalks snaking out behind him like a beacon. It would inevitably lead the mob to him, and in the mood they were in Karr considered it a distinct possibility that they would resort to cruder methods than sterile syringes to extract the *fugue* they so desperately wanted from his body.

In an effort to break the trail Karr ducked into a squat building with tall, narrow windows, but the instant he kicked the heavy door open, he skidded to a halt. The structure was an armory of some kind. Two colonists looked up from charging pulse-rifle clips. Two more in Guard uniforms stood before racks of weaponry.

"Wait!" they called as Karr fled back into the street. "We mean you no harm!"

Karr ran faster. He was not about to entrust his life to unknown colonists in uniforms—anyone could put on a uniform. Behind Karr, a cloud of dust and chaff, rising from the passage of the mob through the polyp fronds, was drawing uncomfortably near. Karr tried another trick. Darting along the side of a recycling-vat yard, he turned left at each corner until he came full circle. Where his noose-like path rejoined itself, a wide swath of crushed fronds crossed in front of Karr. Karr edged forward and peeked out into the swath. To his left, colonists carrying improvised weaponry were disappearing around the recycling vats, hot on his trail. Karr turned right and ran back toward the vivisection lab, his footsteps hidden in the already trampled fronds. His head scanned from side to side, searching for something, anything, that would allow him to extricate himself from the situation. He could hear the cries of the mob echoing from behind the recycling vats; any instant now they would complete the loop around the yard and see him.

Karr spotted a ladder on the side of a building. That would work fine, he decided. Veering toward it, he trampled an especially obvious path to its foot, then carefully retraced his steps back to the wide swath of trampled fronds, and then took a running start and leaped as far as he could into the untouched fronds on the other side.

Karr landed face down next to a *squishy* object.

Deep in the shadows, the reason for the polyp frond overgrowth on the colony island became clear. The parasitic grasses had sprung up around, and were feeding upon, the bodies of humans and Khafra who had fallen in combat. Ravenous tendrils, snaking from every polyp stalk within sight, wormed into a bloated purple cadaver. Karr lay next to it, touching it, its swollen eyes gaping inches from his own. Revolted, he wanted to leap back, but howls of rage rang down the street as the mob completed the loop around the recycling-vat yard and realized Karr's deception. Stampeding feet hammered in his direction. Karr dared not move away from the clammy corpse or the mob would surely spot him—they might spot him anyway. A hundred pairs of eyes seemed to bore into the back of Karr's neck as the rumble neared, but just like clockwork, they spotted the decoy path. Hands and boots clattered, going up the ladder. Other footfalls swarmed around the building on the ground.

"The other side! Cut him off!"

The mob's rumble diminished. Karr rose onto his hands and knees, the movement throwing a different light on the nearby cadaver. Karr suddenly recognized the features. It was the very first colonist who had touched him and then licked the sweat off his hand (a face Karr would never forget). The colonist was frozen in a wide-eyed rictus of agony. It was a pitiable sight; even as Karr hid from the dead boy-man's bloodthirsty brethren, Karr was conscious of the fact that the dead second-generation colonist had not asked to come to a plague-infested planet and die such a gruesome death. Whatever transgressions this fellow human may have made, he had paid the ultimate price for them.

This was a thought process that would not have occurred to Pilot Lindal Karr previous to this ill-fated mission, but his recent first-hand experiences on New Ascension were changing the way he looked at things. The dead man was no longer just an unfortunate number on a roster. Karr actually felt sympathy. On impulse, he reached to close the staring eyes.

That impulse was not a good one.

The face flinched on contact. Karr jerked back as the head abruptly twitched erect on its dead neck, the distended eyes bursting as pungent, lifeless breath howled from a mouth stretching wider and wider. The bloated body split open. Fetid, infectious ichor, in which swam countless tiny, writhing black worms, vomited out of the fissures, splattering Karr and every polyp stalk within ten feet. Karr wiped the vile ejecta from his mouth, nose, and eyes, realizing that he had, no doubt, come face to face with the Scourge and one of the methods it used to propagate itself. Suddenly it was clear why Jenette and the Guards had been so particular about burning their dead quickly.

Karr thanked the Fates that his body was steeped in *fugue*.

Karr crawled off through the fronds, making as little noise as possible and carefully avoiding any further cadavers. Soon he was slinking down an alley and scrambling around a bend between large aquifer extractors, the slow, rhythmic chambers pumping water up from the island's natural reservoirs. Then he was jogging beneath the spoon-shaped scoops of a sensor array, through latticed support structures, and out to the boundary where the colony buildings ended and open fields began.

There, halfway across no-man's land, lay the heavy lifter. Unconsciously, Karr's movements had brought him back towards it, but now he saw how futile that had been. Ferals were swarming over its shattered pieces. Karr didn't see them at first, but longer scrutiny revealed that at least a hundred of the hostile, camouflaged aliens had advanced and were using the hull sections as a forward outpost. Every so often a pulse-rifle shot would *zing* off a ceramite tile and the bullet heads would disappear, but they were no less present or dangerous. And, even if they hadn't been there, and even if Karr could somehow sneak out through the polyp grasses without being seen by the fighting aliens and humans, the lifter was damaged far beyond his ability to jury-rig repairs. It needed weeks, maybe months in a repair dock before it would ever fly again.

Mob cries echoed from behind the aquifer pumps.

Even more harried than before, Karr darted between stacks of high-g containers. Row upon row of the empty things formed a neglected maze at the human edge of no-man's land. It was the perfect place for Karr to get lost. Jog left, right, right, left. Perfect. Oops, a dead end. Turn around and—WHAM! Karr collided with two colonists. Looking like starved children in the shadowy light, they eyed Karr hungrily. One was armed with a large food preparation knife, the other bare-handed. Advancing deliberately, they backed Karr into the dead end. Karr fumbled the cutting beam from his pocket, activating it and aiming for their sunken eyes, but the youths simply shielded themselves with their forearms, ignoring the pain of blisters sizzling up on their flesh. Karr bumped against a solid stack of crates; he could back up no further. The colonists halted three paces away, blocking the only exit.

"Stop wasting it!" the knife-wielder snarled.

Anxious to buy time, if only to catch his breath, Karr clicked off the ineffectual cutter beam and held his hands up. "All right, no problem," he wheeled, vocal cords not yet recovered.

"I said, *stop wasting it!*" the colonist repeated, more agitated.

Confused, Karr looked where they were staring: at his right arm. It glistened black and wet in the dark. His exertions had torn the many cauterized syringe wounds open. Blood dripped onto pavement tubers at his feet.

"Your shirt," the knife-wielder said to his cohort. "Give it to him."

The cohort obediently unzipped his daysuit and pulled his arms out of its sleeves. He then removed an undershirt and tossed it at Karr.

"Put pressure on it," the knife-wielder ordered Karr.

Karr twisted up the questionable bandage and wrapped it around his arm. The second colonist cocked his head as he rezipped his daysuit; riot sounds were spreading out in the distance as the mob frantically searched for Karr.

"Should we tell?"

"Get ours first. Then tell."

"The Body must be Pure."

The knife-wielder grinned. "*Our* bodies must be pure."

The colonists bowed their heads and stacked their fists. The reflex ritual, Karr noted, lasted three heartbeats.

"How will we get it?"

"It is already bleeding."

"How will we subdue it?"

The knife-wielder shifted his blade from a precision, point-up hold, to a point-down power grip. "Any way we can."

Karr had visions of the kitchen knife plunging into his neck. "The Body must be Pure!" he yelled, abruptly stacking his fists over his heart and bowing his head. Both colonists stopped and bowed their heads.

"The Body must be Pure," they intoned.

Karr made a break for it, darting between them, but the reprieve did not last long. All too soon, the colonists were on his heels and while Karr's stamina was flagging, their anticipation of feasting upon the *fugue* in Karr's tissues spurred the colonists to greater speed. Looking back, Karr saw that soon they would have him in their clutches once more.

He unwound the improvised bandage from his arm, stopped and wheeled around.

"Look!" he panted, holding the blood-soaked cloth in plain view. "Enough *fugue* to keep you alive for months, maybe years!" The colonists came to an uncertain stop. "I'll give it to you," Karr said sweetly. "No fighting, no risk of getting wounded, no chance of triggering Scourge onset. Easy pickings."

Like magic, the colonists fixated, reaching out with grasping hands, but just as their fingers were about to close on the bait, Karr flung the dirty rag into the open end of a nearby crate. The colonists wavered for an instant, and then dove for the prize. Karr bolted as they fought over it.

"Mine, mine!"

"No mine! Let go!"

Disoriented, Karr wove through the storage yard maze, trying to find a way out.

That's when he ran into Consul Bragg, literally.

Before Karr knew it, the young man's right hand was clenched around his throat. Bragg's left hand jammed a mauler pistol into Karr's stomach.

"The Body must be Pure!" Karr choked.

An evil grin split Bragg's face. He did not stack his fists or bow his head. "Pilots think they're *so* smart," he said, without taking his eyes off of Karr for an instant. "But they're not smart." Sounds of the mob closing in resounded through the maze about them. Bragg gloated. *"We're* the ones who are smart."

Karr squirmed. Unfortunately, the youth had a very strong grip and any small move on Karr's part found the pistol jabbing harder into his belly.

Bragg leaned in closer, to Karr. "I never liked you."

Karr gasped, uncomfortably. Stifling the impulse to tell Bragg that he never liked him, either, Karr said, "There's no need for us to fight. I'm sure we can come to some sort of mutually beneficial arrangement."

Bragg said, "The arrangement is this: there is just as much *fugue* in your body dead as there is alive." He raised the mauler pistol and pressed it to Karr's temple. *"Make your peace, Pilot."*

Karr felt the mauler pistol's arming rod snap into firing position. He felt Bragg's arm jerk on the weapon. He heard the *crack* of a charge cut the air and waited—in that instant of blinding fear—for *non-existence* as his head vaporized.

Instead, Bragg's cranium vaporized.

Tiny bits of bone and brain streamed off to Karr's right. He looked left. No more than a dozen paces away, where the aisles of storage crates formed an uneven intersection, Jenette stood holding a pulse-rifle in firing position. She blinked, a look of horror on her face. Then, before Karr could say anything, she motioned for Karr to climb the stack of crates next to him, and she took off at a run using the butt of the pulse-rifle against the crates like a stick on a picket fence. Karr scaled the crates. Seconds later a mob of wild-eyed colonists appeared and stampeded off after the receding clatter.

A predatory shape was waiting for Karr atop the crates. It lunged at him.

XLVII

Once we accept our limits, we are forever prisoners to them.

—*Major A. Vidun*
Founder, Pilot Academy

Karr flinched, but the predatory shape was a domestic. Better yet, it was Arrou.

"Want ride?" Arrou asked, offering a perch on his wide back.

Karr lost no time climbing astride Arrou's powerful flanks and grabbing tight to the knots of armor plate at the alien's shoulders.

Below, in the chasms formed by stacked crates, packs of rampaging colonists searched for Karr. From streets beyond the maze, others colonists spotted Karr and Arrou and began to shout and gesticulate in their direction.

"Bad humans coming," said the alien. "Go fast?"

"Five hundred knots," said Karr.

"Five hundred knots! Rraaaarrk!"

Arrou took off. The ride was not exactly comfortable. Various armor plates dug into Karr as Arrou bounded across the top of the crate maze, then leapt down and sprinted along narrow streets, through polyp grass, hurtling over fences, springing into structures through broken windows, and skidding out under half-closed garage doors. Arrou ran a convoluted path that soon had Karr's sense of direction spinning, never mind that of those on their trail. In no time they had lost all sign of pursuit, disappeared beneath dense undergrowth, and secreted themselves into a hiding spot that only a domestic like Arrou would have thought to use.

*   *   *

Karr crouched alone inside the old flitter hull, sitting atop dozens of specimen jars filled with ash. Each one bore a label: Wotan, Jikkawak, Lady, Hastur, Rex. The labels also bore dates, but aside from the year, Karr could not make sense of the non-standard calendar. The latest one was tagged *Trum 53-1-4632,* but there were at least three tiers of jars under Karr, going back many years. Arrou had said the bad humans would not find Karr there, but it was an unsettling place to be.

A projected image from Bob's datacube—one of the few items the colonists had not stripped from Karr when they captured him— provided light. The recording looped endlessly. A disembodied, 3-D Bob head floated above the cube, pinched face, beaky nose, and all.

"This is for my friend, Lindal Karr," the head said. *"A truer pal no one ever had."* Bob's seemed to look right at Karr. Tears welled in Bob's bulgy eyes. *"You're beautiful, buddy. I love you."*

Bob's head shrank as the projected image widened out. Bob was inside Karr's Pilot quarters, on board *Long Reach.* Karr lay on his bunk, in one of his four-month-long sleep periods. Bob, existing in slowtime, sat cross-legged—and buck-ass naked—on the bunk beside Karr.

"Can I say that to you? I love you, man." Bob gave Karr's sleeping image a playful punch on the chin. *"You're the only one that didn't stab Bob in the back."*

Wait and see, Karr thought. Freak.

Tears streamed down Bob's face. His head hung, his voice coming in sporadic, honking sobs. *"I gotta be straight, buddy. I don't think old Bob's going to get out of this. Bob's done some . . . bad things. And he doesn't feel so good right now."* Every crevice, every fold of flesh on Bob's gangly frame was filled with yellow fuzz. Foodyeast immune defenses were at work defending their biosystem, which explained why Bob didn't feel very good. *"No, the odds aren't good for Bob. But you might make it out of this mess, Lindal—if you listen to Bob."* Bob's face became even more pinched than normal as thoughts rattled about in his devious head.

"Bob knows. Bob sees. When nobody knows Bob's around, Bob figures things out."

Bob dug mold out of his ears. Eventually his brain would turn to jelly, he would stop moving, and slowly dissolve into the tissues of the ship. It was a testament to Bob's fortitude that he survived so long.

Bob's face took on a worshipful glow. He caressed Karr's sleeping face. *"You're everything Bob wants to be, buddy. Smart. Honorable. Good looking. Lucky. Problem is, you're also a dupe."* Bob grabbed Karr's sleeping image by the scruff of his ghimpsuit and shook. *"Why? Why? What have the fuckers ever done for you? Nothing!"*

Bob let Karr go, and wept some more.

"Your gut's all out of whack. That's what. Mark my words, if you want to get out of this, you got to turn everything on end. You got to love what you don't want to love and trust what you don't want to trust. Find out what those things are and you're golden, buddy, golden." Bob wavered drunkenly. *"Bob's tired now."*

Bob curled up beside Karr and passed out. The datacube recording clicked back to the beginning. Karr sat quietly in the flitter hulk, ignoring the replay. He was only using the datacube as a light source. Outside the hulk there were people who wanted to eat him and the last thing Karr wished to ponder at that moment was the rantings of a madman.

Digging sounds resonated through the hulk. The hatch opened. Dirt poured in as Arrou's bullet head poked through.

"Arrou back," the alien announced. "Brought Jenette."

Arrou's head darted out once more. Jenette entered, bending over in the cramped space, and sat, looking rather shell-shocked, beside Karr. Since there was no room for a creature of Arrou's bulk inside the skimmer hull, he gently let the hatch back down and, presumably, hid himself from view. Jenette cringed at the sight of Karr's mutilated arm.

"Sorry about that."

"Don't be sorry," said Karr. "It wasn't your fault. You saved my butt. If you hadn't taken that shot, I wouldn't be here right now."

Jenette shivered. "I think I set the shot-torque too high."

"You may have," Karr agreed, recalling how Bragg's head had disintegrated.

"I didn't want to kill him," Jenette said numbly. "I didn't like him, but I didn't want to kill him. But what was I supposed to do? Stand there and let him kill you?"

"I'm glad you didn't. Thank you very much."

"You're welcome," Jenette said despondently.

"Hard decision," Karr said guessing how she must feel. He had made a few of them in his time. "They never get any easier, but sometimes you've got to do what you've got to do. Otherwise nobody will make the tough calls and then where would we be?"

Jenette glared at Karr for a while. He didn't understand why. Her expression became pained and she spoke again.

"There's something I have to tell you," she said. "Back at Gnosis, I may have made a judgment error. In a roundabout way, it's got to do with the situation here at the Enclave. The fighting was fierce. There were heavy losses."

Karr nodded gravely. "I saw what's in the polyp grasses."

Jenette looked equally as grave. "And those are the lucky ones. On this planet there are things worse than death, things that make you wish you were dead. If you die, Scourge eats your body and you explode worms all over the place. But if you get wounded, severely, your immune defenses are compromised and the Scourge attacks. The worms multiply and begin to eat. Millions of the tiny parasites. The pain drives you mad. You lash out, violently. Friends, family, it doesn't matter. Everyone is a target. Your body decays at an accelerated rate, you spread the worms, infecting everything you touch. It's one of the ways Scourge spreads itself."

Karr remembered his first days at the Enclave. "That's why your hospital has bars on the window?"

"Yes," said Jenette.

Karr frowned. "Funny, I don't remember the colonists in the vivisection lab showing any outward sign of injury."

"That's because they weren't injured—those individuals are just cowards . . ." Jenette said disgustedly, her voice trailing off as Bob's recorded chatter interrupted.

"You're beautiful, buddy. I love you."

Leaving the projection as a light source, Karr twisted the volume as low as it would go and turned Bob's face into a corner where the flitter's curving hull sections joined.

"Madman," he muttered. "You were saying, about a judgment error?"

Jenette squirmed uncomfortably. "Let me ask you first, your ship is spawning, what do you plan to do in regards to that?"

"Wait two hundred and thirty-six more days," said Karr simply. "No more meddling. The only reason I tried to shut my ship's engines down when we first arrived at the crash sight was that I thought *Long Reach* was in trouble. Now I know it's all part of a natural reproductive cycle, so it's hands off. That's always been my philosophy as a Pilot anyway. Whenever and wherever possible, let the ship do what it wants. Things work out better that way."

Karr felt good about his position, but it seemed to make Jenette even more uncomfortable.

"Do you remember," she asked, "when I told you about fugueships coming to New Ascension, about the Feral mythology surrounding the Burning Heart of Night and how it relates to your ship spawning?"

"How could I forget?" Karr said fondly.

"Well, I lied," said Jenette.

Karr's face fell. "My ship isn't spawning?"

"Your ship is spawning," Jenette said quickly. "I didn't tell you a *lie* lie. What I told you was true. I just didn't tell you the whole truth."

"So what is the whole truth?" Karr asked.

Jenette winced. "I told you that according to Feral history fugueships spawned on this planet three times, successfully. But . . . what I neglected to mention was that there were at least two other times, and those spawnings failed. Catastrophically. According to the texts, those times the Burning Heart of Night perished before its proper allotment of four-times-four-time-four-times-four days and no new Radiances were birthed. I suppose," Jenette added meekly, "that you would like to know why?"

Hardly daring to breathe, Karr nodded.

"The number of fire pillars was wrong," Jenette continued. "One time the number was five small pillars and another time it was three small pillars and one large pillar."

"What happens when there are four small pillars and one large pillar?" Karr asked in a hush.

"The root texts didn't say," Jenette admitted, looking more remorseful by the word. "There has never been four small pillars and one big pillar before, at least in recorded Feral history. But the texts were very clear that the number of pillars must be exactly four. Four small Radiances and no large Radiance. Otherwise, disaster." Jenette rubbed her temples. "So you see, going back to *Long Reach* now is not a question of meddling. It's a question of setting things right. Something—previous circumstance, bad luck, whatever—has already compromised the spawning and without intervention, well . . ."

Karr gaped speechlessly. *It was all his fault.* His attempts to constrict the flow of thrust through *Long Reach*'s engine nozzles had adversely affected the spawning. That was abundantly clear to him. His ship was headed for a premature death, and it was his fault. Four baby fugueships were going to perish abortively, and it was all his fault. When *Long Reach* was gone there would be only two healthy adult fugueships left in all of human space. Four new spawn would have tripled that number. How much exploration of the galaxy, how many new seeded colonies had Karr wiped from the possible future of the human race with one thoughtless action? Karr's head reeled. It was awful beyond a Pilot's capacity to comprehend.

Jenette tried to explain herself as Karr's brain melted down. "I know I misled you, but I did it because I needed to speak to my father and I knew you would not agree to return if I told you everything, and because I had a hunch things were not going well here at the Enclave . . . and I hope you can see that I was right."

Karr continued to say nothing. Jenette read it as condemnation. "I'm sorry," she said, her lower lip beginning to quiver. "You are the last person I want to lie to, believe me. I understand that you are probably extremely mad right now—I would be—and that I'm probably the last person you want to talk to right now, but, but . . . oh, *fuck it."* Jenette began to sob quietly.

Karr felt for her. Technically, she had betrayed him, but it had been a small betrayal in comparison with the scale of his failure and culpability as a Pilot. In fact, to his self-centered Pilot-mind, Jenette's actions were nearly inconsequential. Karr understood the burden of a Higher Duty, the things it drove you to, the sacrifice and the separation from the wants and needs of normal human existence, the loneliness. Furthermore, crouched there in the skimmer hulk, hiding from Khafra and humans alike, and separated from the comfort of his ship and the enveloping, forgiving, compassion if its *flesh,* Karr's own frail human heart felt very alone, too.

So it was that Karr took an action that he had not taken in hundreds and hundreds of years, an action based on human male–female behavior patterns so deeply rooted that they subverted all of his ingrained Pilot Academy inhibitions and paranoias, an action that surprised himself even as he did it.

Karr gave Jenette a hug.

Jenette buried her face in his shoulder and wept. Karr, socially challenged though he was, had enough sense to keep his mouth shut.

"I promise I'll do everything I can to make this up to you," she said, when she finally extricated herself from his arms.

Karr nodded, still feeling overwhelmed.

"What are we going to do?" Jenette asked.

"I haven't a clue," Karr admitted.

Obviously he had to return to *Long Reach.* Obviously he had to detonate the null-fusion reactor, as originally planned, and snuff out the pillars of fire. Then he would have to somehow descend into his ship and stop it from splitting water into hydrogen and oxygen. He must stop the electrolyzing flow of current through its superconductor core. Perhaps he would then reignite the hydrogen and oxygen which was presumably spewing from four growing, baby fugueships, then the number of flaming pillars would match the Feral prophecy. Hopefully that would set the spawning back on track and *Long Reach's* natural processes of reproduction would take over from there. But how would he get to that point? The human colony certainly did not posses the proper infrastructure to repair the heavy lifter in a timely fashion. And, in any case, its shattered remains lay in Feral hands. He had no way to move a fifty-ton null-fusion reactor a hundred feet, never mind a hundred kiloyards.

It was a pretty bleak situation.

The back of Bob's projected head wavered in the corner. The low volume voice squawked, "... *if you want to get out of this, you got to turn everything on end. You got to love what you don't want to love and trust what you don't want to trust.* ..."

No-man's land was quiet in the predawn air chill. A lone, white-clad figure walked through a field of polyp fronds with its arms up, as if in surrender. As it neared the heavy lifter, Ferals sprang from cover behind it, camouflaged blurs moving in the chest-high stalks.

Jenette crossed her fingers and hoped Karr was right.

Behind Jenette and Arrou was an equally strange situation. Guardsmen aimed their weapons, not outward at the Ferals, but back into the buildings and streets of human-held territory, to hold off Bragg's mob. It was another group of defenders that held the Ferals at bay. They were, of course, the domestics of Jenette's underground network, but Jenette had nothing to do with their sudden courage. It was Patton who rallied and led them because it was Patton who single-handedly devised a strategy to save the human colony by using the instinctual Pact injunction against killing other Pact. Time and time again, even in the short period of time that Jenette had watched the domestics that ringed the human barricades had marched out to drive the Ferals back. No weapons were used, no blood spilt; the domestics themselves were the deterrent to Feral aggression—and the tactic was quite effective. No Ferals had killed a human since Patton's domestics joined Halifax's Guards on the battle lines.

"Mahatma Gandhi," Patton rumbled, "battles of passive resistance, early twentieth century."

Patton and the other domestics were impatient to drive the Ferals back to their side of no-man's land, but Halifax proudly patted his friend's shoulder.

"Patience, soldier. Let's see how this battle plays out."

"Rrrrrr."

Karr stood his ground in the field. Ferals lunged, always in pairs, and then, just as lightning fast, retreated to circle in confused loops about their target. Over and over they attempted to attack the fragile human. None succeeded.

A single large Feral appeared, its glowbuds half white and half blank.

Arrou drew a sharp breath beside Jenette. "Tlalok!"

Tlalok attacked Karr. Both Feral and Pilot tumbled out of sight in the fronds. Several anxious heartbeats later, they reappeared. Karr was unhurt. Tlalok backed off, shaking his muzzle violently. The large Feral suddenly flashed from half white and half blank to full, angry glowbud radiance across his entire four-legged frame. He then threw back his muzzle.

A horrified cry echoed across the battlefield.

PART SIX:

BURNING HEART

XLVII

*Sometimes, hollow winds moan through his fugueship.
Huffff, huffff. Always he wakes up to these uneven
rhythms. Always he feels ill at ease. Huffff, huffff.
Always he slips on a uniform over his ghimpsuit and
shuffles through the nighttime, blue-lit worm-highways
of the ship. He pads over ligaments and bone. Huffff,
huffff. They make a jerky motion under his boots. Birth
canal passages throb around him, but not in their
normal, peaceful way.*

*His sleepy brain imagines that he is a fetus, seeded
in the giant womb of his ship, fermenting, growing into
something . . . other. He walks, walks. Huffff, huffff.
What that other will be he does not know, but he knows
that he has been enwombed before. He remembers, with
memories born of touch and taste and hearing,
memories kept in muscle and bone rather than in
neurons and synapses. He remembers-feels his own
mother slumbering around him when he was a real
fetus, a creature of primordial fish eyes and translucent
organs. He remembers a world of wet, snug love. When
she slept, he slept. When her blood ran fast, his blood
ran fast.*

*And when she had nightmares, he had nightmares.
Huffff, huffff.*

His mother had nightmares a lot.

*Did she sense, even then, the one-in-a-billion
abnormality gestating within her? Did she suspect, did
she have premonitions, as some mothers do, that her
unborn would not birth out the same as all infants?*

His ship shudders. Apprehensions and dreads

*intrude upon his wet-snug. Nightmares in the womb.
That was how they felt then. This is how they feel now.*

But, how can this be, now?

*He wonders, stepping into the brainroom's softly
glowing vault. Pillows of pink cortex swell before him.
The brain is vast compared to him, minuscule compared
to the body it runs. Not enough thinking mass for
intelligence. His wonderful, beloved ship is also a
simple, dumb beast.*

How can a beast of burden have nightmares?

*The brain twitches. He remembers the closed-eye
blinking of a childhood pet. The passage outside jerks
like the inside of a snake. He remembers the pet's paws-
in-quicksand dream running, jerking. That is how it
looked then. This is how it looks now.*

*Stupid or not, idiot or not, his ship is dreaming. He
knows it. Bad dreams. Long bad dreams. His eight
fuguetime hours versus its four realtime months.*

*What nightmares does a fugueship have, a half
million living tons, alone on its pathways between stars,
old enough to have seen human planetary civilizations
rise and fall, but too unknowing and innocent to notice
or care?*

*He remembers that innocence is not always bliss,
childhood damp ultra-fears, who-loves-me-desperation
monsters, abandonment dream-abominations. He does
not analyze them this way—that is too painful to
remember—that is just how the memories feel. Most of
all he remembers the wanting to wake up, the striving to
be free of the somnolent torments.*

Huffff, huffff.

Make it stop, mommy.

*But mommy and daddy sold you for a shiny new life,
and you're not a part of it. These are the nightmares of
an adult-child.*

*The adult-child goes to the beast-of-burden brain.
He presses down on the moist suede cortex, smoothing,
stroking, cooing in his mind, if not with his voice
emulator.*

There, there. It's going to be all right. Everything is going to be all right.

The jerking in the hall outside subsides. He spreads out, face down, maximum touching.

We're safe. We're okay.

The twitching of the cortex calms.

Together they weather their dreams.

Heat.

Pressure.

More than its great, dumb mind remembers, ever.

Crushing it in, from all around.

Heaviness.

No floating, no drifting,

No flying between diamonds of light.

Only weight and wet darkness.

And food, all around.

Gorging.

It wanted to come here, it feels.

But it is sick. Something is wrong.

Something missing.

The tiny good feeling.

So long the tiny good was with it,

So long the sickness was gone,

It felt only content.

But now the tiny good is gone,

There is an empty feeling where it was.

And now sickness is back, escalating.

It feels itself swelling,

Parts of it twisting and stretching,

Buzzing, plating, growing, out of its control.

It is afraid. It wants the changing to stop.

It wants its tiny good back . . .

Only, it cannot call for help.

What, after all, is *calling?*

It can only want and hurt.

It can only fear.

XLVIII

My solution to the Feral problem? Nuke 'em till they glow, then shoot 'em in the dark. They already glow in the dark? Oh, yeah, I forgot.

—Rebecca "Liberty" Toland,
Drunken Reflections on Being
a New Ascension Guard

Karr screamed and screamed and screamed. For three days. Most of his uniform was stripped away. His limbs were stretched and bound in the egg-shaped cell with the glowing white walls. Tlalok attempted everything he could think of. He attempted beating. He attempted suffocating. He attempted peeling skin. And more.

"Why don't you just kill me?" Karr groaned as the torment stretched on.

"Because Tlalok is *bonded* to the blank-one Karr!" Tlalok howled, so distressed that he did not even care that he was using foul blank-one words.

Karr screamed externally. Tlalok screamed internally.

It was unthinkable, unbearable, irredeemable. But it was true. Tlalok was once again bonded to a blank-one. All the awful memories of the time when Tlalok had been enslaved before came flooding back. It was as if all the intervening years of freedom had never existed, except as a fading daydream.

Tlalok could not kill Karr. Nor could Tlalok beat, temporarily suffocate, or peel Karr's skin. The instinctual injunction against harming one's bondmate was too strong.

"How? How?" Tlalok roared. "Tlalok has exchanged no Pact with Karr!"

"It's the *fugue* in my blood," Karr mumbled through battered, swollen lips. "It's related to your immune venom. It must have bound us together when we first met, when you tried to kill me and you tasted my blood."

Karr told Tlalok what Jenette had told him about the Burning Heart of Night, fugueships, Pact, and how she believed fugueships had brought immune venom to New Ascension.

Tlalok did not want to hear it.

Tlalok's needle teeth pierced pink skin and injected a large amount of immune venom to ensure the continuation of Karr's discomfort. Immune venom caused no pain when exchanged between Khafra, so there was no instinctual injunction against using it on a bondmate. But when injected into a blank-one it caused great amounts of pain. Tlalok knew this from first-hand experience of Sacrament. He also knew that if enough immune venom reached a blank-one's brain, then that blank-one would begin to feel pleasure. That's what normally happened, but Karr did not react to Tlalok's immune venom as a normal blank-one would have reacted. Tlalok was forced to inject large amounts to cause Karr pain. It was an extravagant expenditure of Tlalok's immune venom. The bright side was that no matter how much Tlalok injected, Karr felt only pain and never pleasure.

Karr screamed with renewed vigor.

Tlalok brooded. He had told Kitrika. That had been hard; Tlalok was ashamed, but she deserved to know why she had been spurned. She was brave and just. She had fought by Tlalok's side ever since—and in spite of—their abortive tryst. She deserved to know the truth.

She had said nothing when he told her what he would do to Karr, but it was a silence that spoke volumes.

<<Kitrika does not approve of torturing blank-ones?>> Tlalok had asked defensively.

<<Kitrika does not approve or disapprove,>> Kitrika had responded, <<as long as Tlalok is not also torturing Tlalok.>>

Tlalok had not heeded her subtle warning. Now, three days later, he felt like a furnace stoked too hot and about to melt down.

"If *fugue* is Pact," Tlalok growled at Karr, "and the blank-one

Karr is full of *fugue, then why does the blank one Karr feel pain from Tlalok's Pact?"*

"I don't know," Karr admitted through clenched teeth. "The Pact form of *fugue* must have mutated. It *has* to have mutated, since it survives and reproduces itself outside of a fugueship biosystem . . . which is technically impossible."

Tlalok throbbed black and red. "Tlalok does not care about technical impossibilities! Tlalok cares only to eradicate every single blank-one from the face of Tlalok's planet!"

Karr squinted at Tlalok with reddened eyes. "I guess we deserve it. Humans have behaved badly on this planet . . . and that includes me."

"The blank-one Karr killed Lleeala!" Tlalok snarled in confirmation.

"Llee-aaa—la," Karr repeated, trying to replicate the windy pronunciation of the Khafra name. "Was that your bondmate? Lleee—*gack!"*

Tlalok's talons closed about Karr's neck, closing off his airflow and digging in painfully.

"The blank-one Karr will not speak Lleeala's beloved name!"

Karr nodded his head in quick, tiny bobs of acquiescence. Tlalok eased his grip.

Karr croaked at Tlalok as his throat opened up again. "What a puzzle . . . you want to eradicate all blank-ones from your planet. You almost succeed, but just when you're about to finish the Enclave off, domestics enter the battle and stop you. Because Pact shall not kill Pact?"

"Because Pact shall not kill Pact," Tlalok repeated sullenly.

"Even though you call domestics no-Pact, which doesn't make sense to me. But you can't kill them, so you can't kill the blank-ones they defend. And you and your hunters can't kill me because I taste like Pact and, worse for you, you and I are actually bonded. Sounds like a Tora'okkan stand-off to me," said Karr.

Tlalok did not understand Karr's reference, but he grasped the meaning. "The blank-one Karr talks too much."

Karr's face contorted as he struggled to think through his pain.

"So what makes a blank-one?" he persisted. "What makes a blank-one different from a Khafra?"

"No Radiance, no Balance, no Pact," said Tlalok.

"Which means that I am no longer a blank-one, even though I am imBalanced and blank?" Karr asked. "There is Pact in my blood, and that's all that matters?"

"Yes," Tlalok allowed after thinking for some time. "Does not matter. Blank-one or not blank-one, Feral or domestic, once there is Pact all else unimportant."

"Then if that is the case," Karr said, "I propose to help you eradicate all blank-ones from your planet."

Karr told Tlalok how he could do that.

"No," Tlalok said immediately.

"Don't you want to stop humans from murdering and kidnapping?" Karr challenged, using arguments he had heard Jenette use. "Don't you want to put a stop to Sacrament?"

"Yes," Tlalok begrudged. "Of course."

"Then what is the problem?"

"Problem is . . ." Tlalok began, choosing his words carefully, "what the Pilot Karr proposes will stop wrongs that happen *now,* but will not right the wrongs that happened *before.* The Balance will stop tipping, but the Balance must be leveled. Vengeance must be served, to pay for all who died without fulfilling Pact."

"That is your duty?" Karr asked. "To find vengeance?"

Tlalok nodded his head once, human style.

Karr's human eyes became sad. "I understand duty. Someone must pay for all the Lleealas."

Tlalok nodded his head again.

Karr took a deep breath. "Then I will pay."

"But the human Karr is Pact," Tlalok rumbled impatiently, "Tlalok cannot—"

"*I* can do it," Karr said, cutting him off. "After the Burning Heart, I can . . . *sacrifice* myself to right the Balance, and satisfy your duty . . . if you agree."

Tlalok did not know what to think, let alone what to choose. Never before had a blank-one made such a proposal to Tlalok. It was hard for Tlalok to believe that he, the self-appointed avenger against blank-ones, would want to cooperate with a blank-one, let alone this blank-one. But then, as Karr had so artfully pointed out by using Tlalok's own Pact logic against him, Karr was not a blank-one, but *human*. And Pact. And Tlalok must do what must be done. What was right was right, even if he did not like it. But could the human Karr be believed?

It was at that point that Tlalok remembered the last thing Kitrika had said as Tlalok left her to enter the egg-shaped chamber. <<Remember Tlalok, blank-ones speak with the language of lies, but even the blank-one language of lies will speak truth if there is enough suffering behind it.>>

Suddenly, Tlalok's choice was easy.

Tlalok tortured Karr for another three days. Then, and only then, when the human's story did not change, did Tlalok relent and agree to Karr's proposal.

XLIX

Sunset, six days later.

The passageway descended through layers and layers of ghutzu root. Karr followed it down to a grotto where stacks of equipment and glowbars on tripod stands surrounded the null-fusion reactor. Cables snaked from null-regulator sinks and other diagnostic devices to various apertures on the elephantine hourglass. Dr. Bigelow and Guardsman Skutch were hard at work rigging the reactor, leaning in through two of its many access hatches. Karr did not disturb the two humans, but observed, trying to discern if all was going according to plan.

"I've worked out the sequence for shaping the blast," Hutch was saying in a muffled voice.

"Are you certain?" Bigelow responded, equally muffled. "The fields must drop in precisely the right order to shape the detonation up and away from the Pilot's ship."

"Had to increase the figures in the formula by a factor of ten thousand, but it should work . . ."

Karr felt a chill. *Was he doing the right thing?*

Hutch leaned out of the reactor to get a different tool and spotted Karr. "Pretty amazing what a few thousand Ferals can do, hunh?" the Guard quipped, apparently far more confident in his equations than Karr was with his own plans.

"Yes," Karr agreed without enthusiasm. Hordes of the aliens had dragged the reactor to its present location by sheer force of numbers, pulling on a web of lines half a kiloyard long. Now that mass of Ferals was above Karr, using their immune venom to stimulate the growth of dense, fire-resistant ghutzu over the top of the reactor grotto. The protective mound thickened at the rate of one foot per hour. Presently it was the height of a seven-story building. Karr hoped that would be thick enough because it wasn't going to get a lot thicker than that before its protective capabilities were put to the test.

"You brought it, I see," Skutch noted.

"Yes," said Karr, holding up his Gattler. "This won't affect the plan, will it?"

Skutch walked over to Karr and took the Gattler. "Not a chance. There's enough juice in this reactor to snuff out your fire, and then some." Skutch attached the Gattler to one of the many cables connecting to the reactor. The multitool began to bleep happily, its powerpaks recharging. "Where you're going, I figure you might need to use a cutting beam."

Skutch returned to work. Karr stepped over to Bigelow, who was taking readings with a hand-held scan-tap and holding another complicated instrument in his teeth. Bigelow noticed Karr's presence, but kept on at his task and, for a while, Karr waited patiently.

"Will it work?" Karr asked when he finally could restrain himself no longer.

Bigelow shot Karr a sweaty look and removed the tool from his mouth. "The difficulties," he pronounced, his fingers moving with artful precision and speed, testing, tuning, and realigning the reactor's innards, "are a matter of scale rather than probability. The reactor is more than capable of producing the desired pyrotechnics. Not, however, before the null-core is operating at full capacity, a process which alone will take eight more hours. Furthermore, while it is commonly assumed that null-fusion processes are held in check by a single null-field, that is not strictly true. In fact, there are some one thousand two hundred and ninety-six separate nodes, which are divided into twenty-four separate sectors. Each and every one of those nodes generates a portion of the field and each and every one of them must be examined and brought up to specifications. I estimate sixteen hours to completion."

Karr tapped his subdermal chronometer. "Ten hours and counting down."

"Ten hours?" Bigelow repeated. His pudgy hands faltered on a recalcitrant regulator of some kind. Sparks popped. He yanked back and sucked his fingers. *"Ten* hours . . . ?"

Karr's comset activated.

"It's time," Jenette's voice buzzed.

"On my way."

Karr turned away and started back up the passage.

"Wait!" called Bigelow.

Karr looked back. Bigelow and Skutch had expressions best described as those of condemned men who had just received the sentence of a brainwiping.

"Don't you want to know if we can be done in that amount time?" the scientist asked.

"No," Karr said, grimly rubbing one of the many torture marks visible on his neck. He strode away. *"I've got to love what I don't want to love and trust what I don't want to trust."*

A setting sun impaled itself upon the pillars of the Burning Heart of Night. The orb deflated as it sank, surrendering its essence to those radiant skewers, rimming the waves around Gnosis blood red. Kthulah had a clear view of the ill omen from the uppermost slopes of the floating mountain city: the number of Radiances was not four. Four was the number of the Prophecy. The Prophecy said a Pact would come. The Prophecy said that that Pact would make the number of the Radiances four and save a piece of the light. Pact had gathered. Pact had awaited. But *the* Pact had not come. What was Kthulah to do? What would come of the fourth Gift, the Gift of Gamut? Kthulah feared for the Balance. He feared for all that was precious to Pact. A *decision* was imminent. Kthulah did not know what that decision was yet, but he felt it in his bones, a momentous decision, requiring the wielding of much power and a reciprocal punishment such as . . . such as Kthulah shuddered to think upon.

<<The>>

<<Intruder>>

<<Comes>>

<<Soon,>> the Judges warned, from their customary positions

at the corner of Kthulah's square platform, which had been moved
out from its normal position within the tree-sheltered bowl.

Kthulah turned from looking inward at the Burning Heart to
looking outward from the pillars of fire, his gaze following the
lengthening shadows of sunset. Just beyond Gnosis, which was at
a distance of one exact horizon span from the center of the Burning Heart of Night, the rest of the Pact fleet formed a vast double-
tiered ring, sealing off the pillars of Radiance from outside forces.
Sailtrees on the many blockading islands jutted up into the Burning Heart's flaring red light like so many blood-soaked teeth. Further out beyond the blockade, sparkling, radiant words were being
relayed from where the black line of the ocean met a quickly darkening sky.

<<Kthulah of Gnosis! Kthulah of Gnosis!>> the flashing words
said. <<This is Jenette of the blank-ones. Jenette of the blank-ones
craves audience with Kthulah of Gnosis. Jenette of the blank-ones
begs audience with Kthulah of Gnosis.>>

Kthulah could feel the *decision* creeping closer to him, but he
was not yet ready to face it.

<<Battle approaches, blank-one Jenette,>> he replied neutrally.
<<Kthulah has no time for enemies.>>

Kthulah's words were relayed out. More words were relayed
back.

<<Blank-ones and Pact are not enemies,>> Jenette's signals
protested. <<Pact seek to do good. Blank-ones seek to do good.
Please, let us not fight.>>

<<Blank-ones seek to harm the Burning Heart of Night. That
makes blank-ones Kthulah's enemies.>>

Jenette argued, <<Blank-ones seek to heal the Burning Heart of
Night. Blank-ones seek to make the number of Radiances the sacred number of four. Pact want this too, the blank-one Jenette
knows this, so say the Roots of Wisdom, so says the Prophecy.>>

Kthulah objected, <<The Roots of Wisdom say a *Pact* must
heal the Burning Heart, not blank-ones.>>

<<Perhaps . . .>> Jenette's light words faltered, so that Kthulah
could not properly read the inflection of the colors. <<Perhaps a

Pact does come to heal the Burning Heart. Perhaps the blank-one Jenette brings that Pact.>>

Kthulah responded with challenging hues. <<*Perhaps?* A Pact comes, yes or no. Not perhaps.>>

<<Yes, then.>>

<<Name the Pact.>>

Jenette's words flashed meekly. <<The blank-one Jenette cannot . . . Kthulah would not believe it. Kthulah must trust. Please. Let us not fight. Khafra and blank-ones must cooperate. There can be only one outcome from fighting: the Burning Heart will perish.>>

Kthulah was angry with himself. He had felt a surge of hope at the possible coming of the prophesied Pact, even though the promise came from a blank-one, whom no sane Pact would trust even if they *did* speak the radiant language of truth. He abruptly ended the communication. <<Wrong, blank-one. Kthulah sees two outcomes. The Pack of Gnosis fights and defends the Burning Heart of Night, or the Pack of Gnosis fights and perishes trying.>>

The renegade ring-island bludgeoned through ocean waves like an ancient Terran dreadnaught. Ferals manned the island's sailtrees, spreading maximum surface of leaf-sail to the wind. Human soldiers and pulse cannons bristled along its broad flanks. It was an unlikely sight, the product of an even more unlikely alliance: Tlalok's fierce Ferals, colony humans loyal to Jenette (those of the non-loyal, Pilot-consuming variety had stayed behind on the decimated Enclave island), and a few precious scores of domestics were all united to save the fugueship, *Long Reach*, the Burning Heart of Night.

Karr stood at the center of that maelstrom upon a dome of fire-insulating ghutzu. Ferals swarmed over the mound, like a nest of disturbed insects, stabbing their long teeth into the roots and injecting growth-stimulating immune venom. Tendrils sprouted and entwined before Karr's very eyes. Karr had to keep shifting his boots to keep from being rooted to the spot. Shy of being up in a sailtree, however, it was the best vantage point on the island. Karr had a clear view downwind, where the Feral battle lines were com-

ing into view, their islands stretched across the western horizon
from one end to the other, steadfastly maintaining their position by
tacking against the wind, first one way and then the other, as
Tlalok's island charged directly downwind at them.

Beside Karr, Jenette lowered the starlure and switched it off.
Her arms hung slack at her sides, defeated.

"How are you holding up?" Karr asked quietly.

"I'm fine," Jenette replied, keeping a brave front. "I didn't really expect to convince him."

Karr had not been asking about Kthulah. Jenette's father had
been found with his heart ripped out. She had found out during
Karr's six-day *interaction* with Tlalok. Karr did not know how she
was taking it. There had been precious little opportunity to speak
to her during the preceding, highly stressful days. Ferals and Enclave humans had now been allied for three days; they had been
enemies for far longer. Enmity on both sides was in constant danger of erupting and it was a testament to Jenette's diplomatic abil-
ities that she kept the two sides focused and more or less working
together. Outwardly she appeared to be under control, but Karr did
not know how she was holding up, inwardly. It would be disastrous if she broke and succumbed to grief at any point in the next
few critical hours. Karr did not get an opportunity to ask further
questions and set his mind at ease, however. Tlalok was also atop
the ghutzu mound with Karr and Jenette; Karr was wary of how
the fierce alien would react to any mention of Prime Consul Olin
Tesla.

And Karr was downright afraid of how Tlalok would react to
what Karr must say next.

"Night is coming," Karr said, marshaling his nerve.

Tlalok's glowering head swung to face Karr.

Karr held up a black sack, which he had been clutching behind
his back.

Simultaneously, Jenette spoke into her comset. "Relay command: Ferals put *protection* hoods on."

"Urr, protection hoods on," came the replies of numerous
Khafra voices. A flashing of light code then erupted, single points
of light in the island's sailtrees stuttering as domestics stationed

there translated and relayed the command to all the Ferals on the island—all the thousands and thousands of Ferals of Tlalok's horde, who were crowded onto the single floating island.

Karr felt the eyes of all those Ferals turn in his direction as he continued to offer the sack to Tlalok. Jenette used the word *protection* to describe the hoods which had been distributed to the Ferals, but the aliens were not fooled; the sacks might be made of a special human-manufactured fabric which blocked light while allowing sound and air to pass freely, and they might also all have a single human glowbead affixed in the lining to lessen the utter darkness within, but they were *blinding* hoods, plain and simple. The Ferals did not care if it had taken a phenomenal human effort to construct so many in such a limited time; they did not care that if they did not don the sacks, the Burning Heart of Night would surely perish. The Ferals did not want to put them on and they would not put them on if their leader did not put his on.

And none was more loath to don a blinding hood than Tlalok.

"The human Karr will never truly grasp what he asks," the large alien growled. In the following seconds, Karr feared that Tlalok would break their covenant then and there, that suddenly the thousands and thousands of predatory aliens would revolt and cut Jenette's sixteen hundred Enclave humans to shreds. But Tlalok abruptly snatched the hood from Karr's grasp and pulled it over his head. Karr sighed with relief as he then heard the reassuring rustle of thousands more hoods being pulled over thousands more Feral heads.

Wind moaned through the sailtrees.

The blinded juggernaut continued its charge downwind.

The Clash of Radiance erupted.

The islands of the Feral blockade lost headway and drifted at the mercy of air and sea currents as countless incandescent points flared along their shores and on scattered scouting vessels arrayed across the ocean. Kthulah unleashed the might of his Radiance. Cloud bellies reflected artillery round flashes, broadsides of light volleyed toward Tlalok's island, but not a single one of Tlalok's Ferals submitted to the power of Kthulah's radiant commands. They surely would have, except that they could not submit to that

which they could not see. Harder and harder Kthulah tried to win
the battle of light. Even Karr, an illiterate in the alien language,
could see the urgency building in Kthulah's display and its single-
minded focus on making Tlalok's Ferals submit.

That was fine by Karr. The longer and harder Kthulah and his
Ferals fought, the less chance they had of noticing anything else.
Karr could not help glancing back to a luminescent wake, which
was spreading out behind Tlalok's island. Fifty yards back, barely
discernible on either side of the v-shaped trail, were two shadowy
blots, each a few dozen yards across, each rimmed by faint cres-
cents of ocean froth.

Enclave domestics, who wore no blinding-hoods, responded to
the Clash of Radiance, flashing ineffectually in reaction to the entrancing lights. However, when the Clash came to an end, those
domestics were no longer affected. The domestics' bonds to their
humans were too strong for Kthulah to break, just as Arrou's bonds
to Jenette had been too strong to be broken by the Clash of Radiance that he had witnessed from high up in a shooting-star palm
along the shore of FI-716.

"Maintain heading. Maintain speed," Jenette's voice commanded in Arrou's comset.

Arrou's blood was still afire from the euphoria of the Clash of
Radiance; he had enjoyed a particularly spectacular view from
halfway up the island's leading sailtree. Trying to calm his racing
heart, he concentrated on translating Jenette's human words into
Khafra verbal language.

<<Keep wind at backs! Keep leaves fully unfurled!>>

Teeth clattered affirmatively inside blinding hoods near Arrou
and the verbal command was relayed by Ferals up and down that
sailtree's mighty bole—just as it was also being translated by domestics and relayed by Ferals in all the other sailtrees on Tlalok's
island. The four hundred hunters in Arrou's tree held their positions, heads motionless in the featureless black hoods, glowbuds
rippling faintly with both fear and determination. They were brave.

They were blind; Arrou was their eyes.

That was a position of great responsibility, Arrou knew. It made him edgy. Ferals did not like or trust domestics and Arrou wanted very much to prove that they were wrong about domestics. He fidgeted, scrubbing his claws on the tree branch he was perched upon.

The Feral closest to Arrou in the tree, the Feral appointed by Tlalok to speak for all the Pact in the tree, was a female. Trim and graceful of body, her glowbuds sparkled sharply, like ice under stars. Arrou felt that she was somehow observing him despite the hood over her head.

<<What is your name?>> she asked him.

<<Arrou,>> he replied.

<<Do not be nervous, Arrou. Tlalok has placed trust in you.>>

Arrou did not know if he believed that. Probably the female was just trying to be nice. Not that there was anything specifically wrong with being nice, he decided.

<<What is your name?>> he asked her back.

<<Kitrika,>> she replied.

<<Does *Kitrika* trust Arrou?>> he asked.

Kitrika thought about it. <<Yes,>> she decided.

Arrou believed her, since Kitrika not only spoke her vote of trust, but also flashed it on her glowbuds, the radiant language of truth, and that calmed Arrou's worries.

<<Thank you Kitrika. Arrou will try to be as brave as the Khafra of Tlalok's pack.>>

The female's colors smiled enigmatically. <<Try only to be as brave as Arrou. Then you will be brave.>>

Tlalok's island continued its charge at Kthulah's blockade.

The battle lines did not stay disorganized long after the Clash of Radiance fizzled. The islands swung into the wind once more, tightening their spacing as more islands crowded in from further along the blockade to meet the intruder. None of the islands were very large; these were the nimblest, fastest sailing islands in Kthulah's armada, but the numbers were daunting. Plus, they were not content to play a waiting game. They immediately began to close against the wind, tacking diagonally to the north and then back to the south in an effort to take the battle to their enemy. At the end of each leg, light code staccatoed from one island to another along the tips of high trees and the islands heaved around in perfect synchrony. The rustle of many leafy sails going slack and then snapping back taut to the wind was audible across the ocean even at a distance of three kiloyards.

Tlalok's island battleship mustered four, perhaps five knots with the wind at its back, pushing its sailtrees forward, so that if Arrou looked straight down he was actually over water and not island. Kthulah's fleet managed far less speed tacking against the wind, but the speeds meant little. The opposing factions would meet.

Arrou's gut tightened.

He hoped Pilot Karr's trick would work.

The gap between closed to two kiloyards.

Wind speed surged and ebbed. The rhythmic thunder of Tlalok's island plowing through ocean swells counted off the minutes.

The gap narrowed to one kiloyard.

Arrou could now make out individual Ferals, swarming at the forward edges of their islands, ready to spill onto the shores of the blockade-runner the instant the opposing sides made contact.

Five hundred yards. Four hundred yards.

"Get ready, get ready," Jenette warned on the comset.

Three hundred yards.

"Now!" Jenette ordered. "Let her drift!"

<<Lose wind, lose wind!>> Arrou translated.

His sailtree—and all the others on Tlalok's island—came alive with activity. Thousands of Feral forepaws, Kitrika's included, felt for and located stems where sail leaves anchored to horizontal branches. Teeth injected immune venom into those junctures, easily piercing through the blinding hood fabric and into the wood. The large, green leaves immediately twisted up tight. With no surfaces to grab hold of, wind rushed past unfettered. Sailtrees swayed back up to vertical. Tlalok's island lost headway fast.

A roar arose from Kthulah's fleet as his countless Ferals saw their enemies apparently lose nerve and falter.

Halifax's gravelly voice buzzed on the comset. "Main towlines away! Skimmer teams away!"

Behind Tlalok's island, where the two dark shapes had been

trailing along, two filaments glinted briefly and fell slack, dropping into the frothing water. Six plumes of spray then erupted, three ahead of each dark shape; the sound of six turbine engines revving up reached Arrou's perch. With the dark shapes in tow, the skimmers circled around opposite sides of Tlalok's island, breaking out from its shadow into the glare of the Burning Heart. Short towlines could now be seen, stretching back from two groups of three skimmers each to two small skrag islands, each less than one hundred feet in diameter.

The two skimmer teams joined up in front of Tlalok's island and proceeded to charge at the Feral battle lines.

<<What do you see?>> Kitrika asked.

<<Brave humans,>> Arrou said, without truly answering her question. He was glad Kitrika did not know what the humans were really up to. The six tiny machines dragging two pathetic skrag islands at Kthulah's armada did not make an impressive sight. As the skimmer teams closed to within two hundred yards of the blockade, the nearest Feral islands altered their direction so as to be on a course that would overrun and crush the skimmers and skrags.

Halifax's spoke on the comset again, yelling over the howl of turbines and the crash of waves. "On my mark. Three, two, one—mark!"

"Fire in the hole!" buzzed Guard voices Arrou did not recognize.

FOOM! FOOM!

White plumes flared from the skrag islands as charges preset by Guardsman Skutch ignited. Sheets of hungry green flame climbed skyward, devouring stockpiles of incendiary fuel. Candles of viridian spark flurried back and up from fires that swelled ten times larger than the skrag islands they originated from.

Confusion flashed discordantly across the blockade lines. Sail-trees on the Feral islands suddenly heaved over, groaning, dragging the islands of the fleet to either side of the oncoming menace. A gap grew in the first battle line as one island swerving caused the next in line to veer off, and so on, like falling dominoes.

The fire-skrags passed through the first battle line.

"Full speed ahead," Jenette ordered. "Full speed ahead!"

<<Grab wind, grab wind!>> Arrou yelled.

Again Kitrika and the other Ferals on his tree injected immune venom into sail-leaf stems. This time the green sheets unfurled, billowing out and catching the wind. The sailtrees on the island groaned, leaning forward once more as the island picked up speed and was soon churning along after the skimmers and fire-skrags.

Radiance flickered as leaders on the Feral fleet rallied their forces, but by the time the islands began to turn back inward, in a vain attempt to reform the first battle line, Tlalok's island was charging through the gap. Another cheer arose in the night, this time it was not from Kthulah's Ferals but from the humans on Tlalok's island, and Arrou, who tilted back his head and howled right along with them.

L

At the darkest, most desperate point of our lives, that is where we find out what we are truly made of.

—*from the private journals of Olin Tesla*

Tlalok's hood-blinded Ferals did not rejoice with the noisy humans and domestics. Neither did Jenette. She had direct experience with Kthulah and the Ferals of Gnosis; the fire-skrags had taken them by surprise, but they were too sophisticated to react the same way twice.

Tlalok's island, lead by the skimmers and the flaming skrags, charged at Kthulah's second battle line.

True to Jenette's fears, the Ferals of that second line reacted with none of the disarray shown by the first. The chain of islands splits, tacking away to the north and south, forming a gap in the path of the burning skrags. When the breach was wide enough to allow the fire-skrags to pass harmlessly through, the Feral islands tacked back inward on exactly the right angle to intercept Tlalok's island.

Jenette did not know what Kthulah's Ferals would do with Tlalok's Ferals if the opposing forces met, but she knew that her fellow humans would fight to the bitter end. They had gambled everything on this daring plan. They would succeed and live or fail and die. It was as simple as that. Many of both species would perish. *For the greater good.* Her father would have approved. Jenette hated it. She felt trapped.

Furious, she looked around the reactor mound.

Tlalok stood immobile, legs splayed and head down, a barely

perceptible clenching of muscles visible under his thick armor plate. Unpredictably his head would jerk erect, his teeth splaying, stretching the blinding-hood fabric tight, and an ominous rumble would resonate through the alien's torso as he fought his deep-rooted hatred of the hood.

Karr, to Jenette's surprise, was focused on winding a small length of microfiber string around his left index finger. Once in a while, he peeked up at the unfolding sea battle, but mostly he stared at the string. When it was all coiled up around his finger, he methodically uncoiled it, at which point he started the obsessive process all over again.

"What are you doing?" she hissed at Karr.

"Nothing," he responded without looking up.

With growing annoyance, Jenette waved an arm at the battle unfolding ahead of them. "Don't you see what's happening out there?"

"Yes," Karr said, pointedly not looking up from his winding and unwinding. "And there is *absolutely* nothing I can do about it. I helped make the plan. Now it is in motion. Capable humans and aliens are executing it. I need to let them do their jobs. That's what you told me back on Coffin Island. And you were right. I must *trust.*" Karr gritted his teeth. "Does it drive me crazy to stand here doing nothing? Emphatically, *yes!* That's why I'm taking this action which affects nothing, meddles with nothing, interferes with nothing. I'm going to wind this string around my finger until we break through the Feral lines or don't. Either way, I figure there will be plenty to keep me occupied at that point."

There was a crazy logic to Karr's explanation, Jenette had to admit.

"Got another piece of string?" she asked.

"No, sorry."

Upon the ocean, the contest continued to unfold. The humans piloting the tow-skimmers were not beaten yet. The two teams split up, veering toward the closing pincers of the blockade line. The lead island on the northern pincer rapidly broke off, its Ferals throwing sail-leaves aback, heeling the island around to avoid the roaring, rapidly approaching the plume of green flame and, in the process, forcing the islands following it to break off also. The lead island on the southern pincer was a different story, however. It was closing fast with Tlalok's island and its Ferals had no intention of veering off from their target. The quadrupeds strobed with displeasure as a fire-skrag was towed into their path. Orders crackled across the island's bulk and the living mass took evasive measures, first tacking one way and then, abruptly, another, but the skimmers pulling the skrag made a course correction for every action the Ferals took. The skimmers were barely strong enough to pull the skrag; they could move no faster than the Feral island, but the skimmers could turn in any direction they needed to, unlike the Ferals who were restricted by the direction of the wind.

The Feral island, the skimmers, the fire-skrag, and Tlalok's island formed a short, straight line. From Jenette's point of view, the roaring green plume from the skrag made it hard to see the skimmers and the Feral island. Fluctuations in the wind brought the stinging smell of incendiary fuel to her nostrils. Pulse-cannons along the shore of Tlalok's island hummed as Guards powered the killing machines up in anticipation of combat.

Who, Jenette wondered, would blink first?

Jenette glanced back at Karr. He was winding the microfiber string so tightly around his finger that the tip was turning purple.

Kthulah's Ferals blinked first. Strong instincts to nurture and protect the islands that they lived upon spurred the Ferals into action. Hordes of the glowing aliens, who had bunched up along the island's shoreline, scattered. Light blurs swirled along sailtree limbs and organic sail-leaves abruptly changed angles as the Khafra tried to swerve away from the fire-skrag.

"Too late," Jenette whispered.

Through the billowing green skrag flame, Jenette saw tiny human forms move in the skimmers. The sound of turbines changed as the skrag was cast off. Plumes of water curved out into clear view as the nimble vessels darted out from between the imminent collision of the Feral island and the fire-skrag. The fire-skrag plowed on, losing headway, but still headed toward the Feral island. The aliens attempted a sharper turn. Overstrained sail-leaves tore free and fluttered off into blood-red night, like flocks of startled flying creatures.

The flaming skrag struck, spinning down the side of the Feral island, leaving trails of green napalm wherever contact was made. Stress faults shot through the skrag and it broke up, fragments spreading across the ocean like a burning minefield. Feral islands down the line veered off in panic. The second island in line snagged against the third, the fourth, and fifth islands, unable to spill speed from their sails in time, plowed into them. Ghutzu tore, sailtrees toppled, distant Ferals screamed.

The high slopes of Gnosis provided a clear view. The outer blockade line was breached. The inner line was in disarray. The island full of blank-ones and treacherous Pact was winding its way through flaming green island fragments while the blank-one water machines joined together and began to pull the remaining fire-skrag toward Gnosis. The blank-ones intended to impede any last-ditch attempts by Kthulah to cut their island off. It was a wasted effort. The island of Gnosis moved ponderously, with the dignity of its weight and the Wisdom of its Roots. Before it could so much as turn around, the intruders would make good their escape.

<<In the time>>

<<Of the Burning Heart of Night>>

<<Perhaps even the most profane>>

<<Is sacred,>> the Judges offered, penitent gray forms with their single cobalt glowbuds shining between black eye orbs.

Kthulah's muzzle pinched with concern. <<Kthulah can make no sense of it.>>

<<The Burning Heart>>

<<Needs not>>

<<To be comprehended>>

<<Only preserved,>> the Judges said in unison.

<<Yet the number of Radiances is not four,>> Kthulah said spreading the four thumbs on his paw. <<And Pact do not know how to set the count right.>>

<<It>>

<<Is true>>

<<The Roots of Wisdom>>

<<Have forgotten,>> the Judges admitted sadly. Their heads tilted, pondering all sides of the Balance.

<<Perhaps,>>

<<The blank-one Jenette>>

<<Was>>

<<Correct>> the Judges wondered.

<<Perhaps>>

<<There was>>

<<Only losing and dying>>

<<In fighting.>>

<<No,>> Kthulah said, saddened by the loss of so many of his brave Pact. <<There was honor, too. No savages can say that on this night, the Pack of Gnosis did not defend the Prophecy.>>

<<But>>

<<What>>

<<Of that>>

<<Prophecy?>> the Judges flashed, trying unsuccessfully to make sense of their tallies of black and white beads.

<<A>>

<<Decision>>

<<Must be>>

<<Made.>>

Kthulah felt the aches of all the many decisions he had made in the course of his allotted years. It never seemed to end. Kthulah wished the Judges would accept his answer of silence. They did not. They shook their bead-laden staves at him, unsatisfied.

<<Soon,>> Kthulah said, <<Soon.>>

LI

All is not as is seems.
Expect the unexpected.
Don't be afraid of a little pain.

—Reflections of a Fugueship Pilot,
Lindal Karr

Snap. Secure the backup line to a kilnsuit pintle. Click-clack. Insert new cartridges into the Gattler. Rrrrrrzzzk-chuk. Lock fishbowl helmet into position.

The null-fusion reactor lay on its side, looming behind Karr, Dr. Bigelow, and Tlalok; the cavity surrounding the gunmetal hourglass was lit only by a soft purple glow from its perfectly tuned null-field. Karr was in his kilnsuit, suspended over a deep well shaft that connected the insulated cavity to the ocean depths beneath Tlalok's island. Filament lines ran up from carabiners on Karr's chest to a pulley at the apex of a tripod rig that squatted over the shaft. The lines then ran down to a winch unit. Both that winch and the null-fusion reactor were connected to a timing device. Red digital numerals on its face were counting down.

Seventeen minutes, forty-nine seconds to go.

At one minute to go, the winch would begin spooling out filament. Karr would drop down through the ghutzu shaft and into the water where *Long Reach* lay. At zero minutes, zero seconds, the null-fusion reactor itself would overload, at which point it would not be a good idea to be a living organism anywhere in its vicinity.

None of the three sentients in the cavity spoke much. Dr. Bigelow was scurrying around the reactor doing last minute triple-checks of null-nodes and detonator cabling. Tlalok sat beside the timing counter, watching it and the humans most distrustfully.

Jenette stood on the trailing shore of Tlalok's island. Sailtrees and the reactor mound stood out in stark silhouette against the fugueship fires. At a distance of two kiloyards out, the four smaller pillars of hydrogen flame, rotating slowly around a massive central pillar, blotted out half the sky. Jenette felt as though she were inside a blast furnace. Searing convection currents hammered at her back, sucking leaves and other loose debris over the ground and ocean and pulling Tlalok's island faster and faster toward its doom; roaring flames thundered in her ears, making thinking hard and talking all but impossible.

Jenette cupped her hands over her comset pickup and yelled, "Pilot Karr, what is your status?"

"Physical preparations are complete," Karr's voice buzzed back. "Dr. Bigelow is taking his last looks as we speak."

"Tell him to hustle it up," Jenette yelled. "The evacuation is underway."

Hordes of humans, Ferals, and domestics were streaming down to the island's shore where they boarded rafts and paddleboards and anything else that could float. The ocean behind Jenette was black with vessels, many of them being towed by lines spider-webbing out from three of the remaining six colony skimmers (Colonel Halifax was in one of those machines, doing his best to oversee the chaotic retreat). Several thousand bipeds and quadrupeds were crammed onto the remains of a fire-skrag, its incendiary fuel having long since gone out. Two more skimmers towed that mass toward safety.

Evacuating humans looked back at the Burning Heart of Night full of apprehension. Feral expressions were torn between the beauty of the mighty Radiances and the horror of abandoning an island that many of them had lived upon, and nurtured, for their entire lives; many of the aliens had to be forcibly removed by their kindred.

Jenette stood with Arrou, Skutch, Liberty, and Grubb beside the sixth skimmer as the last straggling evacuees reached the shore.

Dr. Marsh and a cluster of med-techs and domestics carried a wailing Panya Hedren into the skimmer. The poor woman had chosen a most inopportune time to go into labor; the Enclave hospital would have been a much better place for her, if it wasn't for the fact that Bragg's mob had been left in control of the colony island, and they were very angry with Panya because she had helped Karr escape their clutches. Burke, Tengen, Rusty, and two young domestics, who Jenette had so recently assigned to the human couple, hurried into the skimmer behind Panya. All of them looked very concerned.

"Bigelow and Tlalok need to get their butts up here ASAP," Jenette's voice buzzed in Karr's helmet ten minutes later.

"Understood," Karr replied. He activated his suit's external speaker. "You two heard that?"

Bigelow nodded distractedly; his attention was fixated on an out of the way panel underneath the reactor.

Tlalok was glowering at Karr. "Do not die killing the False Radiance. Remember, the human Karr's life is already forfeit to Tlalok."

"I'll keep that in mind," Karr said, glumly wishing he could stop thinking about the depths of the well that gaped under his boots, *and* stop worrying about whether Dr. Bigelow's calculations were correct. If the sequential negation of null-fields did not actually shape the exploding reactor core energies as promised, Karr and *Long Reach* would be rendered down to their component molecules. It was a good thing he could not disconnect himself from the winch filaments without assistance, or he might have succumbed to the impulse to flee the reactor cavity gibbering idiotically with fear.

Dr. Bigelow paid no attention to the exchange between Karr and Tlalok. Even more fixated than before, he bent over, reached as far as he could under the curving reactor casing, and swiped a finger across the offending panel. It came away coated in sickly white ichor. Bigelow sniffed and recoiled from the awful aroma.

"Ugh. Whatever can this be?"

A heavy clunk sounded from behind the reactor, like a hatch

falling open. Bigelow tensed, slowly straightening up and leaning as far as he could around the end of the reactor, but before he could determine what had made the noise, the gentle purple of the null-field began to pop and sputter.

The ghutzu cavity was abruptly bathed in searing white light.

Bigelow screamed and threw his arms over his eyes. Karr clenched his eyes tight against the painful brilliance. A split second later his helmet blacked out as the molecules in the transparent bubble automatically went opaque. Thick green afterimages filled Karr's vision in the resulting darkness.

"Who's screaming?" Jenette demanded on the comset. "What's happening?"

"Unknown null-field malfunction, blinding us," Karr said through gritted teeth. "Don't know what caused it—"

"Null foe! Null foe! Null foe!" shrieked a voice.

A heavy, screeching object plowed into Karr. Karr swung from the filaments that suspended him, caroming into and dislodging one of the legs of the tripod rig. For an awful instant, Karr thought he would plummet into the well shaft, entangled in filaments, but he and the heavy object crashed to one side of the hole, the plates of his kilnsuit locking up against the force of impact. Whatever had knocked Karr down then dislodged itself and took off on four legs. Karr tried to move, but he was thoroughly entangled in filaments and tripod legs.

In a series of gradual steps, Karr's helmet began to let light back in. It stopped when the intensity of light was just below the threshold of human discomfort.

The null-field was glowing like the surface of a star. Objects around it were hard for Karr to discern, ghosts in fog. A few feet out of Karr's reach, the timing device was overturned, its emergency shut-off knob depressed, its display no longer counting down. Tlalok stood stock still in the stark radiance, his snout raised at an awkward angle. Bigelow . . . where was Bigelow? There! Squinting hard, Karr could just make out the large man, feeling his way around one end of the reactor, apparently trying to locate the source of the earlier noise and, presumably, regain control of the berserk null-field.

"Bigelow wait!" Karr yelled, trying to free himself. "There's something in here with us!"

The scientist froze apprehensively. "Something *benevolent . . . ?*"

"One of those in-human things from Coffin Island, I think—look out!"

A quadrupedal shape had appeared on the reactor above Bigelow. In a flash of motion, it crabbed down the casing, grabbed the large human, and, with an astonishing burst of strength, dragged Bigelow out of sight behind the end of the reactor.

Karr heard a brief scuffle.

Bigelow began to shriek.

And shriek and shriek and shriek.

Karr flailed around inside his kilnsuit, but the tangle of high-g filaments held him firmly incapacitated.

"Tlalok, help him!" Karr yelled.

"So beautiful, so beautiful . . ." the nearby alien moaned, paralyzed by the bright light.

Bigelow's shrieks rose in volume and pitch, becoming a white noise composed of pure, unrelenting agony.

Karr thrashed harder, fumbling with unwieldy kilnsuit gloves to untangle himself as seconds and then minutes elapsed, but still he could not aid the scientist.

Karr's comset blared with Jenette's frantic questions. "We're burning up out here! Will somebody please tell me what the hell is going on?"

Tlalok's island was within one kiloyard of the central column of fugueship fire; Jenette and the others in the skimmer were wrapped in silvery, heat-reflective blankets. One of the four smaller flame pillars had rotated into the path of the reactor-bearing island. Trees burst into flame on its leading shore, ignited by sheer, ambient heat. The flame pillar passed, missing by less than a quarter or a kiloyard. Swarms of embers and cinders spiraled along in its wake.

And all the while horrible screaming sounded from Jenette's comset.

"They're in trouble!" she yelled to the others. "We've got to help!"

"No way!" Liberty yelled back, grabbing Jenette before the impulsive Consul could jump out of the skimmer and start running back inland. "It's half a mile to the entrance of the mound alone! You'll never make it!"

Skutch backed Liberty up. "She's right. No human can run there and back before the reactor goes up!"

"We should scram, and fast!" Dr. Marsh yelled, taking a moment from tending Panya to put in her two cents.

Jenette and the Guards exchanged confused, anxious looks. No one wanted to abandon Karr or Bigelow or Tlalok. But no one knew what to do, either.

"Arrou will go," Arrou announced.

"No," Jenette said, suddenly wishing she had not made such a suggestion in the first place.

"Arrou runs fast on four legs," Arrou pressed. "Jenette knows. Arrou makes it there, helps Karr and Bigelow and Tlalok, and runs back fast."

Jenette looked back and forth between the nearing, central column of flame and her best friend. If she just gave the order, the skimmer could whisk them all to safety. Those under the reactor mound were as good as dead anyway. If she sent Arrou in she was probably sending him to his death for no good reason. But then that was playing it safe, bean counting, measuring the value of one life against another—and that was not Jenette's way.

She swatted Arrou on the rump.

The alien bounded out of the skimmer, galloping, each leg striking the ground with such force that he kicked up little clouds of debris. A trail of them followed him inland, three melon-sized plumes, then a fist-sized plume—where his stunted right forepaw touched down—then three melon-sized plumes and a fist-sized plume. . . .

<<Light be upon you, Arrou,>> Jenette prayed, in a voice too quiet for the others to hear over the roaring of hydrogen flame.

Karr managed to wrench the Gattler free from the tangle of filaments. Agonizingly, slowly, he began the process of isolating the tangled loops one at a time and severing them with precisely aimed bursts of cutting beam.

Bigelow had stopped screaming. Karr feared the worst.

Finally, the last filament fell away. Karr staggered to his feet. Through the space formed by the pinched waist of the null-fusion reactor and the ghutzu floor of the cavity, Karr saw a body fall to the ground. It was hard to make out in the dazzling light, but it crawled on four legs and its hide glistened like tooled leather. Karr didn't know how Bigelow had overcome the in-human, but he raised the Gattler, increasing the cutting beam power setting, and took a step closer, ready to blast the creature out of existence. However, there was then more movement around the end of the reactor to Karr's right. A large form, bracing itself against the casing with its arms, staggered into view. Karr recognized Bigelow's rotund shape instantly. The scientist was in rough shape. Even in the bright glare Karr could see that Bigelow's clothing had been shredded off; his head hung low on his chest; blood dripped copiously from many orderly lacerations running up and down his legs and arms, bisecting his belly and chest, slashing around his ankles, wrists and neck. Karr moved to help.

The crawling form behind the reactor moaned.

Bigelow lurched on his two legs, grabbing frantically for a handhold on the reactor, and almost fell. Karr lent an arm for support.

"You need to get out of here!" Karr said. "Can you walk?"

Bigelow nodded and took another step, and slipped again. Karr grabbed tightly. *Bigelow's arm skin sloughed off in Karr's hand. Like a sleeve parting at the seam, it came free.* Bigelow groaned, a horrible deep sound. His tortured face tilted up, exposing raw meat sockets where eyes ought to be. Tattered facial flesh hung limp where the vile in-human had tortured him. Still, it was a miracle Bigelow was alive.

Wavering, Bigelow motioned Karr closer, as if he wanted to whisper to Karr. Letting the Gattler dangle by its shoulder strap, Karr took hold of the large man with both hands and leaned close.

Bigelow's face exploded.

A dozen foot-long, radial teeth shot out, first stretching and then tearing right through Bigelow's distorted cheek and forehead flesh like an evil flower opening. The blades clamped down on Karr's helmet as hands with far too many thumbs and talons reached out, clutching and ripping the Gattler out of Karr's arms. Karr realized the enormity of his misidentification as he was then seized and slammed into the reactor casing.

It was not Dr. Bigelow.

It was an in-human wearing Bigelow's bloody skin! And the body on the ground behind the reactor . . . ? Karr stole a second look as it raised a shuddering, pleading, five fingered hand into view. *That* was Dr. Bigelow, his flesh flayed off, his muscles, veins and inner organs glistening and throbbing, his lipless mouth opening wide and howling in anguish.

The in-human creature attacked. It might have been weak compared to Arrou or any other healthy Khafra, but compared to a scrawny human in a cumbersome spacesuit, the in-human was woefully strong. It could not break through the kilnsuit—and it tried very hard to do that—but it could toss Karr about the ghutzu cavity with shocking ease. The suit's interlocking plates braced against each impact, but Karr felt each blow. He could not sustain the battering forever. At some point he would pass out, which was bad enough, but very soon after that the island carrying the reactor would collide with the main hydrogen fire that raged over top of *Long Reach*. He and Bigelow and Tlalok would all die for nothing if Karr could not somehow regain control of the situation by then.

Halfway up the insulating ghutzu mound Arrou reached the tunnel opening. The island was very hot around him; succulent plants were withering in front of his very eyes. So he really wanted to plunge down the passage into its sheltered and cooler air, but he clawed to a halt at the entrance. Down in the far distance, bright, white radiance was flaring up from the reactor chamber and Arrou remembered Jenette mentioning that bright light was blinding Karr and Bigelow and Tlalok. Even though the light looked very beautiful (enticing, in fact), Arrou dared not charge down into it. Otherwise he would end up helpless and needing rescue just like they did. Arrou spun around, searching for anything that might help him deal with that problem.

A solution was not hard to find. Tlalok's island was littered with blinding hoods, where Tlalok's Ferals had ripped them off after doing their part to break through Kthulah's blockade. Arrou took in a stiflingly hot breath. *Now was his chance to show if he could be as brave as Tlalok's Ferals.* Before he could change his mind, he snatched up a blinding hood, pulled it over his head and bounded down the tunnel.

Karr lay in a battered heap to one side of the brilliant chamber as Arrou burst in. The in-human looked up from shredding detonator cables and attacked. Before Karr could utter a word of warning, the two Khafra were at each other's throats. Both Arrou and the in-human were blinded—one by a hood, the other by self mutilation—but whereas Arrou was severely handicapped by the lack of sight, the in-human had spent decades honing its other senses and scored several ferocious hits on Arrou in quick succession. Initially, Karr could not understand why Arrou was neither incapacitated by the null-field light, nor fighting as well as he should have been able to against the in-human, but then Karr perceived the ungainly hood over Arrou's head.

Karr turned up the volume on his kilnsuit's external speaker and began shouting instructions. "To your left, now above you, that's it, duck . . . !" Arrou began to hold his own, dodging the in-human's attacks. Karr heaved himself to his feet, panting; the kilnsuit had definitely not been designed for strenuous activity at a full g-load. A quick glance around the floor did not reveal where his Gattler had fallen, so Karr concentrated on helping Arrou. "Two paces behind you, spin, that's it—now strike!"

Arrou wound up and unleashed a massive backhand. The in-human flew through the air, landing between Karr and the well shaft. The creature levered itself erect on its bulbous joints, but did not immediately counter strike. Instead, it felt around on the ground. Its paws closed on a long, cylindrical object. Rising up on its hind legs, the in-human lifted a multibarreled device to its shoulders and aimed at Arrou.

"Its got the Gattler!" Karr yelled as the in-human pulled the trigger, activating the cutting beam. Ghutzu vaporized under Arrou's feet as he narrowly leapt out of the way. The in-human shot again. Its aim was horribly accurate, considering that it was only using its sense of hearing to acquire its targets. This time the beam grazed Arrou's armored back. Arrou bounded blindly around the cavity, but Karr could see that it was only a matter of time before the in-human got lucky and bull's-eyed Arrou.

Karr charged at the in-human's back. *Clunk, clunk, clunk, clunk,* his heavy kilnsuit joints sounded. *WHAM!* Karr's impact knocked the in-human over the well shaft. Karr himself teetered on the edge. The in-human fell, whirling in midair. One of its claws grabbed Karr's leg. Karr could not move; the kilnsuit had momentarily locked up from the collision. The in-human's weight yanked. Karr lost his balance and felt himself begin to fall. The pit seemed to reach up, a hungry, swallowing mouth.

He and the in-human plummeted out of view.

"Get out! Leave me!" Bigelow's voice choked on Jenette's comset.

"Not right, not right! Come with, come with!" she heard Arrou protest in the background.

"Do as he says, Clarence!" Jenette ordered.

"No," Bigelow gasped. "I can't—*I won't*—live like this. Get *him* out of here, Arrou. . . ."

Click. The comset went dead.

"We've got to get out of the blast zone!" Liberty yelled into Jenette's ear.

Jenette shook her head. "Arrou's coming!"

"He can't make it!" Liberty objected.

"He'll make it!"

But even as Jenette uttered the words, she did not believe them. Another of the smaller pillars of fire was thundering toward Tlalok's island, and this time there would be no near miss.

Arrou struggled to carry Tlalok up the tunnel. The Feral was even bigger than Arrou. Arrou could not move very fast with such a heavy weight on his back, and the fact that he could not see just made matters worse.

<<No, no,>> Tlalok protested meekly, <<too beautiful . . . stay, stay. . . .>>

Halfway up the passage, Arrou ripped the blinding hood off his head and threw it away. Dazzling light poured up from behind him, teasing him to stop and take a look at its beauty, maybe even go back. But Arrou must not look back, not for the light, not even for his friend Dr. Bigelow. Arrou had touched his friend Dr. Bigelow and found out what the in-human had done to him. Arrou felt very bad about that. If only he had not shown the abomination mercy back on Coffin Island. He wished, he wished . . . but wishing was useless! All that was left was *doing.* Now all Arrou could do was respect Bigelow's wishes—and get out.

The island shuddered under Arrou's legs. Something big had collided with it. *BOOM!*

The tunnel mouth was getting closer. Tlalok began to struggle on Arrou's back. Arrou wondered if he was strong enough to knock Tlalok out, but, unexpectedly, Tlalok spoke coherently.

<<Put Tlalok down. Tlalok can walk.>>

Tlalok could walk. As distance made the null-field radiance weaker and weaker, Tlalok even began to run. The two Khafra broke out of the tunnel at a full gallop.

The surface of the island was bathed in blood-red light, the ground lurching as one of the four small columns of hydrogen fire rammed against it, carving into it and hammering up cyclones of sparks. Flaming debris rained down around Arrou and Tlalok, exploding on impact and setting shriveled vegetation on fire. Arrou and Tlalok bounded down the mound of ghutzu as the island began to spin, grinding around the flaming spear, rotating ever nearer to the central inferno. Red hot hail pelted their backs. Smoke stung their eyes. The heat of the air sawed at their throats and lungs.

Land waves rippled out from the impacting pillar of fire, kicking the ground up under their feet. Tlalok, not yet fully recovered from his encounter with the null-field Radiance, faltered. Arrou nipped at his heels to keep him going. Somehow, running through the rolling hills and valleys, evading scorched, heavy tree trunks that swung at them like giant pendulums, they made it to the shore—but there was no skimmer! Arrou clawed the ground in frustration.

<<Arrou's blank-one has abandoned us,>> Tlalok rumbled, as if he had expected such a betrayal all along.

<<No,>> said Arrou, searching the nearby ocean in the hope that the skimmer was close and they would be able to swim out after it. <<Jenette not abandon Arrou.>> Of course, even as he flashed his thoughts, he remembered that Jenette *had* abandoned him once before. He tried to tell himself that that time was different, that she had been trying to save his life—however misplaced that sentiment had been—and that she would never abandon him to die, but he wasn't doing a good job convincing himself. The longer he searched, the more hopeless it seemed.

The island lurched hard. Arrou watched a particularly large land wave ripple across the island. The ground under him and Tlalok was sucked down as it rolled toward them and then they were riding up its steep face and then looking out from high atop its crest.

And there was the skimmer!

Off, clockwise, along the shore, there were Jenette and the Guards, desperately waving heat-shield blankets to attract attention. Arrou realized he had somehow become disoriented in the run down from the tunnel. The skimmer was where it was supposed to be—and so was Jenette. With a howl of relief, Arrou took a fix on the vehicle and lead Tlalok diagonally through the hills and troughs of land waves. In very little time they were in the right location. The skimmer was floating a dozen yards off shore to keep from being battered to pieces by the island's pistoning shoreline. Liberty gunned the skimmer's turbine engine, circling the craft closer to the two Khafra. Arrou and Tlalok sprang onto its near wing. Their claws skittered on the wet surface. Skutch and Grubb reached out and heaved Tlalok inside. Arrou half leapt, half crashed into the inner hull beside them.

The island spun free of the flame pillar. It and the skimmer were now within the orbit that the small pillars took around the large one.

"Go, go, go!" screamed Jenette. "Hit it!"

Liberty applied full power. The skimmer's speed ramped up and it rose onto its stubby, ground-effects wings. Exposed human skin began to burn and blister as Liberty steered a path outward, equidistant between two of the small columns of flame.

The null-field was dim once more; it had been an easy task for Bigelow to correct the in-human's amateurish sabotage. The scientist sat cross-legged under the pinched midsection at the reactor's waist, a Buddha of exquisite agony, his life fluids seeping away. Teeny-tiny buzzers swarmed over him, attracted by the sickly sweet smell of a meal, tickling his internal organs with their dozens of scurrying legs.

In each hand Bigelow held a wire. The ends were frayed. He did not allow them to touch.

The time was near. Bigelow could feel it. The cavity shook from the colossal impact of the island against the central column of fugueship fire. The room shuddered more violently as, Bigelow deduced, the island was being sucked in and consumed by the great inferno. Even the mound of fire-resistant ghutzu would be burning now, his shielding becoming weaker by the heartbeat.

He must wait.

His mind became calm. A few lines of a favorite poem played upon his tongue.

"And you, my father, there on the sad height,

"Curse, bless, me now with your fierce tears, I pray—"

The temperature soared. He felt the air being sucked out of the chamber. He must hold off. Until he was as near to the center of the inferno as possible.

"Do not go gentle into that good night,"

"Rage, rage against the dying of the light."

The island began to tilt.

Bigelow touched the wires together.

The island, a ragged crescent tearing itself apart upon the pillar of fugueship fire behind Jenette, disappeared. The world abruptly went out of focus. A ghostly cloud of shockwave exploded, rising up and out as it expanded over the ocean, hammering away the clouds above. Out of where the island had been, seeming to fold itself out of a dimension which originated somewhere behind Jenette's head, a null-sun erupted, evil and black, ringed with purple, swelling, boiling, snuffing out the Burning Heart of Night. This was the power of that-which-should-not-be, the power humans stole from that the awful, angry void of pre-creation. It rose, mushrooming, its antediluvian hunger greedily devouring all matter in its path.

"Sonofabitch," Jenette heard Skutch gasp beside her. *"That's* an explosion."

At which point an overspill of the blast, an infinitesimal portion of the total unleashed energy, which had not been diverted up and away from the ocean surface by Bigelow's careful null-field shaping, smashed down on the skimmer.

LII

*Play the curveballs destiny throws at you. Do not
mourn for what-could-have-beens and if-onlies. Do
what is right, no matter what the cost.*

                             —from the speeches of Olin Tesla

Karr sank, tumbling out of control, deeper and deeper into the boiling water. The in-human clutched Karr's kilnsuit, the gouts of ferocious bubbles tearing at its ghastly costume as convection currents drew the two of them inexorably toward the fugueship fires. Five orange plumes became visible through the hellish gloom, huge and smearing up from the depths like the tails of spinning, underwater comets. The colors grew hotter and brighter as the distance decreased. In no time, Karr was amidst the fires. An eddy caught him and the in-human and spun them back and forth between plumes of instant incineration.

And then there was *nothing*.

Hard hitting. Black. Enveloping. The death throes of the null-fusion reactor. Blotting out the world from above and sucking the life out of the submerged fires. Karr's kilnsuit went rigid. His helmet cracked along a thousand fracture lines. The proximity of such a voracious *nonexistence* overwhelmed him, seeming to tug at the very threads of his DNA, as if to unravel all trace of his ever having been alive at all. Karr and the in-human were separated.

At length, his sense of self returned.

The laminated layers of his helmet were fractured, but fortunately no water was leaking in. Through that transparent bubble, in a faint gloom seeping down from above, Karr saw the huge and slowly rotating mass of his fugueship. Four bulbous forms sprouted from its grub-shaped midsection, rocket-shaped stamens in the heart of a titanic bloom, each one over half a kiloyard long; each of these booster-spawn making its own plume of water split into hydrogen and oxygen gas. Karr's heart quickened. Here was a vision no other human had seen before: a fugueship reproducing. In spite of the circumstances that he found himself in, Karr could not help but feel a pang of paternal pride. Look what his *Long Reach* had done! It was almost as if the spawn were his children too. He suddenly felt some of the emotions that normal humans feel as they live their normal lives, falling in love, reproducing, seeking out a piece of immortality in the form of their blood descendants. Karr longed to be Pilot for each of the four, to watch them grow, protecting them from harm, sheltering them from sorrow, letting them fly free through the stars . . . and he certainly did not wish to be the cause of their premature deaths, that was for sure. More than ever he knew he had to set the spawning to rights, to do whatever he had to do to set *Long Reach's* normal reproductive process back on track and make the number of hydrogen fires four—as demanded by the Feral prophecy of the Burning Heart of Night.

A petulant current ended Karr's ruminations, seizing and hammering him against *Long Reach*, scraping him down the side of the immense hull. His arms flailed, fingers striving ineffectually to get a grip on the slick surface as he plummeted into the deep.

The Null was gone. Horror.

His new skin was gone. Torn away by the angry water. Inbigelow was dead before even beginning to live. Desolation.

After pulling himself into the strange, new place, he could not move very well. He hurt all over. One of his hind legs did not work anymore.

And yet . . . the in-human was not overcome.

"Ooooooooooh," he cooed.

He felt salvation as he lay prostrate. It throbbed through the fleshy walls, the pulse of a fusion furnace far, far greater than the Null had ever been. This new Null was so big that the in-human could stretch out his arms and not feel the walls of the passage around him, and he sensed that it was much bigger, even, than that. It was a Null with Pact flowing through its veins! That part he did not care for. He remembered what Pact was from the before-time, before his transformation to in-human. The smell of this Null-Pact made him feel strangely *slow*, in a way that he could not understand, and he did not like that, either. But he did not let those things bother him much. What, after all, was a bit of filthy Pact compared to the power of this new Null?

The Null was dead, long live the Null!

This Null he would keep Safe. This Null he would not fail—no matter what skin he bore. Uncoiling a dirty loop from around his neck, the in-human unfolded the last remnants of his old in-robert mask. He stretched it over his head as best he could. He was not hidden very well from the Balance, but at least he had a name, and therefore a purpose.

Hobbling three-legged through pools of fugueship blood, in-robert wormed his way deeper into the ship.

Karr clawed in through an iris-valve at the end of a bilge duct and collapsed onto the floor in a small alley between cartilage arches. Fugueship ichor streaked and stained his already cracked helmet. He could not see a thing. He unlocked the fishbowl and removed it. The smell of jasmine—of familiarity, of duty, of travel between the rainbow lights of distant stars—swamped Karr. He felt lightheaded for a while as his body absorbed and reaccustomed itself to the *fugue* in the air. Then, using the light of a glowstrip that he had brought to facilitate moving around inside the darkened hulk, Karr removed the other ungainly segments of his kilnsuit and stacked them in a fleshy alcove for safekeeping.

The passages Karr wound through were distorted, squeezed, and twisted by the pressures of gravity and water on a creature designed to live in zero gravity, but they were not spasming dangerously as they had been the last time he was on board. *Long Reach* seemed to have found a new, tenuous state of equilibrium. It was still dying, Karr could see, but no longer imminently. Walls no longer wept blood. Infectious patches no longer made walking treacherous. His ship was dying a death by increments, a slow withering. It was not a reassuring prognosis, but at least it meant Karr had a chance to redeem himself as a Pilot, to make up for the ignorant meddling which had jeopardized the lives of his wonderful ship and its even more wonderful spawn. And, most importantly, to save them. He just needed to keep them alive for two hundred and twenty-four realtime days more, until the prophesied *escape* of the Burning Heart of Night. After that, Karr did not know what would happen, but he had placed his faith in the Ferals and their knowledge and prophesies. They believed that everything would all work out, so he believed.

Trust.

"Don't worry," Karr said, easily falling into his old habit of reassuring dialogue with the ship. "Everything is going to be all right, somehow."

Perhaps there was hope after all.

Karr recognized a few landmarks. He was on Bloodflower Boulevard. He followed it down, toward the bow of the ship, where he was pleasantly surprised to find areas where implanted power and light sources still functioned and, not too long after that, he discovered the remains of his old quarters, now looking like a heap of discarded child's blocks. Turning the glowstrip off with a sharp squeeze and stuffing it into a pocket, Karr dug through the jumble of white cubicles. He located and donned a clean ghimpsuit. Normally, a ghimpsuit was not necessary in slowtime. But then again, normally, a Pilot was not trying to function under the pull of one full gravity and Karr figured he could use all the help he could get.

Karr did not waste any time looking for a clean uniform to go over the ghimpsuit. He had no Gattler, and acquiring one was his next priority. After several hours of hunting around the ship, he decided there were no more of the multitools in any of the usual storage dumps. However, he was able to jury-rig one from a stockpile of replacement cartridges and parts. All it had was cutting beam and needle shooting barrels, no surgical foam, adhesive, or ultrasonic projector, but with any luck it would serve Karr's purposes. With apprehension growing in his gut, Karr set off to find *Long*

Reach's chain of large vertebrae and the superconductor core that paralleled them.

Somewhere between the spare parts storage containers and his goal, he felt a heavy impact to the back of his head and his world faded out.

The fires were out.

Humans, domestics, and Ferals huddled together on paddle-boards, skimmers, and skrag island fragments that dotted the ocean. Bruised and battered and wet, they made no sound. Only the labor cries of a single human female broke the dark night. The Burning Heart was gone. The great null-shadow had devoured it. And no one of either species was sure if that was good or bad, or what would happen next.

Dawn broke over the shell-shocked sentients, bringing warmth and glorious radiance, but also bringing Kthulah's armada. The great fleet encircled the survivors. The floating mountain that was the island of Gnosis bore down upon the clustered blockade-breakers and Prophecy violators, coming to visit its judgment upon them.

Karr awoke on his back, his head pounding, his wrists and feet burning. Overhead was a dome of cartilage, glowing a faint salmon pink. Beneath and puffing up around him, were warm pillows of neural tissue. He was in the brainroom. Lifting his head he saw human implanted control consoles, shorted out and lifeless now, which ringed the pear-shaped room. And he also saw the reason his extremities hurt; he was affixed to *Long Reach*'s large cerebral cortex. *Qi* needles were driven right through his wrists and ankles, deep into the convoluted brain tissue. How strange was this, he wondered, as a small movement on his part brought extreme jolts of discomfort, to be crucified in the place where he had always felt the strongest bond between Pilot and fugueship? He had been brought to face the judgment of the ship he had so badly wronged.

But by whom?

Off in a corner, Karr saw his jury-rigged Gattler, carelessly discarded. Closer, pacing as best it could with what looked like a shattered leg, was Karr's jailer and accuser, the in-human.

"Big Null, Big Null," it muttered obsessively. "Must keep Big Null safe. Must, must, must."

Two things about the creature immediately affronted Karr. The first was its very presence. How could it have survived the long minutes submerged in the boiling water, and then the blast, albeit diffused, of the null-fusion reactor? The in-human had appeared half-dead before Karr knocked it into the well shaft to save Arrou. Now it looked positively undead. Its skin was seared black, cracking and showing pink and bloody wherever its hide bent or flexed.

The second thing that affronted Karr, in the extreme, was that the in-human was not collapsed in a *fugue*-coma. In fact it was moving around, talking, and Karr could understand it.

"This one must keep the Big Null safe," it muttered. "But how, when the Big Null does not want to be safe? How? In-robert does not know?"

"In-robert?" Karr heard himself repeating dully. "In-robert, in-robert . . . ?" Why did that name sound so familiar. Why did it bother him so much? Then it hit Karr. "In-*bob?* Your name is in-*BOB!*"

The deranged creature swung its muzzle to face Karr. "Friends sometimes call in-robert that for short."

Karr couldn't take it anymore. He pitched a fit.

"I will not accept this! This is more coincidence than one Pilot can stand!" How could it be, to be plagued, over the span of twenty-seven light years and two subjective months, by not one but two insane creatures, one a human and one an alien, who were both immune to the paralyzing effects of *fugue*—and both of whom were named Bob! What were the odds of it? Once in a billion? One in a billion, billion? It could not be! "I do not accept this!" Karr screamed at the universe.

"In-bob does not accept it either," the creature said, with a pained look on the face under its awful mask. "In-bob must keep the Big Null safe. That is clear. The Big Null is Purpose. The Purpose must be obeyed. The Big Null must be safe. But the Big Null does not want to be safe. So how can the Purpose be obeyed? How can in-bob keep safe the Big Null if it does not want to be safe?"

Karr thrashed, despite the pain it cause his skewered feet and wrists. "Shut up! Shut up, you deranged creature! You're not making any sense!"

In-bob hobbled closer.

"It wants to die," in-bob said, distraught. "In-bob does not know why, but the Big Null wants to die."

The way the creature swung its head around the brainroom, as if looking around with its eyeless sockets, Karr suddenly understood what it meant by the Big Null. It meant *Long Reach*. A shiver coursed down his spine.

"How do you know that?" Karr asked quietly. "How do you know it wants to die?"

"It speaks to in-bob," the in-human said in an awed gurgle.

"It does not," Karr objected. "It doesn't speak. It has no vocal apparatus. And besides, it is a dumb beast of burden."

"No, no," the in-human argued. "It has no mouth, but in-bob knows what it thinks. In-bob *feels* it." The inhuman leaned against *Long Reach's* giant cortex, its Khafra paws splayed wide, as if prostrate before a god, its head bowed, earpits pressing into the soft tissue as if listening, like a human might listen to a seashell. "It is not dumb. It is Pilots that are dumb if they think that. The Big Null needs, feels, knows. Its thoughts are simple, but true, mostly . . . except that it wants to die." In-bob stood up, pursing his cone of teeth pensively. "And except that it won't let in-bob kill the Pilot." In-bob leaned over Karr and snapped his teeth petulantly. "It says Pilot is friend; that is why Pilot is allowed to call this one in-bob, for short. In-bob wants to kill Pilot anyway, but it says no."

"It does? It said that to you?"

"It *feels* that to in-bob," the in-human said, its muzzle curling in disgust as it explained further. "It *feels* better when it feels the Pilot. It isn't lonely when it feels the Pilot. It isn't afraid when it feels the Pilot. It wants the Pilot to be always and never go away. Foolish, foolish Big Null. Why does the Big Null want to die, Pilot? Why?"

"I don't know," Karr stammered, hardly able to speak.

Epiphany.

Karr's ship knew that he existed. It had feelings about him. It felt bad when he was gone and safe when he was near. It did not want him to die. Karr felt hot tears on his cheeks. He had always known that he loved his ship, but he had never known that it loved him too.

In-bob glowered, oblivious to the human's emotions. "Little Nulls are killing it. That must be it. That's what in-bob thinks. Little Nulls are sucking Big Null's life out. Little Nulls must die."

Abruptly, the in-human scuttled out of the brainroom.

Karr continued to weep. Epiphany followed epiphany. *His ship wanted to die.* The mad alien was right, Karr knew. In his own limited way, Karr also sensed the moods of his ship; he could not deny what he felt, crucified upon and half enveloped by his ship's cortex. Karr sensed sadness, but mostly acceptance, and even a little anticipation of the end to his ship's centuries-old journey through time and space.

It was an untenable situation for a Pilot. It was his Duty to do everything in his power to keep his ship alive. He wanted more than anything to keep his ship alive.

But he must kill his ship.

He loved it, therefore he must set it free.

Thirty long, long minutes later, the resorbing *qi* needles that in-Bob had mistakenly used to nail Karr to *Long Reach*'s cortex dissolved. Karr got up, moving numbly. "I guess we're not going to be all right after all," he said, with the sad caress of a hand where his bipedal imprint was slowly disappearing from *Long Reach*'s brain. When it was gone, he picked up his improvised Gattler and exited the room.

The *decision* was upon him. Kthulah felt it in his bones.

The blank-one Jenette had requested an audience. Kthulah had obliged. The *decision* impelled him to confront his fate face-to-face and on four legs. Sixty-four hunters, black with silver stripes running down necks, backs, and limbs, rowed a pyramid-shaped barge. Kthulah's four-sided throne sat at the apex; the Judges sat at the throne's four sacred corners as the barge slid through silvery waves to meet the half-burned skrag where the blank-one Jenette, the traitor Tlalok, and the rest of the Prophecy violators awaited. The renegade Pact and blank-ones looked strikingly similar to Kthulah as he neared. Eyes stared, defeated but defiant, from both pink blank faces and iridescent leathery muzzles. Both four-legged and two-legged creatures, sworn enemies only a pawful of days before, now stood shoulder to shoulder, ready to face judgment together, without reserve or cowardice.

<<Only a common enemy was needed to unite such bitter foes,>> Kthulah flashed softly to the Judges. <<If only that enemy had found Pact and blank-ones many years sooner . . . >>

<<If only>>

<<That enemy>>

<<Had not turned out to be>>

<<Kthulah,>> the Judges observed.

Kthulah flinched, but knew the truth of it. He was the enemy who had united these foes. He, the Keeper of the Roots of Wisdom, Radiance of the Pack of Gnosis. He, who believed in winning wars by not fighting battles. What irony!

The bitter smell of charred ghutzu stung Kthulah's mouth and eyes as the barge drew up against the skrag. The traitor Tlalok and the blank-one Jenette stood foremost on its blackened shore. Tlalok bowed his head, not in submission, but in the respect one hunter gives another, and his Khafra followed suit. As did Jenette, who motioned for her blank-ones and No-pact to do the same.

So many noble passions, Kthulah reflected. So many misguided failures. Was Kthulah himself one of those?

<<The Burning Heart of Night>>

<<Is>>

<<No>>

<<More,>> the Judges flashed solemnly.

<<The time>>

<<Of Kthulah's>>

<<Decision>>

<<Is now.>>

Karr stood as close to the center of his ship as any human could stand without actually being incinerated. Here, striated rust and feeder cores the color of ivory branched out from the curving swell of the fugueship's fusion furnace, carrying current that fed both broken sections of its superconductor core.

It was a simple thing to do, really, Karr tried to tell himself. Just aim and fire.

This was probably his all fault, too. Probably, Karr reasoned, the superconductor core naturally failed during the spawning process. Probably that was why Feral prophecy demanded four *radiances* and not five. But Pilot Lindal Karr had always paid particular attention to the superconductor and its conduit, since without it *Long Reach* could not generate a ramfield or feed, and therefore not fulfill its destiny, wandering between stars. Even now Karr could see the heads of many non-resorbing *qi* needles, which he had implanted over the course of hundreds of years. They were still doing their job by stopping any deterioration of the superconductor dead in its tracks.

It was a thing no Pilot should ever have to do.

It would kill his ship. He understood that as strongly as any human could understand a concept. The only question was how soon? Would the spawning proceed? Would the baby fugueships be saved? He did not know.

Trust.

Karr raised the Gattler and fired. A cutting beam shot out, wide and just long enough to sever the superconductor connections. Two measured sweeps and it was over. Dissolved. Rendered ineffective. Somewhere in the distance, Karr heard a resounding *crack*, as of a large amount of electricity discharging. *Long Reach* did not even shudder, so he paid it no attention.

LIII

Now comes the time
When all bonds
Are broken
And all Pacts made anew.

—the Judges of Gnosis

Lightning sparked in the daytime sky. An immense flash hammered up from the tranquil surface of the ocean, high into the atmosphere. Thunder boomed over those on the water, deafening Pact, blank-one, and No-Pact alike, followed a split second later by the roar of hydrogen and oxygen igniting. Four pillars of Radiance reappeared.

<<The Prophecy>>

<<Has been>>

<<Set>>

<<To Balance!>> the Judges exclaimed.

Kthulah shuddered. The Burning Heart of Night had not perished! The fourth gift of Radiance, the gift of Gamut, might yet come to pass. <<Kthulah has made his decision,>> he flashed for all to see. <<The Burning Heart has been healed. Blank-ones and No-pact, and traitor Pact are absolved of actions against Prophecy.>>

A groan of relief sounded from Tlalok's Khafra. The assembled blank-ones showed signs of relief also, when Jenette's bonded No-pact finished translating for them.

<<However,>> Kthulah continued, <<Blank-ones and No-pact,

and traitor Pact, must leave, never to return to the bounds of the Radiance of Gnosis, never——>>

<<Wait! Stop!>> Jenette pleaded with her device full of starlight.

The sixty-four hunters on Kthulah's barge tensed, ready to attack and squelch such a sacrilegious interruption of their leader, but the Judges held up their staves, rattling loops of black and white beads, which they never stopped tallying.

<<Let>>
<<The>>
<<Blank-one>>
<<Speak!>> they declared.
<<The Balance>>
<<Demands>>
<<To know>>
<<Her mind!>>

The hunters backed down. Gathering courage, the blank-one Jenette continued.

<<This is not the time for separations,>> she flashed. <<This is the time for reparations. This is the time for new beginnings. Kthulah is wise. Does Kthulah not see that blank-ones and those sworn to revenge against blank-ones have found accord?>>

<<Kthulah sees,>> Kthulah acknowledged.

<<Then why can there not be accord between all Khafra and blank-ones? Why can there not be enjoinings instead of separations?>>

<<Because Kthulah has seen too many trustings become betrayings,>> Kthulah flashed in sad colors. <<Too many Khafra have passed at blank-one hands without fulfilling Pact.>>

<<Many blank-ones, who did not wish to betray Pact, have passed, too,>> Jenette countered. <<And yet blank-ones are willing to risk a new trust.>>

<<Pact have too much to lose if such a new trust fails.>>

<<And blank-ones do not? All blank-ones that came to heal the Burning Heart came at the risk of their lives. There will be no more Sacrament. We are decided. There will be only honorable peace, or honorable death. Is that not enough of a guarantee?>>

A committed rumble sounded from the assembled blank-ones as Jenette's No-pact translated her words. Kthulah was touched. He wanted to make a peace, but he could not alone bring himself to take such a gamble. Too much suffering had resulted from such a decision twenty years ago.

<<What does the Balance say?>> Kthulah asked the Judges.

The ascetic Khafra huddled to decipher the meaning hidden in their white and black loops of beads. They argued amongst themselves, becoming more and more agitated. When the four finally arose, the single blue dots in the center of their foreheads—which signified their commitment to live perfectly Balanced, on the knife-edge between life and Radiance, or death and Shadow— these dots had been swelled by shock to clearly discernible disks of glowing glowbuds.

Kthulah had never seen so strong a reaction from the four.

<<Look>>

<<For>>

<<A>>

<<Sign!>> they proclaimed.

As one, the heads of every Khafra and blank-one in sight swiveled, looking, searching, seeking. A hush descended. Not even the distant cry of blank-one pain, which Kthulah had been hearing in the background for some time now, intruded into the expectant quiet. The crowd on the charred skrag island shifted. It began to part, in a wave of motion from its center out to its shore. Equally confused as Kthulah, Tlalok and the blank-one Jenette also stepped aside as the parting of bodies reached them.

Two blank-ones, a large male and a fatigued female assisted by other females and No-pact, made their way into Kthulah's view. The large male and the fatigued female each held two cloth-swathed bundles in their arms. Standing reverently, they held the bundles up for Kthulah to see. The two blank-ones spoke.

Jenette's No-pact translated, <<The blank-ones Burke and Panya offer gifts to Kthulah to make Pact and bind the peace between Khafra and blank-ones.>>

Kthulah squinted with his old eyes. The bundles were newly born blank-one nurslings!

<<The sacred>>
<<Number>>
<<Of>>
<<Four!>> the Judges exclaimed. Their talons flew over their loops of beads.
<<It!>>
<<Is!>>
<<The!>>
<<Sign!>>
A warmth enveloped Kthulah's old heart. The Balance was wise. Here was the portent to end all of Kthulah's uncertainty. He bowed his wizened head.
<<So it is decided. So it shall be done.>>

After the superconductor was disconnected, things really began to change inside *Long Reach*. Muscles, unneeded bones, entire systems of organs began to shrivel and resorb, their amino acids, minerals and other life-sustaining building blocks diverted to the of the nourishment and development of the spawn. Spaces began to open up in the normally crowded and constricted inner hull. Karr had no time for the sorrow he felt watching this process. He focused on one thing and one thing only.

He must locate and terminate in-bob.

It required no leap of genius to know where the in-human could be found. The creature's last words had made that clear enough. *Little Nulls are sucking Big Null's life out. Little Nulls must die.*

Working his way back up to the midsection of the fugueship, Karr located four critically strong junctures in *Long Reach*'s rib system, from which the fugueship spawn sprouted. Of course Karr could not see the booster-rocket shape of the baby fugueships as they appeared from outside the parent ship. Karr saw only the business end of the spawn: the growing superconductor cores, the blast nozzles which would channel the thrust necessary to set the spawn free of New Ascension's gravity well, the angle of umbilical arteries and veins and other conduits carrying nutrients from *Long Reach* to the spawn.

The first spawn was uninjured. Karr found the second in distinctly different condition. Its umbilical connections were ripped and torn. *Long Reach*'s lifeblood pumped out of them, collecting in growing ponds. The spawn was perishing. Karr consulted his subdermal chronometers. It had only been five realtime hours since in-bob had left the brainroom. That was not much time in comparison to a two hundred and fifty-six day spawning cycle. The spawn had a slight bluish tinge to its tissues, Karr saw, but perhaps the damage could still be reversed.

Karr set to work, repairing wounded umbilicals by first pinning the severed ends together with *qi* needles, and then hand applying surgical adhesive from a Gattler canister that he broke open with a pry bar. When all the veins and arteries were reconnected, there were still many leaks, so he retrieved a barrel of quick drying flexicrete, which he had seen while searching the storage units, mixed it up, and applied it over the entire traumatized area with a shovel. The improvised cast worked. The leaks were plugged. The booster-spawn began to look healthier right away.

"Bad, bad Pilot," hissed a voice behind Karr.

Karr whirled to see in-bob perched on a raised juncture of two gigantic ribs. The creature fell onto Karr, slashing and biting, and slamming Karr to the ground. Dagger sharp teeth gnashed inches from Karr's jugular, held back only by the stock of Karr's Gattler. Karr kicked his boot heels into the creature's fractured rear leg. Shrieking in agony, in-bob fell back. Karr swung the Gattler to bear, fumbling to activate the cutting beam. He fired, but not before the blind in-human attacked again, slashing with a forearm and knocking Karr's aim off. The cutting beam burned a hole in a cluster of enormous glands nearby. The sacks ruptured, inundating Karr and in-bob in ejecta; both of them disappeared under the flood and came up choking, *fugue*-rich fluid in their eyes, throats, and nasal passages. Karr attempted to stand, but he was suddenly dizzy and fell. He could not seem to focus on the in-human. He struggled to his feet again, this time keeping his balance, and raising the rudimentary Gattler to his shoulders, but he still could not take proper aim at in-bob. The creature's four-legged form seemed to blur in and out of view, first standing, nearly paralyzed, and then streaking out of sight. The strange phenomena repeated several times before Karr figured it out.

He and in-bob had become saturated in *fugue*.

They were transitioning into fuguetime, where one subjective day equaled one realtime year. The freezing and streaking away was a side effect of the differing rates at which their dissimilar physiologies were adjusting to the change. Karr felt ill and then, as that sensation passed, great weight. He felt as though the gravity of a gas giant was pressing down on him. His slow moving muscles were overwhelmed. The ghimpsuit was all that kept him from collapsing into a feeble pile of skin and bones.

Karr scanned around for in-bob, but the creature was gone. The only evidence of its having been there at all was a blood-streaked trail winding up away from the base of the booster-spawn, out into a connecting passage. Karr determined that the spawn had not been effected by the rupture of *fugue*-containing glands and then lumbered off along in-bob's track. The ghimpsuit actually emitted a scorched electrical odor as it strained toward the limit of its capabilities to keep his body functioning in the high gravity environment.

Thwak, thwak, thwak, thwak.

Kthulah's Radiance was fading, one blow at a time. Sixty-four for forgiving actions against Prophecy.

Thwak, thwak, thwak, thwak.

Sixty-four for allowing traitor Pact to remain, unostracized, within the bounds of the Radiance of Gnosis.

Thwak, thwak, thwak, thwak.

Two hundred and fifty-six for making peace with blank ones.

Thwak, thwak, thwak, thwak.

Five hundred and twelve for allowing blank-one nurslings to make Pact.

Thwak, thwak, thwak, thwak.

One hundred and twenty-eight more for passing his own sacred Pact on to two of the nurslings (the doing of which had given him much contentment).

Thwak, thwak, thwak, thwak.

One thousand and twenty-four in all. The Judges wept as they administered the punishment.

Thwak, thwak, thwak, thwak.

Kthulah had not quite made the sixteen thousand days of his forty allotted years, and he had not seen the escape of the Burning Heart of Night, but he had lived a life worthy of the Roots of Wisdom and he had passed without shadow in his heart.

Thwak, thwak, thwak . . . thwak.

The Judges of Gnosis glowed with the crimson stigmata of grief.

The trail of blood and *fugue* soon dried up. Karr followed the dusty residue. A few subjective minutes later, even the residue was gone, resorbed by the ship's realtime biological processes. Karr kept going. In-bob's tracks had been heading clockwise around *Long Reach* toward the next booster-spawn. There was little question in Karr's mind that the creature would reach its objective. He only hoped that the in-human's adjustment to fuguetime had maintained a steady progression from weaker to stronger *fugue*-states. If there had been any aberration in the change, any regressions back toward realtime, in-bob might have had weeks or even months in which to act while Karr dawdled along in fuguetime. In which case, all the spawn were already dead and Karr just did not know it yet.

Days and weeks elapsed. Clashes of Radiance came and went. But none who had been drawn by the Prophecy, or who gathered seeking a second chance at life from the fugueship, left. No one died, either, not even Panya Hedren, who came down with fullblown Scourge after giving birth. Jenette saw to it that Dr. Marsh and the best Feral healers pooled their knowledge; the mother of the Sacred Sign infants could not be allowed to perish. It was a near thing, but Panya was still alive on the two hundred and fifty-sixth sunrise after Tears had fallen from the sky, two hundred and forty sunrises after the blossoming of the Burning Heart of Night.

On that morning, humans and Khafra ringed the four pillars of flame as closely as they dared in their many vessels large and small, to await, they hoped, the fulfillment of Prophecy. Through that clear morning, nothing occurred, but then as New Ascension's sun reached the highest point in the sky overhead, the pillars of Radiance suddenly began to dwindle.

They fizzled completely.

A great submerged rumbling began to vibrate the mirror-like surface of the ocean. Every assembled sentient felt as though its heart was in the back of its throat.

In-bob was failing. Horror, horror!

He could not keep the Big Null safe. It was dying. The Little Nulls were sucking out its life. The cursed Null-Pact had stopped him. It slowed him down too much. He could barely breathe. He could not move upon his legs. All he could do was crawl, like a spineless thing, his mind fogged by pain, inch after labored inch. And when he got to the third of the Little Nulls, he could not rip and shred as he had before, but only slither up to it and begin to gnaw with his teeth into its body at a point above one of the nozzle cones. Chew and chew and chew. He must kill it. He must. Hours of pain. Then he broke through the Little Null's thick, strong hide. Foul chemical powder spilled out. In-bob choked. He could not burrow deeper, but he could make the hole bigger. He chewed and chewed and chewed some more.

The Big Null began to vibrate. Something bad was happening. Something smelled. Protesting neck muscles dragged his head around to smell better. In-bob smelled Pilot. And he smelled the sterile odor of the Pilot's weapon. It would be aiming at him now. He could not see it or hear it. But in-bob knew. That was what others always wanted to do to in-bob. Kill him. *Why had the Big Null not let in-bob kill the Pilot? Why did it want to die? Why did it want in-bob to fail?* In-bob wept, burbling in self-pity as the Pilot fired. In-bob felt more stabs of pain in his already agonized body. Metal pins nailed in-bob to the Little Null. He could not move.

The shaking of the Big Null increased. The roar of three Little Nulls coming to life rattled in-bob's bones. *WHAM! WHAM! WHAM!*

Fire started below in-bob, sputtering impotently from the nozzle cones. In-bob felt the heat. The Little Null was trying to wake up and escape with the Big Null's life, as the other three were. But it couldn't. Perhaps in-bob had succeeded after all!

But then in-bob smelled ozone. The smell of a cutting beam. The Little Null had somehow been freed; in-bob felt it begin to move. The smell of Pilot disappeared. In-bob felt the nozzle fire below dim growing stronger. Fire also began to spew from the hole he had chewed in the Little Null's body. The foul tasting powder was igniting. In-bob felt the Little Null move. Something separated.

The Little Null was free!

The fire surged. In-bob felt fleeting subjective sensations of realtime events, almost too fast to comprehend. He was moving through water, his extremities burning off from the force of the Little Null's fire, his armored body disintegrating. Then he felt sunlight and thin air. It was a waking nightmare. One that ended, not in escape or saving the Big Null, but in sudden, utter disintegration.

Fugueship spawn burst out of the ocean. Three missile shapes rode roaring thrust up to the stars. Smoke spewed out behind each of them; differing wind directions in the upper layers of New Ascension's atmosphere tugged the exhaust trails into luminous zigzags. As foretold, the Radiances were escaping.

But only three.

A fourth Radiance followed, spinning an erratic path skyward, trying to catch up with the others. It wobbled faster and faster as it rose, tearing itself apart, then suddenly exploding, raining fragments of itself—and thick clouds of *fugue*—down over the onwatching blank-ones and Pact upon the ocean.

A piece of the light had been saved.

Gravity was in revolt. The sensation of up jerked in one unlikely direction and then another. Karr tumbled helplessly, careening into the *ceiling*, slamming against the *deck*, falling into a *wall*. Bam! Thok! Krak! Muscle sheet bulkheads and girder-rib struts battered his frail human form. *Long Reach* was lazily tumbling in the realtime ocean, but the fuguetime equivalent was merciless in its vigor. Angry bruises sprawled across Karr's flesh where his new ghimpsuit could not absorb the damage. Finally, a sickening lurch changed the orientation of *down* while Karr was in midair—causing Karr a final, painful impact—and *Long Reach* settled in its familiar maw-down orientation. Karr's world was still not motionless, however. The deck vibrated under Karr's battered limbs—no doubt his accelerated perception of the ship bobbing on languid ocean waves. For a while the massage felt good, but the oscillation was soon more than his ravaged senses could handle. Nausea. Karr needed out, fresh air and solid ground, or at least the relative stillness of the ocean in realtime.

He had to get out of all of this *fugue*!

Karr crawled along a vibrating tunnelway, up a cartilage-lined shaft and back to the duct where he had so recently entered his ship. Retrieving the jumbled pieces of his kilnsuit and helmet from the floor, he put them on. Karr used a *qi* needle to force the entry duct open. He half expected water to explode in, but the iris-portal relaxed uneventfully and he squirmed out, down through its tight birth canal, struggling to get out.

Karr burst out onto *Long Reach*'s exterior a few yards above sea level. Deep indigo and bright, sky blue strobed as night and day whirled around Karr with ungodly speed. Yellow light flared, morning shadows shortened and arched around, lengthened, blending with dusk and then stars wheeled giddily around New Ascension's south polar star. Night . . . day . . . night . . . day. . . . It was kind of pretty. Karr had expected that. What he had not expected was the strange wall of green and gray which grew up from the horizon in every direction around him, up from the ocean itself, and which then hammered in at him, abruptly entombing him in motionless darkness.

LIV

*Doing mission time is like doing a puzzle. You love the
ship. You love the mission. But nothing changes. Each
year is a day, but each day feels like ten years. Pieces
of the puzzle cut themselves loose. Friends, family,
entire planets disappear. The crux of the problem is, you
somehow have to let them go and do your Duty. And
then when that time of Duty is all over you have to
build a new picture, without falling into negative things
and using only the remaining mixed up pieces.*

> —Bondir Malda
> Pilot, fugueship Kismet,
> One month after retirement

It was ghutzu, of course, the root matter that formed the structure
of New Ascension's floating islands. Karr had anticipated the apparent acceleration of the world around him, but had completely
forgotten about the already hyper-accelerated rate of plant growth
on the planet. That, together with the explosion of the fourth
spawn, which doused the local area in *fugue*, and which he would
learn about later) produced the apparently instantaneous phenomena of his entrapment. Brown-gray root tendrils pressed in tight
against his helmet bowl, looking like so many crowded worms in
the faint light of in-suit readouts; they pried into the helmet's many
fractures, widening the cracks enough for air to leech into the suit.
They kept Karr immobilized, except for what little movement he
could make inside the kilnsuit itself. It was a claustrophobic moment. Fortunately, a warning gage began to blink, distracting Karr.
Fugue concentration was diminishing in the atmosphere within the

suit. He steeled himself as *fugue* level dropped to zero. Soon enough his body wrenched, kept from doubling over by the confined space. *Fugue* withdrawal hit, the familiar throbbing, thought-obliterating torment of a thousand hangovers. It seemed to last forever, Karr's perception popping in and out of realtime so that a hundred times the torment ended, but then resurged and stretched on again—as Karr knew it always did—which made the experience worse, for there was no naive hope of a quick reprieve, only the resigned knowledge that he must tough it out.

Finally, Karr vomited in the kilnsuit.

Vacuum slots automatically sucked the mess away.

Realtime.

And with it, the temporary euphoria.

Even though morbid thoughts wandered loose in Karr's head, he giggled. He was entombed under the ground, no trace of light visible. No one could possibly know where he was. He was completely on his own. He could not scratch his nose, let along dig himself out. Aaaaah, quite humorous! How long would it take to starve to death underground? No, he corrected, thirst would kill him before starvation set in. He made a lighthearted attempt to use the suit's comset. The device appeared to be in working condition, but there was no response on any of the colony channels. Where was everybody? Had the null-fusion explosion gone awry and vaporized them? If not, why weren't they looking for him. *Didn't they know he was buried alive? Buried alive?* Karr laughed hysterically. Time passed. Later, when the giddiness passed, Karr screamed and thrashed. Eventually, exhaustion set in and he slipped into a sort of waking coma, the last vestiges of his reason shutting off the unnecessary parts of his mind, as it also rationed sips of water from the supply nipple and turned off non-vital insuit systems.

A lot of unpleasant realtime passed.

A very long subjective time later, there was a crackling from within the kilnsuit, followed by a scorched plastic smell and a dimming of readout diodes. Karr turned off all the suit systems, vital and non-vital.

Karr began to hallucinate.

It was stuffy, hard to breathe. There were scratching sounds, as of insect legs or rodent teeth, gnawing. They got nearer, making his skin crawl. He could almost feel the unseen swarms taking bites out of his boots, his life-support powerpak, countless hungry things filling his suit, drowning him in crawly bodies. And there were blades! Sharp, raking knives, slashing at Karr from the dark. Zing! Zing! Searing gashes of light opened before his oxygen starved face. Karr clenched his eyes tight against the illusory brilliance. The blades tore at his cocoon. His helmet bubble collapsed, raining fragments into his suit.

Whoosh! Fresh air rushed in.

"Kruff, kruff, kruff?" asked the blades.

Karr shook his head, inhaling deeply. Gradually, his head cleared. He was not hallucinating. He was at the bottom of a burrow. Above, framed against a patch of blue sky, was an unfamiliar Feral.

"Kruff, kruff, kruff?" it repeated.

"I'm all right," Karr said with a thick tongue. He did not expect the Feral to understand, but a response seemed appropriate. "Just stuck," he added.

The Feral reacted as if it understood and began to burrow around Karr, freeing first his shoulders, then each arm, and working on downward. Karr flinched as tooth and claw slashed uncomfortably near his face, but the Feral was precise in its aim. Karr choked on root dust and itchy debris fell inside the kilnsuit, but that was the worst of it. A few rest breaks later, the Feral had chewed and ripped enough ghutzu away to grasp Karr under his arms and, digging in with its rear legs, drag him out of the pit.

Karr rolled onto his back, coughing and blinking. He was on a wide mound looking skyward. *Long Reach*'s stern protruded into his field of view like a great religious obelisk.

Karr elbowed himself up.

A foreign world met his gaze. Rich, green turf sloped down from the fugueship, forming gently rolling hills that stretched off into the distance, dotted here and there with tousled patches of jungle growth, but never showing a sign of coastline, sinkhole, or ocean. What Karr had assumed was a ring-island was not a ring-island at all, or even several islands crammed together, but a small continent, sprawling as far as his eyes could see.

Things had changed while he was entombed.

"Where are we?" Karr wondered at the sight.

Now the Feral spoke a word that he recognized. "Gnosis."

"Gnosis?" Karr repeated. "All this? Gnosis?"

"Gnosis," the Feral repeated and pointed off to Karr's right. In that direction on the horizon was a pyramid shape, almost exactly as large as the portion of *Long Reach* that protruded above the ground. Once that pyramid had been the island of Gnosis. Now it was the mountain of Gnosis.

"How can this be?" Karr asked, looking around, incredulous.

The Feral, who Karr noted was rather small and delicate for a Khafra, did a strange thing. It bowed down before him on forelegs, eyes averted, its glowbuds glittering like metallic gold, and uttered more alien words.

"Ghrrikitakadishtriss."

The Feral stayed prostrate for some time. Karr couldn't make sense of the behavior, other that the fact that is seemed to be thanking him for something. Touching the alien gently on its head, he urged it to its feet. "No, no. Don't thank me. Thank *you* for digging me out." Karr pointed at the nearby pit as the Feral rose to its feet trying to understand. Karr decided to try another strategy. "Karr, Karr," he said, thumping his chest like a fool. "Karr. Understand?"

The alien pulsed happily. *"Pilot* Karr," it said in a windy voice. Then, with a twinkle in its eyes, it thumped its own chest, rather theatrically, and said, "Kıtrıka."

"Aaaah!" said Karr, remembering that this was the female who hung around with Tlalok. "I'm pleased to make your re-acquaintance, Kitrika." Karr looked around. There was no Tlalok to be seen, but there were other Khafra scattered about the manicured-looking landscape. They were pacing individually, heads to the ground sniffing, or gathered together digging clusters of holes in the new earth. "I don't suppose you've seen Jenette or Arrou, have you?" Karr asked.

Kitrika made an effort to shrug like a human.

Karr checked out his fugueship. It did not look dead yet, he reflected, wondering how long it would take a creature, whose blood was *fugue*, to die. Weeks? Months? He hoped not years. It appeared to be rooted into the living continent. He stripped off his kilnsuit and walked up to it. Its pulses were weaker than normal, but steady. Its exterior flesh, once raw and bloody after planetfall, was thickening into rough hide. Perhaps it could still be kept alive—NO! Pulling back a shuddering hand, Karr told himself that he must resist the urge to prolong its life. *Long Reach* wanted to die. He must respect that. He must let it die.

Forcing himself to turn away, Karr set off down the slope in search of other humans. Kitrika followed.

Their wanderings took them past several solitary, digging Ferals before encountering a group that was pulling a naked human out of a freshly burrowed pit. Karr hurried over to look. It was a man Karr did not recognize. The Ferals had cut him out of his clothes in order to extract him from the ghutzu. Based on the shreds of uniform cloth in the pit, Karr concluded the man was a Guard. He lay limp and his skin was bluish and clammy. It would have been easy to assume he was dead, except that Karr was quite familiar with the signs of *fugue*-coma. As he had done to so many colonists in *Long Reach*'s dreamchamber, Karr bent and checked the Guard's vital signs.

"Peculiar," Karr said, resisting the urge to look back at his distant ship. *Long Reach* could not possibly be exuding enough *fugue* to put the man into suspended animation. If it had been, Karr would still be in fuetime. "In fact, impossible."

The Ferals, who were of the sophisticated sort who held patterns immobile on their glowbuds like body paint or badges of rank, gestured for Karr to follow. There was nothing else to do for the Guard but let the *fugue*-coma run its course, so Karr arranged him in a comfortable position and walked along with the quadrupeds.

Over a small rise, around a copse of shooting-star palms and on into a bowl between several rolling hills they went. Lying at the bottom of the depression was physical evidence that answered Karr's confusion. The segments had originally been ring or pipe shaped, between ten to twenty feet in diameter and six to ten feet

tall. Now they were twisted and charred. Quite a few were missing, probably having fallen to the bottom of the ocean, still the Ferals had done a reasonable job of placing the sections into a
semblance of their original, missile-like, shape, right down to po-
sitioning the remains of a bulging nose cone on the proper end.

A Feral with white accents on its paws pantomimed objects
rushing skyward. "Frrooooosh, froooooosh, frooooosh, frooooosh—
FOOOOOM!" It pantomimed an explosion and debris spreading
out and fluttering down.

Karr needed no further explanation. One of the booster-spawn
had not survived the attempt to escape its birth planet's gravity
well—most likely the one in-bob had chewed the hole in. The
burned segments were all that remained of a baby fugueship. It
was sad, but Karr did not allow himself to be too morose. The dead
spawn was part of a larger, near miraculous scenario, he reminded
himself. Up, far beyond New Ascension's azure stratosphere there
were three baby fugueships. Probably they were making their way
to CG-423's single gas giant, to feed and grow strong on the fodder of its atmosphere and rings. That was a glorious thing in itself,
but in addition to that, the last spawn's demise had spread an enormous amount of *fugue* in the area around its parent ship. The local
flora, having evolved over tens of millennia, constantly battling
Scourge to stay alive, had been unexpectedly freed of that struggle. It had suddenly been able to use all of its energy to grow at a
phenomenal rate. The death of the spawn had lead to the birth of
an entire continent.

"It seems a worthy trade," Karr decided quietly.

At which point Kitrika and White Paws and the other Ferals
again prostrated themselves before him.

"Ghrrikitakadishtriss."

Karr and the Ferals wandered.

The Ferals spent their time sniffing for buried *fugue* dreamers.
Sometimes they dug up humans. Many times they unearthed other
creatures: large grazing animals, small fuzzy beasts, serpentine
things, all in suspended animation. The Ferals did not eat any of
the helpless creatures, but laid them in groups of their own kind

and returned to sniffing and digging with unflagging dedication. It was, Karr noted, as if the Ferals were midwives to the rebirth of their world, and in this role they somehow could not kill.

Karr was not of much use. His olfactory senses were insignificant next to the Ferals. He could not dig through roots with his bare, feeble human hands, nor could he accelerate the revival of dreamers from *fugue*-coma. Karr had gone through withdrawal quicker than they because his body had suffered the process so many times. He did not know why the Ferals had come out so much quicker than he, nor what it was about the local fauna that allowed it to keep on growing instead of being paralyzed, but as he wasn't likely to discover those answers soon, he didn't worry about it much.

With nothing else to do, and a strong desire to be alone, Karr split off from the Ferals. Kitrika stayed with the others, helping as Karr could not.

A few days went by.

The new land was vast and beautiful. Flowers of untold numbers in different shapes and colors grew in fields, gems on green velvet. The color brushed off on Karr's legs like wet paint and rich perfumes arose, temporarily overpowering the smell of fresh-grown soil, which pervaded the continent. While there were no creatures to make noise, the new world was full of sounds, for the flora continued to grow rapidly in the Scourge-free environment, so fast that it made a soothing, rustling whisper, which eased Karr to sleep each evening. Every morning he would twist free of the growth that had blanketed him over night. Karr ate fruits shaped like barbells and drank water collected in plants formed like pitchers. His loose goal was to find open ocean. He wasn't sure why, but the water was still there, deep under all the ghutzu. If he closed his eyes and stood motionless, Karr could feed the ocean's movements, ever so slight, like a faint ground tremor on Solara. And it was somehow important to see it.

One afternoon, Karr spotted a great platinum arc on the horizon. He did not know what he had expected to see when he arrived, but there was only endless open water, reflecting clouds and sky in its alien, mirror-like surface. That sight was comforting, though, to know that New Ascension was still the ocean world Karr had seen from orbit, a silvery-blue sphere peppered with green ring-islands—and one large green continent. Pilot Lindal Karr had not screwed things up too badly. Perhaps that was what he had wanted to see.

Karr was sitting in a patch of yellow flowers, staring over nearby cliffs down at the ocean and listening to the trees grow when he saw her. She stepped out from behind a hillock, young and lithe, her short hair grown a bit wild and looking more yellow-blonde than Karr remembered it being before. The crystal starlure hung from her neck and it was her only garment. She did not see Karr at first, but moved sprightly through sights, sounds, and sensations of the world reborn around her, seeing with childlike eyes, gasping and reveling at each new discovery. She ran and dove into a heap of soft blooms.

"Jenette! Consul!" Karr called as she rolled in glittering pollen.

"Lindal!" she cried, a smile splitting her face. She rushed through the flowers, threw her arms around him and gave him a big hug.

"Ouch," Karr flinched.

"Oops," Jenette giggled, drawing back with an expression of exaggerated regret. "Sooorrr-y." She removed the spiky starlure and dropped it into the flowers. She gave Karr another hug and then twirled giddily in the sunlight. "I've had the most wonderful dreams, Lindal!"

Karr nodded knowingly, non-Pilots dreamed heavily under *fugue*. "I'm sure you have."

"Everything was perfect," Jenette bubbled on, "all beautiful and peaceful and utopian. And then I woke up and it was all true!" She stopped spinning. Her attention fixed on Karr, her thoughts turning mischievous. "I bet you'd look pretty good without those silly tights on."

"Pardon?"

Jenette paced sultrily closer. "That geeksuit. . . ."

"Ghimpsuit."

"Whatever. Take it off."

Karr blushed, acutely aware that Jenette wore nothing more than a few streaks of pollen. Saffron smudges curved fully where a young woman should curve fully and stretched long where a young woman should stretch long. Her breasts sat high and perfect. Her ;hips beckoned seductively. Karr's breath became shallow and rapid.

"I don't think you really mean that," he said quickly.

"I don't? Why wouldn't I mean what I say?"

"Because you're sick."

"I feel great."

Karr stumbled backward as she drew nearer. "Oh?" he stammered. "You didn't feel sick after waking up, not at all?"

"Weellll," Jenette admitted, "at first I threw up. But I feel fabulous now." She grabbed hold of Karr's ghimpsuit. "How does this unfasten?"

"Never mind that," Karr objected. "You are suffering from post-*fugue* euphoria. If you just wait a while, it will pass."

"I don't want it to pass."

"But it's not real."

"It's as real as we want to make it."

"It's biochemically induced!"

Jenette abruptly seized Karr's face in her hands. "Look here, gloomy-man, do you love me or not?"

Karr gulped. He glanced around, but there was no one around to help him. He could not even see his ship, the emotional anchor of most of his adult life; it was blocked by a cluster of newly grown trees. He was truly on his own. "Ummm . . ."

"Not the right answer."

"I suppose . . . that is, I guess—"

"Nope. Unacceptable." Jenette shook Karr's head from side to side. "Try again."

Karr sighed. "I don't want to take advantage. I don't want you to do anything you might regret later."

Jenette fixed an icy Tesla stare on him. "Don't think, Pilot Lindal Karr, that just because I feel euphoric that I would do anything I don't want to do. *I'm not a little girl.*"

"No," Karr agreed, sweating. "I can see that you're not."

"So?"

"So . . ." Karr said, abruptly resembling the sad and vulnerable little boy who was taken from the Planet of Industry so many centuries ago. "So, I love you."

"That's better," Jenette said, kissing him hard, "because I love you, too."

LV

Three things being a Pilot will do for you: It will take you to a crossroads. It will harden you. It will kill you.

> —Bondir Malda's suicide note,
> two months after retirement from Kismet

Jenette dreamed:

The proto-man lays before her, in its clothes of white, the color of true love. She has taken good care of it. The seam around its cranium hardly shows. In a jar nearby is its boy-brain. She sweeps the container to the floor. Crash. That won't be necessary any longer.

She opens a ceramite chest. Within, cradled in satin, is a shiny, new brain. Long she searched for it. Hardships she surmounted to acquire it. Tears she cried to feed it. And now it is just right.

It is a man-brain.

She unlocks the man-body's head. Places the man-brain in the empty cavity. Seals it up.

Now the man-body is alive. Now she cannot play with it like a toy. It has its own will. Its own wants. Its own—she hopes—lusts. Now they must play together, woman body to man-brain, man-body to woman-brain, or not play at all.

It grabs her. She is afraid, but excited, too. How will this dream end?

It ends in blossoms.

Her lips wandered over his lips. Exposing, teasing, pressing. He enwrapped her in his arms and she entwined him in her legs, pressing him into her. They moved in the yellow sunlight, caressing, moving with one another as yellow flowers changed color and bloomed white around them, unfurling. Velveteen petals and stems caressed them, changing in perfume as their passion peaked and renewed, reinventing and reinvigorating. The woman, the man, and the field of blossoms made love as the planet made life about them.

Karr held Jenette tightly when it was at last over.

"I've found my home," he said.

Liberty, naked and looking disheveled, wandered into view. Karr lay on his back with Jenette draped lazily over him, both equally as unclothed as the Guard. She spotted the couple and waved.

"I've had sex!" she shouted, sauntering over and looking like the cat that ate the canary. "Six times!" she elaborated. "With three different guys! And they *wanted* to. I think the lot of them grew balls overnight. Not that I'm complaining!"

"I'm glad," Karr said, smiling rather stiffly. Liberty was a stunning, heavily framed woman. Muscles rippled when she moved. Karr had an unsettling image of her popping his head between her strong legs like a grape.

"Thanks," said Liberty. She clenched a fist victoriously. "It was great! Say," she added, on a second thought, "you two are cute. You wouldn't want to, you know, have some fun . . . ? Nah, didn't think so. Catch you later!"

Liberty sauntered on, presumably in search of her next conquests.

"It's pretty amazing about the Khafra," Jenette commented in an idle moment, later.

"What is?"

"How they didn't fall asleep from the *fugue*."

"They didn't?"

"Nope. Not a single one of them."

"Wow," said Karr. That explained why in-bob had not fallen into *fugue*-coma inside of *Long Reach*. It wasn't because of a billion in a billion chance. It was because he was part of an entire race of potential Pilots. *"Wow,"* Karr repeated. It made sense. Immune venom was related to *fugue*. Khafra had to be resistant to its paralyzing effects, otherwise every Khafra Karr had ever encountered would have been lying in suspended animation. He knew of some Pilot Academy instructors who would love to know about New Ascension's secret.

"I've got one for you," Karr said. "The Ferals think that it was me who caused the last fugueship-spawn to explode. It wasn't. It was in-bob." Karr told Jenette the story of the minutes leading up to the spawning.

"A Pact saved a piece of the light after all," Jenette observed. "A *real* indigenous Pact, not a doppelganger Pact like you. The Prophecy was right. The Judges will be happy to know that."

"Maybe we should tell somebody."

"Mmm," Jenette replied, a purr entering her voice, "but we don't have to tell them right away, do we?"

"Decidedly not," Karr said in response to her naughty, roaming fingers.

They resumed playing dueling reproductive games with the flowers.

A few *duels* later, Tlalok appeared, striding into view with the Judges scurrying along behind him. He honed in on Jenette and Karr like a heat seeking missile.

"Human Karr, human Jenette," Tlalok greeted. "Tlalok has been searching for you."

Jenette said, "Hello, oh Keeper of the Roots of Wisdom, oh Radiance of the Pack of Gnosis."

"I guess that means he succeeded Kthulah?" Karr mumbled to Jenette.

Jenette nodded.

"Congratulations," Karr said, a bit awkwardly, to Tlalok; Karr was still a bit intimidated by the fierce Khafra. Tlalok bowed his head slightly. "And please thank Kitrika for digging me out," Karr added.

"Urrkurrkurrk," Tlalok rumbled. His colors formed unsettled, regret-tinged splotches.

Jenette hissed at Karr. "The Radiance of the Pack of Gnosis must have no bondmate. All lesser-radiant Khafra offer up small amounts of Pact to keep him, and the Judges, alive. That way Khafra leaders are sort of bonded to those they lead. It keeps them Balanced."

"Ah," said Karr, not understanding, and not truly wanting to, either. Alien mysticism was always a brain-bender.

"Developments unfold," Tlalok said, impatiently, to Jenette. "Forces of Gnosis have captured traitor humans on Jenette's home island."

Jenette, who had been quite relaxed, was suddenly all business. "How many?" she asked, sitting up and brushing pollen off her breasts and thighs.

Tlalok was oblivious to the humans' state of undress. His muzzle curled into an expression of dislike. *"All* of them, as far as Tlalok knows." His colors became hopeful. "Shall Tlalok kill them for Jenette?"

"No, no," Jenette said quickly.

"Tlalok would not be inconvenienced."

"I must talk to them," Jenette insisted in a friendly manner.

Tlalok was clearly disappointed. He turned his attention to Karr. "The human Karr owes Tlalok a sacrifice."

Karr felt as though the newly formed ground had been pulled out from under him. At long last he had found a place to *belong.* It wasn't perfect, with the death of his ship always nagging somewhere in a corner of his mind, but it was as good as it had ever been. And now this.

"Tlalok will collect now," the alien said. "Not for the original reasons. For new reasons. Tlalok has seen that he was wrong about some things. Wrong about the False Radiance. Wrong about humans. The Balance has righted itself, as wise Kthulah once told a savage it would. Humans and Khafra can exist in harmony. And it is good. Tlalok must quell his instincts to fight. Tlalok must not lead the Pack of Gnosis back into imBalance. The new harmony must endure. But . . . Tlalok hears whispers. Other humans are saying that the '*fugue*' from the 'fugueship-spawn' will wear off. And when it does old human needs will be as strong as before. Is this true?"

"It is true," Karr admitted.

"It must not be," Tlalok said firmly. "There must be another source of *fugue* for humans!"

Tlalok was talking about *Long Reach*, Karr realized. He felt sick to his stomach at where he saw Tlalok's reasoning headed. "The Burning Heart of Night must die. It wants to die. It deserves to die. Even your Prophecy says it must."

"Let the Prophecy be cursed!" Tlalok swore. "Tlalok will make new Prophecy."

The Judges looked on calmly. Fortunately for them, they would never be able to hear, let along understand, human language. Karr hung his head.

"Can the Pilot Karr not extend the Burning Heart's life?" Tlalok demanded.

"Maybe," Karr answered truthfully.

"Then maybe will have to be enough," Tlalok decided. "This is the sacrifice Tlalok demands."

"When?" Karr asked simply.

"Now," said Tlalok.

Karr turned to Jenette. It was doubly awful. He must now go against the wishes of his beloved ship and keep it alive long after its natural time to die was passed. And he was losing Jenette. He would return to his ship, to fuguetime. Days would pass, perhaps even months; he did, after all, know his Pilot skills very well. He might be able to keep *Long Reach* alive and in torment for a very long time. When he came out again, Jenette would be gone.

"You will be keeping us all alive while our scientists search for a cure," Jenette said, equally aware of what was about to happen, and just as sad.

Karr took her hands and clasped them in his own.

"Come with me," he asked. "You will go to sleep, and dream pleasant dreams, and wake up and it will be like no time has passed. We can continue our lives just like nothing happened. . . ."

One look at Jenette's ice-blue, watering eyes was enough for Karr to see that such a fantasy could not be.

Jenette was a prisoner of her duty as much as Karr was a prisoner of his, and she knew it.

No matter how hard she had fought it, it had found her. Just like her father always said it would. His dying words were a trap that had snapped tightly about her. *She must do what she thought was right, always. She must make the hard decisions. And she must be responsible for every single human on the planet she must guide, cajole, manipulate, threaten, and punish—but never abandon.*

Jenette had not promised her father that she would abide by those principals, but now she found that it did not matter. He had ingrained them into her by example. She could not now abandon those traitor humans back on the Enclave, no matter how repugnant their behavior had been, no matter how much she wanted to go with Karr—and she wanted to go with Karr very, very much. No, she had to find a way to bring those errant humans back into the fold, to drag them kicking and screaming into the new harmony forged between humans and Ferals.

She was, after all, a Tesla.

"I cannot," she said to Karr.

Karr kissed her and left with Tlalok. The Judges lingered, sensing the grief of their new human friend. Consulting their tallies, they sighed,

<<Choices seldom>>
<<Become easier>>
<<Only more>>
<<Inevitable >>

Arrou sat in the middle of the field, tearing up grass.

He was free.

The *fugue* in the exploding fugueship-spawn had given freedom to all domestics, and all Ferals too. *It was the time when all bonds are broken, all Pacts made anew.* Most Ferals were now rebonding with their bondmates, reaffirming old attachments with new vigor. But Arrou did not know what to do. He was concerned about his friend Jenette. He still cared about her. That would never change. But he did not have to go and find her *right now*. It was enough for him to have heard from Liberty that Jenette was all right. He would, of course, go and see Jenette soon. But first he must sort through his confusion.

Arrou had never wanted to be free.

In his estimation, everyone served something, it was just a matter of what. The trick was to find the right thing to serve. He had been lucky before; that choice had been made for him. So why fight to be free from that which he would have chosen anyway? But now he must choose for himself. What would he do? Probably, he would help Jenette, he decided. There was still much to be done to make things right. Probably she would still want his help. It would just be in a slightly different way from how he had helped her before. That made him feel a bit better. If it did not completely fill the strange void that his new freedom left in his heart, then, well . . . maybe he just needed to be patient.

Arrou kept pulling grass, pawful by pawful, slowly turning on his haunches to reach more stalks.

A female feral appeared prowling across the field. It was Kitrika. She padded closer and observed Arrou's activity. Arrou had denuded all plant growth an arm's length from himself in every direction.

<<Arrou has made a circle of nothing,>> Kitrika flashed.

<<Yes, sorry.>>

<<Do not be sorry. It is a blessing. What does Arrou bless?>>

Arrou thought he had no answer, but one popped into his head and he said it, <<Bigelow. Arrou blesses his brave friend Bigelow.>> The scientist's death had troubled Arrou much lately. He told Kitrika how he had spared in-robert's life and what the in-human had done to Bigelow.

<<Then it is appropriate for Arrou to bless his friend for being so brave. And to forgive himself for making the wrong choice for all the right reasons.>>

Arrou sighed. <<Too bad the circle will not last long.>> New Ascension plant growth would fill the raw ghutzu ring in no time once Arrou stopped plucking it. Green shoots were already squirming into the brown circle.

Kitrika sparkled sympathetically. <<Silly. That is the idea: a purification, clearing away the old to make way for the new. Watch.>>

Kitrika moved a few paces from Arrou. Raking her powerful rear talons across the ground, and spinning on her forepaws, she rapidly cleared a large circle of nothing.

<<That's how Kitrika and Kitrika's friends make circles of nothing when they are kits.>>

<<Oooh, that good,>> Arrou said. <<Fast. What Kitrika blesses?>>

<<Hapfelumps.>>

<<Hapfelumps?>>

<<Yes,>> Kitrika flashed mirthfully, <<for tasting so good.>>
"Urrr?"

In short order, Kitrika made circles of nothing for *sunny days, pushing friends into cold sinkhole bogs when they aren't expecting it's and sleeping late.* Eventually Arrou's mood lightened, he laughed and, using Kitrika's faster technique, made nothing circles for being *high-up, telling embarrassing secrets about people you don't like,* and especially for *going fast.*

Lastly, they made a big one together, rotating in opposite directions and bumping together where the circle closed upon itself.

<<What this one for?>> Arrou asked as the dust settled.

<<*New friends,*>> Kitrika said coyly.

Karr stepped up to the iris-portal. He turned back, looking around, but no one was there besides Tlalok and the Judges. Jenette was watching, hiding in a copse of distant jungle plants, but she did not wave or otherwise give away her position. She hated drawn-out good-byes. Squaring his shoulders, Karr stepped into his ship and out of her life.

PART SEVEN:

BALANCE

LVI

*When wind blows through scattered farfalla grasses,
they do not hold its whispers after it has gone. When
wild clouds dance over ocean, the water does not retain
shadows after clouds have passed. So too our hearts
must be full only when an event occurs and rest, void,
when the matter ends.*

—*Feral Wisdom*

Prime Consul Jenette Tesla stepped out of the heavy lifter's passenger module and drew an apprehensive breath of night air. She felt like a different person.

Twenty years of hard choices had done it.

How many of those choices had been good? More than half, she hoped. . . . She moved to the side railing, gripping its cool ceramite. Certainly rebuilding the heavy lifter counted as one of the good choices; and then using it to recover the robotic factory from the remains of Coffin Island. Those, in turn had lead to the glittering sprawl of streetglobes, hab complexes, and industrial nodes that the lifter now flew over. After the escape of the Burning Heart, there had been less than three thousand human colonists. Now, two decades later, there were more than twenty thousand, co-mingled with countless Khafra, living and working symbiotically. There were a few individualistic humans and Ferals who refused to participate, but that was their choice—and everyone lived with the consequence of their choice, as Jenette knew all too well.

Was decision possible without regret, she wondered?

A pneumatic door *shushed* open. Footfalls approached. Jenette caught the reflection of radiant words in the lifter's handrail.

<<There is always>>
<<Time to reconsider>>
<<Right up to>>
<<The very end,>> four voices flashed.

Jenette turned to face four bipeds, Kayli, Shona, Soren, and Gall Hedren. They were Pact humans; their hair had fallen out and their follicles turned into glowbuds. And they were *special* Pact-humans. These quadruplets, who had cemented the peace between humans and Khafra, were also heirs to the wisdom of Balance, trained by the four Khafra Judges whom Jenette had come to know so well. Where the old Judges had blocked their earpits to block out the impure verbal language of secrets, one each of the four Pact-human Judges blocked a different sense: sight, sound, taste, or smell. That way at least one of their number was always immune to an imBalancing influence, no matter what sense it originated from; they also meditated upon the voids caused by the loss of those senses, hoping to become wise.

The old Judges were gone. A very old Tlalok had dispatched these Pact humans, their successors, to serve as witness for him this night when the air felt expectant, as if awaiting the coming of an electrical storm. But the only storm was within Jenette.

Jenette said to them, "Changing one's mind is a woman's prerogative." Kayli and Shona smiled, faintly. *"And* a Prime Consul's," Jenette continued. "But I will not change mine tonight. I will make my choice. The only unknown is how it will be received."

All four Pact-human Judges nodded and tallied their beads.

In many ways, Jenette reflected, New Ascension humans were becoming more Khafra than the Khafra were becoming human. Two-thirds of the newest human generation had made Pact. The rest survived on *fugue* and had not made the mutation, but even they cold not avoid the alien influence around them. Within the next generation, New Ascension science and technology would be predominantly human, as it was now, but the culture . . . that would be something altogether different. A fusion of human, Pact-human, and Khafra. It was the fourth and final prophesied gift: the Gift of Gamut. The future that grew out of it would be a *just* future, Jenette knew. Balanced. Better. Jenette had fought for it at every opportunity.

But, after this night, would she have a part to play in it?

Jenette's hand went to a breast pocket, feeling through the fabric to a vial secreted within. It held one-half of the answer to her question. The lifter's destination held the other. Apart of Jenette feared to reach that destination; Kayli, Shona, Soren, and Gall were not the only ones who had changed.

What would *he* think of what she had become?

Time passed, brooding. Settled areas dropped behind. The continent grew dark beneath the lifter as it plunged toward the heart of Gnosis. That heart appeared, lit by four spectral crescent moons in the sky, a great somber mass of bone and hide, pallid and undead looking, rising from the wild preserves surrounding it. At its foot, was a single, tiny mourner.

Jenette's heart leapt into her throat. *The reports were true!*

The lifter set down. Automated boarding stairs unfolded.

Before she could change her mind, Jenette climbed to the ground. She adjusted her close-fitting burgundy jumpsuit, which she had picked out especially for this night, and walked the fifty paces to the mourning figure. Its head shifted at the patter of her approaching boots.

"Hello," said a voice from long ago.

The sound swept Jenette into the past; into a tumultuous time, a formative time, perhaps a best-of-times. Many of the twists and turns of her life were anchored in that brief period. She would have liked to savor the reverie, but all too quick, she was back firmly in the present, staring at the white-uniformed back. *Please don't turn around. Don't look.* Jenette resisted the urge to flee.

She cleared her throat. "I heard a rumor you might be here."

"I have always been here. . . ."

For twenty years Jenette and all non-Pact humans had depended on the fugueship, every six months making a pilgrimage to breathe *fugue*-thick air in chambers just inside its hull, to fall into *fugue*-coma and then be carried back out by Khafra. *Long Reach* had always been there to keep them alive. And Pilot Lindal Karr had always been there, too. No one saw him, even the slowtime

Khafra, but they knew he was there. Jenette felt it keenly at each visit, so near and yet so far. But now that was changing. The vast *cosmosaurus planetos* was still, its heartbeats quieted.

Long Reach was dead.

Karr's head hung low. A Gattler lay on the turf beside him, its life-prolonging barrels and spheres untouched.

"No more tricks," he said. "No more cheats. The suffering ends here."

Age.
Great age.
Many feelings,
More sweet than bitter,
It feels as it slips away.
The new parts of itself are long gone,
To float and fly in diamonds of light,
As it once did.
As is right.
It is weary, so weary.
There is pain,
As ending settles upon it.
It has already ended, it senses, long ago.
It is just catching up.
It is not afraid.
The tiny good has not gone.
The tiny good makes the emptiness less.
But the tiny good does not make the hurting less.
Soon, it hopes, the pain will go.
Soon the all-pressing-down weight will go.
Final comfort tempts it.
And it wants to be tempted.
Do not hold me back, tiny good!
Let me go!

Karr's hands twitched, but he did not reach for the Gattler. "I stopped keeping it alive a couple days ago." Karr confessed quietly. "I owed it that much, after all I put it through."

Jenette reached out as if to comfort Karr, but withdrew at the last second. It was so confusing, what he must feel, what she felt . . . and feared.

Karr said, "I'm sorry, Jenette."

"For what?"

"There's no more *fugue*."

"Oh, that. Don't be." Jenette fumbled into her breast pocket and withdrew a medical vial. "Our scientists finally biofactured a vaccine."

Karr turned around.

His expression was not as Jenette expected. Dried tears stained his face, but there were no tears now. Karr's countenance was philosophical, weary, as if from long hardship, but accepting. He stared at the vial of vaccine.

"That is a great relief."

And then he looked at Jenette. Her throat tightened as he stared. She wanted to speak, anything to distract him from looking at her. She wanted to tell him about the fugueship-spawn, how satellite scans showed they were feeding and growing large on the local gas giant's rings. She wanted to tell him how the colony had rebuilt its beacon and sent a message to the rest of the human universe, and that a message had returned ten years later from a Major Vidun. She wanted to tell Karr how that major and a certain Dr. Uttz were moving the Pilot Academy permanently to New Ascension to take advantage of a planet full of Pilot candidates, so that when the fugueship-spawn became full grown fugueships, they would not have to wander the galaxy alone. She wanted to tell Karr how much she had missed him, and how she desperately wanted him to say how much he had missed her, and that he still loved her. And she wanted to throw her arms around him and for him to hug her back and tell her that it was all over and now they would never be apart again. But Karr's mouth gaped open, and the longer he stared, the wider it gaped.

"It feels like only twenty days to me," he said at last in a hush. "But it's not, is it? Everything changed while I was gone."

Jenette's vision swam. Karr reached out to her, but she slapped his arm away.

"Don't touch me!"

"Jenette, what—?"

"I'm *old!*" she sobbed. "I'm old and weak and wrinkled and disgusting! Don't tell me you don't see it because I can tell by the look on your face. I'm twenty years older and you're young and handsome and exactly the same! And you don't love me anymore, and I don't blame you because I'm old . . . old!" She was becoming an *ancient*, like Colonel Halifax and Dr. Yll and her father before they died. It was beyond horrible. Jenette wept uncontrollably.

Karr reached out again, this time weathering her blows to grasp her shoulders. "Wait a minute—ouch! Stop hitting! Stop! Don't you think you're overreacting? Maybe just a little?"

Jenette settled a little, but continued to glare at Karr. "Don't tell me any lies Lindal Karr! Don't tell me age doesn't matter to you!"

"Okay," Karr said, not seeming to have the energy to get worked up about it. "That's fair. Age does matter to me, but not in the way you think." She started to squirm again. "Sssh. Think about it. How old were you when we first met? Well?"

"You know very well that I was twenty-three standard years," Jenette spat.

"And how old did I say you looked then, by off-world standards?"

Jenette scowled, "Fifteen?"

"Exactly," Karr agreed. "Fifteen. And now, twenty years later, do you know how old you look, by off-world standards?"

"I don't know," Jenette said quietly. "Old?"

"Thirty-five," said Karr. "And a very young thirty-five at that. It must be the residual effects of all those hormone inhibitors. Don't you get it? I'm thirty-six. Your age is perfect."

"But I'm really forty-three. I'm still older than you."

Karr's mouth twisted, not quite into a full-blown smile. Karr's emotions had been beaten and bruised—were still being beaten and bruised—too much, for that. But it was a start. "Jenette, I'm *eleven hundred years old*. You have a long way to go before you're older than me!"

Jenette sniffed, liking his logic, but still suspicious. "But the look on your face when you first saw me . . . ?"

"I simply couldn't believe how good you look as a full grown woman," Karr said. "I still can't. *You're so beautiful. . . .*"

"Really? No patronizing and no pity?"

"Absolutely. I am too weary to beat around the bush."

Jenette's eyes grew big. She leaned up and planted a long, tender kiss on Karr's lips, which he did not seem to mind.

A throaty *urrrrr* carried through the night from the heavy lifter. "About time."

Karr squinted at the alien in the cockpit. "Arrou?"

"Arrou-Two," Jenette corrected.

Karr blinked. Had he been gone that long? Yes, he supposed, he had. "Don't you mean Arrou *the second?*"

Jenette shrugged. "I tried to explain it to them, but they wouldn't listen." She disengaged from Karr's embrace, so as to face the lifter, but stayed close. "There's also a Kitrika-Two, a Jenette-Two and a Karr-Two. They liked the sound of it."

"*Who* liked the sound of it?" Karr asked, feeling as though his brain was running at half-speed.

For an answer, Jenette keyed a comset on her collar. It bleeped and in response two old Khafra stepped out of the lifter's passenger module. "Arrou and Kitrika, of course. Duh."

The old male raised his bullet snout and called out. "Five hundred knots!"

Karr called back. "It's good to see you, old friend."

"Arrou glad to see Karr, too. Arrou has lots of questions. Arrou flies satellites into orbit when Jenette not using lifter for *personal* trips. Hrrrrmmmph."

Karr might have chuckled at the alien's annoyance, but water began to bubble behind him. He spun around. *Long Reach* was sinking. No doubt its iris-valves had relaxed, and the ship was filling full of water.

This was the final sadness Karr had been bracing for. He hurried over and held his head and hands as close as possible to the descending wall of hide. Karr had spent his time away from the realtime world learning from a strange source: in-bob. It had taken some effort, some forgetting of old, regimented beliefs and the learning of new, more intuitive ones, but Pilot Lindal Karr could

now *feel* the moods, if not the exact thoughts of his ship. It was not
as hard as he had imagined. You just had to open yourself up, to
trust. While Karr had been keeping *Long Reach* alive, against its
desire and at great pain to it, he had spent a lot of time practicing
to open himself up and trust and listen to what it would be feeling
at this exact moment. . . .

> *It is floating away,*
> *Into the Light jewels of ending.*
> *But it does not forget.*
> *Gratitude it feels, as warm* nothing *embraces it.*
> *The hard, recent times are already forgotten,*
> *A speck of discomfort in a life of contentment.*
> *A wish it makes,*
> *For the tiny good it leaves behind:*
>
> *Do not be alone,*
> *Do not be afraid,*
> *Forever be un-sad,*
> *Forever and always.*
> *Ending comes.*

That was what Karr had needed to hear. *Forgiveness.* It was the
end of an era. Now Karr's life could move on.

"I'm not a Pilot anymore," he said, looking at the water-filled
hole in the ground.

"Are you sad?" Jenette asked.

"Yes. But I will try not to be. *Long Reach* would not want me
to be sad."

"No," Jenette agreed.

Jenette looked at Karr.

Karr looked at Jenette.

"I expect the colony elected you Prime Consul."

"They did."

"I expect that's a position that doesn't leave very much time left
over."

"It doesn't," Jenette grinned. "But I resigned yesterday."

Karr managed a grin, too.

"So," Jenette asked, "what do you want to do?"

Karr looked from the hole in the ground, with the light of four lonely moons dancing on its surface, over to the heavy lifter. With a last farewell in his heart, he turned his back on the hole and held out his hand.

Jenette took it, willingly.

"Come on," Karr said, "we have a lot of catching up to do."

Julie E. Czerneda

THE TRADE PACT UNIVERSE

*"Space adventure mixed with romance...
a heck of a lot of fun."* –Locus

Sira holds the answer to the survival of
her species, the Clan, within the multi-
species Trade Pact. But it will take a
Human's courage to show her the way.

A THOUSAND WORDS FOR STRANGER

0-8867-7769-0

TIES OF POWER

0-8867-7850-6

TO TRADE THE STARS

0-7564-0075-9

Available wherever books are sold,
or call to order 1-800-788-6262

DAW14